W9-BQJ-263

THE YEAR'S BEST DARK FANTASY AND HORROR

2013 Edition

August 2014

STILLWATER

PUBLIC LIBRARY

Stillwater, Minnesota 55082

OTHER ANTHOLOGIES EDITED BY
PAULA GURAN

Embraces
Best New Paranormal Romance
Best New Romantic Fantasy
Zombies: The Recent Dead
The Year's Best Dark Fantasy & Horror: 2010
Vampires: The Recent Undead
The Year's Best Dark Fantasy & Horror: 2011
Halloween
New Cthulhu: The Recent Weird
Brave New Love
Witches: Wicked, Wild & Wonderful
Obsession: Tales of Irresistible Desire
The Year's Best Dark Fantasy & Horror: 2012
Extreme Zombies
Ghosts: Recent Hauntings
Rock On: The Greatest Hits of Science Fiction & Fantasy
Season of Wonder
Future Games
Weird Detectives: Recent Investigations
The Mammoth Book of Angels and Demons

THE YEAR'S BEST DARK FANTASY AND HORROR

2013 Edition

EDITED BY PAULA GURAN

PRIME BOOKS

THE YEAR'S BEST DARK FANTASY AND HORROR: 2013

Copyright © 2013 by Paula Guran.

Cover design by Stephen H. Segal & Sherin Nicole.
Cover art by Andre Kiselev.

All stories are copyrighted to their respective authors,
and used here with their permission.
An extension of this copyright page can be found on pages 525-527.

Prime Books
www.prime-books.com

Publisher's Note:
No portion of this book may be reproduced by any means, mechanical,
electronic, or otherwise, without first obtaining the permission of the
copyright holder.

For more information, contact Prime Books:
prime@prime-books.com

ISBN: 978-1-60701-396-6

Contents

For Navi—
Who currently makes my life and work
both more bearable and, at times, more challenging.

INSTRUCTIONS FOR USE

Paula Guran

—◆—

A. Flip back a few pages or look at the cover. Note the words in the title: *The Year's Best*.

1.   Please be aware that a *year's best* or *best of the year* or *best new* or *some other variation on this phrase* anthology (*anthology*, in this case, meaning: "a collection of selected literary pieces" published within a calendar year) cannot be taken to mean exactly what it says. It really means the book contains "some of the best of this type of short(ish) fiction as (a) found and read by, (b) within the personal definition of (insert type of fiction covered), (c) in consideration of certain factors of content as determined by, and (d) obtainable for reprint by the individual identified as the editor (not entirely without variables imposed by the publisher including, but not exclusively, how many pages) of said volume." More or less.

2.   The editors I know—and, I am fairly certain, those I don't—who undertake these gigs take the responsibility very seriously. They strive to (a) give recognition to writers who have produced outstanding fiction and (b) offer readers some guidance, as well as (c) good value for their investment (in both time and money). Said editors work very hard to live up to the not exactly lofty honor (and seldom very remunerative) of being arbiters of excellence.

3.   You may not always agree with their choices. That is your prerogative. Consider, debate, have your own opinion, but do not (a) condemn them for their definitions or their tastes, or (b) assume they believe their choices to be the *only* "bests."

B. Now, consider the words: *dark fantasy* and *horror*.

1.   Note: Both are highly debatable and constantly changing literary terms. So are labels like "science fiction," "speculative fiction," "magic realism," "surrealism," "suspense thriller," "mystery," et cetera. Outside of the realm of the written word, the meaning of both are further confused, diluted, and twisted as they also are used to describe other media that convey stories to audiences.

2.   Aforementioned "literary" and/or "genre" terms have been used/are used both correctly and incorrectly as marketing labels for various types of fiction and other media. Business is business. One cannot be a purest.

3.   A dark fantasy or horror story might be only a bit unsettling or perhaps somewhat eerie. It might be revelatory or baffling. You might be "scared" or simply unsettled—or not. It can also simply be a small glimpse of life seen "through a glass, darkly."

4.   Darkness itself can be many things: nebulous, shadowy, tenebrous, mysterious, paradoxical (and thus illuminating) . . . and more.

5.   Fantasy takes us out of our mundane world of consensual reality and gives us a glimpse or a larger revelation of the possibilities of the "impossible."

6.   Fantasy is sometimes, but far from always, rooted in myth and legend. (But then myths were once believed to be part of accepted reality. If one believes in the supernatural or the magical, is it still fantasy?) It also creates new mythologies for modern culture and this can affect us, become a part of who and what we are.

7.   Horror *is* an affect. It is something we feel, an emotion. What we react to, respond to emotionally differs from individual to individual. In fact, to paraphrase those figures of legend, Sir Paul and Saint Lennon, we can't tell you what we see when we turn out the light, but we know it is ours.

8.   Horror is also about finding, even seeking, that which we do not know. When we encounter the unknowable we react with emotion. And the unknowable, the unthinkable need not be supernatural. We constantly confront it in real life.

In consideration of the above, I offer no definitions. I do offer you a diverse selection of dark fiction that I would call dark fantasy and/or horror all published within the calendar year 2012.

Elements of "the dark" and horror are increasingly found in modern stories that do not conform to established tropes. What was once mainstream or "literary" fiction frequently treads paths that once were reserved for "genre." Stories of mystery and detection mixed with the supernatural are more popular today than ever and although they may also be amusing and adventurous, or have upbeat endings, that doesn't mean such stories have not also taken the reader into stygian abysses along the why. Horror is also interwoven—essentially—into many science fiction themes. What post-apocalyptic fiction can be nothing but lightness and cheer? Ultimately, the reader may come away with a hopeful attitude, but not until after having to confront some very scary scenarios and face some very basic fears. Darkness seeps naturally into weird and surreal fiction too. The strange may be mixed with whimsy, but the fanciful does not negate the shadowy

The stories selected for this year often take twists and turns into the unexpected. Disquietude, disintegration, and loss (of many things, including one's mind, memories, or love) evoke fear in some. Human treachery can be more terrifying than anything supernatural, or so strong it calls the unnatural into being. A deviant murderer's monstrosity can go beyond the mere taking of a life, what is thought to be monstrous may not be at all, or monsters can wear the face of injustice. And, of course, we are often the monsters ourselves (or they live just next door.) The dead can be vengeful and terrifying, but they also find peace or help the living. A child's world can be a frightening place, but then children can be quite frightening themselves.

These stories take us back to the past (be it historical, altered, or completely imagined), into a few futures, keep us in the present, and sometimes take us outside of time altogether. You'll visit, among other places, China, Mexico, Russia, Japan, India, Scotland, an English country estate or two, and places that are not places at all.

Along the way, remember when we journey through the darkness, sometimes we emerge better for the journey—more alive, more knowing than when we embarked.

Or not.

C. Read, turn pages, consume.

D. Thanks.

Paula Guran
11 May 2013
National Twilight Zone Day

The dead cannot stay. They are decay, ruination. Things falling apart . . .
But I will tell you a secret, a secret only I know . . .

NO GHOSTS IN LONDON

Helen Marshall

This is a sad story, best beloved, one of the few stories you don't know, one of the few stories which I have kept to myself, locked up tight between cheek and tongue. Not a rainy-day story, no, not a bedtime story, but another kind of story: a sad story, as I said, but also a happy story, a story that is not all one thing at once and so, in the way of these things, a true story. And I have not told you one of those before. So hush up, and listen.

Gwendolyn had worked for the old manor house, Hardwick Hall, ever since her mum died. She knew all the stones in the manor house by heart, the ones kept rough and out of the reach of tourists, the ones smoothed by feet or hands, the uneven bits of the floor underneath the woven rush mat, the inward curves on the stairs; she knew the ghosts who had taken up residence in the abandoned upstairs rooms—dead sons and murdered lovers, a suicide or two, and the children who had died before reaching the age of ten. It was *her* home in many ways, the manor where her mum had worked. Her home. And though she longed to go off to university in the Great City of London, since childhood she had felt the Hall's relentless drawstrings tugging tight as chain-iron around her. The kind, best beloved, that all young people feel in a place that is very, very old.

There was duty, of course. The old duchess's bones creaked like a badly set floorboard when winter came to Derbyshire, and she was wary of strangers, wary of people since her brother's sons had died in the war, wary of everyone except for the sad-eyed, long-jowled bulldog, Montague, who would sit by her side and snuffle against her ancient brocade skirt as she sewed. The duchess's memory was moth-eaten with age, and the only faces that made sense to her were those that had been in her company for some time. As her mother had. As Gwendolyn had. And Gwendolyn found it easy to love the old woman, to love her pink-tongued companion. To love Hardwick Hall.

So there was love as well, which as we all know, best beloved, is as tight a drawstring as any. But love is not always happiness, particularly when you are young, and lovely, and just a bit lonely.

After she buried her mum in the spring in a ceremony that was sweet and sad and comforting with all the manor staff in attendance, Gwendolyn put on her mum's apron and she tended the gardens and organized the servants, keeping them straight, letting them know there was still a firm hand about the place. Yes, my love, this is one of the sad bits but, hush, it was not so very sad as it might have been, for Gwendolyn had been loved by her mother very much, and, in the way of these things, that matters.

So. Gwendolyn stayed, and she minded the manor and all was well for the most part. The servants came to respect her, as they had her mum, to mind what she told them. The only people who didn't attend to her properly were the ghosts. Oh, Gwendolyn would cajole, she would bribe, she would beg, she would order. But hers was a young face, and she was not a blood relation to them. She was a servant herself, and lacked, at that stage, a servant's proper knowledge of how to subtly, secretly, put the screws to her master. Her mum had known how it was done—but her mum had kept many secrets to herself, as all mothers do, sure in the knowledge that there would be time later to pass them on.

Damien, the crinkle-eyed cowherd who minded the animals of the estate and drove the big tractor, the kind of man who was father and grandfather rolled into one, insisted that such things could not be forced. "Ghosts are an unruly lot," he would say to her. "Can't shift too much around at once. They'll take a shine yet, bless."

Shyly, Gwendolyn asked, "Will she ever . . . ?"

But she did not finish and Damien looked away as men do when they are sad and do not want to show it. Then he took her hand very carefully, as if it were one of the fine porcelain figures the duchess kept in her study. "I do not think so, love. *Their* kind"—meaning the ghosts, of course—"they stay for fear, or for anger, or for loneliness. Your mum, bless, she had none of that in her bones and too much of the other stuff. She'd have found somewhere better to rest herself, never you fear."

Gwendolyn smiled a little, and she got on about the business of managing the place as best she could. But after a particularly bad day, when mad old William, the former count of Shrewsbury, had given her such a nasty shock that she had twisted her ankle on the uneven stairs, Gwendolyn decided enough was enough. It was one thing to have to deal with the tourists that filtered in every summer—they were strangers—but the ghosts were something closer to family. She missed her mum badly, but it was just too hard to shut herself away from a world glimpsed in strange accents and half-snatched conversations, a world enticing as any unknown thing is to a girl who lives among the dead, only to face the scorn and distemper of the closest thing to relatives she still had.

"I can't abide it," she confessed in a whisper to Damien as she cast her sad gaze over the roses clinging to the south wall of the garden where she had scattered her mother's ashes. "They never acted up like this for mum."

"Your mum, bless, she had more iron in her blood than the fifth cavalry had on their backs. Even those roses grow straighter and bloom brighter for fear of disappointing her."

"I wish she were here," Gwendolyn said.

"I know, love, I know."

And so Gwendolyn packed her belongings into an old steamer trunk her mum had bought but never used, and she bid the duchess goodbye in the afternoon, as the sun slanted through the window into the blue room and lit up the silk trimmings so that they shone. Montague lay curled in a corner, breathlessly twitching in sleep, his tongue lolling like the edge of a bright pink ribbon. The duchess plucked at the needlework, fingers mindlessly unpicking what she had done, her only sign of agitation as she smiled a soft smile and bid Gwendolyn go. Then she cast her sad, milky eyes downwards, and patted Montague on the head with a kind of familiarity and gentleness that Gwendolyn never saw in the hurried, boisterous jostling of the tourists.

Gwendolyn did not look away then, though she desperately wanted to, because when you love someone, best beloved, and you know you will not see them again then, in the way of these things, you have to look.

Gwendolyn gritted her teeth and she looked until she couldn't bear the weight of that ancient gaze any longer. Then she bent over, and kissed the old woman's forehead, skin as light as brown paper wrapping, so that she could feel the hard bone of the skull underneath.

Then Gwendolyn turned, and in her turning something heavy seemed to fall away from her: the afternoon sun slanting through the window seemed full of hope and promise and if, here, it fell on only the aged, the dying and the dead and there, somewhere, it might also be falling upon things that glittered with their own newness. If she had been listening, Gwendolyn might have heard a whispered goodbye, and: "Please, my darling, do not come back." But with the sorry task of farewells done, Gwendolyn's mind was already ten miles ahead of her feet.

London was the place she had seen in that afternoon-sun vision, a city sharp with hope, glass and steel glittering above streets paved with crisp-wrappers and concrete. She loved the cramped and smelly Tube ride, the tangle of lines that ran beneath the city, the curved cramped space where she would be crowded against men in clean-cut jackets, some slumped over so their backs curved along with the frame, girls dressed in leather, or chiffon, sitting demurely or hurling insults at one another with complete abandon. She loved the cluttered streets, the brown brick walls and white-trimmed windows. Everything was pressed so closely together she could put out both arms and touch the walls on either side of her dormitory room.

There were no ghosts in London, best beloved, not where the living took up so much space. Her roommate, Cindy—you wouldn't like her, she was a lithe, long-legged girl from America who liked to wear heavy perfume and talk to her boyfriend in New York until ungodly hours of the morning—looked at her oddly when she spoke of them.

"We don't have anything like that back home," she'd say in a thick accent that seemed to misplace all the vowels and leave only the consonants in place. "In America, we like to get on with it, you know, lose the baggage."

Gwendolyn liked the idea of getting on with it. Losing the baggage. She liked living without ghosts. She was a city girl now, a Londoner, a girl from London, and she gave herself to the city, let the city transform her the way all cities transform the people who inhabit them. She started wearing heavy perfume and putting on thick, black mascara that promised to give her THE LONDON LOOK, make her eyelashes—formerly stubby and mouse-brown like mine, yes, just like that—long and curving with 14X the volume. Like a movie star, Gwendolyn thought, staring at the fringe of it, the way it curled up away from her eyes in an altogether pleasing manner. She got herself a boyfriend, learned something about snogging, got herself another and learned something about the things that come after snogging.

Gwendolyn wanted to be very like Cindy with her know-it-all attitude and her keen sense of how to get on with things. Soon enough the boyfriend back in New York had disappeared entirely, replaced by one from Oxford or Cambridge—she couldn't remember which, only that his college was one of the better ones, one of the *rich* ones. Cindy didn't shed a tear. "What's the point?" Cindy asked. "He's back home. No use crying over what's not here."

Gwendolyn liked that as well, and she said it over in her mind many times, "No use crying." This was some relief in and of itself, for the mascara made crying a sticky, abysmal business. No one in London cried. You couldn't pull off THE LONDON LOOK unless you kept your eyes bone dry. Soon Gwendolyn could pass rose bushes without ever thinking about the flowers on the south wall, the ones that grew straighter and brighter than any other in the garden. The roses in London were much smaller anyway, cramped into the gardens of townhouses or clinging to what light they could in the cracks between stones. They weren't proper roses, but sickly little things with barely any color at all. No, it was very rarely now that Cindy would pull Gwendolyn aside, squinting, and tell her to fix up her face, the mascara was running.

The duchess paid for her education, discreetly of course, and Gwendolyn promised herself she would write in thanks, but she never did. She started with a major in French, but Cindy advised against that—"Don't trust the French here, do they?"—so she switched over to Psychology.

It wasn't until graduation (in Art History, not Psychology after all) several years later that Gwendolyn received a letter from the post. Cindy was preparing to move back to Chicago where she would be engaged to a fellow with an MBA from Harvard (not the Oxford fellow, after all) and had invited Gwendolyn to come with her and try out the Second City—for that's what they called Chicago in America. London had been Gwendolyn's first city, and if Cindy taught her anything it was that you could never stay with your first, could you? Not with cities. Not with men.

That sounded like a fine enough plan to Gwendolyn, and Chicago seemed like a fine enough place with its aboveground rail service and broad city sidewalks and gleaming steel towers, a place even newer than London. But then the letter came with its rich, velvety paper and the four stamped eglantine roses on the envelope. Gwendolyn felt her fingers shaking as she opened it.

It regretted to inform her of the passing of Lady Sirith of Hardwick Hall, twentieth Duchess of Shrewsbury, Patron of the Silver Garter, and a list of other titles that Gwendolyn only half-remembered. It was customary for a member of the family to sit in mourning at the manor and as she had no living family, the duchess requested that Gwendolyn do the necessary duties. Of course, continued the letter in a quite majestic manner, the terms of her bequest were *quite clear* and should Gwendolyn not arrive in three days' time, she would be required to pay back the sum spent on her education.

Cindy pooh-poohed and turned up her tiny mouth in a moue when Gwendolyn shared the news. "What an old bitch," she said, "threatening to make you pay all that money. It's just as well she's in the worm trough."

Gwendolyn nodded her head, but kept silent. The four roses had sparked a long-neglected sense of familial obligation in her, and she thought that maybe it was proper to visit her mum's grave one last time, to say a proper goodbye, before the government claimed the old manor for a fully renovated heritage center.

Her bags were already packed, so she saw Cindy off to the airport and then rode the Tube (still cramped, still noisy, still flush with warm bodies crowding up against one another) to King's Cross Station where she boarded a train heading to Derbyshire.

Gwendolyn stared out the window, fidgeting sometimes, watching the rolling hills and quilted landscape with increasing apprehension, and asking all the kinds of questions young people ask when they go home again. Would Damien still be there, carrying toffee in his pocket for all those long years, just in case she returned? Would she still know the stones, the places to avoid on the stairs, the tricky bumps on the floor? Would the air smell the same, the sun cast its light just so, the tourists still flash their cameras and chatter on with noisy, Yankee excitement? But most of all, would the roses still grow straighter and brighter on the south wall than anywhere else in the garden? They were warm thoughts, sad thoughts, and when her mascara began to run, Gwendolyn wiped her face raw.

When she pulled into the station, Damien met her with a car from the estate. He looked nervous, picked at the dirt on his clothes with broad, flat fingers and smiled hastily, before averting his eyes away from her. He spoke a little on the ride to the manor house of inconsequential things, little threads that wound around Gwendolyn, picking out her absence, not with cruelty, but with a thousand stories resumed midway whose characters were no longer familiar.

"And the ghosts?" Gwendolyn asked at one point. Damien only looked at her queerly and pursed his lips.

Finally, the car turned past the property fence, sped past the visitor car park, and arrived at the gates. "Your dress looks quite pretty." He smiled almost shyly. "New London fashion, I'd be guessing." Then he was tipping his hat ever so slightly, as if he couldn't decide if she were family or royalty, before disappearing entirely.

Gwendolyn walked the grounds like a nervous cat, feet delicately treading the path. She tiptoed past the lavender and lilac, remarked at the blush of poppies that had sprouted at odd intervals along the sides of the path, and finally turned the corner, past the old wrought-iron bench where honeymooners liked to get their picture taken, towards the south wall.

She was relieved to see that Damien had spent most of his efforts there. Even if the rest of the gardens looked a little shabbier, a little wilder than she had last seen them, the roses on the south wall still bloomed like giant, delicate clouds in hues that ranged from pink to orange-edged cream and yellow. They were beautiful, and looking at them, Gwendolyn felt tears welling up and she was glad the mascara was gone, that it couldn't make a dark muddle of her face.

And at last, Damien returned to take her to see the duchess.

The light was just starting to fade from the Blue Room, best beloved, leaving half- glimmers of turquoise and aquamarine like seashells on a beach. The air was warm from the afternoon sun, but there the duchess sat, unaffected, in her favorite seat, threadbare skin revealing the gnarls and whorls of ancient bones in her hands as she worked with a needle and thread at the stitching she always kept with her.

"My lady?" Gwendolyn asked softly, waiting at the door to be acknowledged as she'd been taught once, a long time ago, the proper forms of address feeling as odd as the unlearned French in her mouth.

The old woman's head nodded, and Gwendolyn approached, her feet already beginning to remember the soft give of the rush matting. But then those sad, milky eyes turned on her with a long, terrible stare and she said in a drawn-out, lisping voice that Gwendolyn barely recognized: "*Who are you?*"

I know, love, this is one of the sadder parts. So you may hold my hand if you wish, if that might make it easier for you to hear.

So. The duchess. She demanded of Damien in her lisping, stranger voice: "I don't know who this woman is. Why is she here?" The hands continued to work at the cloth, and Gwendolyn looked down to watch the threads unraveling, yes, just so, one by one, as she pulled at them, leaving only little holes in the silk where the needle had bound them in.

"My children lay unborn in a dead woman's womb, my brother's children unburied in the North Sea, at Normandy, on the banks. I asked for my blood, my bones, the children of my ancestors. *Who is this one?*"

And Damien replied: "It's Gwendolyn, my lady. I'm sorry."

At hearing her name, Gwendolyn turned behind her, but her gaze was blinded by a bolt of blue, the last light of the dying sun. She couldn't see the old cowherd's face.

"She is nothing. She wears strange clothes, speaks with a strange tongue. She is none of mine."

And, oh, best beloved, pick, pick, pick went her fingers until the cloth practically fell apart in her hands.

Gwendolyn felt something unraveling inside her, and though she knew it was *she* who had made herself the stranger, it hurt terribly to be recognized as such. She fled the room, stumbling past Damien and down the uneven stairs, half tripping, half leaping until her toes touched gravel, and beyond that, the soft grass of the gardens. And there, she stood, by the south wall, sobbing, while the roses quavered around her in the breeze.

She wasn't alone then, no, Damien stood beside her. "The dead are a hard lot," he said. His face looked sad. "They've been picking the place apart like vultures since you left."

But in that moment he was neither father nor grandfather enough to comfort her. "There aren't any ghosts in London," Gwendolyn whispered. And then: "I don't want any more ghosts."

"I know, love." He said softly, and his hands were as cold and chilly as any dead man's when he touched her.

Afterward: "You'll be leaving in the morning then?"

"Yes. But I must sit my vigil first. Blood or no blood."

Vultures, Damien had called them, best beloved, picking apart the seams of things. Gwendolyn saw it everywhere. The tables lay in pieces in the games room, the joints torn out, the curtains frayed to rags and trailing threads where they brushed the floor, the library littered with pages, paper from the new books—the history ones Duchess Hardwick collected from the Folio Society—and parchment from the very old ones, which had not been sent off to the Bodleian to pay the death duties over the last generations. The place smelt musty, and the flakes of gilt and paint glittered in the air.

This was what the ghosts had done. This was what ghosts *were*, my love—decay, ruination, things falling apart, coming undone, the terrible passage of time.

Gwendolyn felt an awful longing for the city, the ache that comes into the heart of all young people who leave and come home and wish they could leave again. But Gwendolyn could not leave. There was duty still to be done. The vigil.

And so, with a heavy heart, she took up the old duties once again—to clean, to mend, to care for—and Gwendolyn began to pick up the pages, to shuffle them back into the correct sequence, often squinting at the pencil folio notes in the corners made by visiting scholars to make sure she got it as correct as possible. She set the pages between the wooden boards in which they had originally been bound. She tried to forgive the ghosts for the destruction of her home and the bright, wondrous things she had loved as a child. She tried not to hate them.

It was only when she found the body of poor, dead Montague—flies crawling around the place where his stomach had been ripped open—that she began to recognize the queer feeling in the pit of her stomach as fear.

Ghosts could be something else, she remembered. They were not always kind.

Gwendolyn knelt beside the poor beast—hush now, darling, I know, I know, but it is how it happened in the story—and she stroked his once-silky coat, and said gentle things to him about loyalty and love. She unbuckled the collar from around his neck, and carried his body out to the garden to bury.

There was a spade lying by the south wall, where the roses grew straight and bright, as if one among them at least had known what ought to be done. She had not done much physical labor during her time in London, and her arms had forgotten much of their strength. By the end, her back ached, and dirt lined the insides of her fingernails. But, there, in front of her, was a hole approximately three feet by three feet. She feared digging deeper. She did not want to disturb the roses.

She laid Montague's limp body in the ground, and scattered the petals of four roses over top. It hurt her to pluck them, but she thought there ought to be something beautiful to mark the grave, even if he was just a dog.

The ghosts had gathered to watch. They wore silks and velvets, jewels in their hair and some of them had weapons buckled to their sides. They were beautiful and aristocratic, with faces that bore some resemblance to the duchess, but, their fingers—oh, my darling!—their fingers were *red*, and there was something wild in their eyes.

They parted, albeit angrily and with brooding looks, when she started on the path back into the manor, but part they did for she was sitting vigil and they knew she was not too be touched.

That night, Gwendolyn labored at putting right all the things in the house. There was much she could not do, but she did as she could. And the ghosts watched. And they muttered. And when they did not mutter they stared at her with their grim eyes and their red, red fingers, until finally Gwendolyn felt something hot and bright flash through her, and it was anger.

"You did this, all of you! You loved this place, protected it for hundreds of years and then you tore it apart. Why? Why?"

At first, there was a long silence.

And then one answered: "We have no kin. We are alone, so very alone."

And another: "To pass the time."

And a third: "There was no one to tell us not to."

And, at last, the duchess spoke: "Because this is a place for the dead. We do not want strangers sleeping in the beds our children slept in, touching our things. I wish this place were dust, and we were dust in our graves, and all the forests of the world rotted down to skeleton leaves."

"You were a kinder person when you were alive," Gwendolyn replied at last.

"You were my closest-to-kin, and you left. It is not for you to judge."

Gwendolyn nodded slowly. Her hands were filthy from mending books, collecting strands of silk for repair, and from digging one lonely grave in the garden. They were servants' hands, calloused, scoured now of polish and perfection; and Gwendolyn knew they were her mother's hands, best beloved, hands that had been bound in service—and love—to this household. And Gwendolyn looked at her hands, and she looked at the hands of the ghosts—red, still, with Montague's blood—and she began to speak:

"In London, there are no ghosts."

Angry stares at that, and bloody fingers twitching. Gwendolyn did not care though. She hated their self-loathing, their spoiled faces, and the cold indifference that had settled into their expressions. Once, they had been a kind of family, familiar, comforting when her mum died. But these were different people, and Gwendolyn hated them. "In London, the dead are buried and gone in a fortnight, and the people ride the Tube every morning to work and every evening home, and they cannot breathe but for the press of bodies around them. In London they eat their dead. They burn them up in cigarettes and automobile crashes and pipe bombs. They screw them away with perfect strangers they despise the next day. They sniff the dead, snort them, inject them into veins. In London, they use up the dead. They feed their bodies to the city that neither loves them nor remembers them. I was happy there. In London. Where they carry around their ghosts inside, and the only harm they can do is to themselves."

And she looked at them, and her gaze was as terrible as theirs.

"I'm going home now."

That was what she said to them, best beloved, to all those dead sons, murdered lovers, and aged monarchs, and she turned away from them and she began to walk. Slowly, carefully, but proudly. Only when she stood last of all before the ghost of Duchess Hardwick—powerful, fierce as a lioness, the way the portraits showed her back before age had bent her spine back in on its self like an old coat hanger—did she stop.

"He loved you," Gwendolyn said. "He loved you without question, and you tore him apart." And there was no ghost for that little dog and Gwendolyn was glad of it. She met the duchess's eyes and they were hard and they were cold—the kind of eyes, best beloved, that command obedience and fear, the kind of eyes that order death, the kind of eyes that are death's ally—and she stared down those eyes until, at last, it was the duchess who turned away.

"Take us back to the city," she said. "Let the city devour us."

And Gwendolyn nodded.

The ghosts murmured, shook their gory fingers, but the duchess raised her hand and there was nothing more to be said, for she was, perhaps, the greatest of them and also, perhaps, the most terrible.

Then they began to file past Gwendolyn, one by one, the dead sons, the murdered lovers, faces that had comforted her at her mother's funeral, faces she had known from her childhood, faces that had loved her once, in their own way, and she had loved as well. Last came crinkle-eyed Damien, and his fingers were red too, but he kept them hidden in shame.

"Not you," she said, but he shook his head sadly.

"These grounds are no longer mine to keep," he told her. Gently. In the voices of a father, and a grandfather. "And I would like to see the city."

"You wouldn't like it," Gwendolyn said softly. "It's a cruel place for the dead."

"Aye," he said. "Most places are." He made a move to join the others, but stopped. "Care for your mother's grave, love. It is a hard thing to be dead and alone."

Then Gwendolyn really did cry, and they were large, proper tears, the kind you can only cry when family is around. And she sobbed until her nose was red, and her face was a road map of dust trails.

The ghosts took the morning train back to London, and as it snaked its way amongst the hills and clumped villages of the English countryside, Gwendolyn found them on their best behavior. They chatted amiably about the city in their days, meeting Queen Elizabeth and that firebrand Mary, Queen of Scots. How it might have changed, what they had heard about the smog. They seemed happy almost. Excited. Like children going to the fair.

Gwendolyn listened a little, but mostly she sat with Damien and told him all about her life at university. She left out the parts about snogging, because, my darling, that is the way of these things, and besides she thought that maybe he knew all about what growing up meant.

Finally, best beloved—and I know you must be tired, my girl, you have held on for such a long time and you have listened well—they alighted at King's Cross, and one by one the dead sons, and the murdered lovers, and the aged duchess disappeared into the press of people boarding the Tube for work. It would be quick, Gwendolyn knew. The city was a cold, indifferent place. It had eaten all of its own ghosts long ago, and would be hungry for more.

Only Damien remained. Gwendolyn smiled, shy again, afraid, sad. "Will you go too?" she asked.

"Aye, love. It's long past time I did something with these old bones. I've followed that lot around so long, I'll be half-mad without them."

"You could stay," she said.

"I shan't, though. Your heart only has room for one ghost, Gwen, love, and you must keep her safe from the city, and from us."

Gwendolyn nodded, and she reached out to touch him, to offer a final gesture of goodbye—but it was too late, too late as all goodbyes are. Particularly the ones that matter. And when he vanished, it was amongst a group of giggling school girls come to the city for the weekend to celebrate their A-levels.

She knew she was supposed to be sad, but the funny thing was, in the end, she wasn't anymore. The sadness was gone with the ghosts—for that, my best

beloved, is the way of things. It has always been the way of things. The dead
cannot stay. They are decay, ruination. Things falling apart. They cannot stay,
my bright, beautiful girl—my Gwendolyn. My best beloved. But I will tell you
a secret, a secret only I know—the secret that makes this a happy story, after
all, and not a sad one, or a scary one, or even a hurtful one. As Gwendolyn left
King's Cross, she felt a kind of weight settling in her chest, a good weight like
a rosebush anchoring into her stomach and sprouting beautiful blossoms, pink,
orange-tipped, yellow, into the dark spaces inside her.

It is time, best beloved. I have held you and I have loved you, but my fingers
are cold and dead: you cannot hang on to me forever. You are young, as *that*
Gwendolyn was, as her mother was before her, and you are destined for places
that sparkle with their own newness. Those places would devour me. What is
warm and bright for the living is hateful to the dead. It is the way of things.
Always. Even thus. Look once, my love, my little girl, because when you love
someone, and you know you will not see them again, then you *must* look. And
then carry me with you. Inside. Where I can take root and grow. Where my
hands will stay clean.

Helen Marshall is an author, poet, and bibliophile. Her poetry and fiction
have been published in *ChiZine, Paper Crow, Abyss and Apex, Lady Churchill's
Rosebud Wristlet,* and *Tor.com* among others. A collection of her poems—
Skeleton Leaves—was published in 2011 and her collection of short stories—
Hair Side, Flesh Side—was released in 2012. Currently, she is pursuing a PhD
in medieval studies at the University of Toronto.

The bottle was supposed to save the world,
but did just the opposite.

FAKE PLASTIC TREES

Caitlin R. Kiérnan

"You're not sleeping," Max said. "You're still having nightmares about the car. When you're awake, it's what you think about. I'm right, Cody, aren't I?"

"Mostly," I told him, and then neither of us said anything else for a while. We sat together and stared at the ugly red river. It was Max finally spoke up and broke the silence.

"Well, I was thinking," he said, "maybe if you were to write it down. That might help, I was thinking."

"It might not, too," I replied. "I already saw Dr. Lehman twice. I did everything he said, and that didn't help. How's writing it down supposed to help?"

"Well, it might," he said again. "You can't know until you try. Maybe you could get the bad stuff you saw out of your head, like when you eat spoiled food and throwing up helps. See, that's what I'm thinking."

"Maybe you ought to think less, Max. Besides, where am I supposed to get anything to write it on?"

He promptly handed me the nub of a pencil and some paper he'd torn out of the *H–G* volume of an encyclopedia in the Sanctuary library. I yelled at him for going and ruining books when there aren't so many left to ruin.

"Cody, we can always put the pages back when you're done," he said impatiently, like I should have thought of that already without him having to explain it to me. "Only, they'll be better than before, because one side will have your story written on them."

"Who's gonna want to read my story?" I asked.

"Someone might. Someday, someone might. Anyway, that's not the point. Writing it's the point."

Sitting there on the riverbank, listening to him, it began to make sense, but I didn't tell him that, because I didn't feel like letting him know I didn't still think he was full of shit, and because I still don't think I can do this. Just because it's my story doesn't mean I can put it into words like he wants.

"At least try," he said. "Just you take a day or two and give it a go." I told him I had too much to do in the greenhouses, what with the beans and corn coming on ripe, and he said he'd take my shifts and no one would even care because there's so little work right now at pumps and filters in the hydroplant.

"Oh, and while you're at it, put in how things went wrong with the world, so when things get better, people will know how it all happened."

I said that was just dumb. Other people have already written it down, what went wrong. The smart people, the people who weren't four years old on the first day of THE END OF THE WORLD.

I stared at the shiny encyclopedia pages in my hands. If they'd been ripped out of a real encyclopedia, words would already have been printed on both sides, but they were just copies got made right after THE EVENT. See, that's how the olders always talk about it, and they say certain words and phrases like THE BEFORE and THE AFTER and THE EVENT and THE GOO as if they were being said all in capital letters. I stared at the pages, which were at least real paper, made from real wood pulp, and I told him if I do this I get more than a kiss. Max said sure, why not, so long as you're honest, and he kissed me then and told me I was prettier than any of the other girls in Sanctuary (which is bullshit), and then he left me alone at the edge of the river. Which is where I'm sitting now. Sitting, writing, stopping to toss a rock that's still a rock into the sludgy crimson river that isn't still a river because most of the water went FACSIMILE twelve years ago.

The river moves by about as slowly as I'm writing this down, and I count all the way up to fifty-three before the rock (real rock) actually sinks out of sight into the not-water anymore. At least the river still moves. Lots of them went too solid. I've seen rivers that stopped moving almost right after THE EVENT. These days, they just sit there. Red and hard. Not moving, and I've even walked on a couple. Some people call them Jesus Streams. Anyway, I walked all the way across a broad Jesus Stream on a dare. But it wasn't much of a dare since I got a good dose of SWITCH OFF in me right away, back when I was four.

Okay. Fine, Max. So I'm doing this even though it's stupid.

And you better not welch on that bet or I'll kick your ass, hear that? Also, I'm not writing much about what happened. I shouldn't waste my time writing any of that stuff. I don't care what Max says, because that's all down on paper somewhere else. I don't even know most of it, anyway, that EVENT three-quarters of my whole life ago. What I know for sure doesn't take long to set down. I learned what they bother to teach about THE GOO in classes. They don't teach all that much because why bother telling us about THE BEFORE and WHAT WENT WRONG so we got THE EVENT, when what we need to be learning is how to run the hydros and keep the power on, horticulture, medicine, engineering, and keeping the livestock alive (Max's dad used to oversee the rat cages before he was promoted to hydro duty, or Max would still be feeding pellets to rats and mice and guinea pigs). But, okay, Max:

This Is What They Teach You

Twelve years ago, in THE BEFORE, there were too many people in the world, and most of them were starving. There wasn't enough oil. There wasn't enough clean water. There wasn't enough of much of anything because people kept having babies almost as fast as the rats do. They'd almost used up everything. There were wars (we don't have those anymore, just the rovers and sneaks), and there were riots and terrorists. There were diseases we don't have anymore. People started dying faster than anyone could hope to bury them, so they just piled up. I can't imagine that many people.

Ma'am Shen says there were more than nine billion people back then, but sometimes I think she surely exaggerates.

Anyway, in the year 2048, in a LOST PLACE called Boston, in a school the olders call MIT, scientists were trying to solve all these problems, all of them at once. Maybe other scientists in other parts of the world at some other schools and some of THE COMPANIES were also trying, but SWITCH ON happened at MIT in Boston, which was in a place called New England. SWITCH ON, says Ma'am Shen, started out in a sort of bottle called a beaker. It gets called THE CRUCIBLE sometimes, and also SEAL 7, that one particular bottle. But I'll just call it the bottle.

Before I started writing this part, I made Max go back to the library and copy down some words and numbers for me on the back of one of these pages. I don't want to sound more ignorant than I am, and it's the least he could do. So, in the bottle, inside a lead box, were two things: a nutrient culture and nano-assemblers, which were microscopic machines. The assemblers used the culture to make copies of themselves. Idea was, make a thing you could eat that continuously made copies of itself, there'd be plenty enough food. And maybe this would also work with medicine and fuel and building materials and everything nine billion people needed. But the assemblers in the bottle were a TRIAL.

So no one was sure what would happen. They made THE GOO, which Max's notes call polyvinyl chloride, PVC, but I'll call it plastic, 'cause that's what it's always called when people talk about it.

People don't talk about it much, though I think they might have back before the SWITCH OFF really started working.

Okay, lost my train of thought.

Oh, right. The bottle at MIT. The bottle that was supposed to save the world, but did just the opposite. The assemblers (or so say Max's notes, and I can hardly read his handwriting) during the TRIAL were just four at the start, and four of them made four more of them. Those eight, though, because the production was exponential, made eight more assemblers. Thirty-six made seventy-two made 144 made 288 made 576 copies, then 1,152, 2,304, 4,608, and this was just in one hour. In a day, there were . . .

I don't know, Max didn't write that part down.

The assemblers went ROGUE and obviously the bottle wasn't big enough to hold them. Probably not after a few million, I'm thinking. It shattered, and they got out of the lead box, and, lo and behold, they didn't need the culture to make copies of themselves.

Just about anything would do. Glass (the bottle). Stone. Metal (the lead box). Anything alive. Water, like the river. Not gases, so not air.

Not water vapor, which is one reason we're not all dead. The other reason, of course, is SWITCH OFF, which was made at another lab, and that one was in another LOST PLACE called France. People got injected with SWITCH OFF, and it was sprayed from the air in planes, and then bombs of SWITCH OFF were dropped all over. THE EVENT lasted two weeks. When it was more or less over, an estimated seventy-eight percent of the global biomass and a lot of the seas, rivers, streams, and the earth's crust had stopped being what it was before and had become plastic. Oh, not all crimson, by the way. I don't know why, but lots of different colors.

I didn't know all these numbers and dates. Max's notes. What I know: my parents died in THE EVENT, my parents and all my family, and I was evacuated to Sanctuary here in Florida on the shores of the St. Johns crimson plastic river. I don't think much more than that matters about THE EVENT. So this is where I'm gonna stop trying to be like the vandalized encyclopedia and tell the other story instead.

The story that's *my* story.

Isn't that what Max wanted me to start with?

My Story
(Cody Hernandez's Story)

I'm discovering, Max, that I can't tell my story without telling lots of other little stories along the way.

Like what happened the day that's still giving me the bad dreams, that was almost a year ago, which means it was about five years after most of the Army and the National Guard soldiers left us here because all of a sudden there were those radio transmissions from Atlanta and Miami, and they went off to bring other survivors back to Sanctuary. Only, they never brought anyone back, because they never came back, and we still don't know what happened to them. This is important to my story, because when the military was here with us, they kept a checkpoint and barricades on the east side of the big bridge over the St. Johns River, the Sanctuary side. But after they left, no one much bothered to man the checkpoint anymore, and the barricades stopped being anything more than a chain-link fence with a padlocked gate.

So, the story of the Army and National Guard leaving to find those people, I had to get that out to get to my story. Because I never would have been able to climb over the fence if they hadn't left. Or if they'd left but come back. They'd have stopped me. Or I'd probably never even have thought about climbing over.

Back in THE BEFORE, the bridge was called the Mathews Bridge. Back in THE BEFORE, Sanctuary wasn't here, and where it is was part of a city called Jacksonville. Now, though, it's just the bridge, and this little part of Jacksonville is just Sanctuary. About a third of the way across the bridge, there's an island below it. I have no idea if the island ever had a name. It's all plastic now, anyway, like most of the bridge. A mostly brown island in a crimson river below a mostly brown plastic bridge. Because of what the sunlight and weather do to polyvinyl chloride—twelve years of sunlight and weather—chunks of the bridge have decayed and fallen away into the slow crimson river that runs down to the mostly-still-crimson sea. The island below the bridge used to be covered with brown plastic palmetto trees and underbrush, but now isn't much more than a scabby-looking lump. The plastic degrades and then crumbles and is finally nothing but dust that the wind blows away.

I wanted to know what was on the other side. It's as simple as that.

I considered asking Max to go with me, Max and maybe one or two others. Maybe the twins, Jessie and Erin (who are a year older than me and Max), maybe Beth, too. There are still all the warning signs on the fence, the ones the military put there. But people don't go there. I suspect it reminds them of stuff from THE BEFORE that they don't want to be reminded of, like how this is the only place to live now. How there's really nowhere else to ever go. Which might be why none of the olders had ever actually *told* me to stay away from the bridge. Maybe it simply never occurred to them I might get curious, or that any of us might get curious.

"What do you think's over there?" I asked Max, the day I almost asked him to come with me. We were walking together between the river and some of the old cement walls that used to be buildings. I remember we'd just passed the wall where, long time ago, someone painted the word NOWHERE. Only, they (or somebody else) also painted a red stripe between the *W* and the *H*, so it says NOW HERE, same as it says NOWHERE.

"Nothing," he replied. "Nothing's over there anymore," and Max shaded his eyes from the bright summer sun. Where we were, it's less than a mile across the river. It's still easy to make out where the docks and cranes used to be. "You can see for yourself, Cody. Ain't nothing over there except what the goo left."

Which is to say, there's nothing over there.

"You never wonder about it, though?"

"Why would I? Besides, the bridge ain't safe to cross anymore." Max pointed south to the long span of it. Lots of the tall trusses, which used to be steel, have dropped away into the sludgy river a hundred and fifty feet below. Lots of the roadway, too. "You'd have to be crazy to try. And since there's nothing over there, you'd have to be extra crazy. You know what suicide is, right?"

"I think about it sometimes, is all. Not suicide, just finding out what's over there."

"Same damn difference," he said. "Anyway, we ought'a be getting back." He turned away from the river and the bridge, the island and the other side of the river. So that's why I didn't ask Max to cross the bridge with me. I knew he'd say no, and I was pretty sure he'd tell one of the olders, and then someone would stop me. I followed him back to the barracks, but I knew by then I was definitely going to climb the chain-link fence and cross the bridge.

Oh, I almost forgot, and I want to put this in, write down what I can recall of it. On the way home, we came across Mr. Benedict.

He was sitting on a rusty barrel not far from the NOW|HERE wall. In THE BEFORE, Mr. Benedict—Mr. Saul Benedict—was a physicist. He's one of our teachers now, though he isn't well and sometimes misses days. Max says something inside his head is broken. Something in his mind, but that he isn't exactly crazy.

Anyway, there he was on the barrel. He's one of the few olders who ever talks much about THE GOO. That afternoon, he said hello to me and Max, but he had that somewhere-else tone to his voice. He sounded so distant, distant in time or in place. I don't know. We said hello back. Then he pointed to the bridge, and that sort of made me shudder, and I wondered if he'd noticed us staring at it. He couldn't have overheard us; we were too far away.

"It doesn't make sense," he said.

"What doesn't make sense?" Max asked him.

"It should have fallen. Steel and concrete, that's one thing.

Iron, steel, precompressed concrete, those materials, fine. But after the bots were done with it . . . that bridge, it should have collapsed under its own weight, even though, obviously, its not nearly as heavy or dense now as it was before. Plastic could never bear the load."

This is the thing about Saul Benedict: he asks questions no one ever asks, questions I don't understand half the time. If you let him, he'll go on and on about how something's not right about our understanding of THE EVENT, how the science doesn't add up right. I've heard him say the fumes from the outgassing plastic should have killed us all years ago. And how the earth's mass would have been changed radically by the nano-assemblers, which would have altered gravity. How lots of the atmosphere would have been lost to space when gravity changed. And how plate tectonics would have come to a halt. Lots of technical science stuff like that, some of which I have to go to the library to find out what he means.

I'm pretty sure very few people bother to consider whether or not Mr. Benedict is right. Maybe not because they believe the questions are nonsense, but because no one needs more uncertainty than we have already. I'm not even sure I spend much time on whether or not he's making sense. I just look up words to see what the questions mean.

"But it *hasn't* fallen down," Max protested, turning back toward the bridge. "Well, okay. Some pieces broke off, but not the whole bridge."

"That's just the problem," Mr. Benedict said. "It hasn't fallen down. You do the math. It would have fallen *immediately*."

"Max is terrible at math," I told Mr. Benedict, and he frowned.

"He doesn't apply himself, Cody. You know that don't you, Max? You don't apply yourself. If you did, you'd be an exemplary student."

We told him we were late for chores, said our until laters, and left him sitting on the rusty barrel, muttering to himself.

"Nutty old fart," Max said, and I didn't say anything.

Before I went to cross the bridge, I did some studying up first. In the library, there's a book about the city that used to be Jacksonville, and I sat at one of the big tables and read about the Mathews Bridge. It was built in 1953, which made it exactly one hundred years old last year. But what mattered was that it's about a mile and a half across. One morning, I talked Mr. Kleinberg at the garage into lending me his stopwatch, and I figured out I walk about three miles an hour, going at an easy pace. Not walking fast or jogging, just walking. So, barring obstructions, if I could go straight across, it would only take me about half an hour. Half an hour across, half an hour back. Maybe poke about on the other side (which, by the way, used to be called Arlington) for a couple of hours, and I'd be back before anyone even noticed I'd gone. For all I knew, other kids had already done it. Even more likely, some of the olders.

I picked the day I'd go—July 18, which was on a Friday. I'd go right after my morning chores, during late-morning break, and be sure to be back by lunch. I didn't tell Max or anyone else. No one would ever be the wiser. I filled a canteen and I went.

It was easy getting over the fence. There isn't any barbed wire, like on some of the fences around Sanctuary. I snagged my jeans on the sharp twists of wire at the top, but only tore a very small hole that would be easy to patch. On the other side, the road's still asphalt for about a hundred yards or so, before the plastic begins.

Like I said, I'd walked on THE GOO before, so I knew what to expect. It's very slightly springy, and sometimes you press shallow footprints into it that disappear after a few minutes. On the bridge, there was the fine dust that accumulates as the plastic breaks down.

Not as much as I'd have expected, but probably that's because the wind blows it away. But there were heaps of it where the wind couldn't reach, piled like tiny sand dunes. I left footprints in the dust that anyone could have followed.

I glanced back over my shoulder a few times, just to be certain no one was following me. No one was. I kept to the westbound lane. There were cracks in the roadway, in what once had been cement. Some were hardly an inch, but others a foot or two across and maybe twice as deep, so I'd have to jump over those. I skirted the places where the bridge was coming apart in chunks, and couldn't help but think about what all Mr. Benedict had said. It shouldn't be here. None of it should still be here, but it is. So what don't we know? How *much* don't we know?

I walked the brown bridge, and on either side of me, far below, the lazy crimson St. Johns River flowed. I walked, and a quarter of a mile from the fence, I reached the spot where the bridge spans the island. I went to the guardrail and peered over the edge. I leaned against the rail, and it cracked loudly and dropped away. I almost lost my balance and tumbled down to the crimson river. I stepped back, trying not to think about what it would be like to slowly sink and drown in that. . . .

And I thought about turning around and heading back. From this point on, I constantly thought about going back, but I didn't. I walked a little faster than before, though, suddenly wanting to be done with this even if I still felt like I had to *do* it.

I kept hearing Max talking inside my head, saying what he'd said, over and over again.

Since there's nothing over there, you'd have to be extra crazy.
You know what suicide is, right?
Ain't nothing over there except what THE GOO left.

It took me a little longer to reach the halfway point than I thought it would, than my three-miles-an-hour walking had led me to believe it would. It was all the cracks, most likely. Having to carefully jump them, or find ways around them. And I kept stopping to gaze out and marvel at the ugly wasteland THE GOO had made of the land beyond the Mathews Bridge. I don't know if there's a name for the middle of a bridge, the highest point of a bridge. But it was right about the time I reached that point that I spotted the car. It was still pretty far off, maybe halfway to the other end. It was skewed sideways across the two eastbound lanes, on the other side of the low divider that I'm sure used to be concrete but isn't anymore.

But all the cars were cleared off the bridge by the military years ago. They were towed to the other side or pushed into the crimson river. There weren't supposed to be any cars on the bridge. But here was this one. The sunlight glinted off yellow fiberglass and silver chrome, and I could tell the nano-assemblers hadn't gotten hold of it, that it was still made of what the factory built it from. And I had two thoughts, one after the other: Where did this car come from? And, Why hasn't anyone noticed it? The second thought was sort of silly because it's not like anyone really watches the bridge, not since most of the Army and National Guard went away.

Then I thought, How long's it been there? And, Why didn't it come all the way across? And, What happened to the driver? All those questions in my head, I was starting to feel like Saul Benedict. It was an older car, one of the electrics that were already obsolete by the time THE EVENT occurred.

"Cody, you go back," I said out loud, and my voice seemed huge up there on the bridge. It was like thunder. "You go back and tell someone. Let them deal with this."

But then I'd have to explain what I was doing way out on the bridge alone.

Are you enjoying this, Max? I mean, if I've let you read it. If I did, I hope to hell you're enjoying it, because I'm already sweating, drops of sweat darkening the encyclopedia pages. Right now I feel like that awful day on the bridge. I could stop now. I could turn back now. I could. I won't, but I *could*. Doesn't matter. I'll keep writing, Max, and you'll keep reading.

I kept walking. I didn't turn back, like a smarter girl would have done. A smarter girl who understood it was more important to tell the olders what I'd found than to worry about getting in trouble for being out on the bridge. There was a strong gust of wind, warm from the south, and the dust on the bridge was swept up so I had to partly cover my face with my arm. But I could see the tiny brown dust devils swirling across the road.

Right after the wind, while the dust was still settling, I came to an especially wide crack in the roadway. It was so wide and deep, and when I looked down, the bottom was hidden in shadow. It didn't go all the way through, or I'd not have been able to see down there. I had to climb over the barricade into the eastbound lane, into the lane with the car, to get around it. I haven't mentioned the crumbling plastic seagulls I kept finding. Well, I figured they'd been seagulls. They'd been birds, and were big enough to have been seagulls. They littered the bridge, birds that died twelve years ago when I was four. Once I was only, I don't know, maybe twenty-five yards from the car, I stopped for a minute or two. I squinted, trying to see inside, but the windows were tinted and I couldn't make out anything at all in there.

The car looked so shiny and new. No way it had been sitting out in the weather very long. There weren't even any pieces of the plastic girders lying on it, no dents from decayed and falling GOO, so it was a newcomer to the bridge, and I think that scared me most of all. By then, my heart was pounding—thumping like mad in my chest and ears and even the tip ends of my fingers—and I was sweating. Not the normal kinda sweat from walking, but a cold sweat like when I wake up from the nightmares of this day I'm writing about. My mouth was so, so dry. I felt a little sick to my belly, and wondered if it was breathing in all that dust.

"No point in stopping now," I said, maybe whispering, and my voice was huge out there in all the empty above and below and around the Mathews Bridge. "So when they ask what I found, I can tell them all of it, not just I found a car on the bridge." I considered the possibility that it might have been rovers, might be a trap. Them lying there in wait until someone takes the bait, then they ask for supplies to let me go. We hadn't seen rovers—looters—in a year or so, but that didn't mean they weren't still out there, trying to get by on the scraps of nothing they found and whatever they could steal. Lower than the sneaks, the rovers. At least the sneaks never kill anyone. They just slip in and rob you when no one's looking. Ma'am Shen says they're all insane, and I expect that's the truth of it. I wished I'd brought a knife (I have a lock-blade I keep in my footlocker), but that was dumb, 'cause rovers carry guns and bows and shit. What good's a knife for a fifteen-year-old girl out on her own, so exposed she might as well be naked. No chance but to turn around and run if things went bad.

I shouted, "Anybody in there?" At the very top of my voice I shouted it. When no one answered, I shouted again, and still nobody answered me. I hadn't thought they would, but it didn't hurt to try.

"You don't need to be scared of me," I called out. "And I ain't got nothing worth stealing." Which I knew was dumb because if it was rovers they wouldn't be after what I *had* on my person, but what they could get for me.

No one called back, and so I started walking again.

Pretty soon, I was close enough I could make out the plates on the front of the vehicle—Alabama, which we all thought was another LOST PLACE, since that's what the Army guys had told us. On the map of what once was the United States hanging on the wall in the library, Alabama was colored in red, like all the LOST PLACES (which is most of the map). But here was a car from Alabama, and it couldn't have been sitting on the bridge very long at all, not and still be so shiny and clean. Maybe I counted my footsteps after shouting and not getting an answer, but if so, I can't remember how many I took.

There was another southerly gust, and more swirling dust devils, and this time the bridge seemed to sway just a little, which didn't make my stomach feel any better.

Then I was finally at the car. Up close, it was a little dirtier than it had seemed from far away. There were a few dents and dings, a little rust, but nothing more than that. None of the tires were even flat. I stared at the tinted windows and waited for rovers to jump out and point their weapons at me, but that didn't happen. For the first time, I considered the possibility that the doors might all be locked, and I didn't even have anything to break out the windows.

I looked past the car at the ruins of Arlington, and considered just sticking to my plan, forget the car for now, poke around over there a bit, then head home again. And yeah, tell the olders about the car and take whatever punishment I'd have coming.

I leaned forward, peering in through the glass, but the tinting was too dark even right up on it like that. I gripped the driver's side door handle, and it was very hot from the Florida sun. It was hot enough I almost pulled my hand back, but only almost. Instead, I gave it a quick twist to the left, and the tumblers clicked. Which meant it wasn't locked after all.

I took a deep breath and pulled up on the door. It came open easy as pie—like the olders say. It lifted, rising above my head, above the roof. The hinges didn't even squeak. There was only a soft whoosh from hydraulics and pistons. Scalding air spilled out of the car.

You know exactly what I found in there, Max? It seems wicked to write it down on these "borrowed" encyclopedia pages. It seems wrong, but I'll do it anyhow. Just in case you're right, because yeah, I want the dreams to stop. Dead people don't have dreams.

Dead people probably don't have anything at all, so it's stupid me worrying like this, hesitating and drawing it out.

The door opened, and there were two people inside.

There was what was left of two people.

Like the might-have-been seagulls, THE GOO had gotten to them, and they were that same uniform shade of bluish green all live things go when the nano-assemblers get hold of them.

I stepped back immediately and turned my head away. I even thought I might puke. It's not that I'd never seen a person who'd died that way; it's just I hadn't seen any in a long, long time, and you forget. Or I'd forgotten. I covered my mouth, not wanting to be sick and have to see my half-digested breakfast spattered all over the road at my feet. I leaned forward, hands on knees, and took deep breaths and counted to thirty. Someone taught me to do that whenever I'm afraid I might be about to throw up, count to thirty, but I can't remember who it was. Not that it matters.

When I felt a little better, 1 looked again. The woman was sitting with her back to the door, and her arms were wrapped tightly around the gift. The woman's fingers disappeared into the gift's hair—hair and hand all one and the same now. I figured they drove as far as they could, drove until they were too far gone to keep going. It takes hours and hours for the infected to die. Like the seagulls, the weather hadn't been at them, and the woman and the gift looked like they'd just been popped fresh out of a mold, like the molds they use in the machine shop to turn non-GOO plastic into stuff we need. Every single detail, no matter how fragile, was still intact. Their plastic eyebrows, each hair, their eyes open and staring nowhere at all. Their skin was almost exactly the color of Ma'am Lillian's teal-zircon pendant. Only completely opaque instead of translucent.

Their clothes and their jewelry (I noticed the woman's silver earrings), those hadn't changed at all. But it didn't strike me odd until later, like the car being okay didn't really strike me odd, though it should have.

I still felt dizzy even if the first shock of seeing them was fading. Even if I was just seeing them now, not seeing them and wanting to run away. I reached inside the car and touched the back of the woman's neck. I shouldn't have, but I did. It was just a little bit tacky from the heat, a little soft, and I left fingerprints behind.

I thought, You leave them out here long enough, shut up and baking inside that car, they'll melt away to shapeless globs long before the plastic has a chance to get brittle. I thought that, and pulled my hand back. I was relieved to see none of the PVC had come off on my fingers. But I rubbed them on my jeans anyway. I rubbed until it's a wonder my skin didn't start bleeding.

They looked like dolls.

They looked almost like the mannequins in the busted shop windows inside Sanctuary.

But they'd both been alive, flesh and bone and breathing, and it couldn't have been more than a few days before. A week at the most. I stared at them. I wondered which of them died first. I wondered lots of stuff there's not much point writing down. Then I glanced into the backseat. And right then, that's when I thought my heart my might stop, just stop beating like the girl's and the woman's had finally stopped beating. There was a cardboard box in the back, and there was a baby in a blanket inside the box. I don't know how the hell it was still alive, how it had been spared by THE GOO or by the heat inside the car, but it was still alive. It looked at me. I saw it was sick, from the broiling day trapped in the automobile, but goddamn it was alive. It saw me and began to bawl, so I rushed around to the other side of the car and opened that door, too. I lifted the cardboard box out careful as I could and set it on the bridge, and then I sat down next to it. I screwed the lid off my canteen and sprinkled water on its forehead and lips. I finally pushed back the blanket and took the baby in my arms. I'd never, ever held a baby. We don't have many in Sanctuary. And the ones we do have, the dozen or so, not just any kid can go picking them up. Just the mothers and fathers, the nurses and doctors. The baby's face was so red, like she'd been roasting alive in there, so I sprinkled more water on its cheeks and forehead. It's eyes were glassy, feverish, and it didn't cry as loudly as I thought it should have been crying. I sat there and rocked it, shushing it, the way I'd seen people do with babies. I sat there trying to remember a lullaby.

No need to draw this part out, Max.

The baby, she died in my arms. She was just too hot, and I'd come along too late to save her from the sun. Maybe me sprinkling the water on her had been too much. Maybe just seeing me had been too much. Maybe she just picked then to die. And I wanted to cry, but I didn't. I don't know why. I knew I ought to, and I still know I ought to have, but I just sat there holding her close to me like she wasn't dead. Like she was only asleep and was gonna wake up. I sat there staring at the blue-green plastic people in the front seat, at the sky, at the car.

In my bad dreams, there are wheeling, screeching gulls in that blue-white sky, and it goes on forever, on out into space, into starry blackness, down to blue skies on other worlds without women and men and youngers, where none of these things have ever happened and where THE EVENT hasn't occurred and THE GOO will never reach. Where it's still THE BEFORE, and will never be THE AFTER.

God and Jesus and angels and a day of judgment of wicked men, they all live and breathe inside the Reverend Swales's black book, and in the songs we sing on Sundays. Many other gods and devils live in other holy books. But on the bridge that day, there was no god. In my dreams, there is no god. And I don't pray anymore. I don't think much of those who do.

You're saying, Now that's not what happened, Cody. I can hear you, Max. I can hear you grumbling, plain as day, "Cody Marlene Hernandez, you're mixing it all up, and you're doing it on purpose. That wasn't the deal, you welcher."

Fine, you win.

I scrounged about and found a couple of other things inside the cardboard box. I hardly looked at them, just stuffed them into my pack. Carrying the dead baby in her blanket, I walked back across the bridge, quickly as I could, quicker than I'd come. It was a lot harder getting over the fence with her in my arms, but I managed. I didn't drop her. I'd have fallen before I ever dropped her.

I spent a week in quarantine, just in case. Five men went out onto the bridge and brought back the plastic woman and the girl and buried them in the cemetery. They buried the baby there, too, after Doc Lehman did his autopsy. No one ever scolded me or yelled or revoked privileges for going out there. I didn't have to ask why. You get punished, you don't have to get punished all over again.

What I'm Writing Down Later

Me and Max sat between the crimson river and the NOW|HERE wall, and I let him read what I wrote on the back of the torn-out encyclopedia pages. He got pissed near the end, and just like I thought he would, called me a welcher.

"The baby always dies in my dreams," I told him, when he finally shut up and let me talk again.

"I didn't say, 'Write what's in your dreams.' I said, 'Write what happened.'"

"It seemed more important," I told him, and tossed a piece of gravel at the river. "What haunts me when I sleep, how it might have gone that day, but didn't. How it probably *should* have gone, but didn't."

"Yeah, but you went and killed that baby."

"No I didn't. My nightmares kill the baby, not me. Almost every time I sleep, the nightmares kill the baby."

He chewed his lip the frustrated way he does sometimes.

"Cody, I just ain't never gonna understand that. You *saved* the baby, but you go and have bad dreams about the baby dyin'. That's stupid. You waste all this energy gettin' freaked out about something didn't even happen except in a dream, and dreams ain't real. I thought writin' the truth, *that* would make you better. Not writing down lies. That's what I don't understand."

"You weren't there. You didn't hold her, and her so hot, and you so sure she was already dead or would be dead any second."

"I just won't ever understand it," he said again.

"Okay, Max. Then you won't ever understand it. That's fair.

There's a lot about myself I don't understand sometimes. Doesn't matter the dreams don't make sense. Only matters it happens to me. It's all too complicated. Never black-and-white, not like SWITCH ON and SWITCH OFF, not like THE BEFORE and THE AFTER. I fall asleep, and she dies in my arms, even though she didn't."

He glared at the pages, chewing his lips and looking disgusted, then handed them back to me.

"Well, you don't win," he said. "You don't get any more than kisses 'cause you didn't even talk about the map or the book, and because you killed the baby."

"I don't care," I replied, which was true.

"I was just trying to help you."

"I know that, Max. Don't you think I know that?" He didn't answer my question. Instead, he said, "I'm going home, Cody. I got chores. So do you, welcher." I told him I'd be along soon. I told him I needed to be alone for a while (which is when I'm writing this part down). So I'm sitting here throwing gravel at the sludgy crimson river people used to call the St. Johns River.

What Really Happened
(For Max)

Outside my dreams, the baby didn't die. The olders figured the car had only driven through Arlington and out onto the bridge the night before I found it. They guessed the girl and the woman got sick a couple of days before that, probably before they even got to Florida. They figured, too, the baby would have died of heat prostration and thirst if I hadn't found it when I did. "You did right," Ma'am Shen whispered in my ear when no one was watching or listening in. "Even if that wasn't your intent, you did right." We never found out the baby's name, so they named it Cody, after me.

The olders found something in the baby's blood. It's like SWITCH OFF, they say, but it's different. It's like SWITCH OFF, but it works better. You breathe it out, and it shuts off the nano-assemblers all around you. Maybe, they say, that's why the car didn't change, and why the woman and the girl's clothes and jewelry wasn't converted, too. But these new bots, they can't turn stuff back the way it was before.

And yeah, there was a map. A map of the United States and Mexico and

Canada. Most of the cries had big red X's drawn on them. Montreal, up in Canada, had a blue circle, and so did San Francisco and a few little towns here and there. A red line was drawn from Birmingham, Alabama all the way to Pensacola. Both those cities had red X's of their own. I found the red pencil in the box with the baby. And I found pages and pages of notes. In the margins of the map, there was a list of countries. Some in red, some in blue.

Turns out the woman was a microbiologist, and she'd been studying when the sanctuary in Birmingham was breached. That's what she'd written in her notes. They read us that part in class.

"The containment has been breached." I also know the notes talk about the nanites evolving, and about new strains the SWITCH OFF doesn't work on, and new strains of SWITCH OFF that shut down THE GOO better than before, like what kept the baby alive. They know the scientist also wrote about how THE EVENT isn't over because the bots are all evolving and doing things they weren't designed to do.

Of course, they also weren't designed to eat up the whole world, but they did.

Saul Benedict still frowns and asks his questions, and he says everything's even more uncertain than it was before I found the car.

But me, I look at that baby, who's growing up fine and healthy and breathing those new bots out with every breath, and sometimes I think about going out onto the bridge again with a can of spray paint and writing *HOPE HERE* in great big letters on the side of the car. So if maybe someone else ever comes along, someone who isn't sick, they'll see, and drive all the way across the bridge.

The *New York Times* recently hailed **Caitlín R. Kiernan** as "one of our essential writers of dark fiction." Her novels include *The Red Tree* (nominated for the Shirley Jackson and World Fantasy awards) and *The Drowning Girl: A Memoir* (winner of the James Tiptree, Jr. Award, nominated for the Nebula, Locus, Shirley Jackson, Mythopoeic, and Bram Stoker awards). To date, her short fiction has been collected in thirteen volumes, most recently *Confessions of a Five-Chambered Heart, Two Worlds and In Between: The Best of Caitlín R. Kiernan (Volume One)*, and *The Ape's Wife and Other Stories*. Currently, she's writing the graphic novel series Alabaster for Dark Horse Comics and working on her next novel, *Red Delicious*.

*He looked out his side window and down and saw the creature running
alongside, the movement of its four legs a blur, its face perfectly human.*

A NATURAL HISTORY OF AUTUMN

Jeffrey Ford

A blue afternoon in autumn, Riku and Michi drove south from Numazu in his
silver convertible along the coast of the Izu Peninsula.

The temperature was mild for the end of October, and the air was clear,
the sun glinting off Suruga Bay. She wore sunglasses and, to protect her hair, a
yellow scarf with a design of orange butterflies. He wore driving gloves, a black
dress shirt, a loosened white tie. The car, the open road, the rush of the wind
made it impossible to converse, and so for miles she watched the bay to their
right and he the rising slopes of maple and pine to their left. Just outside the
town of Dogashima, a song came on the radio, "Just You, Just Me," and they
turned to look at each other. She waited for him to smile. He did. She smiled
back, and then he headed inland to search for the hidden onsen, Inugami.

They'd met the previous night at The Limit, an upscale hostess bar. Riku's
employer had a tab there and he was free to use it when in Numazu. He'd
been once before, drunk and spent time with a hostess. Her conversation had
sounded rote, like a script; her flattery grotesquely opulent and therefore flat.
The instant he saw Michi, though, in her short black dress with a look of
uncertainty in her eyes, he knew it would be a different experience. He ordered
a bottle of Nikka Yoichi and two glasses. She introduced herself. He stood and
bowed. They were in a private room at a polished table of blond wood. The
chairs were high-backed and upholstered like thrones. To their right was an
open-air view of pines and the coast. She waited for him to smile and eventually
he did. She smiled back and told him, "I'm writing a book."

Riku said, "Aren't you supposed to tell me how handsome I am?"

"Your hair is perfect," she said.

He laughed. "I see."

"I'm writing a book," she said again. "I decided to make a study of
something."

"You're a scientist?" he said.

"We're all scientists," she said. "We watch and listen, take in information, process it. We spin theories by which we live."

"What if they're false?"

"What if they're not?" she said.

He shook his head and took a drink.

They sat in silence for a time. She stared out past the pines, sipping her whisky. He stared at her.

"Tell me about your family," said Riku.

She told him about her dead father, her ill mother, her younger sister and brother, but when she inquired about his parents, he said, "Okay, tell me about your book."

"I decided to study a season, and since autumn is the season I'm in, it would be autumn. It's a natural history of autumn."

"You've obviously been to the university," he said.

She shook her head. "No, I read a lot to pass the time between clients."

"How much have you written?"

"Nothing yet. I'm researching now, taking notes."

"Do you go out to Thousand Tree Beach and stare at Fuji in the morning?"

"Your sarcasm is intoxicating," she said.

He filled her glass

"No, I do my research here. I ask each client what autumn means to him."

"And they tell you?"

She nodded. "Some just want me to say how big their biceps are but most sit back and really think about it. The thought of it makes all the white-haired ojiisans smile, the businessmen cry, the young men a little scared. A lot of it is the same. Just images—the colorful leaves, the clear cold mornings by the Bay, a certain pet dog, a childhood friend, a drunken night. But sometimes they tell me whole stories."

"What kind of stories?"

"A very powerful businessman—one of the other hostesses swore he was a master of the five elements—once told me his own love story, about a young woman he had an affair with. It began on the final day of summer, lasted only as long as the following season, and ended in the snow."

"What did you learn from that story? What did you put in your notes?"

"I recorded his story as he'd told it, and afterward wrote, 'The Story of a Ghost.'"

"Why a ghost?" he asked.

"I forget," she said. "And I lied—I attended Waseda University for two years before my father died."

"You didn't have to tell me," he said. "I knew when you told me you called the businessman's story, 'The Story of a Ghost.'"

"Pretentious?" she asked. He shrugged.

"Maybe . . . " she said and smiled.

"Forget about that," said Riku. "I will top that make-inu businessman's exquisite melancholy by proposing a field trip." He sat forward in his chair and touched the tabletop with his index finger. "My employer recently rewarded me for a job well done and suggested I use, whenever I like, a private onsen he has an arrangement with down in Izu. I need only call a few hours in advance."

"A field trip?" she said. "What will we be researching?"

"Autumn. The red and yellow leaves. The place is out in the woods on a mountainside, hidden and very old-fashioned, no frills. I propose a dohan, an overnight journey to the onsen, Inugami."

"A date," she said. "And our attentions will only be on autumn, nothing else?"

"You can trust me when I say, that is entirely up to you."

"Your hair inspires confidence," she said. "You can arrange things with the house on the way out."

"I intend to be in your book," he said and prevented himself from smiling.

After hours of winding along the rims of steep cliffs and bumping down tight dirt paths through the woods, the silver car pulled to a stop in a clearing, in front of a large, slightly sagging farmhouse—minka style, built of logs with a thatched roof. Twenty yards to the left of the place there was a sizeable garden filled with dying sunflowers, ten-foot stalks, their heads bowed. To the right of the house there was a slate path that led away into the pines. The golden late-afternoon light slanted down on the clearing, shadows beginning to form at the tree line.

"We're losing the day," said Riku. "We'll have to hurry."

Michi got out of the car and stretched. She removed her sunglasses and stood still for a moment, taking in the cool air.

"I have your bag," said Riku and shut the trunk.

As they headed for the house, two figures appeared on the porch. One was a small old woman with white hair, wearing monpe pants and an indigo Katazome jacket with a design of white flames. Next to her stood what Michi at first mistook for a pony. The sight of the animal surprised her and she stopped walking. Riku went on ahead. "Grandmother Chinatsu," he said and bowed.

"Your employer has arranged everything with me. Welcome," she said. A small, wrinkled hand with dirty nails appeared from within the sleeve of the jacket. She beckoned to Michi. "Come, my dear, don't be afraid of my pet, Ono. He doesn't bite." She smiled and waved her arm.

As Michi approached, she bowed to Grandmother Chinatsu, who only offered a nod. The instant the young woman's foot touched the first step of the porch, the dog gave a low growl. The old lady wagged a finger at the creature and snapped, "Yemeti!" Then she laughed, low and gruff, the sound at odds with her diminutive size. She extended her hand and helped Michi up onto the porch. "Come in," she said and led them into the farmhouse.

Michi was last in line. She turned to look at the dog. Its coat was more like curly human hair than fur. She winced in disgust. A large flattened pug face, no snout to speak of, black eyes, sharp ears, and a thick bottom lip bubbling with drool. "Ono," she said and bowed slightly in passing. As she stepped into the shadow beyond the doorway, she felt the dog's nose press momentarily against the back of her dress.

In the main room there was a rock fireplace within which a low flame licked two maple logs. Above hung a large paper lantern, orange with white blossoms, shedding a soft light in the center of the room. The place was rustic, wonderfully simple. All was wood: the walls, the ceiling, the floor. There were three ancient carved wooden chairs gathered around a low table off in an alcove at one side of the room. Grandmother led them down a hallway to the back of the place. They passed a room on the left, its screen shut. At the next room, the old lady slid open the panel and said, "The toilet." Further on, they came to two rooms, one on either side of the hallway. She let them know who was to occupy which by mere nods of her head. "The bath is at the end of the hall," she said.

Their rooms were tatami style, straw mats and a platform bed with a futon mattress in the far corner. Each of them, in turn, quickly cleansed themselves in the bath, and then, putting on robes and sandals, met in the hallway. As they passed through the main room of the house, Ono stirred from his spot by the fireplace, looked up at them, and snorted.

"Easy, easy," said Riku to the creature. He stepped aside and let Michi get in front of him. Once out on the porch, she said, "Ono is a little scary."

"Only a little?" he asked.

Grandmother appeared from within the plot of dying sunflowers and called that there were towels in the shed out by the spring. Riku waved to her as he and Michi took the slate path into the pines. Shadows were rising beneath the trees and the sky was losing its last blue to an orange glow. Leaves littered the path and the temperature had dropped. The scent of pine was everywhere. Curlews whistled from the branches above.

"Are you taking notes?" he called ahead to her.

She stopped and waited for him. "Which do you think is more autumnal—the leaves, the dying sunflowers, or Grandmother Chinatsu?"

"Too early to tell," he said. "I'm withholding judgment."

Another hundred yards down the winding path they came upon the spring, nearly surrounded by pines except for one spot with a view of a small meadow beyond. Steam rose from the natural pool, curling up in the air, reminding Michi of the white flames on the old lady's jacket. At the edge of the water, closest to the slate path, there was ancient stonework, a crude bench, a stacked rock wall covered with moss, six foot by four, from which a thin waterfall splashed down into the rising heat of the onsen.

"Lovely," said Michi. Riku nodded.

She left him and moved down along the side of the spring. He looked away as she stepped out of her sandals and removed her robe, which she hung on a nearby branch. He heard her sigh as she entered the water. When he removed his robe, her face was turned away, as if she were taking in the last light on the meadow. Meanwhile, Riku was taking Michi in, her slender neck, her long black hair and how it lay on the curve of her shoulder, her breasts.

"Are you getting in?" she asked.

He silently eased down into the warmth.

When Michi turned to look at him, she immediately noticed the tattoo on his right shoulder, a vicious swamp eel with rippling fins and needle fangs and a long body that wrapped around Riku's back. It was the color of the moss on the rocks of the waterfall.

Riku noticed her glancing at it. He also noticed the smoothness of her skin and that her nipples were erect.

"Who is your employer?" she asked.

"He's a good man," he said and lowered himself into a crouch, so that only his head was above water. "Now, pay attention," he said and looked out at the meadow, which was already in twilight.

"To what?" she asked, also sinking down into the water.

He didn't respond and they remained immersed for a long time, just two heads floating on the surface, staring silently and listening, steam rising around them. At last light, when the air grew cold, the curlews lifted from their branches and headed for Australia. Riku stood, moved to a different spot in the spring, and crouched down again. Michi moved closer to him. A breeze blew through the pines, a cricket sang in the dark.

"Was there any inspiration?" he asked.

"I'm not sure," she said. "It's time for you to tell me your story of autumn." She drew closer to him and he backed up a step.

"I don't tell stories," he said.

"As brief as you want, but something," she said and smiled.

He closed his eyes and said, "Okay. The autumn I was seventeen, I worked on one of the fishing boats out of Numazu. We were out for horse mackerel. On one journey we were struck by a rogue wave, a giant that popped up out of nowhere. I was on deck when it hit and we were swamped. I managed to grab a rope and it took all my strength not to be drawn overboard, the water was so cold and powerful. I was sure I would die. Two men did get swept away and were never found. That's my Natural History of Autumn."

She moved forward and put her arms around him. They kissed. He drew his head back and whispered in her ear, "When I returned to shore that autumn, I quit fishing." She laughed and rested her head on his shoulder.

They dined by candlelight, in their robes, in the alcove off the main room of the farmhouse. Grandmother Chinatsu served, and Ono followed a step behind, so that every time she leaned forward to put a platter on the table, there was the dog's leering face, tongue drooping. The main course was thin slices of raw mackerel with grated ginger and chopped scallions. They drank sake. Michi remarked on the appearance of the mackerel after Riku's story.

"Most definitely a sign," he said.

They discussed the things they each saw and heard at the spring as the sake bottle emptied. It was well past midnight when the candle burned out and they went down the hall to his room.

Three hours later, Michi woke in the dark, still a little woozy from the sake. Riku woke when she sat up on the edge of the bed.

"Are you all right?" he asked.

"I have to use the toilet." She got off the bed and lifted her robe from the mats. Slipping into it, she crossed the room. When she slid back the panel, a dim light entered. A lantern hanging in the center of the hallway ceiling bathed the corridor in a dull glow. Michi left the panel open and headed up the hallway. Riku lay back and immediately dozed off. It seemed only a minute to him before Michi was back, shaking him by the shoulder to wake up. She'd left the panel open and he could see her face. Her eyes were wide, the muscles of her jaw tense, a vein visibly throbbing behind the pale skin of her forehead. She was breathing rapidly and he could feel the vibration of her heartbeat.

"Get me out of here," she said in a harsh whisper.

"What's wrong?" he said and moved quickly to the edge of the bed. She kneeled on the mattress next to him and grabbed his arm tightly with both hands.

"We've got to leave," she said.

He shook his head and ran his fingers through his hair. It wasn't perfect anymore. He carefully removed his arm from her grip and checked his watch. "It's three a.m.," he said. "You want to leave?"

"I demand you take me out of this place, now."

"What happened?" he asked.

"Either you take me now or I'll leave on foot."

He gave a long sigh and stood up. "I'll be ready in a minute," he said. She went across the corridor to her room and gathered her things together.

When they met in the hallway, bags in hand, he asked her, "Do you think I should let Grandmother Chinatsu know we're leaving?"

"Definitely not," she said, on the verge of tears. She grabbed him with her free hand and dragged him by the shirtsleeve down the hallway. As they reached the main room of the house, she stopped and looked warily around.

"Was it the dog?" he whispered. The coast was apparently clear, for she then dragged him outside, down the porch steps, to the silver car. "Get in," he said. "I have to put the top up. It's too cold to drive with it down."

"Just hurry," she said, stowing her overnight bag. She slid into the passenger seat just as the car top was closing. He got in behind the wheel and reached over to latch the top on her side before doing his.

Michi's window was down and she heard the creaking of planks from the porch. She leaned her head toward her shoulder and looked into the car's side mirror. There, in the full moon's light, she could see Grandmother Chinatsu and Ono. The old lady was waving and laughing.

"Drive," she shrieked.

Riku hit the start button, put the car in gear, and they were off into the night, racing down a rutted dirt road at fifty. Once the farmhouse was out of sight, he let up on the gas. "You've got to tell me what happened," he said.

She was shivering. "Get us out of the woods first," she said. "To a highway."

"I can't see a thing and I don't remember all the roads," he said. "We might end up lost." He drove for more than an hour before he found a road made of asphalt. His car had been brutalized by the crude paths and branches jutting into the roadway. There would be a hundred scratches on his doors. During that entire time, Michi stared ahead through the windshield, breathing rapidly.

"We're on a main road. Tell me what happened," he said.

"I got up to use the toilet," she said. "And I did. But when I stepped back out into the hallway to return, I heard a horrible grunting noise. I swear it sounded like someone was choking Grandmother Chinatsu to death in her room. I moved along the wall to the entrance. The panel was partially open, and there was a light inside. The noise had stopped so I peered in, and there was the shriveled old lady on her hands and knees on the floor, naked. Her forearms were trembling, her face was bright red, and she began croaking. At first I thought she was ill, but then I looked up and realized she was engaged in . . . sexual relations."

"Grandmother Chinatsu?" he said and laughed. "Who was the unlucky gentleman?"

"That disgusting dog."

"She was doing it with Ono?"

"I almost vomited," said Michi. "But I could have dealt with it. The worst thing was Ono saw me peering in and he smiled at me and nodded."

"Dogs don't smile," he said.

"Exactly," she said. "That place is haunted."

"Well, I'll figure out where we are eventually, and we'll make it back to Numazu by morning. I'm sorry you were so frightened. The field trip seemed a great success until then."

She took a few deep breaths to calm herself. "Perhaps that was the true spirit of autumn," she said.

" 'The Story of a Ghost,' " he said.

The silver car sped along in the moonlight. Michi was leaning against the window, her eyes closed. Riku thought he was heading for the coast He took a tight turn on a narrow mountain road and something suddenly lunged out of the woods at the car. He felt an impact as he swerved, turning back just in time to avoid the drop beyond the lane he'd strayed into.

Michi woke at the impact and said, "What's happening?"

"I think I grazed a deer back there. I've got to pull over and check to see if the car is okay."

Michi leaned forward and adjusted the rearview mirror so she could look out the back window.

"Too late to see," he said. "It was a half-mile back." He eased down on the brake, slowing, and began to edge over toward the shoulder.

"There's something chasing us," she said. "I can see it in the moonlight. Keep going. Go faster."

He downshifted and took his foot off the brake. As he hit the gas, he reached up and moved the mirror out of her grasp so he could see what was following them.

"It's a dog," he said. "But it's the fastest dog I ever saw. I'm doing forty-five and it's gaining on us."

They passed through an area where overhanging trees blocked the moon.

"Watch the road," she said.

When the car moved again into the moonlight, he checked behind them and saw nothing. Then they heard a loud growling. Each searched frantically to see where the noise was coming from. Swerving out of his lane, Riku looked out his side window and down and saw the creature running alongside, the movement of its four legs a blur, its face perfectly human.

"Kuso," he said. "Open the glove compartment. There's a gun in there. Give it to me."

"A gun?"

"Hurry," he yelled. She did as he instructed, handing him the sleek nine-millimeter. "You were right," he said. "The place was haunted." He lowered his side window, switched hands between gun and wheel. Then, steadying himself, he hit the brake. The dog looked up as it sped past the car—a middle-aged woman's face, bitter, with a terrible underbite and a beauty mark beneath the left eye, riding atop the neck of a mangy gray mutt with a naked tail. As soon as it moved a foot ahead of the car, Riku thrust the gun out the window and fired. The creature suddenly exploded, turning instantly to a shower of salt.

"It had a face," he said, maneuvering the car out of its skid. "A woman's face."

"Don't stop," she said. "Please."

"Don't worry."

"Now," she said, "who is your employer? Why would he send you to such a place?"

"Maybe if I tell you the truth it'll lift whatever curse we're under."

"What is the truth?"

"My employer is a very powerful businessman, and I have heard it said that he is also an Onmyoji. You know him. In a moment of weakness he told you a story about an affair he had. Afterward, he worried that you might be inclined to blackmail him. If the story got out, it would be a grave embarrassment for him both at home and at the office. He told me, spend time with her. He wanted me to judge what type of person you are."

"And if I'm the wrong kind of person?"

"I'm to kill you and make it look like an accident," he said.

"Are you trying to scare me to death, you and the old woman?"

"No, I swear. I'm as frightened as you are. And I couldn't harm you. Believe me. I know you would never blackmail him."

She rested back against the car seat and closed her eyes. She could feel his hand grasp hers. "Do you believe me?" he said. In the instant she opened her eyes, she saw ahead through the windshield two enormous dogs step onto the highway thirty yards in front of the car.

"Watch out," she screamed. He'd been looking over at her. He hit the brake before even glancing to the windshield. The car locked up and skidded, the headlights illuminating two faces—a man with a thin black mustache and wire-frame glasses, whose mouth was gaping open, and a little girl, chubby, with black bangs, tongue sticking out. On impact, the front of the car crumpled, the air bags deployed, and the horrid dogs burst into salt. The car left the road and came to a stop on the right-hand side, just before the tree line.

Riku remained conscious through the accident. He undid his seatbelt and slid out of the car, brushing glass off his shirt. His forehead had struck the rearview mirror, and there was a gash on his right temple. He heard growling, and pushing himself away from the car, he headed around to Michi's side. A small pot-bellied dog with the face of an idiot, sunken eyes, and swollen lower lip was drooling and scratching at Michi's window. Riku aimed, pulled the trigger, and turned the monstrosity to salt.

He opened the passenger door. Michi was just coming around. He helped her out and leaned her against the car. Bending over, he reached into the glove compartment and found an extra clip for the gun. As he backed out of the car, he heard them coming up the road, a pack of them, speeding through the moonlight, howling and grunting. He grabbed her hand and they made for the tree line.

"Not the woods," she said and tried to free herself from his grasp.

"No, there's no place to hide on the road. Come on."

They fled into the darkness beneath the trees, Riku literally dragging her forward. Low branches whipped their faces and tangled Michi's hair. Although ruts tripped them, they miraculously never fell. The baying of the beasts sounded only steps behind them, but when he turned and lifted the gun, he saw nothing but night.

Eventually they broke from beneath the trees onto a dirt road. Both were heaving for breath, and neither could run another step. She'd twisted an ankle and was limping. He put one arm around her, to help her along. She was trembling; so was he.

"What are they?" she whispered.

"Jinmenken," he said.

"Impossible."

They walked slowly down the road, and stepping out from beneath the canopy of leaves, the moonlight showed them, a hundred yards off, a dilapidated building with boarded windows.

"I can't run anymore," he said. "We'll go in there and find a place to hide." She said nothing.

They stood for a moment on the steps of the place, a concrete structure, some abandoned factory or warehouse, and he tried his cell phone. "No reception," he said after dialing three times and listening. He flipped to a new screen with his thumb and pressed an app icon. The screen became a flashlight. He turned it forward, held it at arm's length, and motioned with his head for Michi to get close behind him. With the gun at the ready, they moved slowly through the doorless entrance.

The place was freezing cold and pitch black. As far as he could tell there were hallways laid out in a square, with small rooms off it to either side.

"An office building in the middle of the woods," she said.

Each room had the remains of a western-style door at its entrance, pieces of shattered wood hanging on by the hinges. When he shone the phone's light into the rooms, he saw a window opening boarded from within by a sheet of plywood, and an otherwise empty concrete expanse. They went down one hall and turned left into another. Michi remembered she had the same app on her phone and lit it. Halfway down that corridor, they found a room whose door was mostly intact but for a corner at the bottom where it appeared to have been kicked in. Riku inspected the knob and whispered, "There's a lock on this one."

They went in and he locked the door behind them and tested its strength. "Get in the corner under the window," he said. "If they find us, and the door won't hold, I can rip off the board above us and we might be able to escape outside." She joined him in the corner and they sat, shoulders touching, their backs against the cold concrete. "We're sure to be safe when the sun rises."

He put his arm around her and she leaned into him. Then neither said a word, nor made a sound. They turned off their phones and listened to the dark. Time passed, yet when Riku checked his watch, it read only 3:30. "All that in a half-hour?" he wondered. Then there came a sound, a light tapping, as if rain was falling outside. The noise slowly grew louder, and seconds later it became clear that it was the sound of claws on the concrete floor. That light tapping eventually became a clatter, as if a hundred of the creatures were circling impatiently in the hallway.

A strange guttural voice came from the hole at the bottom corner of the door. "Tomodachi," it said. "Let us in."

Riku flipped to the flashlight app and held the gun up. Across the room, the hole in the bottom of the door was filled with a fat, pale, bearded face. One eye was swollen shut and something oozed from the corner of it. The forehead was too high to see a hairline. The thing snuffled and smiled.

"Shoot," said Michi.

Riku fired, but the face flinched away in an instant, and once the bullet went wide and drilled a neat hole in the door, the creature returned and said, "Tomodachi."

"What do you want?" said Riku, his voice cracking.

"We are hunting a spirit of the living," said the creature, the movement of its lips out of sync with the words it spoke.

"What have we done?" said Michi.

"Our hunger is great, but we only require one spirit. We only take what we need—the other person will be untouched. One spirit will feed us for a week."

Michi stood up and stepped away from Riku. He also got to his feet. "What are you doing?" she said. "Shoot them." She quickly lit her phone and shone it on him.

Instead of aiming the gun at the door, he aimed it at her. "I'm not having my spirit devoured," he said to her.

"You said you couldn't hurt me."

"It won't be me hurting you," he said. She saw there were tears in his eyes. The hand that held the gun was wobbling. "I'm giving you the girl," he called to the Jinmenken.

"A true benefactor," said the face at the hole.

"No," she said. "What have I done?"

"I'm going to shoot her in the leg so she can't run, then I'm going to let you all in. You will keep your distance from me or I'll shoot. I have an extra clip, and I'll turn as many of you to salt as I can before you get to me."

Turning to Michi, he said, "I'm so sorry. I did love you."

"But you're a coward. You don't have to shoot me in the leg," she said. "I'll go to them on my own. My spirit's tired of this world." She moved forward and gave him a kiss. Her actions disarmed him and he appeared confused. At the door, she slowly undid the lock on the knob. Then, with a graceful, fluid motion, she pulled the door open and stepped behind it against the wall. "Take him," he heard her call. The Jinmenkin bounded in, dozens of them, small and large, stinking of rain, slobbering, snapping, clawing. He pulled the trigger till the gun clicked empty, and the room was filled with smoke and flying salt. His hands shook too much to change the clip. One of the creatures tore a bloody chunk from his left calf and he screamed. Another went for his groin. The face of Grandmother Chinatsu appeared before him and devoured his.

The following week, in a private room at The Limit, Michi sat at a blond-wood table, staring out the open panel across the room at the pines and the coast. Riku's employer sat across from her. "Ingenious, the Natural History of Autumn," he said. "And you knew this would draw him in?"

She turned to face the older man. "He was a unique person," she said. "He'd faced death."

"Too bad about Riku," he said. "I wanted to trust him."

"Really, the lengths to which you'll go to test the spirit of those you need to trust. He's gone because he was a coward?"

"A coward I can tolerate. But he said he loved you, and it proved he didn't understand love at all. A dangerous flaw." He took an envelope from within his suit jacket and laid it on the table. "A job well done," he said. She lifted the envelope and looked inside.

A cold breeze blew into the room. "You know," he said, "this season always reminds me of our time together."

As she spoke she never stopped counting the bills. "All I remember of that," she said, "is the snow."

Jeffrey Ford is the author of the novels *The Physiognomy, Memoranda, The Beyond, The Portrait of Mrs. Charbuque, The Girl in the Glass, The Cosmology of the Wider World*, and *The Shadow Year*. His story collections include *The Fantasy Writer's Assistant, The Empire of Ice Cream*, and *The Drowned Life*. The collection *Crackpot Palace* is his latest book. Ford is the recipient of the World Fantasy Award, Nebula, Shirley Jackson Award, Edgar Allan Poe Award, and the Grand Prix de l'Imaginaire. A professor of literature and writing for over twenty-five years, he now lives in Ohio with his wife and two sons, and writes full time. Learn more about his work at www.well-builtcity.com.

*Great-Grandmother peered closely at me, her own skull
weaving slightly from side to side, like a snake's head . . .*

GREAT-GRANDMOTHER IN THE CELLAR

Peter S. Beagle

I thought he had killed her.

Old people forget things, I know that—my father can't ever remember where he set down his pen a minute ago—but if I forget, at the end of *my* life, every other thing that ever happened to me, I will still be clutched by the moment when I gazed down at my beautiful, beautiful, sweet-natured idiot sister and heard the whining laughter of Borbos, the witch-boy she loved, pattering in my head. I *knew* he had killed her.

Then I saw her breast rising and falling—so slowly!—and I saw her nostrils fluttering slightly with each breath, and I knew that he had only thrown her into the witch-sleep that mimics the last sleep closely enough to deceive Death Herself.

Borbos stepped from the shadows and laughed at me.

"*Now* tell your father," he said. "Go to him and tell him that Jashani will lie so until the sight of my face—and only my face—awakens her. And that face she will never see until he agrees that we two may wed. Is this message clear enough for your stone skull, Da'mas? Shall I repeat it, just to be sure?"

I rushed at him, but he put up a hand and the floor of my sister's chamber seemed to turn to oiled water under my feet. I went over on my back, flailing foolishly at the innocent air, and Borbos laughed again. If *shukris* could laugh, they would sound like Borbos.

He was gone then, in that way he had of coming and going, which Jashani thought was so dashing and mysterious, but which seemed to me fit only for sneak thieves and housebreakers. I knelt there alone, staring helplessly at the person I loved most in the world, and whom I fully intended to strangle when—oh, it had to be *when*!—she woke up. With no words, no explanations, no apologies. She'd know.

In the ordinary way of things, she's far brighter and wiser and simply *better* than I, Jashani. My tutors all disapproved and despaired of me early on, with good reason; but before she could walk, they seemed almost to expect my sister to perform her own *branlewei* coming-of-age ceremony, and prepare both the ritual sacrifice and the meal afterward. It would drive me wild with jealousy—especially when Father would demand to know, one more time, why I couldn't be as studious and accomplished as Jashani—if she weren't so ridiculously decent and kind that there's not a thing you can do except love her. I sometimes go out into the barn and scream with frustration, to tell you the truth . . . and then she comes running to see if I'm hurt or ill. At twenty-one, she's two and a half years older than I, and she has never once let Father beat me, even when the punishment was so richly deserved that *I'd* have beaten me if I were in his place.

And right then I'd have beaten *her*, if it weren't breaking my heart to see her prisoned in sleep unless we let the witch-boy have her.

It is the one thing we ever quarrel about, Jashani's taste in men. Let me but mention that this or that current suitor has a cruel mouth, and all Chun will hear her shouting at me that the poor boy can't be blamed for a silly feature—and should I bring a friend by, just for the evening, who happens to describe the poor boy's method of breaking horses . . . well, that will only make things worse. If I tell her that the whole town knows that the fellow serenading her in the grape arbor is the father of two children by a barmaid, and another baby by a farm girl, Jashani will fly at me, claiming that he was a naive victim of their seductive beguilements. Put her in a room with ninety-nine perfect choices and one heartless scoundrel, and she will choose the villain every time. This prediction may very well be the one thing Father and I ever agree on, come to consider.

But *Borbos* . . .

Unlike most of the boys and men Jashani ever brought home to try out at dinner, I had known Borbos all my life, and Father had known the family since his own youth. Borbos came from a long line of witches of one sort and another, most of them quite respectable, as witches go, and likely as embarrassed by Borbos as Father was by me. He'd grown up easily the handsomest young buck in Chun, straight and sleek, with long, angled eyes the color of river water, skin and hair the envy of every girl I knew, and an air about him to entwine hearts much less foolish than my sister's. I could name names.

And with all that came a soul as perfectly pitiless as when we were all little and he was setting cats afire with a twiddle of two fingers, or withering someone's fields or haystacks with a look, just for the fun of it. He took great care that none of our parents ever caught him at his play, so that it didn't matter what I told them—and in the same way, even then, he made sure never to let Jashani see the truth of him. He knew what he wanted, even then, just as she never wanted to believe evil of anyone.

And here was the end of it: me standing by my poor, silly sister's bed, begging her to wake up, over and over, though I knew she never would—not until Father and I . . .

No.

Not ever.

If neither of us could stop it, I knew someone who would.

Father was away from home, making arrangements with vintners almost as far north as the Durli Hills and as far south as Kalagira, where the enchantresses live, to buy our grapes for their wine. He would be back when he was back, and meanwhile there was no way to reach him, nor any time to spare. The decision was mine to make, whatever he might think of it afterward.

Of our two servants, Catuzan, the housekeeper, had finished her work and gone home, and Nanda, the cook, was at market. Apart from Jashani, I was alone in our big old house.

Except for Great-Grandmother.

I never knew her; neither had Jashani. Father had, in his youth, but he spoke of her very little, and that little only with the windows shuttered and the curtains drawn. When I asked hopefully whether Great-Grandmother had been a witch, his answer was a headshake and a definite *no*—but when Jashani said, "Was she a demon?" Father was silent for some while. Finally he said, "No, not really. Not exactly." And that was all we ever got out of him about Great-Grandmother.

But I knew something Jashani didn't know. Once, when I was small, I had overheard Father speaking with his brother Uskameldry, who was also in the wine grape trade, about a particular merchant in Coraic who had so successfully cornered the market in that area that no vintner would even look at our family's grapes, whether red or black or blue. Uncle Uska had joked, loudly enough for me to hear at my play, that maybe they ought to go down to the cellar and wake up Great-Grandmother again.

Father didn't laugh, but hushed him so fast that the silence caught my ear as much as the talk before it.

Our cellar is deep and dark, and the great wine casks cast bulky shadows when you light a candle. Jashani and I and our friends used to try to scare each other when we played together there, but she and I knew the place too well ever to be really frightened. Now I stood on the stair, thinking crazily that Jashani and Great-Grandmother were both asleep, maybe if you woke one, you might rouse the other . . . something like that, anyway.

So after a while, I lit one of the wrist-thick candles Father kept under the hinged top step, and I started down.

Our house is the oldest and largest on this side of the village.

There have been alterations over the years—most of them while Mother was alive—but the cellar never changes. Why should it? There are always the casks, and the tables and racks along the walls, for Father's filters and preservatives and other tools to test the grapes for perfect ripeness; and always the same comfortable smell of damp earth, the same boards stacked to one side, to walk on should the cellar flood, and the same shadows, familiar as bedtime toys. But there was no sign of anyone's ancestor, and no place where one could possibly be hiding, not once you were standing on the earthen floor, peering into the shadows.

Then I saw the place that wasn't a shadow, in the far right corner of the cellar, near the drainpipe. I don't remember any of us noticing it as children—it would have been easy to miss, being only slightly darker than the rest of the floor—but when I walked warily over to it and tapped it with my foot, it felt denser and finer-packed than any other area. There were a couple of spades leaning against the wall further along. I took one and, feeling strangely hypnotized, started to dig.

The deeper I probed, the harder the digging got, and the more convinced I became that the earth had been deliberately pounded hard and tight, as though to hold something down.

Not hard enough: whatever was here, it was coming up now. A kind of fever took hold of me, and I flung spadeful after spadeful aside, going at it like a rock-*targ* ripping out a poor badger's den.

I broke my nails, and I flung my sweated shirt away, and I dug.

I didn't hear my father the first time, although he was shouting at me from the stair. "What are you doing?" I went on digging, and he bellowed loud enough to make the racks rattle, *"Da'mas, what are you doing?"*

I did not turn. I was braced for the jar of the spade on wood, or possibly metal—a coffin either way—but the sound that came up when I finally did hit something had me instantly throwing the instrument away and dropping down to half sit, half kneel on the edge of the oblong hole I'd worried out of the earth. Reaching, groping, my hand came up gripping a splintered bone.

Great-Grandmother! I flung myself face down, clawing with both hands now, frantic, hysterical, not knowing what I was doing. Fingerbones . . . something that might have been a knee, an elbow . . . *a skull*—no, just the top of a skull . . . I don't think I was quite sane when I heard the voice.

"Grandson, stop . . . stop, before you really do addle my poor old bones. Stop!" It was a slow voice, with a cold, cold rustle in it: it sounded like the wind over loose stones.

I stopped. I sat up, and so did she.

Then Father—home early, due to some small war blocking his road—was beside me, as silent as I, but with an unfriendly hand gripping the back of my neck. Great-Grandmother wasn't missing any bones, thank Dran and Tani, our household gods, who are twins. The skull wasn't hers, nor the fingers, nor any of the other loose bones; she was definitely whole, sitting with her fleshless legs bent under her, from the knees, and her own skull clearing the top of my pit to study me out of yellowish-white empty eye sockets. She said, "The others are your Great-Aunt Keshwara. I was lonely."

I looked at Father for the first time. He was sweating himself, pale and swaying. I realized that his hand on my neck was largely to keep me from trembling, and to hold himself upright. "You should not have done this," he said. He was almost whispering.

"Oh, you should never have done this." Then, louder, as he let go of me, "Great- Grandmother."

"Do not scold the boy, Rushak," the stone rustle rebuked him. "It has been long and long since I saw anything but dirt, smelled anything but mold. The scent of fear tells me that I am back with my family. Sit up straight, young Da'mas. Look at me." I sat as properly as I could on the edge of a grave. Great-Grandmother peered closely at me, her own skull weaving slightly from side to side, like a snake's head. She said, "Why have you awakened me?"

"He's a fool," Father said. "He made a mistake, he didn't know . . . "

Great-Grandmother looked at him, and he stopped talking. She repeated the question to me.

How I faced those eyeless, browless voids and spoke to those cold, slabby chaps, I can't tell you—or myself—today. But I said my sister's name— "Jashani"—and after that it got easier. I said, "Borbos, the witch-boy—he's made her sleep, and she won't wake up until we give in and say he can marry her. And she'd be better off dead."

"What?" Father said. "How—"

Great-Grandmother interrupted, "Does she know that?"

"No," I said. "But she will. She thinks he loves her, but he doesn't love anybody."

"He loves my money, right enough," Father said bitterly. "He loves my house. He loves my business."

The eye sockets never turned from me. I said, "She doesn't know about these things . . . about men. She's just *good*."

"Witch-boy . . . " The rusty murmur was all but inaudible in the skeletal throat. "Ah . . . the Tresard family. The youngest."

Father and I gaped at her, momentarily united by astonishment. Father asked, "How did you . . . ?" Then he said, "You were already . . . " I thanked him silently for being the one to look a fool.

Great-Grandmother said simply—and, it might have been, a little smugly—"I listen. What else have I to do in that hole?" Then she said, "Well, I must see the girl. Show me."

So my great-grandmother stepped out of her grave and followed my father and me upstairs, clattering with each step like an armload of dishes, yet held firmly together somehow by the recollection of muscles, the stark memory of tendons and sinews. Neither of us liked to get too close to her, which she seemed to understand, for she stayed well to the rear of our uncanny procession. Which was ridiculous, and I knew it then, and I was ashamed of it then as well. She was family, after all.

In Jashani's chamber, Great-Grandmother stood looking down at the bed for a long time, without speaking. Finally she said softly, almost to herself, "Skilled . . . I never knew a Tresard with such . . . " She did not finish.

"Can you heal her?" The words burst out of me as though I hadn't spoken in years, which was how I felt. "She's never hurt a soul, she wouldn't know how—she's foolish and sweet, except she's very smart, it's just that she can't imagine that anyone would ever wish her harm. *Please*, Great-Grandmother, make her wake up! I'll do anything!"

I will be grateful to my dying day that Jashani couldn't hear a word of all that nonsense.

Great-Grandmother didn't take her empty eyes from my sister as I babbled on; nor did she seem to hear a word of the babble. I'm not sure how long she stood there by the bed, though I do recall that she reached out once to stroke Jashani's hair very lightly, as though those cold, fleshless fingers were seeing, tasting . . .

Then she stepped back, so abruptly that some bones clicked against other bones, and she said, "I must have a body." Again Father and I stared stupidly at her. Great- Grandmother said impatiently, "Do you imagine that I can face your witch-boy like this? One of you—either one—must allow me the use of his body. Otherwise, don't waste my time." She glowered into each of our pale faces in turn, never losing or altering the dreadful grin of the long-dead.

Father took a long breath and opened his mouth to volunteer, but I beat him to it, actually stepping a bit forward to nudge him aside. I said, "What must I do?"

Great-Grandmother bent her head close, and I stared right into that eternal smile. "Nothing, boy. You need do nothing but stand so . . . just so . . . "

I cannot tell you what it was like. And if I could, I wouldn't.

You might ask Father, who's a much better witness to the whole affair than

I, for all that, in a way, I *was* the whole affair. I do know from him that Great-Grandmother's bones did not clatter untidily to the floor when her spirit—soul, essence, life-force, *tyak* (as people say in the south)—passed into me. According to Father, they simply vanished into the silver mist that poured and poured into me, as I stood there with my arms out, dumb as a dressmaker's dummy. The one reasonably reliable report I can relay is that it wasn't cold, as you might expect, but warm on my skin, and—of all things—almost *sweet* on my lips, though I kept my mouth tightly shut. Being invaded—no, let's use the honest word, *possessed*—by your great-grandmother is bad enough, but to swallow her? And have it taste like apples, like *fasteen*, like cake? I didn't think about it then, and I'm not thinking about it now. Then, all that mattered was my feeling of being crowded to the farthest side of my head, and *hearing* Great-Grandmother inside me saying, dryly but soothingly, "Well done, Da'mas—well done, indeed. Slowly, now . . . move slowly until you grow accustomed to my presence. I will not hurt you, I promise, and I will not stay long. Slowly . . . "

Sooner or later, when he judged our anguish greatest, Borbos would return to repeat his demand. Father and Great-Grandmother-in-me took it in turns to guard Jashani's chamber through the rest of that day, the night, and all of the following day. When it was Father's turn, Great-Grandmother would march my body out of the room and the house, down the carriageway, into our orchards and arbors; then back to scout the margins again, before finally allowing me to replace Father at that bedside where no quilt was ever rumpled, no pillow on the floor. In all of this I never lost myself in her. I always knew who I was, even when she was manipulating my mouth and the words that came out of it; even when she was lifting my hands or snapping my head too forcefully from side to side, apparently thrilled by the strength of the motion.

"He will be expecting resistance," she pointed out to us, in my voice. "Nothing he cannot wipe away with a snap of his fingers, but enough to make you feel that you did the best you could for Jashani before you yielded her to him. Now put that thing down!" she lectured Father, who was carrying a sword that he knew would be useless against Borbos, but had clung to anyway, for pure comfort.

Father bristled. "How are we to fight him at all, even with you guiding Da'mas's hand? Borbos could appear right now, that way he does, and what would you do? I'll put this old sword away if you give me a spell, a charm, to replace it." He was tired and sulky, and terribly, terribly frightened.

I heard my throat answer him calmly and remotely, "When your witch-boy turns up, all you will be required to do is to stand out of my way." After that Great-Grandmother did not allow another word out of me for some considerable while.

Father had not done well from his first sight of Jashani apparently lifeless in her bed. The fact that she was breathing steadily, that her skin remained warm to the touch, and that she looked as innocently beautiful as ever, despite not having eaten or drunk for several days, cheered him not at all. He himself, on the other hand, seemed to be withering before my eyes: unsleeping, hardly speaking, hardly comprehending what was said to him. Now he put down his sword as commanded and sat motionless by Jashani's bed, slumped forward with his hands clasped between his knees. A dog could not have been more constant, or more silent.

And still Borbos did not come to claim his triumph . . . did not come, and did not come, letting our grief and fear build to heights of nearly unbearable tension. Even Great-Grandmother seemed to feel it, pacing the house in my body, which she treated like her own tireless bones that needed no relief, though I urgently did.

Surrounded by her ancient mind, nevertheless I could never truly read it, not as she could pick through my thoughts when she chose, at times amusing herself by embarrassing me. Yet she moved me strangely once when she said aloud, as we were crouched one night in the apple orchard, studying the carriageway, white in the moon, "I envy even your discomfiture. Bones cannot blush."

"They never need to," I said, after realizing that she was waiting for my response. "Sometimes I think I spend my whole life being mortified about one thing or another. Wake up, start apologizing for everything to everybody, just on the chance I've offended them." Emboldened, I ventured further. "You might not think so, but I have had moments of wishing I were dead. I really have."

Great-Grandmother was silent in my head for so long that I was afraid that I might have affronted her for a second time. Then she said, slowly and tonelessly, "You would not like it. I will find it hard to go back." And there was something in the way she said those last words that made pins lick along my forearms.

"What *will* you do when Borbos comes?" I asked her. "Father says you're not a witch, but he never would say exactly what you were. I don't understand how you can deal with someone like Borbos if you're not a witch."

The reply came so swiftly and fiercely that I actually cringed away from it in my own skull. "I am your great-grandmother, boy. If that is not all you need to know, then you must make do as you can." So saying, she rose and stalked us out of the orchard, back toward the house, with me dragged along disconsolately, half certain that she might never bother talking to me again.

My favorite location in the house has—naturally enough—always been a place where I wasn't ever supposed to be: astride a gable just narrow enough for me to pretend that I was riding a great black stallion to glory, or a sea-green *mordroi* dragon to adventure. I cannot count the number of times I was beaten, even by Mother, for risking my life up there, and I know very well how foolish it is to continue doing it whenever I get the chance. But this time it was Great-Grandmother taking the risk, not me, so it plainly wasn't my fault; and, in any case, what could I have done about it?

So there you are, and there you have us in the night, Great-Grandmother and I, with the moon our only light, except for the window of Jashani's chamber below and to my left, where Father kept his lonely vigil. I was certainly not about to speak until Great-Grandmother did; and for some while she sat in silence, seemingly content to scan the white road for a slim, swaggering figure who would almost surely not come for my sister that way.

I ground my teeth at the thought.

Presently Great-Grandmother said quietly, almost dreamily, "I was not a good woman in my life. I was born with a certain gift for . . . mischief, let us say . . . and I sharpened it and honed it, until what I did with it became, if not as totally evil as Borbos Tresard's deeds from his birth, still cruel and malicious enough that many have never forgiven me to this day. Do you know how I died, young Da'mas?"

"I don't even know how you lived," I answered her. "I don't know anything about you."

Great-Grandmother said, "Your mother killed me. She stabbed me, and I died. And she was right to do it." I could not take in what she had said. I felt the words as she spoke them, but they meant nothing. Great-Grandmother went on. "Like your sister, your mother had poor taste in men. She was young, I was old, why should she listen to me? If I am no witch, whatever it is that I am had grown strong with the years. I drove each of her suitors away, by one means or another. It was not hard—a little pointed misfortune and they cleared off quickly, all but the serious ones. I killed two of those, one in a storm, one in a cow pen." A grainy chuckle. "Your mother was not at all pleased with me."

"She knew what you were doing? She knew it was you?"

"Oh, yes, how not?" The chuckle again. "I was not trying to cover my tracks—I was much given to showing off in those days.

But then your father came along, and I did what I could to indicate to your mother that she must choose this one. There was a man in her life already, you understand—most unsuitable, she would have regretted it in a month. The cow pen one, that was." A sigh, somehow turning into a childish giggle, and ending in a grunt.

"You would have thought she might be a little pleased this time."

"Was that why she . . . ?" I could not actually say it. I felt Great-Grandmother's smile in my spine.

"Your mother was not a killer—merely mindless with anger for perhaps five seconds. A twitch to the left or right, and she would have missed . . . ah, well, it was a fate long overdue. I have never blamed her."

It was becoming increasingly difficult to distinguish my thoughts—even my memories—from hers. Now I remembered hearing Uncle Uska talking to Father about waking Great-Grandmother again, and being silenced immediately. I knew that she had heard them as well, listening underground in the dark, no soil dense enough to stop her ears.

I asked, "Have you ever come back before? To help the family, like now?"

The slow sigh echoed through our shared body. Great-Grandmother replied only, "I was always a fitful sleeper." Abruptly she rose, balancing more easily on the gable than I ever did when I was captaining my body, and we went on with our patrol, watching for Borbos. And that was another night on which Borbos did not come.

When he did appear at last, he caught us—even Great-Grandmother, I think—completely by surprise. In the first place, he came by day, after all our wearying midnight rounds; in the second, he turned up not in Jashani's chamber, nor in the yard or any of the fields where we had kept guard, but in the great kitchen, where old Nanda had reigned as long as I could remember. He was seated comfortably at her worn worktable, silky and dashing, charming her with tales of his journeys and exploits, while she toasted her special *chamshi* sandwiches for him. She usually needs a day's notice and a good deal of begging before she'll make *chamshi* for anybody.

He looked up when Great-Grandmother walked my body into the kitchen, greeting us first with, "Well, if it isn't Thunderwit, my brother-to-be. How are those frozen brains keeping?" Then he stopped, peered closely at me, and began to smile in a different way. "I didn't realize you had . . . company. Do we know each other, old lady?"

I could feel Great-Grandmother studying him out of my eyes, and it frightened me more than he did. She said, "I know your family. Even in the dirt I knew you when you were very young, and just as evil as you are now. Give me back my great-granddaughter and go your way."

Borbos laughed. It was one of his best features, that warm, delightful chuckle. "And if I don't? You will destroy me? Enchant me? Forgive me if I don't find that likely. Try, and your Jashani slumbers decoratively for all eternity." The laugh had broken glass in it the second time.

I ached to get my hands on him—useless as it would have been—but Great-Grandmother remained in control. All she said, quite quietly, was, "I want it understood that I did warn you."

Whatever Borbos heard in her voice, he was up and out of his seat on the instant. No fiery whiplash, no crash of cold, magical thunder—only a scream from Nanda as the chair fell silently to ashes. She rushed out of the kitchen, calling for Father, while Borbos regarded us thoughtfully from where he leaned against the cookstove. He said, "Well, my goodness," and twisted his fingers against each other in seeming anxiety. Then he said a word I didn't catch, and every knife, fork, maul, spit, slicer, corer, scissors, and bone saw in Nanda's kitchen rose up out of her utensil drawers and came flying off the wall, straight for Great-Grandmother . . . straight for me . . . for us.

But Great-Grandmother put up my hand—exactly as Borbos himself had done when I charged him on first seeing Jashani spellbound—and everything flashing toward us halted in the air, hanging there like edged and pointed currants in a fruitcake. Then Great-Grandmother spoke—the words had edges, too; I could feel them cutting my mouth—and all Nanda's implements backed politely into their accustomed places. Great-Grandmother said chidingly, "Really."

But Borbos was gone, vanished as I had seen him do in Jashani's chamber, his laughter still audible. I took the stairs two and three at a time, Great-Grandmother not wanting to chance my inexperienced body coming and going magically. Besides, we knew where he was going, and that he would be waiting for us there.

He was playing with Father. I don't like thinking about that: Father lunging and swinging clumsily with his sword, crying hopelessly, desperate to come to grips with this taunting shadow that kept dissolving out of his reach, then instantly reappearing, almost close enough to touch and punish. And Jashani . . .

Jashani so still, so still . . .

Borbos turned as we burst in, and a piece of the chamber ceiling fell straight down, bruising my left shoulder as GreatGrandmother sprang me out of the way. In her turn, she made my tongue say *this*, and my two hands do *that*, and Borbos was strangling in air, on the other side of the chamber, while my hands clenched on nothing and gripped and twisted, tighter and tighter . . . but he got a word out, in spite of me, and broke free to crouch by Jashani's bed, panting like an animal.

There was no jauntiness about him now, no mocking gaiety.

"You are no witch. I would know. What *are* you?"

I wanted to go over and comfort Father, hold him and make certain that he was unhurt, but Great-Grandmother had her own plans. She said, "I am a member of this family, and I have come to get my great-granddaughter back from you. Release her and I have no quarrel with you, no further interest at all. Do it now, Borbos Tresard."

For answer, Borbos looked shyly down at the floor, shuffled his feet like an embarrassed schoolboy, and muttered something that might indeed have been an apology for bad behavior in the classroom. But at the first sound of it, Great-Grandmother leaped forward and dragged Father away from the bed, as the floor began to crack open down the middle and the bed to slide steadily toward the widening crevasse. Father cried out in horror.

I wanted to scream; but Great-Grandmother pointed with the forefingers and ring fingers of both my hands at the opening, and what she shouted hurt my mouth. Took out a back tooth, too, though I didn't notice at the time. I was too busy watching Borbos's spell reverse itself, as the flying kitchenware had done.

The hole in the floor closed up as quickly as it had opened, and Jashani's bed slid back to where it had been, more or less, with her never once stirring. Father limped dazedly over to her and began to straighten her coverlet.

For a second time Borbos Tresard said, "Well, my goodness." He shook his head slightly, whether in admiration or because he was trying to clear it, I can't say. He said, "I do believe you are my master. Or mistress, as you will. But it won't help, you know. She still will not wake to any spell, except to see my face, and my terms are what they always were—a welcome into the heart of this truly remarkable family. Nothing more, and nothing less." He beamed joyously at us, and if I had never understood why so many women fell so helplessly in love with him, I surely came to understand it then. "How much longer can you stay in the poor ox, anyway, before you raddle him through like the death fever you are? Another day? A week? So much as a month? My face can wait, mother—but somehow I don't believe you can. I really don't believe so."

The bedchamber was so quiet that I thought I heard not only my own heart beating but also Jashani's, strong but so slow, and a skittery, too-rapid pulse that I first thought must be Father's, before I understood that it belonged to Borbos. GreatGrandmother said musingly, "Patience is an overrated virtue." And then I also understood why so many people fear the dead.

I felt her leaving me. I can't describe it any better than I've been able to say what it was like to have her in me. All I'm going to say about her departure is that it left me suddenly stumbling forward, as though a prop I was leaning on had been pulled away. But it wasn't my body that felt abandoned, I know that. I think it was my spirit, but I can't be sure.

Great-Grandmother stood there as I had first seen her. Lightning was flashing in her empty eye sockets, and the pitiless grin of her naked skull branded itself across my sight. With one great heron-stride of her naked shanks she was on Borbos, reaching out—reaching out . . .

I don't want to tell about this.

She took his face. She reached out with her bones, and she took his face, and he screamed. There was no blood, nothing like that, but suddenly there was a shifting smudge, almost like smoke, where his face had been . . . and there it was, somehow *pasted* on her, merged with the bone, so that it looked *real*, not like a mask, even on the skull of a skeleton. Even with the lightning behind her borrowed eyes.

Borbos went on screaming, floundering blindly in the bedchamber, stumbling into walls and falling down, meowing and snuffling hideously; but Great-Grandmother clacked and clattered to Jashani's bedside, and peered down at her for a long moment before she spoke. "Love," she said softly. "Jashani. My heart, awaken. Awaken for me." The voice was Borbos's voice.

And Jashani opened her eyes and said his name.

Father was instantly there, holding her hands, stroking her face, crying with joy. I didn't know what those easy words meant until then. Great-Grandmother turned away and walked across the room to Borbos. He must have sensed her standing before him, because he stopped making that terrible snuffling sound.

She said, "Here. I only used it for a little," and she gave him back his face.

I didn't really see it happen. I was with my father and my sister, listening to her say my name.

When I felt Great-Grandmother's fleshless hand on my shoulder, I kissed Jashani's forehead and stood up. I looked over at Borbos, still crouched in a corner, his hands pressed tightly against his face, as though he were holding it on. GreatGrandmother touched Father's shoulder with her other hand and said, impassively, "Take him home. Afterward."

After you bury me again, she meant. She held onto my shoulder as we walked downstairs together, and I felt a strange tension in the cold clasp that made me more nervous than I already was.

Would she simply lie down in her cellar grave waiting for me to spade the earth back over her and pat it down with the blade? I thought of those other bones I'd first seen in the grave, and I shivered, and her grip tightened just a bit.

We faced each other over the empty grave. I couldn't read her expression any more than I ever could, but the lightning was no longer playing in her eye sockets. She said, "You are a good boy. Your company pleases me."

I started to say, "If my company is the price of Jashani . . . I am ready." I *think* my voice was not trembling very much, but I don't know, because I never got the chance to finish. Both of our heads turned at a sudden scurry of footsteps, and we saw Borbos Tresard charging at us across the cellar. Head down, eyes white, flailing hands empty of weapons, nevertheless his entire outline was crackling with the fire-magic of utter, insane fury. He was howling as he came.

I automatically stepped into his way—too numb with fear to be afraid, if you can understand that—but Great-Grandmother put me aside and stood waiting, short but terrible, holding out her stick-thin arms. Like a child rushing to greet his mother coming home, Borbos Tresard leaped into those arms, and they closed around him. The impact caught Great-Grandmother off balance; the two of them tumbled into the grave together, struggling as they fell. I heard bones go, but would not gamble they were hers.

I picked up a spade, uncertain what I meant to do with it, staring down at the tumult in the earth as though it were something happening a long way off, and long ago. Then Father was beside me with the other spade, frantically shoving *everything*—dirt and odd scraps of wood and twigs and even old wine corks from the cellar floor—into the grave, shoveling and kicking and pushing with his arms almost at the same time. By and by I recovered enough to assist him, and when the hole was filled we both jumped up and down on the pile, packing it all down as tightly as it would go. The risen surface wasn't quite level with the floor when we were done, but it would settle in time.

I had to say it. I said, "He's down there under our feet, still alive, choking on dirt, with her holding him fast forever. Keeping her company." Father did not answer, but only leaned on his spade, with dirty sweat running out of his hair and down his cheek. I think that was the first time I noticed that he was an inch or so shorter than I. "I feel sorry for him. A little."

"Not I," Father said flatly. "I'd bury him deeper, if we had more earth."

"Then you would be burying Great-Grandmother deeper, too," I said.

"Yes." Father's face was paper-white, the skin looking thin with every kind of exhaustion. "Help me move these barrels."

Thanks to classic works such as *The Last Unicorn, Tamsin,* and *The Innkeeper's Song,* **Peter S. Beagle** is acknowledged as one of America's greatest fantasy authors. In addition to stories and novels he has written numerous teleplays and screenplays, including the animated versions of *The Lord of the Rings* and *The Last Unicorn,* plus the "Sarek" episode of *Star Trek: The Next Generation.* He is also a poet, lyricist, and singer/songwriter. In 2007, Beagle won the Hugo and Nebula Awards for his original novelette, "Two Hearts." For more details see conlanpress.com and facebook.com/petersbeagle.

He had the impression of something huge in front of him, something vast hanging over him, like a wave, only solid, ready to crash down . . .

RENFREW'S COURSE

John Langan

"So this is the wizard," Neil said.

"Supposedly," Jim said.

Six feet tall, the statue had been carved from wood that retained most of its whiteness, even though the date cut into its base read *2005*, seven years ago. Jim thought the color might be due to its not having been finished—splinters stood out from the wood's uneven surface—but didn't know enough about carpentry to be certain.

"Looks kind of Gandalf," Neil said.

He was right. The wide-brimmed hat, long beard, staff and robe, all suggested Tolkien's character, an impression the squirrel at the figure's left foot, fox behind its right, owl on its shoulder did little to argue.

"I know," Jim said. "It's like that statue of William Wallace—did I tell you about that? They wanted to put up a new statue of Wallace—somewhere out near Stirling, I think—so what did the artist come up with? Mel Gibson in *Braveheart*."

"No wonder there're so few Jews in Scotland."

"Apparently, the real guy was much stranger."

"Gibson? I know," Neil said, starting up the hill towards the dirt path that would take them into the nature preserve.

"No, the wizard." Once he had caught up to Neil and they were walking under the tall pine and oak, Jim continued, "In one story, the King of France was causing some kind of difficulty for the local merchants—an embargo, I think. Michael Renfrew mounted his iron horse and in a single bound crossed the distance from Kirkcaldy to Paris. When he showed up at the French palace, its doors flew open for him. The King's guards found their swords red hot in their hands. Needless to say, Louis-the-whatever changed his mind, and quickly, at that."

"An iron horse, huh?"

"Legend says you can still see its hoofprint on the cliff it leapt off."

To their right, separated from them by dense rows of pine, a stone tower raised its crenellated head above the tree line. "See?" Jim said, pointing to it. "Over there—that's Renfrew's keep."

"Which has seen better days."

"It's like seven hundred years old."

"So's Edinburgh Castle, isn't it?"

"Anyhoo," Jim said, "Renfew only stayed there part of the time. He was the court astrologer for the Holy Roman Emperor."

Neil grunted. No longer angry about the Rose incident, neither was he all the way over it. Had he been familiar with Scotland, he might have gone off for a few days on his own, left Jim to worry about what he was up to, whom he was having long, heartfelt conversations with over steaming mugs of chai. The trip, however, had been Jim's baby, a chance to share with Neil the place in which he'd passed the summers of his childhood while also promoting his surprisingly successful book. Neil could not make sense of the timetables for the trains or buses, and as for driving on the other side of the road, forget it. He had no choice but to remain with Jim and his revelation about his *affaire de coeur* with Rose Carlton, which he had dealt with from inside a roiling cloud first of anger, then pique. Jim met this change in their personal weather the way he always did, the way he always had, by talking too much, filling the charged air with endless facts, opinion, speculation.

Not for the first time, the irony of his book's title, *The Still Warrior*, struck him. How often had he urged his students at the dojo not to be afraid of their own quiet, of remaining in place, controlling their sparring bouts by forcing their opponents into committing to action first? It was a perspective he'd spent one hundred and forty-eight pages applying to a wide range of activities and situations, and based on the early sales figures, it was a viewpoint in which a significant portion of the reading public was interested. Look at his life off the dojo's polished hardwood, though, and he might as well have been writing fiction, fantasy rooted in the deepest wish fulfillment. Especially when it came to Neil, he was almost pathologically unable to leave things be, let the kinks and snarls in their relationship work themselves out, as the vast majority of them likely would. Instead, he had to plan excursions like this one, a walk along a nature path that was supposed to bring them . . . what? Closer? "You can't make a scar heal any faster," Neil had said, which Jim wasn't sure he believed but which Neil certainly did.

Ahead, the path was intersected by a secondary trail slanting up from the right. The new trail was little more than a disturbance in the forest's carpet of needles, but Neil turned onto it. "Hey," Jim said.

"I want to see where this goes."

Neil knew he wouldn't argue. *Prick*. Jim followed him off the main path . . .

. . . and was seized by a vertigo so extreme he might have been standing at the edge of a sheer cliff, rather than a not-especially steep trail. He leaned forward, and it was as if he were on the verge of a great abyss, an emptiness that was coaxing him forward, just one more step . . .

A hand gripped his arm. "Hey—you all right?" The voice was high, familiar.

Vision swimming, Jim said, "I don't," and heard the words uttered in a different voice—in what sounded like the voice on his and Neil's videos of their old vacations, his voice of ten years ago.

The hand steadying him belonged to a young man—to Neil, he saw, Neil as he had been when Jim had met him at a mutual friend's Y2K party. His hair was down to his shoulders and, as was the case when he let it grow, both curlier and a shade closer to strawberry blond. The lines on his face were not cut as deep, and his skin was pale from a life lived in front of the computer. Mouth tucked into the smirk that had first caught Jim's notice, he said, "Steady," and released Jim's arm.

Jim raised his right hand and brushed the half-dozen earrings that climbed his ear. He could feel his own hair ponytailed along the back of his neck. "Oh my God," he said.

"What is it?" Neil said.

"I—don't you—"

"Maybe the mushrooms weren't such a good idea."

"Mushrooms?" Jim said, even as he was thinking, *Yes, mushrooms, because that's the kind of shit you do now, at twenty-five, psilocybin and pot and occasionally hash and once in a great while a little E, because you're still five years away from the ambush of turning thirty, when you'll throw away all this stuff and more besides—soda, fast food, desserts—in favor of Shotokan karate seven days a week, fifty-two weeks a year. That's the future: right now, you're pursuing your private version of the systematic derangement of the senses.*

"Man," Neil said, "I guess those things were strong. I've never seen you like this before. Wish they would do something for me." He waved his hand in front of his eyes. "Nada."

"We—how did we get here?"

"We walked."

"No, I mean Kirkcaldy—Scotland."

"Wow."

"How did we get here?"

"Easy, there, easy," Neil said. "Work exchange, remember? I'm over here six weeks, that guy—Doug Moore, right?—is enjoying life in NYC. You tagged along because—well, because you're cute and I like you. Okay?"

Of course that was the case. The moment Jim heard Neil's explanation, he realized he already knew it. Cheeks burning, he said, "Okay. I'm sorry, it's just—those were some strong mushrooms."

"Yeah?"

"Yeah. I was having this whole fantasy that you and I were here, only, in the future."

"The future, huh? What were we like?"

"I had written this really popular book. We were here promoting it. You were . . . still programming, I think."

"Oh, so you're the famous writer and I'm just some computer nerd. Very nice."

"Hey, you were my computer nerd."

"Flattery."

"It's gotten me everywhere."

"You're feeling better."

"I guess."

"Good." The expression on Neil's face looked as if it might portend sex, a quickie amidst the trees, but he turned and continued down the secondary path. As Jim followed, he said, "Before you went all freaky, you were talking about the wizard, old Michael Renfrew."

"I was? Yeah, I suppose I was. Look to your right, ahead and you'll see Renfrew's keep."

"Where? Oh, yeah. What part is that?"

"Must be near the base. That's—I think that's a doorway. Hard to tell through the trees."

"So what about Renfrew?"

"Did I tell you about the iron horse?"

"And the King of France, yeah."

"There's a story about him and the Devil."

"Oh?"

"Or *a* devil: I can't remember which. At some point, he summoned a devil. I'm not sure why. Maybe for knowledge, or maybe to prove his power. It's one of those things magicians do all the time in old stories. Anyway, dealing with this guy was more dangerous than your run-of-the-mill evil spirit. If Renfrew could name a single task the devil could not perform, then he could make whatever use of him he wished for a year and a day. If not, the devil would pull him down to hell."

"And?"

"Renfrew took him to the beach, and commanded him to weave a rope out of sand."

"Not bad. What did he have the devil do for him?"

"The story doesn't say. It's more concerned with him outsmarting the devil than with Renfrew using him for his personal gain."

"Maybe that was how he got the iron horse."

"Could be."

"Anything else?"

"Not really. He's supposed to have had something to do with this book, *Les mystères du ver*, but I'm not sure what."

"*Les*—what?"

"*Les mystères du ver*: *The Mysteries of the Worm*. It's some kind of evil book, Satanic Bible, witch's spell list, that sort of thing."

"*The Mysteries of the Worm*, huh? No wonder you're interested in this guy."

"Worm? Try snake."

"Somebody's overcompensating."

"Merely stating the facts."

Neil did not answer, and Jim could not think of a way to extend their banter that did not sound forced, banal. *It's all right*, he told himself. *Silence is all right. You don't always have to be talking.* Wasn't that one of the things that had attracted him to Neil in the first place, his ability to be comfortable in his own quiet? Even in the length of time they'd been together, hadn't he learned that Neil's sometimes prolonged periods of silence rarely had anything to do with them, that he was usually turning over some work-related problem? He didn't feel the need to fill the air with words, and if that made Jim anxious, that wasn't Neil's fault, was it?

Plus, the sex is fantastic.

Maybe fifteen feet in front of Neil, the path leveled off and was met by another, slanting down from the right to join theirs at an acute angle. When Neil turned at the junction and started up it, Jim said, "Hey."

"Come on," Neil said. "This should take us back to the main trail."

No arguing with that. This track appeared clearer than the one they'd just descended, more sharply-defined. He followed onto it and it was as if he'd tried to walk up a wall. The path rose above him, impossibly high; he staggered backwards, dropped onto his ass. The path loomed overhead, a dark strip of ground about to fall on him, and—

A silhouette leaned in front of him. "What happened?" The voice was flat, familiar.

Struggling against the urge to throw his hands in front of his face, to protect himself from the collapse of dirt and rock, Jim said, "I don't," and was shocked to hear the fragment delivered in a voice whose underlying tones were his but which had been roughened, broadened.

The outline before him resolved into Neil, but a different Neil, a Neil whose face might have received the attentions of a makeup artist instructed to advance his age by twenty, twenty-five years. His hair was crew-cut short. His skin was grooved across the forehead, beneath the eyes, to either side of the mouth. Under the open collar of his shirt, a faded line of green ink scaled the left side of his neck, the edge of a tattoo, Jim knew—remembered. Were he to look into a mirror, he would see its twin on the left side of his neck, a memento of the aftermath of the Rose Carlton incident, when he and Neil had sought a way to reaffirm their bond. The eclipse had been Jim's idea, a symbol that, whatever events might darken their relationship, they would pass.

(Except that he'd developed a staph infection, which the tattooist, a mutual acquaintance, had spent days insisting could not be happening—he ran a clean shop—until Jim had wound up in the hospital, tethered to an IV antibiotic drip for a week. Nor had Neil moved past Rose, not really: Every time an argument escalated to a certain pitch, he reached for her like a favorite weapon.)

"You all right?" Neil asked, the words tinted with something resembling concern.

He's worried about my heart, Jim thought. *The infection affected my heart, weakened it.* (*What the hell is happening to me?*) "Fine," he said, climbing to his feet. "I'm fine, just . . . a little lightheaded." (*Is this some kind of long-term aftereffect of being sick? Did it mess with my head?*) He gestured at the path. "Go on."

"You're sure?"

"Go."

"Take it easy," Neil said. "This isn't a race." Nonetheless, he hurried to keep in front. "Okay?" he called over his shoulder.

"Great."

After a minute of trudging up the thick, rocky earth, Neil said, "Do you feel like continuing the story?"

"Story?"

"Story, chapter, whatever you want to call it. 'Renfrew and the Giant.'"

Almost before he knew he was speaking them, Jim found the words at his lips. "Having endured Renfrew's displays of power, the Giant was less than impressed by his offer of an alliance between them. He said, 'Little man, you have already shown me that I have nothing to fear from you. Why should I cast my lot in with yours?'

"Although obviously exhausted, Renfrew stood straighter and answered,

'Because you have everything to benefit if you do, and everything to lose if you do not.'

"At this, the Giant laughed, and it was the sound of an avalanche, of boulders crashing into one another. 'Little man,' he said, 'your boldness does you credit. I will eat you quickly.' He reached one enormous hand toward the wizard.

"Renfrew did not flinch. He said, 'I know your name—your true name.'

"The Giant's hand halted, inches from Renfrew. His vast brow lowered. 'Impossible,' he said. 'I hid that where no man—no one might find it, ever.'

"'Yes,' Renfrew said, 'in a cavern under a lake watched over by three mountains, locked inside a brass casket guarded by a basilisk. I have been there.'

"The Giant's hand retreated. He said, 'You read of this in one of your wizard's books.'

"Renfrew said, 'The sole means to open the casket is the tooth of a hydra, which is in the basilisk's stomach. The casket contains a pale blue egg resting on a white pillow. To touch the egg is like touching a furnace; to hear its shell crack is like hearing your own death. Within the egg, there is a stone into which has been carved a single word.'

"The Giant's hand had retreated all the way to his great mouth.

"Renfrew said, 'That word is *Mise*.'"

Neil said, "Meesh?"

"I think that's how it's pronounced. It's Gaelic, means, 'I am.'"

"I am?"

"Yeah. The original story doesn't say what the Giant's true name was, only that Renfrew had discovered it and used it against him. I thought about making it something like 'stone' or 'mountain,' but that seemed too obvious."

"Why?"

"Well, giants are big, you know; if you were going to associate them with anything, it would be a mountain."

"I guess."

"Anyway, it made sense to me that the Giant's name would be his life, so, 'I am.'"

"If you say so. Just as long as this one brings another big advance."

Jim said, "Karen's pretty optimistic. Post-Harry Potter, wizards and magic are big business in kids' publishing," even as he was thinking, *Karen Lowatchee, your agent, who repped you on* The Still Warrior *and, when the heart thing made you scale back karate, suggested you try fiction. She'd liked the chapters on karate for kids, said they showed a real grasp of tween psychology. She was the one who came up with the* Jenny Ninja *series title, and got you the big advances for the last two. Neil calls her "Glenda the Good Bitch"; she calls him "Microsoft."*

"What happens next?" Neil said.

"In the chapter? Renfrew turns the Giant into his keep."

"That's it?"

"That's what happens in the original legend."

"Yeah, but—couldn't he have used the Giant, first?"

"Invaded England with him?" Jim said.

"Something."

"I don't know. I kind of like the idea of Renfrew living inside the Giant, wandering around him, listening to the echo of his thoughts, his dreams."

"Sounds pretty creepy, if you ask me."

"And what's wrong with that?"

"Isn't this book supposed to be for kids?"

"It's YA," Jim said, "Young Adult. Older kids."

Over the tops of the pines to their right, Renfrew's keep raised its ragged crown. "See," Jim said, pointing at it, "the windows look like eyes."

"What has eyes like that?"

"It's supposed to be a monster."

"Aren't giants big people?"

"Not all of them. The ancient Greeks described giants with a hundred arms."

"Where do you get this stuff?"

"Depends. The ancient Greek stuff's available all over the place. Information on Renfrew is harder to come by. Mostly, I use that website, Blackguide.com."

"The one that crashed the computer?"

"I told you, it wasn't that: It was all the porn you'd been looking at."

"Very funny."

Neil's pace slowed. In front of him, their path intersected another sloping steeply down from the right. As he stepped onto it, Jim said, "Hey."

"I'm pretty sure this'll lead back to the beginning of the trail," Neil said.

This place isn't that big. I'm sure if I kept on a straight line, I'd come out on a side street, eventually. However discouraging the prospect of an even more strenuous climb was, though, the inevitable spat that would result from him not following Neil, not to mention the two or three days after that before the situation returned to normal, prompted him up the new path. As he did, his vision went dark. He had the impression of something huge in front of him, something vast hanging over him, like a wave, only solid, ready to crash down on him. He wanted to cry out, but his tongue was dead in his mouth; his heart lurched like a racehorse stumbling mid-stride.

Somewhere close by, an old man's voice said, "What is it? What's the matter with you?" The words vibrated with rage, barely controlled.

What's Neil's father doing here? Jim thought. He tried to speak. "Mr. Marshall—"

"Don't Mr. Marshall me. I know who I am. I'm still lucid."

The host of the questions the outburst raised was silenced by the clearing of Jim's sight, which revealed Neil's face inches from his. Its angry expression was almost parodic: eyes wide and staring under lowered brows, top lip arched, teeth visible, chin jutting forward. It was also the face of a man in his mid-seventies. Neil's hair was white, as were his eyebrows; both hair and brows were thick, bushy. The lines across his forehead, to either side of his mouth, appeared cut right down to the bone, while his skin looked loose, its grip on his skull slipping. His gaze was fierce yet unfocused, as if he were unable to pinpoint the source of his rage; already, his lips were retreating from their snarl into the tremors that shook them incessantly.

The Alzheimer's, Jim thought. *That was the first symptom: before the memory loss, the mood swings, that spasm was telling us what was on the way.*

"What happened to you?" Neil said. "Is it your heart? Are you having another heart attack?" The emotion under his words was sliding into panic.

"I'm fine," Jim said. "Just caught up in . . . " *What? What do I call whatever's happening to me? (And, by the way, what the hell is happening to me? Is this some kind of stroke?)* "In a rather vivid day dream, I suppose—a memory, really, of one of our past visits here."

"Oh? Was that before or after you fucked Rose?"

"I didn't—"

"Yes, yes, that's what you always say; what you've always said."

"But you've never believed me, have you?"

"I don't know what I believe. I'm the one whose brain is disintegrating, remember?"

"It isn't," Jim started, then stopped. Technically speaking, Neil's brain wasn't disintegrating, but there were worse ways to describe what was happening to his personality, to the aggregate of memories and attitudes that composed Neil. Anyway, Neil already had turned his back on him and was striding up the path. The disease might be wrecking his mind, but so far, his vitality was undiminished. Jim labored not to fall too far behind.

Neil said, "Do you remember the end of Renfrew's story?"

"Do you mean my book, or the legend?"

"Which was which?"

"My book ends with Renfrew entering the cave at Wemyss in search of the path to the Graveyard of the Old Gods. He leaves Thomas, his apprentice, in charge until his return, which doesn't take place during Thomas's very long life, or that of his apprentice, or that of any of the men and women who have come since. However, the book says, that doesn't mean that, one day, the old wizard won't emerge from the mouth of the cave, squinting at the light, and begin the long walk back to his old home."

"That wasn't it."

"You want the legend, then. That ends with a group of the Covenanters coming armed to Renfrew's keep in order to arrest him on charges of sorcery. When they arrived, though, they found the place deserted, as if no one had lived there for decades, or longer."

"That isn't it, either."

"I don't—there's a tradition, a kind of afterword to the legend proper, that if you follow a certain course through the woods around Renfrew's keep—and if certain conditions are right: the stars are in alignment, that sort of thing; I think an eclipse is supposed to figure into the equation, somehow—then Renfrew himself will appear to you and offer to teach you what he knows. Is that what you were thinking of?"

"Yes," Neil said.

Jim waited for Neil to add something more; when he did not, he said, "What makes you ask?"

"Ask what?"

"About Renfrew's course?"

"What about it?"

"You just asked me to tell you about it."

"I did." Neil shrugged. "I don't remember that."

There was no point in anger; though buttressed by his meds, Neil's short-term memory was far from perfect. Jim said, "You know what I was thinking?"

"How much longer you have to wait before you can put me in a home?"

"What? No, I told you, I'm not going to put you in a home."

"That's what you say now."

"That's what I have said—what I've been saying ever since you were diagnosed."

For a change, he hoped the silence that greeted his reassurance meant the subject of their debate had slipped through the sieve of Neil's immediate recollection. His quiet seemed to imply that it had, another moment caught in the plaque crusting his neurons, then he said, "I hope you and Rose will have the decency to wait until all my things have been moved out for her to move in."

"Neil—"

"It would be nice if you could wait until I'm in the ground, but I'm guessing I could hang on for a while, and you certainly aren't getting any younger. Neither is she; although she isn't as old as we are, is she? Maybe she'll be inclined to do the decent thing, but you won't, will you?"

"I'm sorry: I can't talk to you when you're like this."

Neil lengthened his stride, mountain-goating up the path. Jim didn't bother chasing after. Better to hang back and hope that, by the time he caught up, Neil's thunderstorm of emotions would have passed; though he wasn't sure what he rated the chances of that as. It had been years, almost a full decade, since he and Rose had seen one another, and that had been by accident, a chance encounter at the Union Square Barnes & Noble that had led to nothing more than the occasional e-mail. If he hadn't told Neil about the meeting, or the correspondence, it was because, long after his whatever-you-wanted-to-call-it with her had receded in his memory, in Neil's mind, it was a flame only recently and poorly extinguished, whose smoldering embers might yet ignite again. He would have made too much of the e-mails in which Jim told Rose about his visit to the set of the Renfrew film, Rose told him about her recent trip to Paris with her ninety-two year old mother, mountained the molehills into a secret, ongoing affair. In the wake of Neil's illness, he supposed he had been writing to her more frequently, but his correspondence with all his friends and family had increased as his communication with Neil had grown more erratic.

He was almost at the top of the path. He had climbed higher than he'd realized; to his right and over his shoulder, he could look down on the roofless top of Renfrew's keep. To his relief, Neil was standing waiting for him. "There you are," Jim said—panted, really.

"Here I am," Neil said. His expression was almost kindly. "Need a minute?"

"Half a minute," Jim said, leaning forward. "Neil—"

At Neil's feet, their path formed an acute angle with another climbing up from the right. As he started down it, Jim said, "Hey."

"I can see the place where we started," Neil said, pointing.

Jim squinted. Was that the white of the wizard's statue? They would have to descend from here somehow, he supposed, and this new path, crossed by tree roots that formed an irregular staircase, was probably the best option he could expect. He stepped down and it was like dropping into a well. There was the sensation of falling straight down, and the impression of everything flying up all around him, and the sound of roaring filling his ears. Terror swept through his chest, his head, made them sickeningly light. He flailed his arms. There was nothing under his feet; he was falling.

Something crashed into him from the front. He heard an *Oof!*, felt his direction change. Now he was moving forward, his arms and legs caught with someone else's, tangled, the pair of them thudding and scraping against rock and dirt. He rolled over and under, over and under his companion, then landed hard on his back, his right kidney shouting at the rock it came down on. Above him, the sky was a blue bowl someone had set spinning. He closed his eyes, and when he opened them, Neil was leaning over him. There was a cut high on his forehead leaking blood onto his brow, but aside from that and some dirt, his face was the same as it had been at the start of this strange walk, thirty-nine and looking it. "You klutz," he said. "Karate master, my ass."

Jim flung his arm around him, flinching as his back complained. "I'm sorry," he said into Neil's shoulder. "Are you okay?"

"You mean, aside from the gaping wound in my head? Yeah, I'm peachy."

Jim released him. "I am so sorry," he said as he struggled to his feet. "I just . . . I slipped."

"And you couldn't miss me on the way?"

"I didn't want you to feel left out."

Fighting it, Neil smirked. "You are such an asshole."

"But I'm your asshole."

"Enough shit comes out of you, anyway."

"Ah, I'm sure a little single malt will help."

"First sensible thing you've said all day."

They had rolled almost halfway down the path; no surprise, given the bruises Jim could feel ripening under his shirt, his jeans, the scrapes visible on Neil's arms, his neck. He supposed he should be grateful neither of them had broken a limb, or been concussed. At least Neil had been right about this path returning them to the entrance to the nature preserve: through the trees, the wizard's statue stood a pale beacon. As Neil stepped from tree root step to tree root step, Jim weighed telling him about his . . . what would he call them? Hallucinations? Visions? Waking dreams? Maybe "experiences" was the best word for them. Whatever: it was on the tip of his tongue to say that he had just relived their life together when they'd first met, then seen them at points another twenty and forty or so years in the future. *When I'm the author of a series of successful children's books and he's in mid-stage Alzheimer's, not to mention still obsessing over Rose Carlton: yes, that would go over splendidly.*

Neil was drawing away from him. Strangest of all was that, now that the two of them were their proper selves, he was not more upset by what he had just been through, his experiences. (That still wasn't the right word, but it would do for the moment.) While he had been at each of those other times, the moment had been as real as anything—that he had been wrenched from this specific point in his life had seemed as odd, as disorienting, as any other detail. Returned to the age at which he had entered the nature preserve—the age he was supposed to be—Jim found his and Neil's alternate selves suddenly distant, novels he'd read years ago, their plots dim weights resting in the depths of his memory.

So what was all that? Some kind of projection? Easy enough to trace the roots of at least some of it to the current state of his and Neil's relationship. Future

Neil's fixation on the Rose business arose from Jim's anxiety that, as time went on, he wouldn't be able to relinquish it. Jim's continued success as a writer was simple wish-fulfillment (although his agent had praised the sections of his book dealing with kids). Neil's grandfather had suffered from Alzheimer's, which his father was showing early symptoms of; from there, it was a short jump to imagining Neil eventually overtaken by it.

The vividness of everything, though, he could not account for. He had indulged in enough hallucinogens in his younger years; could this have been a delayed consequence of that? It seemed unlikely, but what was more likely? The place was the site of a ley line that produced brief time-distortions? *Funny how all the tourist info fails to mention that.*

To his right, the lower stretch of Renfrew's keep was visible through the trees. Ahead, Neil was already at the statue. Legs protesting, Jim picked up his pace. Neil had stopped in front of the sculpture, and appeared to be speaking to it. *That can't be good. Did I say neither of us was concussed?*

Jim did not see the man with whom Neil was talking until he was next to him. Standing on the other side of the statue, the man had been obscured from Jim's view by it. A head shorter than either of them, he wore his reddish hair short and a dark suit over an open-collared white shirt. Jim wasn't much for estimating the cost of things, but even he could recognize the quality of the man's clothes, which made the stains on his jacket cuffs, his shirt, all the more conspicuous. The man raised his eyes to Jim, and their green notice was a physical thing, a heaviness passing over him. "You're Jim," he said in a voice that was soft, accentless.

"Yes," Jim said, extending his hand. "You are . . . ?"

The man's hands were in his trouser pockets; he kept them there. "Renfrew."

"Like—" Jim gestured at the sculpture.

"The very same," the man said, "though the likeness is a poor one."

"Wait—what?" Jim glanced at Neil, who was watching the man intently. "I'm sorry: I thought you were saying—"

"I was." The man withdrew his hands from his pockets. Blue flames licked the unburned skin of the left; while a slender emerald snake coiled around the right.

"Jesus!" Jim leapt back.

"Not quite."

"What is this?"

Neil said, "We completed the course."

"You did." The man—Renfrew?—nodded. "Per the terms of a contract that is older than any of us, I am here to offer one of you my tutelage."

"One of us," Jim said. "What about the other?"

"The price of tuition," Renfrew said. "A gesture of commitment."

"Okay, that's enough," Jim said.

"Take me," Neil said.

"What?"

"Very interesting," Renfrew said.

"Neil what are you saying?"

"The Alzheimer's: that's a sure thing?" Neil said.

"Sure enough," Renfrew answered.

"And you can cure it?"

"I have been this age for a very long time," Renfrew said. "You need never meet that old man in the mirror."

"Are you kidding me?" Jim said. "Are you listening to yourself?"

"And there's no other way?" Neil said.

"There are many other ways, if you know where and how to find them. This is my way."

"I'm sorry," Neil started, but Jim cut him off: "This is insane."

"There was a link," Neil said, "on the Blackguide site. I clicked on it, and it led to an account by a guy who had walked this course in the 1930s with his brothers. With each new turn of the path, the three of them were at a different point in their lives: younger, then older, then much older. When they arrived back at the beginning, Renfrew was waiting for them."

"So all that was real?" Jim said.

"Real enough," Renfrew said.

"I thought if we could follow the course, then I could see how things would turn out—if we'd still be together; if we'd be happy; if Rose would still be around. I didn't expect—oh, Christ," Neil said. "Do you have any idea what it's like—no, you don't; how could you? Everything—you're aware that something is wrong, deeply wrong—you can feel it in everything around you—and you're sure you know what it is, what's the matter, but you can't remember it. And then you can remember, and you realize that the problem isn't with what's outside, it's with what's inside, and you know it's only a matter of time until you forget again and the whole process starts over." His eyes swam with tears.

"Neil, honey, it's okay," Jim said. "I'll be there for you."

"No," Neil said. "Don't you get it? I can't—I won't go through that. Now that I know—now that you know, how could you ask me to?"

"So instead you're going to . . . how does that story end, the one about the guy and his brothers?"

"The younger brother accepted Renfrew's offer. He and Renfrew disappeared, and when the older brother returned home, it was as if his brother had never existed. He was the only one who had any memory of him."

"Weren't there three of them? What happened to the other brother?"

"He vanished, too. No one remembered him, either."

Jim's mouth went dry. "The price of tuition."

"Speaking of which," Renfrew said, "we really need to move this along."

"You aren't going to do this," Jim said.

"What choice do I have?"

"You could choose me—choose us."

"Are you sure you don't want to make me an offer?" Renfrew said.

"Me?" Jim said. "I thought Neil—"

"Was here first, yes, but that's more a recommendation than a rule. I'm curious to learn how your convictions fare when the situation is reversed."

Neil's mouth moved, but no sound issued from it.

"Well?" Renfrew said.

His fear seemed outside him, an acrid saturation pressing on him from all sides at once; nonetheless, Jim was able to say, "Fuck you." The frown that darkened Renfrew's face was a small pleasure. Jim looked at Neil, who was staring at the ground. "What I had with Rose—it was never as bad as you thought it was, and when I said it was over, it was."

"For you, maybe."

Renfrew swept his left arm up and down, blue fire trailing from his fingertips, tracing a seam in the air that opened into something like a door. He nodded at Neil, who crossed to and stepped through it without another word. Jim was as astonished by his lack of a parting remark as anything.

"Now," Renfrew said, extending his right hand at Jim. The serpent wrapped around it raised its wedge-shaped head and regarded him lazily. The space behind the wizard darkened, full of an enormous shape. Jim thought, *How did the keep*—and realized that what had stepped closer was not the keep, or, not anymore. It arched towards him, impossible mouth open to consume him, all of him, not only the flesh and bones it would grind between teeth like boulders, but his past, his present, his future, his very place in the world. He wished his fear would leave him, but he supposed it was better than the serrated edge of Neil's betrayal waiting beneath it. At least he could keep his eyes open; at least he would not turn away from the emptiness, the silence, descending on him.

John Langan's latest collection of stories, *The Wide, Carnivorous Sky and Other Monstrous Geographies*, was recently published by Hippocampus Press. He is the author of a novel, *House of Windows*, and collection *Mr. Gaunt and*

Other Uneasy Encounters. His short fiction has appeared in several anthologies, including *Wastelands, The Living Dead, By Blood We Live, Poe, Supernatural Noir, Blood and Other Cravings, Ghosts by Gaslight, Fungi, A Season in Carcosa,* and *Black Wings II.* He's also published stories in *The Magazine of Fantasy & Science Fiction, Lightspeed,* and *Postscripts.* With Paul Tremblay, he co-edited the anthology, *Creatures: Thirty Years of Monsters.* He teaches courses in creative writing and gothic fiction at SUNY New Paltz, and lives in upstate New York with his family.

He screamed and struggled against the wave of ancient voices,
but inhuman force turned him back to face the horrors . . .

END OF WHITE

Ekaterina Sedia

Coronet Kovalevsky had never expected to find that land was finite. It seemed so abundant to him when he was younger, something you could never possibly run out of—or run off of—that the very suggestion seemed ludicrous. Yet there he was in the summer of 1919, teetering on the precipice of the Crimean peninsula, with very little idea of what to do after Wrangel's inevitable defeat and his own presumed tumble into the Black Sea. He had decided that he would not join the Bolsheviks—not so much out of any deeply held belief but rather because of his inherent disposition to avoid any large amounts of soul-overhauling work. He appeared committed and idealistic from the outside, even though inside he knew it was mere laziness and ennui.

So he lingered with the rest of his regiment in the small Crimean town (more of a village, if one was to be honest) named N., close to the shore, away from the invading Red armies and the dry, fragrant steppes that smelled like thyme and sun. At first, the officers kept to themselves, spending their days playing cards in the town's single tavern, and waiting for the news from the front. The evacuations of Murmansk and Arkhangelsk had already started, and the British hospital near N. promised the same opportunities for salvation, if the things didn't go the way Wrangel wanted them to. They waited for the fighting, for some way to end this interminable standoff. Kovalevsky hoped that his demise would be quick and, if not glorious, then at least non-embarrassing.

But the days were warm, the house he stayed in had white curtains on its tiny windows, cut like embrasures in thick clay walls—walls that retained pleasant coolness long into the afternoon heat. A split-rail fence half-heartedly guarded long rows of young sunflowers and poppies, with more mundane potatoes and beets hidden behind them, and a couple of chickens scratched in the dust of the yard. It was not unpleasant, if overly rustic.

The owner of the clay-walled, thickly whitewashed house was one Marya

Nikolavna, a small and disappearing kind of woman who seemed neither overjoyed nor appalled to have an officer quartering in her house; but nonetheless she frequently brought him homemade kvas and ripe watermelons, their dark green skins warm from the sun and their centers cold as well water, red and crumbling with sugar. She did not complain when Olesya started to come by.

Oh, Kovalevsky could tell that there was gypsy blood in Olesya—there was wildness about her, in the way the whites of her eyes flashed in the dusk of his room, the way her pitch-black braid snaked down her back, its tip swinging hypnotic as she walked. It took him a while, however, to recognize that it wasn't just the wild gypsy fire that smoldered hot and low in her blood, it was something else entirely that made her what she was.

It was a cloudy, suffocating kind of day in July, when everything—man, beast, and plant—hunkered close to the ground and waited for the relief of a thunderstorm. Unease charged the air with its sour taste, and Kovalevsky, feeling especially indisposed to getting out of bed that day, watched Olesya pad on her cat-soft feet across the wide floorboards, her half-slip like a giant gardenia flower, her breasts, dark against the paler skin stretched over her breastbone, lolling heavily. She opened the curtains to peer outside, the curtain of her messy black hair falling over half her back. Her profile turned, silver against the cloudy darkened glass. "It's going to rain," she said, just as the first leaden drops thrummed against the glass and the roof, formed dark little craters in the dust, pummeled the cabbage leaves like bullets.

And just as if the spell of heavy, lazy air was lifted, Olesya straightened and bounded out the door, shrieking in jubilation.

Kovalevsky, roused from his languid repose by the sound as well as the breaking heat, sat up on the bed, just in time to see Olesya running across the yard. He cringed, imagining her running through the village like that, half naked—not something he would put beyond her—as she disappeared from view. She soon reappeared, fists full of greenery, and came running inside, her wet feet slapping the floor and the black strands of her hair plastered to her skin, snaking around her shoulders like tattoos.

"What's this?" Kovalevsky asked, nodding at the tangled stems in her fist beaded with raindrops.

"This is for you," she said as she tossed a few poppies, their capsules still green and rubbery, at his bed. "And this"—she held up dark, broad leaves and hairy stems of some weed he didn't know—"this is for me."

She found his penknife on the bed table and drew crisscrossing lines on the green poppy capsules, until they beaded with white latex. Kovalevsky watched, fascinated—the drops of rain, the drops of white poppy blood . . . it made sense then when Olesya drew the blade along the pad of her left thumb, mirroring the beaded trail in red. And in this cut, she mashed a dark green leaf, closing her eyes. She then wadded up the rest of the leaves and stuck them behind her cheek, like a squirrel. She tossed the pearled poppy capsules at Kovalevsky. "Here."

He wasn't naïve, of course—he just didn't feel any particular need for additional intoxicants. But under Olesya's suddenly wide gaze, her pupils like twin wells, he drew the first capsule into his mouth and swallowed, undeterred by its grassy yet bitter taste.

His sleep was heavy, undoubtedly aided by the monotone of the rain outside and by the drug in his blood. He dreamed of waves and of Olesya, of her bottomless eyes. He dreamed of her wrapping his head in her white underskirts so that he became blind, mute, and deaf, and his mouth filled with suffocating muslin. He woke up, coughing, just as the moon looked into his room through the opened curtains and opened window. Olesya was gone—of course she was, why wouldn't she be? Yet, he was uneasy, as he stared at the black sky and the silver moon. He imagined it reflecting in the sea, just out of sight, in parallel white slats of a moon road. It was so bright, the large fuzzy stars in its proximity faded into afterimages of themselves.

The opium still clouded his senses and his mind, and he lolled on the border between sleep and wakefulness, his mouth dry and his eyelids heavy, when fluttering of curtains attracted his attention. He peered into the darkness and managed to convince himself that it was just the wind, a trick of light, but just as he started to drift off, a spot in the darkness resolved into an outline of a very large and very black cat, who sat on the floor by the foot of his bed, its green eyes staring.

Now, the cats as such were not an unusual occurrence—like any place that grew crops, the village was besotted by mice, and cats were both common and communal, traveling from one barn to the next yard, from a hay loft of one neighbor to the kitchen of another. They were welcomed everywhere, and their diet of mice was often supplemented by milk and meat scraps (but never eggs: no one wanted the cats to learn to like eggs and start stealing them from under hens). Yet, this cat seemed particularly audacious, as it sat and stared at Kovalevsky. He stared back until his eyelids fluttered and gave out, and he felt himself sinking into his drugged sleep again; through the oppressive fog, he felt the cat jump up on the bed and he was surprised by its heft—the bed gave and moaned as the beast, soft-pawed, kneaded and fussed and finally curled next to his thigh.

The next morning came with no traces of the strange cat's presence—or Olesya's, for that matter. Kovalevsky felt rested, and decided to visit the only drinking establishment the village possessed—indicated only by a faded and yet unusually detailed sign depicting a black goat with what seemed to be too many limbs, a fancy often found in rustic artists. The tavern was located in the same building as N.'s only hotel; it was a wide, low room housing a series of rough tables and serving simple but filling fare—borscht and dumplings swimming in butter and sour cream, then black bread and pickled beets and herring. This is where most of the officers spent their days—at least, those who had not been lucky enough to take up with one of the local sirens.

To his surprise, the tavern was quiet; the owner, a well-fed and heavily mustachioed Ukrainian named Patsjuk, lounged at the table nearest to the kitchen.

Kovalevsky asked for tea and bread and butter, and settled at the wide table by the window. The grain of the rough wooden slats was warm under his fingertips, a tiny topographic map, and he closed his eyes, feeling the ridge, willing them to resemble the terrain they had covered. There was just so much of it—on foot and horseback, on the train, sleeping in the thin straw, next to the peasants and lost children crawling with typhoid lice. The railroads and the regular roads (highways, dirt paths, streets) went up and down and up again, wound along and across rivers, through the mountains, through forests—and his fingers twitched as he tried to remember every turn and every elevation, until Patsjuk brought him his tea and warm bread, peasant butter (melted and solidified again into yellow grainy slabs) piled on the saucer like stationary waves.

"Where's everyone?" Kovalevsky asked. His tea smelled of the same heavy greenery that tainted Olesya's breath last night, and he wondered about where she went—to what Sabbath.

Patsjuk shrugged and leered. "Wouldn't know. Your colonel was by the other day, but he's just about the only one who even comes anymore. I suspect the rest discovered the moonshiners, or some other nonsense abomination." He spat.

Kovalevsky nodded—Colonel Menshov was just the type to keep to the straight and narrow, away from any shady liquor, very much the same way as the rest of the regiment were likely to do the exact opposite. Kovalevsky could only assume that he hadn't heard anything of the matter due to his recent discovery of novelty intoxicants, of which Olesya was not the least.

One needed intoxicants at the times like these—at the times when one's army was all but squeezed between the pounding waves and the impossible, unturnable tide of the Reds, and the matters of being compressed like that (and where would one go under such circumstances) seemed impossible to ponder, and Kovalevsky tried his best to let his gaze slide along the ridges and the valleys of the yellow butter, to distract his uneasy mind from things that would make it more uneasy. To his good luck, an outside distraction soon presented itself.

Colonel Menshov walked into the dining room, in a less leisurely step than the circumstances warranted—in fact, he downright trotted in, in an anxious small gait of a man too disturbed to care about outward appearances. "Kovalevsky!" he cried, his face turning red with anguish. "There's no one left!"

"So I heard," Kovalevsky said. He slid down the long, grainy wooden bench to offer Menshov a seat. "Patsjuk here says they fell in with the moonshiners."

"Or Petliura got them," Patsjuk offered from his place behind the counter unhelpfully.

"What Petliura?" Menshov, who just sat down, bolted again, wild-eyed, his head swiveling about as if he expected to see the offender here, in the tavern.

"He's joking, I think," said Kovalevsky. "Symon Petliura is nowhere near these parts."

"In any case, it's just you and me." Menshov waved at Patsjuk. "If you have any of that moonshine you've mentioned, bring me a shot of your strongest."

Kovalevsky decided not to comment, and waited until Menshov tossed back his drink, shuddered, swore, and heaved a sigh so tremulous that the ends of his gray mustache blew about. "What happened?" he said then.

"Darkness," Menshov said. "Not to mention, everyone except you is missing."

"They'll come back."

"I'm not so sure." Menshov gestured for Patsjuk to hurry with another drink. "Demons and dark forces are in this place, you hear? It's crawling with the unclean ones."

Kovalevsky looked at Patsjuk, who busied himself pouring a murky drink from a large glass bottle, and appeared to be doing everything in his power to avoid eye contact. Kovalevsky guessed that he probably played not a small part in straying Menshov off the straight and narrow.

"What led you to that conclusion?" Kovalesky asked.

"Cats," Menshov said, and waved his arms excitedly. "Haven't you seen them? Giant black cats that walk on hind legs? These are no cats but witches."

Kovalevsky felt a chill creeping up his spine, squeezing past the collar of his shirt and exploding in a constellation of shivers and raised hairs across the back of his head. He remembered the nightmare weight of the cat, and Olesya's smolder stare, her hands as she cut the poppies, how they bled their white juice . . . He shook his head. "There was a cat in your house?"

"Last night." Menshov slumped in his seat. "The awful creature attacked me as I slept—I woke and was quick enough to grab my inscribed saber. I always have it by my bed."

"Naturally," Kovalevsky said.

"The cat—and it was large, as large as a youth of ten or so—swiped at my face, and I swung my saber at its paw. It howled and ran out through the window, and its paw . . . it stayed on the floor. God help me, it's still there, I didn't have the bravery to toss it or to even touch it. Come with me, I'll show you, and you'll see that this is a thing not of this world—that it has no right to be at all."

Kovalevsky followed, reluctant and fearful of the possibility that Menshov was neither drunk nor addled. The fact that he even entertained the thought showed to him how unhinged he had become—then again, months of retreat and the trains crawling with lice would do it to a man. He wondered as he walked down the dusty street, large sunflowers nodding behind each split rail fence, if the shock of the revolution and the war had made them (everything) vulnerable—cracked them like pottery, so even if they appeared whole at the casual glance, in reality they were cobwebbed with hairline fissures, waiting only for a slightest shove, a lightest tap, to become undone and to tumble down in an avalanche of useless shards.

Menshov stopped in front of a fence like every other, the wood knotted and bleached by the sun, desiccated and rough, and pushed the gate open. It swung inward with a long plaintive squeal, and Kovalevsky cringed. Only then did he become aware of how silent the village had become—even in the noon heat, one was used to hearing squawking of chickens and an occasional bark of a languid dog.

"You hear it too?" Menshov said. "I mean, don't hear it."

"Where's everyone? Everything?"

There was no answer, and one wasn't needed—or even possible. The house stood small and still, its whitewashed walls clear and bright against the cornflower-blue of the sky, the straw thatched roof golden in the sunlight. Kovalevsky knew it was cool and dry inside, dark and quiet like a secret forest pool, and yet it took Menshov's pleading stare to persuade him to step over the threshold into the quiet deep darkness, the dirt floor soft under his boots.

He followed Menshov to the small bedroom, vertiginously like Kovalevsky's own—square window, clean narrow bed covered with a multicolored quilt—his heart hammering at his throat. He felt his blood flow away from his face, leaving it cold and numb, even before he saw the grotesque paw, a few drops and smudges of blood around it like torn carnations. But the paw itself pulled his attention—it was black and already shriveling, its toes an inky splash around the rosette of curving, sharp talons, translucent like mother-of-pearl. If it was a cat's paw, it used to belong to one very large and misshapen cat.

"My God," Kovalevsky managed, even as he thought that with matters like these, faith, despite being the only protection, was no protection at all. His mind raced, as he imagined over and over—despite willing himself to stop with such foolish speculation—he imagined Olesya leaving his house that morning, the stump of her human arm dripping with red through cheesecloth wrapped around it, cradled against her lolling breast.

"Unclean forces are at work," Menshov said. "And we are lost, lost."

Kovalevsky couldn't bring himself to disagree. He fought the Red and the Black armies, and he wasn't particularly afraid of them—but with a single glance at the terrible paw, curling on the floor in all its unnatural plainness, resignation took hold, and he was ready to embrace whatever was coming, as long as it was quick and granted him oblivion.

He tried to look away, but the thing pulled at his glance as if it was a string caught in its monstrous talons, and the more he looked, the more he imagined the battle that took place here: in his mind's eye, he saw the old man, the hilt of the saber clutched in both hands as if he became momentarily a child instead of a seasoned warrior, his naked chest hairless and hollow, backing into the corner. And he saw the beast—the paw expanded in his mind, giving flesh and image to the creature to which it was attached. It was a catlike thing, but with a long muzzle, and tufted ears and chin. It stood on its stiff hind legs, unnaturally straight, without the awkward slumping and crouching usually exhibited by the four-legged beasts, its long paws hanging limply by its sides for just a second, before snatching up and swiping at Menshov.

Kovalevsky always had vivid imagination, but this seemed more than mere fancy—it was as if the detached paw had the power to reach inside his eyeballs somehow and turn them to hidden places, making him see—see as Menshov staggered back, the saber now swinging blindly. He propped his left hand against the bedpost, gaining a semblance of control, just as the monster reached its deformed paw and swept across Menshov's bare shoulder, drawing a string of blood beads across it.

The old man hissed in pain and parried, just as the creature stepped away, hissing back in its low throbbing manner. With every passing second, Kovalevsky's mind imagined the creature with greater and greater clarity, just as the still-sane part of him realized that the longer he stared at the accursed paw, the closer he moved to summoning the creature itself.

He clapped his hand over his eyes, twisting away blindly. Whatever strange power had hold of him deserved the name Menshov gave it—it was unclean and ancient, too old for remembering and cursed long before the days of Cain.

Menshov's mind was apparently on a similar track. "If we die here," he said, quietly, "there's no way for us but the hellfire."

"Would there be another way for us otherwise?"

Menshov stared, perturbed. "We've kept our oath to the Emperor. We fought for the crown, and we fought with honor."

"That's what I mean." Kovalevsky forced his gaze away from the paw and turned around, as little as he liked having it behind his back. "Come now, let's see who else can we find. And as soon as we do, we best leave—if they let us, if we can."

They searched for hours—but no matter how many doors they knocked on, only empty shaded coolness greeted them, as if every house in the village had been gutted, hollowed of all human presence, and left as an empty decoration to await a new set of actors. And the more they saw of it, the more convinced Kovalevsky grew that the buildings must've been like that—empty, flat— before they'd moved in. Where were the villagers? And, most importantly, where was Olesya? Was she just a vision, a sweet nightmare created from his loneliness and fear, aided by the soothing latex of the poppies in the yard and Patsjuk's dark green tea?

"Was it always like this?" Menshov said when the two of them finally stopped, silent and sweating. "Do you remember what this place was like when we first got here?"

Kovalevsky shook his head, then nodded. "I think it was . . . normal. A normal village."

He remembered the bustling in the streets, the peasants and the noisy geese, bleating of goats, the clouds of dust under the hooves of the White Army's horses when they rode in. Did they ride in or did they walk? If they rode, where were the horses—gone, swept away with everything else?

And then he remembered—a memory opened in his mind like a fissure—he remembered the view of the village and how quiet it was, and how he said to a man walking next to him (they must've been on foot, not horseback) that it was strange that there was no smoke coming from the chimneys. And then they walked into the village, and there was bustle and voices and chimneys spewed fat white smoke, and he'd forgotten all about it. "Maybe not so normal," he said. "I remember not seeing any smoke when we first approached."

Menshov nodded, his gray mustache shaking. "I remember that too! See, it was like an illusion, a night terror."

"The whole town?" Kovalevsky stopped in his tracks, his mind struggling to embrace the enormity of the deception—this whole time, this whole village . . . It couldn't be. "What about Patsjuk and his tavern? We were just there. Is it still . . . ?"

"Let's find out."

As they walked back, the dusty street under their feet growing more insubstantial with every passing moment, Kovalevsky thought that perhaps this all was the result of this running out of land—running out of the world. After all, if there was no place left for the White Army, wouldn't it be possible that some of them simply ran and tripped into some nightmare limbo? It seemed likely, even.

The tavern stood flat and still, and it seemed more like a painting than an actual building—it thinned about the edges, and wavered, like hot air over a heated steppe. Illusion, unclean forces.

Patsjuk sat on the steps, and seemed real enough—made fatter, more substantial by the fact that Olesya perched next to him, her round shoulder, warm and solid under her linen shirt, resting comfortably against the tavern's owner's. Both her hands were intact, and Kovalevsky breathed a sigh of relief, even if he wasn't sure why.

She grinned when she saw Kovalevsky. "There you are," she said. "See, you took my medicine, took my poison, and now you're lost. The loving goat-mother will absorb you, make you whole again."

Menshov grasped Kovalevsky's shoulder, leaned into him with all his weight. "Why?" he said.

A pointless question, of course, Kovalevsky thought. There were never any whys or explanations—there was only the shortage of land. By then, the ground around them heaved, and the dead rose, upright, the nails of their hands still rooting them to the opened graves, their eyes closed and lips tortured. The streets and the houses twisted, and the whole world became a vortex of jerking movement, everything in it writhing and groaning—and only the tavern remained still in the center of it.

Kovalevsky's hand, led by a memory of the time when he cared enough to keep himself alive, moved of its own volition, like a severed lizard's tail, and slid down his leg and into his boot, grasping for the horn handle of the knife he always had on him. He hadn't remembered it, but his body had, and jerked the knife out, assuming a defensive, ridiculous posture. He swiped at the air in front of him, not even trying for Patsjuk's belly, then turned around and ran.

His boots sunk into the road as if it were molasses, but he struggled on, as the air buzzed around him and soon resolved into bleating of what seemed like a thousand goats. Transparent dead hands grasped at him, and the black thing, more goat than a cat now, tried to claw its away out of his skull. Kovalevsky screamed and struggled against the wave of ancient voices, but inhuman force turned him back, back, to face the horrors he tried to run from.

So this is how it is, Kovalevsky thought, just as Olesya's face stretched into a muzzle, and her lower jaw hinged open, unnaturally wide. Without standing up, she extended her neck at Menshov. The old man grasped at his belt, uselessly, looking for his saber, even as Olesya's mouth wrapped around his head.

On the edge of his hearing, Kovalevsky heard whinnying of the horses off in the distance, and the uncertain, false tinny voice of a bugle. The Red Armies were entering the town of N.; he wondered briefly if the same fate awaited them—but probably not, since they were not the ones rejected by the world itself.

Kovalevsky closed his eyes then, not to see, and resigned himself to the fact that his run was over, and at the very least there would be relief from the sickening crunch that resonated deep in his spine, from the corpses and their long fingernails that dragged on the ground with barely audible whisper, and from the tinny bugle that was closing on him from every direction.

Born and raised in Moscow, **Ekaterina Sedia** now resides in the Pinelands of New Jersey. She is the author of four critically acclaimed novels, *The Secret History of Moscow*, *The Alchemy of Stone*, *The House of Discarded Dreams*, and *Heart of Iron*. Her short stories have been published in periodicals such as *Analog*, *Baen's Universe*, *Subterranean*, *Fantasy*, and *Clarkesworld*, as well as numerous anthologies, including *Haunted Legends* and *Magic in the Mirrorstone*. Her first collection of short fiction, *Moscow But Dreaming*, was published last year. She is also the editor of *Paper Cities* (World Fantasy Award winner), *Running with the Pack* and *Bewere the Night*, *Willful Impropriety*, *Circus: Fantasy Under the Big Top*, and *Bloody Fabulous*.

Miss Sycorax has been making some very strange calls...

WHO IS ARVID PEKON?

Karin Tidbeck

Despite the well-known fact that it's the worst time possible, everyone who needs to speak to a governmental agency calls on Monday morning. This Monday was no exception. The tiny office was buzzing with activity, the three operators on the day shift bent over their consoles in front of the ancient switchboard.

On Arvid Pekon's console, subject 1297's light was blinking. He adjusted his headset, plugged the end of the cord into the jack by the lamp and said in a mild voice:

"Operator."

"Eva Idegård, please," said subject 1297 at the other end.

"One moment." Arvid flicked the mute switch and fed the name into the little computer terminal under the wall of lamps and jacks. Subject 1297 was named Samuelsson, Per. Idegård, Eva was Samuelsson's case worker at the unemployment insurance office. He read the basic information (*1297 unemployed for seven months*), listened to the voice sample, and flicked the mute switch again.

"Gothenburg unemployment insurance office, Eva Idegård," Arvid said in a slightly hoarse alto voice.

"Hi, this is Per Samuelsson," said Per. "I wanted to check what's happening with my fee." He rattled off his personal registration number.

"Of course," said Arvid in Eva Idegård's voice.

He glanced at the information in the registry: *last conversation at 1.43 PM, February 26: Subject's unemployment benefits were lowered and insurance fee raised because of reported illness but no doctor's certificate. (Subject did send a doctor's certificate—processed according to randomized destruction routine §2.4.a.)*

"You'll have to pay the maximum insurance fee since we haven't received a doctor's certificate," said Arvid.

"I sent two of them in the original," said Per. "This isn't right."

"I suppose one could think that," said Arvid, "but fact remains that we haven't received them."

"What the hell do you people do all day?" Per's voice was noticeably raised.

"You have a responsibility to keep informed and send the right information to the unemployment benefit fund, Per," Arvid said, in a soft voice.

"Bitch. Hag," said Per and hung up.

Arvid removed his headset, massaged the sore spot it left above his right ear. He wrote in the log: *2.07 PM, March 15: Have explained the raised fee.*

"Coffee break?" said Cornelia from the terminal to his right.

The light by subject 3426 was blinking when Arvid sat down again.

"Operator," said Arvid, calling the details up on his screen. There was no information except for a surname: Sycorax, Miss. He hadn't seen this subject before.

"Hello?" said a voice. It was thin and flat.

"Yes, hello."

"I would like to be put through to my dead mother," said Miss Sycorax.

"Just a moment." Arvid muted the call. "Dead mother? How am I supposed to imitate her dead mother?" he said to his terminal. He peeked for the guidelines that should be popping up next to Miss Sycorax's name. There was nothing. Then he saw his hand rise up and flick the mute switch, and a sonorous voice burst out of his mouth. "Hello?"

"Mother, is that you?" said Miss Sycorax.

"Darling! Hello there. It's been a while, hasn't it?"

"Finding a good connection to Hell isn't easy, Mother."

Arvid fought to press his lips together. Instead they parted, and his mouth said: "It's lonely down here."

"Not much I can do about that, Mother," Miss Sycorax replied.

"Can't you come visit, just for once?" said Arvid, his voice dolorous. He desperately wanted to rip his headset off, but his hands lay like limp flippers in his lap.

"Well, if you're only going to be whiny about it I think we can end this conversation," Miss Sycorax said, tartly.

Arvid called her just that—tart—in her dead mother's voice. His ear clicked. Miss Sycorax had hung up. Arvid's hands were his own again. He took his headset off with shaky hands and looked around. At the next terminal, Cornelia was talking to subject 2536 (*Persson, Mr., talking to an old friend from school in Vilhelmina*), twirling a lock of dark hair around her pencil as she spoke to the subject in an old man's voice. When she ended her call, Arvid stood up from his chair.

"I'll be leaving early," he said.

"Oh. Are you all right?" Cornelia asked, reverting to her melodic Finno-Swedish.

Arvid looked for any sign that she had overheard him talking in a dead person's voice, but thought he saw nothing but concern in her liquid brown eyes.

"Migraine, I think." Arvid took his coat from the back of the chair. "Migraine, I have a migraine."

"Go home and rest," said Cornelia. "It happened to me a lot when I was new. It'll get better, I promise." She turned back to her terminal to take a new call.

Arvid punched out and left the office. Outside, yellow afternoon light slanted through the street. As Arvid unlocked his bicycle, a woman in a phone booth next to the bicycle stand was arguing with some- one. Arvid caught the words "unemployment" and "fee." He wondered briefly if that was Cornelia's call; she was unyielding in her case worker personas.

Arvid did feel better the next day. By nine-o'-clock coffee, he felt more or less normal. As he entered the break room, he saw that Konrad, the senior operator, was carefully laying out pale cakes on a plate. Cornelia was stirring an enormous mug of coffee.

"Kubbar!" said Konrad. "I made them last night."

Arvid picked a cake from the plate and bit into it. It was dry and tasted of ammonia and bitter almonds. Cornelia was sniffing at hers. "How are they?" Konrad asked. He was watching Arvid eagerly. "I haven't made these for years. I was wondering if I got the proportions right."

"It's different," Arvid managed. He washed the cake down with some coffee.

"It tastes like cyanide shortbread," stated Cornelia. "Very Agatha Christie."

"Heh," said Konrad. He took a cake for himself and tasted it. "Your generation isn't used to ammonia cakes, I suppose."

Arvid had another cake. The ammonia taste was strangely addictive.

"I have a question for you," Arvid said after a moment. "You've been here the longest. How are the subjects picked, really?"

Konrad shrugged and bit into his third *kubbe*. "No idea," he said. "I signed an NQ-NDA, just like you."

Arvid looked at Cornelia, who was chewing. She jerked a thumb at Konrad and nodded.

"So nobody knows?" said Arvid.

"The manager does, I expect," Konrad replied. "But don't you ever wonder?"

"No Questions, No Disclosure, son. I'm not about to bite the hand that feeds me. Besides, all you need to know is in the work description. We take calls to governmental agencies . . . "

" . . . and calls to persons the subjects don't know very well," Arvid filled in. "But—"

"And follow instructions. That's all there is to it. That's all you need to know. The manager relies on our discretion, Arvid. NQ-NDA."

Arvid sighed. "All right. What did you do before you got this job, anyway?"

"Stage actor," said Konrad. He picked a fourth *kubbe* from the plate. "Mhm?" he said, pointing at Arvid with the cake.

"Ventriloquist." Arvid nodded at Cornelia. "You?"

"Book audiotapes," said Cornelia.

Konrad swallowed. "See there, three crap jobs you can't make a living off of. Isn't it nice to be able to pay rent and eat good food?"

"I guess," said Arvid.

"You're new here. When you get over that starving artist thing, when you're my age, you'll agree that it's nice to be able to eat roast beef." Konrad pushed the plate toward Arvid. "Here, have another *kubbe*."

It was one week later, just after lunch, that Miss Sycorax's lamp started blinking again. Arvid hesitantly took the call.

"Hello," said the flat voice of Miss Sycorax.

"Where would you like to be connected?" said Arvid. "I want to be connected to the Beetle King."

"I see," said Arvid and muted Miss Sycorax. He cast a frantic glance at Cornelia, who was deeply involved in yet another call with subject 9970, Anderberg. Mrs. Cornelia frowned and waved him off. He returned to Miss Sycorax.

"Miss, I'm afraid I really can't connect you to anyone by the name of hello, my little pupa." A rustling voice forced its way out of his mouth mid-sentence.

"There you are," Miss Sycorax said. "I have a request."

"Anything for my little sugar lump," hummed Arvid.

"Aww, shucks," said Miss Sycorax.

"Your wish?"

"There are bugs crawling all over me."

"I know! Isn't it wonderful?" crowed Arvid.

"Hm. Yes, perhaps. In any case," she went on, "I'd like them to take some time off. I'm developing a rash."

"A rash, yes? An eczema."

"Yes. It's flaking a bit."

"And that isn't very pleasant."

"No. It itches."

"Well," said Arvid, "where should I send them off to, then?"

"Anywhere you like," said Miss Sycorax. "But for example, I don't like the old woman in the corner store. Or the man who sells sticky window-pane-climbing dolls in Old Town."

"Ahah."

"I don't like the switchboard operator either."

"Let's say then," said Arvid, "that we dismiss the little critters until you feel better."

"Good."

"And you let me know when you start feeling lonely again."

"Okay."

"Goodbye, honeycomb."

"Goodbye, your Majesty."

When the Beetle King's voice had left him, Arvid sagged back in his chair.

"I might have gone mad," he told the terminal. He put his coat on and left the office.

When he came into the office the next day, Arvid found a stag beetle sitting on his terminal. It hissed angrily when he shooed it off, and crawled in under the desk where it refused to move. Shortly after morning coffee, a cockroach settled on his rules-and-regulations binder. Arvid left it alone.

Cornelia was more drastic about it. She had sat down in her chair to find the stuffing colonized by flour beetles. She was currently in the backyard, setting fire to the seat. The whole office smelled like insulin. Konrad sat at his terminal at the other end of the office, observing with great interest a dung beetle struggling with some cookie crumbs. No one was taking the incoming calls.

"Shouldn't we call pest control?" said Arvid.

"Can't get through," said Konrad, eyes on the beetle. "I heard something on the radio about a bug invasion in Old Town."

"Maybe it's the season for it," said Arvid.

"This dung beetle," said Konrad, "this beetle shouldn't be here at all. It's African. A very pretty specimen, actually." He gave it a piece of cookie to wrestle with.

Cornelia entered the office with a new chair. At the same time, the light by Miss Sycorax's number started blinking. Arvid considered not picking up. But Cornelia sat down and put her headset on, and Konrad tore himself away from the dung beetle, and there was no longer an excuse not to work. He pushed the button.

"Operator."

"Hello," said the flat voice.

"Yes, hello."

"I want to be put through to Arvid Pekon," said Miss Sycorax.

"Arvid Pekon," Arvid repeated. His finger flicked the mute switch up and down.

"Arvid," said his voice.

A slap woke him up. Cornelia's round eyes were staring worriedly into his. She turned her head to look over at Konrad's looming silhouette. They grabbed Arvid's arms and dragged him up into his chair.

"You had us worried there," said Cornelia. "You fainted," Konrad explained.

"What happened?" asked Arvid. The buzzing in his head made it difficult to hear the other two. His face tingled.

"Oops. Head between your knees," said Konrad.

"What happened?" asked Arvid of the linoleum.

"You talked to 3426 for almost an hour and then you fell off your chair," said Cornelia.

"But I took the call just now."

"No, you've been going on for an hour."

"What did I talk about?"

Cornelia was silent for a moment. She was probably glaring at him. "You know we don't listen to each other's calls."

"Yes," mumbled Arvid to the floor.

A hand landed on his shoulder. "You should probably go home," said Konrad.

"I think I have to talk to the manager," said Arvid.

The door to the manager's office had an unmarked window of opaque glass. Arvid knocked on the glass. When there was no reply, he carefully pressed down the door handle and stepped inside. The room was smaller than he remembered it, but then again it was only his second time in here. There were no shelves or cabinets, just the enormous mahogany desk that covered most of the room. The desk was bare save for a telephone and a crossword puzzle magazine. Behind the desk, doing a crossword puzzle with a fountain pen, sat the manager in her powder blue suit and immaculate gray curls. She looked up as Arvid opened the door and smiled, her cheeks drawing back in deep folds.

"Egyptian dung beetle, six letters?" said the manager.

Arvid opened his mouth.

"S-C-A-R-A-B," said the manager. "Thank you." She closed and folded the magazine, put it aside and leaned back into her chair. She smiled again, with both rows of teeth.

Arvid waited.

"You have neglected to log three calls this month, Arvid," the manager said. "Subject 3426 at 2.35 PM on March 15; subject 3426 at 1.10 PM on March 21; subject 3426 at 4.56 PM on March 30. Why is this, Arvid?"

"I'm having a bit of trouble," said Arvid and shifted his weight from side to side.

"Trouble." The manager was still smiling, cheeks folded back like accordions.

"I think I may be having a nervous breakdown."

"And that's why you haven't logged your calls."

"This is going to sound insane," said Arvid.

"Go on," said the Manager.

Arvid took a deep breath. "Subject number 3426 . . . "

"Miss Sycorax," supplied the Manager.

"Miss Sycorax," Arvid continued, "has been making some very strange calls."

"Many of our subjects do."

"Yes, but not like her. Something's off."

"I see."

"Eh, I don't know," he said. "Maybe I need some time off."

"If you think you're having a nervous breakdown, Arvid," said the Manager, "I'll book an appointment with the company doctor and let him decide. We need to know if it's a workplace injury, you know. Oh, and do talk to Cornelia. She's the union representative."

"I will."

"All right, Arvid. Go on home. I'll have the doctor's office call you this afternoon." The Manager smiled at him with both rows of teeth.

At the switchboard, Konrad and Cornelia were back at work. Cornelia was doing her best to ignore a little army of ants who were marching in a circle around her desk. Konrad and the dung beetle, on the other hand, seemed to have become fast friends. The dung beetle was rolling a sticky ball of masticated cookie crumbs.

Arvid sat down in his chair and stared at the terminal. After some hesitation, he put his headset on. Then he put a call through to Miss Sycorax.

"Hello," said Miss Sycorax after the third ring.

"Hello," echoed Arvid.

"Hello."

"This is the operator," Arvid managed.

"Oh."

Arvid took a deep breath. "Who is this Arvid Pekon you wanted to be put through to?"

At the other end of the line, Miss Sycorax burst into laughter. The sound made Arvid cower in his chair.

"It's a funny name," she said. "Pekon, it sounds like a fruit. Like plums or pears. Or like someone from China. Or like a dog breed."

"Who is Arvid Pekon?" Arvid repeated.

"There is no Arvid Pekon," Miss Sycorax replied.

"Yes there is!"

"No there isn't. I thought there was, but then I realized I was mistaken."

Arvid disconnected and tore his headset off.

"I'm right here!" he yelled at the cockroach on the inbox. "Look!" He banged his fist on the desk so hard that it tingled. "Would I be able to do that if I wasn't here?"

Something crackled. He looked down at his hand, which was lying in shards on the desk. The tingling sensation spread up his arm, which shuddered and then exploded in a cloud of dust.

"Where did Arvid go?" Cornelia asked Konrad a little while later.

"Who?" Konrad was looking at a ball of cookie crumbs on his desk, having no clear idea of how it got there. He popped it in his mouth.

Cornelia shook her head. "I don't know what I'm on about. Never mind."

"Coffee break?" said Konrad. "I've brought Finnish shortbread."

Originally from Stockholm, Sweden, **Karin Tidbeck** (karintidbeck.com) now lives in Malmö. She's published fiction in Swedish since 2002 and in English since 2010. Tidbeck debuted with the short story collection *Vem är Arvid Pekon?* in 2010, followed by the novel *Amatka* in 2012. Her English publication history includes *Weird Tales*, *Shimmer Magazine*, *Unstuck Annual*, and the anthology *Odd?*. Her first book in English, the short story collection *Jagannath: Stories*, was published last year and won the Crawford Award and was shortlisted for the Tiptree Award. Tidbeck's also written articles and essays on computer games, roleplaying, and interactive arts. She currently works for a writers' interest organization and occasionally teach creative writing. "Who is Arvid Pekon?" has been made into a short film by Patrik Eriksson.

"Stories can educate just as much as facts," Miss Mailer says.
"They teach us how to live, and how to think."

IPHIGENIA IN AULIS

Mike Carey

Her name is Melanie. It means "the black girl," from an ancient Greek word, but her skin is mostly very fair so she thinks maybe it's not such a good name for her. Miss Justineau assigns names from a big list: new children get the top name on the boys' list or the top name on the girls' list, and that, Miss Justineau says, is that.

Melanie is ten years old, and she has skin like a princess in a fairy tale: skin as white as snow. So she knows that when she grows up she'll be beautiful, with princes falling over themselves to climb her tower and rescue her.

Assuming, of course, that she has a tower.

In the meantime, she has the cell, the corridor, the classroom and the shower room.

The cell is small and square. It has a bed, a chair and a table in it.

On the walls there are pictures: in Melanie's cell, a picture of a field of flowers and a picture of a woman dancing. Sometimes they move the children around, so Melanie knows that there are different pictures in each cell. She used to have a horse in a meadow and a big mountain with snow on the top, which she liked better.

The corridor has twenty doors on the left-hand side and eighteen doors on the right-hand side (because the cupboards don't really count); also it has a door at either end. The door at the classroom end is red. It leads to the classroom (duh!). The door at the other end is bare gray steel on this side but once when Melanie was being taken back to her cell she peeped through the door, which had accidentally been left open, and saw that on the other side it's got lots of bolts and locks and a box with numbers on it. She wasn't supposed to see, and Sergeant said "Little bitch has got way too many eyes on her," but she saw, and she remembers.

She listens, too, and from overheard conversations she has a sense of this place in relation to other places she hasn't ever seen. This place is the block. Outside the block is the base. Outside the base is the Eastern Stretch, or the Dispute Stretch. It's all good as far as Kansas, and then it gets real bad, real quick. East of Kansas, there's monsters everywhere and they'll follow you for a hundred miles if they smell you, and then they'll eat you. Melanie is glad that she lives in the block, where she's safe.

Through the gray steel door, each morning, the teachers come. They walk down the corridor together, past Melanie's door, bringing with them the strong, bitter chemical smell that they always have on them: it's not a nice smell, but it's exciting because it means the start of another day's lessons.

At the sound of the bolts sliding and the teachers' footsteps, Melanie runs to the door of her cell and stands on tiptoe to peep through the little mesh-screen window in the door and see the teachers when they go by.

She calls out good morning to them, but they're not supposed to answer and usually they don't. Sometimes, though, Miss Justineau will look around and smile at her—a tense, quick smile that's gone almost before she can see it—or Miss Mailer will give her a tiny wave with just the fingers of her hand.

All but one of the teachers go through the thirteenth door on the left, where there's a stairway leading down to another corridor and (Melanie guesses) lots more doors and rooms. The one who doesn't go through the thirteenth door unlocks the classroom and opens up, and that one will be Melanie's teacher and Melanie's friends' teacher for the day.

Then Sergeant comes, and the men and women who do what Sergeant says. They've got the chemical smell, too, and it's even stronger on them than it is on the teachers. Their job is to take the children to the classroom, and after that they go away again. There's a procedure that they follow, which takes a long time. Melanie thinks it must be the same for all the children, but of course she doesn't know that for sure because it always happens inside the cells and the only cell that Melanie sees the inside of is her own.

To start with, Sergeant bangs on all the doors, and shouts at the children to get ready. Melanie sits down in the wheelchair at the foot of her bed, like she's been taught to do. She puts her hands on the arms of the chair and her feet on the footrests. She closes her eyes and waits. She counts while she waits. The highest she's ever had to count is 4,526; the lowest is 4,301.

When the key turns in the door, she stops counting and opens her eyes. Sergeant comes in with his gun and points it at her. Then two of Sergeant's people come in and tighten and buckle the straps of the chair around Melanie's wrists and ankles. There's also a strap for her neck: they tighten that one last of all, when her hands and feet are fastened up all the way, and they always do it from behind. The strap is designed so they never have to put their hands in front of Melanie's face. Melanie sometimes says, "I won't bite." She says it as a joke, but Sergeant's people never laugh. Sergeant did once, the first time she said it, but it was a nasty laugh. And then he said, "Like we'd ever give you the fucking chance, sugarplum."

When Melanie is all strapped into the chair, and she can't move her hands or her feet or her head, they wheel her into the classroom and put her at her desk. The teacher might be talking to some of the other children, or writing something on the blackboard, but she (unless it's Mr. Galloway, who's the only he) will usually stop and say, "Good morning, Melanie." That way the children who sit way up at the front of the class will know that Melanie has come into the room and they can say good morning, too. They can't see her, of course, because they're all in their own chairs with their neck-straps fastened up, so they can't turn their heads around that far.

This procedure—the wheeling in, and the teacher saying good morning, and then the chorus of greetings from the other kids—happens seven more times, because there are seven children who come into the classroom after Melanie. One of them is Anne, who used to be Melanie's best friend in the class and maybe still is except that the last time they moved the kids around (Sergeant calls it "shuffling the deck") they ended up sitting a long way apart and it's hard to be best friends with someone you can't talk to. Another is Steven, whom Melanie doesn't like because he calls her Melon-Brain or M-M-M-Melanie to remind her that she used to stammer sometimes in class.

When all the children are in the classroom, the lessons start. Every day has sums and spelling, but there doesn't seem to be a plan for the rest of the lessons. Some teachers like to read aloud from books. Others make the children learn facts and dates, which is something that Melanie is very good at. She knows the names of all the states in the United States, and all their capitals, and their state birds and flowers, and the total population of each state and what they mostly manufacture or grow there. She also knows the presidents in order and the years that they were in office, and she's working on European capitals. She doesn't find it hard to remember this stuff; she does it to keep from being bored, because being bored is worse than almost anything.

Melanie learned the stuff about the states from Mr. Galloway's lessons, but she's not sure if she's got all the details right because one day, when he was acting kind of funny and his voice was all slippery and fuzzy, Mr. Galloway said something that worried Melanie. She was asking him whether it was the whole state of New York that used to be called New Amsterdam, or just the city, and he said, who cares? "None of this stuff matters anymore, Melanie. I just gave it to you because all the textbooks we've got are twenty years old."

Melanie persists, because New Amsterdam was way back in the eighteenth century, so she doesn't think twenty years should matter all that much. "But when the Dutch colonists—" she says.

Mr. Galloway cuts her off. "Jesus, it's irrelevant. It's ancient history! The Hungries tore up the map. There's nothing east of Kansas anymore. Not a damn thing."

So it's possible, even quite likely, that some of Melanie's lists need to be updated in some respects.

The children have classes on Monday, Tuesday, Wednesday, Thursday, and Friday. On Saturday, the children stay locked in their rooms all day and music plays over the PA system. Nobody comes, not even Sergeant, and the music is too loud to talk over. Melanie had the idea long ago of making up a language that used signs instead of words, so the children could talk to each other through their little mesh windows, and she went ahead and made the language up, or some of it anyway, but when she asked Miss Mailer if she could teach it to the class, Miss Mailer told her no really loud and sharp. She made Melanie promise not to mention her sign language to any of the other teachers, and especially not to Sergeant. "He's paranoid enough already," she said. "If he thinks you're talking behind his back, he'll lose what's left of his mind." So Melanie never got to teach the other children how to talk in sign language.

Saturdays are long and dull, and hard to get through. Melanie tells herself aloud some of the stories that the children have been told in class.

It's okay to say them out loud because the music hides her voice. Otherwise Sergeant would come in and tell her to stop.

Melanie knows that Sergeant is still there on Saturdays, because one Saturday when Ronnie hit her hand against the mesh window of her cell until it bled and got all mashed up, Sergeant came in. He brought two of his people, and all three of them were dressed in the big suits, and they went into Ronnie's cell and Melanie guessed from the sounds that they were trying to tie Ronnie into her chair. She also guessed from the sounds that Ronnie was struggling and making it hard for them, because she kept shouting and saying, "Let me alone! Let me alone!" Then there was a banging sound that went on and on and Sergeant shouted, "Shut up shut up shut up shut up shut up!" and then other people were shouting, too, and someone said, "Christ Jesus, don't—" and then it all went quiet again.

Melanie couldn't tell what happened after that. The people who work for Sergeant went around and locked all the little doors over the mesh windows, so the children couldn't see out. They stayed locked all day.

The next Monday, Ronnie wasn't in the class anymore, and nobody seemed to know what had happened to her. Melanie likes to think that Ronnie went through the thirteenth door on the left into another class, so she might come back one day when Sergeant shuffles the deck again.

But what Melanie really believes, when she can't stop herself from thinking about it, is that Sergeant took Ronnie away to punish her, and he won't let her see any of the other children ever again.

Sundays are like Saturdays except for the shower. At the start of the day the children are put in their chairs as though it's a regular school day, but instead of being taken to the classroom, they're taken to the shower room, which is the last door on the right, just before the bare steel door.

In the shower room, which is white-tiled and empty, the children sit and wait until everybody has been wheeled in. Then the doors are closed and sealed, which means the room is completely dark because there aren't any lights in there. Pipes behind the walls start to make a sound like someone trying not to laugh, and a chemical spray falls from the ceiling.

It's the same chemical that's on the teachers and Sergeant and Sergeant's people, or at least it smells the same, but it's a lot stronger. It stings a little, at first. Then it stings a lot. It leaves Melanie's eyes puffy, reddened and half-blind. But it evaporates quickly from clothes and skin, so after half an hour more of sitting in the still, dark room, there's nothing left of it but the smell, and then finally the smell fades, too, or at least they get used to it so it's not so bad anymore, and they just wait in silence for the door to be unlocked and Sergeant's people to come and get them.

This is how the children are washed, and for that reason, if for no other, Sunday is probably the worst day of the week.

The best day of the week is whichever day Miss Mailer teaches. It isn't always the same day, and some weeks she doesn't come at all. Melanie guesses that there are more than five classes of children, and that the teachers' time is divided arbitrarily among them. Certainly there's no pattern that she can discern, and she's really good at that stuff.

When Miss Mailer teaches, the day is full of amazing things. Sometimes she'll read poems aloud, or bring her flute and play it, or show the children pictures out of a book and tell them stories about the people in the pictures. That was how Melanie got to find out about Agamemnon and the Trojan War, because one of the paintings showed Agamemnon's wife, Clytemnestra, looking really mad and scary. "Why is she so mad?" Anne asked Miss Mailer.

"Because Agamemnon killed their daughter," Miss Mailer said. "The Greek fleet was stuck in harbor on the island of Aulis. So Agamemnon put his daughter on an altar, and he killed her so that the goddess Artemis would give the Greek fleet fair winds and help them to get to the war on time."

The kids in the class were mostly both scared and delighted with this, like it was a ghost story or something, but Melanie was troubled by it. How could killing a little girl change the way the winds blew? "You're right, Melanie, it couldn't," Miss Mailer said. "But the Ancient Greeks had a lot of gods, and all kinds of weird ideas about what would make the gods happy. So Agamemnon gave Iphigenia's death to the goddess as a present, and his wife decided he had to pay for that." Melanie, who already knew by this time that her own name was Greek, decided she was on Clytemnestra's side. Maybe it was important to get to the war on time, but you shouldn't kill kids to do it. You should just row harder, or put more sails up. Or maybe you should go in a boat that had an outboard motor.

The only problem with the days when Miss Mailer teaches is that the time goes by too quickly. Every second is so precious to Melanie that she doesn't even blink: she just sits there wide-eyed, drinking in everything that Miss Mailer says, and memorizing it so that she can play it back to herself later, in her cell. And whenever she can manage it, she asks Miss Mailer questions, because what she likes most to hear, and to remember, is Miss Mailer's voice saying her name, Melanie, in that way that makes her feel like the most important person in the world.

One day, Sergeant comes into the classroom on a Miss Mailer day.

Melanie doesn't know he's there until he speaks, because he's standing right at the back of the class. When Miss Mailer says, " . . . and this time, Pooh and Piglet counted three sets of footprints in the snow," Sergeant's voice breaks in with, "What the fuck is this?"

Miss Mailer stops, and looks round. "I'm reading the children a story, Sergeant Robertson," she says.

"I can see that," Sergeant's voice says. "I thought the idea was to educate them, not give them a cabaret."

"Stories can educate just as much as facts," Miss Mailer says.

"Like how, exactly?" Sergeant asks, nastily.

"They teach us how to live, and how to think."

"Oh yeah, plenty of world-class ideas in *Winnie-the-Pooh*." Sergeant is using sarcasm. Melanie knows how sarcasm works: you say the opposite of what you really mean. "Seriously, Gwen, you're wasting your time. You want to tell them stories, tell them about Jack the Ripper and John Wayne Gacy."

"They're children," Miss Mailer points out.

"No, they're not," Sergeant says, very loudly. "And that, that right there, that's why you don't want to read them *Winnie-the-Pooh*. You do that, you start thinking of them as real kids. And then you slip up. And maybe you untie one of them because she needs a cuddle or something. And I don't need to tell you what happens after that."

Sergeant comes out to the front of the class then, and he does something really horrible. He rolls up his sleeve, all the way to the elbow, and he holds his bare forearm in front of Kenny's face: right in front of Kenny, just an inch or so away from him. Nothing happens at first, but then Sergeant spits on his hand and rubs at his forearm, like he's wiping something away.

"Don't," says Miss Mailer. "Don't do that to him." But Sergeant doesn't answer her or look at her.

Melanie sits two rows behind Kenny, and two rows over, so she can see the whole thing. Kenny goes real stiff, and he whimpers, and then his mouth gapes wide and he starts to snap at Sergeant's arm, which of course he can't reach. And drool starts to drip down from the corner of his mouth, but not much of it because nobody ever gives the children anything to drink, so it's thick, kind of half-solid, and it hangs there on the end of Kenny's chin, wobbling, while Kenny grunts and snaps at Sergeant's arm, and makes kind of moaning, whimpering sounds.

"You see?" Sergeant says, and he turns to look at Miss Mailer's face to make sure she gets his point. And then he blinks, all surprised, and maybe he wishes he hadn't, because Miss Mailer is looking at him like Clytemnestra looked in the painting, and Sergeant lets his arm fall to his side and shrugs like none of this was ever important to him anyway.

"Not everyone who looks human is human," he says.

"No," Miss Mailer agrees. "I'm with you on that one." Kenny's head sags a little sideways, which is as far as it can move because of the strap, and he makes a clicking sound in his throat.

"It's all right, Kenny," Miss Mailer says. "It will pass soon. Let's go on with the story. Would you like that? Would you like to hear what happened to Pooh and Piglet? Sergeant Robertson, if you'll excuse us? Please?"

Sergeant looks at her, and shakes his head real hard. "You don't want to get attached to them," he says. "There's no cure. So once they hit eighteen . . . "

But Miss Mailer starts to read again, like he's not even there, and in the end he leaves. Or maybe he's still standing at the back of the classroom, not speaking, but Melanie doesn't think so because after a while Miss Mailer gets up and shuts the door, and Melanie thinks that she'd only do that right then if Sergeant was on the other side of it.

Melanie barely sleeps at all that night. She keeps thinking about what Sergeant said, that the children aren't real children, and about how Miss Mailer looked at him when he was being so nasty to Kenny.

And she thinks about Kenny snarling and snapping at Sergeant's arm like a dog. She wonders why he did it, and she thinks maybe she knows the answer because when Sergeant wiped his arm with spit and waved it under Kenny's nose, it was as though under the bitter chemical smell Sergeant had a different smell altogether. And even though the smell was very faint where Melanie was, it made her head swim and her jaw muscles start to work by themselves. She can't even figure out what it was she was feeling, because it's not like anything that ever happened to her before or anything she heard of in a story, but it was like there was something she was supposed to do and it was so urgent, so important, that her body was trying to take over her mind and do it without her.

But along with these scary thoughts, she also thinks: Sergeant has a name, the same way the teachers do. The same way the children do.

Sergeant has been more like the goddess Artemis to Melanie up until now; now she knows that he's just like everyone else, even if he is scary.

The enormity of that change, more than anything else, is what keeps her awake until the doors unlock in the morning and the teachers come.

In a way, Melanie's feelings about Miss Mailer have changed, too.

Or rather, they haven't changed at all, but they've become stronger and stronger. There can't be anyone better or kinder or lovelier than Miss Mailer anywhere in the world; Melanie wishes she was a Greek warrior with a sword and a shield, so she could fight for Miss Mailer and save her from Heffalumps and Woozles. She knows that Heffalumps and Woozles are in *Winnie-the-Pooh*, not the *Iliad*, but she likes the words, and she likes the idea of saving Miss Mailer so much that it becomes her favorite thought. She thinks it whenever she's not thinking anything else.

It makes even Sundays bearable.

One day, Miss Mailer talks to them about death. It's because most of the men in the Light Brigade have just died, in a poem that Miss Mailer is reading to the class. The children want to know what it means to die, and what it's like. Miss Mailer says it's like all the lights going out, and everything going real quiet, the way it does at night—but forever. No morning. The lights never come back on again.

"That sounds terrible," says Lizzie, in a voice like she's about to cry.

It sounds terrible to Melanie, too; like sitting in the shower room on Sunday with the chemical smell in the air, and then even the smell goes away and there's nothing at all forever and ever.

Miss Mailer can see that she's upset them, and she tries to make it okay again by talking about it more. "But maybe it's not like that at all," she says. "Nobody really knows, because when you're dead, you can't come back to talk about it. And anyway, it would be different for you than it would be for most people because you're . . . "

And then she stops herself, with the next word sort of frozen halfway out of her lips.

"We're what?" Melanie asks.

"You're children," Miss Mailer says, after a few seconds. "You can't even really imagine what death might be like, because for children it seems like everything has to go on forever."

There's a silence while they think about that. It's true, Melanie decides. She can't remember a time when her life was any different from this, and she can't imagine any other way that people could live. But there's something that doesn't make sense to her, in the whole equation, and so she has to ask the question.

"*Whose* children are we, Miss Mailer?"

In stories, she knows, children have a mother and a father, like Iphigenia had Clytemnestra and Agamemnon. Sometimes they have teachers, too, but not always, and they never seem to have Sergeants. So this is a question that gets to the very roots of the world, and Melanie asks it with some trepidation.

Miss Mailer thinks about it for a long time, until Melanie is pretty sure that she won't answer. Then she says, "Your mom is dead, Melanie. She died before . . . She died when you were very little. Probably your daddy's dead, too, although there isn't really any way of knowing. So the army is looking after you now."

"Is that just Melanie," John asks, "or is it all of us?"

Miss Mailer nods slowly. "All of you."

"We're in an orphanage," Anne guesses. The class heard the story of Oliver Twist once.

"No. You're on an army base."

"Is that what happens to kids whose mom and dad die?" This is Steven now.

"Sometimes."

Melanie is thinking hard, and putting it together, inside her head, like a puzzle. "How old was I," she asks, "when my mom died?" Because she must have been very young, if she can't remember her mother at all.

"It's not easy to explain," Miss Mailer says, and they can see from her face that she's really, really unhappy.

"Was I a baby?" Melanie asks.

"A very tiny baby, Melanie."

"How tiny?"

"Tiny enough to fall into a hole between two laws."

It comes out quick and low and almost hard. Miss Mailer changes the subject then, and the children are happy to let her do it because nobody is very enthusiastic about death by this point. But Melanie wants to know one more thing, and she wants it badly enough that she even takes the chance of upsetting Miss Mailer some more. It's because of her name being Greek, and what the Greeks sometimes used to do to their kids, at least in the ancient times when they were fighting a war against Troy. At the end of the lesson, she waits until Miss Mailer is close to her and she asks her question really quietly.

"Miss Mailer, were our moms and dads going to sacrifice us to the goddess Artemis? Is that why we're here?"

Miss Mailer looks down at her, and for the longest time she doesn't answer. Then something completely unexpected and absolutely wonderful happens. Miss Mailer reaches down and she strokes Melanie's hair.

She strokes Melanie's hair with her hand, like it was just the most natural and normal thing in the world. And lights are dancing behind Melanie's eyes, and she can't get her breath, and she can't speak or hear or think about anything because apart from Sergeant's people, maybe two or three times and always by accident, nobody has ever touched her before and this is Miss Mailer touching her and it's almost too nice to be in the world at all.

"Oh, Melanie," Miss Mailer says. Her voice is only just higher than a whisper.

Melanie doesn't say anything. She never wants Miss Mailer's hand to move. She thinks if she could die now, with Miss Mailer's hand on her hair, and nothing changed ever again, then it would be all right to be dead.

"I—I can't explain it to you," Miss Mailer says, sounding really, really unhappy. "There are too many other things I'd have to explain, too, to make sense of it. And—and I'm not strong enough. I'm just not strong enough."

But she tries anyway, and Melanie understands some of it. Just before the Hungries came, Miss Mailer says, the government passed an amendment to the Constitution of the United States of America. It was because of something called the Christian Right, and it meant that you were a person even before you were born, and the law had to protect you from the very moment that you popped up inside your mom's tummy like a seed.

Melanie is full of questions already, but she doesn't ask them because it will only be a minute or two before Sergeant's people come for her, and she knows from Miss Mailer's voice that this is a big, important secret. So then the Hungries came, Miss Mailer said—or rather, people started turning into Hungries. And everything fell to pieces real fast.

It was a virus, Miss Mailer says: a virus that killed you, but then brought you partway back to life; not enough of you to talk, but enough of you to stand up and move around and even run. You turned into a monster that just wanted to bite other people and make them into Hungries, too. That was how the virus propagated itself, Miss Mailer said.

So the virus spread and all the governments fell and it looked like the Hungries were going to eat everyone or make everyone like they were, and that would be the end of the story and the end of everything. But the real people didn't give up. They moved the government to Los Angeles, with the desert all around them and the ocean at their back, and they cleared the Hungries out of the whole state of California with flamethrowers and daisy cutter bombs and nerve gas and big moving fences that were on trucks controlled by radio signals. Melanie has no idea what these things are, but she nods as if she does and imagines a big war like Greeks fighting Trojans.

And every once in a while, the real people would find a bunch of Hungries who'd fallen down because of the nerve gas and couldn't get up again, or who were stuck in a hole or locked in a room or something.

And maybe one of them might have been about to be a mom, before she got turned into a Hungry. There was a baby already inside her.

The real people were allowed to kill the Hungries because there was a law, Emergency Ordnance 9, that said they could. Anyone could kill a Hungry and it wouldn't be murder because they weren't people anymore.

But the real people weren't allowed to kill the unborn babies, because of the amendment to the Constitution: inside their moms, the babies all had rights. And maybe the babies would have something else, called higher cognitive functions, that their moms didn't have anymore, because viruses don't always work the same on unborn babies.

So there was a big argument about what was going to happen to the babies, and nobody could decide. Inside the cleared zone, in California, there were so many different groups of people with so many different ideas, it looked like it might all fall apart and the real people would kill each other and finish what the Hungries started. They couldn't risk doing anything that might make one group of people get mad with the other groups of people.

So they made a compromise. The babies were cut out of their mommies. If they survived, and they did have those function things, then they'd be raised, and educated, and looked after, and protected, until one of two things happened: either someone came up with a cure, or the children reached the age of eighteen.

If there was a cure, then the children would be cured.

If there wasn't . . .

"Here endeth the lesson," says Sergeant.

He comes into Melanie's line of sight, right behind Miss Mailer, and Miss Mailer snatches her hand away from Melanie's hair. She ducks her head so Melanie can't see her face.

"She goes back now," Sergeant says.

"Right." Miss Mailer's voice is very small.

"And you go on a charge."

"Right."

"And maybe you lose your job. Because every rule we got, you just broke."

Miss Mailer brings her head up again. Her eyes are wet with tears.

"Fuck you, Eddie," she says.

She walks out of Melanie's line of sight, very quickly. Melanie wants to call her back, wants to say something to make her stay: *I love you, Miss Mailer. I'll be a warrior for you, and save you.* But she can't say anything, and then Sergeant's people come. Sergeant's there, too. "Look at you," he says to Melanie. "Fucking face all screwed up like a tragedy mask. Like you've got fucking feelings."

But nothing that Sergeant says and nothing that Sergeant does can take away the memory of that touch.

When she's wheeled into her cell, and Sergeant stands by with his gun as the straps are unfastened one by one, Melanie looks him in the eye. "You won't get fair winds, whatever you do," she tells him. "No matter how many children you kill, the goddess Artemis won't help you." Sergeant stares at her, and something happens in his face. It's like he's surprised, and then he's scared, and then he's angry. Sergeant's people can see it, too, and one of them takes a step toward him with her hand halfway up like she's going to touch his arm.

"Sergeant Robertson!" she says.

He pulls back from her, and then he makes a gesture with the gun.

"We're done here," he says.

"She's still strapped in," says the other one of Sergeant's people.

"Too bad," says Sergeant. He throws the door open and waits for them to move, looking at one of them and then the other until they give up and leave Melanie where she is and go out through the door.

"Fair winds, kid," Sergeant says.

So Melanie has to spend the night in her chair, still strapped up tight apart from her head and her left arm. And it's way too uncomfortable to sleep, even if she leans her head sideways, because there's a big pipe that runs down the wall right there and she can't get into a position that doesn't hurt her.

But then, because of the pipe, something else happens. Melanie starts to hear voices, and they seem to be coming right out of the wall. Only they're not: they're coming down the pipe, somehow, from another part of the building. Melanie recognizes Sergeant's voice, but not any of the others.

"Fence went down in Michigan," Sergeant says. "Twenty-mile stretch, Clayton said. Hungries are pushing west, and probably south, too. How long you think it'll be before they cut us off?"

"Clayton's full of shit," a second voice says, but with an anxious edge. "You think they'd have left us here, if that was gonna happen? They'd have evacuated the base."

"Fuck if they would!" This is Sergeant again. "They care more about these little plague rats than they do about us. If they'd have done it right, we didn't even need to be here. All they had to do was to put every last one of the little bastards in a barn and throw one fucking daisy cutter in there. No more worries."

It gets real quiet for a while after that, like no one can think of anything to say. "I thought they found a cure," a third voice says, but he's shouted down by a lot of voices all at the same time. "That's bullshit." "Dream on, man! Onliest cure for them fuckin' skull-faces is in this here clip, and I got enough for all,"

"They did, though," the third voice persists. "They isolated the virus. At that lab in Houston. And then they built something that'll kill it. Something that'll fit in a hypo. They call it a *phage*."

"Here, you, skull-face." Sergeant is putting on a funny voice. "I got a cure for you, so why'n't you come on over here and roll up your sleeve? That's right. And all you other cannibal motherfuckers, you form an orderly line there."

There's a lot of laughter, and a lot of stuff that Melanie can't hear clearly. The third voice doesn't speak again.

"I heard they broke through from Mexico and took Los Angeles." Another new voice. "We ain't got no government now. It's just the last few units out in the field, and some camps like this one that kept a perimeter up. That's why there's no messages anymore. No one out there to send them."

Then the second voice comes in again with, "Hell, Dawlish. Brass keep their comms to theirselves, like always. There's messages. Just ain't any for you, is all."

"They're all dead," Sergeant says. "They're all dead except us. And what are we? We're the fucking nursemaids of the damned. Drink up, guys. Might as well be drunk as sober, when it comes." Then he laughs, and it's the same laugh as when he said, "Like we'd ever give you the chance." A laugh that hates itself and probably everything else, too.

Melanie leans her head as far to the other side as it will go, so she can't hear the voices anymore.

Eddie, she tells herself. Just Eddie Robertson talking. That's all.

The night is very, very long. Melanie tells herself stories, and sends messages from her right hand to her left hand, then back again, using her sign language, but it's still long. When Sergeant comes in the morning with his people, she can't move; she's got such bad cramps in her neck and her shoulders and her arms, it feels like there's iron bars inside her.

Sergeant looks at her like he's forgotten up until then what happened last night. He looks at his people, but they're looking somewhere else.

They don't say anything as they tie up Melanie's neck and arm again.

Sergeant does. He says, "How about them fair winds, kid?" But he doesn't say it like he's angry, or even like he wants to be mean. He says it and then he looks away, unhappy, sick almost. To Melanie, it seems like he says it because he has to say it; as though being Sergeant means you've got to say things like that all the time, whether that's really what you're thinking or not. She files that thought next to his name.

One day, Miss Mailer gives Melanie a book. She does it by sliding the book between Melanie's back and the back of the wheelchair, and tucking it down there out of sight. Melanie isn't even sure at first that that's what just happened, but when she looks at Miss Mailer and opens her mouth to ask her, Miss Mailer touches a finger to her closed lips. So Melanie doesn't say anything.

Once they're back in their cells, and untied, the children aren't supposed to stand up and get out of their chairs until Sergeant's people have left and the door is closed and locked. That night, Melanie makes sure not to move a muscle until she hears the bolt slide home.

Then she reaches behind her and finds the book, its angular shape digging into her back a little. She pulls it out and looks at it.

Homer. The *Iliad* and *The Odyssey*.

Melanie makes a strangled sound. She can't help it, even though it might bring Sergeant back into the cell to tell her to shut up. A book! A book of her own! And *this* book! She runs her hands over the cover, riffles the pages, turns the book in her hands, over and over. She smells the book.

That turns out to be a mistake, because the book smells of Miss Mailer. On top, strongest, the chemical smell from her fingers, as bitter and horrible as always: but underneath, a little, and on the inside pages a lot, the warm and human smell of Miss Mailer herself.

What Melanie feels right then is what Kenny felt, when Sergeant wiped the chemicals off his arm and put it right up close to Kenny's face, but she only just caught the edge of it, that time, and she didn't really understand it.

Something opens inside her, like a mouth opening wider and wider and wider and screaming all the time—not from fear, but from need. Melanie thinks she has a word for it now, although it still isn't anything she's felt before. Sometimes in stories that she's heard, people eat and drink, which is something that the children don't ever do. The people in the stories need to eat, and then when they do eat they feel themselves fill up with something, and it gives them a satisfaction that nothing else can give. She remembers a line from a song that Miss Justineau sang to the children once: *You're my bread, when I'm hungry.*

So this is hunger, and it hurts like a needle, like a knife, like a Trojan spear in Melanie's heart or maybe lower down in her stomach. Her jaws start to churn of their own accord: wetness comes into her mouth. Her head feels light, and the room sort of goes away and then comes back without moving.

The feeling goes on for a long time, until finally Melanie gets used to the smell the way the children in the shower on Sunday get used to the smell of the chemicals. It doesn't go away, exactly, but it doesn't torment her in quite the same way: it becomes kind of invisible just because it doesn't change. The hunger gets less and less, and when it's gone, all gone, Melanie is still there.

The book is still there, too: Melanie reads it until daybreak, and even when she stumbles over the words or has to guess what they mean, she's in another world.

It's a long time after that before Miss Mailer comes again. On Monday there's a new teacher, except he isn't a teacher at all: he's one of Sergeant's people. He says his name is John, which is stupid, because the teachers are all Miss or Mrs. or Mister something, so the children call him Mr. John, and after the first few times he gives up correcting them.

Mr. John doesn't look like he wants to be there, in the classroom. He's only used to strapping the children into the chairs one by one, or freeing them again one by one, with Sergeant's gun on them all the time and everything quick and easy. He looks like being in a room with all the children at the same time is like lying on an altar, at Aulis, with the priest of Artemis holding a knife to his throat.

At last, Anne asks Mr. John the question that everybody wants to ask him: where the real teachers are, "There's a lockdown," Mr. John says. He doesn't seem to mind that the children have spotted him for a fake. "There's movement west of the fence. They confirmed it by satellite. Lots of Hungries coming this way, so nobody's allowed to move around inside the compound or go out into the open in case they get our scent. We're just staying wherever we happened to be when the alarm went. So you've got me to put up with, and we'll just have to do the best we can."

Actually, Mr. John isn't a bad teacher at all, once he stops being scared of the children. He knows a lot of songs, and he writes up the words on the blackboard; the children sing the songs, first all at once and then in two-part and three-part harmonies. There are lots of words the children don't know, especially in "Too Drunk to Fuck," but when the children ask what the words mean, Mr. John says he'll take the Fifth on that one. That means he might get himself into trouble if he gives the right answer, so he's allowed not to; Melanie knows this from when Miss Justineau told them about the Bill of Rights.

So it's not a bad day, at all, even if they don't have a real teacher. But for a whole lot of days after that, nobody comes and the children are alone. It's not possible for Melanie to count how many days; there's nothing to count. The lights stay on the whole time, the music plays really loud, and the big steel door stays shut.

Then a day comes when the music goes off. And in the sudden, shocking silence the bare steel door slams open again, so loud that the sound feels like it's shoving its way through your ear right inside your head. The children jump up and run to their doors to see who's coming, and it's Sergeant—just Sergeant, with one of his people, and no teachers at all.

"Let's do this," Sergeant says.

The man who's with him looks at all the doors, then at Sergeant.

"Seriously?" he says.

"We got our orders," Sergeant says. "What we gonna do, tell them we lost the key? Start with this bunch, then do B to D. Sorenson can start at the other end."

Sergeant unlocks the first door after the shower room door, which is Mikey's door. Sergeant and the other man go inside, and Sergeant's voice, booming hollowly in the silence, says, "Up and at 'em, you little fucker."

Melanie sits in her chair and waits. Then she stands up and waits at the door with her face to the mesh. Then she walks up and down, hugging her own arms. She's confused and excited and very, very scared.

Something new is happening. She senses it: something completely outside of her experience. When she looks out through the mesh window, she can see that Sergeant isn't closing the doors behind him, as he goes from cell to cell, and he's not wheeling the children into the classroom.

Finally her door is unlocked. She steps back from it as it opens, and Sergeant and the other man step inside. Sergeant points the gun at Melanie.

"You forget your manners?" he asks her. "Sit down, kid." Something happens to Melanie. It's like all her different, mixed-up feelings are crashing into each other, inside her head, and turning into a new feeling. She sits down, but she sits down on her bed, not in her chair.

Sergeant stares at her like he can't believe what he's seeing. "You don't want to piss me off today," he warns Melanie. "Not today."

"I want to know what's happening, Sergeant," Melanie says. "Why were we left on our own? Why didn't the teachers come? What's happening?"

"Sit down in the chair," the other man says.

"Do it," Sergeant tells her.

But Melanie stays where she is, on the bed, and she doesn't shift her gaze from Sergeant's eyes. "Is there going to be class today?" she asks him.

"Sit in the goddamn chair," Sergeant orders her. "Sit in the chair or I swear I will fucking dismantle you." His voice is shaking, just a little, and she can see from the way his face changes, suddenly, that he knows she heard the shake. "Fucking—fine!" he explodes, and he advances on the chair and kicks it with his boot, really hard, so it flies up into the air and hits the wall of the narrow cell. It bounces off at a wild angle, hits the other wall and crashes down on its back. Sergeant kicks it again, and then a third time. The frame is all twisted from where it hit the wall, and one of the wheels comes right off when Sergeant kicks it.

The other man just watches, without saying a word, while Sergeant gets his breath back and comes down from his scary rage. When he does, he looks at Melanie and shrugs. "Well, I guess you can just stay where you are, then," he says.

The two of them go out, and the door is locked again. They take the other kids away, one by one—not to the classroom, but out through the other door, the bare steel door, which until now has marked the farthest limit of their world.

Nobody comes, after that, and nothing happens. It feels like a long time, but Melanie's mind is racing so fast that even a few minutes would feel like a long time. It's longer than a few minutes, though. It feels like most of a day.

The air gets colder. It's not something that Melanie thinks about, normally, because heat and cold don't translate into comfort or discomfort for her; she notices now because with no music playing and nobody to talk to, there's nothing else to notice. Maybe it's night. That's it. It must be night outside. Melanie knows from stories that it gets colder at night as well as darker.

She remembers her book, and gets it out. She reads about Hector and Achilles and Priam and Hecuba and Odysseus and Menelaus and Agamemnon and Helen.

There are footsteps from the corridor outside. Is it Sergeant? Has he come back to dismantle her? To take her to the altar and give her to the goddess Artemis?

Someone unlocks Melanie's door, and pushes it open.

Miss Mailer stands in the doorway. "It's okay," she says. "It's okay, sweetheart. I'm here."

Melanie surges to her feet, her heart almost bursting with happiness and relief. She's going to run to Miss Mailer. She's going to hug her and be hugged by her and be touching her not just with her hair but with her hands and her face and her whole body. Then she freezes where she is.

Her jaw muscles stiffen, and a moan comes out of her mouth.

Miss Mailer is alarmed. "Melanie?" She takes a step forward.

"Don't!" Melanie screams. "Please, Miss Mailer! Don't! Don't touch me!"

Miss Mailer stops moving, but she's so close! So close! Melanie whimpers. Her whole mind is exploding. She drops to her knees, then falls full-length on the floor. The smell, the wonderful, terrible smell, fills all the room and all her mind and all her thoughts, and all she wants to do is . . .

"Go away!" she moans. "Go away go away go away!" Miss Mailer doesn't move.

"Fuck off, or I will dismantle you!" Melanie wails. She's desperate.

Her mouth is filled with thick saliva like mud from a mudslide. She's dangling on the end of the thinnest, thinnest piece of string. She's going to fall and there's only one direction to fall in.

"Oh God!" Miss Mailer blurts. She gets it at last. She rummages in her bag, which Melanie didn't even notice until now. She takes something out—a tiny bottle with yellow liquid in it—and starts to spray it on her skin, on her clothes, in the air. The bottle says *Dior*. It's not the usual chemical: it's something that smells sweet and funny. Miss Mailer doesn't stop until she's emptied the bottle.

"Does that help?" she asks, with a catch in her voice. "Oh baby, I'm so sorry. I didn't even think . . . "

It does help, a little. And Melanie has had practice at pushing the hunger down: she has to do it a little bit every time she picks up her book.

This is a million times harder, but after a while she can think again and move again and even sit up.

"It's safe now," she says timidly, groggily. And she remembers her own words, spoken as a joke so many times before she ever guessed what they might actually mean. "I won't bite."

Miss Mailer bends down and sweeps Melanie up, choking out her name, and there they are crying into each other's tears, and even though the hunger is bending Melanie's spine like Achilles bending his bow, she wouldn't exchange this moment for all the other moments of her life.

"They're attacking the fence," Miss Mailer says, her voice muffled by Melanie's hair. "But it's not Hungries, it's looters. Bandits. People just like me and the other teachers, but renegades who never went into the western cordon. We've got to get out before they break through. We're being evacuated, Melanie—to Texas."

"Why?" is all Melanie can think of to say.

"Because that's where the cure is!" sobs Miss Mailer. "They'll make you okay again, and you'll have a real mom and dad, and a real life, and all this fucking madness will just be a memory!"

"No," Melanie whimpers.

"Yes, baby! Yes!" Miss Mailer is hugging her tight, and Melanie is trying to find the words to explain that she doesn't want a mom or a dad, she wants to stay here in the block with Miss Mailer and have lessons with her forever, but right then is when Sergeant walks into the cell.

Three of his people are behind him. His face is pale, and his eyes are open too wide.

"We got to go," he says. "Right now. Last two choppers are loaded up and ready. I'm real sorry, Gwen, but this is the last call."

"I'm not going without her," Miss Mailer says, and she hugs Melanie so tight it almost hurts.

"Yeah," Sergeant says. "You are. She can't come on the transport without restraints, and we don't got any restraints that we can use. You come on, now."

He reaches out his hand as if he's going to help Miss Mailer to her feet. Miss Mailer doesn't take the hand.

"Come on, now," Sergeant says again, on a rising pitch.

"I'm not leaving her," Miss Mailer says again.

"She's got no—"

Miss Mailer's voice rises over Sergeant's voice, shouts him into silence. "She doesn't have any restraints because you kicked her chair into scrap metal. And now you're going to leave her here, to the mercy of those animals, and say it was out of your hands. Well damn you, Eddie!" She can hardly get the words out; she sounds like there's no breath left in her body. "Damn—fuck—rot what's left of your miserable fucking heart!"

"I've got to go by the rules," Sergeant pleads. His voice is weak, lost.

"Really?" Miss Mailer shouts at him. "The rules? And when you've ripped her heart out and fed it to your limp-dick fucking rules, you think that will bring Chloe back, or Sarah? Or bring you one moment's peace? There's a cure, you bastard! They can cure her! They can give her a normal life! You want to say she stays here and rots in the dark instead because you threw a man-tantrum and busted up her fucking *chair*?"

There's a silence that seems like it's never going to end. Maybe it never would, if there was only Sergeant and Miss Mailer and Melanie in the room: but one of Sergeant's people breaks it at last. "Sarge, we're already two minutes past the—"

"Shut up," Sergeant tells him. And then to Miss Mailer he says, "You carry her. You hold her, every second of the way. And you're responsible for her. If she bites anyone, I'm throwing you both off the transport."

Miss Mailer stands up with Melanie cradled in her arms, and they run. They go out through the steel door. There are stairs on the other side of it that go up and up, a long way. Miss Mailer is holding her tight, but she rocks and bounces all the same, pressed up against Miss Mailer's heart. Miss Mailer's heart bumps rhythmically, as if something was alive inside it and touching Melanie's cheek through her skin.

At the top of the stairs, there's another door. They come out into sudden cold and blinding light. The quality of the sound changes, the echoes dying suddenly. Air moves against Melanie's bare arm. Distant voices bray, almost drowned out by a mighty, droning, flickering roar.

The lights are moving, swinging around. Where they touch, details leap out of the darkness as though they've just been painted there. Men are running, stopping, running again, firing guns like Sergeant's gun into the wild, jangling dark.

"Go!" Sergeant shouts.

Sergeant's men run, and Miss Mailer runs. Sergeant runs behind them, his gun in his hand. "Don't waste rounds," Sergeant calls out to his people. "Pick your target." He fires his gun, and his people fire, too, and the guns make a sound so loud it runs all the way out into the dark and then comes back again, but Melanie can't see what it is they're firing at or if they hit it. She's got other stuff to worry about, anyway.

This close up, the smelly stuff that Miss Mailer sprayed on herself isn't strong enough to hide the Miss Mailer smell underneath. The hunger is rising again inside Melanie, filling her up all the way to the top, taking her over: Miss Mailer's arm is right there beside her head, and she's thinking *please don't please don't please don't* but who is she pleading with? There's no one. No one but her.

A shape looms in the darkness: a thing as big as a room, that sits on the ground but rocks from side to side and spits dirt in their faces with its deep, dry breath and drones to itself like a giant trying to sing. It has a door in its side; some of the children sit there, inside the thing, in their chairs, tied in with straps and webbing so it looks like a big spider has caught them. Some of Sergeant's people are there, too, shouting words that Melanie can't hear. One of them slaps the side of the big thing: it lifts into the air, all at once, and then it's gone.

Sergeant's arm clamps down on Miss Mailer's shoulder and he turns her around, bodily. "There!" he shouts. "That way!" And they're running again, but now it's just Sergeant and Miss Mailer. Melanie doesn't know where Sergeant's people have gone.

There's another one of the big rocking things, a long way away: a *helicopter*, Melanie thinks, the word coming to her from a lesson she doesn't even remember. And that means they're outside, under the sky, not in a big room like she thought at first. But even the astonishment is dulled by the gnawing, insistent hunger: her jaws are drawing back, straining open like the hinges of a door; her own thoughts are coming to her from a long way away, like someone shouting at her through a tiny mesh window: *Oh please don't please don't!*

Miss Mailer is running toward the helicopter and Sergeant is right behind. They're close to it now, but one of the big swinging lights turns and shows them some men running toward them on a shallow angle.

The men don't have guns like Sergeant does, but they have sticks and knives and one of them is waving a spear.

Sergeant fires, and nothing seems to happen. He fires again, and the man with the spear falls. Then they're at the helicopter and Miss Mailer is pulled inside by a woman who seems startled and scared to see Melanie there.

"What the fuck?" she says.

"Sergeant Robertson's orders!" Miss Mailer yells.

Some more of the children are here. Melanie sees Anne and Kenny and Lizzie in a single flash of one of the swinging lights. But now there's a shout and Sergeant is fighting with somebody, right there at the door where they just climbed in. The men with the knives and the sticks have gotten there, too. and the sticks have gotten there, too.

Sergeant gets off one more shot, and all of a sudden one of the men doesn't have a head anymore. He falls down out of sight. Another man knocks the gun out of Sergeant's hand, but Sergeant takes his knife from him somehow and sticks it into the man's stomach.

The woman inside the copter slaps the ceiling and points up—for the pilot, Melanie realizes. He's sitting in his cockpit, fighting to keep the copter more or less level and more or less still, as though the ground is bucking under him and trying to throw him off. But it's not the ground, it's the weight of the men swarming on board.

"Shit!" the woman moans.

Miss Mailer hides Melanie's eyes with her hand, but Melanie pushes the hand away. She knows what she has to do, now. It's not even a hard choice, because the incredible, irresistible human flesh smell is helping her, pushing her in the direction she has to go.

She stops pleading with the hunger to leave her alone; it's not listening anyway. She says to it, She stops pleading with the hunger to leave her alone; it's not listening anyway. She says to it, instead, like Sergeant said to his people, *Pick your target.*

And then she jumps clear out of Miss Mailer's arms, her legs propelling her like one of Sergeant's bullets.

She lands on the chest of one of the men, and he's staring into her face with frozen horror as she leans in and bites his throat out. His blood tastes utterly wonderful: he is her bread when she's hungry, but there's no time to enjoy it. Melanie scales his shoulders as he falls and jumps onto the man behind, folding her legs around his neck and leaning down to bite and claw at his face.

Miss Mailer screams Melanie's name. It's only just audible over the sound of the helicopter blades, which is louder now, and the screams of the third man as Melanie jumps across to him and her teeth close on his arm. He beats at her, but her jaws are so strong he can't shake her loose, and then Sergeant hits him really hard in the face and he falls down.

Melanie lets go of his arm, spits out the piece of it that's in her mouth.

The copter lifts off. Melanie looks up at it, hoping for one last sight of Miss Mailer's face, but it just disappears into the dark and there's nothing left of it but the sound.

Other men are coming. Lots of them.

Sergeant picks up his gun from the ground where it fell, checks it.

He seems to be satisfied.

The light swings all the way round until it's full in their faces.

Sergeant looks at Melanie, and she looks back at him.

"Day just gets better and better, don't it?" Sergeant says. It's sarcasm, but Melanie nods, meaning it, because it's a day of wishes coming true.

Miss Mailer's arms around her, and now this.

"You ready, kid?" Sergeant asks.

"Yes, Sergeant," Melanie says. Of course she's ready.

"Then let's give these bastards something to feel sad about." The men bulk large in the dark, but they're too late. The goddess Artemis is appeased. The ships are gone on the fair wind.

Mike Carey is the author of the Felix Castor novels and (along with Linda and Louise Carey) *The Steel Seraglio*. He has also written extensively for comics publishers DC and Marvel, including long runs on X-Men, Hellblazer, and Ultimate Fantastic Four. He wrote the comic book *Lucifer* for its entire run and is the co-creator and writer of the ongoing Vertigo series The Unwritten. He received a 2013 Edgar nomination for "Iphigenia in Aulis."

*Fate held her in its grasp for four decades. It makes her crave
the slick feel of hot gun metal in her hand . . .*

SLAUGHTERHOUSE BLUES

(Based on Nick Cave's "O'Malley's Bar" from *Murder Ballads*)

Tim Lebbon

He walks in through the front door, still tall, still thin, and her heart flutters like a frantic raven's wing in her chest. For a second she thinks she's going to drop dead and that all those years would have been for nothing. She breathes deeply and closes her eyes, keeping his image in her mind's eye (though for a blink he's younger and more beautiful, and he still has the ability to smile), and the drunken old fuck Max leans into her and asks *wassa madda*. She shoves Max away and looks again, and by now he's at the bar, pulling up a stool, ordering a drink, and she notices something wrong with his hands.

Brady, the bartender and owner, pours the man a whiskey, and she hears the familiar story for the millionth time.

"Drunk at the Slaughterhouse before?"

The man shakes his head, and she frowns. *Surely he has,* she thinks. But then she starts to remember, and it's as if his reappearance is polishing her memories, making them clean and crisp and sharp where down through the years they've become tarnished with age and overuse.

"Well, keep your head down if you hear anyone call it O'Malley's." Brady is already laughing in anticipation of his old, old joke. "That's an old name now." He chuckles, sounding like a bronchial pig. "We change the name of this place every time there's a massacre!" He starts laughing out loud, and a few people around the bar join in. Max is one of them, even though he's too far gone to have understood a word.

She stares right at the man, and for a moment she thinks it's all going to happen again. He's reaching into his jacket—

(what *is* wrong with his hands?)

—and a rush of memory and emotion overcomes her: fear and excitement, terror and delight. But he brings out only his wallet, awkwardly, and drops a twenty onto the bar. Brady smiles because he knows the guy's staying for a while.

She smiles, too. He's here again. She's been waiting for this day for over forty years.

He didn't take a drink because he never had the time. She was standing in the corner over by the pool table when she saw him enter, a place where real ladies didn't hang out, and the guy she'd been watching potting ball after ball stood up and propped the end of the cue on his shoe. A cigarette hung from the corner of his mouth, smoke curling up into his watering eye. He was too cool to move it away.

The man was tall and deadly and he walked directly to the bar without taking a single look around the room. That would haunt her for some time—the fact that he'd not even considered who would die when the shooting began—and he told O'Malley he was thirsty.

Shooting the barman before he had a chance to drink, the man turned around and started to say his words.

Her knees went weak and she hit the boards. Not through fear or shock— though both of those emotions were playing their own particular notes across her body—but from surprise at how fucking *loud* the gunshot had been.

She remained where she was behind the pool table, hearing the new shots and the crumple of bodies, the man's words and his measured footsteps, and thinking to herself, *He's come to rescue me.* She really believed that. He was here for her, and anyone who got in his way would find themselves—

Henry, the guy she'd been watching play pool and who she'd be- gun thinking she might fuck behind the bar later, took a bullet in the chest. He flipped back and his trousers exploded, spilling guts and bowels and blood across the polished wooden floor.

She stopped breathing then, and only started again when she'd crawled into the ladies' toilet and was propped up in one of the stalls. *Did he see me come in here?* she wondered. *Did he hear me? See the door open? Catch sight of me in the bar mirror while he was killing someone else?* She sat there shaking, wondering and hoping that he had.

For years she'd felt that she had nothing to live for.

He's come to rescue me.

She stands and walks across to the ladies' room. The bar is much different now, of course. Back then it was been a smoky, dark place, where the subdued conversation was countered by the sound of O'Malley polishing and shelving his glasses, smashing empty bottles down the chute into the cellar, or arguing loudly about the latest news event. He'd been a cantankerous old bastard, changing his opinions depending on the weather or the angle of the sun, or just so he could counter whoever dared argue with him. The floor was bare wood, polished here and there but still wearing through and presenting dangerous trip hazards for those who'd had a few too many. The furniture was mismatched, the ceiling yellowed by cigarette smoke, the same nicotined color as most of the patrons. Now the bar is all glass and chrome, with full-height mirrors behind the bar itself, and casual leather seats scattered around in mock-random fashion. The pictures on the walls are modern art prints instead of rural landscapes, and though Brady still makes his jokes about the massacre, it's no longer a visible, palpable part of this place's history. Its name has changed more than once since then, its décor many times more, and it might as well be somewhere else entirely.

She remembers, though, and Brady knows who she is. Sometimes she thinks he only lets her stay because she spends most of her time and all of her money in here.

As she pushes open the door to the ladies' room—it's still in the same place in relation to the bar, though the pool table disappeared back in the eighties to make way for a salad bar—she glances at the seated man's back. His hair is short, not long, and gray, not black. His shoulders are hunched instead of straight and proud. But she could never forget that profile. And as he lifts the whiskey glass to his lips, she knows it's the very first time he's taken a drink in this place.

She sits in the cubicle, a woman pushing sixty who is feeling as excited and giddy as that girl who'd hidden away forty years before. She'd known he was being released, because there was a small piece about it in the local rag a week before. It concentrated on old Meredith Bellows, whose son had his brains smashed out across the bar with an ashtray.

And then she decides it's time to go out and see him. There's something she has to ask, the same question that was on her mind when she cowered here many years earlier.

She takes a deep breath, pushes the door open, and approaches the bar.

She waited in the toilet cubicle for quite some time, listening to the screaming and shooting and the wet thudding sounds of him smashing someone's brains out. She was shivering and sweating, and it took a while for her to pluck up the courage to open the door and go back out. *He's a gentleman,* she thought. *He won't come into the ladies' room, so I'll have to go out there to him.* She imagined the look on his face when he finally saw her, the recognition of identical pain, and she hoped she'd see the bullet coming.

She crept to the door and placed her ear against it, frowning. No more gunshots.

"Fear me!" he shouted, and her knees went weak again and she pissed herself, just a little. She grabbed the door handle and twisted, and then she heard the muffled sound of police loudhailers. When she opened the door it creaked, letting in the stench of blood and shit and insides turned out.

To begin with she couldn't see him, he was standing so still. There were bodies splayed around the bar, only bodies, no one moving, and gun smoke hung in the air in place of cigarette smoke, butts now extinguished by vomit and blood. The pool table was red. O'Malley grinned bloody and dead from behind the bar.

Then she saw him, and he saw her, and he lifted his gun and smiled.

"Do I know you?" she asks.

He sighs, but doesn't turn around. "Mind if I take a seat?"

Still no answer.

Shaking, sweating, more nervous than she's ever been before, she pulls out the bar stool next to his and sits down. And then she gets a proper look at his hands. They've been mutilated, fingers cut off below the second knuckle, leaving only the index finger and thumb on his right hand. The wounds look old and gnarled, and necessitate him picking up his glass with a delicate, almost formal precision.

"Why didn't you kill me?" she whispers.

He freezes completely. He stops breathing, his eyes glaze over, and his one remaining thumb halts the gentle tattoo it has been playing against the bar top. She believes then that if she exhales across his head, her alcohol breath will not even shift one of his short hairs. He's paused in time between blinks and breaths, and she wonders what she has done.

Then he turns slowly to look at her and recognition dawns. It brings little emotion with it. Regret, maybe, for not killing her . . . or at least she hopes that's what the sadness means. No surprise, no shock that she should be here waiting for him after forty years, but of course not, because they're made of the same flesh and blood now, aren't they?

"Why?" she prompts.

He blinks, then turns back to the bar and lifts the glass to his lips. Draining it in one go, he places it on the bar again and goes to leave. "Wait!" she says. She grabs his arm. He looks down at her hand and she lets go, ashamed of her presumptuous contact. "Please!"

"I recall that's just what you said last time we met." He walks away from her towards the door, and she sees Brady watching the old man go, a confused frown twisting his face.

"I have no free will!" she shouts. He stops then, halfway to the door, and every other patron in the bar looks at her, and at him. He's the center of attention in that place again, but this time no one knows why. Not even Brady, who has a place on the wall around the corner of the bar where he keeps photographs of everyone the man killed that day in what Brady says is in honor but which she knows is just a twisted way to try and attract more attention to the slaughter . . . not even Brady knows his face.

"And you think that makes us the same?" he asks softly.

She nods. Holds up her hands, trying clumsily to bend down her fingers, fisting them in so that he can see himself reflected in her.

He scoffs, comes back to the bar and sits beside her again. She can barely believe this is happening. He came back and she almost lost him again, and now here he is sitting beside her on purpose, ordering another drink, and this time it's a large one.

"You?" he asks, nodding at her glass. She cannot speak, and it's lucky that Brady knows her usual.

She looks at the side of his head. If he'd sat on the other side she wouldn't have seen, and maybe he's done it on purpose, because now she's sure she can make out the subtle, circular barrel burn. *He's showing me,* she thinks. *He* wants *me to see.* He takes a casual drink and looks at himself in the bar mirror, and she lets herself think that for a while longer.

That smile, she thought, because there was something familiar in there, something knowing and understanding, a mad grin that she could see through to the level certainties possessed by the killer on the other side.

She reached out one tentative hand past the doorjamb, keeping the rest of her body hidden away. *Like a shy naked woman wearing a mask,* she thought, and his grin widened as he pressed the barrel of the gun hard against his temple.

He turned away from her then, staring at the bar's shattered front window. *He didn't waste a bullet.* She counted the shots in her mind and the bodies sprawled motionless or twitching before her. A bullet must have passed right through one of O'Malley's patrons, and she wondered whose blood it was speckling a thousand shards of glass on the sidewalk outside.

He took one step forward, and the mechanized police voices grew louder.

"Please!" she said. *Please don't do it please don't go please kill me.* She wasn't sure exactly what she meant, but that one word attracted his glance again.

"Drop your weapon and come out! Keep your hands above your head!"

"Please," she said again, because now the man was utterly motionless, his eyes half closed and his hand still holding the gun to his temple. Then he seemed to come to a decision. He looked at her and grinned again, dropped the gun, and walked from the bloodied bar.

Something slumped within her. She might have been fooled that it was a sense of relief, but she knew herself too well for that, had dis- covered things about herself while bent over behind this place letting the latest bad boy have her, walking through the dismal town at noon with false smiles veering away, sitting alone in her parents' house because they'd died and left her only with her own damaged self. It *wasn't* relief she felt, but sadness. Sadness that this moment had passed, and it had been the best of her life. Nothing that followed could ever equal this. Her heart was thundering, blood pulsed at her ears, and the door swung closed behind him. There was shouting and the scraping of feet across the sidewalk, but that was somewhere else.

She looked down at the gun he'd used. It was big and long, the barrel thicker than most guns she'd seen. It had landed pointing at her, spilled blood from fat Vincent West running into a floorboard joint and not quite touching it. She stared into its mouth and knew it would fire no more.

"Anyone left alive in there?" a scared voice called. One of the young cops from the town, younger than her.

No, she thought, *no one alive in here,* and she walked toward the gun.

It was still warm as she clasped her hand around the barrel. She closed her eyes and breathed in the gun smoke, distinguishing it from the blood and insides because it was pure and honest, not tainted and sick. The gun was heavy and hard in her hand. She was feeling her death, and inside this thing was the bullet that should have penetrated her and brought her everything she wanted.

She began to wonder, and the door burst open.

"We've got a live one!" the cop shouted, and she almost laughed at the deluded young fool.

"I can't believe you came back," she says.

"I can't believe you're still here."

"Where else would I go?"

He shrugs and glances at her. His eyes aren't what they use to be. Not dead, exactly, but . . . tempered. Something has sucked that extravagant life from him and left him normal.

"I kept your gun," she says.

"No you didn't." He frowns at her, and almost looks unsettled. She glances down at her hand and remembers the heat of the barrel. Her skin is old and creased now, yellowed by smoke and made thin by decades of alcohol abuse. She can almost see her blood flowing, and it mocks her.

"What happened to your fingers?" she asks. "Prison?"

"Prison." He picks up his glass again, a difficult movement that is nevertheless confident. She wonders how he can do everything that needs doing with only two fingers.

"Why did they do it?"

"They didn't. I did." He falls quiet as Brady walks past them behind the bar, casting a curious glance at the mutilated man. He looks at her too, and she feigns drunkenness so she doesn't have to focus. *This is my moment,* she thinks, *don't fuck it up, Brady.* She remembers the man blasting O'Malley in the throat and the musical jingle of glass that accompanied the echo, and smiles.

"You did it to yourself."

"One finger for everyone in the bar that day," he says, lifting his fingerless left hand. "I was countin'."

She frowns and starts going over all the names she knows. She can barely remember their voices or faces any more, their personalities or what they meant to her, but their names are as familiar as this man's face in her dreams. She counts, and quickly passes ten.

"I stopped," he says. "Started cutting, then lost my nerve. Had to have something left, didn't I? Drink, wipe my ass, jerk off. Surprising how much you can do with just a thumb and index finger." He drinks some more, and she stares at his stumps.

"Get you another?" Brady asks. He's been hovering.

"'Nother double. And one for the lady." Brady pours their drinks.

"Have you come back to finish things?" she asks, because it's pressing, this need to know. She hasn't waited forty years to die, but the memory of how she felt back then is suddenly fresh and sharp.

"Why so keen to die?" he asks, once Brady is out of earshot. He actually leans closer to her, turning to face her fully for the first time, and his stale breath is as familiar to this place as gun smoke. "If I'd done you back then, think of all you'd've missed."

"All I would have missed," she says, and she tries to hold back the bitter laughter. There must have been good times, but Max catches her eye then and tries to wink, and he's far too drunk and he does so with both eyes. He doesn't open them again; drifts off, slumps sideways, snoring. "All I would have missed." She looks around the bar at the other patrons, a few of whom she recognizes. Funny, how someone can drink in the same place with the same people for so long and never exchange a word with them. The old black woman who always sits by the door, keeps her hat on and a scarf around her neck, just about to leave as she polishes off most of a bottle of whiskey. The younger guy in the back, nursing a half-full glass for hours on end because he only ever has enough begging money for one. She gave him a hand job in the men's toilet once, but she has never known his name.

"You don't know what you did to me back then," she says, suddenly bitter. "You left me that day, abandoned me, and I was between blinks. Between breaths." Her voice is rising. "I was winded by what I saw and what you did to me—"

"Lady, I didn't do anythin' to you."

"Yes!" she shouts, and then Brady is there telling her to can it. She closes her eyes and breathes in deeply

. . . and the gun smoke had started to clear. She sat on a stool by the bar as the medics checked her over, and the police stared dumbfounded at what they'd walked in on, and a detective fired questions at her that she could not hear. They mumbled some soothing words from which she took no comfort at all, then someone grabbed her arm and guided her outside.

The sun hit her. She hadn't even known it was daylight. Every breath she took belonged to someone else. Every step along the sidewalk was somewhere she was never meant to go. She was living on borrowed time, and payback would not come for many, many years.

"Where is he?" she asked.

"It's okay, Ma'am, he can't hurt you—"

"Where is he?"

"He's being taken to the—"

"Where is he?"

A pause. "He's gone."

"Where is he?"

They stopped answering her then, but she didn't stop asking. She *never* stopped asking.

He takes another drink, and this time she buys the round. Brady is becoming suspicious; he knows something is happening, but he can't tell what. He hates that in his own bar. He thinks he's the king.

"So why have you come back?" she asks.

"Not for what you think."

"What is it you think I think?"

He laughs. It's not the sound made by a mass murderer. "Lady," he says, "you're an open book."

"You owe me," she says, and she's holding back the tears. "You stole something from me, and you owe me. I didn't lie, you know. I have no free will, 'cause you stole it back then. With everything I saw, everything you did . . . I was only a girl!"

"I spared your life." He's almost sneering now, or perhaps his face is distorted through her tears. Then he leans in close and says, "And I knew very well what I was doing."

"What? What?" But he has gone. She watches him leave and goes to follow, but she falls from the stool, burning her elbows on the polished floor. Brady has come around the bar and he's helping her up, and the stupid fucking idiot still doesn't know, still doesn't understand who's been sitting at his bar drinking his best whiskey.

"That was *him*," she says.

"Who?" Brady asks.

And she leaves it at that, because perhaps he'd been a ghost after all.

She leaves the bar and stands outside. From the sidewalk the Slaughter-house looks like any one of a hundred bars in a hundred cities. There's nothing to show what happened in there, and though the façade is almost the same as it was back then, the new windows and paintwork have given it more of an upbeat feel. Its face is as different as hers, except that this place now looks even younger. She stares at herself in its window, her image vague and insubstantial, and she is old. The massacre she witnessed has not been all her life is about, but it has been a large part of it. She's made that so. Much as she tried to lay responsibility on his stooping shoulders, she has no one to blame but herself.

Someone inside the bar returns to their seat with a drink—Max, or the old woman—and their image seems to ripple through her own reflection.

Maybe I've been in there ever since, she thinks. *Maybe he shot me before he pressed the gun's hot barrel to his temple.* The idea has occurred to her a thousand times over the years, but now that she's seen what he has become it takes on a convincing weight. Would he really have turned into something like that anywhere other than in her haunted dreams? Would a man so tall and proud and handsome, so full of vitality and purpose, have done that to himself? The barrel would have cooled down too much to burn him, wouldn't it . . . unless he'd fired it one more time before turning the empty gun on himself? She closes her eyes and tries to remember the bullet coming for her, and when she opens them again and looks along the street, she sees him.

He is walking slowly, as if his unbalanced hands mess with his stability. People weave around him like they would a drunk, but he isn't drunk. Maybe they see him for what he is. Perhaps they know him like she does.

She turns and walks the other way, because even if she hurries to catch up, he can never be what she wants. *I have no free will,* she said, and she feels fate directing her still. It held her in its grasp for four decades, preparing her for the here and now. It makes her crave the slick feel of hot gun metal in her hand, and when she's too drunk to travel to the range, she makes do with cold.

Time pulling her toward home, she leaves O'Malley's behind for the last time. It became the Slaughterhouse many years ago. Lining the street, she sees plenty of other places ready to change their names.

The author of more than two-dozen novels and many works of short fiction, **Tim Lebbon** won the Bram Stoker Award for Short Fiction for his short story "Reconstructing Amy" and his novel *Dusk* won the August Derleth Award from the British Fantasy Society for best novel. His novelization of the movie *30 Days of Night* became a *New York Times* bestseller and won a Scribe Award. His most recent novels are *Star Wars: Dawn of the Jedi: Into the Void* and *Reaper's Legacy.* He lives in Goytre, Monmouthshire with his wife and two children.

Science and magic together are more powerful,
are greater weapons, than they are apart . . .

ENGLAND UNDER THE WHITE WITCH

Theodora Goss

It is always winter now.

When she came, I was only a child—in ankle socks, my hair tied back with a silk ribbon. My mother was a seamstress working for the House of Alexandre. She spent the days on her knees, saying Yes, madame has lost weight, what has madame been doing? When madame had been doing nothing of the sort. My father was a photograph of a man I had never seen in a naval uniform. A medal was pinned to the velvet frame.

My mother used to take me to Kensington Gardens, where I looked for fairies under the lilac bushes or in the tulip cups.

In school, we studied the kings and queens of England, its principal imports and exports, and home economics. Even so young, we knew that we were living in the waning days of our empire. That after the war, which had taken my father and toppled parts of London, the sun was finally setting. We were a diminished version of ourselves.

At home, my mother told me fairy tales about Red Riding Hood (never talk to wolves), Sleeping Beauty (your prince will come), Cinderella (choose the right shoes). We had tea with bread and potted meat, and on my birthday there was cake made with butter and sugar that our landlady, Mrs. Stokes, had bought as a present with her ration card.

Harold doesn't hold with this new Empress, as she calls herself, Mrs. Stokes would tell my mother. Coming out of the north, saying she will restore us to greatness. She's established herself in Edinburgh, and they do say she will march on London. He says the King got us through the war, and that's good enough for us. And who believes a woman's promises anyway?

But what I say is, England has always done best under a queen. Remember Elizabeth and Victoria. Here we are, half the young men dead in the war, no one for the young women to marry so they work as typists instead of having homes of their own. And trouble every day in India, it seems. Why not give an Empress a try?

One day Monsieur Alexandre told my mother that Lady Whorlesham had called her impertinent and therefore she had to go. That night, she sat for a long time at the kitchen table in our bedsit, with her face in her hands. When I asked her the date of the signing of the Magna Carta, she hastily wiped her eyes with a handkerchief and said, As though I could remember such a thing! Then she said, Can you take care of yourself for a moment, Ann of my heart? I need to go talk to Mrs. Stokes.

The next day, when I ran home from school for dinner, she was there, talking to Mrs. Stokes and wearing a new dress, white tricotine with silver braid trim. She looked like a princess from a fairy tale.

It's easy as pie, she was saying. I found the office just where you said it was, and they signed me right up. At first I'm going to help with recruitment, but the girl I talked to said she thought I should be in the rifle corps. They have women doing all sorts of things, there. I start training in two days.

You're braver than I am, said Mrs. Stokes. Aren't you afraid of being arrested?

If they do arrest me, will you take care of Ann? she asked. I know it's dangerous, but they're paying twice what I was making at the shop, and I have to do something. This world we're living in is no good, you and I both know that. Nothing's been right since the war. Just read this pamphlet they gave me. It makes sense, it does. I'm doing important work, now. Not stitching some Lady Whortlesham into her dress. I'm with the Empress.

In the end, the Empress took London more easily than anyone could have imagined. She had already taken Manchester, Birmingham, Oxford. We had heard how effective her magic could be against the remnants of our Home Forces. First, she sent clouds that covered the sky, from horizon to horizon. It snowed for days, until the city was shrouded in white. And then the sun came out just long enough to melt the top layer of snow, which froze during the night. The trees were encased in ice. They sparkled as though made of glass, and when they moved I heard a tinkling sound.

Then, she sent wolves. Out of the mist they came, white and gray, with teeth as sharp as knives. They spoke in low, guttural voices, telling the Royal Guards to surrender or have their throats ripped out. Most of the guards stayed loyal. In the end, there was blood on the snow in front of Buckingham Palace. Wolves gnawed the partly frozen bodies.

Third and finally came her personal army, the shop girls and nursemaids and typists who had been recruited, my mother among them. They looked magnificent in their white and silver, which made them difficult to see against the snow. They had endured toast and tea for supper, daily indignity, the unwanted attention of employers. Their faces were implacable. They shot with deadly accuracy and watched men die with the same polite attention as they had shown demonstrating a new shade of lipstick.

Buckingham Palace fell within a day. On the wireless, we heard that the King and his family had fled to France, all but one of his sisters, who it turned out was a sympathizer. By the time the professional military could mobilize its troops, scattered throughout our empire, England was already hers to command.

I stood by Mrs. Stokes, watching the barge of the Empress as it was rowed down the Thames. She stood on the barge, surrounded by wolves, with her white arms bare, black hair down to her feet, waving at her subjects.

No good will come of this, you mark my words, said Mr. Stokes.

Hush! Isn't she lovely? said Mrs. Stokes.

You have seen her face in every schoolroom, every shop. Perhaps in your dreams. It is as familiar to you as your own. But I will never forget that first glimpse of her loveliness. She looked toward us, and I believed that she had seen me, had waved particularly to me.

The next day, our home economics teacher said, From now on, we are not going to learn about cooking and sewing. Instead, we are going to learn magic. There was already a picture of our beloved Empress over her desk, where the picture of the King used to be.

At first, there were resistance movements. There were some who fought for warmth, for light. Who said that as long as she reigned, spring would never come again. We would never see violets scattered among the grass, never hear a river run. Never watch young lovers hold each other on the embankment, kiss each other not caring who was watching. There was the Wordsworth Society, which tried to effect change politically. And there were more radical groups: the Children of Albion, the Primrose Brigade.

But we soon learned that our Empress was as ruthless as she was beautiful. Those who opposed her were torn apart by wolves, or by her girl soldiers, who could tear men apart with their bare hands and were more frightening than any wolves. Sympathizers were rounded up and imprisoned, encased in ice. Or worse, they were left free but all the joy was taken from them, so that they remained in a prison of their own perpetual despair.

Her spies were everywhere. Even the trees could not be trusted. The hollies were the most dangerous, the most liable to inform. But resistance groups would not meet under pines, firs, or hemlocks. In many households, the cats were on her side. Whispers of disloyalty would bring swift retribution.

And many said, such traitors deserved punishment. That winter was good for England, that we needed cold, needed toughening. We had grown soft after the war, allowed our dominions to rebel against us, allowed the world to change. But she would set things right. And so the resistance movements were put down, and our soldiers marched into countries under a white flag that did not mean surrender. Those who had tried to be free of us were confronted with winter, and sorceresses, and wolves. Their chiefs and rajahs and presidents came to London, bringing jewels and costly fabrics to lay before her feet, and pledged their loyalty.

Our empire spread, as indeed it must. A winter country must import its food, and as winter spreads, the empire must expand to supply the lands under snow, their waters locked in ice. That is the terrible, inescapable logic of empire.

I was a Snowflake, in a white kerchief with silver stars. Then, I was an Ice Maiden. The other girls in school nodded to me as I walked by. If they did not wear the white uniform, I asked them why they had not joined up yet, and if they said their parents would not let them, I told them it was their responsibility to be persuasive. I won a scholarship to university, where I was inducted into the Sisterhood of the Wolf.

My den mother encouraged me to go into the sciences. Scientists will be useful to the Empress in the coming war, she said. Science and magic together are more powerful, are greater weapons, than they are apart. And there is a war coming, Ann. We hear more and more from our spies in Germany. A power is rising in that part of the world, a power that seeks to oppose the reign of the Empress. Surely not, I said. Who would oppose her? A power that believes in fire, she said. A fire that will burn away the snow, that will scorch the earth. That does not care about what we have already achieved—the security, the equality, the peace we will achieve when her empire spreads over the earth.

When I graduated, the Empress herself handed me a diploma and the badge of our order. My mother, who had been promoted to major-general, was so proud! All of us in the Sisterhood had been brought to Buckingham Palace, in sleighs drawn by reindeer with silver bells on their antlers. We waited in a long room whose walls were painted to look like a winter forest, nibbling on almond biscuits and eating blancmange from silver cups with small bone spoons. At last, we were summoned into her presence.

You have seen our beloved Empress from far away, from below while she stands on a balcony, or from a sidewalk as she is drawn through the city streets in her sleigh. But I have met her, I have kissed her hand. It was white and cold, with the blue veins visible. Her grip was strong—stronger than any man's, as she was taller than any man. Her face was so pale that I could only look at it for a moment without pain. Her black hair trailed on the floor.

You have done well, she said to me, and I could hear her voice in my head as well as with my ears. To hear that voice again, I would consent to being torn apart by wolves.

You have never seen, you will never see, anything as magnificent as our Empress.

Where did she come from? Some say she came from the stars, that she is an alien lifeform. Some say that she is an ancient goddess reborn. Some say she is an ordinary woman, and that such women have always lived in the north: witches who command the snows.

The question is whispered, in secret places where there are no hemlocks, no cats: does human blood flow in her veins? Can our Empress die?

I met Jack in the basic physical training program required for all recruits to the war effort. My mother had used her influence to have me chosen for the Imperial Guard, the Empress's personal girl army, which could be deployed throughout the empire. After basic training, I was going to advanced training in the north, and then wherever the war effort needed me. He was a poet, assigned to the Ministry of Morale. He had been conscripted after university—this was in the early days of general conscription. He was expected to write poetry in praise of the Empress, and England, and those who served the empire. But first, we all had to pass basic training.

We stayed in unheated cabins, bathed in cold water, all to make us stronger, to bring the cold inside us. Each morning, we marched through the woods. The long marches, hauling weapons and equipment through the snow, were not difficult for me. I had been training since my university days, waking at dawn to run through the snow or swim in the icy rivers with the Sisterhood. But he was not as strong as I was. He would stumble over roots or boulders beneath the snow, and try to catch himself with chilled, chapped hands—the woolen gloves we had been issued were inadequate protection against the cold. I would help him up, holding him by the elbow, and sometimes I would carry part of his equipment, transferring it into my pack surreptitiously so the Sergeant did not see me.

Why are you so kind to me, Ann? he asked me once. Someone has to be, I said, smiling.

The other girls laughed at him, but I thought his large, dark eyes were beautiful. When he looked at me, I did not feel the cold. One day, I sat next to him at dinner. He told me about Yorkshire, where he was born—about the high hills, the sheep huddled together, their breaths hanging on the air.

Perhaps I should have been more like my father, he said. It was my headmaster at school who first read my poems and told me to apply for a scholarship. There I was, a farmer's son, studying with the children of ministers and generals, who talked about going to the palace the way I talked about going to the store. I kept to myself, too proud or ashamed to approach them, to presume they might be my friends. But my tutor sent my poems to the university literary magazine, and they were published. Then, I was invited to join the literary society. I thought it was an honor—until we all received letters from the war office. So here I am, losing my toes to frostbite so I can write odes for the dead in Africa—or for the war they say is coming.

We all believed that war was coming. The newspapers were already talking about a fire rising in the east, burning all before it.

It's a great honor to write for the Empress, I said.

Yes, of course it is, he said after a moment. He looked at me intently with those dark eyes. Of course, he said again, before finishing the thin broth with dumplings that we were told was Irish stew.

We spent more and more time together, huddled in the communal showers when we could, telling each other about our childhoods, the foods we liked, the books we had read. We wondered about the future. He hoped that after his compulsory service, he could work as a schoolteacher, publish his poems. I did not know where I would be assigned—Australia? South America? There was always unrest in some part of the empire.

One day, the sergeant said to me, Ann, I'm not going to tell you what to do. I'm just going to warn you—there's something not right about Jack Kirby. I don't know what it is, but Thule—who was her wolf—can't stand him. I don't think a general's daughter should show too much interest in that boy. You don't want anyone questioning your loyalty, do you?

Her words made me angry. He was going into the Ministry—wasn't that good enough? That night, we met in the showers. I don't want to talk, I said. I kissed him—slid my hands under his jacket, sweater, undershirt. His body was bony, but I thought it had its own particular grace. He told me that I was beautiful, breathing it into my neck as we made love, awkwardly, removing as few layers of clothing as possible. You're beautiful, Ann—I hear it in my mind and remember the warmth of his breath in that cold place. There had been others, not many, but he may as well have been my first. He is the one I remember.

During our week of leave, he asked me to come home with him, to Yorkshire. His father met us at the train station. He was a large, quiet man who talked mostly of sheep. Look at these pelts, he told me. Feel the weight of them. Didn't use to get wool like this, in Yorkshire. It's the perpetual winter as does it. Grows twice as thick and twice as long. But he grumbled about the feed from the communal granaries—not as nourishing as the grass that used to grow on the hillsides, never seen such sickly lambs. And the wolves—not allowed to shoot them anymore. Those who complained were brought before a committee.

We had suppers of Yorkshire pudding and gravy, and walked out over the fields holding hands. I asked Jack about his mother. She had died in the influenza epidemic, which he had barely survived. That was before the coming of the Empress. I could see, from the photograph of her on the bureau, that he had inherited her delicacy, her dark eyes and thick, dark hair. Late at night, when his father was asleep, he would sneak into the guest room and we would make love under the covers, as quietly as possible, muffling our laughter, whispering to one another.

The day before we were to return from leave, his father told him that a ewe was giving birth in the snow. She had become trapped in a gully, and could not be lifted out in her condition. There was no chance of bringing her into the barn, so he and his father, one of the two farm hands, and the veterinarian went out, grumbling about the cold.

I wandered through the house, then sat in his room for a while, looking through the books he had read as a child. Books from before the Empress came, and from after—*Prince Frost and the Giants*, the Wolf Scout series, the *Treasury of English Poems* we had all studied in school. I can't tell you why I chose to look though the battered old desk he had used as a schoolboy. It was wrong, a base impulse. But I loved him, and on this last day before we went back to the camp, I wanted to feel close to him. I wanted to know his secrets, whatever they were—even if they included love letters from another girl. I tortured myself for a moment with that thought, knowing how unlikely it was that I would find anything but old school books and pens. And then I pulled open the drawer.

In the desk was a notebook, and in the notebook were his poems—in his handwriting, with dates at the tops of the pages indicating when they had been written. The latest of them was dated just before camp. They spoke of sunlight and warmth and green fields. Next to the notebook was a worn copy of one of the forbidden books: *The Complete Poetical Works of Wordsworth*. I opened to the page marked with a ribbon and read,

> *I wandered lonely as a cloud*
> *That floats on high o'er vales and hills,*
> *When all at once I saw a crowd,*
> *A host, of golden daffodils . . .*

I slammed the book shut. My hands were shaking. I remembered what the sergeant had said: You don't want anyone questioning your loyalty, do you?

By the time Jack, his father, and the other men had returned, I was composed enough to seen almost normal. That night, he came to my room. We made love as though nothing had happened, but all the time I could hear it in my head: *I wandered lonely as a cloud—a host of golden daffodils.* I remembered daffodils. I could almost see them, bright yellow against the blue sky.

The next morning, as Jack and his father were loading our bags into the sleigh that would take us to the train station, I told them I had forgotten something. I ran back into the house, up the stairs and into Jack's room, then quickly slid the notebook and book into my backpack.

When we arrived back at camp, I went to the sergeant and denounced Jack Kirby as a traitor.

I told myself that I was doing the right thing. He would be sent for reeducation. He would become a productive citizen, not a malcontent longing for what could never be. Perhaps some day he would even thank me.

He was sent to a reeducation camp in the north of Scotland. I graduated from basic training, went on to advanced training for the Imperial Guard, and was eventually given my wolf companion, Ulla. Together, we were sent to France, where the war had already started. We were among the first to enter Poland. We were in the squadron that summoned ice to cover the Black Sea so our soldiers could march into Turkey. My den mother had been right: science and magic together created powerful weapons. It took five years, but the fire in the east was defeated, and our empire stretched into the Russian plains, into the deserts of Arabia.

When I returned to England, I asked for Jack's file. It told me that he had died in the camp, shortly after arriving. The causes of death were listed as cold and heartbreak.

During the Empress's reign, England has changed for the better, some say. There is always food in the shops, although it has lost its flavor. Once, carrots were not pale, like potatoes. Cabbages were green. They were not grown in great glass houses. The eggs had bright yellow centers, and all meat did not taste like mutton. Once, there were apple trees in England, and apples, peaches, plums were not imported from the distant reaches of our empire, where winter has not yet permanently settled. There was a sweetness in the world that you have never tasted. There was love and joy, and pain sharp as knives, rather than this blankness.

Our art, our stories, our poems have changed, become ghosts of their former selves. Mothers tell their daughters about Little White Hood and her wolf companion. About Corporal Cinder, who joined the liberation army and informed on her wicked sisters.

Our soldiers move on from conquest to conquest, riding white bears, white camels. Parts of the world that had never seen snow have seen it now. I myself have sent snowdrifts to cover the sands of the Sahara, so we could deploy our sleighs. I have seen the Great Pyramid covered in ice, and crocodiles lying lethargic on ice-floes in the Nile.

Our empire stretches from sea to sea to sea. Eventually, even the republics that now fight against us will come under our dominion. And then perhaps the only part of the world that has not bowed down to our Empress, the wild seas themselves, will be covered in ice. What will happen to us then, when there are no more lands to send provisions to the empire? I do not know. Our Empress has promised us a perfect world, but the only perfection is death.

You have heard stories of primroses and daffodils, and you do not believe them. You have heard that there were once green fields, and rivers that ran between their banks, and a warm sun overhead. You have never seen them, and you believe they are merely tales. I am here to tell you that they are true, that in my childhood these existed. And cups of tea that were truly hot, and Christmas trees with candles on their branches, and church bells. Girls wore ribbons in their hair rather than badges on their lapels. Boys played King Arthur or Robin Hood rather than Wolf Scout.

I'm here to tell you that the fairy tales are true.

And that, sitting in this secret place, looking at each other in fear, wondering who among you is an informant, you must decide whether to believe in the fairy tales, whether to fight for an idea. Ideas are the most powerful things— beauty, freedom, love. But they are harder to fight for than things like food, or safety, or power. You can't eat freedom, you can't wield love over another.

You are so young, with your solemn faces, your thin bodies, nourished on pale cabbage and soggy beef and slabs of flavorless pudding! I do not know if you have the strength. But that, my children, you will have to find out for yourselves.

Your leaders, who have asked me here tonight, believe that winter can end, if you have the courage to end it. They are naive, as revolutionaries always are. Looking at your faces, I wonder. You have listened so intently to an old soldier, a woman who has seen much, felt much, endured. I have no strength left to fight, either for or against the Empress. Everyone I have ever loved—my mother, Mrs. Stokes, Jack Kirby, Ulla—is dead. I have just enough strength to tell you what the world was once, and could be again: imperfect, unequal, and in many ways unjust. But there was warmth and light to counteract the cold, the darkness.

What do I believe? Entropy is the law of the universe. All things run down, all things eventually end. Perhaps, after all, she is not an alien, not a witch, but a universal principal. Perhaps all you can do is hold back the cold, the darkness, for a while. Is a temporary summer worth your lives? But if you do not fight, you will never feel the warmth of the sun on your cheeks, or smell lilacs, or bite into a peach picked directly from the tree. You will never hold each other on the embankment, watching the waters of the Thames run below. The old stories will be forgotten. Our empire will spread over the world, and it will be winter, everywhere, forever.

Theodora Goss was born in Hungary and spent her childhood in various European countries before her family moved to the United States. Her publications include the short story collection *In the Forest of Forgetting* (2006); *Interfictions* (2007), a short story anthology coedited with Delia Sherman; *Voices from Fairyland* (2008), a poetry anthology with critical essays and a selection of her own poems; and *The Thorn and the Blossom* (2012), a novella in a two-sided accordion format. She has been a finalist for the Nebula, Locus, Crawford, and Mythopoeic Awards, as well as on the Tiptree Award Honor List, and has won the World Fantasy Award.

All roads lead to death. Aokigahara is death. All roads lead to Aokigahara . . .

THE SEA OF TREES

Rachel Swirsky

Not ten minutes in, I spot yellow electrical tape strung through the trees. Recent, not tattered. I grab, hold on hand-over-hand as I scramble over roots and rocks. Good to have a touch-connection to the way out. If you don't know the way back, the trees might lure you and keep you.

The forest is all shadows. Clinging mist damps the sunlight. Light penetrates at strange angles, casting a glow over lichen-covered roots, shredded bark and rotting logs.

To the left: a rope suspended from a branch that's too weak to support a man's weight. Hung by someone stupid or indecisive or playing a prank. Hope that's not all I'll find today.

To the right: a second tape trail branching into the shadows.

Better stick to the trail I'm on for now. Hope it pays off.

A few meters later: a woman's compact on the ground. Kick it; watch it bounce end over end, mirror flashing. It leaves an indentation in the soil. It's lain undisturbed awhile. Good. Makes it more likely I've gotten here before the suicide watch. I slip the compact into my pack.

I'm feeling really good right now. This is a bingo. Can already see *yurei* shadows hiding behind trunks. Not long dead, this one, not with ghosts still gathering.

The scent of mandarin oranges precedes a *yurei* flashing next to me. She's all floating with no feet. Her Edo-style white burial kimono casts a shadow on the lichen.

Black hair sweeps to her waist, equally covering the back and front of her head. Impossible to locate her face. Tendrils curl toward me entreatingly.

This *yurei*'s been around as long as I have. Likes jokes. Minor pranks. She's harmless.

"*Your life is a precious gift from your parents,*" she says. "*Please think about your parents, siblings, and children.*"

"*Ha.*"

She's quoting the signs that are posted at the edge of the forest in a weak attempt to turn back the suicidal before they add to the body count among the trees. Who gets this far to be stopped by a sign?

Tendril of hair grasps my shoulder. I bug-shudder it off. "*You know that's not why I'm here.*"

"*Don't keep it to yourself,*" she says, still quoting. "*Talk about your troubles.*"

"*Only trouble I've got right now is where to find good scavenge.*"

The *yurei* rotates slowly in the air. A raven lock gestures down the trail I've been following.

"*Thief-girl.*" She uses her derisive pet name for me. "*That one's got nothing. Couldn't even take a train back to Tokyo.*"

Another tendril points back to the tape fork.

"*That one came with everything he's got. Red tent under a big tree.*"

Her tone is too helpful. Suspicious. This *yurei* likes barbs and mischief. She's not sugar unless she's hiding something.

"*Not gone yet, is he?*" I ask.

Ends of her hair curl up in a shrug. "*Neck's broken. Wait ten minutes.*"

All right. I open my hydration pack. Drink.

Yurei keeps floating by. Can't tell where her eyes are behind all that hair, but she's watching me.

"*You want something?*" I ask.

She bobs silently.

Sigh. "*Go ahead.*"

She floats closer. Tendrils of hair reach out like tentacles. I grit my teeth as she feels my face like a blind person. Hair feels like hair feels, but this hair moves like hair shouldn't. Body knows that. Body does not like being touched by the dead.

The scent of mandarin oranges lingers as her hair withdraws. "*Just wanted to remember,*" she says. "*What it's like. To touch skin that wants to live.*"

I wipe my mouth, reseal the hydration pack. "*It'll be ten by the time I get there. Thanks for the tip.*"

You can call this place Aokigahara or you can call it Jukai, the sea of trees. Either way, it's haunted.

The forest grew eight hundred and fifty years ago after an eruption of Mount Fuji. Green things sank their roots after the lava cooled.

The woods are very quiet. Little lives here except for ghosts and people on their way to joining them. Wind scarcely blows. Mists hang. Overhead, branches and leaves tangle into a roof underneath which the world is timeless and directionless.

Everything is trapped.

Everything is waiting.

A pair of tennis shoes, sitting alone.

Pants, voluminous over leg bones.

A suicide note nailed to a tree: "Nothing good ever happened in my life. Don't look for me."

The *yurei*, watching.

The man hanging above the red tent smells like the shit his bowels just released. He has three gold teeth, an expensive watch, brand-name trainers, and a pack of money. I'm unclear on the point of taking cash into the forest, but people do what they do.

Good scavenge, that's sure. Most people have nothing when they come here to die. Easier to feel empty when your bank account's the same.

Scissors, nail clippers, a comb. Copy of Wataru Tsurumi's *Complete Manual of Suicide*. Half of everyone who comes here carries that. Stupid book. Stupider people. Can't even reject their lives without instructions.

I'm about to toss it back when I hear a crunch in the undergrowth.

Nearby.

Damn it.

Snap to my feet. Pull on my pack. Now I notice what greed blinded me to: where are the *yurei* around this fresh death? Other living people must be on their way. Scared the ghosts off.

That *yurei* must have known. She trying to get me caught?

The suicide watch is not going to be friendly when they realize I'm looting. I scramble, searching for a tree to climb. No way they won't have heard me by now, but some are superstitious, might put noises down to *yurei* without really looking.

I hear the smack of someone tripping. The swearing that follows is in American English.

"Damn it to bugfucking, motherfucking hell!"

I can see her now. American tourist wearing a downy red sweatshirt over jeans with sandals of all stupid things. Half-empty hydration pack hangs from her backpack. Either she can't ration or she's been hiking awhile.

Young. Maybe fifteen, sixteen. Makeup and clothes are all-American, but can't conceal Japanese eyes. Probably another fucking Nisei looking for her roots.

I push into the shadows, thinking I'll wait her out, but it turns out that despite being clumsy and unprepared, she's not stupid.

"*Sumimasen,*" she says. "*Eigo hanashimasuka?*"

She wants to know if I speak English. I have no intention of letting her know I do. *"Gomen nasai. Eigo ga wakarimasen."*

"Figures," she mutters. "Just another slant-eyed motherfucker with half a brain."

I can't stop my snarl in time. She cracks a grin.

"Ha! Thought you did!"

No point denying it. "What do you want?"

"I'm lost."

I point over her shoulder at the tape path. "You can get out that way."

She squints. "I recognize you. In town. I stopped to use my phone. You were on the corner."

"Sorry, wasn't me."

"Someone pointed you out. They said there aren't many women who spend time up here. They said an *onryo* follows you around."

People should set up shop and charge for gossip the way they toss other people's stories around. Everyone figures it's fair game if there's a ghost.

I gesture at the trees. "You see an *onryo*?"

"They didn't say it followed you all the time."

I cross my arms. "What do you want?"

"I need to find a *yurei*."

I point to the newly hanged man. "Wait around."

"No. I need to find a particular *yurei*. I need to find my father."

Here's the thing about me: I came to Aokigahara when I was twenty-two, the year my *onryo* came for me. I've been here seven years since. Sure, I leave the trees, but I'm always here.

I make my living scavenging. Selling valuables. Or, most of the time, not finding anything valuable and then hunting down buyers with too much death on their minds, people who want to thrill themselves with a hint of the haunted by buying detritus that once belonged to a suicide. Combs. Glasses. Rope from a noose. Remnants of lives abandoned.

I don't need much to live, but I earn less. That's why I listen when the American girl caps her plea with, "I'll pay."

"How much?"

The figure she names is enough to buy a day or two in the forest looking for a ghost.

I won't even have to find her father. Just spend some time searching, then turn up any ghost at all. She'll never tell the difference.

Still, I can't help pressing further. See what she's made of.

I sling my backpack off my shoulder. "Sounds like a deal."

She smiles. Gestures to herself. "I'm Melon."

I give her an oddball eye. She laughs.

"Mom thinks nature names sound Japanese."

I exchange mine. "Nao."

"Cool. Where do we start?"

"Nowhere today. It's getting late."

It's early evening; we could go a couple hours. But I want to stop here.

I unpack my sleeping bag. "I'll be fine on the ground."

She nods.

I add, "You take the tent."

I grin as I point. The red tent still smells like the sweat and piss of the man swinging from the tree. The girl looks up. His shadow falls over her, black as bruises. She swallows fast.

Breaking her gaze from the dead man's eyes, she crouches to unzip the flap.

"Look comfy?" I ask.

She glances back. Her too-earnest American face has a closed, hard set.

"Looks fine."

She crawls in. I'm not unimpressed.

Two a.m. The ghost hour.

The whistling of wind wakes me. The sound comes alone, unaccompanied by breeze.

Then she's there. My Sayomi. My *onryo*.

Dead lips on mine. Cold fingers stroking my thighs. Prehensile tendrils of hair circling my waist, teasing my nipples, trailing my spine.

Creep-shudder, gullet to gut. Body does not like being touched by the dead.

But my Sayomi. Body likes being touched by my Sayomi.

Timeless at twenty-one. Smooth-cheeked, willow-bodied, bloodlessly pale. Eyes shining with tears a decade old.

A long skirt flows to her ankles, Western-style but cut from white-flowered silk. Low-cut lace shows the apple-tops of her breasts. Lipstick stains her mouth; she opens to moan; blood-color smears her teeth.

She dressed up to die, my Sayomi.

Ashen tongue in my mouth like a cold lump of meat. Hair busy undoing the zip of my jeans, her obi-style waistband. Night air breathes cold on flesh usually hidden.

She pushes me to the ground, roots sharp in my back. Sayomi on top of me. Her hair parting my lips. Her fingers inside me.

I moan.

She always makes me moan.

The creeping horror of her hair. The unchanging beauty of her face.

My body tightens. That moment, near arriving. Her unfinished business with me nearly resolved.

It takes a great deal of will to shove her away before it comes.

She screams. Her hair ties itself in angry knots. I squirm out from underneath. Her fingernails claw the dirt where I've been.

Someday, I won't get away.

Someday I won't want to.

I gain my feet. Her hair stretches for my wrists and ankles. Her eyes are wide and guileless even as she tries to drag me down.

It would be so easy to give in.

Clouds shift. Across her moonlit face, a shadow swings.

I look up. The hanged man. Socks on his dangling feet, robbed of their expensive trainers.

The red tent. The American girl. I'd forgotten where I was.

Desire vanishes.

Sayomi pounds her fists on the air. She screams again. This time, the sound dissolves her. It becomes a windless whistle as she blows away.

Back in the silence of the sea of trees, all I can hear is my ragged breath.

I pull up my jeans. The girl's face peeps through the tent flap. I politely look away, but she won't give me the courtesy of silence.

She asks, "Was that the *onryo*?"

I shrug. She knows it was.

"Why is she a pile of bones?"

I sigh. "There's an old ghost story. A lonely scholar lives in his house, pining away, until one day a beautiful woman visits at night. He lets her in. They make love. In the morning, she leaves, and the scholar gets sick. Every night after that, she comes to him. They make love, she gives him pleasure, and he gets weaker."

The girl's watching eyes are bright like Sayomi's, but tearless.

"One night, the scholar's worried neighbor looks through the window," I continue. "He sees the scholar in bed with a skeleton. He tells the scholar what he saw, and that night, when the ghost arrives, the scholar knows what she is. But he doesn't see a pile of bones. When he looks at her, he sees a woman."

"What happened to the scholar?"

"He died."

Silence. Then, "What does your *onryo* look like?"

I shrug again.

"Did you know her? When she was alive?"

That's enough. I don't listen to whatever she asks next.

• • •

A girl may love a girl, but eventually both become women.

One goes to university in America. The other studies in Fukuoka. Each misses the other, but one is distracted by learning English and sunbathing by Lake Michigan and eating cafeteria lunches. For the other, Fukuoka is what Fukuoka has always been, but drained of joy. Joy that will never return for girls who've grown into women.

Even across the boundary of life and death, flesh may yearn for flesh. But when the dead pleasure the living, they pull them to their side, as the ghost woman pulled her scholar.

As a ghost, Sayomi doesn't talk, but just before she died, she sent an e-mail. I didn't receive it until after she was gone. Sometimes it feels as if it were written by her ghost.

Come to Aokigahara, she wrote. *We'll finish things there.*

I wake before the girl does.

Three *yurei* gather around the hanged man. Clawed hands emerge from hair-veils to peck at the corpse. Spectral fingers leave no marks, but the man's body swings back and forth despite the lack of wind. Slowly at first and then faster and faster. The branch creaks as if caught in a hurricane. The *yurei* make noises I've never heard. Part shriek and part scratch, simultaneously the sounds of predators and of terrified things.

I pull the girl out of the tent. Gesturing for silence, I point to the raven-like *yurei*. The girl's not stupid; she follows my lead, packing without a word. We back away, careful not to make noise with our feet.

When we're a distance removed, she asks, "What was that?"

I feign nonchalance. "Don't know."

Hope she'll think I'm saying *Don't know and it doesn't matter* instead of *Don't know and I thought I knew everything about* yurei.

Not sure she buys my dismissive shrug. She keeps her own counsel for once.

When she does talk again, it's about something else. She pulls a photo from her pack. "This is my father."

I expect a generic, smiling face, but the photo shows a corpse. Dried flesh on bones. A tidy button-down drapes over shoulders that look like a coat hanger. Hair clumps on remnants of scalp. Part of the nose and cheek remain, but not enough to make a face.

She points to the background. "See those rocks? I thought maybe you'd recognize them."

Tourists.

"It's a big forest," I answer.

"Not that big."

"Big enough."

She should know what I mean without my having to tell her: with all the ghosts here, the sea of trees is as big as it wants to be.

The girl looks like she wants to stomp her feet. "Then how are you going to find him!"

"Wander. Watch the trees." She still looks pissed. I add, "If we keep going deeper, he'll find you."

If he wants to find her.

If someone else doesn't find us first.

She bites her lips. Gazes abstractly at distant trees. "Do you think he'll talk to me?"

"*Yurei* like to talk."

I shouldn't say more since her optimism is what's paying me, but I can't stop myself.

I add, "No telling what he'll say."

We're still in familiar forest. I can navigate. Would be better to follow tape trails, but I don't want the strange *yurei* to find us too easily.

Once we're moving steadily, the girl starts talking.

"My mother met my father while she was backpacking the summer after college. He was older than she was. They didn't stay in touch, but she had his name. Last year when I turned sixteen, she said I was old enough to figure out for myself what to do with it. So I tracked down his family. They told me he'd died, but they wouldn't say anything else."

"He committed suicide," I assume.

"The suicide watch found him here." Melon's voice is thick. She tugs the strap of her backpack so she has an excuse to hesitate. "They sent me photos."

"What makes you think he became a *yurei*?"

"I read online that the first night after they bring the bodies back, someone from the suicide watch sleeps next to them. In the morgue or wherever they take them. To make sure their souls can rest."

"No one slept next to him?"

"I don't know. I didn't ask. But in the photo of him, of his body . . . you can see that he's been . . . that's he's already . . . "

"Rotted."

She stiffens. Doesn't protest. "No one slept with him then. On the real first night."

Quiet, there, in the sea of trees. Just me and her. Me and her and her sadness.

I ask, "Did he know about you?"

"Mom told him. Before I was born." Her tone changes. Last night's hard look returns to her face. "I know what you're asking. No. He never tried to get in touch with me. It doesn't matter. I care even if he didn't. I have to know where I came from."

I don't think much of Melon's reasons, but I like her conviction. I also like the fact that even though I can see she's tired and sore, she hasn't complained.

"Why do you speak English?" she asks.

"I went to college in America."

"Where?"

"Northwestern."

"Oh!" she says. Then, quietly, "I've read a lot about Chicago."

Something mournful there. Something unsaid. Maybe something to do with why she's seventeen and hiking alone half a world from where she grew up, searching for a father she never knew.

I'm so grateful that she's keeping something to herself for once that I leave it alone.

We're past where most suicides go, but we find footprints so I stop. Gives the girl a chance to rest. Gives me a chance to keep my profits up.

Result: a bag half buried between roots. I shake off loose soil. Dig through canned food and hygiene products.

The girl asks, "Why'd they bring all that in?"

"Some people stay a long time before they do anything."

"Saying goodbye to the world?"

"Or making up their minds."

At the bottom of the bag, a *mokume-gane* wedding band. Dirty. Sized for a small man or a large woman.

The girl watches the light pick a glint from beneath the grime. "How sad."

I push the ring into my pocket.

Melon continues, "It makes sense to want to say goodbye to the world before you leave it."

Mist drifts through motionless leaves. Trees creep slowly, invisibly, toward the masked sun.

"This place is like a graveyard," she says.

"Whole world is. At least here, it looks like what it is."

We go on. Evening draws closer. Silent and navy instead of silent and white.

I almost lead the girl toward a cave I know when I feel sudden trepidation. I stop abruptly. "Shh!" I hiss to forestall the girl's question.

A *yurei*, crouched between trees. He hovers midair, hair parting over his nose and sweeping down in two dark curtains. His exposed jaw stretches all the way to the ground: a gaping maw the size of a door. Black, open, waiting to swallow us into hungry dark.

I pull the girl backward for several meters before I dare turn. We move swiftly through the trees. Takes a while. Navy turns darker. Still doesn't feel safe.

The girl gets sick of following. Demands, "Where are we going?"

I look back through the dark, toward where the mouth gapes. *Yurei* like ravens. *Yurei* waiting to swallow us down.

I've lost my nerve.

"We should get out," I say.

"Why?"

"Something's wrong. Something's bringing out the darkest."

In the last light, she looks lost and lonely. Her voice is all breath. "Maybe it's me."

Melon's stupid and young and American. Annoying as she is, I can't imagine what about her would draw darkness from ghosts.

Chill on my nape, though. Says maybe I'm wrong.

Melon asks, "Can you get us out this late?"

It's almost black. Moonlight casts faint silhouettes across nearby trunks.

We're far away from electrical tape and signs entreating us not to end our lives.

I could get us out. I think. But I don't want to be wrong.

"We'll talk in the morning," I say.

Moonlight reveals her guileless grin.

Two a.m.

The sound of wind without wind.

Sayomi.

Me on the ground in my sleeping bag. Crisp, night smells. The girl nearby.

Doesn't matter who's watching. Nothing stops Sayomi's devouring kisses. Hair embraces me. Meat-lump tongue laps at my lips. She wants to pull me out through my mouth. Fill her ribcage with my heart. Fill her bones with my marrow.

I want her too.

Legs scissoring. Pelvises matched. Lips to lips. Pleasure fluttering. Hovering. Rising. I should go with her. I should let her make me come. I should come; I should go; at least then I'd be somewhere.

No. Not now. Not tonight, with the girl watching. There will always be another night to let Sayomi suck me down.

I shove Sayomi away. She screams. Hair lashes my face, leaves stinging marks that will last till morning.

"No." I shove again.

Hair winds around my throat. Pulls tight. An ethereal glow lights the whiteness of her skin. Her teeth are bared, her weeping eyes bloodshot. She strains as her hair cinches tighter.

Throat hot. Lungs searing. I'm suddenly hyper-aware of air on my face, on my thighs—air I can't breathe.

Sayomi's never gone this far before.

Even as her hair strangles me, strands of it separate to move beneath my waist. The burning cinch. The gentle stroke. Each sensation sharpens the other.

My vision sparks. Blue. White. Fading. Can't even struggle.

A rock streaks past Sayomi's cheek, clatters on the ground behind her. She can't be hurt like that anymore, but she recoils with surprise. Her hair withdraws from me, moving reflexively to protect her like a shield. I can just make out Sayomi's eyes behind the veil. Angry. Betrayed.

Air chokes my throat. I grasp my neck. Pain all the worse now that I have oxygen to feel it.

Hands on my back, checking to see if I'm all right. Melon's hands. "Nao!" she exclaims.

Sayomi looks down at us and screams again, that hair-to-heel scream that scatters her into the night.

"I tried not to watch," Melon says.

I clutch my burning throat.

"Her bones are white. I thought you had to be dead a long time for your bones to bleach like that."

Her voice trembles. Her eyes are afraid. Maybe she's realizing the danger now. These aren't American ghosts you can banish with water and chanting. They're *yurei*. They take what they want.

I knew Sayomi was dead as soon as I read her e-mail. She was long gone by the time I arrived in Aokigahara.

I've spent years reconsidering all the times we'd spent together after I left for school. The phone calls made when one or the other of us should have been sleeping. The e-mails complaining about classwork. The summer after my second year when I came home and we went hiking but we got too tired to climb and so we laid down near the mountain's base instead, holding each other's hands and watching the sky.

I should have heard the plaintive tone in her voice on the train heading back. "You'll always come back for me, won't you?" She was staring out the window, not even able to look at me. I hadn't understood what that meant.

I didn't give her what she needed then so I give her what I can now. Not much: a few kisses, a nightly embrace.

Until I can muster more.

The girl and I are both awake by dawn.

She's angry that I still want to go back. "I need to find my father! You deal with ghosts all the time. I thought you were an expert!"

"That's why I know when to leave."

"You can't just stop! I'm paying you!"

I laugh.

Angry surprise lights her face. American girl, used to money buying power. She doesn't expect *dismissal.*

"This is my only chance! I have to fly back to Nebraska on Tuesday. Who knows if I'll ever get back? I have to find my father! Please! You owe me. You wouldn't even be here if I hadn't rescued you last night!"

I wait for her to run out of shouting.

"I'm heading back," I say. "Come with me or go alone."

Her face goes blank, caught between pride and fear.

I throw her a bone.

"Maybe we'll find your father on the way out."

When we glimpse sunlight, the trees thicken.

Down past the rocks, the trees thicken.

Along every path, the trees thicken.

Each time, I turn heel and try another way. My heartbeat goes faster. My mouth dries. I tell myself I'm only lost. I'll find the way.

But I already know. There is no way.

The trees have claimed us.

I don't tell Melon. It would only scare her. She'll eventually work it out.

Maybe by then I'll know what to do.

The girl's frightened inhalation warns me to halt.

I'm about to step out from underneath the canopy's shadow. In front of us, a lightning-struck tree has fallen across its sisters, creating a small clearing.

Encroaching on its boundaries, dozens of *yurei.* Flocking. Screeching.

It's daytime, but shadows swarm around the ghosts, creating temporary dark. Some hold torches aloft in locks of their hair. Firelight picks out undertones of blue and green in their white kimonos. They swoop and dart like carrion-eaters, all suddenness with no grace.

Leaders emerge into the clearing. Pass through. There are many, many more behind.

The girl trembles. Goosebumps prick my skin.

Any moment, they could smell us. They may already be watching behind their hair. Clawed hands could part their veils at any instant.

Hundreds stream by until, at last, the grimacing legion is gone, shadows and firelight with them, leaving behind mist and silent trees.

The girl starts forward into the clearing. No! I throw my arm out to stop her. She cringes as she glimpses what I've seen.

One last *yurei* sitting on the lightning-charred stump.

The air is so cold. My exhalations are ice.

The *yurei*'s scent drifts toward us.

Mandarin oranges.

Relief instantly warms me. "Don't worry," I tell the girl. "I know this one."

The *yurei*'s head rotates toward our approach. Her body remains motionless. If she had a living neck, it would snap.

"*Thanks for your advice the other day,*" I say acidly in Japanese.

"A moment, please!" she replies in English. "Consult the police before you decide to die."

The girl gasps. Her expression shows fear.

"Don't worry," I repeat. "This one always quotes the signs. She thinks it's a joke."

Melon trembles. She braces her hands protectively across her stomach. I think but don't say, *You're the one who wanted to meet a ghost.*

"We can't get out," I tell the *yurei*.

She switches to Japanese. "*All roads lead to Aokigahara.*"

Melon breathes raggedly. I can't tell how much she understands.

"Hardly anything leads to Aokigahara."

"*All roads lead to death. Aokigahara is death. All roads lead to Aokigahara.*"

"*You are not being helpful!*" I reply angrily in Japanese.

"*The forest wants you.*"

"*I've been here a hundred times! Why does it want me now?*"

I glare at the *yurei*. I know her pricks and pranks. She's keeping something to herself.

The girl breaks in, using halting Japanese. "*Please! I need to find my father. Can you help me?*"

The *yurei* turns again, that neck-snapping turn. "Your name is Melon."

Her English is very bad.

"Yes," Melon says. She's afraid, but it doesn't silence her.

The *yurei* calls back to me, "*You come a hundred times alone and once with this one. What do you think is different?*"

Melon looks between us, confused. The Japanese is too fast for her. "Please," she repeats. "My father's name is Manabu. He died here."

"Why should I help you?" the *yurei* grumbles. She adds in Japanese, "*She doesn't have anything I want.*"

"*She has the same thing you get from me,*" I say. "*She has skin that wants to live—*"

The words aren't entirely out of my mouth before I realize what the *yurei* is implying.

I gape at Melon. "What did you really come here to do?"

Melon hasn't understood our words, but she knows how to read my shocked eyes. She tenses. I move forward to catch her, but I'm too late. She flees.

The *yurei* rises to watch her go. Her hovering form casts a sharp shadow across the lightning-struck log.

For a moment, I'm too confused to pursue. Everything is going wrong. The trees closing in. Sayomi refusing to let go.

"*One girl wants to die,*" the yurei says. "*One girl is marked by a ghost. Both belong to us.*"

"What do I do? How do I get out?"

"*The trees have been waiting to claim you. They won't let you out while they're feeding on her.*"

"Then I'll chop them down! Damn it! What do I do?"

The *yurei* says nothing. She won't help. She got what she wanted yesterday and now she's watching her prank play out.

Damn her. I run past, following Melon.

"*Please reconsider!*" the yurei calls after me. "*Think of your family!*"

Melon's still walking when I find her, but she's turned herself in circles and hasn't made it far.

She jumps when she feels my hand on her pack. She struggles to keep me from pulling it off, but I'm stronger and her straps are loose.

Inside: gear, clothes, hygiene items—and there: I rattle an enormous bottle of analgesics.

"What's wrong with you?" I ask. "Why do you think you need these?"

I push the lid down and twist. Throw the open bottle. Pills rain down in a hyperbola.

I grab another. Melon fights me for it. I twist free of her grip. Scatter another pill rain.

"Do whatever you want!" she shouts. "You think I need pills? Look where we are!"

Bottle of vodka at the bottom of the pack to wash it down. I dump it. Make some mud.

Melon stomps off. Leaving her pack behind. Leaving me behind. I jog after. Catch her in a couple steps.

"Poison's not even a good way to do it. Stick to rope. It's faster."

"Thanks for the advice."

"I'm not giving you advice! How old are you? Sixteen?"

"Seventeen."

"What the hell is wrong with you at seventeen that you think you need to come here?"

She whips around to face me. The ferocious movement makes me stagger back.

"You think I can't have problems because I'm seventeen? My mother ran off. Okay? She ran off to Chicago when I was seven and left me in Omaha with my grandparents. They don't even like kids. Last year, she comes home just long enough to give me my father's name. Only time I've seen her since I was twelve. So I take the money I've been saving for college and I buy a trip here. To meet my father's family. But they don't want me either! Who am I to them? Some kid from another country? I'm here to find my father!"

Spit from her shouting lands on my face. I'm too stunned to answer. Not used to people emptying themselves. Not to me, the woman with the *onryo* who spends too much time with the dead.

At last, I think of words. "You think you're going to find family here?" I gesture at the trees. "Make a family of ghosts?"

"Why not? You're fucking one."

She can see that hurts. She's happy to have landed a punch.

"Leave me alone," she says.

"The trees won't let me." I hate to say it, but it's true. "I already half belong to them. They won't let me leave without you."

Doubt flickers across Melon's face. She didn't intend to force me to die with her.

I push at her weakness. "Your father. Will you promise not to kill yourself if I help you find him?"

She hesitates. Nods. I can see from the flicker in her eyes that it's not a real promise. She'll still kill herself to stay with him if she can.

As long as she's with me, I've got time to convince her otherwise.

• • •

We retrieve her pack and walk in silence.

The girl's shoes squeak as we walk uphill. Our unwashed smell clings to our clothes.

Why do I care if Melon dies and takes me with her? I've been here seven years, flirting with death. Letting death kiss me. Waiting for her to bring me to a height I can't safely leap down from.

I always knew Sayomi would take me eventually, but not now, I never wanted it now. Seven years of soon, later, someday.

Maybe I never wanted to die at all.

We tread on springy feathers of lichen. Creepers wind around tree trunks like *yurei* hair, beautiful and confining. Fingerlike branches point in a thousand different directions.

Between trees, a shadowed mass blooms where there should be day.

The horde of ghosts.

I grab Melon's elbow. I know where to find her father.

Ghosts' shadows blacken the narrow, winding twists between trees. We run toward them as they stream toward us. Within moments, we're engulfed in dark.

I scream into the mass of ghosts. "We're looking for her father! You know where he is!"

Torchlight illuminates Melon's upturned face. She's all flickers and contrasts.

Something changes in the flow of ghosts. They move around us as if we're an island, leaving an empty space. A *yurei* floats into the opening.

Melon's father.

He wears the button-down shirt from the picture, faded and grayed. Too-long slacks drape over his feet—if he has feet. Empty cuffs hang two feet above the ground.

He doesn't have tumbling hair like traditional *yurei*, but what hair he has obscures his eyes. Impossible to tell where he's looking. What he's thinking.

"Manabu?" Melon's voice shakes.

The ghost's words scrape against each other like pumice stones. "*I was alone.*"

"Speak in English?" Melon pleads.

"*They didn't think I could do it. They thought I was a coward.*"

"Please. I know you used to speak English with my mother. She can't even say *domo arigato*."

"*No one would hire me. I spent all day in the park.*"

A wind that affects nothing else blows around him. His clothing streams away from his body. Sometimes it presses tight against him, revealing the outline of his skeleton. His hair remains motionless, concealing his face.

I shout at Melon, "He's not even listening to you!"

She ignores me. "I'm your daughter! From America! I knew you'd understand me. You know what it's like to be alone."

"I told my mother I'd talk to her landlord about the plumbing. She said I didn't have anything else to do. She pestered me until I said yes. She called my cell phone while I was sitting in the park. 'Why haven't you done it yet? You can't even talk to the landlord.' She didn't think I could do it. She thought I was a coward."

"Please! I don't understand! Talk to me in English!"

"I had an interview that day. Maybe I'd have gotten the job. Who knows? I went to the landlord. I told him to fix my mother's plumbing. He said he'd get to it. I slammed him against the wall and told him, 'Get to it now.' He didn't think I was a coward then."

"Your . . . your mother's toilet . . . ?"

"He said he was going to call the police. I told him, 'Go ahead.' They could find me in the park. I left his house, but I didn't go to the park. I bought a train ticket instead."

I grab urgently for Melon's hand. "He's stuck! Listen! It's what they're like. They're fixed . . . fixed on loneliness, on kissing someone, on playing games . . . "

"I was alone. They didn't think I could do it."

Her father has reached the end of his story that is also the beginning. He's repeating himself now, but Melon's still listening to him, not me. *Yurei* stream around us, their hair growing longer and shorter as the torchlight flickers.

I have to do something to get her attention.

I fumble in my pocket. The *mokume-gane* wedding ring. Polished by my worrying fingers, it glistens. I hurl it toward the *yurei.*

They descend, magpies after something shiny. Claws emerge from hair. Wordless, screaming voices rise.

"You see?" I shout. "That's all they are! Picking after scraps of lives *they chose* to leave behind!"

One snatches the ring. It disappears under the veil of her hair. Others screech.

Melon's father drones. *"They thought I was a coward. No one would hire me."*

I rip open my pack and pull out the trash. Scissors, nail clippers, comb, compact.

I throw them toward the trees. Where each item falls, flocks of *yurei* descend.

"I spent all day in the park. I told my mother I'd talk to her landlord about the plumbing."

"It might make sense to kill yourself if you thought it would stop the pain. But look at them! It doesn't stop! It just keeps going!"

"She said I didn't have anything else to do."

"There's no family here! Look at them!"

Two *yurei* attack each other in the air. Their claws rake toward each other's throats.

"They'll tear each other apart for a shred of something living!"

"She pestered me until I said yes. She called my cell phone while I was sitting in the park. 'Why haven't you done it yet?'"

It's not enough. Melon's gaze is still on her father. Full of longing. Full of hope.

I grab for a side pocket of her pack. She wrenches away, but I snatch the zipper. Open it, pull out what I saw her tuck there: the photo of her father's corpse.

I throw it at the ghost's feet. At once, he falls silent. As he recognizes himself, he becomes an arrow of greed and obsession. He dives to retrieve it, Melon forgotten.

"Do you see?" I ask. "Do you understand?"

I see the moment when Melon's gaze hardens. She turns away from her father. I grab her hand.

Wordlessly, we run through fire-lit dark, terrain rough beneath our feet. We stumble over roots and rocks. Barely manage not to fall.

The howling *yurei* horde pursues. I pull more trash from my pack. Strew it behind us. It slows them down, but they're still too close.

Melon shrugs off her pack. Abandons it.

I follow her lead and throw the expensive stuff. The trainers from the hanged man. A fan of money.

Our temporary lead widens. We glimpse sunlight through the trees. Burst into day so bright it makes us blink.

The shadows speed behind us. We've nothing else to throw.

From ahead, a drifting scent: mandarin oranges.

There she is, floating above the fork of a tree, the twisted thing that tangled me in this. I want to snarl. I want to punish her. But she's our only chance.

"Please!" I shout. "We need to get out!"

She doesn't rotate toward my voice. Was already facing us. Was probably watching all along.

She asks, *"The usual price?"*

"Yes!"

She floats toward us. Dread pricks the back of my neck.

"Why are you helping now?" I ask.

"*Now there are two of you to pay.*"

In front of us: her hair extending toward our bodies. Behind us: the *yurei* horde blocking out the light. Her hair reaches us before the horde does. Wraps us in its cocoon.

Tendrils tangle my eyelashes. Intrude into my ears, my nostrils. Horrible bug-shudder of dead-touch all over. Inescapable. We're buried alive in her hair.

Joy sparks her split ends like static electricity. Will she ever let us go?

Eventually, the hair unwinds. I can move my fingers. My limbs. She unveils my sight last. The *yurei* horde is gone, passed while we were hidden.

"Thanks," I say.

There's acid in my tone. It's hard to thank someone after they risk your life. Gratitude in my tone too. Hard not to be grateful after someone saves you.

She floats a meter away from us. Her hair is back to its normal length, sweeping to her knees, no longer voluminous enough to engulf two people.

"*Consider your parents, your siblings, your children,*" she says. "*Tell the police about your troubles.*"

A lock of her hair separates from the rest. Points to a gap between trees.

"*End of a tape road there,*" she says. "*It'll get you out.*"

She rotates to watch us leave.

"I wonder who she was," Melon says. "Maybe she's from old Japan. Like her kimono."

"Hard to say."

"Maybe she's the first one who died in the forest."

"Maybe."

Melon and I sit in the parking lot. During the day, it's filled with tourist buses. Now, no one else is here.

We'll go back to town soon. Now we need rest.

"What am I going to do?" Melon asks plaintively.

Hard to answer a question like that. So painfully honest.

"You should call your grandparents."

"They don't care."

"They might."

She shakes her head. Looks away.

"Someone will care."

Her voice is quiet. "Yeah, right."

She inhales raggedly as if she's going to cry, but she doesn't. She doesn't say anything either.

Speaking feelings is hard for me, but I try. "You'll be happy. Someday. Even for a few minutes. It's more than the ghosts get." Remembering what the *yurei* said in the forest, I add, "All roads lead to Aokigahara. You may as well walk slowly."

The words leave a too-sweet aftertaste. Sentimental. But they make Melon smile.

Maybe a little sweetness will keep her from dying so young.

Isn't that why I've spent seven years in Aokigahara? Wishing to stop a girl from dying young?

We sit quietly for a few more minutes before we walk to town. I sit by while she places an international collect call to her grandparents.

Two a.m.

Wind whistles without blowing.

My Sayomi.

She coils hair around my wrists. Draws me closer.

She's different. Almost transparently pale. So cold that her embrace is like spring rain: sudden, drenching, cold.

Hair strips my clothes. Winds between my thighs. A humid smell rises between us. Tears and desire mingle on our skins.

She opens me. Begins her caress. Cold: both shocking and exquisite.

We half-embrace, half-struggle on the floor of my single room. Same as we've been for seven years. Caught between yearning and anger.

Does she blame me? For leaving? For failing to see what I should have seen?

Do I blame her for drawing me back? For tangling me in death while I still lived?

I push my fingers between her thighs. In her midst, a spot of warmth. She tenses as I find it.

Hair simultaneously pushes me away and draws me closer. Its tips tie themselves in knots. Sayomi's expression is furious, rapturous, relieved.

All things I'm feeling too.

My tongue, melting her ice.

Her cold numbing my lips.

We shiver together as she comes.

At the apex, she screams. For once, it's not rage. It's consummation. It's expiation. It's catharsis.

As the sound dissolves her, I know she won't return. Her ghost form dissipates, leaving behind only bleached, white bones.

My Sayomi.

I curl myself around her skeleton. It's no longer as cold as ice, only as cold as death.

I sleep there, on the floor, with what's left of her, just as the suicide watch sleeps beside the bodies they bring back. For one night at least, someone must stay to console the newly dead. To ease their loneliness as best we can before morning.

When we have to go on.

Rachel Swirsky holds an MFA from the Iowa Writers Workshop. Her fiction has appeared in numerous magazines, anthologies, and year's best compilations. She's been nominated for the Hugo Award, the Locus Award, the Sturgeon Award, and the World Fantasy Award, and in 2011, her novella "The Lady Who Plucked Red Flowers Beneath the Queen's Window" won the Nebula Award. *Through the Drowsy Dark*, a slim volume of feminist short stories and poetry, is her first collection.

And I fear that I am going mad, for I cannot just be growing old. If I have failed in this one task, oh God, then only let me do this thing . . .

THE MAN WHO FORGOT RAY BRADBURY

Neil Gaiman

I am forgetting things, which scares me.

I am losing words, although I am not losing concepts. I hope that I am not losing concepts. If I am losing concepts, I am not aware of it. If I am losing concepts, how would I know?

Which is funny, because my memory was always so good. Everything was in there. Sometimes my memory was so good that I even thought I could remember things I didn't know yet. Remembering forward . . .

I don't think there's a word for that, is there? Remembering things that haven't happened yet. I don't have that feeling I get when I go looking in my head for a word that isn't there, as if someone must have come and taken it in the night.

When I was a young man I lived in a big, shared house. I was a student then. We had our own shelves in the kitchen, neatly marked with our names, and our own shelves in the fridge, upon which we kept our own eggs, cheese, yoghurt, milk. I was always punctilious about using only my own provisions. Others were not so . . . there. I lost a word. One that would mean, "careful to obey the rules." The other people in the house were . . . not so. I would go to the fridge, but my eggs would have vanished.

I am thinking of a sky filled with spaceships, so many of them that they seem like a plague of locusts, silver against the luminous mauve of the night.

Things would go missing from my room back then as well. Boots. I remember my boots going. Or "being gone," I should say, as I did not ever actually catch them in the act of leaving. Boots do not just "go." Somebody "went" them. Just like my big dictionary. Same house, same time period. I went to the small bookshelf beside my face (everything was by my bed: it was my room, but it was not much larger than a cupboard with a bed in it). I went to the shelf and the dictionary was gone, just a dictionary-sized hole in my shelf to show where my dictionary wasn't.

All the words and the book they came in were gone. Over the next month they also took my radio, a can of shaving foam, a pad of notepaper, and a box of pencils. And my yoghurt. And, I discovered during a power cut, my candles.

Now I am thinking of a boy with new tennis shoes, who believes he can run forever. No, that is not giving it to me. A dry town in which it rained forever. A road through the desert, on which good people see a mirage. A dinosaur that is a movie producer. The mirage was the pleasure dome of Kublai Khan.

No . . .

Sometimes when the words go away I can find them by creeping up on them from another direction. Say I go and look for a word—I am discussing the inhabitants of the planet Mars, say, and I realize that the word for them has gone. I might also realize that the missing word occurs in a sentence or a title. *The _____ Chronicles. My Favorite _____ .* If that does not give it to me I circle the idea. Little green men, I think, or tall, dark-skinned, gentle: Dark they were and Golden-eyed . . . and suddenly the word *Martians* is waiting for me, like a friend or a lover at the end of a long day.

I left that house when my radio went. It was too wearing, the slow disappearance of the things I had thought so safely mine, item by item, thing by thing, object by object, word by word.

When I was twelve, I was told a story by an old man that I have never forgotten.

A poor man found himself in a forest as night fell, and he had no prayer book to say his evening prayers. So he said, "God who knows all things, I have no prayer book and I do not know any prayers by heart. But you know all the prayers. You are God. So this is what I am going to do. I am going to say the alphabet, and I will let you put the words together."

There are things missing from my mind, and it scares me.

Icarus! It's not as if I have forgotten all names. I remember Icarus. He flew too close to the sun. In the stories, though, it's worth it. Always worth it to have tried, even if you fail, even if you fall like a meteor forever. Better to have flamed in the darkness, to have inspired others, to have *lived*, than to have sat in the darkness, cursing the people who borrowed, but did not return, your candle.

I *have* lost people, though.

It's strange when it happens. I don't actually *lose* them. Not in the way one loses one's parents, either as a small child, when you think you are holding your mother's hand in a crowd and then you look up, and it's not your mother . . . or later. When you have to find the words to describe them at a funeral service or a memorial, or when you are scattering ashes on a garden of flowers or into the sea.

I sometimes imagine I would like my ashes to be scattered in a library. But then the librarians would just have to come in early the next morning to sweep them up again, before the people got there.

I would like my ashes scattered in a library or, possibly, a funfair. A 1930s funfair, where you ride the black . . . the black . . . the . . .

I have lost the word. Carousel? Rollercoaster? The thing you ride, and you become young again. The Ferris wheel. Yes. There is another carnival that comes to town as well, bringing evil. "By the pricking of my thumbs . . ."

Shakespeare.

I remember Shakespeare, and I remember his name, and who he was and what he wrote. He's safe for now. Perhaps there are people who forget Shakespeare. They would have to talk about "the man who wrote to be or not to be"—not the film, starring Jack Benny, whose real name was Benjamin Kubelsky, who was raised in Waukegan, Illinois, an hour or so outside Chicago. Waukegan, Illinois was later immortalized as Green Town, Illinois, in a series of stories and books by an American author who left Waukegan and went to live in Los Angeles. I mean of course, the man I am thinking of. I can see him in my head when I close my eyes.

I used to look at his photographs on the back of his books. He looked mild and he looked wise, and he looked kind.

He wrote a story about Poe, to stop Poe being forgotten, about a future where they burn books and they forget them, and in the story we are on Mars although we might as well be in Waukegan or Los Angeles, as critics, as those who would repress or forget books, as those who would take the words, all the words, dictionaries and radios full of words, as those people are walked through a house and murdered, one by one: by orang-utan; by pit and pendulum; for the love of God, Montressor . . .

Poe. I know Poe. And Montressor. And Benjamin Kubelsky and his wife, Sadie Marks, who was no relation to the Marx Brothers and who performed as Mary Livingston. All these names in my head.

I was twelve.

I had read the books, I had seen the film, and the burning point of paper was the moment where I knew that I would have to remember this. Because people would have to remember books, if other people burn them or forget them. We will commit them to memory. We will become them. We become authors. We become their books.

I am sorry. I lost something there. Like a path I was walking that dead-ended, and now I am alone and lost in the forest, and I am here and I do not know where here is any more.

You must learn a Shakespeare play: I will think of you as Titus Andronicus.

Or you, my friend, you could learn an Agatha Christie novel: you will be *Murder on the Orient Express*. Someone else can learn the poems of John Wilmot, Earl of Rochester, and you, whoever you are, reading this, you can learn a Dickens book, and when I want to know what happened to Barnaby Rudge, I will come to you. You can tell me.

And the people who would burn the words, the people who would take the books from the shelves, the firemen and the ignorant, the ones afraid of tales and words and dreams and Hallowe'en and people who have tattooed themselves with stories and Boys! You Can Grow Mushrooms in Your Cellar! and as long as your words which are people which are days which are my life, as long as your words survive, then you lived and you mattered and you changed the world and I cannot remember your name.

I learned your books. Burned them into my mind. In case the fire- men come to town.

But who you are is gone. I wait for it to return to me. Just as I waited for my dictionary or for my radio, or for my boots, and with as meager a result.

All I have left is the space in my mind where you used to be. And I am not so certain about even that.

I was talking to a friend. And I said, "Are these stories familiar to you?" I told him all the words I knew, the ones about the monsters coming home to the house with the human child in it, the ones about the lightning salesman and the wicked carnival that followed him, and the Martians and their fallen glass cities and their perfect canals. I told him all the words, and he said he hadn't heard of them. That they didn't exist.

And I worry.

I worry I was keeping them alive. Like the people in the snow at the end of the story, walking backwards and forwards, remembering, repeating the words of the stories, making them real.

I think it's God's fault.

I mean, he can't be expected to remember everything, God can't. Busy chap. So perhaps he delegates things, sometimes, just goes, "You! I want you to remember the dates of the Hundred Year's War. And you, you remember Okapi. You, remember Jack Benny who was Benjamin Kubelsky from Waukegan, Illinois." And then, when you forget the things that God has charged you with remembering, bam. No more okapi. Just an okapi-shaped hole in the world, which is half-way between an antelope and a giraffe. No more Jack Benny. No more Waukegan. Just a hole in your mind where a person or a concept used to be.

I don't know.

I don't know where to look. Have I lost an author, just as once I lost a dictionary? Or worse: Did God give me this one small task, and now I have failed Him, and because I have forgotten him he has gone from the shelves, gone from the reference works, and now he only exists in our dreams . . .

My dreams. I do not know your dreams. Perhaps you do not dream of a veldt that is only wallpaper but that eats two children. Perhaps you do not know that Mars is Heaven, where our beloved dead go to wait for us, then consume us in the night. You do not dream of a man arrested for the crime of being a pedestrian.

I dream these things.

If he existed, then I have lost him. Lost his name. Lost his book titles, one by one by one. Lost the stories.

And I fear that I am going mad, for I cannot just be growing old. If I have failed in this one task, oh God, then only let me do this thing, that you may give the stories back to the world.

Because, perhaps, if this works, they will remember him. All of them will remember him. His name will once more become synonymous with small American towns at Hallowe'en, when the leaves skitter across the carpet like frightened birds, or with Mars, or with love. And my name will be forgotten.

I am willing to pay that price, if the empty space in the bookshelf of my mind can be filled again, before I go.

Dear God, hear my prayer.

A . . . B . . . C . . . D . . . E . . . F . . . G . . .

Neil Gaiman is the *New York Times* bestselling author of novels *Neverwhere, Stardust, American Gods, Coraline, Anansi Boys, The Graveyard Book,* (most recently) *The Ocean at the End of the Lane,* and (with Terry Pratchett) *Good Omens*; the Sandman series of graphic novels; and the story collections *Smoke and Mirrors* and *Fragile Things*. He has won numerous literary awards including the Hugo, the Nebula, the World Fantasy, and the Stoker Awards, as well as the Newbery medal.

Witches in books are old and bent over, with ugly warts. The woman on the screen has a smooth, soothing voice, red, red lips, and sparkling eyes . . .

THE EDUCATION OF A WITCH

Ellen Klages

Lizzy is an untidy, intelligent child. Her dark hair resists combs, framing her face like thistles. Her clothes do not stay clean or tucked in or pressed. Some days, they do not stay on. Her arms and face are nut-brown, her bare legs sturdy and grimy.

She intends to be a good girl, but shrubs and sheds and unlocked cupboards beckon. In photographs, her eyes sparkle with unspent mischief; the corner of her mouth quirks in a grin. She is energy that cannot abide fences. When she sleeps, her mother smooths a hand over her cheek, in affection and relief.

Before she met the witch, Lizzy was an only child.

The world outside her bedroom is an ordinary suburb. But the stories in the books her mother reads to her, and the ones she is learning to read herself, are full of fairies and witches and magic.

She knows they are only stories, but after the lights are out, she lies awake, wondering about the parts that are real. She was named after a princess, Elizabeth, who became the queen of England. Her father has been there, on a plane. He says that a man's house is his castle, and when he brings her mother flowers, she smiles and proclaims, "You're a prince, Jack Breyer." Under the sink—where she is not supposed to look—many of the cans say M-A-G-I-C in big letters. She watches very carefully when her mother sprinkles the powders onto the counter, but has not seen sparkles or a wand. Not yet.

2

Lizzy sits on the grass in the backyard, in the shade of the very big tree. Her arms are all over sweaty and have made damp, soft places on the newsprint page of her coloring book. The burnt umber crayon lies on the asphalt driveway, its point melted to a puddle. It was not her favorite. That is purple, worn down to a little stub, almost too small to hold.

On the patio, a few feet away, her parents sit having drinks. The ice cubes clink like marbles against the glass. Her father has loosened his tie, rolled up the sleeves of his white go-to-the-office shirt. He opens the evening paper with a crackle.

Her mother sighs. "Wish this baby would hurry up. I don't think I can take another month in this heat. It's only the end of June."

"Can't rush Mother Nature." More crackle, more clinks. "But I *can* open the windows upstairs. There's a Rock Hudson movie at the drive-in. Should be cool enough to sleep when we get back."

"Oh, that would be lovely! But, what about—" She drops her voice to a whisper. "Iz-ee-lay? It's too late to call the sitter."

Lizzy pays more attention. She does not know what language that is, but she knows her name in most of the secret ways her parents talk.

"Put her in her jammies, throw the quilt in the back of the station wagon, and we'll take her along."

"I don't know. Dr. Spock says movies can be very frightening at her age. *We* know it's make-believe, but—"

"The first show is just a cartoon, one of those Disney things." He looks back at the paper. "*Sleeping Beauty.*"

"Really? Well, in that case . . . She loves fairy tales."

Jammies are for after dark, and always in the house. It is confusing, but exciting. Lizzy sits on the front seat, between her parents, her legs straight out in front of her. She can feel the warm vinyl through thin cotton. They drive down Main Street, past the Shell station—S-H-E-L-L—past the dry cleaners that gives free cardboard with her father's shirts, past the Methodist church where she goes to nursery school.

After that, she does not know where they are. Farther than she has ever been on this street. Behind the car, the sun is setting, and even the light looks strange, glowing on the glass and bricks of buildings that have not been in her world before. They drive so far that it is country, flat fields and woods so thick they are all shadow. On either side of her, the windows are rolled down, and the air that moves across her face is soft and smells like grass and barbecue. When they stop at a light, she hears crickets and sees a rising glimmer in the weeds beside the pavement. Lightning bugs.

At the Sky View Drive-In they turn and join a line of cars that creep toward a lighted hut. The wheels bump and clatter over the gravel with each slow rotation. The sky is a pale blue wash now, streaks of red above the dark broccoli of the trees. Beyond the hut where her father pays is a parking lot full of cars and honking and people talking louder than they do indoors.

Her father pulls into a space and turns the engine off. Lizzy wiggles over, ready to get out. Her mother puts a hand on her arm. "We're going to sit right here in the car and watch the movie." She points out the windshield to an enormous white wall. "It'll be dark in just a few minutes, and that's where they'll show the pictures."

"The sound comes out of this." Her father rolls the window halfway up and hangs a big silver box on the edge of the glass. The box squawks with a sharp, loud sound that makes Lizzy put her hands over her ears. Her father turns a knob, and the squawk turns into a man's voice that says " . . . concession stand right now." Then there is cartoon music.

"Look, Lizzy." Her mother points again, and where there had been a white wall a minute before is now the biggest Mickey Mouse she has ever seen. A mouse as big as a house. She giggles.

"Can you see okay?" her father asks.

Lizzy nods, then looks again and shakes her head. "Just his head, not his legs." She smiles. "I could sit on Mommy's lap."

" 'Fraid not, honey. No room for you until the baby comes." It's true. Under her sleeveless plaid smock, her mother's stomach is very big and round and the innie part of her lap is outie. Lizzy doesn't know how the baby got in there, or how it's going to come out, but she hopes that it will be soon.

"I thought that might be a problem." He gets out and opens the back door. "Scoot behind the wheel for a second."

Lizzy scoots, and her father puts the little chair from her bedroom right on the seat of the car. Its white painted legs and wicker seat look very wrong there. But he holds it steady, and when she climbs up and sits down, it *feels* right. Her feet touch flat on the vinyl, and she can see *all* of Mickey Mouse.

"Better?" He gets back in and shuts his door.

"Uh-huh." She settles in, then remembers. "Thank you, Daddy."

"What a good girl." Her mother kisses her cheek. That's almost as good as a lap.

Sleeping Beauty is Lizzy's first movie. She is not sure what to expect, but it is a lot like TV, only much bigger, and in color. There is a king and queen and a princess who is going to marry the prince, even though she is just a baby. That happens in fairy tales.

Three fairies come to bring presents for the baby. Not very good ones—just beauty and songs. Lizzy is sure the baby would rather have toys. The fairies are short and fat and wear Easter colors. They have round, smiling faces and look like Mrs. Carmichael, her Sunday School teacher, except with pointy hats.

Suddenly the speaker on the window booms with thunder and roaring winds. Bright lightning makes the color pictures go black-and-white for a minute, and a magnificent figure appears in a whoosh of green flames. She is taller than everyone else, and wears shiny black robes lined with purple.

Lizzy leans forward. "Oooh!"

"Don't be scared." Her mother puts a hand on Lizzy's arm. "It's only a cartoon."

"I'm not." She stares at the screen, her mouth open. "She's *beautiful*."

"No, honey. She's the witch," her father says.

Lizzy pays no attention. She is enchanted. Witches in books are old and bent over, with ugly warts. The woman on the screen has a smooth, soothing voice, red, red lips, and sparkling eyes, just like Mommy's, with a curving slender figure, no baby inside.

She watches the story unfold, and clenches her hands in outrage for the Witch, Maleficent. If the whole kingdom was invited to the party, how could they leave *her* out? That is not fair!

Some of this she says a little too out loud, and gets Shhh! from both her parents. Lizzy does not like being shh'd, and her lower lip juts forward in defense. When Maleficent disappears, with more wind and green flames, she sits back in her chair and watches to see what will happen next.

Not much. It is just the fairies, and if they want the baby princess, they have to give up magic. Lizzy does not think this is a good trade. All they do is have tea, and call each other "dear," and talk about flowers and cooking and cleaning. Lizzy's chin drops, her hands lie limp in her lap, her breathing slows.

"She's out," her father whispers. "I'll tuck her into the back."

"No," Lizzy says. It is a soft, sleepy no, but Very clear. A few minutes later, she hears the music change from sugar-sweet to pay-attention-now, and she opens her eyes all the way. Maleficent is back. Her long slender fingers are a pale green, like cream of grass, tipped with bright red nails.

"Her hands are pretty, like yours, Mommy," Lizzy says. It is a nice thing to say, a compliment. She waits for her mother to pat her arm, or kiss her cheek, but hears only a soft *pfft* of surprise.

For the rest of the movie, Lizzy is wide, wide awake, bouncing in her chair. Maleficent has her own castle, her own mountain! She can turn into a dragon, purple and black, breathing green fire! She fights off the prince, who wants to hurt her. She forces him to the edge of a cliff and then she—

A tear rolls down Lizzy's cheek, then another, and a loud sniffle that lets all the tears loose.

"Oh, Lizzy-Lou. That was a little *too* scary, huh?" Her mother wipes her face with a tissue. "But there's a happy ending."

"Not happy," Lizzy says between sobs. "He *killed* her."

"No, no. Look. She's not dead, just sleeping. Then he kisses her, and they live happily ever after."

Lizzy wails. "Not her. *Mel*ficent!"

They do not stay for Rock Hudson.

3

"Lizzy? Put your shoes back on," her mother says.

Her father looks up over *Field and Stream*. "Where are you two off to?"

"Town and Country. I'm taking Lizzy to the T-O-Y S-T-O-R-E."

"Why? Her birthday's not for months."

"I know. But everyone's going to bring presents for the baby, and Dr. Spock says that it's important for her to have a little something, too. So she doesn't feel left out."

"I suppose." He shrugs and reaches for his pipe.

When her mother stops the car right in front of Kiddie Korner, Lizzy is so excited she can barely sit still. It is where Christmas happens. It is the most special place she knows.

"You can pick out a toy for yourself," her mother says when they are inside. "Whatever tickles your fancy."

Lizzy is not sure what part of her is a fancy, but she nods and looks around. Kiddie Korner smells like cardboard and rubber and dreams. Aisle after aisle of dolls and trucks, balls and blocks, games and guns. The first thing she sees is Play-Doh. It is fun to roll into snakes, and it tastes salty. But it is too ordinary for a fancy.

She looks at stuffed animals, at a doll named Barbie who is not a baby but a grown-up lady, at a puzzle of all the United States. Then she sees a *Sleeping Beauty* coloring book. She opens it to see what pictures it has.

"What fun! Shall we get that one?"

"Maybe."

It is too soon to pick. There is a lot more store. Lizzy puts it back on the rack and turns a corner. *Sleeping Beauty* is everywhere. A Little Golden Book, a packet of View-Master reels, a set of to-cut-out paper dolls, a lunchbox. She stops and considers each one. It is hard to choose. Beside her, she hears an impatient puff from her mother, and knows she is running out of time.

She is about to go back and get the coloring book when she sees a shelf of bright yellow boxes. Each of them says P-U-P-P-E-T in large letters.

"Puppets!" she says, and runs over to them.

"Oh, look at those! Which one shall we get? How about the princess? Isn't she pretty!"

Lizzy does not answer. She is busy looking from one box to the next, at the molded vinyl faces that peer out through cellophane windows. Princess, princess, princess. Prince. King. Fairy, fairy, prince, fairy, princess—and then, at the end of the row, she sees the one that she has not quite known she was looking for. Maleficent!

The green face smiles down at her like a long-lost friend.

"That one!" Lizzy is not tall enough to grab the box; she points as hard as she can, stretching her arm so much it pulls her shoulder.

Her mother's hand reaches out, then stops in mid-air.

She frowns. "Are you sure? Look, here's Flora, and Fauna and—" She pauses. "Who's the other one?"

"Merryweather," Lizzy says. "But I want *her*!" She points again to Maleficent.

"Hmm. Tell you what. I'll get you all *three* fairies."

That is tempting. But Lizzy knows what she wants now, and she knows how to get it. She does not yell or throw a tantrum. She shakes her head slowly and makes her eyes very sad, then looks up at her mother and says, in a quiet voice, "No thank you, Mommy."

After a moment, her mother sighs. "Oh, *all* right," she says, and reaches for the witch.

Lizzy opens the box as soon as they get in the car. The soft vinyl head of the puppet is perfect—smiling red lips, yellow eyes, curving black horns. Just as she remembers. Beneath the pale green chin is a red ribbon, tied in a bow. She cannot see anything more, because there is cardboard.

It takes her a minute to tug that out, and then the witch is free. Lizzy stares. She expected flowing purple and black robes, but Maleficent's cotton body is a red plaid mitten with a place for a thumb on both sides.

Maybe the black robes are just for dress-up. Maybe this is her bathrobe. Lizzy thinks for a few minutes, then decides that is true. Plaid is what Maleficent wears when she's at home, in her castle, reading the paper and having coffee. It is more comfortable than her Work clothes.

4

On Saturday, Lizzy and her mother go to Granny Atkinson's house on the other side of town. The women talk about baby clothes and doctor things, and Lizzy sits on the couch and plays with her sneaker laces. Granny gets out a big brown book, and shows her a picture of a fat baby in a snowsuit. Mommy says *she* was that baby, a long time ago, but Lizzy does not think that could be true. Granny laughs and after lunch teaches Lizzy to play gin rummy and lets her have two root beers because it is so hot.

When they pull into their own driveway, late in the afternoon, Lizzy's mother says, "There's a big surprise upstairs!" Her eyes twinkle, like she can hardly wait.

Lizzy can't wait, either. She runs in the front door and up to her room, which has yellow walls and a window that looks out onto the driveway so she can see when Daddy comes home. She has slept there her whole life. When she got up that morning, she made most of her bed and put Maleficent on the pillow to guard while she was at Granny's.

When she reaches the doorway, Lizzy stops and stares. Maleficent is gone. Her *bed* is gone. Her dresser with Bo Peep and her bookcase and her toy chest and her chair. All gone.

"Surprise!" her father says. He is standing in front of another room, across the hall, where people sleep when they are guests. "Come and see."

Lizzy comes and sees blue walls and brown heavy curtains. Her bed is next to a big dark wood dresser with a mirror too high for her to look into. Bo Peep is dwarfed beside it, and looks as lost as her sheep. The toy chest is under a window, Maleficent folded on top.

"Well, what do you think?" Her father mops his face with a bandana and tucks it between his blue jeans and his white T-shirt.

"I *liked* my room," Lizzy says.

"That's where the baby's going to sleep, now." Her mother gives her a one-arm hug around the shoulders. "*You* get a big-girl room." She looks around. "We will have to get new curtains. You can help me pick them out. Won't that be fun?"

"Not really." Lizzy stands very still in the room that is not her room. Nothing is hers anymore.

"Well, I'll let you get settled in," her father says in his glad-to-meet-you voice, "and get the grill started." He ruffles his hand on Lizzy's hair. "Hot dogs tonight, just for you."

Lizzy tries to smile, because they are her favorite food, but only part of her mouth goes along.

At bedtime, her mother hears her prayers and tucks her in and sings the good-night song in her sweet, soft voice. For that few minutes, everything is fine. Everything is just the way it used to be. But the moment the light is off and the door is closed—not all the way—that changes. All the shadows are wrong. A street-light is outside one window now, and the very big tree outside the other, and they make strange shapes on the walls and the floor.

Lizzy clutches Maleficent under the covers. The witch will protect her from what the shapes might become.

5

"When do you get the baby?" Lizzy asks. They are in the yellow bedroom, Lizzy's real room. Her mother is folding diapers on the new changing table.

"Two weeks, give or take. I'll be gone for a couple of days, because babies are born in a hospital."

"I'll go with you!"

"I'd like that. But this hospital is only for grown-ups. You get to stay here with Teck."

Teck is Lizzy's babysitter. She has a last name so long no one can say it. Lizzy likes her. She has white hair and a soft, wrinkled face and makes the best grilled cheese sandwiches. And she is the only person who will play Candy Land more than once.

But when the baby starts to come, it is ten days too soon. Teck is away visiting her sister Ethel. Lizzy's father pulls into the driveway at two in the afternoon with Mrs. Sloupe, who watches Timmy Lawton when his parents go out. There is nothing soft about her. She has gray hair in tight little curls, and her lipstick mouth is bigger than her real one.

"I'll take your suitcase upstairs," he tells her. "You can sleep in our room tonight."

Her mother sits in a chair in the living room. Her eyes are closed, and she is breathing funny. Lizzy stands next to her and pats her hand. "There there, Mommy."

"Thank you, sweetie," she whispers.

Daddy picks her up and gives her a hug, tight and scratchy. "When you wake up in the morning, you're going to be a big sister," he says. "So I need you to behave for Mrs. Sloupe."

"I'll be very have," Lizzy says. The words tremble.

He puts her down and Mommy kisses the top of her head. Then they are gone.

Mrs. Sloupe does not want to play a game. It is time for her stories on TV. They can play after dinner. Dinner is something called chicken ala king, which is yellow and has peas in it. Lizzy only eats two bites because it is icky, and her stomach is scared.

Lizzy wins Candy Land. Mrs. Sloupe will not play again. It is bedtime. But she does not know how bedtime works. She says the now-I-lay-me prayer with the wrong words, and tucks the covers too tight.

"Playing fairy tales, were you?" she says, reaching for Maleficent. "I'll put this ugly witch in the toy chest, where you can't see it. Don't want you having bad dreams."

Lizzy holds on to the puppet with both arms.

"Well, aren't you a queer little girl?" Mrs. Sloupe says. "Suit yourself." She turns off the light and closes the door, all the way, which makes the shadows even more wrong. When Lizzy finally falls asleep, the witch's cloth body is damp and sticky with tears.

Her father comes home the next morning, unshaven and bleary. He picks

Lizzy up and hugs her. "You have a baby sister," he says. "Rosemary, after your mother's aunt." Then he puts her down and pats her behind, shooing her into the living room to watch *Captain Kangaroo*.

Lizzy pauses just beyond the hall closet, and before he shuts the kitchen door, she hears him tell Mrs. Sloupe, "She was breech. Touch and go for a while, but they're both resting quietly, so I think we're out of the woods."

He takes Mrs. Sloupe home after dinner, and picks her up the next morning. It is three days before Teck arrives to be the real babysitter, and she is there every day for a week before he brings Mommy and the baby home.

"There's my big girl," her mother says. She is sitting up in bed. Her face looks pale and thinner than Lizzy remembers, and there are dark places under her eyes. The baby is wrapped in a pink blanket beside her. All Lizzy can see is a little face that looks like an old lady.

"Can we go to the playground today?"

"No, sweetie. Mommy needs to rest."

"Tomorrow?"

"Maybe next week. We'll see." She kisses Lizzy's cheek. "I think there's a new box of crayons on the kitchen table. Why don't you go look? I'll be down for dinner."

Dinner is a sack of hamburgers from the Eastmoor Drive-In. At bedtime, Mommy comes in and does all the right things. She sings *two* songs, and Lizzy falls asleep smiling. But she has a bad dream, and when she goes to crawl into bed with Mommy and Daddy, to make it all better, there is no room. The baby is asleep between them.

For days, the house is full of grown-ups. Ladies and aunts come in twos and threes and bring casseroles and only say hi to Lizzy. They want to see the baby. They all make goo-goo sounds and say, "What a little darling!" At night, some men come, too. They look at the baby, but just for a minute, and do not coo. They go out onto the porch and have beers and smoke.

The rest of the summer, all any grown-up wants to do is hold the baby or feed the baby or change the baby. Lizzy doesn't know why; it is very stinky. She tries to be more interesting, but no one notices. The baby cannot do a somersault, or say the Pledge of Allegiance or sing "Fairy Jocka Dormy Voo." All she can do is lie there and spit up and cry.

And sleep. The baby sleeps all the time, and every morning and every afternoon, Mommy naps with her. The princess is sleeping, so the whole house has to stay quiet. Lizzy cannot play her records, because it will wake the baby. She can't jump on her bed. She can't even build a tall tower with blocks because if it crashes, it will wake the baby. But when the baby screams, which is a lot, no one even says Shhh!

Lizzy thinks they should give the baby back.

"Will you read to me?" she asks her mother, when nothing else is happening.

"Oh . . . not now, Lizzy-Lou. I've got to sterilize some bottles for Rosie. How 'bout you be a big girl, and read by yourself for a while?"

Lizzy is tired of being a big girl. She goes to her room but does not slam the door, even though she wants to, because she is also tired of being yelled at. She picks up Maleficent. The puppet comes to life around her hand. Maleficent tells Lizzy that she is very smart, very clever, and Lizzy smiles. It is good to hear.

Lizzy puts on her own bathrobe, so they match. "Will you read to me?" she asks. "Up here in our castle?"

Maleficent nods, and says in a smooth voice, "Of course I will. That would be lovely," and reads to her all afternoon. Even though she can change into anything she wants—a dragon, a ball of green fire—her eyes are always kind, and every time Lizzy comes into the room, she is smiling.

On nights when Mommy is too tired, and Daddy puts Lizzy to bed, the witch sings the good-night song in a sweet, soft voice. She knows all the words. She whispers "Good night, Lizzy-Tizzy-Toot," the special, only-at-bedtime, good-dreams name.

Maleficent loves Lizzy best.

6

Lizzy is glad when it is fall and time for nursery school, where they do not allow babies. Every morning Mrs. Breyer and Mrs. Huntington and Mrs. Lawton take turns driving to Wooton Methodist Church. When her mother drives, Lizzy gets to sit in the front seat. Other days she has to share the back with Tripper or Timmy.

She has known Timmy her whole life. The Lawtons live two doors down. They have a new baby, too, another boy. When they had cocktails to celebrate, Lizzy heard her father joke to Mr. Lawton: "Well, Bob, the future's settled. My two girls will marry your two boys, and we'll unite our kingdoms." Lizzy does not think that is funny.

Timmy is no one's handsome prince. He is a gangly, insubstantial boy who likes to wear sailor suits. His eyes always look as though he'd just finished crying because he is allergic to almost everything, and is prone to nosebleeds. He is not a good pick for Red Rover.

The church is a large stone building with a parking lot and a playground with a fence around it. Nursery school is in a wide, sunny room on the second floor. Lizzy climbs the steps as fast as she can, hangs up her coat on the hook under L-I-Z-Z-Y, and tries to be the first to sit down on the big rug in the middle of the room, near Mrs. Dickens. There are two teachers, but Mrs. Dickens is her favorite. She wears her brown hair in braids wrapped all the way around her head and smells like lemons.

Lizzy knows all the color words and how to count up to twenty. She can write her whole name—without making the Z's backward—so she is impatient when the other kids do not listen to her. Sometimes she has to yell at them so she can have the right color of paint. The second week of school, she has to knock Timmy down to get the red ball at recess.

Mrs. Dickens sends a note home, and the next morning, the next-door neighbor comes over to watch the baby so Lizzy's mother can drive her to school, even though it is not her turn.

"Good morning, Lizzy," Mrs. Dickens says at the door. "Will you get the music basket ready? I want to talk to your mother for a minute."

Lizzy nods. She likes to be in charge. But she also wants to know what they are saying, so she puts the tambourine and the maracas in the basket very quietly, and listens.

"How are things at home?" Mrs. Dickens asks.

"A little hectic, with the new baby. Why?"

"New baby. Of course." Mrs. Dickens looks over at Lizzy and puts a finger to her lips. "Let's continue this out in the hall," she says, and that's all Lizzy gets to hear.

But when they make Circle, Mrs. Dickens pats the right side of her chair, and says, "Come sit by me, Lizzy." They sing the good-morning song and have Share and march to a record and Lizzy gets to play the cymbals. When it is time for Recess, Mrs. Dickens rings the bell on her desk, and they all put on their coats and hold hands with their buddies and walk down the stairs like ladies and gentlemen. For the first time, Mrs. Dickens is Lizzy's buddy, and no one gets knocked down.

On a late October morning, Lizzy's mother dresses her in the green wool coat, because it is cold outside. It might snow. She runs up the stairs, but the coat is stiff and has a lot of buttons, and by the time she hangs it up, Anna Von Stade is sitting in *her* place in the circle. Lizzy has to sit on the other side of Mrs. Dickens, and is not happy. Timmy sits down beside her, which does not help at all.

"Children! Children! Quiet now. Friday is a holiday. Who knows what it is?"

Lizzy's hand shoots straight up. Mrs. Dickens calls on Kevin.

"It's Halloween," he says.

"Very good. And we're going to have our own Halloween party." "I'm going to be Pinocchio!" David says.

"We raise our hand before speaking, David." Mrs. Dickens waggles her finger at him, then waits for silence before she continues. "That will be a good costume for trick-or-treating. But for *our* party, I want each of you to come dressed as who you want to be when you grow up."

"I'm going to be a fireman!"

"I'm going to be a bus driver!"

"I'm going—"

Mrs. Dickens claps her hands twice. "Children! We do not talk out of turn, and we do not talk when others are talking."

The room slowly grows quiet.

"But it is good to see that you're all so enthusiastic. Let's go around the circle, and everyone can have a chance to share." She looks down to her right. "Anna, you can start."

"I'm going to be a ballerina," Anna says.

Lizzy does not know the answer, and she does not like that. Besides, she is going to be last, and all the right ones will be gone. She crosses her arms and scowls down at the hem of her plaid skirt.

"I'm going to be a doctor," Herbie says.

Fireman. Doctor. Policeman. Teacher. Mailman. Nurse. Baseball player. Mommy. Lizzy thinks about the lady jobs. Nurses wear silly hats and have to be clean all the time, and she is not good at that. Teacher is better, but two people have already said it. She wonders what else there is.

Tripper takes a long time. Finally he says, guess I'll be in sales."

"Like your father? That's nice." Mrs. Dickens nods. "Carol?"

Carol will be a mommy. Bobby will be a fireman.

Timmy takes the longest time of all. Everyone waits and fidgets. Finally he says he wants to drive a steam shovel like Mike Mulligan. "That's fine, Timmy," says Mrs. Dickens.

And then it is her turn.

"What are you going to be when you grow up, Lizzy?"

"Can I see the menu, please?" Lizzy says. That is what her father says at the Top Diner when he wants a list of answers.

Mrs. Dickens smiles. "There isn't one. You can be anything you want."

"Anything?"

"That's right. You heard Andrew. He wants to be president someday, and in the United States of America, he can be."

Lizzy doesn't want to be president. Eisenhower is bald and old. Besides, that is a daddy job, like doctor and fireman. What do ladies do besides mommy and nurse and teacher? She thinks very hard, scrunching up her mouth—and then she knows!

"I'm going to be a witch," she says.

She is very proud, because no one has said that yet, no one in the whole circle. She looks up at Mrs. Dickens, waiting to hear, "Very good. Very creative, Lizzy," like she usually does.

Mrs. Dickens does not say that. She shakes her head. "We are not using our imaginations today. We are talking about real-life jobs."

"I'm going to be a witch."

"There is no such thing." Mrs. Dickens is frowning at Lizzy now, her face as wrinkled as her braids.

"Yes there is!" Lizzy says, louder. "In 'Hansel and Gretel,' and 'Snow White,' and 'Sleeping—'"

"Elizabeth? You know better than that. Those are only stories."

"Then stupid Timmy can't drive a steam shovel because Mike Mulligan is only a story!" Lizzy shouts.

"That's *enough*!" Mrs. Dickens leans over and picks Lizzy up under the arms. She is carried over to the chair that faces the corner and plopped down. "You will sit here until you are ready to say you're sorry."

Lizzy stares at the wall. She is sorry she is sitting in the dunce chair, and she is sorry that her arms hurt where Mrs. Dickens grabbed her. But she says nothing.

Mrs. Dickens waits for a minute, then makes a noise and goes back to the circle. For almost an hour, Lizzy hears nursery school happening behind her: blocks clatter, cupboards open, Mrs. Dickens gives directions, children giggle and whisper. This chair does not feel right at all, and Lizzy squirms. After a while she closes her eyes and talks to Maleficent without making any sound. Out of long repetition, her thumb and lips move in concert, and the witch responds.

Lizzy is asking when she will learn to cast a spell, how that is different from spelling ordinary W-O-R-D-S, when the Recess bell rings behind her. She makes a disappearing puff with her fingers and opens her eyes. In a moment, she feels Mrs. Dickens's hand on her shoulder.

"Have you thought about what you said?" Mrs. Dickens asks.

"Yes," says Lizzy, because it is true.

"Good. Now, tell Timmy you're sorry, and you may get your coat and go outside."

She turns in the chair and sees Timmy standing behind Mrs. Dickens. His hands are on his hips, and he is grinning like he has won a prize.

Lizzy does not like that. She is not sorry.

She is *mad*.

Mad at Mommy, mad at the baby, mad at all the unfair things. Mad at Timmy Lawton, who is right here.

Lizzy clenches her fists and feels a tingling, all over, like goosebumps, only deeper. She glares at Timmy, so hard that she can feel her forehead tighten, and the anger grows until it surges through her like a ball of green fire.

A thin trickle of blood oozes from Timmy Lawton's nose. Lizzy stares harder and watches blood pour across his pale lips and begin to drip onto his sailor shirt, red dots appearing and spreading across the white stripes.

"Help?" Timmy says.

Mrs. Dickens turns around. "Oh, dear. Not again." She sighs and calls to the other teacher. "Linda? Can you get Timmy a washcloth?"

Lizzy laughs out loud.

In an instant, Lizzy and the chair are off the ground. Mrs. Dickens has grabbed it by the rungs and carries it across the room and out the classroom door. Lizzy is too startled to do anything but hold on. Mrs. Dickens marches down the hall, her shoes like drumbeats.

She deposits Lizzy with a thump in the corner of an empty Sunday School room, shades drawn, dim and chilly with brown- flecked linoleum and no rug.

"You. Sit. There," Mrs. Dickens says in a voice Lizzy has not heard her use before.

The door shuts and footsteps echo away. Then she is alone and everything is very quiet. The room smells like chalk and furniture polish. She lets go of the chair and looks around. On one side is a blackboard, on the other a picture of Jesus with a hat made of thorns, like the ones Maleficent put around Sleeping Beauty's castle.

Lizzy nods. She kicks her feet against the rungs of the small chair, bouncing the rubber heels of her saddle shoes against the wood. She hears the other children clatter in from Recess. Her stomach gurgles. She will not get Snack.

But she is not sorry.

It is a long time before she hears cars pull into the parking lot, doors slamming and the sounds of many grown—up shoes on the wide stone stairs.

She tilts her head toward the door, listens.

" . . . Rosemary? Isn't she adorable!" That is Mrs. Dickens.

And then, a minute later, her mother, louder. "Oh, dear, *now* what?"

Another minute, and she hears the click-clack of her mother's shoes in the hall, coming closer.

Lizzy turns in the chair, forehead taut with concentration. The tingle begins, the green fire rises inside her. She smiles, staring at the doorway, and waits.

Ellen Klages was born in Ohio, and now lives in San Francisco. Her short fiction has appeared in anthologies and magazines including *The Magazine of Fantasy and Science Fiction*, *Black Gate*, and *Firebirds Rising*. Her story, "Basement Magic," won the Best Novelette Nebula Award. Several of her other stories have been on the final ballot for the Nebula and Hugo Awards. She was a finalist for the John W. Campbell Award. Her young adult novels—*The Green Glass Sea* and sequel *White Sands, Red Menance*—were both award winners and her collection, *Portable Childhoods*, was nominated for a World Fantasy award. She has also written four books of hands-on science activities for children (with Pat Murphy, et al.) for the Exploratorium museum in San Francisco.

*There weren't supposed to be any of his kind anymore, though. Them
and the dragons, they were on the extinct list, right? . . .*

WELCOME TO THE REPTILE HOUSE

Stephen Graham Jones

It didn't start the way you might think.

This is where I kind of pause, look off, bite my lip into my mouth so I can
come up with the next big lie. With what my dad, talking loud for my little
sister, would call Jamie Boy's next big excuse.

Let me try it again: it started pretty much exactly the way you'd think a
thing like this would get going.

I was twenty-two, still flashing my high-school diploma at job interviews.
Still doing stuff like stealing an extra bag of ice from the cooler if the clerk's
not eyeballing me. Hiding a litter of mismatched puppies for the weekend for
my friend Dell, and not asking any questions. Bumming smokes outside the
bars, but sometimes having my own pack.

I was just getting into tattoos, too. Not on me—my arms had been choked
blue not four months after I moved into my own place—but *from* me. That
was the idea, anyway. I wasn't officially apprenticing anywhere, and nobody'd
offered their skin to me yet, but I'd always been drawing. My notebooks from
junior high are like a running autobiography in doodles, and I'd worked one
summer applying decals and pinstriping at my uncle's bodyshop, and finally
graduated to window tint before he trusted me with the front-door keys.

He should have known better.

But, tats, they were kind of the same as those junior high notebooks.
They were the one thing I could concentrate on. Just for hours. Planning,
sketching, tracing. For now I was practicing on the back of my right calf,
the side of my left I could reach. Snakes and geckos mostly, though I could
feel a dragon curled up inside me, waiting for the right swatch of skin. I've
talked to the grizzly old-timers, the real gunslingers of the wild west of body
art, and they say you go through phases. You get stuck on something, and
talk all your clients into it. What you're trying to do is get it right, what's in

your head. You want to get it right and make it permanent, and then watch it walk away.

Like I say, though, tattooing was strictly a sideline, and, as I couldn't afford supplies, it probably wouldn't have been just superhygenic for me to draw on anybody, either. It was just me so far, so I guess that didn't matter too much. But I could already see myself ten years down the road. My own shop, a girlfriend with my ink reaching north out of her bra, circling her shoulder, everybody but me having to imagine what the full image was.

Anyway, where it started: one night, to pay me back for the thing with the puppies, Dell's on my phone, has a shiny new job.

"Seriously, *morgue* attendant?" I said, turning away from my living room of three people with names I hadn't all-the-way caught.

"Different," he said.

I told him maybe, sure, but was there two hours after midnight all the same, a cigarette pinched between my thumb and index finger.

"Leave it," Dell said, opening the door on me and looking past in his important way. Into the parking lot.

Saddleview Funeral Chapel and Crematorium.

I rubbed my cherry out on the tall ashtray, followed him in.

On the way through the maze of viewing rooms to get to the back, Dell told me how his uncle got him this gravy gig. His uncle had worked here forever and a day ago, sitting up with dead soldiers mailed back from war. Or, not sitting up, but sleeping in the same room with, like a guard. It was because there had been some political vandalism or something. Anyway, the boss man now had been the boss man then, and remembered Dell's uncle, so here Dell was. His job was to buzz the alley door open for deliveries, and not touch anything.

He was Dell, though, right?

We toured through the cold room. It was slab city, naked dead people everywhere, their usually covered parts not nearly so interesting as I'd kind of been hoping. We put those paper mouth-masks on and felt like mad scientists drifting through the frost, deciding who to bring back, who to let rot.

"Hell yeah," I said through my mask, and, ahead of me, Dell nodded that he knew, he knew.

I told him about who-all'd been at my place earlier, maybe lying a little, and in return, like I owed him here, he asked me for the thousandth time for my little sister's number. Not permission, he'd always assumed he had permission to do what- and whoever he wanted. But he wanted me to middleman it.

"Off limits," I told him, about her, trying to make my voice sound all no-joke. Because it was.

"Fruit on the limb," Dell said, reaching up to pluck her. Except more graphically, somehow. With distinct pornographic intent.

"She's not like us," I said, but before we could get into our usual dance where my sister was involved, the lights dimmed. A second later, a painful buzz filled the place, coming in from all sides, like the walls were speakers.

"Delivery," Dell said. "Hide."

Alone in the room with the dead moments later, I looked around, breathing harder than I was meaning to. All fun and games until one of those bright white sheets slithers off, right? Until somebody sits up.

Finally I held my breath and crawled in under one of the tables, onto that clangy little shelf, some guy's naked ass not two feet over my face, his body bloated with all kinds of vileness.

After ten minutes in which I got terminally sober, the double doors slammed back. They were the same kind restaurants have, that are made for crashing open, that don't even have handles.

A gurney or whatever was rolling through, no legs pushing it. Just exactly what I needed, yeah. Finally it bumped into a cabinet, stopped. I breathed out but then its wheels started creaking again. It lurched its way over to right beside me, parked its haunted self inches from my face. Just far enough away for a hand to flop down in front of my face. It was pale, dead, the beds of the fingernails dark blue.

I flinched back, fell off my shelf, and Dell laughed, stepped off the belly of the new dead dude he'd been using like a kneeboard.

I flipped him off, pushed him away and lit up a cigarette. Not like anybody in there was going to mind. Dell took one too and we leaned back against stainless steel edges, reflected on our lives.

Another lie.

What he did was haul a laser tag kit up from his locker.

It was the best war ever, at least until, trying to duck my killshot, he crashed a cart over, a dead lady spilling out, sliding to a stop at a cabinet.

I read her toe tag, looked up to her face.

On her inner thigh was a chameleon.

Everything starts somewhere, Dad.

Before you get worried, no, this isn't some necro-thing about to happen. I never asked Dell what those puppies were for, but I'm pretty sure he'd nabbed them from about twelve different backyards—people in the classifieds give their addresses over so willingly—and would guess he sold them from a box in the mall parking lot. Meaning they all have good lives now. He wasn't sacrificing them out on some lonely road or anything. He wasn't trying to conjure up a buddy to rape dead women with.

However, if what he was looking for was somebody to trade him rides and cigarettes and ex-girlfriends' numbers for some quality time alone in his cold room with a tat gun, well: there I was.

When you're looking to hire onto a parlor, to rent a booth—hell, even just to lure a mentor in—one thing you've always got to have, it's an art book. A portfolio. What you can do, your greatest hits, the story of your craft.

Problem is, every two-bit dropout can pull something like that together.

But. What if, say, you'd moved to the city only a couple of months ago. And had always just done ink for friends, but were looking to go legit, now. And, what? Did I snap pics of any of those mythically good tats?

Yeah, yes, I did.

Here.

Play with the hue a bit on your buddy's computer, and a gecko crawling up a dead guy's shoulder, his skin will look so alive. And there won't even be any rash, any blood. Like you've got that light of a touch.

At first Dell would only let me practice on the bodies that were queued up for the oven, as that would erase evidence of our non-crime, but one night he left me alone to make a burger run—it's cliché that morgue attendants are always eating sloppy food, but I guess it's cliché for a reason—and I unplugged my gun, plugged it back in under the table of this woman I was pretty sure had been a yoga instructor. And recently.

Her skin was tight, springy. Most of the dead, I was having to really stretch their flesh out, then get Dell to hold it tight while I snapped the pic, so that night's lizard wouldn't look like it was melting off.

With her, though. I was just halfway through the iguana's tail by the time Dell got back.

He had to let me finish, because who conks with only ten percent of a tattoo done, right?

It was a beauty, too. Just like in my head, I made the tongue curl the opposite direction the tail was, for symmetry. And where it was reaching, only her boyfriend would ever know.

Pretty as it was, though, I didn't get any burgers—this was Dell's punishment (like I would want to eat something his hands had been touching on)—and, to make him laugh, I inked X's over the eyes of the guy at the front of the line for the oven. He was skinny, pale with death, still cold from the freezer, his two gunshot wounds puckered up like lips. He looked like a punk reject from 1977.

Dell shook his head, walked away smiling. I could see his reflection in all the stainless steel, and, as it turned out, Dell's uncle's reference didn't mean much when the boss man's just-dead, honor-student, choir-singing, yoga-bunny niece he'd been saving for the morning to embalm *personally* turned up with an evil bug-eyed lizard of some kind trying to crawl up her side, its tongue reaching up to circle her nipple in the most lecherous fashion.

Some people got no sense of art, I mean.

Dell in particular.

Like he had to, he came over, did what he needed to do to my face, to my television and my lamp. The television wasn't mine, but I wasn't saying anything. And then, so I would remember, he dug my tattoo gun up from my backseat, came back in and pulled me off the couch by the shirt I wasn't wearing, sat on my arms with his knees so he could drill some bathroom-wall version of a penis into my chest. Or maybe it was a novelty sprinkler, or a leaky cowboy hat, I don't know.

Chances are I could have bucked him off, but I kind of deserved it too, I guessed. Though if he'd been a real friend, he would have lit a cigarette for me. And maybe done a better job.

When he was done he threw my rig into the corner, slammed through my screen door, told me to forget his number if I knew what was good for me.

I spent the next two days turning his punishment tattoo into a Texas bluebonnet, because that's where I'd been born. At least that was the new story I was going to have ready.

How a flower was going to fit with the iguana theme I'd been studying on lately, I had no idea, but maybe it didn't matter so much either. Soon I wasn't going to have any skin left.

A week passed, then another, and, standing outside a bar one night with my shirt already gone, I saw the last girl Dell had been shacking up with. I'd taken her to prom once upon a time, when prom still existed. She was riding by on the back of another guy's motorcycle. Really pressing herself into him. Glaring us all down.

"She thinks we care?" I said to whoever was beside me.

"Probably thinks we did it," whoever it was said back, taking a deep drag and holding it, holding it.

I narrowed my eyes, looked over through her smoke: Sheila. From when I was a community-college student for three weeks.

"Story?" I said, offering her one from my pack.

She held it sideways, ran her fingers along the white paper and sneered about it like she always did, like she hated cigarettes, like she was just smoking them to kill them. But she threaded it behind her ear all the same. Your monkey's always whispering to you, I guess.

She shrugged, told me about Dell.

He'd been found not just normal-dead, like OD'd or stabbed or drowned in vomit in a bed across town. No, he'd been like *exploded* behind a club. A dental-records-only kind of thing. Smeared on the brick, important footsteps leading away, the whole trip.

I *eek*ed my mouth out, stood on the stoop for more smokes than I'd meant.

The bluebonnet on my chest was waving with each inhale.

I went home, watched it in the mirror. Added red buds in the blue, in *memorium*. I think that's the word.

When I searched Dell up on the newspaper site, two hits came up.

One was his obituary, the funeral I'd missed, and the other hit was about impropriety with the dead.

The blotter had nothing at all about the late-night, involuntary tattoo on the owner's car-wrecked niece—I guess I could have been famous, started a career right there—but it did mention how Saddleview was getting the funeral home version of an audit. Evidently, one month it had taken in more bodies than it had buried.

I shook my head, clicked away. Dell.

He'd probably got the orders wrong. Pushed one too many into the oven one night, then tried to fix the manifest, had to burn a to-be-buried stiff as well.

It didn't have anything to do with me, anyway.

That part of my life was over.

Lie number ten-thousand, there, I guess. But who's keeping count.

As for why Dell had turned inside-out behind the bar, I had no clue. He'd always been high-strung. In junior high, he'd always been the first one to put his lips to the freon tube, the first one to spray thinner into the rag, press it against his mouth, so I figured it was some accumulated chemical reaction. Something the military would probably pay big bucks to the get the formula for. They should have been monitoring us the whole time. Every night, we were out there, experimenting.

And, just because Dell was gone, that didn't mean the lab was closed.

One night maybe three weeks after he funeral where I probably should been a pallbearer, there we all were, miles out of the city, in a field with a bonfire, like the bonfire had always been there, waiting. There were sparks and, when the wood started to run out, everybody had to donate one article of clothing. And then two.

It was interesting in a decline-of-the-world kind of way. I was kicked back in a lawn chair, zoned out, just mellow, my shirt burning, keeping us all warm.

I was watching this one girl named Kelly, already down to her pink clamshell bra, and thinking I might have to wait this situation out when another car pulled up and we all kind of sighed.

Too many cars meant the cops wouldn't be far behind.

Then, too, depending on who was in that car, it could all be worth it.

I shrugged to myself, leaned back to see who the new victims were going to be: first was a guy who could have been a surf bum in a movie ten years ago, second was his clone, and third was a red-headed girl I thought I knew from somewhere.

When the fourth stepped out, I knew where I knew Red from: my sister's friend from down the street at the old house.

Gigi was here.

"Hey!" my non-buddy Seth called out, dancing behind her, pointing down to her with both hands.

I settled deeper into my chair, looked back to the fire like maybe I could blind myself by staring.

Soon enough she found me, stood there with a silver can in her hand and said, "Dad's been trying to reach you."

"Dell?" I said.

"You were his best friend."

"He was a punk. A wastoid."

"And what are you?"

"You should leave," I told her.

"I'm the one who should be doing things, yeah," she said, and that was it.

For a while some guys were running at the fire and jumping over it, but that was short-lived. It was mostly quiet and surly, at least for me. Just music and muttering, and too many snapshot flashes of my sister with surfer boy two, his arm draped over her in a way that was making me swallow hard.

Before the night was over, there were going to be words. And probably more. But first I'd need to make sure he was eighteen—too old to press charges, according to Dell, who would have learned the hard way.

I was nodding to myself about how it was all going to play out, how I was about to step across to the cable spool they were using like a love seat, and was even halfway counting down in my head when a chainsaw pulled up to our little gathering in the sticks.

It was Dell's ex. On her new guy's motorcycle. She stepped off—dismounted, more like—and he just sat there still holding the grips, inspecting us all, the fire dancing in the black glass of his helmet.

I swallowed, looked away like I'd never seen them, tried not to track Gigi even though I did register the t-shirt she'd had on at one point. It was in the fire. The first chance I got I went to pee in the tall grass, never came back, just stopped at a convenience store, called the party in.

You do what you can to save your little sister, I guess. Even cash your friends in.

In my living room the next morning, still awake—I hadn't planned on coming home this early—I ran my hand over the elaborate, dragon-scaled salamander on the right side of my left calf.

I tried to keep the hair there shaved down, to really show it off, but, running my hand over it, it was crackly. And smelled worse than bad.

I sleuthed through my head, made the necessary connection: this was the leg I'd had kicked up on the cooler, close to the fire. On purpose, to show off my work, show what I could do. I'd even been wetting down the scales with beer when nobody was looking, just waiting for anybody to say anything.

Nobody had.

Instead I'd just curled all the hair on my leg, and singed the heel of my favorite shoe.

Everybody had to have seen, though. It was beautiful, it was crawling, it was alive.

I smoothed it down, passed out on the couch with that lizard warm under my hand, its eyes open for me, wheeling in their orbits, the pupils just slits, like rips you could climb through, into another world.

I should have tried.

I woke at dusk and flinched back hard, deeper into the couch.

There was a black motorcycle helmet on my coffee table. Watching me.

"Recognized your work," a guy said from the kitchen, and punctuated it by closing my refrigerator hard enough to rattle the ketchup.

Dell's ex's new boyfriend.

"Be still my heart," I said, clutching it, sitting up.

"Don't be stupid," he told me, and stepped in, my tub of butter in his left hand, his right index finger smeared glossy yellow.

He ran it into his mouth, pulled his finger out like he was sneaking frosting off somebody's saved-back cupcake.

"Dairy," he said, running his finger along the edge of the tub again, then shaking his head to get his oily bangs out of his face.

I nearly screamed.

His eyes.

There were two crude X's tattooed over them. Two X's I'd done. When he was cold and dead on a rolling cart, two bullets punched through his chest.

"Been looking for someone with your particular . . . talents," he said, downing another fingerful.

I shook my head no, no, saw Dell smeared on a brick wall and stood to crash my way to the screen door, escape out into the night, into some other life.

The boyfriend's helmet caught me in the back like a bowling ball, threw me into the wall by the door, the whole house shaking when I hit.

He turned me over with the toe of his boot, stared down at my chest. Eating butter the whole while.

"Thought you were into reptiles," he said, about my bluebonnet, his accent tuned to the UK station, and just dialed over all the way to it.

I coughed, turned to the side, threw up.

He stepped his boot out of the way.

When I was done he kneeled down, jammed his butter finger into my mouth, smearing yellow all around inside. It was cold, wet, tasteless.

His face so close to mine.

"I'm sorry?" I said.

He laughed, pushed my head down, bouncing it off the carpet.

"You know cow milk is ninety-eight percent the same as cow blood?" he said, dipping his finger into the tub again.

I was just trying to breathe.

He shrugged, said, "Close enough," and set the butter down on a speaker.

From my angle on the floor, he was forever tall, and still pale like a junkie. But he did carry himself something like a British Invasion reject, definitely. Something self-consciously waifish and bad attitude about the way he caved his shoulders in around his chest. The hollow where his stomach should be. His lowslung jeans, like he was just daring you to trace his belt line.

There weren't supposed to be any of his kind anymore, though. Them and the dragons, they were on the extinct list, right? All there were that was even close anymore was all the goths, I guess, the Sandman dreamers, the Bauhaus diehards, the velvet vest crowd who'd read too much Anne Rice, were probably going to grow up into good little steampunk rejects one day.

This boyfriend, though, I had a sense he was their original. That Neil Gaiman had seen him at a party in the UK, that Anne Rice had followed him through the streets of New Orleans one night, that Sid Vicious had taken a cue or two from him.

"This," he said, giving me some jazz hands action over his face, his eyes, those X's, "this isn't just permanent, you know? With me it's kind of forever, now, yeah? Get what I'm saying? What do you think of that, Jamie Boy?"

I pushed myself up against the wall, let some butter dribble from my mouth, down onto the bluebonnet.

"Jamie Boy?" I managed to say.

My dad was the only one who did that.

He just stared at me about that.

"She was nice," he said, falling back onto the couch like it was a throne, licking his lips in the most exaggerated way. "But little sisters are always nice, aren't they?"

"Who told you?"

"You did, telescope eyes."

Meaning he'd followed her home. Thinking that's where I was going to be. And then he'd made do with who *was* there.

I stood, but it was just to fall across the coffee table, into the hall. Not for any window but for the bathroom, for the toilet. To throw the rest of the world I used to know up.

In the shower, exploded, smeared all over the tile, was Dell's ex.

She had a bar of soap stuffed in what was left of her mouth.

"Sorry for the mess," the boyfriend said from the door, his leather pants somehow vulgar. "Got to clean up after you eat, though. If you don't, they come back, all that. I'm sure you've heard."

He was bored with it, trailed off, looking down the hall like at something important.

I knew where he was looking, though.

Four miles over, into the Crane Meadow subdivision. Into what could no longer really be considered a living room, I was pretty sure.

So, monsters are real. Surprise.

For some reason I'd never considered this.

Or—I'm lying again: *one* monster's real, anyway.

And I get the sense that's just how he likes it.

When I was done emptying myself into the toilet, I zombied my way back to the living room, my peripheral vision just a smoky haze.

Instead of killing me like I expected, like I wanted, like I deserved, he slapped a pair of blue nitrile gloves down on the coffee table, told me to rubber up, whirred my gun in his other hand.

I looked down at myself to see what room was left for him to do his damage on.

I had it backwards.

Until thirty minutes before dawn, his left hand cupped around my balls the whole time—he'd crunched a metal thermos into tinfoil, to show what he could do—I worked on his face.

Every tattoo artist has to be able to repair somebody else's work. To cover up a name, fix a mis-spelling, fudge a date. Put a bikini top on that girl, make a pistol into a submarine, a submarine into a flying saucer, a flying saucer into a shadow, all that.

What I was supposed to do was make those dashed-on X's over his eyes into something presentable enough for the coming eternity. Something he wouldn't have to hide behind a helmet, a helmet he could only explain if he had a motorcycle, and he hated motorcycles. Everything went by too fast.

While I did my thing, holding his dead, cold skin tight—I'd had practice—he told me about 1976. How glorious it had been. No cell phone cameras, no bullshit DNA, no credit cards in the system, to track people with. Back then he never woke up in morgues, had to sneak out. Back then he was keeping the morgues *stocked*.

In his raspy singsong voice he told me about concerts and brushes with fame, and about a milkmaid he'd known with blond hair that curled on the side like she was an orthodox Jew, and how that framed her face so perfect, even though, where and when she'd lived, she probably hadn't even known Jews existed. How he never knew her name, only her insides. How she tasted.

Because I didn't have the barber patter down yet, and because this was my first time inking a *face*, I just worked, and kept light on my toes. It wasn't on purpose, but his hand on my balls—going up on your toes is kind of a natural response.

Still, even working fast enough to sweat, I was only able to get one eye done.

I was being careful, I mean.

I handed him the mirror, let him look, my balls still in his hand.

He looked side-to-side at himself and squeezed gently, rolling me like marbles, my spine straightening from it, and then he looked me straight on.

It wasn't bad.

That mime make-up trick, with a tapered, upside-down cross kind of coming through the eyebrow, leaking down onto the cheek? I'd taken some of that and mixed it with the diamond eyes harlequins in comic books have, and filled it all in solid, so that his right eyeball, looking out from all that black, it was seriously wicked. I'd gotten the idea . . . well, first from what I needed to cover that stupid X, but second from a facepaint band I'd seen one night—not KISS, please, and this wasn't a juggalo night, and I've never seen Marilyn Manson live. Reading the show's write-up the next day, though, the show-off reviewer was saying how the lead singer's black-bagged eyes had been an insult to everything The Misfits had ever not stood for.

I didn't know Glenn Danzig's make-up well enough to make the link like the reviewer was—I was always more of a Sex Pistols kind of punk, I guess—but the guy with my balls in his hands seemed to recognize something. "Sick like a *dog*," he said, and held the mirror over to get a proper angle on his face. Run his other hand over the stubble he would probably never grow.

He liked it.

I breathed out for what felt like the first time in hours and he stood up into that one moment of relief I had, his lips right against mine, my balls tighter in his hand now, so that I was practically floating, my eyes watering whether I was telling them to or not.

I turned to the side to let him do what he was going to do and caught the sun, just starting to warm the very top of my gauzy ancient hand-me-down drapes.

"Hey," I said about it.

He hissed, brought his mouth down to my neck, his teeth grazing my skin there, and said, "We finish it tonight," tapping his naked eye, and then him and his black helmet and his perfumed stench were gone, stalking out the back, leaving my kitchen door open behind him, his bike tearing the morning open.

At first I just zoned out there after he was gone, staring at the pattern of the skirt tacked onto the bottom of my couch, pretending it was the curtain of a show I was waiting for. Pretending a tiny actor was about to prance out, ask how I'd liked the show, how I was liking this joke.

I made my way to the bedroom, rang my dad's phone.

No answer.

I shut my eyes, threw the phone into the wall.

Gigi. Gretchen, really, but really Gigi, since she was little.

I'd always felt like I was out here throwing my life way so she could go the other way. Like I was sacrificing myself so she wouldn't have to. Like this was the only way to save her, the only way to be a decent big brother.

It's stupid, I know. But I'm not smart.

My dad could have told you that.

Still, sometimes.

What I've done now, all day, is scrawl a rough X over each eye. And then over every free inch of space I've got left on my body, I've traced out scales, like I'm going to shade them in with color later. On my left side, kind of where I always imagined my heart to be, four of those scales have names on them. Like tombstones.

Mom, Dad, Gigi. Me.

This is the kind of art that would get me space at any parlor in town. The kind of imagery bleeding into meaning that makes real tattoo artists wince.

But that's all over now, I guess.

It's almost dark again.

Soon the chainsaw sound will be dying in the air, the helmet on my couch. A monster kicked back in my easy chair, his right hand between my legs, keeping me honest.

One last job, right?

But it's also my first.

To prepare, and also because I can't help it anymore, I feel my way down to the bathroom, lick what I can off the tile walls of the shower, scraping the rest in with my fingers. Pushing it deep inside.

What's left of Dell's ex is black and dried, but that taste underneath, it's to die for. To kill for. Milk could never be like this, not in a thousand years. Cows got nothing on people.

I wore gloves when I was working on him, yeah, so I wouldn't catch anything that was catching.

But then I used the same needle on myself, and I went deeper than I had to for just the ink to set.

His blood spiked up and down me. All through me, hungry.

For two hours, between one and three, the sun right above the house instead of slashing in through the window, I'm pretty sure I was clinically dead.

And I kind of still am.

Will he be able to smell it on me right away, through the flannel shirt I've put on to cover my new ink, to cover the bluebonnet on my chest that's now my chest cracking open to reveal the real me, crawling out tooth and claw, or will we wait to do this thing until I've driven the needles through his naked eye into what the centuries have left of his brain?

It doesn't matter.

Either way I win.

There always was a dragon curled up inside me, Dad.

Tonight it's going to stand up.

Stephen Graham Jones is the author of sixteen books, now. Most recent are *Zombie Sharks with Metal Teeth* and *Flushboy*. Up soon are *The Least of My Scars* and *The Gospel of Z*. He lives and teaches in Boulder, Colorado. More at demontheory.net.

Her daughter's dream brought back an identical nightmare she herself had experienced in that very room as a girl . . .

GLAMOUR OF MADNESS

Peter Bell

❖

Are there here and there sequestered places which some curious creatures still frequent, whom once on a time anybody could see and speak to as they went about on their daily occasions, whereas now only at rare intervals in a series of years does one cross their paths and become aware of them.—M.R. James

Strange, indeed, are the roots of coincidence—I believe a famous American author wrote a learned book on the subject. Only the other day, having spent the morning ridding the garden of a most irksome weed, I put on the radio only to hear a voice uttering the unruly plant's Latin name. On more than one occasion a long-unseen acquaintance has entered my mind—then they appear round a corner, call on the phone, or send a letter. Could this be second sight? (Celtic blood runs in my veins, after all.) A wise friend, an eminent professor of mathematics, assures me however that a universe in which there were no coincidence would be far stranger; that it could not, indeed, logically exist, if quantum theory is to be believed, with its elevation of the random to a universal principle . . .

I digress. But it is due to chance—the serendipitous bringing together of two distinct events, one recent, the other immersed in the misty past—that I have been minded to compose the following narrative. The discovery afforded me what I believe mathematicians refer to as a "eureka moment." What I have to say hardly rivals Einstein's insights or the resolution of Fermat's Last Theorem, but it will interest those fascinated by the strange and supernatural. There are, indeed, more things in Heaven and Earth than are dreamt of by those tiresome rationalists who would pit Science—surely no more than measurement of a mystical enigma?—against the inexplicable.

In these frenetic days of mobile phones, iPods, and bleeping laptops, few places remain where quiet prevails. Yet a certain tranquility is still to be found within the confines of our more ancient universities during what our wise predecessors aptly used to call "the long."

The tale I recount began in the private rooms of a famous Cambridge college.

Professor Silas B. Dewar, though American, had enjoyed a meteoric career within the English academic world, ultimately achieving the Chair of Psychology at the University of Sussex; a post, moreover, that brought him a consultancy with the Home Office, rumored to exceed, at tax-payer's expense, even his handsome professorial stipend. I was never able to elicit exactly what he did for the Home Office, except that it concerned Broadmoor. Professor Dewar had a particular interest in psychotic behavior, having published a string of eminent papers on the subject, and held firmly to the view that there was a fine line between madness and what our ancestors chose to call possession.

Quite how we got on to the supernatural I do not recall, but as an excellent sherry lowered in the bottle at a bemusing pace, my esteemed colleague told me a curious tale concerning a niece on his wife's side (she being, by the way, English). It ended, sad to relate, in tragedy. Dewar did impart to me the names of the people involved and the location (not so very far from here). Out of respect for surviving relatives, however, I substitute pseudonyms and remain silent about the place. I summarize the professor's anecdote with as much authenticity as memory allows; which, as may be imagined, proceeded in the meandering manner of two middle-aged academics imbibing that most remarkable sherry, whose name, alas, eludes me, but which certainly bettered the Tío Pepe served in the Senior Common Room.

Our conversation occurred not that long ago (though these days never has the phrase *tempus fugit* sounded so apposite, and it may be longer than I recall). The events described took place in the closing years of the last century.

"My niece," Dewar began, "couldn't believe her luck when she acquired the Old Rectory. A rather grand old house, it was in a habitable condition, though in estate agent talk, in need of some upgrading. Ninety-one-year-old Mrs. Seymour had spent the last two years in a care home, and a degree of negligence was apparent—gray squirrels had taken possession of the attic, starlings had torn the roof-felt, there was rising damp in the unheated rooms and so on . . . But it was a snip. Susan's husband, Martin Travers, a merchant banker, easily afforded it out of the year's generous bonus."

Dewar laughed, "Not that we academics would resent him that!"

It occurred to me that the professor probably did very nicely for himself, better than the average academic, much less a humble librarian, but I bit my tongue.

"Friends and relations—envy, of course—asked why Susan needed so spacious a house with only one child. There were mutterings about upkeep, draughts, keeping on top of the garden, the cost of heating and so on. As a matter of fact, Susan would have liked another child but, following a difficult confinement at the age of forty, it was out of the question. So, her eight-year-old daughter, Emma, became the recipient of a form of neurotic maternal over-indulgence.

"A pleasing child, by all accounts, but she had a side that was almost certainly a consequence of that pampering: a propensity towards nervous debility and an over-vivid imagination. This was a source of constant anxiety to her mother. Martin, who inhabited a rarefied plane of high finance, showed little patience towards his wife on this score and maybe he was right. Susan's fussing was no doubt infectious; her obsession, maybe, was creating the very things in the child's mind she sought to pre-empt. The problem was that Susan no longer needed to work. She had given up her career as a music teacher. She had all the time in the world to think while her husband spent twelve hours a day, weekends as well, at the bank or traveling to foreign countries.

"At first, though, the new place was a godsend. There was so much to occupy her time, especially the huge garden. And, enclosed by a high wall, it provided just that security Susan wanted for Emma. But there was another reason why Susan was so delighted to have become mistress of the Old Rectory.

"It was in this very house, you see, that Susan, as a child, had frequently stayed during summer holidays. Mr. Seymour was a cousin of her father. The visits ceased when she was eleven, following a dispute between her mother and the eccentric Mrs. Seymour. Those days, tinged with nostalgia's golden glow and layered with the indelible patina of childhood recollection, Susan always said, were the happiest of her life. Now, as an adult, she had reclaimed her long lost paradise—or so she believed.

"She loved the vastness of the place, so different from her parents' terraced house in Ealing—the spacious rooms and corridors; the grand front staircase, the backstairs by the kitchen, the attic, reached by another stair: a child's fantasy of unending space. Later, when I spoke to her after the tragedy, these memories were the only things that brought animation to her face. Most of all she loved the rambling garden that surrounded the house. She described it to me in detail. The heady scent of the rose bed, she said, lingered in her mind decades later. Coming to live in the house brought all those fine childhood memories flooding back. As we shall see, this was not a good thing. She was pining for a security that would ever stay out of reach.

"Of course, the house and the garden appeared to her adult eye half the size.

And signs of neglect were everywhere. The roses had gone wild, a tangle of thorns with a few sickly blooms; but still, she said, exuding the familiar scent which touched her to the quick. She felt, as often happens when going back years later to a once familiar place, a sense of melancholy running parallel with her elation—though not the disquiet that was in due course to intrude. 'There is about the quality of melancholy,' she said to me, 'a suffusion of its very opposite: happiness in a minor key, like a string quartet by Mozart.' Needless to say, when she tried to convey such sensitive impressions to her husband, they fell on stony ground. Her confidante was always Emma.

"Emma took to the place with the same alacrity as her mother. She seemed eminently happy. Susan was pleased at the way it brought back her own infancy.

Little details, pointed out by Emma, triggered whole chains of recollection; things Susan had locked away without realizing in the attic of her mind." Professor Dewar paused and replenished his glass, then proceeded to extemporize on the complexities of psychiatry. Whilst I hesitate to cast aspersions on a field of scholarship so far removed from my own, nevertheless I cannot help feeling with this sort of thing that, behind a veil of the abstruse, little more is being imparted than could otherwise be worked out by common sense—indeed, in my opinion, frequently departing from common sense.

"You will, understand," Dewar continued, "that we already detect here, beneath a veneer of idyllic bliss, a clear case of infantile regression. Susan, wandering round the garden, bemused at her regained Shangri-la, in fact felt deeply isolated. Her husband, outer-directed towards his work, did not understand her. There was no shortage of cash, but as with many of these *nouveau riches*, material wealth disguised spiritual poverty. Affording the rectory was a material triumph, but it could not buy back Paradise. She sought solace from her isolation by ever thinking back to her childhood; and this explains also her perception of Emma as her only confidante. Over-protective of a child conceived late in life, condemned to be the only one, this fuelled anxieties of loss, making it all the more important to over-mother her; hence the attraction of the self-contained world with its high surrounding wall. This kind of over-protection, you know, manifesting itself in excess love and solicitude, can easily turn into quite the other. The mother, maybe, subconsciously resented the daughter, blaming her for the fact that she could bear no further child."

I stifled a yawn, eyeing him skeptically.

The professor drained his sherry and in defiance of the college's rules and, I suspect these days, the law, lit up a cigarette, and blew the foul effusion in my direction. He fixed me with a knowing look.

"They had been in their new domain about a year when the idyll ceased. It transpired there was a region of the garden which Emma avoided. It was only when pressed that she admitted to a sense there of being watched. The area concerned was near the rear perimeter wall, where a gate led into a plantation of oaks and fir trees. Here, she claimed, she had on occasion seen a cloaked or hooded figure; and once a horrid face peering at her from the gate; that of an oddly dressed woman. 'All pink with pop-out eyes,' she described the face, 'with something white on her head, like maids wore a long time ago.' Each time, she declared, the day had grown dark, 'as if something terrible was going to happen.'

"Anyway, as autumn drew in the incident receded; Emma did not mention the figure again and, outwardly at least, it passed from her mind. It left Susan, however, very jittery. A sense of *déja vu* had seized her when Emma first described her encounter, as did her daughter's premonition of imminent doom. It was, moreover, unsettling to realize the property's inviolable seclusion was compromised, and she pressed her husband to install state-of-the-art security. Henceforth, Emma was discouraged from going into the garden on her own.

"All might have been forgotten had not, towards the end of the winter, a fresh anxiety emerged. I should explain first that Emma's bedroom was at the back of the house, rather a large one for a child. Susan had suggested a smaller room—the very one Susan had slept in as a girl—but Emma had been insistent. Her chosen room had a wide aspect over the garden where it sloped up towards the plantation. Towards the end of February, Emma had the first of several dreadful nightmares. It happened during a stormy night. Susan had been kept awake by the gales and heard her daughter screaming. When she reached her room she found Emma in a distressed state; never had she seen her so terrified. The essence of the dream was thus: Emma believed she had awoken and, looking out of her window, perceived a figure in a cloak stealing across the lawns; then came the sound of plodding up the backstairs and along the passage, followed by a twist of the door-knob. 'She was coming for me, she wants to kill me,' she cried to her mother. When asked to whom she referred, she replied, 'The lady from the wood with the horrid face and the thing on her head.'

"The nightmare, of course, could be dismissed as no more sinister than a throwback to the summer. The noises of the storm had created an illusion of footsteps, stimulating Emma's memory of her fright—that was all. It was, however, not the end of it; though varying in form and sequence the same dream recurred over many weeks. But what bothered Susan most was that her daughter's dream brought back an identical nightmare she herself had experienced in that very room as a girl. It had been on the sole occasion she slept there, when her usual room was being redecorated. That it should have faded from her memory was not so odd. It's not infrequently the mind's habit in conjuring a lost Eden to remove the vision of a serpent.

"The episode distressed Susan out of all proportion. Was it a case of inherited memory? Could her own anxiety have transferred to her daughter? When she raised such ideas with her husband, he accused her, rather, of allowing Emma's fantasies to possess her own mind. The incident honed her neuroticism, reviving her disquiet at Emma's encounters in the garden. Had her daughter perhaps not imagined things but actually espied an interloper? You may recall there had been a lot in the newspapers around that time about the abduction and murder of a child in Epping Forest? Susan began pestering her husband again about installing CCTV cameras around the property.

"Her renewed obsession with security no doubt explained why one afternoon Susan investigated the part of the garden where Emma had been frightened. She looked for the gate, to check it was secure. In the summer it had been partly masked by weeds, but in the bareness of winter it was quite visible. Then she noticed something—something that puzzled her; it seemed inconceivable she had not noticed it before, when they first moved in and certainly last summer. In her childhood, she recalled, a wooden gate had given access to the plantation and beyond into the old Lathom park. Yet there before her was a barred metal gate of relatively late design, though rusting with the years. Obviously, the old one had been long ago replaced. Nevertheless, she could have sworn Emma, too, had specifically referred to a wooden gate. Susan traced the full length of the wall, wondering if she had confused the position, but it was not so.

"Returning to the gate, she found to her dismay that it had no kind of lock at all. It took considerable nerve, she said, but she entered the plantation. She was not sure what she was afraid of or expected to find, but she told of an atmosphere of dread and a darkening of the sky, 'as if something terrible was going to happen'—the very same words, note, that Emma had herself used. The plantation came to an end after thirty or forty yards, and there before her was the other gate affording exit from the wood; many a time as a child she had come along this path which led into the Lathom estate. But not anymore. Bland suburbia confronted her. Neat lawns and mock-historic cottages, a middle-class travesty of old rural England. Disoriented, she hurried back, resolving to instruct a contractor to have the gate removed and the space bricked up.

"Now came Susan's greatest shock. Making her way back, she stumbled on an object in the undergrowth. On inspection it proved to be timber, the remains of the very wooden gate she had, indeed, accurately remembered. More lost recollections came flooding back: there it was, the panel with the curious square aperture, by means of which the catch was disengaged when passing through, where once—just like Emma—she had been scared by a peeking face, and Mrs. Seymour had chided her, saying she had never heard such nonsense. What did it all mean, this strange bequest of fears to her daughter?

"As summer arrived, Susan's state of mind grew worse. On top of her anxieties about Emma, she began to suspect that her husband, on the pretext of lengthy hours at the bank and frequent trips abroad, was having an affair with his secretary. Acquaintances of hers I spoke to later told of widespread neighborhood gossip—nervous breakdown, mental illness. Susan was considered by many to have become very peculiar. Emma became the object of ever more overprotection. She was escorted to and from school. There was no mixing with local children. Within her own home she was a virtual prisoner, scarcely ever out of her mother's sight."

The professor replenished his glass, lit another Dunhill International and lent forward in a melodramatic manner.

"On the eleventh of August, 1999," he declared, "you will recall there occurred a total eclipse of the sun. It was overcast here, dull and oppressive, with little expectation of the once-in-a-lifetime celestial event being visible."

I nodded. I failed to see the relevance of this, but I remembered it well. All that had been apparent was a gathering general gloom, though I recall that, as it lightened, dogs barked and a cock crowed. My father had seen a far more impressive one decades before in the Yorkshire Dales at Giggleswick. But I digress . . .

Dewar continued, unfazed by my faltering attention. This time, I regret to say, I failed to stifle my yawn.

"Susan—if she is to be believed—had fallen asleep in the lounge. Awaking late in the afternoon, she made tea and took a cup up to Emma, whom she had last seen reading in her room. But Emma was not there. Nor was she anywhere to be found in the house. Front and back doors were locked and could not be opened without a key. Emma had no key and no keys were missing. Likewise, windows were firmly secured. There was no sign of a struggle, nor of forced entry, nothing suggesting abduction. The police carried out the usual searches and enquiries, but drew blanks. No one in the area had witnessed anything suspicious. Emma Travers was added to the long list of missing persons."

Professor Dewar up-ended his glass and shook the empty bottle, as if coaxing any reluctant drop he had overlooked. I regarded him somewhat skeptically.

"You wouldn't believe, Dr. Black," he said, catching my frown, "how many people in this little country of yours do disappear every year, and many can't be accounted for in any rational way . . . but this is by no means the end of the story.

"Within days the police called Susan in for questioning, suspecting she'd arranged the abduction of her own child. They knew about the strained relations with her husband. They were also mindful of Susan's mental state, which they had got from her husband and—most improperly—from a doctor she had been seeing about depression. The officers suggested she had staged the abduction out of malice, a way of getting at her husband. She was released, though advised to seek further psychiatric treatment—this is where I came in. I knew her consultant. He thought I might be able to get through to her."

"The police don't sound to have been up to much," I said. "Accusing the victim. A useless search. How long did they carry out their missing persons enquiry?"

Dewar smiled knowingly.

"Shorter than you'd expect," he said. "A week or so later they called in Susan again; in fact they arrested her—this time on suspicion of murder."

"Her mother killed her?" I asked, incredulous.

"That's what they thought. A man from the village had been walking his dog in the plantation. It got off the lead and ran into a fenced-off section of the woods away from the footpath. When he caught up, the dog was digging underneath some shrubs. It unearthed a body. Emma's body. The girl had been strangled."

"And Susan was convicted?" I asked.

"No. Susan was released without charge—eventually. The forensic evidence was problematic. Certainly, the police were incompetent—and that's putting it mildly. Apart from their cursory search, which was negligent enough, they then overplayed their hand. They were convinced that Susan had psychopathic tendencies. They allowed prejudice to override sober judgment. They assumed in advance she was guilty, then in misguided zeal they tried to railroad the evidence. The detective-inspector in charge was desperate to secure a conviction, having failed to carry out an efficient search. He was suspended and later dismissed from the force. The coroner's verdict was murder by person, or persons, unknown. The case remains officially unsolved to this day.

"But I'm not so sure. As you know, I've spent a lot of time with crimes committed by the insane, and I believe—I believed it at the time—that Susan was capable of murder. The police, maybe, could have secured a conviction: they had a motive and persuasive DNA evidence; but it was rumored that the reason the inspector was sacked, was that he had contrived to lose a maverick DNA sample inconveniently suggesting that the strangulation may have been effected by someone other than Susan."

It was now past midnight; I was longing for my bed. The professor appeared intent on endlessly spinning a mystery.

"So was it or wasn't it Susan?"

"As I say, I keep an open mind. But there were classic symptoms. She was becoming deranged, paranoid. And remember, there was an eclipse that day. There are well-documented case histories showing that, as with a full moon, it can push unstably minded people over the edge. Think of all that concentrated gravitational energy when sun, moon, and earth are in alignment!"

Really, this was hard to swallow. I was unclear whether it was meant to be a joke. It occurred to me that Dewar's account had all along been nothing more than a yarn to idle the night hours away over sherry.

"Are you serious?" I retorted. "This sounds more like Universal Studios!"

"Believe me, Dr. Black," Dewar laughed, "there are stranger things at Broadmoor than were ever dreamt of in Hollywood."

"And Susan?" I asked. "What became of her?"

"Tragedy. Daughter murdered. Culprit not found. Arrested by police. Betrayed by her husband. Guilty, perhaps, herself. Who knows what was in her mind? Maybe she did it, yet believed she did not do it. The nursing of contradiction. Guilt and denial—the most lethal of concoctions. It was all too much. Her husband sold up and went off with the secretary—the Old Rectory's an old people's home now. Susan was sectioned, confined to a mental hospital, swiftly deteriorated and was eventually diagnosed a paranoid schizophrenic. Neurosis became psychosis—it happens."

"And is she still confined?" Dewar looked grave.

"No, not anymore, I'm afraid. The following August she took her own life. Leapt from a third story window. The last time I saw her, a week before, she was on another planet. Couldn't get through at all. She looked strange, too, wasted, aetherial, yet oddly youthful, with a kind of wide-eyed glamour."

Dewar lent back with an air of finality. It all seemed rather anticlimactic. And where did the supernatural come in? It seemed more like a locked room mystery, or an episode from Ruth Rendell.

"So that's it?" I asked. "Where's your ghost?"

"Well, I never said there *was* a ghost," he replied; "I merely wished to indicate that there are many inexplicable things in Heaven and Earth."

"But this . . . apparition. The woman that Emma thought she saw? What was that? Is there any story connected with the place?"

"Oh, a couple of vague rumors. I spoke to this chap Higgins, an old man who used to do the garden for Mrs. Seymour. He said his grandfather once told him something about a hooded figure in white in the plantation. And when the new houses at the back were going up a couple of Irish navvies said they'd seen something passing into the wood one night—but that was probably the drink.

"Anyway," Professor Dewar laughed, "isn't this more your line than mine? You're the archivist. I'm only a scientist!"

Following our conversation I made a mental note to check out the local history, but the matter faded from my mind. There were more pressing priorities, notably the needless refurbishing of the college library, ordered against the advice of scholars and librarians alike by the new director of enterprise and innovation. However, as I shall shortly explain, it was directly due to this mammoth exercise that certain papers came to light that mayhap shed light on the murder of Emma Travers. This is what I meant when I spoke of the operations of chance. However, prior to that there was another fortuitous event, without which I might never even have thought about the case again, and probably not made my discovery amidst the disordered archives.

Rarely do I read university tittle-tattle, but I happened to catch, as I placed a recent copy of *The Academic Journal* on the open shelves, the name of Professor Dewar. It was, sad to say, an obituary. The professor, during a Canadian lecture tour, had collapsed in the cocktail lounge, after addressing assembled psychiatrists at the University of Regina; evidently prey to an undiagnosed heart complaint. So, as I persevered with my Promethean task, consigning much material to the stack to make way for computers, my late night chat over sherry with Dewar was very much in mind—as was the provenance of that fine sherry I have never been able to remember the name of, or find again.

An executive decision had been made to store all unpublished pre-nineteenth-century material at a remote site; and it was while shifting these papers that a box came to light. It was in a cupboard blocked by considerable shelving that had been erected over a period I dare not hazard; quite possibly they had rested there unread for a hundred years or more. They pertained to the eighteenth century. The box bore the name of the clergyman then resident at the rectory which later became the Travers' home—the Reverend Mr. Abshire. Much was dross—old sermons, church accounts, Bible quotations, etcetera—and I contemplated dumping all then and there in the skip. At the bottom of the pile, however, I found a handwritten manuscript. It contained in its title a word that, in the light of the Travers murder, caught my attention—*eclipse*. I recalled Dewar's peroration on the phenomenon. The MS's full title was intriguing: *Iniquities & Blasphemies That Did Afflict This Shire At The Time Of The Great Eclipse, In The Year Of Our Lord, 1724.*

The Reverend Mr. Abshire was clearly a man of apocalyptic persuasion who saw the Devil's hand everywhere, and whose opinion of his fellow men followed the less charitable teachings of the Prophets. His account of the supposed consequences of the eclipse smacked more of pagan superstition than Christianity. In the Gog and Magog Hills a calf had been born with two heads. A prize herd of swine had perished after stampeding into a marsh. A baby had died of a baffling ailment at a Grantchester poor house. A man with a pitchfork had run amok in Silver Street. A case of plague had been reported on a remote farm where "did dwell a vile harlot." Abshire was wont to attribute any and every misfortune to the eclipse. Indeed, it was difficult to tell whether he was raging against the workings of Satan or invoking the righteousness of an angry God.

It was as I reached the end of the MS that I knew my Eureka moment. Abshire concluded with a lengthy description of a calamity that had befallen the family of his predecessor at the rectory, the Reverend Mr. Staines. Abshire's account, I should add, was dated 1761.

On May 22nd 1724, the day of the total eclipse—the last one visible in England before the twentieth century—six-year-old Mary Staines was abducted from the rectory. Her body was subsequently discovered inexpertly buried in the oak wood at the property's rear. The perpetrator of the crime was rapidly identified as one Eliza Wilde, who had been employed as a chambermaid at Lathom Hall. The young woman, evidently, had some years before fallen into disgrace after conceiving a child as the result of a romantic liaison with the rector's eldest son, when she was sixteen years old. To avoid scandal her infant was taken at birth into the Porter household, living there as sibling to its own father; and Eliza was exiled from her scene of shame to a distant house owned by the Lathom family in Cumberland. Several years later, however, she was brought back by the new head of the family, who was selling the northern property and did not wish to dispense with the girl's efficient service. Once back, she developed an unfortunate habit. At every opportunity she visited the wood so as to watch her own child playing in the rectory garden; doing so by means of a small gap in the wooden gate leading into it, this surreptitious means of scrutiny being adopted in the mistaken belief that she was hidden from view. So great became her importunity—and her mental state so unstable—that, following numerous warnings, she was dismissed, and was thought to have taken up a position in London. Some weeks later she reappeared on the scene and did the awful deed. She preferred to take her own child's life than see it raised by others. Despite her plight—for she was clearly insane—the court imposed the ultimate penalty. According to Abshire, Eliza Wilde went to the scaffold "with the whites of her eyes rolling most horridly as in a glamour of madness."

Peter Bell has written articles and stories for *All Hallows*, *The Ghosts & Scholars M. R. James Newsletter*, *Wormwood*, *Faunus*, and *Supernatural Tales*; his work has also been published by Ash-Tree Press, Gray Friar Press, Side Real Press, The Scarecrow Press, and Hippocampus Press. He is a historian, a native of Liverpool, an inhabitant of York, and likes to wander the hidden places of Scotland and the North of England. His debut collection, *Strange Epiphanies*, was published by the Swan River Press in 2012.

When you work with magic, you rapidly realize that it is far easier to disrupt
than to create, far more difficult to mend than to destroy.

BIGFOOT ON CAMPUS

Jim Butcher

The campus police officer folded his hands and stared at me from across the table. "Coffee?"

"What flavor is it?" I asked.

He was in his forties, a big, solid man with bags under his calm, wary eyes, and his nametag read DEAN. "It's coffee-flavored coffee."

"No mocha?"

"Fuck mocha."

"Thank God," I said. "Black."

Officer Dean gave me hot black coffee in a paper cup, and I sipped at it gratefully. I was almost done shivering. It just came in intermittent bursts now. The old wool blanket Dean had given me was more gesture than cure.

"Am I under arrest?" I asked him.

Officer Dean moved his shoulders in what could have been a shrug. "That's what we're going to talk about."

"Uh-huh," I said.

"Maybe," he said in a slow, rural drawl, "you could explain to me why I found you in the middle of an orgy."

"Well," I said, "if you're going to be in an orgy, the middle is the best spot, isn't it."

He made a thoughtful sound. "Maybe you could explain why there was a car on the fourth floor of the dorm."

"Classic college prank," I said.

He grunted. "Usually when that happens, it hasn't made big holes in the exterior wall."

"Someone was avoiding the cliché?" I asked.

He looked at me for a moment, and said, "What about all the blood?"

"There were no injuries, were there?"

"No," he said.

"Then who cares? Some film student probably watched *Carrie* too many times."

Officer Dean tapped his pencil's eraser on the tabletop. It was the most agitated thing I'd seen him do. "Six separate calls in the past three hours with a Bigfoot sighting on campus. Bigfoot. What do you know about that?"

"Well, kids these days, with their Internets and their video games and their iPods. Who knows what they thought they saw."

Officer Dean put down his pencil. He looked at me, and said, calmly, "My job is to protect a bunch of kids with access to every means of self-destruction known to man from not only the criminal element but themselves. I got chemistry students who can make their own meth, Ecstasy, and LSD. I got ROTC kids with access to automatic weapons and explosives. I got enough alcohol going through here on a weekly basis to float a battleship. I got a thriving trade in recreational drugs. I got lives to protect."

"Sounds tiring."

"About to get tired of you," he said. "Start giving it to me straight."

"Or you'll arrest me?" I asked.

"No," Dean said. "I bounce your face off my knuckles for a while. Then I ask again."

"Isn't that unprofessional conduct?"

"Fuck conduct," Dean said. "I got kids to look after."

I sipped the coffee some more. Now that the shivers had begun to subside, I finally felt the knotted muscles in my belly begin to relax. I slowly settled back into my chair. Dean hadn't blustered or tried to intimidate me in any way. He wasn't trying to scare me into talking. He was just telling me how it was going to be.

And he drank his coffee old-school.

I kinda liked the guy.

"You aren't going to believe me," I said.

"I don't much," he said. "Try me."

"Okay," I said. "My name is Harry Dresden. I'm a professional wizard."

Officer Dean pursed his lips. Then he leaned forward slightly and listened.

The client wanted me to meet him at a site in the Ouachita Mountains in eastern Oklahoma. Looking at them, you might not realize they were mountains, they're so old. They've had millions of years of wear and tear on them, and they've been ground down to nubs. The site used to be on an Indian reservation, but they don't call them reservations anymore. They're Tribal Statistical Areas now.

I showed my letter and my ID to a guy in a pickup, who just happened to pull up next to me for a friendly chat at a lonely stop sign on a winding back road. I don't know what the tribe called his office, but I recognized a guardian when I saw one. He read the letter and waved me through in an even friendlier manner than he had used when he approached me. It's nice to be welcomed somewhere, once in a while.

I parked at the spot indicated on the map and hiked a good mile and a half into the hills, taking a heavy backpack with me. I found a pleasant spot to set up camp. The mid-October weather was crisp, but I had a good sleeping bag and would be comfortable as long as it didn't start raining. I dug a fire pit and ringed it in stones, built a modest fire out of fallen limbs, and laid out my sleeping bag on a foam camp pad. By the time it got dark, I was well into preparing the dinner I'd brought with me. The scent of foil-wrapped potatoes baking in coals blended with that of the steaks I had spitted and roasting over the fire.

Can I cook a camp meal or what?

Bigfoot showed up half an hour after sunset.

One minute, I was alone. The next, he simply stepped out into view. He was huge. Not huge like a big person, but huge like a horse, with that same sense of raw animal power and mass.

He was nine feet tall at least and probably tipped the scales at well over six hundred pounds. His powerful, wide-shouldered body was covered in long, dark brown hair. Even though he stood in plain sight in my firelight, I could barely see the buckskin bag he had slung over one shoulder and across his chest, the hair was so long.

"Strength of a River in His Shoulders," I said. "You're welcome at my fire."

"Wizard Dresden," River Shoulders rumbled. "It is good to see you." He took a couple of long steps and hunkered down opposite the fire from me. "Man. That smells good." "Darn right it does," I said. I proceeded with the preparations in companionable silence while River Shoulders stared thoughtfully at the fire. I'd set up my camp this way for a reason—it made me the host and River Shoulders my guest. It meant I was obliged to provide food and drink, and he was obliged to behave with decorum. Guest-and-host relationships are damned near laws of physics in the supernatural world: They almost never get violated, and when they do, it's a big deal. Both of us felt a lot more comfortable around one another this way.

Okay. Maybe it did a wee bit more to make me feel comfortable than it did River Shoulders, but he was a repeat customer, I liked him, and I figured he probably didn't get treated to a decent steak all that often.

We ate the meal in an almost ritualistic silence, too, other than River making some appreciative noises as he chewed. I popped open a couple of bottles of McAnnally's Pale, my favorite brew by a veritable genius of hops, back in Chicago.

River liked it so much that he gave me an inquisitive glance when his bottle was empty. So I emptied mine and produced two more.

After that, I filled a pipe with expensive tobacco, lit it, took a few puffs, and passed it to him. He nodded and took it. We smoked and finished our beers. By then, the fire had died down to glowing embers.

"Thank you for coming," River Shoulders rumbled. "Again, I come to seek your help on behalf of my son."

"Third time you've come to me," I said.

"Yes." He rummaged in his pouch and produced a small, heavy object. He flicked it to me. I caught it and squinted at it in the dim light. It was a gold nugget about as big as a Ping-Pong ball. I nodded and tossed it back to him. River Shoulders's brows lowered into a frown.

You have to understand. A frown on a mug like his looked indistinguishable from scowling fury. It turned his eyes into shadowed caves with nothing but a faint gleam showing from far back in them. It made his jaw muscles bunch and swell into knots the size of tennis balls on the sides of his face.

"You will not help him," the Bigfoot said.

I snorted. "*You're* the one who isn't helping him, big guy."

"I am," he said. "I am hiring you."

"You're his *father*," I said quietly. "And he doesn't even know your name. He's a good kid. He deserves more than that. He deserves the truth."

He shook his head slowly. "Look at me. Would he even accept my help?"

"You aren't going to know unless you try it," I said. "And I never said I wouldn't help him."

At that, River Shoulders frowned a little more.

I curbed an instinct to edge away from him.

"Then what do you want in exchange for your services?" he asked.

"I help the kid," I said. "You meet the kid. That's the payment. That's the deal."

"You do not know what you are asking," he said.

"With respect, River Shoulders, this is not a negotiation. If you want my help, I just told you how to get it."

He became very still at that. I got the impression that maybe people didn't often use tactics like that when they dealt with him.

When he spoke, his voice was a quiet, distant rumble. "You have no right to ask this."

"Yeah, um. I'm a wizard. I meddle. It's what we do."

"Manifestly true." He turned his head slightly away. "You do not know how much you ask."

"I know that kid deserves more than you've given him."

"I have seen to his protection. To his education. That is what fathers do."

"Sure," I said. "But you weren't ever *there*. And that *matters*." Absolute silence fell for a couple of minutes.

"Look," I said gently. "Take it from a guy who knows. Growing up without a dad is terrifying. You're the only father he's ever going to have. You can go hire Superman to look out for Irwin if you want to, and he'd still be the wrong guy—because he isn't you."

River toyed with the empty bottle, rolling it across his enormous fingers like a regular guy might have done with a pencil.

"Do you want me on this?" I asked him. "No hard feelings if you don't."

River looked up at me again and nodded slowly. "I know that if you agree to help him, you will do so. I will pay your price." "Okay," I said. "Tell me about Irwin's problem."

"What'd he say?" Officer Dean asked.

"He said the kid was at the University of Oklahoma for school," I said. "River'd had a bad dream and knew that the kid's life was in danger."

The cop grunted. "So . . . Bigfoot is a psychic?"

"Think about it. No one ever gets a good picture of one, much less a clean shot," I said. "Despite all the expeditions and TV shows and whatnot. River's people have got more going for them than being huge and strong. My guess is that they're smarter than humans. Maybe a lot smarter. My guess is they know magic of some kind, too."

"Jesus," Officer Dean said. "You really believe all this, don't you?"

"I want to believe," I said. "And I told you that you wouldn't."

Dean grunted. Then he said, "Usually they're too drunk to make sense when I get a story like this. Keep going."

I got to Norman, Oklahoma, a bit before noon the next morning. It was a Wednesday, which was a blessing. In the Midwest, if you show up to a college town on a weekend, you risk running into a football game. In my experience, that resulted in universal problems with traffic, available hotel rooms, and drunken football hooligans.

Or wait: *Soccer* is the one with hooligans. Drunken American football fans are just . . . drunks, I guess.

River had provided me with a small dossier he'd had prepared, which included a copy of his kid's class schedule. I parked my car in an open spot on the street not too far from campus and ambled on over. I got some looks: I sort of stand out in a crowd. I'm a lot closer to seven feet tall than six, which might be one reason why River Shoulders liked to hire me—I look a lot less tiny than other humans, to him. Add in the big black leather duster and the scar on my face, and I looked like the kind of guy you'd want to avoid in dark alleys.

The university campus was as confusing as all of them are, with buildings that had constantly evolved into and out of multiple roles over the years. They were all named after people I doubt any of the students had ever heard of, or cared about, and there seemed to be no organizational logic at all at work there. It was a pretty enough campus, I supposed. Lots of redbrick and brownstone buildings. Lots of architectural doohickeys on many of the buildings, in a kind of quasi-classical Greek style. The ivy that was growing up many of the walls seemed a little too cultivated and obvious for my taste. Then again, I had exactly the same amount of regard for the Ivy League as I did for the Big 12.

The grass was an odd color, like maybe someone had sprayed it with a blue-green dye or something, though I had no idea what kind of delusional creep would do something so pointless.

And, of course, there were students—a whole lot of kids, all of them with things to do and places to be. I could have wandered around all day, but I thought I'd save myself the headache of attempting to apply logic to a university campus and stopped a few times to ask for directions. Irwin Pounder, River Shoulders's son, had a physics course at noon, so I picked up a notebook and a couple of pens at the university bookstore and ambled on into the large classroom. It was a perfect disguise. The notebook was college-ruled.

I sat near the back, where I could see both doors into the room, and waited. Bigfoot Irwin was going to stand out in the crowd almost as badly as I did. The kid was huge. River had shown me a photo that he kept in his medicine bag, carefully laminated to protect it from the elements. Irwin's mom could have been a second-string linebacker for the Bears. Carol Pounder was a formidable woman, and over six feet tall. But her boy was a head taller than she already, and still had the awkward, too-lean look of someone who wasn't finished growing. His shoulders had come in, though, and it looked like he might have had to turn sideways to walk through doors.

I waited and waited, watching both doors, until the professor arrived, and the class started. Irwin never arrived. I was going to leave, but it actually turned out to be kind of interesting. The professor was a lunatic but a really entertaining one.

The guy drank liquid nitrogen, right there in front of everybody, and blew it out his nose in this huge jet of vapor. I applauded along with everyone else, and before I knew it, the lecture was over. I might even have learned something.

Okay.

Maybe there *were* some redeeming qualities to a college education.

I went to Irwin's next class, which was a freshman biology course, in another huge classroom.

No Irwin.

He wasn't at his four o'clock math class, either, and I emerged from it bored and cranky. None of Irwin's other teachers held a candle to Dr. Indestructo.

Huh.

Time for plan B.

River's dossier said that Irwin was playing football for OU.

He'd made the team as a walk-on, and River had been as proud as any father would be about the athletic prowess of his son. So I ambled on over to the Sooners' practice field, where the team was warming up with a run.

Even among the football players, Irwin stood out. He was half a head taller than any of them, at least my own height. He looked gangly and thin beside the fellows around him, even with the shoulder pads on, but I recognized his face. I'd last seen him when he was about fourteen. Though his rather homely features had changed a bit, they seemed stronger, and more defined. There was no mistaking his dark, intelligent eyes.

I stuck my hands in the pockets of my old leather duster and waited, watching the field. I'd found the kid, and, absent any particular danger, I was in no particular hurry. There was no sense in charging into the middle of Irwin's football practice and his life and disrupting everything. I'm just not that kind of guy.

Okay, well.

I try not to be.

"Seems to keep happening, though, doesn't it," I said to myself. "You show up on somebody's radar, and things go to DEFCON 1 a few minutes later."

"I'm sorry?" said a young woman's voice.

"Ah," said Officer Dean. "This is where the girl comes in."

"Who said there was a girl?"

"There's always a girl."

"Well," I said, "yes and no."

She was blond, about five-foot-six, and my logical mind told me that every inch of her was a bad idea. The rest of me, especially my hindbrain, suggested that she would be an ideal mate.

Preferably sooner rather than later.

There was nothing in particular about her that should have caused my hormones to rage. I mean, she was young and fit, and she had the body of the young and fit, and that's hardly ever unpleasant to look at. She had eyes the color of cornflowers and rosy cheeks, and she was a couple of notches above cute, when it came to her face. She was wearing running shorts, and her legs were smooth and generally excellent.

Some women just have it. And no, I can't tell you what "it" means because I don't get it myself. It was something mindless, something chemical, and even as my metaphorically burned fingers were telling me to walk away, the rest of me was going through that male physiological response the science guys in the Netherlands have documented recently.

Not *that* one.

Well, maybe a little.

I'm talking about the response where when a pretty girl is around, it hits the male brain like a drug and temporarily impairs his cognitive function, literally dropping the male IQ.

And hey, how Freudian is it that the study was conducted in the Netherlands?

This girl dropped that IQ-nuke on my brain, and I was standing there staring a second later while she smiled uncertainly at me.

"Urn, sorry?" I asked. "My mind was in the Netherlands."

Her dimple deepened, and her eyes sparkled. She knew all about the brain nuke. "I just said that you sounded like a dangerous guy." She winked at me. It was adorable. "I like those."

"You're, uh. You're into bad boys, eh?"

"Maybe," she said, lowering her voice and drawing the word out a little, as if it was a confession. She spoke with a very faint drawl. "Plus, I like meeting new people from all kinds of places, and you don't exactly strike me as a local, darlin'."

"You dig dangerous guys who are just passing through," I said. "Do you ever watch those cop shows on TV?"

She tilted back her head and laughed. "Most boys don't give me lip like that in the first few minutes of conversation."

"I'm not a boy," I said.

She gave me a once-over with those pretty eyes, taking a heartbeat longer about it than she really needed. "No," she said. "No, you are not."

My inner nonmoron kept on stubbornly ringing alarm bells, and the rest of me slowly became aware of them. My glands thought that I'd better keep playing along. It was the only way to find out what the girl might have been interested in, right? Right. I was absolutely not continuing the conversation because I had gone soft in the head.

"I hope that's not a problem," I said.

"I just don't see how it could be. I'm Connie."

"Harry."

"So what brings you to Norman, Harry?"

"Taking a look at a player," I said.

Her eyes brightened. "Oooooo. You're a scout?"

"Maybe," I said, in the same tone she'd used earlier.

Connie laughed again. "I'll bet you talk to silly college girls like me all the time."

"Like you?" I replied. "No, not so much."

Her eyes sparkled again. "You may have found my weakness. I'm the kind of girl who likes a little flattery."

"And here I was thinking you liked something completely different."

She covered her mouth with one hand, and her cheeks got a little pinker. "Harry. That's not how one talks to young ladies in the South."

"Obviously. I mean, you look so outraged. Should I apologize?"

"Oh," she said, her smile widening. "I just have to collect you." Connie's eyes sparkled again, and I finally got it.

Her eyes weren't *twinkling*.

They were becoming increasingly flecked with motes of molten silver.

Cutie-pie was a frigging vampire.

I've worked for years on my poker face. Years. It still sucks pretty bad, but I've been working on it. So I'm sure my smile was only slightly wooden when I asked, "Collect me?"

I might not have been hiding my realization very well, but either Connie was better at poker than me, or else she really was too absorbed in the conversation to notice. "Collect you," she said. "When I meet someone worthwhile, I like to have dinner with them. And we'll talk and tell stories and laugh, and I'll get a picture and put it in my memory book."

"Um," I said. "Maybe you're a little young for me."

She threw back her head and gave a full-throated laugh. "Oh, Harry. I'm talking about sharing a meal. That's all, honestly. I know I'm a terrible flirt, but I didn't think you were taking me seriously."

I watched her closely as she spoke, searching for the predatory calculation that I knew had to be in there. Vampires of the White Court—

"Wait," Dean said. "Vampires of the White Castle?"

I sighed. "White Court."

Dean grunted. "Why not just call her a vampire?"

"They come in a lot of flavors," I said.

"And this one was vanilla?"

"There's no such thing as . . . " I rubbed at the bridge of my nose. "Yes."

Dean nodded. "So why not just call 'em vanilla vampires?"

"I'll . . . bring it up at the next wizard meeting," I said.

"So the vampire is where all the blood came from?"

"No." I sighed. "This kind doesn't feed on blood."

"No? What do they eat, then?"

"Life-energy."

"Huh?"

I sighed again. "Sex."

"Finally, the story gets good. So they eat sex?"

"Life-energy," I repeated. "The sex is just how they get started."

"Like sticking fangs into your neck," Dean said. "Only instead of fangs, I guess they use—"

"Look, do you want the story or not?"

Dean leaned back in his chair and propped his feet up on his desk. "Yon kidding? This is the best one in years."

Anyway, I watched Connie closely, but I saw no evidence of anything in her that I knew had to be there. Vampires are predators who hunt the most dangerous game on the planet. They generally aren't shy about it, either. They don't really need to be. If a White Court vampire wants to feed off a human, all she really has to do is crook her finger, and he comes running.

There isn't any ominous music. Nobody sparkles. As far as anyone looking on is concerned, a girl winks at a boy and goes off somewhere to make out. Happens every day.

They don't get all coy asking you out to dinner, and they sure as hell don't have pictures in a memory book.

This was weird, and long experience has taught me that when the unexplained is bouncing around right in front of you, the smart thing is to back off and figure out what the hell is going on. In my line of work, what you don't know can kill you.

But I didn't get the chance. There was a sharp whistle from a coach somewhere on the field, and football players came rumbling off it. One of them came loping toward us, put a hand on top of the six-foot chain-link fence, and vaulted it in one easy motion. Bigfoot Irwin landed lightly, grinning, and continued directly toward Connie.

She let out a girlish squeal of delight and pounced on him.

He caught her. She wrapped her legs around his hips, held his face in her hands, and kissed him thoroughly. They came up for air a moment later.

"Irwin," she said, "I met someone interesting. Can I collect him?"

The kid only had eyes for Connie. Not that I could blame him, really. His voice was a basso rumble, startlingly like River Shoulders's. "I'm always in favor of dinner at the Brewery."

She dismounted and beamed at him. "Good. Irwin, this is . . . "

The kid finally looked up at me and blinked. "Harry."

"Heya, Irwin," I said. "How're things?"

Connie looked back and forth between us. "You know each other?"

"He's a friend," Irwin said.

"Dinner," Connie declared. "Harry, say you'll share a meal with me."

Interesting choice of words, all things considered.

I think I had an idea what had caused River's bad dream. If a vampire had attached herself to Irwin, the kid was in trouble. Given the addictive nature of Connie's attentions, and the degree of control it could give her over Irwin . . . maybe he wasn't the only one who could be in trouble.

My, how little Irwin had grown. I wondered exactly how much of his father's supernatural strength he had inherited. He looked like he could break me in half without causing a blip in his heart rate. He and Connie looked at me with hopeful smiles, and I suddenly felt like maybe I was the crazy one. Expressions like that should not inspire worry, but every instinct I had told me that something wasn't right.

My smile probably got even more wooden. "Sure," I said. "Why not?"

The Brewery was a lot like every other sports bar you'd find in college towns, with the possible exception that it actually was a brewery. Small and medium-sized tanks stood here and there throughout the place, with signs on each describing the kind of beer that was under way. Apparently, the beer sampler was traditional. I made polite noises when I tried each, but they were unexceptional. Okay, granted I was probably spoiled by having Mac's brew available back at home. It wasn't the Brewery's fault that their brews were merely excellent. Mac's stuff was epic, it was legend. Tough to measure up to that.

I kept one hand under the table, near a number of tools I thought I might need, all the way through the meal, and waited for the other shoe to drop—only it never did. Connie and Irwin chattered away like any young couple, snuggled up to one another on adjacent chairs. The girl was charming, funny, and a playful flirt, but Irwin didn't seem discomfited by it. I kept my responses restrained anyway. I didn't want to find out a couple of seconds too late that the seemingly innocent banter was how Connie got her psychic hooks into me.

But a couple of hours went by, and nothing.

"Irwin's never told me anything about his father," Connie said.

"I don't know much," Irwin said. "He's . . . kept his distance over the years. I've looked for him a couple of times, but I never wanted to push him."

"How mysterious," Connie said.

I nodded. "For someone like him, I think the word 'eccentric' might apply better."

"He's rich?" Connie asked.

"I feel comfortable saying that money isn't one of his concerns," I said.

"I knew it!" Connie said, and looked slyly at Irwin. "There had to be a reason. I'm only into you for your money." Instead of answering, Irwin calmly picked Connie up out of her chair, using just the muscles of his shoulders and arms, and deposited her on his lap. "Sure you are.

Connie made a little groaning sound and bit her lower lip.

"God. I know it's not PC, but I've got to say—I am into it when you get all caveman on me, Pounder."

"I know." Irwin kissed the tip of her nose and turned to me.

"So, Harry. What brings you to Norman?"

"I was passing through," I said easily. "Your dad asked me to look in on you."

"Just casually," Irwin said, his dark eyes probing. "Because he's such a casual guy."

"Something like that," I said.

"Not that I mind seeing you," Irwin said, "but in case you missed it, I'm all grown-up now. I don't need a babysitter. Even a cool, expensive one."

"If you did, my rates are very reasonable," Connie said.

"We'll talk," Irwin replied, sliding his arms around her waist.

The girl wasn't exactly a junior petite, but she looked tiny on Irwin's scale. She hopped up, and said, "I'm going to go make sure there isn't barbecue sauce on my nose, and then we can take the picture. Okay?"

"Sure," Irwin said, smiling. "Go."

Once she was gone from sight, Irwin looked at me and dropped his smile. "Okay," he said resignedly. "What does he want this time?"

There wasn't loads of time, so I didn't get all coy with the subject matter. "He's worried about you. He thinks you may be in danger."

Irwin arched his eyebrows. "From what?"

I just looked at him.

His expression suddenly turned into a scowl, and the air around grew absolutely thick with energy that seethed for a point of discharge. "Wait. This is about Connie?" I couldn't answer him for a second, the air felt so close. The last time I'd felt this much latent, waiting power, I'd been standing next to my old mentor, Ebenezar McCoy, when he was gathering his strength for a spell.

That pretty much answered my questions about River Shoulders's people having access to magical power. The kid was a freaking dynamo of it. I had to be careful. I didn't want to be the guy who was unlucky enough to ground out that storm cloud of waiting power. So I answered Irwin cautiously and calmly.

"I'm not sure yet. But I know for a fact that she's not exactly what she seems to be."

His nostrils flared, and I saw him make an effort to remain collected. His voice was fairly even. "Meaning what?"

"Meaning I'm not sure yet," I said.

"So what? You're going to hang around here butting into my life?"

I held up both hands. "It isn't like that."

"It's just like that," Irwin said. "My dad spends my whole life anywhere else but here, and now he thinks he can just decide when to intrude on it?"

"Irwin," I said, "I'm not here to try to make you do anything. He asked me to look in on you. I promised I would. And that's all."

He scowled for a moment, then smoothed that expression away. "No sense in being mad at the messenger, I guess," he said. "What do you mean about Connie?"

"She's . . . " I faltered, there. You don't just sit down with a guy and tell him, "Hey, your girlfriend is a vampire, could you pass the ketchup?" I sighed. "Look, Irwin. Everybody sees the world a certain way. And we all kind of . . . well, we all sort of decide together what's real and what isn't real, right?"

"Magic's real," Irwin said impatiently. "Monsters are real. Supernatural stuff actually exists. You're a professional wizard."

I blinked at him, several times.

"What?" he asked, and smiled gently. "Don't let the brow ridge fool you. I'm not an idiot, man. You think you can walk into my life the way you have, twice, and not leave me with an itch to scratch? You made me ask questions. I went and got answers."

"Uh. How?" I asked.

"Wasn't hard. There's an Internet. And this organization called the 'Paranet' of all the cockamamie things that got started a few years ago. Took me like ten minutes to find it online and start reading through their message boards. I can't believe everyone in the world doesn't see this stuff. It's not like anyone is trying very hard to keep it secret."

"People don't want to know the truth," I said. "That makes it simple to hide. Wow, ten minutes? Really? I guess I'm not really an Internetty person."

"Internetty," Irwin said, seriously. "I guess you aren't."

I waved a hand. "Irwin, you need to know this. Connie isn't—"

The pretty vampire plopped herself back down into Irwin's lap and kissed his cheek. "Isn't what?"

"The kind to stray," I said, smoothly. "I was just telling Irwin how much I'd like to steal you away from him, but I figure you're the sort who doesn't play that kind of game."

"True enough," she agreed cheerfully. "I know where I want to sleep tonight." Maybe it was unconscious, the way she wriggled when she said it, but Irwin's eyes got a slightly glazed look to them.

I remembered being that age. A girl like Connie would have been a mind-numbing distraction to me back then even if she hadn't been a vampire. And Irwin was clearly in love, or as close to it as he could manage through the haze of hormones surrounding him. Reasoning with him wasn't going to accomplish anything—unless I made him angry. Passion is a huge force when you're Irwin's age, and I'd taken enough beatings for one lifetime. I'd never be able to explain the danger to him. He just didn't have a frame of reference . . .

He just didn't know.

I stared at Connie for a second with my mouth open.

"What?" she asked.

"You don't know," I said.

"Know what?" she asked.

"You don't know that you're . . ." I shook my head, and said to Irwin, "She doesn't know."

"Hang on," Dean said. "Why is that significant?"

"Vampires are just like people until the first time they feed," I said. "Connie didn't know that bad things would happen when she did."

"What kinda bad things?"

"The first time they feed, they don't really know it's coming. They have no control over it, no restraint—and whoever they feed on dies as a result."

"So she was the threat that Bigfoot dreamed about?"

"I'm getting to it."

Irwin's expression had darkened again, into a glower almost exactly like River Shoulders's, and he stood up.

Connie was frowning at me as she was abruptly displaced.

"Don't know wh—oof, Pounder!"

"We're done," Irwin said to me. His voice wasn't exactly threatening, but it was absolutely certain, and his leashed anger all but made the air crackle. "Nice to see you again, Harry. Tell my dad to call. Or write. Or do anything but try to tell me how to live my life."

Connie blinked at him. "Wait . . . wait, what's wrong?" Irwin left a few twenties on the table, and said, "We're going."

"What? What happened?"

"We're going," Irwin said. This time, he did sound a little angry.

Connie's bewilderment suddenly shifted into some flavor of outrage. She narrowed her lovely eyes, and snapped, "I am not your pet, Pounder."

"I'm not trying to . . . " Irwin took a slow, deep breath, and said, more calmly, "I'm upset. I need some space. I'll explain when I calm down. But we need to go."

She folded her arms, and said, "Go calm down, then. But I'm not going to be rude to our guest."

Irwin looked at me, and said, "We going to have a problem?"

Wow. The kid had learned a lot about the world since the last time I'd seen him. He recognized that I wasn't a playful puppy dog. He realized that if I'd been sent to protect him, and I thought Connie was it. And he'd just told me that if I did, he was going to object. Strenuously. No protests, no threats, just letting me know that he knew the score and was willing to do something about it if I made him. The guys who are seriously capable handle themselves like that.

"No problem," I said, and made it a promise. "If I think something needs to be done, we'll talk first."

The set of his shoulders eased, and he nodded at me. Then he turned and stalked out. People watched him go, warily.

Connie shook her head slowly, and asked, "What did you say?"

"Um," I said. "I think he feels like his dad is intruding on his life."

"You don't say." She shook her head. "That's not your fault. He's usually so collected. Why is he acting like such a jerk?"

"Issues," I said, shrugging. "Everyone has a parental issue or two."

"Still. It's beneath him to behave that way." She shook her head. "Sometimes he makes me want to slap him. But I'd need to get a chair to stand on."

"I don't take it personally," I assured her. "Don't worry."

"It was about me," she said quietly. "Wasn't it? It's about something I don't know."

"Um," I said.

It was just possible that maybe I'd made a bad call when I decided to meddle between River and his kid. It wasn't my place to shake the pillars of Irwin's life. Or Connie's, for that matter. It was going to be hard enough on her to find out about her supernatural heritage. She didn't need to have the news broken to her by a stranger, on top of that. You'd think that, after years as a professional, I'd know enough to just take River's money, help out his kid, and call it a night.

"Maybe we should walk?" I suggested.

"Sure."

We left and started walking the streets of downtown Norman. The place was alive and growing, like a lot of college towns: plenty of old buildings, some railroad tracks, lots of cracks in the asphalt and the sidewalks. The shops and restaurants had that improvised look that a business district gets when it outlives its original intended purpose and subsequent generations of enterprise take over the space.

We walked in silence for several moments, until Connie finally said, "He's not an angry person. He's usually so calm. But when something finally gets to him . . . "

"It's hard for him," I said. "He's huge and he's very strong and he knows it. If he loses control of himself, someone could get hurt. He doesn't like the thought of that. So when he starts feeling angry, it makes him tense. Afraid. He's more upset about the fact that he feels so angry than about anything I said or did."

Connie looked up at me pensively for a long moment. Then she said, "Most people wouldn't realize that."

I shrugged.

"What don't I know?" she asked.

I shook my head. "I'm not sure it's my place to tell you."

"But it's about me."

"Yeah."

She smiled faintly. "Then shouldn't I be the one who gets to decide?"

I thought about that one for a moment. "Connie . . . you're mostly right. But . . . some things, once said, can't be unsaid.

Let me think about it."

She didn't answer.

The silence made me uncomfortable. I tried to chat my way clear of it. "How'd you meet Irwin?"

The question, or maybe the subject matter, seemed to relax her a little. "In a closet at a party. Someone spiked the punch. Neither of us had ever been drunk before, and . . . " Her cheeks turned a little pink. "And he's just so damned sexy."

"Lot of people wouldn't think so," I noted.

She waved a hand. "He's not pretty. I know that. It's not about that. There's . . . this energy in him. It's chemical. Assurance. Power. Not just muscles—it's who he is." Her cheeks turned a little pink. "It wasn't exactly love at first sight, I guess. But once the hangover cleared up, that happened, too."

"So you love him?" I asked.

Her smile widened, and her eyes shone the way a young woman's eyes ought to shine. She spoke with calm, simple certainty. "He's the one."

About twenty things to say leapt to my mind. I was going to say something about how she was too young to make that kind of decision. I thought about how she hadn't been out on her own for very long, and how she had no idea where her relationship with Irwin was going to lead. I was going to tell her that only time could tell her if she and Irwin were good for one another and ready to be together, to make that kind of decision. I could have said something about how she needed to stop and think, not make blanket statements about her emotions and the future.

That was when I realized that everything I would have said was something I would have said to a young woman in love—not to a vampire. Not only that, but I heard something in her voice or saw something in her face that told me that my aged wisdom was, at least in this case, dead wrong. My instincts were telling me something that my rational brain had missed.

The kids had something real. I mean, maybe it hadn't gotten off on the most pure and virtuous foot, but that wasn't anything lethal in a relationship. The way they related to one another now? There was a connection there. You could imagine saying their names as a unit, and it *fit*: ConnieandIrwin. Maybe they had some growing to do, but what they had was real.

Not that it mattered. Being in love didn't change the facts.

First, that Connie was a vampire. Second, that vampires had to feed. Third, they fed upon their lovers.

"Hold on," Dean said. "You missed something."

"Eh?"

"Girl's a vampire, right?"

"Yeah.

"So," Dean said. "She met the kid in a closet at a party. They already got it on. She done had her first time."

I frowned. "Yeah."

"So how come Kid Bigfoot wasn't dead?"

I nodded. "Exactly. It bothered me, too."

The girl was in love with Irwin, and it meant she was dangerous to him. Hell, she was dangerous to almost everyone. She wasn't even entirely *human*. How could I possibly spring something that big on her?

At the same time, how could I *not*?

"I should have taken the gold," I muttered to myself.

"What?" she asked.

That was when the Town Car pulled up to the curb a few feet ahead of us. Two men got out of the front seat. They wore expensive suits and had thick necks. One of them hadn't had his suit fitted properly—I could see the slight bulge of a sidearm in a shoulder holster. That one stood on the sidewalk and stared at me, his hands clasped in front of him. The driver went around to the rear passenger door and opened it.

"Oh," Connie said. "Marvelous. This is all I need."

"Who is that?" I asked.

"My father."

The man who got out of the back of the limo wore a pearl gray suit that made his thugs' outfits look like secondhand clothing. He was slim, a bit over six feet tall, and his haircut probably cost him more than I made in a week. His hair was dark, with a single swath of silver at each temple, and his skin was weathered and deeply tanned. He wore rings on most of his manicured fingers, all of them sporting large stones.

"Hi, Daddy," Connie said, smiling. She sounded pleasant enough, but she'd turned herself very slightly away from the man as she spoke. A rule of thumb for reading body language is that almost no one can totally hide physical reflections of their state of mind. They can only minimize the signs of it in their posture and movements. If you mentally exaggerate and magnify their body language, it tells you something about what they're thinking.

Connie clearly didn't want to talk to this man. She was ready to flee from her own father should it become necessary.

It told me something about the guy. I was almost sure I wasn't going to like him.

He approached the girl, smiling, and after a microhesitation, they exchanged a brief hug. It didn't look like something they'd practiced much.

"Connie," the man said, smiling. He had the same mild drawl his daughter did. He tilted his head to one side and regarded her thoughtfully. "You went blond. It's . . . charming."

"Thank you, Daddy," Connie said. She was smiling, too. Neither one of them looked sincere to me. "I didn't know you were in town. If you'd called, we could have made an evening of it."

"Spur-of-tne-moment thing," he said easily. "I hope you don't mind."

"No, of course not."

Both of them were lying. Parental issues indeed.

"How's that boy you'd taken up with? Irving."

"Irwin," Connie said in a poisonously pleasant tone. "He's great. Maybe even better than that."

He frowned at that, and said, "I see. But he's not here?"

"He had homework tonight," Connie lied.

That drew a small, sly smile out of the man. "I see. Who's your friend?" he asked pleasantly, without actually looking at me.

"Oh," Connie said. "Harry, this is my father, Charles Barrowill. Daddy, this is Harry Dresden."

"Hi," I said brightly.

Barrowill's eyes narrowed to sudden slits, and he took a short, hard breath as he looked at me. He then flicked his eyes left and right around him, as if looking for a good place to dive or maybe a hostage to seize.

"What a pleasure, Mr. Dresden," he said, his voice suddenly tight. "What brings you out to Oklahoma?"

"I heard it was a nice place for perambulating," I said. Behind Barrowill, his guards had picked up on the tension. Both of them had become very still. Barrowill was quiet for a moment, as if trying to parse some kind of meaning from my words. Heavy seconds ticked by, like the quiet before a shootout in an old Western.

A tumbleweed went rolling by in the street. I'm not even kidding. An actual, literal tumbleweed. Man, Oklahoma.

Then Barrowill took a slow breath and said to Connie, "Darling, I'd like to speak to you for a few moments, if you have time."

"Actually . . . " Connie began.

"Now, please," Barrowill said. There was something ugly under the surface of his pleasant tone. "The car. I'll give you a ride back to the dorms."

Connie folded her arms and scowled. "I'm entertaining someone from out of town, Daddy. I can't just leave him here." One of the guard's hands twitched.

"Don't be difficult, Connie," Barrowill said. "I don't want to make a scene."

His eyes never left me as he spoke, and I got his message loud and clear. He was taking the girl with him, and he was willing to make things get messy if I tried to stop him.

"It's okay, Connie," I said. "I've been to Norman before. I can find my way to a hotel easily enough."

"You're sure?" Connie asked.

"Definitely."

"Herman," Barrowill said.

The driver opened the passenger door again and stood next to it attentively. He kept his eyes on me, and one hand dangled, clearly ready to go for his gun.

Connie looked back and forth between me and her father for a moment, then sighed audibly and walked over to the car.

She slid in, and Herman closed the door behind her.

"I recognize you," I said pleasantly to Barrowill. "You were at the Raith Deeps when Skavis and Malvora tried to pull off their coup. Front row, all the way on one end in the Raith cheering section."

"You have an excellent memory," Barrowill said.

"Got out in one piece, did you?"

The vampire smiled without humor. "What are you doing with my daughter?"

"Taking a walk," I said. "Talking."

"You have nothing to say to her. In the interests of peace between the Court and the Council, I'm willing to ignore this intrusion into my territory. Go in peace. Right now."

"You never told her, did you?" I asked. "Never told her what she was."

One of his jaw muscles twitched. "It is not our way."

"Nah," I said. "You wait until the first time they get twitterpated, experiment with sex, and kill whoever it is they're with. Little harsh on the kids, isn't it?"

"Connie is not some mortal cow. She is a vampire. The initiation builds character she will need to survive and prosper."

"If it was good enough for you, it's good enough for her?"

"Mortal," Barrowill said, "you simply cannot understand. I am her father. It is my obligation to prepare her for her life. The initiation is something she needs."

I lifted my eyebrows. "Holy . . . that's what happened, isn't it? You sent her off to school to boink some poor kid to death. Hell, I'd bet you had the punch spiked at that party. Except the kid didn't die—so now you're in town to figure out what the hell went wrong."

Barrowill's eyes darkened, and he shook his head. "This is no business of yours. Leave."

"See, that's the thing," I said. "It is my business. My client is worried about his kid."

Barrowill narrowed his eyes again. "Irving."

"Irwin," I corrected him.

"Go back to Chicago, wizard," he said. "You're in my territory now."

"This isn't a smart move for you," I said. "The kid's connected. If anything bad happens to him, you're in for trouble."

"Is that a threat?" he asked.

I shook my head. "Chuck, I've got no objection to working things out peaceably. And I've got no objection to doing it the other way. If you know my reputation, then you know what a sincere guy I am."

"Perhaps I should kill you now."

"Here, in public?" I asked. "All these witnesses? You aren't going to do that."

"No?"

"No. Even if you win, you lose. You're just hoping to scare me off." I nodded toward his goons. "Ghouls, right? It's going to take more than two, Chuck. Hell, I like fighting ghouls. No matter what I do to them, I never feel bad about it afterward." Barrowill missed the reference, like the monsters usually do.

He looked at me, then at his Rolex. "I'll give you until midnight to leave the state. After that, you're gone. One way or another."

"Hang on," I said, "I'm terrified. Let me catch my breath."

Barrowill's eyes shifted color slightly, from a deep green to a much paler, angrier shade of green-gold. "I react poorly to those who threaten my family's well-being, Dresden."

"Yeah. You're a regular Ozzie Nelson. John Walton. Ben Cartwright."

"Excuse me?"

"Mr. Drummond? Charles . . . in Charge? No?"

"What are you blabbering about?"

"Hell's bells, man. Don't any of you White Court bozos ever watch television? I'm giving you pop reference gold, here. Gold."

Barrowill stared at me with opaque, reptilian eyes. Then he said, simply, "Midnight." He took two steps back before he turned his back on me and got into his car. His goons both gave me hard looks before they, too, got into the car and pulled away.

I watched the car roll out. Despite the attitude I'd given Barrowill, I knew better than to take him lightly. Any vampire is a dangerous foe—and one of them with holdings and resources and his own personal brute squad was more so. Not only that but . . . from his point of view, I was messing around with his little girl's best interests. The vampires of the White Court were, to a degree, as dangerous as they were because they were partly human. They had human emotions, human motivations, human reactions. Barrowill could be as irrationally protective of his family as anyone else.

Except that they were also *inhuman*. All of those human drives were intertwined with a parasitic spirit they called a Hunger, where all the power and hunger of their vampire parts came from.

Take one part human faults and insecurities and add it to one part inhuman power and motivation. What do you get?

Trouble.

"Barrowill?" Officer Dean asked me. "The oil guy? He keeps a stable. Of congressmen."

"Yeah, probably the same guy," I said. "All vampires like having money and status. It makes their lives easier."

Dean snorted. "Every vampire. And every nonvampire."

"Heh," I said. "Point."

"You were in a fix," he said. "Tell the girl, you might wreck her. Don't tell her, and you might wreck her and Kid Bigfoot both. Either way, somebody's dad has a bone to pick with you."

"Pretty much."

"Seems to me a smart guy would have washed his hands of the whole mess and left town."

I shrugged. "Yeah. But I was the only guy there."

Forest isn't exactly the dominant terrain in Norman, but there are a few trees, here and there. The point where I'd agreed to meet with River Shoulders was in the center of the Oliver Wildlife Preserve, which was a stand of woods that had been donated to the university for research purposes. As I hiked out into the little wood, it occurred to me that meeting River Shoulders there was like rendezvousing with Jaws in a kiddy wading pool—but he'd picked the spot, so whatever floated the big guy's boat.

It was dark out, and I drew my silver pentacle amulet off my neck to use for light. A whisper of will and a muttered word, and the little symbol glowed with a dim blue light that would let me walk without bumping into a tree. It took me maybe five minutes to get to approximately the right area, and River Shoulders's soft murmur of greeting came to me out of the dark.

We sat down together on a fallen tree, and I told him what I'd learned.

He sat in silence for maybe two minutes after I finished.

Then he said, "My son has joined himself to a parasite."

I felt a flash of mild outrage. "You could think of it that way," I said.

"What other way is there?"

"That he's joined himself to a girl. The parasite just came along for the ride."

River Shoulders exhaled a huge breath. It sounded like those pneumatic machines they use to elevate cars at the repair shop. "I see. In your view, the girl is not dangerous. She is innocent."

"She's both," I said. "She can't help being born what she is, any more than you or I."

River Shoulders grunted.

"Have your people encountered the White Court before?"

He grunted again.

"Because the last time I helped Irwin out . . . I remember being struck by the power of his aura when he was only fourteen. A long-term draining spell that should have killed him only left him sleepy." I eyed him. "But I don't feel anything around you. Stands to reason, your aura would be an order of magnitude greater than your kid's. That's why you've been careful never to touch me. You're keeping your power hidden from me, aren't you?"

"Maybe."

I snorted. "Just the kind of answer I'd expect from a wizard."

"It is not something we care for outsiders to know," he said. "And we are not wizards. We see things differently than mortals. You people are dangerous."

"Heh," I said, and glanced up at his massive form beside mine. "Between the two of us, I'm the dangerous one."

"Like a child waving around his father's gun," River Shoulders said. Something in his voice became gentler. "Though some of you are better than others about it, I admit."

"My point is," I said, "the kid's got a life force like few I've seen. When Connie's Hunger awakened, she fed on him without any kind of restraint, and he wound up with nothing worse than a hangover. Could be that he could handle a life with her just fine."

River Shoulders nodded slowly. His expression might have been thoughtful. It was too dark, and his features too blunt and chiseled to be sure.

"The girl seems genuinely fond of him. And he of her. I mean, I'm not an expert in these things, but they seem to like each other, and even when they have a difference of opinions, they fight fair. That's a good sign." I squinted at him. "Do you really think he's in danger?"

"Yes," River Shoulders said. "They have to kill him now."

I blinked. "What?"

"This . . . creature. This Barrowill."

"Yeah?"

"It sent its child to this place with the intention that she meet a young man and feed upon him and unknowingly kill him."

"Yeah."

River Shoulders shook his huge head sadly. "What kind of monster does that to its children?"

"Vampires," I said. "It isn't uncommon, from what I hear."

"Because they hurt," River Shoulders said. "Barrowill remembers his own first lover. He remembers being with her. He remembers her death. And his wendigo has had its hand on his heart ever since. It shaped his life."

"Wendigo?"

River Shoulders waved a hand. "General term. Spirit of hunger. Can't ever be sated."

"Ah, gotcha."

"Now, Barrowill. He had his father tell him that this was how it had to be. That it had to be that way to make him a good vampire. So this thing that turned him into a murdering monster is actually a good thing. He spends his whole life trying to convince himself of that." River nodded slowly. "What happens when his child does something differently?"

I felt like a moron. "It means that what his father told him was a lie. It means that maybe he didn't have to be like he is. It means that he's been lying to himself. About everything."

River Shoulders spread his hands, palm up, as if presenting the fact. "That kind of father has to make his children in his own image. He has to make the lie true."

"He has to make sure Connie kills Irwin," I said. "We've got to get him out of there. Maybe both of them."

"How?" River Shoulders said. "She doesn't know. He only knows a little. Neither knows enough to be wise enough to run."

"They shouldn't have to run," I growled.

"Avoiding a fight is always better than not avoiding one."

"Disagree," I said. "Some fights should be sought out. And fought. And won."

River Shoulders shook his head. "Your father's gun." I sensed a deep current of resistance in River Shoulders on this subject—one that I would never be able to bridge, I suspected. River just wasn't a fighter. "Would you agree it was wisest if they both fled?"

"In this case . . . it might, yeah. But I think it would only delay the confrontation. Guys like Barrowill have long arms. If he obsesses over it, he'll find them sooner or later."

"I have no right to take his child from him," River Shoulders said. "I am only interested in Irwin."

"Well, I'm not going to be able to separate them," I said. "Irwin nearly started swinging at me when I went anywhere close to that subject." I paused, then added, "But he might listen to you."

River Shoulders shook his head. "He's right. I got no right to walk in and smash his life to splinters after being so far away so long. He'd never listen to me. He's got a lot of anger in him. Maybe for good reasons."

"You're his father," I said. "That might carry more weight than you think."

"I should not have involved you in this," he said. "I apologize for that, wizard. You should go. Let me sort this out on my own."

I eyed River Shoulders.

The big guy was powerful, sure, but he was also slow. He took his time making decisions. He played things out with enormous patience. He was clearly ambivalent over what kind of involvement he should have with his son. It might take him months of observation and cogitation to make a choice.

Most of us don't live that way. I was sure Barrowill didn't. If the vampire was moving, he might be moving now. Like, right now.

"In this particular instance, River Shoulders, you are not thinking clearly," I said. "Action must be taken soon. Preferably tonight."

"I will be what I am," River said firmly.

I stood up from the log and nodded. "Okay," I said. "Me too."

I put in a call to my fellow Warden, "Wild Bill" Meyers, in Dallas, but got an answering service. I left a message that I was in Norman and needed his help, but I had little faith that he'd show up in time. The real downside to being a wizard is that we void the warrantees of anything technological every time we sneeze. Cell phones are worse than useless in our hands, and it makes communications a challenge at times though that was far from the only possible obstacle. If Bill was in, he'd have picked up his phone. He had a big area for his beat and likely had problems of his own—but since Dallas was only three hours away (assuming his car didn't break down), I could hold out hope that he might roll in by morning.

So I got in my busted-up old Volkswagen, picked up a prop, and drove up to the campus alone. I parked somewhere where I would probably get a ticket. I planned to ignore it. Anarchists have a much easier time finding parking spots.

I got out and walked toward one of the smaller dorm buildings on campus. I didn't have my wizard's staff with me, on account of how weird it looked to walk around with one, but my blasting rod was hanging from its tie inside my leather duster. I doubted I would need it, but better to have it and not need it than the other way around. I got my prop and trudged across a short bit of turquoise-tinted grass to the honors dorms, where Irwin lived. They were tiny, for that campus, maybe five stories, with the building laid out in four right-angled halls, like a plus sign. The door was locked. There's always that kind of security in a dorm building, these days.

I rapped on the glass with my knuckles until a passing student noticed. I held up a cardboard box from the local Pizza 'Spress, and tried to look like I needed a break. I needn't have tried so hard. The kid's eyes were bloodshot and glassy. He was baked on something. He opened the door for me without blinking.

"Thanks."

"No problem," he said.

"He was supposed to meet me at the doors," I said. "You see a guy named, uh . . . " I checked the receipt that was taped to the box. "Irwin Pounder?"

"Pounder, hah," the kid said. "He'll be in his room. Fourth floor, south hall, third door on the left. Just listen for the noise."

"Music?"

He tittered. "Not exactly."

I thanked him and ambled up the stairs, which were getting to be a lot harder on my knees than they used to be. Maybe I needed orthopedic shoes or something.

I got to the second floor before I felt it. There was a tension in the air, something that made my heart speed up and my skin feel hot. A few steps farther, and I started breathing faster and louder. It wasn't until I got to the third floor that I remembered that the most dangerous aspect of a psychic assault is that the victim almost never realizes that it's actually happening.

I stopped and threw up my mental defenses in a sudden panic, and the surge of adrenaline and fear suddenly overcame the tremors of restless need that I'd been feeling. The air was thick with psychic power of a nature I'd experienced once before, back in the Raith Deeps. That was when Lara Raith had unleashed the full force of her come hither against her own father, the White King, drowning his mind in imposed lust and desire to please her. He'd been her puppet ever since.

This was the same form of attack, though there were subtle differences. It had to be Barrowill. He'd moved even faster than I'd feared. I kept my mental shields up as I picked up my pace. By the time I reached the fourth floor, I heard the noise the amiable toker had mentioned.

It was sex. Loud sex. A lot of it.

I dropped the pizza and drew my blasting rod. It took me about five seconds to realize what was happening. Barrowill must have been pushing Connie, psychically—forcing her to continue feeding and feeding after she would normally have stopped. He wanted her to kill Irwin like a good little vampire, and the overflow was spilling out onto the entire building.

Not that it takes much to make college kids interested in sex, but in this instance, they had literally gone wild. When I looked down the four hallways, doors were standing wide open. Couples and . . . well, the only word that really applied was *clusters* of kids were in the act, some of them right out in the hall. Imagine an act of lust. It was going on in at least two of those four hallways.

I turned down Irwin's hall, channeling my will into my blasting rod—and yes, I'm aware of the Freudian irony, here.

The carved runes along its length began to burn with silver and scarlet light as the power built up in it. A White Court vampire is practically a pussycat compared to some of the other breeds on the planet, but I'd once seen one of them twist a pair of fifty-pound steel dumbbells around one another to make a point. I might not have much time to throw down on Barrowill in these narrow quarters, and my best chance was to put him down hard the instant I saw him.

I moved forward as silently as I knew how, stepping around a pair of couples who were breaking some sort of municipal statute, I was sure. Then I leaned back and kicked open the door to Irwin's room.

The place looked like a small tornado had gone through it.

Books and clothing and bedclothes and typical dorm room décor had been scattered everywhere. The chair next to a small study desk had been knocked over. A laptop computer lay on its side, showing what I'd once been told was a blue screen of death. The bed had fallen onto its side, where two of the legs appeared to have snapped off.

Connie and Irwin were there, and the haze of lust rolling off the ingénue succubus was a second psychic cyclone. I barely managed to push away. Irwin had her pinned against the wall in a corner. His muscles strained against his skin, and his breath came in dry, labored gasps, but he never stopped moving.

He wasn't being gentle, and Connie apparently didn't mind.

Her eyes were a shade of silver, metallic silver, as if they'd been made of chrome, reflecting the room around her like tiny, warped mirrors. She'd sunk her fingers into the drywall to the second knuckle on either side of her to hang on, and her body was rolling in a strained arch in time with his motion. They were gratuitously enthusiastic about the whole thing.

And I hadn't gotten laid in forever.

"Irwin!" I shouted.

Shockingly, I didn't capture his attention.

"Connie!"

I didn't capture hers, either.

I couldn't let the . . . the, uh, process continue. I had no idea how long it might take, or how resistant to harm Irwin might be, but it would be stupid to do nothing and hope for the best.

While I was trying to figure out how to break it up before someone lost an eye, I heard the door of the room across the hall open behind me. The sights and sounds and the haze of psychic influence had my mental processes running at less than peak performance. I didn't process the sound into a threat until Barrowill slugged me on the back of the head with something that felt like a lump of solid ivory.

I don't even remember hitting the floor.

• • •

When I woke up, I had a Sasquatch-sized headache, my wrists and ankles were killing me. Half a dozen of Barrowill's goons were all literally kneeling on me to hold me down. Every single one of them had a knife pressed close to one of my major arteries.

Also, my pants had shrunk by several sizes.

I was still in Irwin's dorm room, but things had changed. Irwin was on his back on the floor, Connie astride him. Her features had changed, shifted subtly. Her skin seemed to glow with pale light. Her eyes were empty white spheres. Her cheekbones stood out more harshly against her face, and her hair was a sweat-dampened, wild mane that clung to her cheeks and her parted lips. She was moving as if in slow motion, her fingernails digging into Irwin's chest.

Barrowill's psychic assault was still under way, and Connie's presence had become something so vibrant and penetrating that for a second I thought there might have been a minor earthquake going on. I had to get to that girl. I *had* to.

If I didn't, I was going to lose my mind with need. My instant reaction upon opening my eyes was to struggle to get closer to her on pure reflex.

The goons held me down, and I screamed in protest—but at least being a captive had kept me from doing something stupid and gave me an instant's cold realization that my shields were down. I threw them up again as hard as I could, but the Barrowills had been in my head too long. I barely managed to grab hold of my reason.

The kid looked awful. His eyes were glazed. He wasn't moving with Connie so much as his body was randomly shaking in independent spasms. His head lolled from one side to the other, and his mouth was open. A strand of drool ran from his mouth to the floor.

Barrowill had righted the fallen chair. He sat upon it with one ankle resting on his other knee, his arms folded. His expression was detached, clinical, as he watched his daughter killing the young man she loved.

"Barrowill," I said. My voice came out hoarse and rough. "Stop this."

The vampire directed his gaze to me and shook his head.

"It's after midnight, Dresden. It's time for Cinderella to return to her real life."

"You son of a bitch," I snarled. "She's killing him." A small smile touched one corner of his mouth. "Yes. Beautifully. Her Hunger is quite strong." He made a vague gesture with one hand. "Does he seem upset about it? He's a mortal. And mortals are all born to die. The only question is how and in how much pain."

"There's this life thing that happens in between," I snarled.

"And many more where his came from." Barrowill's eyes went chill. "His. And yours."

"What do you mean?"

"When she's finished, we leave. You're dessert."

A lump of ice settled in my stomach, and I swallowed. All things considered, I was becoming a little worried about the outcome of this situation. *Talk, Harry. Keep him talking. You've never met a vampire who didn't love the sound of his own voice. Something could change the situation if you play for time.*

"Why not do it before I woke up?" I asked.

"This way is more efficient," Barrowill said. "If a young athlete takes Ecstasy, and his heart fails, there may be a candlelight vigil, but there won't be an investigation. Two dead men? One of them a private investigator? There will be questions." He shrugged a shoulder. "And I don't care for you to bequest me your death curse, wizard. But once Connie has you, you won't have enough left of your mind to speak your own name, much less utter a curse."

"The Raiths are going to kill you if you drag the Court and the Council into direct opposition," I said.

"The Raiths will never know. I own twenty ghouls, Dresden, and they're always hungry. What they leave of your corpse won't fill a moist sponge."

Connie suddenly ceased moving altogether. Her skin had become pure ivory white, She shuddered, her breaths coming in ragged gasps. She tilted her head back and a low, throaty moan came out of her throat. I've had sex that wasn't as good as Connie sounded.

Dammit, Dresden. Focus.

I was out of time.

"The Council will find out, Chuck. They're wizards. Finding unfindable information is what they do."

He smirked. "I think we both know that their reputation is very well constructed."

We *did* both know that. Dammit. "You think nobody's going to miss me?" I asked. "I have friends, you know."

Barrowill suddenly leaned forward, focusing on Connie, his eyes becoming a few shades lighter. "Perhaps, Dresden. But your friends are not here."

Then there was a crash so loud that it shook the building.

Barrowill's sleek, black Lincoln Town Car came crashing through the dorm room's door, taking a sizable portion of the wall with it. The ghouls holding me down were scattered by the debris, and fine dust filled the air.

I started coughing at once, but I could see what had happened. The car had come through from the far side of this wing of the dorm, smashing through the room where Barrowill had waited in ambush. The car had crossed the hall and wound up with its bumper and front tires resting inside Irwin's room. It had smashed a massive hole in the outer brick wall of the building, leaving it gaping open to the night.

That got everyone's attention. For an instant, the room was perfectly silent and perfectly still. The ghoul chauffeur still sat in the driver's seat—only his head wobbled loosely, leaning at a right angle to the rest of his neck.

"Hah," I cackled, wheezing. "Hah, hah. Heh bah, hah, hah. Moron."

A large figure leapt up to the hole in the exterior wall and landed in the room across the hall, hitting with a crunch only slightly less massive than the car had made. I swear to you, if I'd heard that sound effect they used to use when Steve Austin jumped somewhere, I would not have been shocked. The other room was unlit, and the newcomer was a massive, threatening shadow.

He slapped a hand the size of a big cookie tray on the floor and let out a low, rumbling sound like nothing I'd ever heard this side of an amplified bass guitar. It was music. You couldn't have written it in musical notation, any more than you could write the music of a thunderstorm, or write lyrics to the song of a running stream. But it was music nonetheless.

Power like nothing I had ever encountered surged out from that impact, a deep, shuddering wave that passed visibly through the dust in the air. The ceiling and the walls and the floor sang in resonance with the note and impact alike, and Barrowill's psychic assault was swept away like a sand castle before the tide.

Connie's eyes flooded with color, changing from pure, empty whiteness back to a rich blue as deep and rich as a glacial lake, and the humanity came flooding back into her features. The sense of wild panic in the air suddenly vanished, and for another timeless instant, everything, everything in that night went utterly silent and still.

Holy.

Crap.

I've worked with magic for decades, and take it from me, it really isn't very different from anything else in life. When you work with magic, you rapidly realize that it is far easier to disrupt than to create, far more difficult to mend than to destroy.

Throw a stone into a glass-smooth lake, and ripples will wash over the whole thing. Making waves with magic instead of a rock would have been easy.

But if you can make that lake smooth again—that's one hell of a trick.

That surge of energy didn't attack anything or anybody. It didn't destroy Barrowill's assault.

It made the water smooth again.

Strength-of-a-River-in-his-Shoulders opened his eyes, and his fury made them burn like coals in the shadows—but he simply crouched, doing nothing.

All of Barrowill's goons remained still, wide eyes flicking from River to Barrowill and back.

"Back off, Chuck," I said. "He's giving you a chance to walk away. Take him up on it."

The vampire's expression was completely blank as he stood among the debris. He stared at River Shoulders for maybe three seconds—and then I saw movement behind River Shoulders.

Clawed hands began to grip the edges of the hole behind River. Wicked, bulging red eyes appeared. Monstrous-looking *things* in the same general shape as a human appeared in complete silence.

Ghouls.

Barrowill didn't have six goons with him.

He'd brought them *all*.

Barrowill spat toward River, bared his teeth and screamed, "Kill it!"

And it was on.

Everything went completely insane. The human-shaped ghouls in the room bounded forward, their faces and limbs contorting, tearing their way out of their cheap suits as they assumed their true forms. More ghouls poured in through the hole in the wall like a swarm of panicked roaches. I couldn't get an accurate count of the enemy—the action was too fast. But twenty sounded about right. Twenty flesh-rending, superhumanly strong and durable predators flung themselves onto River Shoulders in an overwhelming wave. He vanished beneath a couple of tons of hungry ghoul. It was *not* a fair fight.

Barrowill should have brought more goons.

There was an enormous bellow, a sound that could only have been made by a truly massive set of lungs, and ghouls exploded outward from River Shoulders like so much hideous shrapnel. Several were flung back out of the building. Others slammed into walls with so much force that they shattered the drywall. One of them went through the ceiling, then fell limply back down into the room—only to be caught by the neck in one of River Shoulders's massive hands. He squeezed, crushing the ghoul's neck like soft clay, and there was an audible pop.

The ghoul spasmed once, then River flung the corpse into the nearest batch of monsters.

After that, it was clobbering time.

Barrowill moved fast, seizing Connie and darting out the door. I looked around frantically and spotted one of the knives the goons had been holding before they transformed. My hands and ankles had been bound in those plastic restraining strips, and I could barely feel my fingers, but I managed to pick up the knife and cut my legs free. Then I put it on the front bumper of the Lincoln, stepped on it with one foot to hold it in place, and after a few moments managed to cut my hands loose as well.

The dorm sounded like a medley of pay-per-view wrestling and the *Island of Doctor Moreau*. Ghouls shrieked. River Shoulders roared. Very, very disoriented students screamed. The wails and floor shook with impact again and again as River Shoulders flung ghouls around like so many softballs. Ghoulish blood spattered the walls and the ceiling, green-brown and putrid-smelling, and as strong as he was, River Shoulders wasn't pitching a shutout. The ghouls' claws and fangs had sunk into him, covering him in punctures and lacerations, and his scarlet blood mixed with theirs on the various surfaces.

I tried to think unobtrusive thoughts, stayed low, and went to Irwin. He still looked awful, but he was breathing hard and steady, and he'd already begun blinking and trying to focus his eyes.

"Irwin!" I shouted. "Irwin! Where's her purse?"

"Whuzza?" Irwin mumbled.

"Connie's purse! I've got to help Connie! Where is her purse?" Irwin's eyes almost focused. "Connie?"

"Oh never *mind*." I started ransacking the dorm room until I found Connie's handbag. She had a brush in it. The brush was liberally festooned with her blond hairs.

I swept a circle into the dust on the floor, tied the hair around my pentacle amulet and invested the circle with a whisper of will. Then I quickly worked the tracking spell that was generally my bread and butter when I was doing investigator stuff. When I released the magic, it rushed down into Connie's borrowed hair, and my amulet lurched sharply Out of plumb and held itself steady at a thirty- or forty-degree angle. Connie went thataway.

I ducked a flying ghoul, leapt over a dying ghoul, and staggered down the hall at my best speed while the blood went back into my feet.

I had gone down one whole flight of stairs without falling when the angle on the amulet changed again. Barrowill had gone down one floor, then taken off down one of the residential hallways toward the fire escape at the far end. He'd bypassed security by ripping the door off its hinges, then flinging it into the opposite wall. Kids were scattering out of the hallway, looking either horrified or disappointed. Some both. Barrowill had reached the far end, carrying his daughter over one shoulder, and was headed for the fire door.

Barrowill had been savvy enough to divest me of my accoutrements, but I was still a wizard, dammit, blasting rod or no. I drew up my will, aimed low, and snarled, "*Forzare!*" Pure kinetic force lashed invisibly through the air and caught Barrowill at the ankles. It kicked both of his feet up into the air, and he took a pratfall onto the floor. Connie landed with a grunt and bounced to one side. She lay there dazed and blinking.

Barrowill slithered back up to his feet, spinning toward me, and producing a pistol in one hand. I lurched back out of the line of fire as the gun barked twice, and bullets went by me with a double hiss. I went to my knees and bobbed my head out into the hall again for a quick peek, jerking it back immediately. Barrowill was picking Connie up. His bullet went through the air where my head would have been if I'd been standing.

"Don't be a moron, Harry," I said. "You came for the kid. He's safe. That's all you were obligated to do. Let it g—oh who am I kidding. There's a girl."

I didn't have to beat the vampire—I just had to slow him down long enough for River Shoulders to catch up to him . . . assuming River did pursue.

I took note of which wing Barrowill was fleeing through and rushed down the stairs to the ground floor. Then I left the building and sprinted to the far end of that wing.

Barrowill slammed the emergency exit open and emerged from the building. He was moving fast, but he also had his daughter to carry, and she'd begun to resist him, kicking and thrashing, slowing him down. She tugged him off balance just as he shot at me again, and it went wide. I slashed at him with another surge of force, but this time I wasn't aiming for his feet—I went for the gun. The weapon leapt out of his hands and went spinning away, shattering against the bricks of the dorm's outer wall. Another blast knocked Connie off his shoulder, and she let out a little shriek. Barrowill staggered, then let out a snarl of frustration and charged me at a speed worthy of the Flash's understudy.

I flung more force at him, but Barrowill bobbed to one side, evading the blast. I threw myself away from the vampire and managed to roll with the punch he sent at my head. He caught me an inch or two over one eyebrow, the hardest and most impact-resistant portion of the human skull. That and the fact that I'd managed to rob it of a little of its power meant that he only sent me spinning wildly away, my vision completely obscured by pain and little silver stars. He was furious, his power rolling over me like a sudden deluge of ice water, to the point where crystals of frost formed on my clothing.

Barrowill followed up, his eyes murderous—and then Bigfoot Irwin bellowed, "Connie!" and slammed into Barrowill at the hip, using his body as a living spear. Barrowill was flung to one side, and Irwin pressed his advantage, still screaming, coming down atop the vampire and pounding him with both fists in elemental violence, his sunken eyes mad with rage. "Connie! Connie!"

I tried to rise but couldn't seem to make it past one knee. So all I could do was watch as the furious scion of River Shoulders unleashed everything he had on a ranking noble of the White Court. Barrowill could have been much stronger than a human being if he'd had the gas in the tank—but he'd spent his energy on his psychic assault, and it had drained him. He still thrashed powerfully, but he was no match for the enraged young man. Irwin slammed Barrowill's nose flat against his face. I saw one of the vampire's teeth go flying into the night air. Slightly too-pale blood began to splash against Irwin's fists.

Christ. If the kid killed Barrowill, the White Court would consider it an act of war. All kinds of horrible things could unfold. "Irwin!" I shouted. "Irwin, stop!"

Kid Bigfoot didn't listen to me.

I lurched closer to him but only made it about six inches before my head whirled so badly that I fell onto my side. "Irwin, stop!" I looked around and saw Connie staring dazedly at the struggle. "Connie!" I said. "Stop him! Stop him!"

Meanwhile, Irwin had beaten Barrowill to within an inch of his life—and now he raised his joined hands over his head, preparing for a sledgehammer blow to Barrowill's skull.

A small, pretty hand touched his wrist.

"Irwin," Connie said gently. "Irwin, no."

"He tried," Irwin panted. "Tried. Hurt you."

"This isn't the way," Connie said.

"Bad man," Irwin growled.

"But you aren't," Connie said, her voice very soft. "Irwin. He's still my daddy."

Connie couldn't have physically stopped Irwin—but she didn't need to. The kid blinked several times, then looked at her. He slowly lowered his hands, and Connie leaned down to kiss his forehead gently. "Shhhh," she said. "Shhhh. I'm still here. It's over, baby. It's over."

"Connie," Irwin said, and leaned against her.

I let out a huge sigh of relief and sank back onto the ground.

My head hurt.

Officer Dean stared at me for a while. He chewed on a toothpick and squinted at me. "Got some holes."

"Yeah?" I asked. "Like what?"

"Like all those kids saw a Bigfoot and them whatchamacalits. Ghouls. How come they didn't say anything?"

"You walked in on them while they were all still trying to put their clothes back on. After flinging themselves into random sex with whoever happened to be close to them. They're all denying that this ever happened right now."

"Hngh," Dean said. "What about the ghoul corpses?"

"After Irwin dragged their boss up to the fight, the ghouls quit when they saw him. River Shoulders told them all to get out of his sight and take their dead with them. They did."

Dean squinted and consulted a list. "Pounder is gone. So is Connie Barrowill. Not officially missing, or nothing. Not yet. But where are they?"

I looked at Dean and shrugged.

I'd seen ghouls in all kinds of situations before—but I'd never seen them whipped into submission. Ghouls fought to the grisly, messy end. That was what they did. But River Shoulders had been more than their match. He'd left several of them alive when he could have killed them to the last, and he'd found their breaking point when Irwin had dragged Barrowill in by his hair. Ghouls could take a huge beating, but River Shoulders had given them one like I'd never seen, and when he ordered them to take their master and their dead and never to return, they'd snapped to it.

"Thanks, Connie," I groaned as she settled me onto a section of convenient rubble. I was freezing. The frost on my clothes was rapidly melting away, but the chill had settled inward.

The girl looked acutely embarrassed, but that wasn't in short supply in that dorm. That hallway was empty of other students for the moment, though. We had the place to ourselves, though I judged that the authorities would arrive in some form before long.

Irwin came over with a dust-covered blanket and wrapped it around her. He'd scrounged a ragged towel for himself though it did more to emphasize his physique than to hide it. The kid was ripped.

"Thank you, Irwin," she said.

He grunted. Physically, he'd bounced back from the nearly lethal feeding like a rubber freaking ball. Maybe River Shoulders s water-smoothing spell had done something to help that.

Mentally, he was slowly refocusing. You could see the gleam coming back into his eyes. Until that happened, he'd listened to Connie. A guy could do worse.

"I . . . " Connie shook her head. "I remember all of it. But I have no idea what just happened." She stared at River Shoulders for a moment, her expression more curious than fearful. "You . . . You stopped something bad from happening, I think."

"Yeah, he did," I confirmed.

Connie nodded toward him in a grateful little motion.

"Thank you. Who are you?"

"Irwin's dad," I said.

Irwin blinked several times. He stared blankly at River Shoulders.

"Hello," River rumbled. How something that large and that powerful could sit there bleeding from dozens of wounds and somehow look sheepish was beyond me. "I am very sorry we had to meet like that. I had hoped for something quieter. Maybe with music. And good food."

"You can't stay," I said to River. "The authorities are on the way."

River made a rumbling sound of agreement. "This is a disaster. What I did . . . " He shook his head. "This was in such awful taste."

"Couldn't have happened to nicer guys, though," I said.

"Wait," Connie said. "Wait. What the hell just happened here?"

Irwin put a hand on her shoulder, and said, to me, "She's . . . she's a vampire. Isn't she?"

I blinked and nodded at him. "How did . . . ?"

"Paranet," he said. "There's a whole page."

"Wait," Connie said again. "A . . . what? Am I going to sparkle or something?"

"God, no," said Irwin and I, together.

"Connie," I said, and she looked at me. "You're still exactly who you were this morning. And so is Irwin. And that's what counts. But right now, things are going to get really complicated if the cops walk in and start asking you questions. Better if they just never knew you were here."

"This is all so . . . " She shook her head. Then she stared at River Shoulders. Then at me. "Who are you?"

I pointed at me, and said, "Wizard." I pointed at River. "Bigfoot." I pointed at Irwin. "Son of Bigfoot." I pointed at her. "Vampire. Seriously."

"Oh," she said faintly.

"I'll explain it," Irwin told her quietly. He was watching River Shoulders.

River held out his huge hands to either side and shrugged. "Hello, son."

Irwin shook his head slowly. "I . . . never really . . . " He sucked in a deep breath, squared off against his father, and said, "Why?"

And there it was. What had to be the Big Question of Irwin's life.

"My people," he said. "Tradition is very important to them. If I acknowledged you . . . they would have insisted that certain traditions be observed. It would have consumed your life. And I didn't want that for you. I didn't want that for your mother. I wanted your world to be wider than mine."

Bigfoot Irwin was silent for a long moment. Then he scratched at his head with one hand and shrugged. "Tonight . . . really explains a lot." He nodded slowly. "Okay. We aren't done talking. But okay."

"Let's get you out of here," River said. "Get you both taken care of. Answer all your questions."

"What about Harry?" Irwin said.

I couldn't get any more involved with the evident abduction of a scion of the White Court. River's mercy had probably kept the situation from going completely to hell, but I wasn't going to drag the White Council's baggage into the situation. "You guys go on," I told them. "I do this kind of thing all the time. I'll be fine."

"Wow, seriously?" Irwin asked.

"Yeah," I said. "I've been in messier situations than this. And . . . it's probably better if Connie's dad has time to cool off before you guys talk again. River Shoulders can make sure you have that time."

Outside, a cart with flashing bulbs on it had pulled up.

"River," I said. "Time's up."

River Shoulders rose and nodded deeply to me. "I'm sorry that I interfered. It seemed necessary."

"I'm willing to overlook it," I said. "All things considered." His face twisted into a very human-looking smile, and he extended his hand to Irwin. "Son."

Irwin took his father's hand, one arm still around Connie, and the three of them didn't vanish so much as . . . just become less and less relevant to the situation. It happened over the course of two or three seconds, as that same nebulous, somehow transparent power that River had used earlier enfolded them. And then they were all gone.

Boots crunched down the hall, and a uniformed officer with a nametag reading DEAN burst in, one hand on his gun.

Dean eyed me, then said, "That's all you know, huh?"

"That's the truth," I said. "I told you that you wouldn't believe it. You gonna let me go now?"

"Oh, hell no," Dean said. "That's the craziest thing I've ever heard. You're stoned out of your mind or insane. Either way, I'm going to put you in the drunk tank until you have a chance to sleep it off."

"You got any aspirin?" I asked.

"Sure," he said, and got up to get it.

My head ached horribly, and I was pretty sure I hadn't heard the end of this, but I was clear for now. "Next time, Dresden," I muttered to myself, "just take the gold."

Then Officer Dean put me in a nice quiet cell with a nice quiet cot, and there I stayed until Wild Bill Meyers showed up the next morning and bailed me out.

Jim Butcher is the *New York Times* bestselling author of the Dresden Files and the Codex Alera series. The fifteenth novel featuring Harry Dresden, *Skin Game*, will be published later this year. Butcher also has a new steampunk series, the Cinder Spires, that will be starting soon. He enjoys fencing, martial arts, singing, bad science-fiction movies, and live-action gaming. He lives in Missouri with his wife, son, and a vicious guard dog. You may learn more at www.jim-butcher.com.

*Neighbors who walk past the house keep on moving; dogs pull their
owners across to the other side of the street . . .*

EVERYTHING MUST GO

Brooke Wonders

*Split-level ranch-style home features a spacious and private fenced backyard with a
covered deck and small dog run.*

The blue-gray house at 1414 Linden Dr. is afraid of the dark. The foreclosure
crisis hit its neighborhood hard, and in house after house, lights wink out and
never turn back on. The house at 1414 waits for new families to move in, and
sometimes they do, but more often than not the owners abandon their property.
Linden Drive grows increasingly desolate, and 1414 clings to the warmth and
safety of its inhabitants, sure that it is too well-loved to be left behind.

Its family owns a dog, an ancient mutt with a gray-frosted muzzle who
spends most of his time in the backyard, sprawled on his side in the brown
grass. The house has long admired the diligence with which the mutt defends
its home. When neighbors pass by with their own dogs, Lucky drags himself
over to the gate connecting his run to the front yard and lets loose a fit of
barking. But one morning in late summer, a man with two collies strolls past,
and Lucky doesn't bark.

Two thick branches of English ivy pull away from 1414's exterior and wend
their way around the corpse. The rusted hinges of its cellar-door croon a lullaby
of creaks and whines as they gape wide to receive Lucky. The house pulls the
vine-choked body deep inside its walls. Tucked between sheets of plaster and
insulation, the dog mortifies; soon the basement reeks of decay. Upstairs, a girl
mourns her lost pet.

East-facing bedroom catches morning light, a bonus in wintertime.

The daughter at fourteen is a folded-up girl of elbows, knobby knees, and
angles a which-way. She loves origami, late into every night creasing out birds

of paradise, pagodas, sea horses, and lotuses that trip from her fingertips. From her ceiling hang a thousand cranes it took her months to fold, multicolored and hopeful, made of wrapping paper, construction paper, butcher paper, wax paper, glitter paper, natural-wood-pulp paper. Origami paper proper she treasures, hoards like allowance money or dragon's gold. The house thinks of the folded-up girl as Paper, and loves her.

Corner bedroom features windows on two sides. Bright and airy!

The son is growing wings. They first appear after his thirteenth birthday party, when his mother burns the cake and then locks herself in the bathroom while his father sits alone in the garage, drinking whiskey and building birdhouses out of scrap. The son packs a suitcase and explains his plans to Paper: he'll escape out his bedroom window, run away to join the circus. His sister talks him out of it, to the house's relief. The boy's wings begin as nubbins protruding from each shoulder blade that ache and ache as he grows. By seventeen, nubbins have grown into a skeletal wing-structure, hollow bones covered in tufted feathers and long pinions, though he cannot yet lift himself off the ground. The house thinks of the winged boy as Bird, and loves him.

Third bedroom, slightly smaller—use it for storage, or turn it into baby's first bedroom.

Their mother has her own workspace wherein she fashions elaborate textile art from found objects, fabric, and yarn. Lately, though, the house has noted a desperate loneliness threaded through her. Husband at work, kids at school, she fritters away her time following the soaps, crocheting blankets only to unravel them. She ties each member of the family to her via thick silken cords, cords whose color changes depending on her mood: crimson for anger, cerulean for disappointment, jet for possessiveness, silver for regret. The house lets these strings tangle throughout the hallways, following the arcing filaments from room to room. The house tries to warm to her, but she's metal-cold, her voice scissor-sharp. The house fears her, and calls her Needle.

Two-car garage.

A grease-stained man who smells of slaughter, their father lives in the garage when he doesn't live at his butcher shop. The house envies him his children's unconditional love: they crouch at his elbows as he shingles a miniature roof, then fight over who gets to help install his latest creation. A neighborhood's worth of elaborately finished birdhouses dot the backyard, attracting flocks of cardinals, rooks, and wrens.

But the house knows where the father keeps his skeletons, round glass secrets full of intoxicating oblivion stashed everywhere: in the trunk of the car, in with the New Year's decorations, beneath the bathroom sink. When the couple'd first moved in, before there were papers or birds between them, he'd kept this secret, and long has the house tracked the ebb and flow of his addiction. It calls him Glass, for the bottles that clink like chains and sing to him from within their hiding places.

Kitchen has no dishwasher but plenty of counter space.

The teens have never seen their parents in the same room at the same time. Needle pours canned green beans and mushroom soup into a casserole dish, then retreats to the pantry just as Glass heads to the fridge for an ice water. Only once he's wandered back to the garage does she reappear. Though the parents play elaborate hide-and-seek, the walls speak; every night the teens lie awake in their beds and listen to their parents argue.

—The mortgage is too expensive; where can we cut back?

—Do we really need another birdhouse?

—We don't need more of your wall blankets, that's for sure.

—It's not a wall blanket, it's fiber-art.

—If we can afford your art, why can't we afford mine?

The house rustles the homemade tapestries that line its walls, drapings heavy with dust and guilt.

Downstairs master bedroom for maximum privacy.

The walls shout louder and louder, the house hating every resonant echo, until the only way the kids can sleep is by pressing palms deep into their ears. As if to compensate for the increase in noise, both parents have begun to fade from view. Their mother flickers in and out like TV static, as if she's trying to switch to a different channel. Their father's skin has become glass, behind which amber alcohol roils.

Bird catches his father getting dressed one morning, the flab of Glass's belly hanging translucent over his belt-buckle. He watches his father remove a fifth of Jack from its sock-drawer hideaway and down a few quick swigs. Through his father's transparent flesh, Bird can see the liquor slide slow down Glass's throat until it joins the tawny liquid sloshing waist-high. Tiny waves break against his bellybutton. The immediate difference is imperceptible, but as the days rush by, Bird watches the amber tide rise from bellybutton to chest to clavicle, until Glass has filled himself up nearly to the brim, his eyes shiny as bottle caps.

Carpeted staircase with banister leads down to the lower level.

The house wakes in the middle of the night to a boot kicking through the safety wall of the stairwell landing. It groans through every vertical beam. Glass stands on the stairs, lamplight refracted through him casting whiskey-colored cracks across the house's interior. Needle's splayed against the banister, eyes rimmed red with crying, her lip split bloody.

The next morning, Glass spackles over the hole. The house, wounded, shrinks ever smaller. Does your room seem tinier than usual? Paper asks Bird one day. Bird nods, but they've gotten older and taller; they aren't children anymore. The house is grateful for these excuses.

All bedrooms have walk-in closets

Paper folds a dollhouse. The first piece of butcher paper she cuts is massive. It creases down into an eleven-room suburban ranch home identical to her own. Then small squares for all the furnishings. She sets it up like a diorama on top of her chest-of-drawers, back in the deepest recesses of her closet where no one else goes. Its white picket fence spills off into darkness, disappearing behind her winter coats. She folds up father, mother, brother, sister, and stuffs them inside. The house notices that a streak of red mars the mother-doll's face. Once her parents have gone to bed, Paper steals matches from the pantry and sets the folded father on fire; he crumbles to ash in her metal waste-bin.

Within the hour, Glass slams out the front door. In his wake, a heavy silken thread lies twitching like a coral snake on the lawn, one crimson end severed and fraying. Needle moves methodically from room to room, packing Glass's belongings into boxes. Gasping cries push past her lips, her sorrow the crackle and shush of a blown speaker, a low rasp on repeat. The house howls wind through its eaves in mourning.

Bird seeks out Paper. Pushing open the door to her bedroom, he finds her sitting inside her closet, folding. She's trying not to cry, the hitch in each inhale synched in time to her mother. Bird catches Paper's hands in his to still their darting movements and flutters his wingtips across her fingers. She begins to comb through his feathers in long, even strokes and her breathing steadies long enough for her to confess her crime. Bird assures her that it couldn't possibly have been her fault, that she had nothing to do with Glass leaving, then helps her dispose of the small pile of new-made origami fathers that litter the floor.

Low ceiling in the living room makes for a cozy living space.

Every piece of furniture stands halved. Of the dining table, only two legs remain, its lacquered surface leaning out over empty space. Half a filament glows dimly within the halved light bulbs inside every light fixture, each under a halved lampshade. The rug is halved, and the refrigerator is definitely halved, as suddenly there's a lot less food in the house. Glass sends money, and so far they've managed to save the house, but Needle struggles to get dinner on the table.

Bird cycles from bedroom to kitchen, twice a day stopping before the half-fridge only to slam it closed in disappointment. The house remembers when it was just a wooden frame, before the contractor had installed its drywall; it imagines Bird must feel something similar: hollowed out and vulnerable.

Paper begins to watch her weight as if she hopes to become parchment, as transparent as her mother. Only the house counts how many times each day Paper locks herself in the bathroom and steps onto the scale. It dislikes the purple veins running so close to the surface of her skin, the curve of her lungs as they contract and expand within her ribcage, her bones visible like an abandoned building exposed to years of bad weather. If Bird notices his sister thinning, he says nothing.

Since Glass left, Bird sleeps on the floor of Paper's room most nights, and they lie awake talking until all hours, imagining the futures they'll have when they finally escape. Bird jokes that together they're a paper bird, one of his sister's folded cranes but with the power of flight. By their powers combined, they could fly far away from home. His broad wings span the room, a comfort. The house worries that the two teens will be divided next—half a Paper, half a Bird. It vows to keep them safe as houses.

Carpeted upstairs hallway means children can run and play in safety.

Paper grooms her brother's wings every day, and they grow in strength, though their pristine blackness is occasionally marred by molt. One morning, while finger-combing near his spine, she notices what the house has known for weeks: that several of his primary feathers have been cut about a third of the way down, at sharp angles.

That night, she pulls down all thousand of the cranes that roost against her ceiling, littering her floor with their rainbow corpses. The house admires her ingenuity, the trap she's laid to catch the wing-clipper.

Crunch, crunch in the dark and Paper leaps up to flick the light-switch. Needle's outline is a staticky blur, but her sewing shears, poised over one black wing, glisten in the sudden brightness.

Bird wakes in a rage. Before his sister's eyes, Bird's features morph into something *else*, someone the house doesn't recognize. Surely this nightmare beast can't be its own winged son? Bird's face twists into a black beak, his fingers curl into talons, and his feathers beat a furious whirlwind. He lunges at his mother, but she vanishes into white noise.

Downstairs half-bath for guests.

Their mother drifts through the hallways, visible only as a human-shaped distortion in space. Paper watches her mother pace, white-gray ants suffusing the outline of a woman. The house wonders why Needle has not yet returned to her textiles. Bins of crewel, quilting and lace clutter the craft room floor, gathering dust. The house finds this odd, as the craft room is the only space that has yet to be plagued by black holes.

Glass's exit left holes strewn everywhere—by the work bench in the garage, in front of the refrigerator, hovering over the couch in the den—and Needle keeps falling into them, a phenomenon that concerns the house. The teens generally avoid the holes, though they've accidentally created a few: Their dad has hidden bottles everywhere, and whenever they find one, it implodes into a new hole, reality warping around an empty center.

One day, while playing find-the-bottle, Paper catches Bird drinking deep from a fifth of whiskey they'd discovered not a week earlier, one she'd thought had burst into the usual hole. She snatches the bottle from his hand and shatters it against the porcelain sink. Bird's face begins to elongate into that horrible beak, skin shifting to barbed feathers, hands to scaled talons, as if he's swallowed a black hole and it's consuming him from the inside.

From the empty silence surrounding them comes the susurrus of their mother's presence. Then mother and son are wrestling on the bathroom floor, him a winged, clawed monster, her a disembodied hush and ten fingernails that rake deep red furrows down his biceps. Paper squeezes her eyes shut tight as fists.

The house knows the three of them can't go on like this, wants to help, and does what it can, battening down the insulation to keep in warmth against oncoming winter.

Master bathroom features two sinks and a separate shower area.

Paper arrives home from school to find the dim outline of her mother seated on the bathroom floor, the under-sink cabinet open and a whiskey bottle next to her. Eyes unseeing, Needle's hands clutch at empty air. A black hole shimmers unreality beneath her. Paper wants to grab her hands and pull her away from the danger, but she's been here before: If she's not terribly careful—the house has watched it happen too many times—she'll be sucked in as well.

Paper sifts through her mother's sundry crafting bins until she finds something she thinks will work: a long skein of heavy cord in pale blue. She makes a lasso of cord and loops it over her mother's shoulders, grips the end, and tugs. Needle tumbles free and the hole blinks out into memory.

Her mother lies comatose, her outline shimmering, a needle held up to light and turned this way and that so its eye flickers into and out of existence. Needle stares through her daughter, and Paper feels as invisible as she'd ever wished to be. She takes her mother's cold hand in hers. Gently she loops blue cord around Needle's bloodless fingers. Round and round it ravels. Paper is painstaking; she threads the skein about her mother's every limb in ever-tightening circles, tugging the cord taut against her mother's incorporeal corpus.

It takes all day and late into the night for Paper to wind cord, thread, yarn, and string—two full bins of material—around her mother's body, a body shaped just like her own will be someday. Wrapped up like a spindle or a mummy, Needle can once again be seen. She meets her daughter's eyes, pupils contracting and expanding in bewilderment.

Needle moves around the house more freely after rejoining the land of the visible, stacking boxes of their father's things in the garage and out of sight, returning to her crafting, even hugging Paper every so often, though Bird still won't go near her. The house, thrilled to have Needle back, stretches happily through the long wires inside its walls, solid in the surety of their connection to the outside world. The house can appreciate ties that bind.

Small attic for extra storage.

Bird's slept in the attic since his mother's attempted pinioning. He tugs the pull-down ladder up behind him each night, just to be sure. Skin mottled with brown tufts of downy feather, face craggy with shadow, he hunches his back under the weight of the full-grown wings arcing over his head. Bird has been working, saving up for his great escape, and he's finally made enough, just six days shy of eighteen.

Paper's stolen her mother's shears; with them, she cuts Bird free of the silvery blue cord binding him to Needle. She holds out a loose twist of yellow embroidery thread, one end attached to the attic furnace. He recoils, hissing, but she pats his arm to reassure him: he's tied only to his childhood home, not to Needle. His eyes are falcon-hooded; nevertheless, he allows her to encircle his wrist with the thread. It glimmers in sunlight, golden bright and joyful. He stands to his full height, aware that he's taller now than their father had been. Stretching dark wings, he's poised to swoop down from the attic window.

The house is having none of this. It bares paned-glass teeth and snaps a sill shut on Bird's boot heel. Bird and Paper cry out, and then she braces herself against the window-frame and yanks upward, and Bird loosens his shoelaces and dives downward, and there's just his black boot stuck in the house's craw as he swoops low, then speeds sky-high. Windows rove wild-eyed; doors slam open and shut, enraged. Their father's frayed red thread is still out on the lawn, its color faded to pink. Paper stares after her brother until the black dot of him winks out against the horizon, yellow thread pulled taut as it spools out thinner and thinner.

All through the night, the house growls and shudders like earthquake, terrified that soon it will be plunged into darkness. It's grown too much like Needle, in her desperation and possessiveness, and too much like Glass, wanting only to be filled. The house's fears form a yawning black hole that encompasses its plot entirely, as if the earth planned to open like a cellar door and suck the neighborhood underground like a hundred birdhouses perched atop quicksand. The house is immobile and has no means of escape, but it's seen the family deal with enough such holes to understand their operations.

The dog is in a state of advanced decomposition when the house coughs Lucky up from its bowels. It's swaddled the body in insulation, but that doesn't much contain the stench; Paper finds the corpse almost immediately. Tugging a sleeve over her nose, she rolls it into the garden with a rusted shovel and leaves it to mulch. By summertime, the remains will be skin and bones and the hydrangea blooms nearby especially lovely.

Paper walks upstairs to stand before her mirror, turning sideways as if reveling in the acute angles she's made of her body. Taking one hand in the other, she folds herself in half, then does it again and again and again. By the time the house realizes, long before it can formulate a plan to stop her, she's disappeared. Her mother finds her that evening, a single sheet of translucent paper, a note explaining what she's done. Needle and the house are left alone.

Large manicured front lawn with mature trees. Please call Arbor Realty to schedule an appointment to view this property.

A mess of bishop's weed obscures the walkway. A lattice trestle covered in ivy creeps upward toward the roof's edge. The house's eyes are shut, mouth closed and locked up tight. Neighbors who walk past keep on moving; dogs pull their owners across to the other side of the street. The house mutters, settles into its cracked foundation. It monitors the single bright yellow thread that arcs into the distance, waiting for any movement on the line, any sign that its winged boy will soon fly home.

Brooke Wonders' fiction has appeared in *Apeiron Review, Clarkesworld, Daily Science Fiction, Electric Velocipede, Mirror Dance, and Monkeybicycle,* among others. She is a graduate of Clarion 2011 and a current PhD candidate at the University of Illinois at Chicago. She blogs at girlwonders.com.

He reeled at what he saw, had to reach out and steady
himself with one hand on the mantel edge. . . .

NIGHTSIDE EYE

Terry Dowling

—◆—

The fact that the guest lounge, ballroom, whatever it had originally been, was devoid of furniture only intensified the feeling of something waiting to happen.

Jared had read the latest tender updates for the old Hydro Majestic Hotel, knew that they all listed the Delfray Room as a minor function room.

"So that's it?" he said, indicating the mantelpiece above the handsome fireplace in the eastern wall.

"That's it," Susan answered, clearly intrigued, possibly even disconcerted at knowing someone who actually wore an eye-patch like the traditional black one over Jared's left eye. Jared was thirty-six, lean enough, his features regular enough, to make him attractive to many women at first glance. The patch lent him an unexpectedly rakish air, friends and colleagues said. Susan Royce was in her late twenties, with ginger hair in a pixie crop, and was clearly taken with him—in spite of the patch, because of it, who could say? Now she led the way across the parquetry floor to the black iron fireplace, looking for a moment as if she were actually going to touch the unadorned marble ledge. "Put anything on it, it ends up on the floor."

Jared did reach out and touch the cold smooth marble. "But not immediately, I understand. It takes time."

"Not immediately, no." Susan seemed interested, well-intentioned. She was a different heritage representative than the one assigned to Martin Rathcar fifteen months before. Without Rathcar's media brouhaha, the scale of that whole publicity circus to draw attention, she may have had only a token briefing on what this evening's proceedings were all about. "But an hour, two hours later. It always happens. Used to take days, weeks, months, but it's much more frequent now, a matter of hours, sometimes minutes. Even heavy weights end up being shifted. They say it's something electro-magnetic, a freak of nature."

"You've seen it?" Jared asked. Though he'd been hoping he'd get Cilla Paul, the same heritage rep Rathcar had dealt with, things seemed to be shaping up well regardless.

"Only on CCTV. I'm still pretty new."

The Delfray Room seemed larger from this angle than it actually was. Being painted a stylish off-white probably helped create that effect. At the far end, the western end near the double doors, four long sash windows were curtained with light brown drapes, gathered back with the same tasseled silken cords as on the other westward-facing windows in the hallways of the old Hydro Majestic. Like those hallway windows, these too looked out over the vastness of the Megalong Valley, gave the spectacular views that had made the place so famous in its heyday. Now the Hydro was in its third year of being closed, officially awaiting restoration to all its former glory as a world-class spa resort if only the appropriate government, licensing, and restoration bodies could agree. Having read the various tender documents, Jared knew how dauntingly expensive it was going to be. The old Victorian and Edwardian buildings made a gentle chevron along the ridgeline, set fifty meters in from the main highway that led across the Blue Mountains from Sydney out to Lithgow, Bathurst, and beyond. It was the sort of white elephant that was so costly to maintain yet too dramatically part of the local landscape and local history to be ignored.

The late-autumn sun had already set beyond the last of the ranges. The famous view was gone from the long windows now, their old panes turned to so many mirror reflections by the light from the Deco wall sconces and the chandelier overhead. The black iron fireplace, clean but inevitably dusty, was the room's most distinctive feature, the mantel a modest afterthought by comparison, even more simple and functional than the CCTV footage had shown it to be.

"The previous owners must have become fed up with the whole thing," Jared said.

Susan nodded. "None of the various management groups ever said much about it but, you know, who wanted the publicity? It could happen at any time. It was always there. And, like I say, it's been getting more frequent."

"Hard to live with."

"They only used the Delfray Room as an overflow room for special occasions, last-minute wedding bookings, that sort of thing. They just made sure they put nothing on the mantel. Records show that the occurrences—you call them 'events,' don't you?—started soon after the hotel was first opened in 1891 as the Belgravia Hotel though very infrequently then. When it became the Hydro, only a few people knew about them. Management had to consider their more refined and sensitive clientele, so hushed things up pretty quickly. There was originally a large mirror mounted over it, quite ornate, so no one really questioned the lack of other adornment."

"Except the occasional guest who suddenly found his drink on the floor."

Susan laughed. "Exactly. The ultimate party trick. I imagine it's a bit like trying to sell or lease out a murder house. Something you just don't mention, just work around as best you can. Mr. Ryan—Jared—if you'll excuse me asking. I understand that you're not blind in that eye. You're just masking it for what's being done tonight. Is what Cilia said true? This whole thing is about seeing what's doing it?"

"That's right."

"You don't mean it's someone? A person? A ghost?"

Jared shrugged. "We can't know. Martin Rathcar proceeded from the certainty that something was doing it—whether resident poltergeist or freak of nature. He found serious funding to develop a method for seeing anomalies like this a different way."

"But the patch. I understand that—"

"Dr. Rathcar called it the Nightside Eye as a media drawcard in 2008, back when the funding proposals went in. Made it sound sexy, mysterious. He got the idea from one of those mythbuster programs on TV."

"Really. How so?"

"It seems veteran seamen aboard sailing ships in the seventeenth, eighteenth, and nineteenth centuries often wore a patch over one eye when they went below-deck. They swapped the patch from one eye to the other so they were nightsighted and could see immediately. It let them find things quickly, stopped them bumping their heads. Very practical."

Susan looked skeptical. "That really happened?"

"It's highly likely. Dr. Rathcar expanded on the idea, kept one eye completely isolated from all the customary vision tasks for nine months, took injections of several quite powerful very specific neurological regulators to intensify the 'nightside' function in that particular optic nerve."

"Biased it?"

"Many claimed so, though the regulators weren't known to be hallucinogens. More like the drugs used in eye surgery, optical trauma events, sight retrieval situations. Increased receptivity and adaptivity. Intensification of the optic process."

"I remember now. Rathcar's the guy from Sydney University who wouldn't say what he saw. He took his own memories with another drug. I remember that interview on *60 Minutes*."

"That's the guy. Martin Rathcar."

"You're doing what he did?"

"As best I can." Jared touched the smooth marble ledge again. There were no frissons, no untoward sensations, nor had he expected any. He took his hand away. "When he injected the Trioparin, took his memories, he breached quite a few legal agreements. He ended up being locked out of his own facilities, forfeited his database and research material. But some preliminary theory was already published. There was even a popular article in *New Scientist* to generate interest. The rest of the procedure was relatively easy to duplicate. The main thing was getting access to the same location he used a year ago. You can see why I'm so grateful to you and your office."

Susan smiled. "Cilla briefed me as well as she could before she left for London. Her mum is unwell—all last minute. She said I just have to be here and watch. Make sure rules are followed."

"You're doing more than you realize. You and the security guards rostered on tonight become impartial observers as well."

"Hey, I like that. Independent witnesses!"

"I'm glad you think so. I wonder if you'd be okay with us using your names in our observation log? It could really help."

"Sure. It's exciting. I'll ask Geoff and Amin later."

"My camera and sound people will be here soon, Sophie and Craig, my volunteer assistants and official witnesses. It's six o'clock now. Once we're set up, we'll begin at 7:00 p.m., the same time Dr. Rathcar did fifteen months ago. We'll do the whole thing twice if we can, put several objects here on the mantel—a plastic bottle, a child's wooden block, a toy train, and simply record what happens. Second time through, if we are lucky tonight and the phenomenon occurs, the moment they're moved, disturbed in any way at all I shift the patch from one eye to the other and see what I get. It shouldn't take long."

"You do that *once* it happens."

"As soon as it happens. As close to. The first time is a control to establish parameters: event frequency and duration, lighting levels, things like that. But the second time round I stand over here by the fireplace and shift the patch, just as Rathcar did."

"But the camcorders will only catch your reactions. Not what you see."

"Right. But whatever we get may match reactions in the CCTV footage from the Rathcar attempt. Rathcar's own footage hasn't been made available yet, but may be released once we do this. Rathcar called out a single word—'Kathy!'—his assistant's name. We don't know why now, and of course he can't tell us."

"Or won't."

"Or won't. But there may be some key detail or other that emerges. Later spectrographic analysis may show even more, who knows?"

"It's all very uncertain," Susan said, looking at him intently, or possibly at the eye-patch that was to play such a key role in what was about to happen.

"True. But it's all we can expect in a situation like this, and hopefully what we do tonight will actually duplicate Rathcar's results, whatever those ultimately were. All we know is that there was an event and that Dr. Rathcar shifted his patch, reacted strongly to something, called out Kathy Nicholls' name, just her first name, then shifted the patch back. It's what he did afterwards that caused the fuss. Gave himself the injection."

"So you're doing this to help Dr. Rathcar."

"In a sense. Not out of some noble motive or anything; I've never even met the man. But I have to allow that he saw something. A respected research scientist took his own memories of what seems to be the key moment in a serious experiment. Grandstanding aside, something probably significant happened to make him do that."

"The resident poltergeist," Susan said.

"I'll settle for that, whatever it is."

"You hope to see it?"

"That's the idea. Hopefully see something."

"So why do it at night? It happens in daylight too. Surely that'd be easier."

Jared had to smile. "Rathcar did it at night, so we do likewise. I think it was Channel 9's idea, having the night-shoot. Spookier. More dramatic."

"I can understand that. The smallest things are scarier at night."

"Exactly."

"But whatever you see may just be sensory overload. All those drugs you mentioned."

"I know. Large-scale perceptual trauma. But those optical regulators aren't known for that, have been deliberately tailored to avoid it in fact. And here are my long-suffering volunteers!"

Sophie Mace and Craig Delmonte had appeared at the doorway to the Delfray Room, laden with camcorders, audio equipment and a portable lighting stand, assisted by Geoff and Amin, the security guards rostered on for the evening.

Jared and Susan walked back to the double doors, where Jared completed the introduce tions then helped the security men carry in chairs and a table so Craig and Sophie could set up their video monitors just inside the entrance. Susan left them to it, going outside to discuss the evening's schedule with the guards.

"Give us twenty minutes to get the settings,' Craig said.

"Won't take long."

"Listen, Craig—"

"Jared. Let's do this like we discussed. You're pumped, I can tell. It's only natural. Go for a walk and calm down! Sophie and I can handle this."

"Right."

They had talked about it, about remaining composed, focused, letting others help. This footage would be seen, closely scrutinized. Objectivity and detachment were everything.

Jared stepped out into the corridor, walked the short distance to the corner and turned left into the long axial hallway for the whole wing. It was dimly lit, and so quiet, stretching off into shadow at its farthest reaches. Jared started along it, moving soundlessly on the old carpet, with locked doors to his left and long darkened windows to the right. He knew that beyond the steady mirror reflections in those panes the land fell away over sheer crags, buttresses, blurrings of eucalypts, a great gulf of darkness, all invisible now. In daylight it was the sort of panoramic view that caught your breath, weakened you in the knees, made any attempts to capture it in photographs impossible. Photographs never caught the scale, the dimension, the vast uncaring emptiness.

Now that he was finally doing it, everything seemed intensely unreal, and he had to counter that feeling. He took several deep breaths, made himself consider where he was. The old spa complex was all around him, stretching away like a bleached wishbone here by the highway at Medlow Bath, an antique ivory clasp opened and laid out along the ridge, arms pushed back against the incredible drop. The phrase "abandoned in place" had never been more appropriate. This fabulous old hotel was meant to be restored, maintained, feted, if only as something as second-rate yet cherished as the Carrington Hotel in nearby Katoomba. But *used*, for heaven's sake. Though no one was saying so officially, there was already the distinct feeling that it might all prove too hard, that these empty rooms, forgotten lounges, deserted balconies, and silent staircases would stay like this indefinitely, the only thing moving in the halls by day the motes of dust glittering in the westering sunlight, by night the shadows made by the moon as it fell down the sky.

Now and then security guards would come and go, trying the locks, checking the fire-doors, running the aircon in various rooms to counter mildew and mold, helping to replace the fire-extinguishers as they reached their use-by dates, escorting the planning people who seemed to come less and less frequently now.

Jared turned to face his own reflection in one of the long casements, stood distracted by the familiar shape with the eye-patch. For a moment it made him forget the great darkness beyond the glass, but then he forced himself to think of it, savor it: the fact that two things could be true at the same time, his image and the other. It calmed him, anchored him somehow.

When he finally did check his watch, he saw it was 6:51, time to get back. He re-traced his course, returned with the same silent tread to the Delfray Room, welcoming the soft murmur of voices as Sophie and Craig made final adjustments, calmly explaining what they were doing for Susan's benefit. The security guards were off making last-minute checks of the exits.

Everyone knew to leave Jared be now, and he distanced himself, found focus by reviewing how well it had gone so far.

The Rathcar duplication was nearly complete: his taking the exact regulator doses across nine long months, the grooming of the monocular separation followed to the letter. The logistical requirements had been met too: securing the Hydro for the evening, keeping the costs well down. The guards were rostered on anyway. Only Susan had to be paid a fee for the two or three hours it should take, and she had turned out to be so interested that if he'd bothered to arrange to meet beforehand she might well have done it for free.

At 6:56, Jared called for Stand-by. Susan took out her mobile and contacted the security men. "Geoff, get Amin. We're about to start."

The guards appeared in the doorway moments later, took their places on the spare chairs, interested and attentive.

"All right," Jared said. "So everyone is clear on the sequencing, we roll cameras at 7:00 sharp, do the control run to make sure our visitor is with us. We set up our things on the mantel, let our guest have a free go at them. Once it happens, if it happens, we then take the thirty-eight minute break and do it all again, this time with me standing over by the mantel and swapping the patch as soon as I can after the event occurs."

"Is the thirty-eight minutes necessary?" Susan asked.

"Again, it's what Rathcar did. It wasn't planned. He just had more things to coordinate. But we're duplicating his sequencing as closely as possible."

"Understood."

"Okay, Sophie, Craig. It's 6:59. Begin recording. I'll go put the things on the mantelpiece."

Jared did so, once again crossing the empty dance-floor to the fireplace. First he stood the plastic bottle on its end, then set down the wooden block a short distance along from it, finally placed the red toy locomotive. Though tempted to stay by the mantel even for this first run, pulling his patch aside at the first sign of any disturbance, he made himself return to the monitors by the doors.

The vigil proper began at 7:02.

It was exciting at first, full of a new and understandable tension, an intensification of everything. The objects sat there—so ordinary, so comical in that ordinariness, both unreal yet super-real but growing more and more unsettling, even disturbing somehow in their stillness.

As long minutes passed, the waiting soon became unbearable, of course. In most modern cultures, human senses were rarely accustomed to being strained this way. What once might have been essential for hunting and for vigilance in the face of danger and strife now brought only a worrying hypersensitivity. Jared watched the monitors, then the mantel across the room, monitors and mantel, glance up, glance down, the cycle repeating over and over. He found himself afraid to blink, straining to catch the slightest movement, the smallest disturbance, keenly aware of the gulf beyond the windows, of the chill autumn darkness all about them, thought of the empty rooms and hallways, the locked bars and dining rooms, the kitchens, closets, the empty pipes, the utterly still interiors of the hotel outbuildings scattered along the ridge. He imagined movement a dozen, two dozen times, but there was nothing, certainly no confirmation from Craig and Sophie at their monitors, watching the test objects in both long-shot and close-up. Geoff and Amin sat quietly behind him, Susan to his right, close by the monitor screens, no doubt staring too.

Jared had not forbidden talking, but that's what had resulted. There was barely a sound.

Ten minutes became twenty, thirty, and the silence grew to be a layered thing. Sounds not noticed at first gained a striking new intensity: the hum of the recording equipment, the smallest cough, the rhythmic cycle of their breathing, the occasional tick of temperatures shifting, of masonry cooling, old pipes settling, whatever traces came in from the great emptiness beyond the windows.

It was so sudden when it happened—as alarming, dramatic and violent as everyone had said it would be. One moment the objects sat unmoving, exactly as placed. The next they were gone, clattering on the parquetry floor as if an unseen arm had swept them aside.

"First event, 7:46," Craig said for the audio log, then: "Stand by. Stand by. Counting to the thirty-eight minute repeat at 7:47—now!"

Everyone relaxed then, began talking all at once. It was happening. They were in the thirty-eight minute time-out.

To Jared's surprise, one of the security guards, Amin, was suddenly at his elbow, handing him a folded note. "When I started my rounds earlier, Jared, a guy parked out by the highway asked me to give you this the moment something happened."

"What's that?" Jared said, even as he took the note, opened and read it.

Mr. Ryan
I am waiting in front of the Hotel in a white Camry. Please give me fifteen minutes of your time. It is very important that you do so.
                                                                 Martin Rathcar

Jared passed the note to Craig, said: "Keep to the countdown. I'll be back in time." Then he left the Delfray Room, hurried out to the front exit, out through the porte-cochère to where, sure enough, a solitary white Camry was parked by the highway. As Jared approached the vehicle, the passenger window lowered, revealed a man behind the wheel leaning over, smiling.

"Jared Ryan? I'm Martin Rathcar. Thanks for coming out. Please get in for a moment."

Jared dimbed into the passenger seat and they shook hands.

"Dr. Rathcar, I have to say this is truly a surprise! Really quite marvelous! But why are you here?"

Martin Rathcar looked older than his fifty-two years. He sat with his hands on the steering wheel his narrow face partly shadowed, partly lit by the highway lamps. His eyes glittered. "I know you don't have long. My one-time assistant, Kathy Nicholls, let me know that you'd duplicated the monocular separation and were doing this tonight."

"Using your Nightside Eye."

Rathcar gave a wry smile. "To call it that. I enjoyed the theatricality, I suppose."

"I've read all the interviews, all the *available* transcripts."

"That's all there are."

"I accept that. But I thought—since you asked to see me—that there was something you remembered and were prepared to share."

"Jared, I remember nothing of what I saw, just that it was enough to make me obliterate the memory of whatever it was. It's strange to find myself asking you to abandon the whole thing now when I have no memory of what it is I'm warning you away from. Feels a bit silly really, especially when it puts me in the position of wanting more than anything to know exactly what I *did* see. But I have to allow that there were vitally important reasons. Please reconsider going ahead with this.'

The request surprised Jared. "What about your own reply to Sandra Cartwright on *60 Minutes* in July 2009? 'This is science. Learning about the world.'"

"I won't insult your intelligence by giving the line that was put to me in the same interview, that there are things we are simply not meant to know. I still hold with what I said. If we can know it, it's science and there to be known. It's only right that I should wonder now about what I saw that night that led me to take the final step. Theatricality is one thing, melodrama quite another, and I really do hate sounding this way after years of advocating rigorous investigation myself. But it had to have been important. I pretty well committed professional suicide with what I did."

"Surely not. It was always going to be a case of their having to take your word for whatever you saw. You just pissed off a lot of people. Deprived them of an answer to something they would have called inconclusive anyway."

"Which, nevertheless, many say was because I saw nothing. That this was my intention all along."

"Dr. Rathcar—Martin—your reputation, your previous work in perception, suggests otherwise." Jared hesitated. "It really did take your memory of it?' He had never been truly convinced, he realized.

"That's the thing, isn't it? I should have insisted on a second subject doing it with me from the beginning, or at least waited until whatever I saw could be verified in a subsequent procedure. But Trioparin is effective only on recent memory. I was told it affected only an hour, ninety minutes tops. It's like a mindshock that way, very different to Diprovan and other amnesiacs. Whatever I saw made me decide that I could not by any means wait for subsequent verification."

"It bothered you that much."

"I have to allow that it did. I desperately needed to forget. Anyway, the drug worked better than expected. My short-term memory of the twenty-six hours preceding the injection was lost. Twenty-six hours, can you believe it? Far longer than anyone expected. Part of me wants to know what it was I saw, now more than ever given your intentions tonight, I can't deny it. But I have to accept that I gave myself that injection knowing what it was I did."

"But to have arranged for that contingency in the first place, you must have seriously suspected—sensed that something could go wrong. Trioparin is a last-resort trauma amnesiac. Prohibitively expensive."

Rathcar nodded. "At the time I simply allowed that there could be intense trans-perceptual trauma. It seemed entirely likely. You deprive one eye of its normal tasks for months on end, suppress at least three key neurotransmitters in doing so, then suddenly restore sight to that—let's use the pop term—Nightside Eye. Well you know the outcome, though now I wish I'd never mentioned arranging such a precaution. The media seized on it, had a field day."

Though he hadn't automatically expected it, Jared found himself liking this man. "You didn't just accept that whatever you saw might be dismissed as hallucination, hyper-perception. It suggests you *believed* what you saw."

"It does, doesn't it? I'm glad you think so."

"You wanted it *all* gone regardless, though you knew in advance that it would be intolerable for you afterwards. The *not* knowing."

Rathcar gave a forbearing smile. "That's what made me drive up here tonight and ask to see you. Weird position to find myself in, like I say, but I have to allow that it really is as serious, as important, as my subsequent behavior suggests. I was never much given to pranks or over-reaction, believe me."

"But what could it be? What must you have seen—even as a hallucination that could possibly make you want to forget it forever?"

Rathcar sat with his hands on the wheel for a time, staring at nothing. Then, noticing Jared glance at his watch, he continued. "You understand my dilemma. I have to allow that it was either a hallucination for me, something purely subjective, or a reality for us all. They're the alternatives, the least I can claim. But, Jared, you stand to face the problem I faced: failing in your duty as a scientist. I clearly didn't want even the *possibility* of it being real in the objective sense. You see the extremes here, why I can't help but be fascinated with what you're about to do. I knew it might happen in time, but now, tonight, I keep reproaching myself for not seeking corroboration before taking my memories of what I saw."

Jared smiled grimly at the implications. "It really must have been something."

"Well, no matter. At least you're doing it at the same place I did. And I understand you've duplicated my procedures for fostering the Eye precisely."

"That was the whole point, duplicating what you did."

"Again, I'd be lying if I didn't say that I'm fascinated to know what will happen. Maybe I was wrong to do what I did. But that's the other reason I wanted to see you. Would you consider using a lethophoric like Trioparin to take your memories?"

"Frankly, Martin, I'm more the budget operation. You had institutional funding. I can't afford luxuries like that."

Rathcar smiled again. It was a good smile. They truly did like each other. He took one hand from the wheel, patted the pocket of his jacket. "I have some here in case. The last of my supply, pocketed that night, thank goodness. Everything else was confiscated. I'll wait out here in the car."

"Come inside."

"No, I must *not* be in there. You must appear unbiased. But just remember that it's here. I'm here."

"If I do come out to you, you won't ask what I've seen?"

"I'll want to more than anything in the world. But, no. I promise I won't. I must believe in myself to that extent. You say you're not doing this for me, and I believe you. In a sense, I'm not just doing this for you either. It's because I have to trust myself—trust that I acted for the right reasons. I do not need to know what you see. But if you come out and ask for the Trioparin, I will at least know that you've seen something as unbearable and that I was right in doing what I did that night. Right now that means everything."

Jared made it back to the Delfray Room with seven minutes to spare. Both Sophie and Craig wanted to ask about what had happened, but Jared raised a hand.

"He just wanted to wish me luck and try to talk me out of going through with it."

"Really?' Sophie said. "No insights?"

"Unfortunately not a thing," Jared told her. "But we can talk about this later. It's nearly time."

At 8:24, Jared crossed to the fireplace again, retrieved the bottle, the wooden block, and the toy locomotive from the floor where they had fallen, and began setting them back on the mantel making sure that the placing of the train coincided with Craig's three-two-one countdown to 8:25 exactly. Jared then moved to the right of the fireplace, watching the three objects, wondering how long it would be—*if* at all.

It was a different sort of vigil now, of course, marked by a wholly new kind of tension, such a definite—*pressure* was the only word. Jared's breathing was so loud in his ears. He could feel his heart thumping, his pulse racing, was aware again of the silence out in the room, of how far away the others were across the dull sheen of the parquetry. A quick glance showed Sophie and Craig at their monitors, faces ghost-lit just a touch, showed Susan looking up from the screens to him, the screens then him.

Geoff and Amin sat behind them, darker shapes in the open doorway, eyes fixed and glinting.

The pressure became everything. It could happen at any moment, any instant. He felt he could almost guess when. It was like the waiting tension in a game of Snap or that kids' game where closed fists were placed knuckle to knuckle against one another, and the kid who was it got to hit the other's hand before it could be snatched away.

Jared's thoughts raced. What was it? *Who* was it? Was it really something as simple as electro-magnetic fluxes, atmospheric and geomorphic glitches, nothing supernatural at all? Or was there motivation behind it? Purpose? That was the real question here. What was out there drawing ever nearer, was even now preparing to sweep the objects aside, so dramatically, so brutally. Where did it come from? How far did it have to travel to do this simple mindless thing? Is that what the delay meant, or was this poltergeist always here, holding back out of a sense of mischief? But why did it have to be done—this furious sweeping aside? That remained the issue. The real priority wasn't just shifting the patch to see what there was *after* the event, but shifting it in time to catch who or what was doing it *just as it was about to happen!*

It would be departing from Rathcar's procedure, certainly, but this was about finding answers, seeing the process as process. Complete process, with more than just an ending, an outcome. With a beginning, a definite lead-up and possibly—could it be?—with intent.

The pressure *was* building, definitely growing stronger, Jared was sure of it. Something was about to happen, was beginning even now out there in the room, there to be seen if he dared risk it, dared throw it all away on a conviction, this felt certainty, totally unprovable.

Jared felt his hand clench, felt himself preparing to take that risk, commit that violation.

This was what it needed to be! Knowing what it was before it happened, *as* it happened, not afterwards. Seeing the cause, not the effect.

The pressure was too much.

His hand was at the patch, shifting it from one eye to the other, uncovering the different kind of seeing.

Jared reeled at what he saw, had to reach out and steady himself with one hand on the mantel edge.

There was no sign of Susan or the others, none of the equipment, not even the spotlight. The room was crowded, too crowded, with row upon row of dead-white forms, pallid near-human shapes pressing shoulder to shoulder with not a space between them, dozens, hundreds of sexless, minimalist things like mannequins, but with mouths hanging open and dull red eyes fixed mindlessly ahead, looking beyond him, fixed on nothing.

He was frantically registering the enormity of what he was seeing when there was a commotion in the throng, a sudden rippling forward as someone, something came pushing through, finally thrusting aside the figures in the foremost row to stand slavering, heaving. It was another of the pallid shapes, but this one had eyes that were wildly animated, blazing red, and a mouth stretched wide in a grotesque toothless grin.

No sooner was it there than it raised one long white arm and swept everything from the mantel. The familiar clatter echoed in the room, in no way muffled by the crowding forms.

Jared stared in utter dread. It wasn't just the dead-white face, the grinning, gaping mouth, the imbecilic, red-eyed glare.

It was the idiot glee in those eyes, the look of absolute manic delight at having done this single, simple, stupid thing yet again. It was like a puppy waiting for the next throw of a ball a witless automaton for whom only this had meaning.

And worse still was the sense that the rest of the crowding, slack-faced throng had their special things too, tasks waiting to be triggered and just as mindlessly resolved, whatever they were, however long they had to wait, however long it took.

"Susan!" he shouted, not to Sophie or Craig, but to the young woman who was nearest in his thoughts, had been the focus of so much recent attention.

And there she was, visible now, moving from the back of the shapes, moving forward *through* all the still figures, but not alone. One of the pallid, gaping forms moved with her, followed close behind, in attendance, her eager companion.

We all have them, Jared realized. Following, always following, always there, biding their time.

Are they what waits for us? All that is left of us? What simply wears us down, brings us to death, what?

There was no way of knowing. But this was what Rathcar had seen. What Martin Rathcar had understood.

Jared couldn't help himself. He reached up, snatched the patch back over the Nightside Eye so the room, the hotel the world became normal again.

Seemed to.

"What was it?" Susan asked, still moving towards him across the empty, never-empty room. "What did you see?"

"Nothing," Jared managed, giving the beautiful lie. "There was nothing. It was too much of a shock. Just too much disorientation for the brain. It didn't work."

And he gazed out at the welcome emptiness, the normal world, knowing it could never be that again, knowing that Rathcar was right and realizing what had to be done.

If Rathcar had waited, kept his word, was still out by the highway.

Jared ran to the double doors, rushed out to the main entrance. Susan hurried behind. Sophie and Craig abandoned their monitors and ran after him. Geoff and Amin exchanged glances and followed.

Behind them the abandoned equipment hummed quietly.

The things from the mantel lay scattered where they had fallen.

The windows reflected only the empty room, showed not a trace of the darkness beyond the old, old panes.

Terry Dowling is the author of the Ditmar Award-winning Tom Rynosseros saga, as well as *Wormwood, The Man Who Lost Red, An Intimate Knowledge of the Night, Antique Futures, Blackwater Days*, and *Basic Black: Tales of Appropriate Fear* (which won the International Horror Guild Award), *Make Believe: A Terry Dowling Reader, Amberjack: Tales of Fear & Wonder*, and *Clowns at Midnight*. He is editor of several anthologies including the World Fantasy Award-winning *The Essential Ellison*. Find out more about the Australian writer at terrydowling.com.

My life is a torrent of memories and desires, regrets and delusions.
But why do the memories keep changing? Everything can't be true.

ESCENA DE UN ASESINATO

Robert Hood

"Buy a photo?" I say without hope, talking to a rotund man in a business suit. He's stopped to check out the prints stuck on my tatty pin-board, which leans uncertainly on the wall next to me.

"I don't think so," he mutters, on the verge of turning away. But something in the photographs keeps him standing there.

"Some of them aren't bad," he mutters at last.

I shrug, feeling the texture of the brick wall against my back, the cold resistance of the footpath under my arse. I can smell my own sweat and despondency. "Ten dollars. Give an aging ex-photographer a break!"

"How much for that one?" He points at a street scene in a Mexican town. There are two people prominent in the foreground. One is an old woman, the other a masked visage with only the eyes showing. Though the masked man is not always in the photo, he's there now. He's rarely been so close. The intensity in his eyes is unnerving.

"You from Mexico?" I ask.

The man scowls, considering. "My mother was."

"Did she work for the government?"

"Yes, as a matter of fact. Not that it's any of your business."

"You have a wife? Kids?" He nods absently.

"I can't sell you that one," I say, resisting the deep-seated compulsion that urges me to do the opposite. I grip the object hidden in my pocket.

"Why not?"

"The masked man in the picture means you harm."

My potential customer scowls again, more expressively this time. He thinks I'm crazy and he might be right. Yet even if he deserves the ill fortune owning that photograph would bring, I can't do it to him.

"How about another one?" I gesture vaguely at a picture of Mayan ruins. Landscape only. No people. I've never seen anyone in that particular photograph.

The man shrugs. "No thanks." He flicks a coin into the empty camera case I use as a pauper bowl and takes off down the street, looking back once or twice as though afraid I'll follow him.

I feel the anger radiating from the photo of the woman and the masked man. El Roto's eyes burn with frustration.

"I won't let you kill again," I whisper, holding onto the small primitive doll for my life.

August 1999, it's cold, and I'm in Sydney—that ex-colonial metropolis hunkering down in fin de siècle tension between rising ocean and expanding desert interior. Westward, tendrils of suburban indifference spread outward from its heart. I stare through reflections on glass at the city's patterns of artificial light, burnt into the haze and dark. I'm not feeling optimistic.

My exhibition of travel photography—*Susurros del Roto*—opens tonight. There are fewer than thirty people in attendance, one of the them an influential TV talking-head who writes for the *Herald*'s culture pages and is likely to give me a much-needed review if the work either impresses him or he thinks I'm on the rise and wants to hedge his bets. At the moment he's talking to an over-sexed, under-dressed young woman in high heels who's offering him a sultry smile. My most recent girlfriend. I'm hoping Sioni's rather crude allure will get him on side.

"That streetscape is a work of genius, Morley," a middle-aged woman says with undue familiarity, sleazing up to me and waving her umpteenth glass of New Zealand Pinot Noir between the tips of over-painted fingers. I have no idea who she is. "You've absolutely captured the essence of the country's post-revolutionary despair."

The "framed silver gelatin" (aka black-and-white) print she alludes to is one I took a few years ago in Ocosingo, a town in the Chiapas state of Mexico. I can't give an exact date. My notes are less than precise and my memory's a bag with holes. An ordinary street behind the market area, made evocative by shallow depth of field, a splash of darker paint on flimsy-looking walls, and close focus on the wrinkled features of an old woman just appearing out of a doorway. Parts of the street are suspended in her gaze. She looks as though she's about to curse.

"You think so?" I say. "I liked the contrast of the woman's ornate wrinkles against the barren poverty of the buildings. They're akin, yet profoundly separate. Aesthetics, that's all. No politics."

She makes a small coughing sound. "But surely the figure emerging from the shadows at the far end of the street is part of an ongoing discourse on the country's unresolved past?" She squints at me expectantly.

"What figure?" I say, amused. "The street's empty. If anything about that photo is symbolic, it's the emptiness."

"There's definitely a figure there, Mr. Turrand. I can see it clearly. Not its features as such but the general shape. A desperado or something."

I turn toward the photo. "There's nothing . . . " The words fall away. There is something. Behind the face of the old woman, barely distinguishable from the blur of the distant street, lurks a human form. It's unclear whether, as I'd pressed the shutter release, the figure had been moving or was stationary, observing. Nor can I tell where it's looking, though I have an unsettling sense that it's staring straight towards the camera. I've studied that image many times as I prepared the photographs for display, and I'm positive I've never seen that shape before.

I push past the woman, who grunts her own displeasure and begins whining about artistic eccentricity to someone near her. I don't care. I lean close to the print, but the figure is real enough—not simply a simulacra, not a smudge or chemical stain. It's dressed in what appears to be a loose-fitting black poncho gathered in at the waist, with a black hood or scarf tied at the top of the head to form a mask, so that only a light smear of face is visible. It may hold a rifle.

I've seen it before, or something like it.

June 1996. I'm sitting in an ordinary cantina in the township of Ocosingo, brooding over a mug of cheap *comiteco*. I look up as a woman sits at my table. It's unexpected, because there's a sign on the door forbidding entry to policemen, dogs and whores. No one seems bothered by her presence though.

"*Buenas noches*," she says, with a sardonic smile. She's smoking a small cigar.

"Sorry," I say, groping for the words, "I'm not looking for, um, companionship."

Those eyes, that were copal only a moment ago, darken. "You assume I am a *puta*? Why? Because I sit uninvited? Because I talk to a stranger?"

I hadn't expected my crude Spanish to be understood. Her English, however, is fine. I look her over. Her white shirt is open at the neck, but not enough to reveal cleavage, just soft *café con leche* skin. She's wearing baggy black pants. I imagine the small hips, and the firm, reddish-tanned legs they cover. "Are you?" I ask, reverting to English.

"Does it make a difference?"

"Maybe."

Her eyes are darkly luminous, her hair black and cut short around her ears. No obvious make-up, but she's not colorless or plain for all that. With a hat and serape, she'd almost pass for a man from a distance, but up close, her body is distinctly feminine and her face mesmerizing: full lips slightly parted, rounded cheeks, and the centers of the eyebrows, over Frida Kahlo eyes that won't let you off too easily, raised, questioning.

"Care for a drink?"

"I don't drink," she replies and falls silent, staring at me.

I lean a little closer, smelling scented vanilla mixed with white chocolate.

"How can I help you then?"

She shrugs and blows a cloud of smoke over my head. "I sit. I wait."

Now I feel discomfort, even a sense of danger, though she has made no threatening moves. Her rich, unpainted lips caress the cigar with delight, teasingly. After a few moments she reaches down into a pocket in her pants, and I inhale. She fetches some object and places it on the table in front of me. Her hand draws away, leaving it standing there.

The thing is a small rough doll, whether man or woman is unclear. About eight or nine centimeters high, it's dressed in what is meant to be a black serape, head covered in a hood except for a slit from which two eyes peer, sewn in black thread. Hands and visible face are the only white fabric—though a twine made of black-and-white yarns crosses its chest like bandoliers. In its nascent hands it holds a crude rifle made of wood.

"What's this?" I ask.

"Zapatista doll," she murmurs.

I touch it then pull my hand back. "Zapatista?"

She glares critically, but that only makes her more captivating. "You are not very perceptive, are you, Señor Turrand? You photograph but you do not see."

"Well, I don't know what you want me to see—"

"Zapatistas are rebels," she says. "*Bandidos*, if you will. Part of the Ejército Zapatista de Liberación Nacional. They have opposed the oppressive Mexican state since 1994—the tailend of a war that has gone on for many decades. To many they are heroes. The better known of them have been turned into these figures, so." She gestures at the doll. "It is good for tourism."

"Is that right?" I lean closer to the doll, pondering the ubiquitous tradition that transforms social malcontents into celebrities. Robin Hood, Ned Kelly, Phoolan Devi, Ishikawa Goemon, Dick Turpin, Pancho Villa: hero-bandits all.

"Who's this bloke?"

"El Roto." She offers a half-grin. "Once Genaro el Roto, Genaro the Broken, the Lost."

"Is he particularly famous?"

"Famous for being dead. He was shot here in this town during the fighting two years ago, murdered by the government's militia. His first name was indeed Genaro. But his last was a secret, his nom de guerre El Roto, after our famous Mexican outlaw from a century ago. Others have adopted that name now. El Roto lives on in them."

"Others?"

"The fight continues, Señor Turrand. But it is now in the hands of the new generation, with their different methods. This man needs to be freed. Vengeance does not work for the greater good, and he is become a liability. Do you understand?"

I shrug, bewildered by her words and her quiet passion.

She smiles, her sensuality warming me. "You, too, are El Roto. I see it in your eyes."

"If you say so."

"I do. Take it." She gestures at the doll. "I want you to have it." What's she after? I don't know how to respond.

"Those that die without resolution often return," she adds, "and may not serve the best interests of the country. It can be disruptive."

"You mean they become martyrs to the cause?"

"Victims merely. But vengeful ones."

Her burnt honey eyes hold meaning she doesn't speak. "So where was El Roto killed?" I ask, unnerved by the depth of those eyes, which now half close.

"The market square. Along with others." She gestures again. "Take the doll. It is a gift. Take it back with you when you go home, to remind you that not all find peace."

I frown again at the insistence in her tone.

"Take it," she repeats.

"I meant no disrespect."

She watches with curious intensity as I reach out and let my fingers wrap around the doll. When I draw it closer to myself, it's as though she relaxes. I can feel the atmosphere around us lighten.

Her eyes rest on me gently, perhaps sadly now.

"*Más comiteco*, Señor?" Torn from my distraction, I look up into an indifferent, plump and pitted, mustachioed face—the *tabernero*'s.

"No thanks, though the lady might want something."

He looks confused. Perhaps I'd said it incorrectly; my grasp of Spanish and local dialects is horrible, frankly. "Lady?" he queries.

"This one—" I glance across the table to where the alluring woman was sitting, but she's no longer there. Nor can I see her anywhere in the room. Only the chocolatey scent of Ocosingo's fully-bloomed ceiba flowers lingers.

"Señor?"

"She appears to have gone."

Ragged eyebrows bend into a frown. "There are no ladies here, Señor." He shrugs, and adds, "It is prohibited."

"She gave me this." I hold out the doll.

He dismisses it as commonplace, immediately backing away from it. I can tell it worries him.

"What's going on here?" I demand.

"Please leave." His face is hard and serious. Then he turns and shuffles back toward the bar.

I don't bother arguing; I've had enough of this. I drop the doll on the table and head for the door.

January 1994. I'm stumbling through a street off the market square, the bullet lodged in my thigh burning as fiercely as my anger. Around me, the air vibrates with shouting, gunfire and the choking breath of my own fear. From behind, a percussive rifle shot catches up to me, overtakes and echoes along the street ahead.

"Genaro!" Acatl cries and I glance back.

He falls to one knee, hand clutching his shoulder—and beyond him several government militia run toward us, yelling and waving their rifles. I take a hesitant step forward, aware that we are being hemmed in, but not wanting to abandon my friend. Another shot cracks and bounces off the walls to either side. Acatl jerks forward onto his face, the road surface muffling his cry.

I regain my balance and turn to run on, desperation energizing my aching muscles. Bullets explode into the ground to my right, and I leap awkwardly towards the nearest cover, behind some concrete stairs. One more step then my left thigh erupts in pain, throwing me forward. My leg collapses and I crash to the ground.

I'm aware of the thud of heavy boots drawing near. A soldier looms over me. He's breathing heavily.

I glance up at him. "*Bastardo!*" I say, a mere whisper.

The man—large and black against the sky and the eves of shops on the far side of the road—looks down in silence. His face is harsh, and his rifle poised and ready.

I hear the shot and feel near-simultaneous pain in my forehead—a blood-flash before the bullet ruptures my skull.

August 1999, the day after my exhibition's opening night. I've been drinking for hours now, appeasing my own unhappiness through the pursuit of oblivion. The morning newspapers are strewn over the floor of my apartment, torn and crumpled.

"Had enough, Morley?"

Sioni stands in the bedroom doorway, her hair untidy and make-up smeared. She's wearing a Red Hot Chili Peppers T-shirt and nothing else. It'd make me take her straight back to bed if I wasn't so pissed.

I drag my carcass off the sofa, and squint. "So what's with Groban anyway?" I refill my scotch glass. "I saw you playing up to the bastard."

"You told me to."

"'More post-colonial landscapes from Morley Turrand. Yawn.' What sort of a review is that?"

"Is that what he wrote? He told me he liked your snaps." I stand close, so close I can feel the heat of her.

"Likes my *snaps*? I guess the blow-job you gave him in the backroom wasn't up to scratch then."

"Fuck you, Morley."

"Sioni, it's all you're good for. Least you can do is get it right."

She glares, her whipped-puppy eyes moist. She's on the verge. It's so damn easy.

But she fights it. I see the moment of vulnerability pass. "Maybe it's your snaps that are fucked."

Before any reactive synaptic activity can generate a response in my muscles, her fist catches my left cheek, even though she was aiming for my mouth. It wouldn't have been so bad but she's got a silver skull ring on her third finger, Keith Richards-style; one I gave her! I stumble back a bit.

After a moment she looks up at me. Tears glint in her eyes—but they're hot tears, not the lukewarm drizzle of misery. "You want me to be sorry, Morley? Well, I'm sorry you didn't get what you wanted from me. I'm sorry about your career and I'm sorry you're an arsehole. Most of all I'm sorry I've had anything to do with you."

Her words cut through the alcoholic haze. "Sioni, I'm bleeding here—"

"And don't bother to apologize. I'm going as soon as I get dressed. I won't be back."

The bedroom door slams. For a moment I fight an impulse to kick it down, but the fire dies quickly. I don't even try to talk her out of it.

She's as good as her word. Still disheveled but dressed in the red, impossibly sexy silk dress she'd been wearing last night, she emerges from the bedroom about ten minutes later. "I *am* sorry, Sioni," I almost bawl. "It's the bloody alcohol, my head, that dick Groban—"

She gives me little more than a side-glance before turning away. The fact that she doesn't even have the passion left to slam the front door as she leaves paralyzes me.

So I take another swig of scotch and follow up by tossing the glass, half-full though it is, against the wall. It shatters with satisfactory violence.

How long I slump in the chair, mindless with self-pity, I don't know—but I'm pulled out of it by the phone. It's Grace Nye, the gallery owner—the last person I want to talk to. When I left the exhibition at about 11:00, only one or two minor unnumbered pieces had been sold.

"Not good, eh, Grace," I say.

"Not in volume, no—and yes, I noticed Groban's comment this morning." Silence. I'm afraid to say anything.

"But I have one piece of good news. You sold one of the major pieces."

"Good god! Which one?"

"*Escena de un Asesinato*. The street scene with the old woman's face—"

"Really?"

"It was Norma Rivera. You know her? She seemed to know you quite well." I didn't, but I get Grace to describe her and I place her at once.

"The thing is, Morley," Grace continues, "she wanted to take it with her. Number one of the run. Seemed rather obsessive about it."

"I don't usually do that—and besides, the print was flawed." Remembering the phantom shape, I immediately determine to check the other prints.

"Was it? I didn't notice. Anyway, she insisted. Even offered to pay more. I could hardly refuse." Grace tells me how much more and all my objections suddenly dissipate in a cloud of mercenary relief. "Anyway," she continues, "can you bring me another print? Maybe a few of them, just in case. I'll get one framed before we open this afternoon. We might be on a winner there."

"Sure, sure."

As I hang up, I start to shout for Sioni, to tell her the good news. Then I feel my face and remember that she's gone.

June 1996, a few days after I met the woman in the cantina. I've been wandering the countryside around Ocosingo, on this occasion photographing the nearby Mayan ruins at Toniná in a way that I hope will appeal to tourists. *Travel Scene* magazine somehow heard that I'm here in Mexico and tracked me down to the Hotel de Destino. The editor wants me to take some appropriate shots of the area, on commission. I can use the money, so I reluctantly agree to prostitute myself. Now I'm busy playing the backdoor whore. It's not hard. It's what I've always done.

The day is warm, not hot enough to irritate me. It rained last night, lightly, so the air's clear. I'm feeling almost optimistic. I take some panoramic shots of the view then proceed through random clusters of trees toward the detritus of ancient stonework and Toniná's huge central pyramid. It rises from grass and vegetation as though thrust up from underground.

Despite its openness, there's a shadowy quality to Toniná that quickly drags me back into myself after the innocence of the surrounding fields. The ancient ruins are scattered over much of the hillside like the broken corpse of a city, but as I pass a sacrificial altar isolated in an open area of grass, and climb the stairs into the ruins proper, the ornate rubble closes around me and begins to squeeze my soul.

Toniná's antique paths, foundations and walls become a maze-like complex that is, they say, oriented to the night-sky, with occasional openings thick with shadow that lead downward into the earth. But I'm so enmeshed in the details, I can't see the pattern. Friezes solidify out of the rough stonework as I move about, many of them depicting bound and headless prisoners. The most prominent is of King Kan-Xul from nearby Palenque, cowering with rope tied around one constricted arm. Among Toniná's greatest achievements were, apparently, the defeat of Palenque and the capture of the King, who subsequently suffered ten years of humiliation at his captors' hands before execution. So my guidebook tells me.

I come across a sarcophagus carved out of a single large stone, its lid missing and its mortal contents long gone. By now I've lost the bucolic peace I'd found in the green fields and darker green clumps of trees that sweep across the gently rolling land around the hilltop ruins, oppressed by an awareness that what remains longest of civilization are the scars of violence and death. I wonder if the original inhabitant of the sarcophagus is still here somewhere, unwilling to leave. As I take picture after picture, the sun gradually lowers and the light glows eerily.

A breeze picks up as the day dwindles. I've been shooting the outside of a half-buried wall topped by cacti, with three arched doorways leading below ground-level to a labyrinth known as the Palace of the Underworld. Snapping shots as I go, I approach the central opening. Thick darkness beyond it gives me a momentary *frisson* that makes my skin squirm. It's a psychosomatic response, I know, but the shiver is real enough.

Looking through my Minolta, I set up a frame that encompasses only the central archway and surrounding stonework. As the scene comes into focus I'm aware of a figure standing in the internal shadows beyond the rough architrave. I take the shot then pull the camera away from my face, blinking to peer through the lowering sunlight. The opening's about one hundred meters distant, so if someone's there I should be able to see him. But I can't, only that dark gaping hole into the Underworld. Another glance through the camera's viewfinder, using a close-in zoom, reveals nothing. Whoever it was must have stepped backwards into the labyrinth.

I approach the middle doorway, but even standing right at the shadow's edge I can't peer more than a meter or two beyond the entrance. Without consciously acknowledging the fact, I am unable to enter, muscular control drained by an awareness of evil. Instead I discharge the camera's flash, splashing its garish light over the rough internal walls. At the far end of the passage is a male, almost naked, what clothing he wears tattered and meager.

His eyes spark red. I gasp, and step back as the afterimage fades.

"Señor?" comes a voice from behind me. I expel a weak gasp as I turn and stumble to the side. A small man wearing farmer's clothes and a large straw hat squints up at me with sardonic curiosity, as though my reaction is an absurdity he can't quite fathom.

I apologize in my uncertain Spanish. "You, um, surprised me. There was someone . . . In the, um . . . *en el laberinto.*"

He stares in that direction then scowls, his lips twitching like anxious slugs. "*Bandido?*"

I try to explain that the figure seemed like an ancient Mayan, like many of the friezes that depict Toniná's prisoners.

He shrugs incomprehension or indifference then steps into the dark passage. I try to stop him, but he brushes me off and disappears. I hear his feet scraping down the rough path. A minute or two later he returns. His dark pupils peek through a mass of wrinkles, enough to evaluate me.

"*Nada?*" I say. He nods.

"Do they hide here? *Bandidos?* Do they hide in those—?" I gesture toward the darkness.

He says nothing. Either he can't understand me or he thinks me crazy.

After a few moments of silence, irritated by his inaction, I ask him what he'd wanted in the first place.

"Turrand?" The word seems distasteful to him.

"Morley Turrand. *Sí.*"

His long battered hand offers me a Zapatista doll. It looks familiar. I remember leaving it behind in the cantina a few days before.

"Where did you get this?" I ask.

"*Qué?*"

"The doll . . . Zapatista doll? Who gave it to you?"

"*Fantasma,*" he answers without a hint of irony. A ghost? He follows up with a jumble of words I'm too surprised to translate, though I gather he thinks I've been careless.

I ask if he knows who the ghost was.

He says I know her—that is what matters.

"What do you mean?"

"*Fantasma,*" he repeats, pointing at my chest.

June 1996. Sometimes *this* is how I remember meeting the woman. She sits across the table from me, smoking her thin cigarette with calm intensity. She isn't pleased. We have spoken briefly and though she denies being a prostitute I can't imagine why else she would be here.

Offering me the Zapatista doll was an unsettling moment—so familiar, giving me a shiver of déjà vu, and filled with the white chocolate-mixed-with-vanilla fragrance of ceiba. Yet her explanation fascinates me, even if it smacks of unstated intent. I should refuse it and send her away.

"Take the doll," she whispers. "It is a gift. To remind you that not all find peace."

I frown at the insistence in her tone.

"Take it," she repeats.

I grasp the doll despite myself and study the odd crudity of its making to avoid the embarrassment of having obeyed her so easily. Now, however, having accepted her gift, I find myself being drawn to the woman. My skin tingles as though her slim fingers caress my face. I raise my eyes from the doll to stare at her, imagining the small blossom of a body she hides beneath unappealingly masculine clothes. The beginnings of desire stir in my gut.

"Now you want me," she says, "whether or not I am a *puta*."

"If you're a streetwalker, I'm not interested."

Her smile is private and knowing. I feel voyeuristic merely seeing it.

"To pay for sex," she says, "would be an affront to your masculinity, would it?"

"No, that's not—"

"Do not fear, Señor Turrand," she interrupts, "I have not loved for a long time, and would not consider it now except that you interest me."

"I *interest* you?" I say, taken aback by her forthright manner.

"*Sí.* As I *interest* you."

I should be put off by her condescending manner, but the deep tones of her voice vibrate through my mind, overturning denial and stoking the fires of arousal.

"What's your name?" I ask.

"Once, I was called Coronela María de la Luz Espinosa Barrera. Perhaps you have heard of me."

I haven't and she knows it. Her smile makes my heart beat faster.

"Should I?"

"If you cared for more than yourself, perhaps . . . yes. History is *importante*, Señor."

Annoyance rises again, but it only fuels my desire for her. I frown—and the woman laughs. "Just Coronela then."

"Coronela." I taste the word, letting it vibrate in my throat.

"Come!" She takes my hand and pulls me to my feet. The table rattles and the *tabernero* glances our way. I extract money from my pocket and ostentatiously place it under my half-empty glass.

"Enough?" I yell across the room.

He gestures uncertainly, a little befuddled, but doesn't pursue the matter. Coronela leads me out into the street. "Where are we going?" I ask.

"I do not make love on cantina tables. Or in back alleys." She gestures.

"Your hotel, I think." Speechless, I follow.

After a few blocks, she indicates a large space that opens out to our right beyond the buildings at the end of a narrow road. "That is the market," she says. "It is there that many Zapatista rebels died when their peaceful occupation of the township was repressed most violently by Government butchers." She gestures around us. "Here is where Genaro el Roto was murdered. Remember the spot. You must come back and photograph it, no?"

"I guess."

"You will photograph it, won't you, Señor Morley?"

I stare at her accusingly. "How do you know my name, Coronela?" I demand. "How did you know what I do? I never told you."

That secret smile again, advising me that she has no intention of answering my question. "Much depends on you photographing this spot." She grabs my arm and pulls me close, forcing me to look directly into her eyes. Their black depth mesmerizes me. "When you do, you must carry the doll with you."

"The doll?'"

"*Sí*, you must keep it close."

"Okay, okay, I will."

"You must." She lets go.

"Also when you go to Toniná in three days time," she continues, "you must take care what you photograph."

"What d'you mean?"

"There are things in that place, ancient resentments, which you must not capture with your camera. The doll, El Roto—it marks you as his and will keep the others at bay. Stupidly, however, you went there without it."

"*Went there without it?* Look, I've never been to Toniná. I've no intention of going there."

"You will have reason to go to Toniná—and you will go, without protection. But I have righted that error. Now you will take the doll."

"You righted it? Even though I haven't gone there yet?" Her eyes hold me in their silence.

"I don't have a clue what the hell you're talking about," I say.

She doesn't smile as she takes my hand. "Come, I will give you what you think you want. Later you may understand."

June 1996. Toniná. Is this the way it happens? It feels wrong.

I'm photographing the ruins for *Travel Scene* magazine, fairly unenthusiastically, I must confess. I've been at it for several hours already and am now facing a wall with three stone-framed doorways leading to underground tunnels—the Palace of the Underworld. Raising the viewfinder of the Minolta to my eye, I focus on the central passage. A lighter shadow lingers in the internal darkness beyond the rough architrave. I take the shot then pull the camera away from my face, but there's no one there, only that dark gaping hole into the Underworld. Another glance through the camera's viewfinder. Nothing.

I must be imagining things. There aren't even tourists around—I haven't seen anyone all day. Nervously I grip the Zapatista doll, which is in my coat pocket. My breathing calms and once again the day seems ordinary.

I take more shots of the ruins, even forcing myself to get a few inside the structure itself. I find no evidence of other people among its evocative shadows. When I re-emerge from the gloom the atmospheric sunlight has turned into a flat gloaming and I begin the long trek back to Ocosingo. It's dark by the time I get to the hotel.

August, 1999. When I check them, none of the other prints of *Escena de un Asesinato* show any background markings that might be construed as a human being. I take numbers two to ten to Grace at the gallery and she accepts them eagerly. She's hoping that Norma Rivera's excessive enthusiasm for the picture will be the start of a trend. Even if others pay less, the commission will help reduce the loss she clearly expects to make.

"How many are there in the run, Morley?" she asks. I point toward my hand-drawn signature. Under it I've written *2 of 17.* "Only seventeen?"

"That's how you make these things valuable, Grace."

"But we usually extend the run to fifty or or 100."

"I want this to be very collectible."

"Why?"

I frown, not having considered it before. "I don't know. Why not? I burnt the negatives of all the exclusives. There has to be a guarantee of limitation."

"That's ridiculous, Morley. Do you realize what we could lose on a deal like that?"

"It's how I want it."

She gives me a side-glance sneer that says *you think far too highly of yourself,* though she doesn't articulate it further. When I don't respond she turns her gaze toward the picture.

"It's a nice shot, Morley. There's something compelling in it. Why's it called *Escena de un Asesinato*?"

"*Murder Scene*. A revolutionary was killed there in 1994."

She nods thoughtfully. "That explains something the Rivera woman said: *An echo of the last Ocosingo insurgents*. She reckoned there was a bandit further up the street. She was keen to show it to her husband. Couldn't see it myself."

"You couldn't?"

She shrugs, holding up print #2. "Well, can you?"

As I leave her to her business, I feel a sense of disquiet scratching at the insides of my skull. I'm sure there had been a shape there on the street in print #1 of *Escena de un Asesinato*, the suggestion of a bandit-like spectre coming my way. Norma Rivera had seen it. So had I. Why not Grace?

June 1996.

Do I make love with Coronela?

"*You must see, Morley, and if not you, you must let your camera see what is before you.*"

I peer through the lens down a shadowy street, snapping pictures as she directs.

"*There,*" Coronela says, "*El Roto is there. Do you see?*"

Someone is there, in the distance. His eyes are black holes—all three of them, one in his forehead. An old woman with wrinkled skin and withered lips appears in the frame. "*No camera!*" she screeches.

Click.

After we reach the Hotel de Destino, does Coronela come up to my room and with the aggressive lack of subtlety that seems typical of her, does she remove her clothes, place my hands on her skin, encourage arousal in herself and in me? I don't know. I can't remember. There are images in my head, erotic moments, heat and passion, all infused with the ceiba scent, but I don't know if they are memories or simply phantoms of desire.

"*Do you seek love among the dead?*" I hear her whisper in my ear. "*Futile if you don't find it first among the living. Should life get too dark, then in death there will only be profounder darkness.*"

"*There! El Roto is there.*"

Click.

She consumes me, draining any desire to escape. I try to push her away, but instead find myself drawn further and further into the heart of her.

I want to know who she is.

"Coronela María de la Luz Espinosa Barrera was a veteran of the Mexican Revolution of 1910," she tells me. *"She fought with greater distinction than most men, and was awarded a pension once the fighting was done. But she became an exile in her own land, her temperament unsuited to peacetime society's inane mores. She wandered the country like a lost ghost, dressed as a man, abandoned in a time that was no longer her own."*

"And you're this La Coronela, are you?"

She laughs. *"Perhaps. Perhaps not."*

"What do you want from me?"

"There! He watches you from the shadows. Shoot!"

Click.

"What will I do?"

"You will take these pictures back to your land," she says, tapping the camera on the table near me. Her voice is no more definite than breath. *"The doll will protect you, but your actions will feed El Roto's desires."*

Click.

Click.

A black bird flaps against the window and startles me. I open my eyes to the bloody dimness of twilight as it leaks in through tattered curtains.

I'm alone. The sheets are crumpled and sweaty. I untangle myself, needing to use the toilet, and look for my pants. My camera is lying on the floor near my discarded clothes. I check how many pictures have been taken, only to discover the entire roll is spent. I'm sure it was new only an hour before.

Later, when I develop the film, I see I have taken a series of pictures in the streets around Ocosingo's market square. I don't remember doing it.

"These are good," I mutter to myself, knowing I've found the soul of my upcoming exhibition.

August 1999, and it's the day after the opening.

In a display of useless pretension, I seek out Norma Rivera, ostensibly to give her the choice of obtaining an unblemished print for her money, just to be fair. But in truth I don't care about her or fairness. I simply want to see the thing, to assure myself that the figure we both saw at the opening is still there, and not a glitch of memory.

It turns out that Norma Rivera is the wife of Alex Rivera, CEO of Harvest Futures. Their mansion is on the harbor foreshore in an exclusive northside suburb, and I can't even get past the gate. But an intercom device, its far end impersonating some sort of semi-articulate minder, finally listens long enough to discover what I want, and replies with the terse diagnosis: "She's dead."

"Dead?"

I pause, trying to summon either genuine surprise or a modicum of sympathy. Neither comes.

"Um, perhaps I could speak to Mr. Rivera then, if he's not too busy," I say at last, rather tactlessly.

"I'm sorry, sir," the voice replies, "Mr. Rivera is . . . unavailable."

Now a pinprick of apprehension scratches across the inside of my belly. The intercom coughs and faintly I hear a gruff voice: "I'll take care of it." At that moment, I spot a blue flash through the bushes, down the distant end of the curving driveway. A cop car. Of course there'd be police.

"Who is this?" the voice growls.

"I'm a photographer," I manage then add hastily, "Not the press."

He asks me to explain and I do and by the time I've finished there's an officer approaching the gate. I resist the urge to run, experiencing a moment of Hitchcockian paranoia. *I didn't do it*, I want to shout.

The cop opens the gate. "Mr. Turrand?"

I acknowledge the fact and he asks me to accompany him back to the house. He says nothing as we follow the roadway up to Rivera's mansion. The day has become colder, but sweat soaks into my shirt.

Something rather gothic is what I expect from the place, but the house turns out to be modern—all straight lines, glass and hard, functional edges. An incongruously soft-edged man in a dark suit nods in my direction. He approaches and holds out his hand.

"Detective-Inspector Greer," he says. "Thank you for cooperating, Mr. Turrand"

"Ah," I say, shaking his clammy palm, "I have no idea how I can help. I don't even know what's happened."

"They're both dead." His placid eyes stare into mine. I sense his evaluation, though not as a threat.

"That's terrible," I offer, without much conviction. "How?"

"Undecided. Did you know the victims?"

"Victims?"

"Did you know them?"

"No, no, not at all. The woman . . . Mrs. Rivera . . . spoke to me at the opening yesterday. I didn't know who she was. And I've never met the other."

"I see. If you could follow me, I'd like to show you something."

At the door he gives me plastic covers to put over my shoes. "Don't touch anything," he mutters. "We're still examining the scene."

He guides me into an open area that looks out through huge plate-glass windows onto an immaculately kept and spacious yard, leading down to a small wharf and Sydney Harbor beyond. It's the kind of view you see on calendars and has to be worth millions. In the room are more cops, a forensic team with assorted gadgets and bags, and two bodies. Norma Rivera is on the floor, leaning against a white wall with her eyes staring at me, sightless—mouth open as though frozen in the middle of a passionate monologue, all secret in its meaning. There doesn't appear to be a mark on her. A man I assume is Alexander Rivera is spread-eagled on the far side of the room. There's blood pooled around him and before Greer guides me away, artfully obscuring sight of him, I realize that his head is shattered, with blood and gore forming a Jackson Pollock splatter across the polished boards.

"Is this your photograph?" Greer asks.

Norma has already hung it, giving it pride of place on an open wall beside a small bar. But the glass has been shattered and the photograph ruined; it looks as though three bullets have been fired through the print into the wall behind.

"I guess he didn't like it," I say.

"Where was the stain you reckon was on the print?"

"There." I point. "Right where the holes are."

"Do you know of any reason why the victim might have done this?"

"I told you, Inspector, I've never met the man. It was just a picture I took while I was in Mexico a few years ago."

He nods to himself, rubbing at his chin as though what I've just said is the key to some grim insight.

Then he asks if I have any objection to being fingerprinted.

"Am I a suspect?" I ask.

He shrugs. "I very much doubt it. But you did turn up here at the scene and there are procedures."

As one of his underlings takes my fingerprints and particulars, Greer presses me some more, with questions relating to my whereabouts and movements the previous night, perhaps hoping I'll be distracted by the bureaucratic chores and give myself away. He takes down Sioni's contact number so she can corroborate my alibi. I wonder if she will. Finally he decides I'm either innocent or a complete drongo and gets one of his men to show me out.

In the days that follow I discover from one of Grace's PR acquaintances that ballistics indicates it was definitely Alex Rivera who pumped three bullets *into Escena de un Asesinato #1 of 20*—but no other rounds had been fired.

"What about the one that killed him?" I ask. "He was clearly shot in the head."

"Not so, apparently," she replies. "No other bullets anywhere, no chemical residue in the wound, no projectile scoring on the skull fragments. He wasn't shot, or battered to death for that matter. They don't know what caused it. That's what's got them confused."

"I don't understand."

"Incidentally," she adds, "were you aware that he was a native of Chiapas state?"

"What?"

"Born in San Cristóbal, Mexico. Quite a coincidence, eh? Apparently his father was in the Mexican army during the 1920s and fought against the rebels. He may have been ex-militia himself. At any rate the cops suspect that Rivera was a member of one of the larger drug cartels and involved in illegal importation. They think he may have swindled his Mexican bosses. That'd be why he was killed. Retribution."

I'm aware of someone sitting on the bench at my feet, their presence obvious to me though I haven't opened my eyes yet. *Do not resist him*, a female voice whispers. My pulse quickens. I pull my old coat off my head and push myself onto one aching elbow. The night has been cold and my joints are stiff. There's no one there.

"What d'you want of me?" I shout at the empty space, scaring a group of pigeons into panicked flight. An early morning commuter across the park glances in my direction and quickly looks away again. He hurries toward the sounds of traffic beyond the trees.

June 1996. In retrospect, I realize that I can't remember ever feeling Coronela's breath on my skin, hearing her heart beat or sensing her warmth as our bodies press together. Is she still here beside me, I wonder? Was she ever here?

"We avenge our men and ourselves," she whispers. *"It may be the men who die, but it is the women who suffer."*

I want to reach over and touch her, but suddenly I'm afraid of what I'll find. It makes no sense.

The darkness thickens and night palls.

"Why me?" I ask.

Her voice seems to linger, no longer immediate, but more like a memory.

"I'm sorry, Señor Morley," she whispers. In the morning, she's gone.

August/September 1999. A cleaner named Emilio Torres dies in his flat, his skull shattered, though from what investigating officers can't tell. Inconsistencies in the forensic detail run counter to evidence that it might have been the result of a physical blow. Torres wasn't a rich man, and had lived alone, yet he'd felt compelled to buy one of my overpriced *Escena de un Asesinato* prints. He'd limped badly—from an injury sustained during the Chiapas uprising of 1994, he told Grace. That's why he was so fascinated with the photo. She sold him one of the later numbers, unframed. It was found crumpled near his body.

A few days later Gabriel Moreno, owner of a chain of Mexican restaurants, is shot in the head in his home, though no bullet can be found at the scene and nor does forensic analysis reveal sign of a weapon's discharge. He was holding the print of *Escena de un Asesinato* that he'd purchased the previous evening. His wife and son are found dead in other parts of the house, though their bodies reveal no signs of violence at all.

Robert Ortega and his wife die under mysterious circumstances the following evening. They have also bought one of my *Escena de un Asesinato* prints. Ortega has diplomatic connections with the Mexican government, though none of my sources can discover what those connections are. Whatever his job might be, it ensures that the details of his death remain hidden from the press.

I sleep badly. In the night I dream I am running through the streets of Ocosingo, pursued by a man with no face. There is a pattern, I'm sure of that, and I also know that if I can only work out what it is, I can escape the inevitable fate that awaits me. But in my blind panic I can't see the pattern, only chaos. I try to change the dream, knowing the outcome, but am unable to. Inevitably the faceless man will catch me.

Juliana Estranez buys *Escena de un Asesinato #5 of 17*, takes it home and subsequently tries to burn it. She fails and is discovered next day by her cleaner, dead on the floor near the fireplace. There is no sign of violence. Later I learn that her father had been an officer in the Mexican army during the first half of the twentieth century.

Before too long, manic with weariness and fear, I embrace what my rational mind has been avoiding and collect all remaining copies of *Escena de un Asesinato* from Grace. She doesn't understand and I can't explain. We argue.

"At least leave me a couple of them," she pleads.

"I can't."

"What are you going to do with them?"

"Doesn't matter. Just push the other photos, Grace."

"No one wants the others, Morley. They want *Escena de un Asesinato*."

"I'm not selling any more of them. That's it."

In frustration, she points out that this sort of idiosyncratic behavior might be tolerated in the Greats of the Art World, but it isn't going to do a second-rater like me much good at all.

I shrug.

She cancels the exhibition not long after I leave.

I'm too fixated on my absurd belief that the prints are haunted, too terrified of the impossible, to care one way or the other. Back in my studio, I rip the remaining prints of *Escena de un Asesinato* apart, tossing the shreds into a metal waste bin and setting them alight. For a while, as I decimate the run, I don't notice the decrease in room temperature that causes my breath to cloud, despite the flames and the heated air rising from the bin. After four or five prints have turned to ash, it seems as though my strength has leaked away, weariness overtaking me and turning the deepening shadows into a weight I can barely carry. Any blood still flowing through my veins becomes lethargic.

"Leave me alone!" I growl at the shadows that seem to fill the room.

But I've been careless. I don't have the Zapatista doll on me. It lies on a nearby bench, far away, and I glance at it now, fighting despair. My muscles have weakened to the point of almost total incapacity; I fight the feeling, staggering forward with my hand extended. The remaining prints drop from my fingers, scattering across the floor. I stagger. Ambient hiss in my ears becomes louder and louder as the sound of traffic beyond the walls disappears. And then, all around me, yet dim as though echoing from far away, I hear voices shouting in Spanish. I can't make out what they're saying, but the fury they express is unmistakable.

My fingers clasp the doll. Instantly the sounds disappear and my strength returns. The atmosphere lightens.

"Just stay away!' I rasp at the room. "I won't let this continue. "

Holding onto the doll with one hand, I scoop up the scattered prints and one-by-one drop them into the fire. Flame consumes them. But as the last blackens and shrivels, consciousness leaks out of me and I collapse onto the floor.

Living on the streets should make you feel free, but it doesn't. It's like a constant ache, a bone-cold reminder of the human connections that have foresworn you—or that you have foresworn. You are not part of the current that rushes time and the world forward. Rather, you dwell in a psychological billabong of your own, a stagnant backwater where the detritus of your past gathers to groan, to mutate, to drown you.

My life is a torrent of memories and desires, regrets and delusions. But why do the memories keep changing? Everything can't be true.

A cold wind rakes its claws through the park and I shut my eyes and hunker further into my coat. It is old and no doubt smelly, but I'm used to the stink and it's at least thick, the weave tight. It keeps out some of the chill.

Half the time now I can't remember why I burned the photos, what it was that made me imagine that posthumous resentments lingered in dark places within my mind and escaped via memory of that confused three-week visit to Mexico. The ghost of El Roto? I looked him up, back when I had internet access. El Roto—Chucho el Roto—was a bandit active at the end of the nineteenth century. He was famous, an ambiguous hero, a lover of the theatre, a seducer, and a "non-violent" thief, but he died in prison in Veracruz in 1885, possibly beaten to death. Not in the streets of Ocosingo in 1994. The woman I knew, Coronela—she'd said the doll was Genaro el Roto. Not Chucho. The designation "*el roto*"— "broken," "discarded," "abandoned"—has been applied to many unfortunates, many outlaws. What does it mean? Why did he, whoever he is, pick me to be his courier, his "people smuggler"?

You, too, are El Roto, she said.

It wasn't until much later—expelled from my studio and my apartment with whatever prints I could scavenge—when the money was gone, and I was hungry and desperate—that I decided to do what others did and sell my old, unwanted goods on the street. Some spruiked ink drawings, some old comic books, some bits of metal twisted into ornaments. Photographs? Why not? What good are they to me? As I pinned them to a scrap of cardboard in the hope that someone would buy them, one grabbed my attention. I seemed to remember it. *Escena de un Asesinato*. Hadn't I destroyed them all? One of that run, just one, had somehow survived. I couldn't recall why I'd burned the rest.

Why does knowing that one still exists give me the tremors? I clutch at the doll I keep stuffed in my coat pocket till the fear subsides.

Escena de un Asesinato has a strange possessing power, there's no doubt about that. Though I know I shouldn't, I can't help displaying it with the other, harmless prints of Mayan ruins and Chiapas countryside. An overweight man in a brown business suit is staring at me from further down the street. I recognize him, even though I see many people in a day at my railway-entrance post. He's been here before. He shuffles up, hesitant, frowning.

"That photo?' he says. "I want it."

I know which one he's referring to.

"It's not for sale."

Obsession's twitching his muscles. I imagine the fire that scalds his belly and tightens its grip on his heart, so intensely I imagine for a moment that I can see the flames burning away his resistance.

"Fight it," I say, feeling the eyes of the hooded man in the picture drilling the back of my skull.

"What?"

"It's him." I gestured at the image. The eyes are visible through the mask; at that moment their intensity makes me pull away. "It's El Roto," I explain. "He's the one that's making you want the picture."

I force myself to stand, though I feel weak and unsteady. As I lean toward him the man draws back.

"He was murdered," I whisper. "His hatred runs deep."

The man looks panicked and for a moment I believe he's about to run off again.

"He'll kill you," I tell him. "He'll kill your family."

I see the moment he capitulates. El Roto's fire leaps into his eyes. He reaches out and grabs me by the coat, teeth gritted and violence turning his desire into a weapon. "Shut up!" he snarls, and pushes me aside. I'm too weakened to resist. I stumble and fall, cracking my head against the brickwork. Commuters drift past like ghosts, some looking, conflicted, but declining to commit to helping me. I've been exiled from their stable, civilized lives and don't command protection.

Dazed, I watch the man in the business suit grab the picture, but it's too quick and my vision is too blurred for me to tell if there is triumph in the eyes of Genaro el Roto.

"Wait!" I manage, reaching into my coat and extracting the doll. "Take this. It belongs with the picture."

The man stares at it.

"They belong together," I insist, desperate for him to have it. "It'll save you."

For a moment he clutches at his forehead, as though the pressure is already building within his skull. Perhaps, at a level beyond the control of El Roto, he knows I mean what I say, even if my words seem to be nonsense.

He leans down and snatches the rough doll from my outstretched hand.

The undercurrent of guilt that lies beneath El Roto's passion breaks through. I see it on his face.

Then it's gone. The man turns and runs. Perhaps I saved him. I'll never know.

Three days later, I huddle in a disused sewer outfall, listening to the obsessive sounds of my own inner workings. The rush of blood through veins and the tighter hiss of its passage into smaller capillaries leading to the brain. Gurgling from my stomach and intestines, as they struggle to deal with whatever scraps I can find to send to them. The thudding of my heart. The white noise of tinnitus.

It should comfort me perhaps, this symphony of corporeal existence, but instead it fills me with dread. I don't know if they're the sounds of life or reminders of mortality.

Something—a shadow of something—has appeared in the photographs of ancient Mayan ruins that I took one afternoon in Toniná. It's a shape formed from shadows and I think it is coming closer. At first I believed it was El Roto, back to have his revenge on me. But no, this is something different, something more ancient and perhaps more terrible.

I don't know what to do. I'm too weak to resist, and Coronela's protection is gone.

Keep it with you at all times, she'd whispered. So all I can do is sit.

And wait.

Perhaps she'll come back to me—and change my memories once again.

Robert Hood has had over one hundred stories published, as well as three collections, and several novels including four of his Shades series of supernatural young adult novels. He's been nominated for several awards and won two Atheling Awards for Genre Criticism. He co-authored (with David Young) a vampire-oriented, text-based interactive game designed to be played via mobile phone networks. Hood co-edited (with Robin Pen) three anthologies of giant monster stories, the first of which *Daikaiju! Giant Monster Tales* which won a Ditmar Award. He currently lives with his partner, Cat Sparks, and a number of small-c cats on the Illawarra Coast of Australia and serves the Graphic Design/Publications Coordinator of the Faculty of Commerce at Wollongong University. His website is www.roberthood.net.

The old magic seems to be leaving the land. A more powerful
kind of magic has come . . .

GOOD HUNTING

Ken Liu

Night. Half moon. An occasional hoot from an owl.

The merchant and his wife and all the servants had been sent away. The large house was eerily quiet.

Father and I crouched behind the scholar's rock in the courtyard. Through the rock's many holes I could see the bedroom window of the merchant's son.

"Oh, Tsiao-jung, my sweet Tsiao-jung . . ."

The young man's feverish groans were pitiful. Half-delirious, he was tied to his bed for his own good, but Father had left a window open so that his plaintive cries could be carried by the breeze far over the rice paddies.

"Do you think she really will come?" I whispered. Today was my thirteenth birthday, and this was my first hunt.

"She will," Father said. "A *hulijing* cannot resist the cries of the man she has bewitched."

"Like how the Butterfly Lovers cannot resist each other?" I thought back to the folk opera troupe that had come through our village last fall.

"Not quite," Father said. But he seemed to have trouble explaining why. "Just know that it's not the same."

I nodded, not sure I understood. But I remembered how the merchant and his wife had come to Father to ask for his help.

"How shameful!" The merchant had muttered. "He's not even nineteen. How could he have read so many sages' books and still fall under the spell of such a creature?"

"There's no shame in being entranced by the beauty and wiles of a hulijing," *Father had said. "Even the great scholar Wong Lai once spent three nights in the company of one, and he took first place at the Imperial Examinations. Your son just needs a little help."*

"You must save him," the merchant's wife had said, bowing like a chicken pecking at rice. "If this gets out, the matchmakers won't touch him at all."

A *hulijing* was a demon who stole hearts. I shuddered, worried if I would have the courage to face one.

Father put a warm hand on my shoulder, and I felt calmer. In his hand was Swallow Tail, a sword that had first been forged by our ancestor, General Lau Yip, thirteen generations ago. The sword was charged with hundreds of Daoist blessings and had drunk the blood of countless demons.

A passing cloud obscured the moon for a moment, throwing everything into darkness.

When the moon emerged again, I almost cried out.

There, in the courtyard, was the most beautiful lady I had ever seen.

She had on a flowing white silk dress with billowing sleeves and a wide, silvery belt. Her face was pale as snow, and her hair dark as coal, draping past her waist. I thought she looked like the paintings of great beauties from the Tang Dynasty the opera troupe had hung around their stage.

She turned slowly to survey everything around her, her eyes glistening in the moonlight like two shimmering pools.

I was surprised to see how sad she looked. Suddenly, I felt sorry for her and wanted more than anything else to make her smile.

The light touch of my father's hand against the back of my neck jolted me out of my mesmerized state. He had warned me about the power of the *hulijing*. My face hot and my heart hammering, I averted my eyes from the demon's face and focused on her stance.

The merchant's servants had been patrolling the courtyard every night this week with dogs to keep her away from her victim. But now the courtyard was empty. She stood still, hesitating, suspecting a trap.

"Tsiao-jung! Have you come for me?" The son's feverish voice grew louder.

The lady turned and walked—no, glided, so smooth were her movements—towards the bedroom door.

Father jumped out from behind the rock and rushed at her with Swallow Tail.

She dodged out of the way as though she had eyes on the back of her head. Unable to stop, my father thrust the sword into the thick wooden door with a dull *thunk*. He pulled but could not free the weapon immediately.

The lady glanced at him, turned, and headed for the courtyard gate.

"Don't just stand there, Liang!" Father called. "She's getting away!"

I ran at her, dragging my clay pot filled with dog piss. It was my job to splash her with it so that she could not transform into her fox form and escape.

She turned to me and smiled. "You're a very brave boy." A scent, like jasmine blooming in spring rain, surrounded me. Her voice was like sweet, cold lotus paste, and I wanted to hear her talk forever. The clay pot dangled from my hand, forgotten.

"Now!" Father shouted. He had pulled the sword free.

I bit my lip in frustration. *How could I become a demon hunter if I was so easily enticed?* I lifted off the cover and emptied the clay pot at her retreating figure, but the insane thought that I shouldn't dirty her white dress caused my hands to shake, and my aim was wide. Only a small amount of dog piss got onto her.

But it was enough. She howled, and the sound, like a dog's but so much wilder, caused the hairs on the back of my neck to stand up. She turned and snarled, showing two rows of sharp, white teeth, and I stumbled back.

I had doused her while she was in the midst of her transformation. Her face was thus frozen halfway between a woman's and a fox's, with a hairless snout and raised, triangular ears that twitched angrily. Her hands had turned into paws, tipped with sharp claws that she swiped at me.

She could no longer speak, but her eyes conveyed her venomous thoughts without trouble.

Father rushed by me, his sword raised for a killing blow. The *hulijing* turned around and slammed into the courtyard gate, smashing it open, and disappeared through the broken door.

Father chased after her without even a glance back at me. Ashamed, I followed.

The *hulijing* was swift of foot, and her silvery tail seemed to leave a glittering trail across the fields. But her incompletely transformed body maintained a human's posture, incapable of running as fast as she could have on four legs.

Father and I saw her dodging into the abandoned temple about a *li* outside the village.

"Go around the temple," Father said, trying to catch his breath. "I will go through the front door. If she tries to flee through the back door, you know what to do."

The back of the temple was overgrown with weeds and the wall half-collapsed. As I came around, I saw a white flash darting through the rubble.

Determined to redeem myself in my father's eyes, I swallowed my fear and ran after it without hesitation. After a few quick turns, I had the thing cornered in one of the monks' cells.

I was about to pour the remaining dog piss on it when I realized that the animal was much smaller than the *hulijing* we had been chasing. It was a small white fox, about the size of a puppy.

I set the clay pot on the ground and lunged.

The fox squirmed under me. It was surprisingly strong for such a small animal. I struggled to hold it down. As we fought, the fur between my fingers seemed to become as slippery as skin, and the body elongated, expanded, grew. I had to use my whole body to wrestle it to the ground.

Suddenly, I realized that my hands and arms were wrapped around the nude body of a young girl about my age.

I cried out and jumped back. The girl stood up slowly, picked up a silk robe from behind a pile of straw, put it on, and gazed at me haughtily.

A growl came from the main hall some distance away, followed by the sound of a heavy sword crashing into a table. Then another growl, and the sound of my father's curses.

The girl and I stared at each other. She was even prettier than the opera singer that I couldn't stop thinking about last year.

"Why are you after us?" she asked. "We did nothing to you."

"Your mother bewitched the merchant's son," I said. "We have to save him."

"*Bewitched? He's* the one who wouldn't leave *her* alone."

I was taken aback. "What are you talking about?"

"One night about a month ago, the merchant's son stumbled upon my mother, caught in a chicken farmer's trap. She had to transform into her human form to escape, and as soon as he saw her, he became infatuated.

"She liked her freedom and didn't want anything to do with him. But once a man has set his heart on a *hulijing*, she cannot help hearing him no matter how far apart they are. All that moaning and crying he did drove her to distraction, and she had to go see him every night just to keep him quiet."

This was not what I learned from Father.

"She lures innocent scholars and draws on their life essence to feed her evil magic! Look how sick the merchant's son is!"

"He's sick because that useless doctor gave him poison that was supposed to make him forget about my mother. My mother is the one who's kept him alive with her nightly visits. And stop using the word *lure*. A man can fall in love with a *hulijing* just like he can with any human woman."

I didn't know what to say, so I said the first thing that came to mind. "I just know it's not the same."

She smirked. "Not the same? I saw how you looked at me before I put on my robe."

I blushed. "Brazen demon!" I picked up the clay pot. She remained where she was, a mocking smile on her face. Eventually, I put the pot back down.

The fight in the main hall grew noisier, and suddenly, there was a loud crash, followed by a triumphant shout from Father and a long, piercing scream from the woman.

There was no smirk on the girl's face now, only rage turning slowly to shock. Her eyes had lost their lively luster; they looked dead.

Another grunt from Father. The scream ended abruptly.

"Liang! Liang! It's over. Where are you?"

Tears rolled down the girl's face.

"Search the temple," my Father's voice continued. "She may have pups here. We have to kill them too."

The girl tensed.

"Liang, have you found anything?" The voice was coming closer.

"Nothing," I said, locking eyes with her. "I didn't find anything."

She turned around and silently ran out of the cell. A moment later, I saw a small white fox jump over the broken back wall and disappear into the night.

It was Qingming, the Festival of the Dead. Father and I went to sweep Mother's grave and to bring her food and drink to comfort her in the afterlife.

"I'd like to stay here for a while," I said. Father nodded and left for home.

I whispered an apology to my mother, packed up the chicken we had brought for her, and walked the three *li* to the other side of the hill, to the abandoned temple.

I found Yan kneeling in the main hall, near the place where my father had killed her mother five years ago. She wore her hair up in a bun, in the style of a young woman who had had her *jijili*, the ceremony that meant she was no longer a girl.

We'd been meeting every Qingming, every Chongyang, every Yulan, every New Year's, occasions when families were supposed to be together.

"I brought you this," I said, and handed her the steamed chicken.

"Thank you." And she carefully tore off a leg and bit into it daintily. Yan had explained to me that the *hulijing* chose to live near human villages because they liked to have human things in their lives: conversation, beautiful clothes, poetry and stories, and, occasionally, the love of a worthy, kind man.

But the *hulijing* remained hunters who felt most free in their fox form. After what happened to her mother, Yan stayed away from chicken coops, but she still missed their taste.

"How's hunting?" I asked.

"Not so great," she said. "There are few Hundred-Year Salamanders and Six-Toed Rabbits. I can't ever seem to get enough to eat." She bit off another piece of chicken, chewed, and swallowed. "I'm having trouble transforming too."

"It's hard for you to keep this shape?"

"No." She put the rest of the chicken on the ground and whispered a prayer to her mother.

"I mean it's getting harder for me to return to my true form," she continued, "to hunt. Some nights I can't do it at all. How's hunting for you?"

"Not so great either. There don't seem to be as many snake spirits or angry ghosts as a few years ago. Even hauntings by suicides with unfinished business are down. And we haven't had a proper jumping corpse in months. Father is worried about money."

We also hadn't had to deal with a *hulijing* in years. Maybe Yan had warned them all away. Truth be told, I was relieved. I didn't relish the prospect of having to tell my father that he was wrong about something. He was already very irritable, anxious that he was losing the respect of the villagers now that his knowledge and skill didn't seem to be needed as much.

"Ever think that maybe the jumping corpses are also misunderstood?" she asked. "Like me and my mother?"

She laughed as she saw my face. "Just kidding!"

It was strange, what Yan and I shared. She wasn't exactly a friend. More like someone who you couldn't help being drawn to because you shared the knowledge of how the world didn't work the way you had been told.

She looked at the chicken bits she had left for her mother. "I think magic is being drained out of this land."

I had suspected that something was wrong, but didn't want to voice my suspicion out loud, which would make it real.

"What do you think is causing it?"

Instead of answering, Yan perked up her ears and listened intently. Then she got up, grabbed my hand, and pulled until we were behind the buddha in the main hall.

"Wha—"

She held up her finger against my lips. So close to her, I finally noticed her scent. It was like her mother's, floral and sweet, but also bright, like blankets dried in the sun. I felt my face grow warm.

A moment later, I heard a group of men making their way into the temple. Slowly, I inched my head out from behind the buddha so I could see.

It was a hot day, and the men were seeking some shade from the noon sun. Two men set down a cane sedan chair, and the passenger who stepped off was a foreigner, with curly yellow hair and pale skin. Other men in the group carried tripods, levels, bronze tubes, and open trunks full of strange equipment.

"Most Honored Mister Thompson." A man dressed like a mandarin came up to the foreigner. The way he kept on bowing and smiling and bouncing his head up and down reminded me of a kicked dog begging for favors. "Please have a rest and drink some cold tea. It is hard for the men to be working on the day when they're supposed to visit the graves of their families, and they need to take a little time to pray lest they anger the gods and spirits. But I promise we'll work hard afterwards and finish the survey on time."

"The trouble with you Chinese is your endless superstition," the foreigner said. He had a strange accent, but I could understand him just fine. "Remember, the Hong Kong-Tientsin Railroad is a priority for Great Britain. If I don't get as far as Botou Village by sunset, I'll be docking all of your wages."

I had heard rumors that the Manchu Emperor had lost a war and been forced to give up all kinds of concessions, one of which involved paying to help the foreigners build a road of iron. But it had all seemed so fantastical that I didn't pay much attention.

The mandarin nodded enthusiastically. "Most Honored Mister Thompson is right in every way. But might I trouble your gracious ear with a suggestion?"

The weary Englishman waved impatiently.

"Some of the local villagers are worried about the proposed path of the railroad. You see, they think the tracks that have already been laid are blocking off veins of *qi* in the earth. It's bad *feng shui*."

"What are you talking about?"

"It is kind of like how a man breathes," the mandarin said, huffing a few times to make sure the Englishman understood. "The land has channels along rivers, hills, ancient roads that carry the energy of *qi*. It's what gives the villages prosperity and maintains the rare animals and local spirits and household gods. Could you consider shifting the line of the tracks a little, to follow the *feng shui* masters' suggestions?"

Thompson rolled his eyes. "That is the most ridiculous thing I've yet heard. You want me to deviate from the most efficient path for our railroad because you think your idols would be angry?"

The mandarin looked pained. "Well, in the places where the tracks have already been laid, many bad things are happening: people losing money, animals dying, household gods not responding to prayers. The Buddhist and Daoist monks all agree that it's the railroad."

Thompson strode over to the buddha and looked at it appraisingly. I ducked back behind the statue and squeezed Yan's hand. We held our breaths, hoping that we wouldn't be discovered.

"Does this one still have any power?" Thompson asked.

"The temple hasn't been able to maintain a contingent of monks for many years," the mandarin said. "But this buddha is still well respected. I hear villagers say that prayers to him are often answered."

Then I heard a loud crash and a collective gasp from the men in the main hall.

"I've just broken the hands off of this god of yours with my cane," Thompson said. "As you can see, I have not been struck by lightning or suffered any other calamity. Indeed, now we know that it is only an idol made of mud stuffed with straw and covered in cheap paint. This is why you people lost the war to Britain. You worship statues of mud when you should be thinking about building roads from iron and weapons from steel."

There was no more talk about changing the path of the railroad.

After the men were gone, Yan and I stepped out from behind the statue. We gazed at the broken hands of the buddha for a while.

"The world's changing," Yan said. "Hong Kong, iron roads, foreigners with wires that carry speech and machines that belch smoke. More and more, storytellers in the teahouses speak of these wonders. I think that's why the old magic is leaving. A more powerful kind of magic has come."

She kept her voice unemotional and cool, like a placid pool of water in autumn, but her words rang true. I thought about my father's attempts to keep up a cheerful mien as fewer and fewer customers came to us. I wondered if the time I spent learning the chants and the sword dance moves were wasted.

"What will you do?" I asked, thinking about her, alone in the hills and unable to find the food that sustained her magic.

"There's only one thing I *can* do." Her voice broke for a second and became defiant, like a pebble tossed into the pool.

But then she looked at me, and her composure returned. "There's only one thing *we* can do: Learn to survive."

The railroad soon became a familiar part of the landscape: the black locomotive huffing through the green rice paddies, puffing steam and pulling a long train behind it, like a dragon coming down from the distant, hazy, blue mountains. For a while, it was a wondrous sight, with children marveling at it, running alongside the tracks to keep up.

But the soot from the locomotive chimneys killed the rice in the fields closest to the tracks, and two children playing on the tracks, too frightened to move, were killed one afternoon. After that, the train ceased to fascinate.

People stopped coming to Father and me to ask for our services. They either went to the Christian missionary or the new teacher who said he'd studied in San Francisco. Young men in the village began to leave for Hong Kong or Canton, moved by rumors of bright lights and well-paying work. Fields lay fallow. The village itself seemed to consist only of the too-old and too-young, and their mood one of resignation. Men from distant provinces came to inquire about buying land for cheap.

Father spent his days sitting in the front room, Swallow Tail over his knee, staring out the door from dawn to dusk, as though he himself had turned into a statue.

Every day, as I returned home from the fields, I would see the glint of hope in Father's eyes briefly flare up.

"Did anyone speak of needing our help?" he would ask.

"No," I would say, trying to keep my tone light. "But I'm sure there will be a jumping corpse soon. It's been too long."

I would not look at my father as I spoke because I did not want to look as hope faded from his eyes.

Then, one day, I found Father hanging from the heavy beam in his bedroom. As I let his body down, my heart numb, I thought that he was not unlike those he had hunted all his life: they were all sustained by an old magic that had left and would not return, and they did not know how to survive without it.

Swallow Tail felt dull and heavy in my hand. I had always thought I would be a demon hunter, but how could I when there were no more demons, no more spirits? All the Daoist blessings in the sword could not save my father's sinking heart. And if I stuck around, perhaps my heart would grow heavy and yearn to be still too.

I hadn't seen Yan since that day six years ago, when we hid from the railroad surveyors at the temple. But her words came back to me now.

Learn to survive.

I packed a bag and bought a train ticket to Hong Kong.

The Sikh guard checked my papers and waved me through the security gate.

I paused to let my gaze follow the tracks going up the steep side of the mountain. It seemed less like a railroad track than a ladder straight up to heaven. This was the funicular railway, the tram line to the top of Victoria Peak, where the masters of Hong Kong lived and the Chinese were forbidden to stay.

But the Chinese were good enough to shovel coal into the boilers and grease the gears.

Steam rose around me as I ducked into the engine room. After five years, I knew the rhythmic rumbling of the pistons and the staccato grinding of the gears as well as I knew my own breath and heartbeat. There was a kind of music to their orderly cacophony that moved me, like the clashing of cymbals and gongs at the start of a folk opera. I checked the pressure, applied sealant on the gaskets, tightened the flanges, replaced the worn-down gears in the backup cable assembly. I lost myself in the work, which was hard and satisfying.

By the end of my shift, it was dark. I stepped outside the engine room and saw a full moon in the sky as another tram filled with passengers was pulled up the side of the mountain, powered by my engine.

"Don't let the Chinese ghosts get you," a woman with bright blond hair said in the tram, and her companions laughed.

It was the night of Yulan, I realized, the Ghost Festival. *I should get something for my father, maybe pick up some paper money at Mongkok.*

"How can you be done for the day when we still want you?" a man's voice came to me.

"Girls like you shouldn't tease," another man said, and laughed.

I looked in the direction of the voices and saw a Chinese woman standing in the shadows just outside the tram station. Her tight western-style cheongsam and the garish makeup told me her profession. Two Englishmen blocked her path. One tried to put his arms around her, and she backed out of the way.

"Please. I'm very tired," she said in English. "Maybe next time."

"Now, don't be stupid," the first man said, his voice hardening. "This isn't a discussion. Come along now and do what you're supposed to."

I walked up to them. "Hey."

The men turned around and looked at me.

"What seems to be the problem?"

"None of your business."

"Well, I think it *is* my business," I said, "seeing as how you're talking to my sister."

I doubt either of them believed me. But five years of wrangling heavy machinery had given me a muscular frame, and they took a look at my face and hands, grimy with engine grease, and probably decided that it wasn't worth it to get into a public tussle with a lowly Chinese engineer.

The two men stepped away to get in line for the Peak Tram, muttering curses.

"Thank you," she said.

"It's been a long time," I said, looking at her. I swallowed the *you look good.* She didn't. She looked tired and thin and brittle. And the pungent perfume she wore assaulted my nose.

But I did not think of her harshly. Judging was the luxury of those who did not need to survive.

"It's the night of the Ghost Festival," she said. "I didn't want to work any more. I wanted to think about my mother."

"Why don't we go get some offerings together?" I asked.

We took the ferry over to Kowloon, and the breeze over the water revived her a bit. She wet a towel with the hot water from the teapot on the ferry and wiped off her make up. I caught a faint trace of her natural scent, fresh and lovely as always.

"You look good," I said, and meant it.

On the streets of Kowloon, we bought pastries and fruits and cold dumplings and a steamed chicken and incense and paper money, and caught up on each other's lives.

"How's hunting?" I asked. We both laughed.

"I miss being a fox," she said. She nibbled on a chicken wing absent-mindedly. "One day, shortly after that last time we talked, I felt the last bit of magic leave me. I could no longer transform."

"I'm sorry," I said, unable to offer anything else.

"My mother taught me to like human things: food, clothes, folk opera, old stories. But she was never dependent on them. When she wanted, she could always turn into her true form and hunt. But now, in this form, what can I do? I don't have claws. I don't have sharp teeth. I can't even run very fast. All I have is my beauty, the same thing that your father and you killed my mother for. So now I live by the very thing that you once falsely accused my mother of doing: I *lure* men for money."

"My father is dead, too."

Hearing this seemed to drain some of the bitterness out of her. "What happened?"

"He felt the magic leave us, much as you. He couldn't bear it."

"I'm sorry." And I knew that she didn't know what else to say either.

"You told me once that the only thing we can do is to survive. I have to thank you for that. It probably saved my life."

"Then we're even," she said, smiling. "But let us not speak of ourselves any more. Tonight is reserved for the ghosts."

We went down to the harbor and placed our food next to the water, inviting all the ghosts we had loved to come and dine. Then we lit the incense and burned the paper money in a bucket.

She watched bits of burnt paper being carried into the sky by the heat from the flames. They disappeared among the stars. "Do you think the gates to the underworld still open for the ghosts tonight, now that there is no magic left?"

I hesitated. When I was young I had been trained to hear the scratching of a ghost's fingers against a paper window, to distinguish the voice of a spirit from the wind. But now I was used to enduring the thunderous pounding of pistons and the deafening hiss of high-pressured steam rushing through valves. I could no longer claim to be attuned to that vanished world of my childhood.

"I don't know," I said. "I suppose it's the same with ghosts as with people. Some will figure out how to survive in a world diminished by iron roads and steam whistles, some will not."

"But will any of them thrive?" she asked.

She could still surprise me.

"I mean," she continued, "are you happy? Are you happy to keep an engine running all day, yourself like another cog? What do you dream of?"

I couldn't remember any dreams. I had let myself become entranced by the movement of gears and levers, to let my mind grow to fit the gaps between the ceaseless clanging of metal on metal. It was a way to not have to think about my father, about a land that had lost so much.

"I dream of hunting in this jungle of metal and asphalt," she said. "I dream of my true form leaping from beam to ledge to terrace to roof, until I am at the top of this island, until I can growl in the faces of all the men who believe they can own me."

As I watched, her eyes, brightly lit for a moment, dimmed.

"In this new age of steam and electricity, in this great metropolis, except for those who live on the Peak, is anyone still in their true form?" she asked.

We sat together by the harbor and burned paper money all night, waiting for a sign that the ghosts were still with us.

Life in Hong Kong could be a strange experience: from day to day, things never seemed to change much. But if you compared things over a few years, it was almost like you lived in a different world.

By my thirtieth birthday, new designs for steam engines required less coal and delivered more power. They grew smaller and smaller. The streets filled with automatic rickshaws and horseless carriages, and most people who could afford them had machines that kept the air cool in houses and the food cold in boxes in the kitchen—all powered by steam.

I went into stores and endured the ire of the clerks as I studied the components of new display models. I devoured every book on the principle and operation of the steam engine I could find. I tried to apply those principles to improve the machines I was in charge of: trying out new firing cycles, testing new kinds of lubricants for the pistons, adjusting the gear ratios. I found a measure of satisfaction in the way I came to understand the magic of the machines.

One morning, as I repaired a broken governor—a delicate bit of work—two pairs of polished shoes stopped on the platform above me.

I looked up. Two men looked down at me.

"This is the one," said my shift supervisor.

The other man, dressed in a crisp suit, looked skeptical. "Are you the man who came up with the idea of using a larger flywheel for the old engine?"

I nodded. I took pride in the way I could squeeze more power out of my machines than dreamed of by their designers.

"You did not steal the idea from an Englishman?" his tone was severe.

I blinked. A moment of confusion was followed by a rush of anger. "No," I said, trying to keep my voice calm. I ducked back under the machine to continue my work.

"He is clever," my shift supervisor said, "for a Chinaman. He can be taught."

"I suppose we might as well try," said the other man. "It will certainly be cheaper than hiring a real engineer from England."

Mr. Alexander Findlay Smith, owner of the Peak Tram and an avid engineer himself, had seen an opportunity. He foresaw that the path of technological progress would lead inevitably to the use of steam power to operate automata: mechanical arms and legs that would eventually replace the Chinese coolies and servants.

I was selected to serve Mr. Findlay Smith in his new venture.

I learned to repair clockwork, to design intricate systems of gears and devise ingenious uses for levers. I studied how to plate metal with chrome and how to shape brass into smooth curves. I invented ways to connect the world of hardened and ruggedized clockwork to the world of miniaturized and regulated piston and clean steam. Once the automata were finished, we connected them to the latest analytic engines shipped from Britain and fed them with tape punched with dense holes in Babbage-Lovelace code.

It had taken a decade of hard work. But now mechanical arms served drinks in the bars along Central and machine hands fashioned shoes and clothes in factories in the New Territories. In the mansions up on the Peak, I heard—though I'd never seen—that automatic sweepers and mops I designed roamed the halls discreetly, bumping into walls gently as they cleaned the floors like mechanical elves puffing out bits of white steam. The expats could finally live their lives in this tropical paradise free of reminders of the presence of the Chinese.

I was thirty-five when she showed up at my door again, like a memory from long ago.

I pulled her into my tiny flat, looked around to be sure no one was following her, and closed the door.

"How's hunting?" I asked. It was a bad attempt at a joke, and she laughed weakly.

Photographs of her had been in all the papers. It was the biggest scandal in the colony: not so much because the governor's son was keeping a Chinese mistress—it was expected that he would—but because the mistress had managed to steal a large sum of money from him and then disappear. Everyone tittered while the police turned the city upside down, looking for her.

"I can hide you for tonight," I said. Then I waited, the unspoken second half of my sentence hanging between us.

She sat down in the only chair in the room, the dim light bulb casting dark shadows on her face. She looked gaunt and exhausted. "Ah, now you're judging me."

"I have a good job I want to keep," I said. "Mr. Findlay Smith trusts me."

She bent down and began to pull up her dress.

"Don't," I said, and turned my face away. I could not bear to watch her try to ply her trade with me.

"Look," she said. There was no seduction in her voice. "Liang, look at me."

I turned and gasped.

Her legs, what I could see of them, were made of shiny chrome. I bent down to look closer: the cylindrical joints at the knees were lathed with precision, the pneumatic actuators along the thighs moved in complete silence, the feet were exquisitely molded and shaped, the surfaces smooth and flowing. These were the most beautiful mechanical legs I had ever seen.

"He had me drugged," she said. "When I woke up, my legs were gone and replaced by these. The pain was excruciating. He explained to me that he had a secret: he liked machines more than flesh, couldn't get hard with a regular woman."

I had heard of such men. In a city filled with chrome and brass and clanging and hissing, desires became confused.

I focused on the way light moved along the gleaming curves of her calves so that I didn't have to look into her face.

"I had a choice: let him keep on changing me to suit him, or he could remove the legs and throw me out on the street. Who would believe a legless Chinese whore? I wanted to survive. So I swallowed the pain and let him continue."

She stood up and removed the rest of her dress and her evening gloves. I took in her chrome torso, slatted around the waist to allow articulation and movement; her sinuous arms, constructed from curved plates sliding over each other like obscene armor; her hands, shaped from delicate metal mesh, with dark steel fingers tipped with jewels where the fingernails would be.

"He spared no expense. Every piece of me is built with the best craftsmanship and attached to my body by the best surgeons—there are many who want to experiment, despite the law, with how the body could be animated by electricity, nerves replaced by wires. They always spoke only to him, as if I was already only a machine.

"Then, one night, he hurt me and I struck back in desperation. He fell like he was made of straw. I realized, suddenly, how much strength I had in my metal arms. I had let him do all this to me, to replace me part by part, mourning my loss all the while without understanding what I had gained. A terrible thing had been done to me, but I could also be *terrible*.

"I choked him until he fainted, and then I took all the money I could find and left.

"So I come to you, Liang. Will you help me?"

I stepped up and embraced her. "We'll find some way to reverse this. There must be doctors—"

"No," she interrupted me. "That's not what I want."

It took us almost a whole year to complete the task. Yan's money helped, but some things money couldn't buy, especially skill and knowledge.

My flat became a workshop. We spent every evening and all of Sundays working: shaping metal, polishing gears, reattaching wires.

Her face was the hardest. It was still flesh.

I poured over books of anatomy and took casts of her face with plaster of Paris. I broke my cheekbones and cut my face so that I could stagger into surgeons' offices and learn from them how to repair these injuries. I bought expensive jeweled masks and took them apart, learning the delicate art of shaping metal to take on the shape of a face.

Finally, it was time.

Through the window, the moon threw a pale white parallelogram on the floor. Yan stood in the middle of it, moving her head about, trying out her new face.

Hundreds of miniature pneumatic actuators were hidden under the smooth chrome skin, each of which could be controlled independently, allowing her to adopt any expression. But her eyes were still the same, and they shone in the moonlight with excitement.

"Are you ready?" I asked.

She nodded.

I handed her a bowl, filled with the purest anthracite coal, ground into a fine powder. It smelled of burnt wood, of the heart of the earth. She poured it into her mouth and swallowed. I could hear the fire in the miniature boiler in her torso grow hotter as the pressure of the steam built up. I took a step back.

She lifted her head to the moon and howled: it was a howl made by steam passing through brass piping, and yet it reminded me of that wild howl long ago, when I first heard the call of a *hulijing*.

Then she crouched to the floor. Gears grinding, pistons pumping, curved metal plates sliding over each other—the noises grew louder as she began to transform.

She had drawn the first glimmers of her idea with ink on paper. Then she had refined it, through hundreds of iterations until she was satisfied. I could see traces of her mother in it, but also something harder, something new.

Working from her idea, I had designed the delicate folds in the chrome skin and the intricate joints in the metal skeleton. I had put together every hinge, assembled every gear, soldered every wire, welded every seam, oiled every actuator. I had taken her apart and put her back together.

Yet, it was a marvel to see everything working. In front of my eyes, she folded and unfolded like a silvery origami construction, until finally, a chrome fox as beautiful and deadly as the oldest legends stood before me.

She padded around the flat, testing out her sleek new form, trying out her stealthy new movements. Her limbs gleamed in the moonlight, and her tail, made of delicate silver wires as fine as lace, left a trail of light in the dim flat.

She turned and walked—no, glided—towards me, a glorious hunter, an ancient vision coming alive. I took a deep breath and smelled fire and smoke, engine oil and polished metal, the scent of power.

"Thank you," she said, and leaned in as I put my arms around her true form. The steam engine inside her had warmed her cold metal body, and it felt warm and alive.

"Can you feel it?" she asked.

I shivered. I knew what she meant. The old magic was back but changed: not fur and flesh, but metal and fire.

"I will find others like me," she said, "and bring them to you. Together, we will set them free."

Once, I was a demon hunter. Now, I am one of them.

I opened the door, Swallow Tail in my hand. It was only an old and heavy sword, rusty, but still perfectly capable of striking down anyone who might be lying in wait.

No one was.

Yan leapt out of the door like a bolt of lightning. Stealthily, gracefully, she darted into the streets of Hong Kong, free, feral, a *hulijing* built for this new age.

. . . *once a man has set his heart on a* hulijing, *she cannot help hearing him no matter how far apart they are* . . .

"Good hunting," I whispered.

She howled in the distance, and I watched a puff of steam rise into the air as she disappeared.

I imagined her running along the tracks of the funicular railway, a tireless engine racing up, and up, towards the top of Victoria Peak, towards a future as full of magic as the past.

⊰———⊱

Ken Liu's fiction has appeared in The Magazine of *Fantasy &Science Fiction*, *Asimov's*, *Analog*, *Strange Horizons*, *Lightspeed*, and *Clarkesworld*, among other

places. He has won a Nebula, a Hugo, a World Fantasy Award, and a Science
Fiction & Fantasy Translation Award, and been nominated for the Sturgeon
and the Locus Awards. He lives near Boston with his family.

*There was a presence in the cold, peering from the darkened alleys
and discarded refuse, spying from between bricks and mortar . . .*

GO HOME AGAIN

Simon Strantzas

She remembered so little of her father, but what she did was vivid, crystalized
in the fractures of her psyche. His sour breath, his distended gorge rising and
falling as he stared at her, licking his razor lips. If she closed her eyes, she could
almost hear his slurred voice bellowing at her cowering mother. The phantoms
of his presence surrounded her. She knew this was so because every part of her
wanted to break down into sobs. But she would not offer even his memory that
satisfaction. In hindsight, she could remember his withering face, his jaundiced
skin, his waning strength, but none of these things struck her as abnormal.
She was blind to the truth and perhaps always had been. Even when her father
disappeared for good, she did not question it. Ives knew nothing more of life
than that, believed the world was one way and no other. Even if she could
not express the thought, she understood that nothing was permanent, that
everything in the world tended toward chaos. It was the reason fathers died and
black mold infected the only tangible proof they had ever existed at all.

Afterward, once bruises healed and wounds scarred, once Ives was old
enough to understand, her mother told tales of her husband, of his generosity,
of the feats he had accomplished before his death, but Ives understood those
notions could not be reconciled with the shade that haunted her memory—the
man who had glared at her between crib slats, the man whose skin seeped
terminal foulness. They were the true memories, and Ives would be the keeper
of them if her mother could not.

The return to the house had been slowed only by Ives's reluctance and a
basement window swollen shut. So many years spent fleeing only to return
and find nothing had changed. Nothing beyond the creep of fungus across the
walls. Ives shined her flashlight as she carefully trod, part of her scouring the
rubble for any mark of her late father's passing, but she found none. Instead,
only gravity's constant desire to unmake them.

The noxious mold had spread across vacant rooms, swirling around broken fixtures and outlets. It was a bizarre pattern, one she very nearly understood and yet one that remained frustratingly beyond. Part of her longed to touch the spreading cancer, as though that would somehow reveal what had been so deceptively hidden, but she resisted. It was a trap: touching the growth offered no reward she might want. And yet, again, the longing was there, like the ache to leap from the edge of a bottomless gorge, or to thrust a hand deep into the flames of a fire—that urge to experience death, even while running fleet-footed from it.

The floating spores were so thick in the air that Ives could barely breathe. They coated her mouth, slipped down into her lungs—the mere thought scratching her throat, wanting her to cough. Instead, she bit down and stifled the sensation before she inadvertently launched more spores into the air. Her eyes filled with tears, tears for no one but her, for nothing but what life had brought her on a platter and tried to convince her was fruit. But she was no fool; if it were, it would not be so terribly bitter.

Anchorless, her pale mother floundered. With no forethought, she moved them from Montreal to Ottawa, where she believed a new beginning awaited. But her anxieties made the trip along with them, and those few places where she found employment were impossible to maintain. Ives had no better luck entering school mid-stream—her English was poor and their living arrangements were far too mercurial for any allowances to be made. Instead, she remained with her mother and feigned happiness in hopes it would inspire the same. But her mother was not her. She was not strong, and she could do little to keep food on their table, or soon enough a roof over their heads. Ives was barely nine by the time she was sleeping in a parked car with her mother, and nowhere near ten when her mother left to get food and never returned. Ives waited patiently in the car for days, staring at the buildings along the street. It was between their brick she saw the first sign of her life's infection, a small vein of darkness that broke through the mortar like a snake from its skin.

The house fared worse. No one had stepped foot within its skewed walls since Ives and her mother had left in tears. What once was solid became less so—a phantasm fading from notice, invisible to the world around it. Ives, too, nearly passed it on her approach, the overgrown landscape obscuring the drive, and it was only the tug of memories unburied that caused her to slow enough to spot it.

Artwork from Ives's young hands remained affixed to the broken refrigerator, but what shapes she once drew had become a mystery. Lines, spirals, blobs, each so carefully delineated, some arcane pattern whose purpose had been long forgotten. A sorrowful atmosphere pervaded. Within it, a faded table and set of chairs materialized, as though from Ives's half-remembered past. She ran her finger across the surface and left marks in the dust like scars, but the colors beneath were no less muted. She shined her flashlight on the kitchen wall where the black mold expanded outward like a web, spiraling from the cracks and into others, glistening in the harsh light.

Ives imagined the tumors had been black and tuberous, poison growing inside her father, and her mother's loathing for life could have been little different. Both stole everything. Ives had and abandoned her with no hope of survival. But she did survive. The abandoned car was her shelter, her home, and though she knew somewhere deep inside that her mother would never return, she continued to wait. Even when she was discovered by a parking officer, even when she was taken back to the station by child service workers, she silently waited. It was only after she was given a room with other children, asked to sleep and eat and wait with boys and girls whose parents had lost them, that she saw the dark entirety of her life in full relief. She was nothing like those children. She remained alone in her cot, staring at the corners of the walls, no longer waiting for something she finally understood would never come.

What she would not reveal was what she witnessed while inside that locked automobile, waiting for her mother to bring her food. People of different shapes and ages walked by, most ignoring the old car, some peering in the windows. For these, she did as her mother instructed and hid beneath a blanket, remaining perfectly still until she was sure they had gone, and then waiting a time longer. There was more outside the car to worry over, more than scarred men and staggering, hard-faced women. There was a presence in the cold, peering from the darkened alleys and discarded refuse, spying from between bricks and mortar. It wanted her, wanted her as she had never been wanted before. Had she known where to go, she might have run and not looked back.

Dim salvation came in the guise of an aunt she never knew existed, summoned from Sherbrooke by the call of the police. Ives was collected into open arms and taken away, back to that small town to be given the sort of life she never thought possible. There, she was safe, impossibly loved by a woman who had given up on a child of her own, and yet Ives still could not scrape her soul of the crooked house's stain. She lay awake at night in her soft, painted room, wondering whether it was back there that everything had begun to go wrong, if it was there that her infinite choices had been to a single devastating place.

Was that decaying house any different than her? Sickness grew along its foundations, ate away its support, spread in ever-widening circles so as to consume everything around it. Fingers of mold reached out like shadows across the walls, the ceilings, the floors. She could see them quiver in the beam of her flashlight, struggling to be cloaked once again so they would be free to move, to touch, to explore. If she closed her eyes, she could imagine them wrapping around her throat, trying to choke the last dregs of life from her battered body.

She stood at the foot of the uneven stairs to the second floor and felt awash in evocations of childhood more vivid than any before. The flashlight's small circle climbed the treads before her. Ives found herself surprised it did not light the face of her own younger version, perched on the stair halfway between floors with stuffed toy in hand, staring up at what loomed at the summit. A cold chill ran along Ives's legs, the specter of something behind her, but the flashlight found nothing—no haunting spirits of the past, no memories made flesh. Instead, there was an empty sitting room, the plaster of its walls crumbling with neglect.

Three bedrooms with open doors waited at the top of the stairs, but she had no desire to enter any of them. The air smelled of stale earth, and she wondered if she had not erred in returning to the house. What hid in the corners of that forgotten hallway? Were they mere shadows or masses of that black mold, expanding from the bubbling walls as though it were more than simply a fungus, as though it were something from beyond trying to force its way through? Part of her sought an explanation that would bring some modicum of sense to all she had experienced, but inside her head was another voice, wiser and unfamiliar, that wanted her to leave the house and never look back. It was that voice she almost obeyed.

But one door, one room, would not be dismissed. She could feel a force within it drawing her, wordlessly promising the answers she had so long sought. The air had so congealed with dust and spores, as dense and sickening as honey, that she had to push her way slowly through it. With each step forward, her hesitation increased. Every fiber of her being warned her, but she continued, despite knowing she would find nothing to bandage her suffering wounds. Closure was a lie the world wanted to believe. But there could be no closure, no ending, There were no circles, only lines, each with a beginning and an end. And there was nothing between.

As though Ives's vision had once been fogged, suddenly the shape at the center of the room snapped into focus, though Ives did not believe it was possible. It was a crib, her crib—she would forever recognize those slats—but its once-protective shape had been corrupted by teeming black mold. Ives shined her flashlight and saw the mold had spread everywhere, across every wall, every surface, strains of it in a Fibonacci spiral, each tendril recursively spiraling until every surface was inhabited, The black mold pulsed underneath her flashlight like veins of a body, pumping dark ichor throughout. When she traced them back, each strand clearly originated from a single place, one colorless position in the middle of the room. The place where Ives's blackened crib stood.

She could not resist coughing any longer, the dense air accreting in her lungs, and the echo that reflected did not sound proper. It was as though it emerged from another, one who both mocked Ives while striving to become her. Colder, deeper, it lacked any of the nuances of human speech. It was alien. When she turned around once more to point her flashlight beam at what stood behind her, what she found was not merely spore-filled air but something far worse.

It was a shape, darker than the shadows around it. It had no face, no real head of any kind beyond a formless lump. There were no eyes, but it saw her nonetheless. She knew it saw her, for it choreographed its movements with hers. The thing stood nearly her height, was wider than her by half. Where might have hung arms instead grew a bundle of long tendrils, each pulsing and stretching into the black course that erupted from the crib. The surface of the shapes bubbled like molten rock, cauliflower protuberances covering its body. It was not human, but it wanted to be. Wanted to grow legs and arms and a face. Wanted to look her in the eye for some unfathomable purpose. The smell was utterly repulsive, but it was that odor that clarified its origins, led Ives to understand what it was that slouched toward her, waiting to be born. Holes pockmarked its body, visible only in the light's reflection off its glazed surface, and those openings shrank with each advancing step, its strength growing. Terror strangled the words in Ives's throat, but her fractured mind finally put the pieces together. Despite her horrible choking fear, she managed to scream aloud, "Daddy! No!"

But the words aloud revealed their wrongness. The black mold had tricked her, betrayed her, for what reached out and entangled her in its approximate arms was not her father. It could not be. What embraced her in a malodourous grip did so not with anger or resentment, disgust, hate, or vengeance. What took her in its arms was something else. something so foreign to any of those that she did not know if it had a name. But it took her, regardless, and though she struggled like a demon against it, she knew it was too late. She had been infected. The black alien spores within her had finally taken root.

She remained an eternity in its embrace, time itself slowed by the solidified air. Thoughts coursed through her suspended mind, visions of the past feverishly rushing by, stripped of all meaning. She had no control, her resistance paling in the face of the sickly mold's control. She could not breathe, her body struggling for air but unable to expel the mass of spores from her

SIMON STRANTZAS

lungs. The tendrils that bound her absorbed her convulsions. As though in defense, her mind detached itself and fell into a warm state of delirium.

When consciousness returned, it did so gradually. It was only when she finally opened her eyes that the briar of tendrils that trapped her loosened their grip. Ives fell the floor, breathless, black decay spewing from her lungs, and looked up to see that half-formed grotesquery before her start to liquefy, the dark ooze seeping into the cracks between the warped floorboards. Coughing, she found herself reaching toward it, but, as her hand pressed into it, what remained burst like a thin membrane and rained the rest of its foulness onto the thirsty floor.

When Ives finally found strength enough to stand, she did so on wobbly legs. Her chest still burned from what she had experienced; her head ached, full of unsettled memories. She retrieved the flashlight from where it had fallen and used it to discover that no trace of the half-formed thing remained. But there was more that had disappeared. The dark crib in the middle of the room had gone as well. As she shined the light on the walls around her, she saw that the mesh of fungus no longer glistened as it had before. Its color dulled, pieces had already begun to fall away. It was then Ives experienced the vivid realization of how utterly empty the house really was, how devoid of anything that she might care about. It was the debris of another life, remnants of another world that fell further away the faster the warming spores inside of her multiplied and grew. Pieces of wall crumbled around her like an avalanche, but she uneasily stepped over the debris and toward the rickety stairs. With each step she took, more strength returned, her once stumbling steps becoming confident strides. As her fear ebbed, the house's walls began to shrink, returning to a shape more ordinary than her memories once painted. Pieces of the house rained down around her as she strode to the front door. When she reached it she threw it open, letting a flood of daylight sweep into the house.

She stepped outside and marveled. The sun had risen, something the mold-coated windows could no longer keep secret. She stared up at the hanging orb. Though she wanted to look away, she could not. It was too large, too overwhelming, and she felt its intense heat. It burned away the last part of her taking refuge in the crumbling house of her childhood, a house she had built from the bricks of her past. She walked away from it and never looked back.

Simon Strantzas is the author of the critically-acclaimed short story collections *Beneath the Surface*, *Cold to the Touch*, and *Nightingale Songs*, as well as the editor of *Shadows Edge*. His writing has appeared in *The Mammoth Book of*

Best New Horror, and *The Year's Best Dark Fantasy & Horror*, and has been nominated for the British Fantasy Award. He lives in Toronto, Canada, with his wife and an unyielding hunger for the flesh of the living. Find out more at www.strantzas.com.

It was then that he saw the angel. It stood by the tool shed. It did not descend in a cloud, nor announce itself with voices singing . . .

THE BIRD COUNTRY

K. M. Ferebee

Childer killed the boy during the night, quietly, on the bed's Egyptian cotton sheets. On sheets as white as sun lining the back of the Nile, he knelt atop the boy, knees on either side of his chest, and held a pillow over the boy's face until he ceased to breathe. Childer had to check, afterwards, the breath. He checked it with a hand mirror: the Victorian way. If some small exhalation smeared the glass, then Childer would have to cover the face again. It felt sullied the second time around, profane. The path from life to death should be direct and steady. There shouldn't be any detours along the way.

The boy's name was Finn, and he was fair-haired. Sixteen years old. Childer had taken him out for a walk in the fields. The fields fallow this close to winter, stripped of their hay. Finn's breath came in pale, coiled bursts against the frosted air. In the warm molting color of autumn his hair seemed light, his skin translucent. He wore a woolen scarf. His family were Irish, and it was in his manner of speaking, his long soft vowels as he said, "In the old days, of course, people knew what winter meant. Not just a season, but the killing season. When the light and heat go out of things. How do we know we'll get them back? That's a lot of Christian faith, right there."

In the house between night and dawn, as Finn's body cooled beside him on the cotton sheets and the country wind came cold through the cracks in the glass pane, Childer thought about the boy's voice saying these things. He liked its lilt—the foreign liveliness that reminded him of birds moving upwards and downwards in the sky. His own voice was without accent. It troubled him, this absence of a quality others seemed so effortlessly to achieve. He touched Finn's thin white throat, then his bruised-looking lips. The muscles that moved to make sound leave the body were still. Childer closed his eyes, but was unable to sleep. When the light turned a first fragile blue, he rose and donned his work boots. He set a pot of coffee brewing in the kitchen and went to the back garden to dig a grave.

The ground was hard, stiffening already in anticipation of the frost to come. Where his shovel struck no worms curled from the earth; no beetles scurried from lairs disturbed. The soil was dark but slightly chalky. Flecks of mica glittered. It felt dead. He'd tried to tend plants in the garden at first. But he hadn't the gift. Vines withered to slim straw stalks under his hand; roses rotted on the bush and in time were overtaken by thorns. Some part of Childer had thought, had hoped that if he buried the boys among the rose bushes a spark, a transfer of life might occur. But the same knots of thorns remained by the rocky earth of the first two graves. Now he was digging farther off, among the herb beds. Dill and rosemary ran wild, interspersed with weeds. Their scents mingled strangely in the morning air.

Childer hollowed the grave out to three feet and no farther—he didn't see the point of a deep grave. The dead didn't have to live in exile. He hefted a stray clod of dirt. He could feel a cold sweat under his clothes, the kind that hard work in winter produces. The day was just beginning. The sun was rising, a white circle, very far away. He wiped the dirt from his hands.

It was then that he saw the angel. It stood by the tool shed. It did not descend in a cloud, nor announce itself with voices singing. But an angular light seemed to haunt it, a stray white echo of that early sun. It went barefoot. It wore a hooded sweatshirt and ragged jeans. Childer identified it at once as an angel, though he could not have explained this understanding. There was no shadow to it, not even the shortest stretch of darkness. It didn't speak to him.

After a while, Childer leaned the shovel against the back steps and went inside. In the bedroom Finn's body still rested amongst the rumpled cotton sheets. His T-shirt bore the faded legend of a rugby club and a knotted emblem in the shape of a cross. Bruises had flowered on his upper arm, like blurred footprints, a violet shade. Childer lifted the dead boy in his arms. He was not a large man, but Finn had been lightly built. Childer could carry him with ease through the warm kitchen now rich with the smell of coffee, out to the back garden and his grave. Finn fit easily into the space Childer had made for him.

The angel watched inscrutably as Childer took up the shovel and buried the boy. Childer was able to ignore the angel's presence. He concentrated instead on packing the soil in tightly, like he'd been taught to do whilst planting. Seeds displace less soil, though, and no matter how closely he pressed in the dirt there was always a heap left over, a small sad excess hill.

When he had tamped down as evenly as possible the earth over Finn's grave, he found that the angel was still waiting. The time was perhaps eight o'clock by then. Where the angel stood, small green threads were starting to snarl the surface of the earth. New shoots growing fast and thick. From the angel's bare and high-arched feet they hove outwards.

Childer leant the shovel against the back wall and went in to breakfast. The coffee had started to scald slightly. It tasted burnt, which he liked, like something had been boiled out of it, some impurity, and now it was clean. When he looked back over his shoulder he could see the angel in the garden. He grew used to it quickly. Soon he stopped checking to see if it had gone away.

He dreamed of abstract and ordinary things. He dreamed of himself as a child, throwing rocks at crows to scare them away. He dreamed of other birds, starlings. A crowd of them was called a murmuration, after the sound of their wings. When he was a child great clouds of them would gather going into winter, shrouding the sun with their dark bodies, blotting the light like beads in a kaleidoscope tray. Now the climate had changed and the winters were colder. The birds went elsewhere.

Childer dreamt of where the birds might go: a country warmer and brighter, where children went running under the trees. They left little footprints amongst the tall grasses and the air was filled with the sound of their laughter. Starlings sat on their shoulders and made nests out of their fine light hair. It was always winter in this other country, but the winter was not cold. The weather was equanimous. Seeds in the soil stayed dormant. The birds were never moved to migrate away.

The next day, Thursday, he proceeded into town. The morning air was thin and mountainous, suggesting frost. He weighted the bed of his pick-up so it wouldn't skid or flip on bad patches. The best weights for this purpose were worn-out books. Childer used an elderly set of encyclopedias, browned by basement flooding and brittle-leaved. They contained the names of every bird known to man by the books' date of printing, as well as notes of their special markings and migratory diagrams. There were other items in the encyclopedias: information on areas of the world unvisited by Childer, illustrations of plants that he had never seen. A man in one photograph held his hand beside a flower to show the great size of each petal. Palm outwards, fingers rigid and straight. On another page the aurora cut across a northern sky. There had once been such a sunstorm that men could see the aurora where Childer lived, and further south. Prospectors asleep by rivers in the Rocky Mountains awoke to a pale sky and thought it was day. Childer read this account and failed to understand their mistake. He felt sure that the aurora would prove different to the sun's staid dawn. He studied the photograph. The aurora bent like smoke sinking towards the earth instead of rising. Their shapes ringed the landscape in lucent display.

The engine of the pick-up shook at first when he started it, then settled into a steady rhythm. He steered out onto the gravel road. There were fifteen miles between his house and the town, flat and inhabited mostly by birds. This early the neighboring fields were colorless. The scrub by the side of the road was a ghost grass, bleached bluish-gray.

He stopped for a kolache at the edge of town. The night boy at the bakery was still on shift. He handed Childer the paper sack, pastry warm within it. Childer paid in coins so he could put them in the boy's slightly sticky hand. He sat by the front window and watched the boy lift pecan buns from the oven on large flat trays. There was flour smeared across the boy's sweatshirt. He wore a baseball cap pulled low over his forehead. Sleeplessness blued the skin under his eyes. Childer wanted to place his hands on the boy's narrow shoulders. He wanted to lower his head to the boy's neck and smell the sweat and powdered sugar there. He bit into the kolache. Seeds from the raspberry filling stuck in his teeth.

He drove next to the co-op. He was running low on coffee, flour, fruit, and meat. As a precaution he purchased several boxes of plastic trash bags to protect the garden against a later freeze. Sheets and blankets were best to keep the frost out in the dead of winter, their corners weighted with stones or cinder blocks. But in autumn they wetted come dawn and smelled of must and decay. With plastic he could shake the water off. He loaded also a case of beer into the bed of the truck. He liked, come the long winter nights, to sit on the back porch and look out over the tangle of the garden, drinking. The colder it got the cleaner he felt. When sensation ceased in his feet and hands he would go inside, but not before. Then back in the heat he would be clumsy. His fingers, mercifully severed for a moment, forced to re-learn how to feel.

The cashier at the co-op asked him, "Getting ready for the first big freeze?"

"Oh, yeah," Childer answered. "Got to start settling in for the winter."

The cashier wore a nametag that said *Daniel*. He had black hair and a blue tattoo of a star on his wrist, bisected by his sleeve. The ink of the tattoo had faded. It was the color of a summer storm cloud. Childer watched as Daniel bagged the groceries: holding, briefly, each red apple in his careful hands. The blue star flashed as he lifted the bags to Childer. Idly, the boy tugged at his shirt to cover it. Childer found it difficult to move away. In the pick-up, he dissociated the apples from the other groceries. He had not yet decided if he would eat them. He placed them in the passenger seat and from time to time, whilst driving, would touch them as though for reassurance. They had acquired a kind of radiance, visible only to him.

When he arrived home it was after midday. He loaded a few beers into the icebox and stored the rest of the groceries away. The apples he lined up on the kitchen counter. Then, as an afterthought, he took one in his hand and went out to the garden. The angel slept, curled like an animal on the earth. The new greenery formed a pillow under its head. Elsewhere vines had begun touching at the walls of the house with tentative fingers. Childer considered whether he should pry them off, but let them be. He went over to where the angel slept and set the apple beside it. It occurred to him—an impulse quickly stifled—to describe aloud to the angel where the apple had been. Instead he returned to the house. He tore a lined sheet of paper from a spiral notebook and sketched on it in ballpoint pen a star. He had no clear idea what to do with the drawing once it was finished. He folded it twice and tucked it in his pocket. All the rest of the day he was aware of it, reverent, somehow, of what he carried with him. In the grip of the superstition he caught himself minding his words, careful of his actions. He wanted obscurely to prove himself worthy of the star.

Come the next morning, the apple he had left for the angel was gone. Gray clouds gathered overhead, threatening rain. The angel sat cross-legged and gazed up at the sky. The clouds were fast-moving. They seemed to swell close to the earth and then recede. Childer made coffee and took a cup of it out to the back porch. The wind was high, the coffee hot and sweet. A brown bird perched on the packed earth in the garden. Childer could tell it was a mockingbird when it took flight; the fine white bars that marked its feathers stood out against the sullen sky. It seemed to rise and rise, till Childer could not see it. It loosed a single, insensible cry.

"Should be moving on for the winter, anyway," Childer said aloud. He glanced at the angel. "If I built a coop I could keep some, maybe through any season. Have to get a manual on it for next year."

The angel said nothing. It inclined its head. Its eyes were a light shade almost like seawater, suspended between blue and gray. The cashier's tattoo had been that color. Like a bruise in the shape of a star.

"Hard to keep them warm, though," Childer said. "Same with the plants. I try all the tricks they say on the radio. Garden shows. Still lose a few come that first freeze or a hard storm. Some people've got a knack for it, I guess, that I don't have."

The angel blinked. The vines it had produced were climbing the wall. They bore large, dark, insistent leaves. They clutched at the garden fence as well. On the ground, small white flowers had sprung up in clusters like weeds. They grew even over the graves of the boys, where the soil was loose and new. The angel seemed unaware of the effect it was having.

"Reckon we'll see what makes it through the winter," Childer said. He returned to the kitchen, placed his coffee cup in the sink. In the base of the cup some fine slough of sugar remained. He tilted the cup; the sugar took on a shape. Continent-like, a mass of land. In his mind he mapped the contours of it. A private country. A moment later he twisted the tap and washed the whole of it away.

The week went. Once or twice Childer left food for the angel: half a sandwich, a soft- boiled egg. Later, the food had always gone. He assumed the angel ate. On Sunday he drove to the bakery, intending to bring back a box of doughnuts or a coffee cake. The boy from the night shift wasn't working; a teenaged girl had replaced him. Childer found that his appetite waned. He wondered where the boy was, if he were sleeping. He envisioned him buried under a comforter and cotton sheets. His bedroom perhaps smelling sweetly of the bakery. The boy's mouth slightly agape. Childer could not bring himself to buy anything from the girl who manned the counter. He stopped at the filling station for a coffee instead. On the long road home he was tense and restless. The sky overhead seemed to expand. Its goal was to shake him loose from the earth, to lose him. He would drift into it and never see the boy again. It was his memories of each of the boys, his anamnesis of their bodies that formed an anchor of sufficient weight. He worked to recall the night shift boy's short hair curling at the nape of his neck. That warm place which one hand could cover, fingers resting against the back part of the skull. But it had been days since Childer had seen the boy and he could not resolve the image. In his mind the boy's eyes hovered between blue and gray.

When he reached the house he headed to the garden. He felt somehow that he needed to explain. He had wanted to bring the angel an offering, something the boy at the bakery had held in his hands. Instead he had nothing. But when he met the angel's eyes, squinting tenderly against the broad light of day, he knew in an instant that it understood his failure, by instinct, as though they were of one body. It beheld him kindly. For the first time, it extended a hand to him. Childer was reluctant to touch it. When he did, he held his breath. It seemed to him that as long as he was not breathing he could briefly absent himself from the physical plane. Something other than his clumsy flesh would touch the angel's fingers. But if he breathed he called an end to the whole charade. If he could have caused his heart not to beat it would have been better. But his nervous pulse betrayed him.

The angel's hand was cool and slightly gritty. Dirt gathered under the short nails and in the lines of its skin. Childer was overcome by a strong desire to raise the angel's palm to his mouth and taste it. It would taste, he thought, like wet earth after a rain. He folded the angel's fingers into a fist and released it.

"It's getting cold," he said. "You should come inside."

The angel smiled at him and did not reply. Childer stood ineffectually for a moment. He wanted to inspire the angel to movement. What if an ice storm comes, he thought. What if it freezes. On the wall of the house, a stiff wind stirred the ivy as though it were not winter at all. Elsewhere, other plants were pushing up from the dark earth. The rosemary had doubled its radius. There was a desert smell of its spiny leaves.

For the first time, Childer dreamed of Finn. In the dream they were pressed up close against each other, underground, in a grave. The earth was warm and smelled sweet. Childer tasted cedar mulch, wet leaves. His hand, heavy and hot, rested against Finn's ribcage. Childer could feel the faint heart beating beneath. Finn raised a finger to his lips: a secret. His eyes were black, the pupils blown and strange.

Finn touched Childer's mouth with the same cool finger. Soil clotted his fine pale hair. Childer could feel his breath hot against the boy's hand. He was ashamed at his own animal mechanics. Finn's body had a different architecture. He did not need to breathe. When he moved his lips it was not a human voice that came out, foreign-accented and made of air and thin, but the low warble of birdsong. Black and liquid. Based in the throat. Childer closed his eyes and covered the boy's mouth. He could not stand to hear it. He was consumed by envy, by fear of the sin he had committed, the creature that he had made.

A hard freeze came, finally, when the week was halfway through. Childer woke to find long fingers of ice on all the windows. When he walked outside a layer of frost broke under his work boots. He had covered the garden as a precaution but left the area the angel inhabited bare. Now when he went to lift the trash bags he had weighted over the herb beds, he saw that the new growth surrounding the angel was untouched. No frost matted the dark leaves. The angel itself huddled by the tool shed, its hands pulled up against its body. It watched without comment as Childer inspected the garden. There was no ice damage; the plants were vivid and green. Even over the graves of the three boys, wildflowers were thriving. Childer stopped and knelt beside the third grave. When he breathed, his breath hung in the air as though reluctant to leave him. He thought of Finn's breath whitening the mirror. He looked away.

The angel was shivering. "If you're so cold," Childer said, "why don't you just fly away?" For the first time he considered the angel's shoulders, narrow beneath the aged sweatshirt. "Have you not got any wings?"

It made a sad, curious gesture, neither confirmation nor denial. It dug its toes into the hard-packed dirt. Its feet looked bruised, blackened by dust.

Abruptly Childer wanted to wash them. He imagined rinsing the angel's worn body clean.

"Come inside," he offered again. "I can make you some breakfast. You don't have to stay out in the cold."

He waited for the angel to answer. Slowly it dawned on him that this was its answer, that it would not enter the house. Resigned, he got to his feet and left the garden. In the kitchen he cracked three eggs into a frying pan. He cooked them till they were coherent, each yolk a solid globe of sun. He had meant to divide them between himself and the angel, but by the time they were done he found he was no longer hungry. He slid the eggs onto a plastic plate. He thought of making toast, and did so. And bacon. Then added salt and pepper to the eggs. He searched the kitchen for something else he could feed the angel. The last of the apples, turned slightly withered. Half a grapefruit. A hunk of cheese. He carried the crowded plate outside, the eggs still slightly steaming. The angel did not look at him. Childer set the plate on the grass and stepped away. A hollow had opened somewhere within him, in a part of his body that had no name. He felt in his pocket for the star he had drawn. The crumpled paper. It seemed to him not a common five-pointed emblem but a colossal, luminous thing. Large enough to fill the hole, or at least patch it. He pressed it, trembling, into the palm of his hand.

He woke the next day to snow outside his window, thin light flakes barely feathering the breeze. His chest ached, a familiar feeling. The heat had gone out in the night, and the cold was a physical form that pressed against him. Needy, insistent. Nudging him with its icy nose. He drew his arms around himself and regarded, through the window, the descent of the snow. The small flakes died on the fields and road. The earth was not frozen enough to accept them. It would be in another few days.

Outside the sun seemed weak and screened through water. White clouds moved swiftly overhead. He brushed ice from the books weighting the bed of the pick-up; scraped the windscreen clean. The engine heaved when started, like an animal roughly awakened. Childer directed the truck down the road and away.

At sixty or seventy miles per hour he sometimes felt he was no longer limited to his body that other things contained him instead. The long fences with barbed wire starry between their pillars, the animals gut-split by the side of the road. The low grass that clung to the bad soil by the shoulder, the vultures aloft and eyeing their prey. Then the sight of something beautiful would rise up out of the landscape and reduce him. That had been Finn: a hitchhiker, slightly sunburnt at the roadside. Childer's human desire had stirred. Now he increased his speed, hungry for the sense of exaltation. But the world around him played dead.

When he reached the bakery, the night shift boy was still working. Relief swept him like a strong wind, leaving him shaky on his feet. He stood in the warm sweet air of the shop and watched the boy arrange pastries on wax paper. The sleeves of his sweatshirt were pushed up past his elbows, putting the thin bones of his wrists on display. The sweatshirt was hooded and worn, just like the angel's.

The boy looked up. "What can I get for you today?"

"Just a cup of coffee," Childer said. He didn't want the coffee, but he wanted to see the boy make it. Raising the carafe, careful with the hot and fragrant steam. The boy's hands wrapped around the cup, leaving fingerprints, traces. Childer's gaze traveled from the cup to the boy's face. His eyes were gray, his hair wheat-colored. A silver chain cut across the hollow of his throat, where his pulse was beating. Childer could not see what depended from the chain. He wanted to press his thumb there till the pulse slowed and stilled. Till the heart ceded its function, surrendered, abstained.

He had thought to stay and offer the boy a ride home when his shift ended. But indecision gripped him. He felt restless in his own skin. He remembered the angel waiting in the garden. He wondered how he would explain the presence of the boy. The new body the inevitable grave. The earth was hard and to break it would take hours. The angel would watch him, unspeaking. Flowers would crawl from where the boy's body was laid. Childer measured his want against the wan horror of this image: the flowers seething inexorably upwards, pity printed on the angel's luminous face. When he pictured it he could feel his hands raw where they would grip the shovel. The red pain reminding him of what he couldn't bear.

He walked rapidly from the bakery and came to rest with his forehead pressed against the truck's front window. Snow wasn't falling any longer, but the glass was cold, so cold he couldn't feel it. It was a relief. He closed his eyes and pictured birds flying, dozens of them and then thousands, so many he could count them only by the sound of their wings. They flashed before his eyes, dark forms, bound for a new country. He wanted to follow them, but they had no set direction. They moved according to a tropic pull, like plants that navigate towards sunlight, their secret course whispered to them in germination, destination obscure yet somehow plain.

For hours after leaving the bakery he drove without aim. Out in the cropped fields nothing stirred amongst the blunted rows of corn or cotton. The sunlight was closer to silver than gold. He tasted snow on the wind. Once or twice the tires of his truck skidded. He imagined leaving the tarmac, the truck's body flipping, his head snapping against the windscreen before coming to rest. He had weighted the pick-up bed against such an accident, but now he found he wanted it.

When the sun had passed its summit he pulled off on the shoulder and parked the truck. He took the encyclopedias from the pick-up bed and began to tear out their pages in fistfuls, as many pages as he could seize in his hand. They were so thin under his fingers that he was reminded of the shells cicadas left in the summer, clinging like living creatures to the bark of trees. Wind lifted the pages and carried them over the fields until Childer could no longer see them. The photographs of aurora, gone forever; the diagrams of birds and all their migrancies. Floating like foreign snow over distant farms and townships, coming to nest in the bare trees. As each book emptied, he dropped the binding. His hands ached where the paper had cut him, but the cuts were not deep enough to bleed.

The angel was sleeping in the garden. Childer stood over it for a long while, watching. Its unconscious hands gripped at the roots of the plants that grew around it, milkweed and paintbrush and the dark ivy that had now overtaken the house's wall. There was no sign in the garden that snow had fallen. Flowers were blooming, thick and lavish. Their scent intoxicated him. The leaves of the ivy stirred. Childer heard in the sound something that was almost language: a half-speech, subtle and inhuman. He bent and touched the angel's face. Its skin was cold. It didn't waken. He stroked its hair, like he would a child's; covered its mouth, like he had done to Finn in his dream. An edge of sunlight stayed with it, despite the approach of winter. It was the most beautiful thing Childer had seen.

"Why did you come here?" he asked it. His voice cracked on the question. He could not bring himself to imagine the days to come: ivy overgrowing the doors and windows, ryegrass creeping gradually through the cracks in the floor. The scent of summer from the garden, like a ghost of what had gone away. And the angel, lambent in its mercy, like a star whose brightness he could not contain.

He lifted the angel in his arms. Its body was very light. He carried it inside the house, through the kitchen, to the bedroom, where he laid it on the cotton sheets. Tenderly, Childer knelt above it, his knees on either side of its narrow body. He placed a hand against its neck, finding the pulse point.

The angel opened its eyes. It was still slow with sleep. It smiled and tried to raise itself on the bed. Childer prevented it. He applied pressure where he gripped its throat. The angel's smile disappeared. Still it did not struggle. Could it die? Childer wasn't sure. He no longer operated according to logic. Another instinct dictated the actions of his hands. He bore down on the body beneath him. The angel smelled like bruised grass, growing things. Its arms moved convulsively against him, then were still. For a moment Childer saw wings spread out against the Egyptian cotton, wings of a whiteness that put the Nile sun to shame. He turned his head; he couldn't bear their radiance. They were large enough to carry a man away. He pressed his own forehead to the angel's. A ragged sob escaped him. He felt the angel's arms enfold him gently. There would be no release.

K. M. Ferebee's work has appeared or is forthcoming in *The Masters Review, Fantasy Magazine, Strange Horizons, Weird Tales, Lady Churchill's Rosebud Wristlet, Not One of Us,* and *Shimmer.* Her nonfiction work has appeared in *The Brooklyn Rail.* Previously she worked as a professional musician in the United States and Europe. Now she is pursuing new careers. Her interests include foreign languages, the philosophy of time travel, and obscure ethical choices. She lives in Texas.

There were five tiny holes in the sand, each one directly in front
of a toe depression. Claws. And the toes were webbed.

SINKING AMONG LILIES

Cory Skerry

I studied the village of Keyward from the packed gravel by the water. Judging by the skulls roped to the pylons in the estuary, the people here knew how to take care of themselves. But even if there was no fight to be had, perhaps the townsfolk would be interested in the one and only book I had to sell.

I peered at one of the skulls as I passed. It had been there long enough to have lost the lower jaw and most of the teeth; mussels the size of my thumbnails had attached themselves to the sides like bristling purple sideburns.

It was common enough on the coast to tie pirate corpses out for the gulls, but I couldn't help but remember how easily I might have become a pirate myself all those years ago, suddenly homeless with only my learned violence to serve me. I shuddered and renewed the tactic of Floating-Among-Lilies, taking a deep breath and transforming the air into a false pink light that only I could see, caressing the edges of my vision as I exhaled. Thus calmed, I guided my horse along the muddy sand that bordered Keyward.

The town hunched above salt-worn rocks, bisected by a harried stream. The tall, narrow buildings were almost disguised by the pines, but even from the bottom of the hill I could see iron bars on the lower-level windows. Wooden bridges fluttered with laundry, some of it sporting faded, rusty stains. Bandages.

The closest building was a stout inn with a pattern of pale streaks marking the walls. Scars from dismantled scaffolding, I realized when I noticed there were iron grids installed across the upper windows as well.

High above me, a man with a crossbow lazed on a balcony on the second floor. He wasn't rude enough to aim yet, but his eyes were on me. I was an unusual sight, a woman traveling alone.

I waved. He pulled a cord. Perhaps it meant I was friendly; perhaps it was a warning. I thought it best to wait for a greeting.

Expensive defenses like glass, iron, and crossbows meant that Keyward not only had a supernatural threat but they could afford a trained professional to deal with it. I just needed to convince them they'd rather hire me than await the slow mercy of the Assembly of the Divine Lady.

"Good day, cousin."

A man with a dark woolly beard the size of his own head stepped out of the inn, looking down from a wooden terrace that wrapped around the ground floor. Jagged scraps of iron stuck out of the shadows beneath the walk where he stood. The scars from the scaffolding stopped just under the defenses, and I wondered why they'd even bothered putting grids on the windows when anathema would have to get past those enormous iron teeth.

Clusters of gold coins tipped each of his matted ropes of hair. They only fell past his chin, so he hadn't been wealthy for long. Mine were to my waist, and while I had a modest amount of coin woven in, I had never had to cut a single one to use it. I wondered what had prompted him to shave his head and start over. That kind of ostentatious prosperity belonged on a tough street lord in a port city, or at least a mercenary like myself—not an innkeeper on the coast.

Aloud, I only said, "Good day to you, cousin. My second name is Bane. I'm looking for a room."

"My second name's Browan. If you like the place, you can bring your horse 'round back."

We entered through the inn's front door, which held seven different locks and a bar, all of them forged of iron. The windows, too, had been built to keep out anathema—the sills were iron, as were the bars that held the glass panes in place. Keyward could definitely afford my services, and moreover, seemed to need them.

Browan passed me a drink when I asked for his best. "No one in these parts understands what best means," he said. "Something tells me you've traveled enough to advise whether or not it's worth the word."

My eyes wandered over the room as I swilled the brew over my tongue. Stuffed creatures—mostly shore birds and small predators—perched on the rafters; pelts of marine mammals like seals, otter, and beaver hung above the mantel.

"It's darker than I would have brewed it, but if you're not already sending kegs to Kalperry, consider doing so."

"Thank you. Please pardon me if I'm impolite . . . " I knew without a doubt what he would ask. His line of sight wasn't quite meeting my eyes. "Out here, we don't get many westerners. I'm familiar with the Lady's Column. But your mark?"

"It's called the Exit Cross," I said. Or, to some, the Betrayer's Cross, but I kept that to myself. The first line represented the pillars that held up the roof of the Lady's temple. The second intersected it at the center and divided my forehead into quadrants. "I don't serve the Lady."

When Browan rang a bell, an unkempt ghost of a child, all bare feet and shaggy white-blond hair, scurried in and left a tray with thick rye bread, cheese, and an apple. The child darted back out, leaving only an impression of androgyny and fear.

"If not the Lady, who do you serve, cousin? If you don't mind me asking?"

"The people," I said. "I put an end to trouble. I'm not cheap, but I'm well worth the expense." I took a bite of cheese, a bite of apple, and a bite of bread, and chewed them all at once. One, two, fifteen, swallow. A seer had predicted my end in a storm of fire and blood, which I preferred to the ignominious death of choking at table.

"Why would people hire you, instead of sending for the free aid of the disciples of the Fierce Mother?" He sounded genuinely interested.

"The Fierce Mother is slow in her aid," I said wryly. "And no one in her employ has this."

I unbuckled my cloak and withdrew my line of prizes. I coiled the thin linen rope on the table, letting the trinkets form a clinking spiral of teeth and bones and one withered, resin-encapsulated eye.

He sucked in a breath, and pointed at the last. "This?"

"Sandwiel. Kypteri desert. Nothing from the eastern coast, yet, though I saw bandages hanging on the bridges. Perhaps I'll take a prize here."

Browan leaned back and laughed. "Nothing so dramatic as a sandwiel here, I'm afraid. Mackilvie got in a fight with a seal over who owned the fish in his net."

"And the defenses on the walls?"

"That . . . that is for something else," he said. He smiled. "We'll take care of it, though. We have a book on anathema, and it's served us well so far."

"The author?"

He said my name, and I laughed a bittersweet laugh. He clearly didn't believe me, so I pulled my sword partly from its sheath that he might see IMURI BANE engraved in the hilt.

"You'll write yourself out of a job," he said.

"Sadly, never. Knowing their nature doesn't necessarily render someone capable of defeating them. Have you identified the anathema?"

"If I tell you," he teased, "you'll kill it and send us a bill. Think of Keyward as a vacation, cousin."

He showed me to my room, which was an attic loft with a bed near the warm stones of the chimney. Perhaps I would write myself out of a job, but I wasn't going to stop using my bounties to have that book copied again, and again, and again.

Anathema was the blanket term the church encouraged, and it was commonly thought that all anathema were the same: supernatural constructs that could take any form they chose, to torment humanity and tempt us or herd us away from faith. Within the Order of the Fierce Mother, however, we were taught the science of anathema, their anatomy, husbandry, and nature.

I had come to trust in that science. It had saved my life. I'd pushed for posters and books detailing the forms in which anathema could appear, disseminated among the parishes. "Teach them how to classify, discover, and avoid anathema. They should know how to combat these threats," I'd insisted.

High Priest Kellar had smiled at me like a patient father with an unruly child. He responded with the motto of the Order of the Fierce Mother: "It is for us to fight with a sword; they must fight with faith."

"We can't protect them all the time. And it takes us time to answer a summons. We must teach fishermen that a selkie's blood spilled in the sea will certainly raise a storm. They should learn how to extinguish a marshlight, how to lay the fitful dead to rest."

"Without the fear of the dark, Sister Imuri, what need would they have for us, the bringers of light?" Priest Kellar had asked.

Even thinking about it warmed my guts with a familiar anger. I quickly renewed Floating-Among-Lilies to quell the feeling. When my heart was cool again, I excused myself to tend to my horse. Once done, I exited the dim stable and headed back to the inn, toward the kitchen entry. The lines I had thought were scars from scaffolding continued up the walls to the doorjamb, but here they skewed and overlapped, the crosshatching of a mad artist with a knife. Now I could see them for what they were—claw marks.

Something had tried to climb inside, and Browan's mysterious remarks made me suspect it would try again. The scratches weren't deep—it wasn't digging its way through.

It was just writing the promise that it would.

The science of anathema arrayed itself in my thoughts unbidden. I counted the marks—five in each swipe—layered from multiple nights of scratching. They reached as high as a man, avoiding the iron fittings on the window frames and the kitchen door.

Whatever it was, it was as big as me. Something that size wasn't a fair match for ignorant villagers with nothing but a book written by an ex-priest.

I made certain to bar my door when I retired for the night.

I woke to a woman's scream.

The crescent moon was wasting away on the western horizon and a wet smear of light marked the east. Fog blanketed the sea and shore, fading into wisps among the trees, but from my window, I could see dark shapes slithering through the white miasma, and the shouts of men ricocheted through the ravine.

I renewed Floating-Among-Lilies, which had torn in my sleep, leaving me with dreams that were sometimes black-and-white and devoid of emotion and sometimes fiery bursts of passion that seemed to break my heart. I was grateful for the awakening.

With the clawmarks as a warning, I'd slept in my clothes. I donned the thin mail shirt and skirt. As I wiggled my helm into place, my thumbs touched the rusted holes on either side where the holy smith had desecrated his own work by tearing out the wings.

Browan's wife stood in front of the fire, clutching a shapeless bit of cloth in one hand and a knife in the other. In firelight, the hunting trophies looked particularly grisly where they stared down from the walls.

"What's going on?" I asked.

"Anathema stole a child from Fenny Smith." She stared at my scarred armor and the Exit Cross on my forehead. After a moment, she pointed through the window. "Up the south hill, above the smithy."

I strode out the door into the mist and crossed the narrow ravine that divided the town. Watching-as-the-Owl, I peered between the houses wedged onto the steep hillside. If there was danger, I wanted to see it first. Only moths stirred around the smith's windows, though the walls below were scored with now-familiar claw marks. Sobs echoed within.

The door hung open, as if they welcomed the return of the terror now that they were awake and armed. Inside, I found a man weeping as he clung to a woman who seethed in his embrace. In the corner, a bereaved sibling crouched as far from the adults as she could get. She hugged her knees, and her mop of cornsilk hair covered her face.

"I'm sorry," the man whimpered through his sobs. He was huge, shirtless, and though a dark braid thick as a horsetail hung down his back, not a single hair sprouted on his arms. The smith, I guessed.

The woman's hard gaze sharpened on me as I entered. "Who are you?" she spat.

"Imuri Bane," I said.

She shrugged off her husband. The miserly lines around her mouth deepened as she sized me up. "Bane? You deal with anathema, then?"

"For a price."

Only a ghost of grief pained her voice when she asked, "How much is my child's life worth?"

I thought about what I knew, about windows and an abundance of iron, about common townfolk who could afford nice crossbows.

"If the child still lives, eighteen imperial horseheads. If it's dead when I get there, I'll bring you the remains for ten. Either way, I'll kill the anathema and teach you how to stop it next time. Half upfront."

One of the men staring out the windows turned around. A Lady's Column inked the back of his right hand, and he wore a black silk sash around his waist. Mine had been orange, the second-brightest color in the Assembly of the Divine Lady.

His sleek black brows rumpled, but his voice was even when he spoke. "You would charge for a service our Fierce Mother provides for free?"

"If you'd prefer to wait for a Disciple, I won't argue. If the weather holds, they might even get across the mountains before the passes close. Whatever you decide," I said, turning to address the pinch-faced woman and her wet-faced husband, "please decide soon. If you don't require my services, I'm going back to my warm bed."

The sobbing father barked at me. "I have the money, and I'll pay it. I want Keeley home." He turned haunted eyes on me. Swollen and red, they reminded me of the sagging, fleshy anemones that slept during the low tide. "You'll swear it?"

"I swear on the Suffering Sailor's blisters, the rope that bound him, and the storm that freed him." It wasn't the standard oath in Fierwa, but it was serious enough, especially among fishermen.

The parish keeper—he'd have had a Column on both hands if he was a full priest—said nothing, and though his eyes latched into the Exit Cross on my forehead like a hook in a fish, he remained unnaturally composed.

He was Floating-Among-Lilies. I was still doing it myself, so I didn't even smile when I noticed. The practice of distancing your soul from the moment, packing it up and setting it on an invisible shelf, was the first of the difficult Tactics. My teachers had done everything from pricking my face with skewers to throwing a dead, dog-chewed child into my lap. Eventually, I had stopped flinching. I wondered if this parish keeper truly had learned Floating-Among-Lilies or if it was a textbook mockery of my own perfection.

"Browan said he's seen a book of anathema," I said. "Which did this?"

"Anathema are all the same. They take the form that hurts us most. If such a book existed, I wouldn't consult it," the parish keeper said.

I nodded. "I thought you'd refuse to help a child if it went against doctrine." It was a calculated barb—at the moment, I didn't hate him for his simple, pleasant existence or the lack of responsibility on his bony shoulders. I only wanted to be sure I made my bounty.

"You're—you're charging them!"

His incredulity knocked his soul off the shelf. Sinking-Among-Lilies, I thought, but I still didn't smile. I would be smug later, when my emotions weighed so heavily that they forced me to release the Tactic and feel all the stomach-sickening passion it had kept at bay.

"Tell me exactly what happened, and show me where it occurred," I said.

The wife took the lead, climbing a leaning wooden ladder with fitted iron braces. The carpentry was so perfect it was like climbing stairs. The tiny mezzanine held one empty bunk, crafted with the same love and skill as the ladder. No blood, but water droplets dappled the floor. I put my finger in one and tasted it. Salt.

I mentally listed aquatic threats: kelpies, jennies, sharkums, niskies, kraken. The water trail began at the window; when I glanced out, I saw claw scrapes on the sill and, below, something white in the bushes. I dashed outside. It was a ladder, constructed nearly as well as the one I'd just used, but this was of driftwood, bone, and scraps of dark knotted rope that peeled away under my fingernails. Seaweed.

Nothing on my list could do this. Not a jenny, who haunted freshwater. It could only be niskies if there were many, because it would have taken at least ten to carry this ladder, and besides, they were too small to make the marks on the walls. Whatever it was, it had left the ladder behind.

The parents waited in the doorway, their pale faces like sad twin moons.

"Was the anathema interrupted in its task?" I asked.

The wife shook her head. "No. I heard a crash outside, and when Browan got up to investigate, I went up. She was gone."

I went over the ground around the house, but of course their kinfolk had already trampled it into a sea of chopped, muddy boot prints.

I took my soul down and stopped Floating-Among-Lilies, because now I would need my intuition.

It didn't feel much different. I was still working. It wasn't my child, and it wasn't the first, or even the fiftieth, of the children I'd attempted to recover. I vowed it would not be the twenty-seventh I'd lost. The hill sharpened into a cliff as it neared the water. I squinted in the dark. Watching-as-the-Owl, I spotted long horizontal scrapes in the moss on the vertical rock face.

I tiptoed through the fog, silent in my leather-soled boots as I hugged the cliff. The identity of the anathema gnawed at me. I had narrowed it down to sharkums, which built complex cities of coral beneath the waves, but I'd never seen a sharkum leave the water for more than a minute or two. It might be only a clever human predator, transferring the suspicion onto anathema.

Or the anathema might be unlisted, something new.

I found a trail of human footprints, adult, not much larger than mine. I lost them over fucus-furred rocks and found them again, skirting a herd of sleeping, log-like seals. The trail stopped at the rising tide.

Simple, ugly. She'd been put into a boat and floated out into the gray nothing. She'd be sold into slavery, perhaps, or kept for the amusement of a repulsive but unfortunately common paedophile.

I renewed Watching-as-the-Owl and added Unsinging-of-Cats, so if a child cried on the water, or even a paddle sloshed among the waves, I might pick out the wrong notes in the otherwise peaceful symphony of the shore. Nothing.

My eyes fell on the prints one last time as I turned to leave. There were five tiny holes in the sand, each one directly in front of a toe depression. Claws. And the toes were webbed.

Even if the villagers wouldn't tell me what was plaguing them, I would solve their soiled laundry and scarred wood. I would get them a better, uglier skull to display down by the water.

When I returned to the inn, my ears were still sensitive with the Unsinging-of-Cats. Notes of anger filtered out through the inn's stoic cedar walls. As I crept across the bridge, I held my arms out from my sides so the mail wouldn't clink against itself. Even with all my precautions, I could barely hear the conversation, and it ended too soon.

"It's an abomination, Browan. Heresy!" The words rushed into the night air as the parish keeper stormed out the door. Though his face twisted with hate at the sight of me, he passed me by. I stepped inside and found Browan setting out china for breakfast, which wasn't for a few hours yet.

"Couldn't sleep," he said.

"Nothing will happen to a child in this house," I promised. "Does the parish keeper often raise his voice?"

He chuckled, running his thumb along the edge of one hand-painted dish. "He tells me you'll take care of the anathema, on Fenny Smith's gold."

"I'll try," I said. I stared hard at his brown eyes—long-lashed and friendly and covetous of their secrets. I didn't think he would tell me why he was unusually prosperous at his out-of-the-way inn, and his wife likely wouldn't either.

But children had less sense about such things.

I spent the day scouring the foggy shore. In this remote stretch of beach, there were plenty of anathema, but none of them seemed a likely culprit. I saw niskies in the waves. They giggled and blew foam bubbles, and the only corpse they played with today was that of a battered gull. A more stately selkie lounged in seal form on a slab of barnacle-crusted rock—I only knew she wasn't a mere seal because of the fear in her gaze. A real seal was stupid. Fragments of coral structure from a storm-torn sharkum city littered the tideline, but there was no telling how long they had been knocking about in the depths beyond Keyward, or how far away the city might be.

I returned for the mid-day meal with damp sand-filled woolens and a few cuts from prying oysters off of the rocks. These latter were my excuse for entering the back door.

Browan's child was there, as I suspected. It crouched on a pile of sacks by the woodpile, strangely far from the fire's warmth. I decided it was a boy. His snowy hair reached his shoulders, and when he turned his eyes on me, I suddenly dropped my hand to the hilt of my sword.

The parish keeper's talk of abominations hadn't been about me, after all. It was expressly forbidden by the Lady to harbor or treat with anathema; the king's penalty was death, and the Lady's penalty was excommunication. The sour little man had known the whole time.

I kicked myself for observing without thinking. Every adult in Keyward had brown hair, and I'd seen two blond children, unkempt and poorly clothed despite the town's unexplained prosperity. There had only been one bed in Smith's house—the blond child slept on a rumpled blanket while the missing Keeley had a bed.

I took a step toward the blond boy. He pressed himself against the wall, his feet kicking dirty burlap between us. His mouth hung open, panting like a dog's, his sea-gray eyes wide with horror at the sight of all that steel. All that iron. I glanced back at the door frame—the handle was iron, the doorjamb, the hinges, and there were so many iron nails pounded into it that not even the fiercest of adult selkies could hope to claw through.

Suddenly, the furnishings in the main room became a sinister cruelty instead of a strange display of wealth and prowess. Pelts.

The parish keeper was right. This was an abomination. And not just to break the Lady's edicts but to subjugate any living thing, supernatural or not . . .

"I won't hurt you," I said. My voice was so gentle it surprised me. "How many of you were stolen?"

"That's none of your mother-damned business, Prodigal."

Browan stood in the doorway to the common room, his bulk not quite obscuring the raw-eyed smith behind him or a lean woman about my age with a cudgel propped on her shoulder. She looked like she might be Browan's sister.

So the parish keeper had explained what my cross tattoo meant. I took to my feet slowly. I had my sword, and I had a bag of fist-sized oysters. All the rest of my weapons were in my room.

As I rose, the selkie child flashed three fingers at me. The webbing between them had been sliced away, to make his hand seem more human.

The child shrieked as Browan thrust his iron-tipped club toward it, dragging the metal down the boy's leg. It left a streak of bluish-purple, like a scar exposed to the cold.

Browan turned back to me, his brow low and his teeth bared. "Leave town."

"What made you decide to come after me?" I asked. "Is this how you afford your china, Browan? Robbing those who trust your hospitality?"

"Dandla saw you sneak into the kitchen with a bag of treats for my anathema. Leave now, and the most you'll lose is your horse."

I slipped out the door and strode toward the beach. Unsinging-of-Cats would let me know if they followed me, but it was still difficult to control the urge to glance over my shoulder.

I knew they would attempt to murder me—their apostasy and treason were too great of secrets. They were well aware that I was a trained warrior. They would try to take me in the night.

I walked down the stream toward the sea. The entire village was complicit in this grotesque slavery, not to mention the loss of all the belongings that I had been forced to abandon in my room, and there were few places left to hide while I strategized.

The islands, nothing more than dark smears in the dissipating fog, beckoned to me from the bay. Let the men and women of Keyward navigate their way out there in the dark, past the selkies they'd wronged. I had Warmth-of-the-Bear to keep me, at least until morning.

I stole a skiff and two iron-reinforced oars. Fenny Smith's work was fine indeed, and I thought perhaps I might burn it when I was done with it.

I rowed straight out to the islands, a row of jagged black silhouettes rising out of a bed of fog. A fine mist obscured the struggling sun, and as I approached, I found the rocks less friendly than I'd imagined. Rain soaked my clothes and hair. I despaired of finding a way to climb ashore without cracking my bones in the surf before I discovered a slender crescent of sandy beach. It lay submissively at the feet of the sheer cliffs on the tallest island.

Selkies eat birds, so I wasn't surprised when I stepped out of the boat and found a horde of anathema crawling out of crevices in the rocks.

"Why do you intrude, human?" The anathema's voice was like the rain on my skin, smooth and cool and shiver-inducing.

"My conscience," I said.

The anathema who had spoken first cocked its head to the side. "I wasn't aware the thieves of children had such endowments." Its sibilant speech crashed against my ears like the tide on the rocks.

"I've never stolen a child," I said. "But tonight, I will steal three."

The anathema held still, but its gaze slid over my weapons and mail, over the coins dangling in my hair. "If you speak of our children," it said, narrowing its eyes, "you must mean eleven."

My teeth ground against one another for a brief moment before I regained control of myself. Browan brazenly wore the coins of a warrior or a thief king; he mimicked the men who gambled that their deeds were so fierce, so brave, that if you tried to take their hair you'd regret it.

Yet the lying wretches of Keyward had taken every golden disk from the sale of the most helpless of all anathema: a creature enslaved to the holder of its pelt.

"If you go to retrieve our children, we will help. I am Lum."

"I am Imuri. I welcome your help."

"You and I shall swear on fire," said Lum. "It burns us both, and the one who breaks their word will suffer its wrath."

I nodded. They escorted me inside the largest of their caves. It was damp and smelled of salt and stone. I couldn't tell if I was a guest or a prisoner, but the plan we discussed was mostly mine, so perhaps I was a general. A general of anathema, Lady forgive me, but when her followers acted as they did, what were right and wrong but simple words?

In the corner, two human children huddled, terrified of the anathema and not mollified by the woman with a sword who politely sipped cold fish soup while discussing the terms of the children's ransom and the punishment of their parents.

Lum was lanky, with rubbery grayish-white flesh and a mostly human face. I recognized that the skull on the pylon outside Keyward wasn't a man—the sockets were too angular, the breadth of the cheekbones too wide. If there'd been any teeth left, they would have been pointed.

"You know you cannot stay," I said. "They'll find you here, and destroy your home."

"If I cannot keep mine," he replied, "then why should they keep theirs?"

His wife held out a wide flat clamshell that I could have used as a dinner plate. A coal smoldered in the center.

After speaking his oath to me, which I accepted, he placed his palm on the coal and allowed his flesh to sizzle for three seconds before lifting his hand. The air reeked of charred fish and charcoal.

My hand hovered over the coal as I spoke mine, and then my toes curled in my boots at the excruciating pain. One. Two. Three. The sickening scent of baked ham scalded my nostrils. I pulled my hand away and allowed his wife to wrap it in cold seaweed.

It was time to return to Keyward.

• • •

The parish keeper answered the knock at his window holding an iron knife and a handful of salt. He didn't know the difference between selkies and nippers—Browan and Fenny hadn't shared the book with him.

He was the reason I couldn't stop giving away my books. He needed to know that nippers wouldn't be interested in his salt; the grains were too small, and the shining surfaces would hurt their bulbous eyes. It would be better to distract them with a handful of black rice. It could be my fault if he died, or worse yet, if he taught a child the wrong way to defend herself.

Just like it was my fault the villagers had the information that led to the slave trade in selkie pups. Guilt stung me as the thought surfaced again, until Floating-Among-Lilies sagged under the weight of my grief. I had included the most benign of anathema so they might be separated from the more dangerous niskies and sharkums, not so they might be preyed upon.

I was cleaning up my mess, Lady bless me. I would scour it with fire and steel and if I had to, the most dangerous Tactic: Fight-of-the-Crocodile.

"What do you here, Prodigal?" The parish keeper spat the words as if they tasted of his own guilt.

"I found the human children," I said. "For a small fee and an answer, I'll tell you where."

He didn't ask me how he'd know I was telling the truth. He could afford to trust me; with such a successful parish, he had plenty of coins to spare. And he cared about those children because at least in that, he was faithful.

"What answer would you have of me?" he demanded.

"Why haven't you told the Order of this town's sins?"

He shook his head. "I wouldn't see Keyward's children become orphans because of behavior that can yet be changed. And your criminal insistence on solving problems best left to members of the Order hasn't helped reinforce their trust in the Lady."

I kept my last thought to myself, that he had sworn to uphold the Lady's dominion over every other concern. Whether he admitted it or not, it wasn't the Lady's dogma he was defending but her spirit. I smiled for him then, a real smile. I told him the truth—the children were tethered where I said—but I added a lemon-sour lie.

"There are twenty-five selkies waiting there," I said. The words stung my lips like a cat's cratch. "I would have saved them myself and demanded a bounty, but your townfolk have stolen my belongings—"

"Do not speak to me of theft," he snapped. He threw a handful of coins in the dirt and slammed the window shut.

Floating-Among-Lilies, I stepped into the stream and stood still as a sleeping ghost. The parish keeper didn't take long rousing the townfolk. Lanterns flickered to life in their hands, like a nest of wasps radiant with rage. The lights flowed away over the hill.

Only those who couldn't fight were left behind, with a few able but inexperienced youths to protect them; Watching-as-the-Owl allowed me to see them pass through the darkness. They congregated in the smithy, not the parish. Perhaps they wanted the safety of the iron fittings, or perhaps they knew the Lady wouldn't shelter them after what they had done.

I sheltered them in her stead. Their safety was part of the bargain I made. The selkies and I were there to punish, not to torture; we planned to burn wood, not people. The prisons in Keyward would be too easy to use again if we didn't destroy them.

I stepped into the inn's kitchen and whispered for the selkie child who Lum called Izhmir. It was a girl, not a boy, and if I had not been Floating-Among-Lilies, I would have been excited to see her again. She had risked Browan's iron poker to tell me how many of her sestren were captured. Our names were similar.

And she wasn't there.

The smith's house was empty as well; so was the chandler's, where the third selkie child was supposed to be trapped.

I found Lum standing on the bank of the stream. Already, flames flickered on the roofs and walls of the other houses. He stared down the hill at the forge. Yellow light spilled out of the windows, pale and weak compared to the raging flames of the smith's house just a few yards up the hill.

"They've moved the selkie children," I said.

He was silent for a moment. "Show me where my daughter was."

He followed me to the inn, and when I opened the door, his nostrils flexed, as if it smelled of feces or sickness. He jumped over the doorjamb and forced his feet across the iron-nailed boards.

Lum stopped where his daughter had slept, a tiny patch free of poison metal. He shredded the sacks with his claws and began wrapping his feet.

Then he picked up his harpoon, grabbed a piece of firewood in his free hand, and stood between me and the door. Floating-Among-Lilies made this nothing more than a fact. I didn't fear him. I also didn't understand.

"Why?" I asked.

"Our children are hostages in the smithy. The villagers think this makes them safe. No one is safe."

Things scraped against the outside of the walls like large insects. The selkies were setting kindling around the inn. They would burn it down, with me inside. I was reminded why I wrote in my book that no one was to treat with anathema. This incomprehensible betrayal strained at my Floating-Among-Lilies. Curiosity weighed heavily on the invisible shelf above my head.

"I helped you."

"You are the only human who has found our caves. The others stole our children from the shore. You must die, and take your knowledge with you."

"And you?"

"See me keep my oath. I appreciate your help, and for this betrayal, I will suffer the wrath of fire."

"I am the only one who can get your children out of that building," I said. It wasn't a desperate plea; it was the truth. The townfolk would be back soon. I alone, armored and unafraid of iron, could walk into the smithy and disarm the humans who were guarding them.

"We've already said goodbye to them," Lum said.

They were going to burn the smithy, with everyone's children inside.

Floating-Among-Lilies tore apart, sagging and ripping under the weight of my anger. I choked it back, but it was a flood torrent, filled with sharp pieces of regret and guilt. While the calm of the lilies slipped from my grasp, the darkness beneath became real.

I drowned my way down to the last of the Tactics, the only one I had never used before.

Fight-of-the-Crocodile couldn't be practiced among friends, because every blow that weakened one combatant poured strength into the other. I would have less time in which to win, and less strength to flee the flames.

Lum was paths of blood, branches of a cold tree I needed to chop down. He glowed with an aura of oceanic violet; in contrast, a corona of deep orange-amber throbbed around me. Honey-sticky strands of light stretched between us, shifting with our thoughts, our breathing, and the beat of our hearts.

I sallied forward with a series of whirling cuts. Heat stung my throat, but I could only think of opening those veins and spilling that violet ichor.

He jabbed with his harpoon, a powerful thrust that would have punctured my heart if not for my mail overshirt. The bone barbs slid off the metal links. Some orange light sucked into the purple, where it dissipated like blood in water. I sliced his arm before he could draw back, and light swelled around me as he dribbled blood. He was too fast, though, and the cut was shallow.

Lum asked, "What have you done?"

I didn't answer; he'd find out soon enough.

He advanced, swinging the driftwood to force me away from the door. My sword chopped off splinters. I stumbled back, maddened by the tantalizing purple power just out of my reach.

I had forgotten that Lum fought sharks with his harpoon, under the weight of water. His muscles were fast and perfect in the light resistance of the air, though his aim was off, and he coughed heavily, his slimy lungs less prepared than mine for the hot smoke.

I kicked his driftwood and swung my sword, slicing into his arm again, but even though it was a deeper cut, the cost was a harpoon stab in my leg. The aura of his life swelled with my injury. I hobbled backward, my back bumping against the swinging door to the common room.

If they were burning the inn the way I taught them, the roof was already ablaze. Lum smashed the lantern hanging above the big table, and drops of flaming oil spattered across the furniture and floor. I had taught them this as well, how to quicken the fire with oil.

All the trophies above the fire remained but one: Izhmir's pelt. The time I caught Browan's wife by the fire with the limp thing in her hand, she must have been threatening the child with it. If Izhmir's relatives were near, attempting vengeance, the pelt was the only way to control anathema who might otherwise risk a leap to freedom, iron doorjamb or no.

That same twisted scene was probably happening at that very moment, in the confines of the smithy. Three little pelts. Three terrified selkies.

I stabbed my fury toward Lum, connected, pulled free. Gutblood dribbled down the pale line around his waist where he often wore his pelt. He hadn't brought it to the fight, of course—if he was captured, it was better to die than become a slave, like his daughter.

Their nature. It was what I preached, and I knew their weaknesses as well as their strengths. My weakness was the need for my shield. When it was strapped to my arm, it was a part of me. But the townspeople had driven me off without it.

My mooning got me a harpoon punched into my other leg. Now I had two limps. My orange light shrank down toward me; Lum's purple glow expanded. Gritting my teeth against the oozing ache of each step, I stumbled back toward the stairs.

Let him keep me in the house, then. If Browan hadn't pawed through it yet, I might have an armory upstairs, in the attic. I hoped the smoldering roof would hold out long enough for me to find it.

Lum, afraid I'd climb out the window, followed. His coughs slowed him. The smoke was thicker in the stairway. It stung our eyes.

I could no longer kick and still hold my balance, but as I backed up the stairs, I managed to hook the driftwood with my sword hilt and knock it loose.

It thumped down to the ground floor, leaving a flickering shadow that pointed toward us. The flames from the spilled lamp grew, a garden of threatening light.

When I reached the attic room, I slammed the door behind me and locked it. It was only wood, no iron but the handle and hinges, so he threw himself into it over and over. Thump, thump. Purple glow flared along this side of the door and then melted away each time. My orange light wouldn't glow through the door; there wasn't enough left.

Lum would break the wood but perhaps not before the burning roof collapsed on us. I could win that way, if nothing else. My armor heated up, sweat tickled my skin, and the smoke was suffocating me. I rushed for the window like he expected, to breathe fresh air one last time, even if I couldn't escape.

What I saw stopped me.

They hadn't burnt the bridges yet. They were standing on them, watching this building, watching their leader's last brave act. Waiting.

I would choke to death on smoke or be roasted by flames or get stabbed in the back, but the last thing I did would save the smithy and everyone in it. I knew the nature of fire. I knew the nature of the anathema.

I held my breath and scrabbled for my things, in the corner where I'd left them. They'd been pawed through, but my crossbow was still in my saddlebags, and so was the cylindrical leather case where I kept fifteen steel quarrels.

Coughing, squinting, I elbowed out the glass panes and yanked the iron cross out of the window. It was hot enough to leave a scar on my palm to match the ink on my forehead. I threw it down and grasped the crossbow.

This was what I was trained for. I didn't have the strength, I thought, but I loaded and loosed quarrel after quarrel. The iron soared through the night like hunting hawks, each finding the hearts and guts of the selkies on the bridges. Only Lum's life would leak into mine, so my orange light grew thin as I watched the selkies fall and bleed. Their thick blood flowed slowly, too slowly. It might never make it to the water.

Behind me, the door crashed open. I turned in time to knock Lum's harpoon aside with the crossbow. He drew back, coughing. The air was better on the floor, where I lay, but he didn't know this. He thought he was winning if he was still standing. His purple was smaller, but my orange was barely visible.

If I didn't get out then, I never would.

I couldn't stand—my right leg now cramped when I tried—but I could swing my sword. Lum was blinded by smoke, jabbing toward me but missing. I swiped as if chopping wood with an axe. When I hit his leg, a long slab of meat peeled off and flopped down. Blood poured out.

The branching tree inside his body crumpled as he fell to the floor; the purple fluid drained him to a dry husk. And the glow moved into mine, feeding the orange light. It flared, I think, but maybe that was the fire. The flames were orange like my aura. Like the silk sash I had worn long ago. The flames were mine, too.

I lay beside Lum, my mail shirt scalding my skin where it touched, but I couldn't do anything but cough. I heard howls ripping through the world, through the flames, but I didn't know if they were Lum's, or the other selkies, or the villagers, or wolves who had smelled cooked meat and come to feast. There was a rumbling I thought might be Lum coughing, but I couldn't force my eyes open anymore.

In the midst of the choking inferno, just before I passed out, I felt something cold and wet. I knew it couldn't be real, but I was no longer Floating-Among-Lilies, so I hoped.

When I faded back, the world was different. I coughed, but instead of smoke, I inhaled air like that of the mountain passes: crisp, fresh. It stank of charred thatch and wet pine needles. Rain stung my face, driven by a howling wind, and I wondered if I had fallen out the window after all.

But the floor beneath my cheek was wood, and warm, and when I cracked my eyes, I saw the broken door, burning just beyond Lum's motionless body. Even as I watched, the wind forced the door off its hinges. It splashed into a puddle in the center of the floor, extinguishing the flames. The roof had been burned by fire and torn away by wind.

In my book, it said you must not spill the blood of a selkie in salt water, for it would cause a storm. I had spilled several pints, all carried to the sea by the stream.

Most of the town was dark. Watching-as-the-Owl, I saw that even with the downpour, it was still ruined. Blackened beams stabbed at the sky, supporting webs of charred timber. I glanced down toward the smithy. The roof was dark; there were a few tiny flames struggling on the outside, but the storm had quenched the worst of it.

I gathered my belongings and climbed down the side of the building. From the back porch, I jumped onto the stable roof, which wasn't burned at all. My horse whinnied—he hated the scent of the fire and the uncomfortable force of the storm, but he was unharmed.

I put my hood up, but it did no good. The wind was a wild thing, intent on badgering me in whatever way it could. It slapped my face with the coins in my hair, flung water into my ears and even up my nose. Without Watching-as-the-Owl, I wouldn't have been able to see my way to the smithy.

I carried a bar for prying the lids off of coffins, and I used it to crack the door off of the smithy. Rain poured in through the roof in places, where the fire had burned through before the storm.

"The three blond children are coming with me, back to the sea," I said. "Anyone who tries to stop them will also go into the sea."

The selkie children were bound with their hands behind their backs. They looked sickly amidst all the iron. Izhmir didn't smile, but when she looked at me, her gray eyes were silver with hope.

One of the young men who was supposed to be guarding the prisoners cut them free. Browan's wife looked as if she might try to throw the seal pelt in the fire, but the parish keeper hissed at her, and she grudgingly handed it to Izhmir. When the other children had their pelts, I shepherded them down to the water, and I told them the truth.

Two of them shed their clothes, tugged their skins on, and disappeared into the maelstrom. Izhmir watched them first, and then she tore off her human clothes. I was shivering under the sky's onslaught, but she tied her pelt around her waist as if it was only a spring breeze and the rain was the heat of the sun.

"I want to see your book," she said.

I wondered if selkies age the same as we do. Was she older than she seemed? I thought on it for a moment, and then I reached in my jacket. If she ruined the book, I could make another. I knew it well. And I would deserve it, after my volume had caused the slavery and destruction of so many of her people.

She picked through the pages from the back of the book to the front, using her index finger instead of her thumb the way a human would. Her hands still moved as if she had webbing instead of scars.

The storm shrieked around us while she perused the book. I realized I didn't even know if she could read, or if she was amazed by the pictures, or if she could even see in the darkness. The few flashes of lightning couldn't be enough.

Suddenly, she recited from the book, her voice clear and sharp as a ship's bell. " . . . and if they find their pelt, they will return to the sea. Because of this weakness, selkies avoid humans when possible. They will not attack unless directly provoked, such as by sealers with harpoons. It is best to remain uninvolved."

She turned to stare at me, and we studied each other's faces in the blue darkness. The hollows around her eyes were black, her mouth expressionless. My own mouth fought me, trying to cry instead of speak.

I managed to say, "I'm sorry."

Izhmir dropped the book in the sand. She draped the pelt over her head like a hood, and her body seemed to flow upward even as the pelt lowered toward the ground. By the time her round belly hit the sand beside the book, she was a seal. An orphaned seal, because of me. She dove into the surf.

I clumsily mounted my poor wet horse. I had one chance to escape the wrath of Keyward, and it was in the arms of this equally furious storm.

For hours, the horse and I trudged back the way we came, inland, away from the force of the gale. Finally, I spied a fallen tree near the road. It had blown over in another storm, long ago, and we sheltered behind the giant fan of its gnarled roots.

When I unrolled the old sailcloth I used as a tent, I saw Izhmir crouched against the edge of the roots, her head tipped back and her mouth open. Rain beaded on her lips and splashed directly onto her eyes, but she didn't blink it away.

She had followed me through miles of shrieking wind and stinging rain. I was crippled by the cold as much as my wounds. If it was revenge she sought, she could have it.

"I thought you went into the water," I said. With the webs cut from her fingers and her hair over her ears, only another Bane could recognize she wasn't human.

"I did. Then I came back out."

She crawled over and peered at the wounds on my thighs. They glared up, like two wet red eyes. My body accused me of poor judgment. The wounds said I should have floated out of Keyward on a bed of lilies, not stayed to defend children who weren't mine, weren't even human.

One of those children turned her large, pale eyes up to me.

"Why did you go into the smithy." It wasn't a question, the way she said it. That was fitting, because what I had to say wasn't an answer.

"It's been a long time since I stopped floating above everything. I'd forgotten what it's like to swim along with everyone else, to feel currents instead of merely watching them."

"You find pearls only when you sink," Izhmir offered.

I fingered my line of prizes where it poked against my wet skin, jewelry created of blood and bone. How many times had I passed the opportunity to add something more beautiful to my memories?

"Yes," I said. "I could do with more of those."

Cory Skerry lives in the Northwest U.S. in a spooky old house that he doesn't like to admit is haunted. When he's not peddling (or meddling with) art supplies, he's writing, reading submissions at *Tor.com* or copy-editing for

Shimmer Magazine, and often off exploring with his sweet, goofy pit bulls. He's a graduate of both Viable Paradise and Clarion West, and his work has appeared in *Strange Horizons*, *Fantasy/Lightspeed*, and *Beneath Ceaseless Skies*, among others. For more of his stories, visit coryskerry.net.

And, sure enough, the most evil, cold-blooded thing
in his memory was there . . .

DOWN IN THE VALLEY

Joseph Bruchac

Bones, Theo Buck had told him. That was all they found.

Sucked clean of every bit of flesh. So white they mistook them for ice when they saw them and the bottom of the stream that led down into the cedar swamp.

How many went missing?

Seven, Theo said, tapping his walking stick on the ground. The Horsemen were no damn help. Just come in and poked around and then said it had to have been a bear. But there was no tooth marks on them bones.

So what can I do that the Mounties can't? John Sundown said.

Since it wasn't really a question, Theo Buck just looked sideways at him and nodded.

John Sundown readjusted the weight of the heavy pack and the rifle as he looked down into the valley. The wind that came up the rocky draw into his face was warm. It carried with it the aroma of new growth, despite the thin snow that clung to the ridges. He recognized the scents of familiar spring plants, the same ones that used to grow near the streams back down on his own reservation—back before the dam was built.

He took a deep breath. Gettin' too old for this.

Come here, the voice said again.

Not a voice you hear with your ears. Well, maybe not that old.

The valley on the other side of the low range of white-capped Ontario hills seemed just as deserted as he'd been told it would be. The streams that flowed down there still had a plenty of trout in them. But no deer sign since he'd started to climb. No rabbits spooked from the brush. And no smells of smoke as there would have been if there were any people still down there. Even though it had been the favored hunting grounds for half the Anish families hereabouts, no one had set foot in the valley since they'd found the bones of Bill Mink and both his boys at the edge of the bigger of the two cedar swamps.

John Sundown raised his chin and drew in an even deeper breath through his nose. And he caught the faintest trace of another scent, a scent that was *majid*. In English *majid* might be translated as *bad*. But English didn't do the old word justice.

The eight years he'd been forced to stay at the Indian Industrial School hadn't taken away his language or dulled his senses. They might have split him from family, cut his hair, stuffed him into a uniform and thrown him into the guardhouse every time he forgot and spoke a word of Algonquin but all that they were able to strip away from him was on the outside.

They thought he'd been civilized. Even the English Master, Mr. Asa Poundshaw never suspected. Boston-bred, the meanest teacher at the school, bald Poundshaw whipped any brown-skinned boy or girl who failed to show proper respect or mispronounced a word. But John Sundown learned fast. He knew who to be afraid of and what he needed to do after his first brutal beating, followed by three days in the cold guardhouse on bread and water. By the time Sundown had been at school for two months, whenever Poundshaw turned his cold fishy gaze to look down his long nose at John, all he saw was a little Indian boy nodding his head in what seemed to be perfect agreement. It was not easy for John to swallow down his anger, to hide the fear that the terrified beating of his heart would give him way. And perhaps Poundshaw suspected that John Sundown's conversion had been a little too fast. But there were far too many other obviously recalcitrant Indian boys and girls for him who needed to feel the civilizing stroke of his cane.

His last two years there, John Sundown had been more than a model example for the civilizing hand of at the government boarding school. A true dawn-of-the-twentieth-century Indian. Perfect class attendance for four straight terms, second string running back on the Indian football team, member of the school orchestra (playing the cello). One of John Sundown's poems extolling his teachers was published in the *Monthly Arrow*—whose Boston-born editor apparently not only lacked an eye for irony but also had not (like John Sundown) looked up the word "acrostic" in *Webster's Dictionary*.

> *For all that school has given freely*
> *Unto this red lad forest bred*
> *Callow before he did receive*
> *Kind instructions, a pat upon his head.*
> *Yea, let me heap up grateful praise*

On those who generously granted
Unto me kindly Wisdom's gaze.

He hadn't even spoken a word of protest when he was sent out—like all the other able-bodied Indian students—to be a low-paid field worker at one of the white farms in the countryside around the school that made use every summer of cut-rate red labor. Where sometimes a vulnerable young native boy or girl might be used in another way.

John Sundown shook his head at that memory. Figured for sure school had killed the Indian in me.

That had been the mistake of Old Hans, the hulking owner of the farm where John had been "outed," as they called that system of semi-slave labor. He'd assumed that John Sundown was just another little Indian boy he could take advantage of out behind his cow barn. But John's being quiet and reliable at his chores hadn't meant that he was either vulnerable or slow. One of the little tricks you learn playing football against Ivy League boys— Harvard linemen who knew where to jam a knee at just the right time—had come in handy when he felt the ham-like hand of Hans on his shoulder.

John Sundown smiled at the thought of how Old Hans had limped for a week afterwards—and kept a respectful distance away from him for the rest of that summer.

He shaded his eyes against the rising light of the late June sun with his left hand. This valley was at least a mile wide, maybe four miles long. A river flowing through it. Marsh lands and a little lake at the far end where the cliffs came down. Spruce, hemlock, balsam and pine on the higher slopes, then birch and beech, cherry and oak and maple. Everything here seemed just about right—at first glance—for him to locate what he was looking for. He'd find the useful plants his grandmother had taught him about when he was little, before the Indian agent had him shipped off down to Pennsylvania. The land down there ought to be right for all kinds of medicines, even the ginseng that they'd pay a hefty price for back down in the States, and then ship it off to the Far East where it was used as a medicine for just about any ailment. Ginseng roots were worth their weight in gold. And just like gold, ginseng drew greedy men to Indian lands to dig it out. So now it is rare and worth even more.

They never gathered medicine the way we do, John thought. He touched the tobacco pouch at his side. He was only four when Grama Sabbatis put a handful of tobacco in his palm.

Put that down there by the roots. Don't hurry. Show your respect and thanks. Explain how we need its help. Ask permission before you pull it up.

That plant had seemed to jump into his hand after he did that. And they only took that one plant, not even the biggest one of the family of plants they found growing there. That way there would always be more of that medicine when they needed it.

Healing was like that. You had to take it slow, be patient. And there was a lot of healing he had to do. It was hard to believe how much he'd seen in the last few years. Two years of college at Dickinson after Carlisle. Then enlisting when America entered the war.

He'd been in France, a member of the Expeditionary Force, when it had come to him. Come to him after the blast deafened him and threw him twenty feet through the air. Come while the shrapnel was still so hot in his thigh he could smell his own flesh burning.

The voice came. He'd never heard it before, but he recognized it. It was the same voice his Grama told him she first heard when she was twelve winters.

Wake up, it said. You have a job now. You must help heal the people.

A voice as everyday and as matter of fact as that of one of his superior officers. But an inhuman voice, one without breath, spoken inside his mind.

First, stay alive. Lead your men.

He had done that. He got up. Moving faster than any man should with German steel lodged in his thigh, he'd roused his company. Black men, every one of them. The Army would never have assigned white men to be led by an Indian, even one who was an officer and had gone to engineering school. Then John Sundown had led them down the trenches, across the no-man's land of night, safely away from the gas attack that flowed in behind them like a yellow burning fog over the flat marsh land, its long fingers strangling and suffocating those who had not followed him.

The armistice came a week later. Like tens of thousands of other soldiers in a dozen different uniforms, he had limped away from the bitter land they'd watered with their blood. Packed his kit bag, threw in a few souvenirs, boarded a troop ship at Brussels. A month later he was back home in Maine on his grandmother's porch.

Slowly he drank the tea she'd made for him from the same tin cup given him since John was a little child.

I'm here to help, Nokomis, he said. They both smiled after he said that. Even though she had ninety winters, she could still split wood as good as a man half her age, and there were as many on Indian Island who feared her as there were those who respected her.

If a bear in the woods runs into Grama Sabbatis, it was said, that bear turns and runs for its life.

It's good you come here for help, Nosis, she said.

Then they both sat for a while listening to the river . . . and his breath which still rasped every now and then.

You heard the voice, she finally said. He nodded.

Good.

Summer began to walk away towards the south and the wind held a hint of the northland's breath. The leaves were falling. John hunted birds and small animals for food. Deer were all gone now from around Indian Island. He worked a few odd jobs in the town to get flour, sugar and coffee. Cut wood, kept the stove burning, grew stronger. By the time of the Freezing Moon, his lungs were clear again. His hip no longer ached every time he drew a breath. That was when the moon was as full of light, as a wise old woman's face. His grandmother told him stories as she had done when he was little. Her words were as healing the clean air, the familiar land beneath his feet, the music of the good river flowing near her cabin.

When early the Moon of Maple Sugar came, they tapped the seven maples by the edge of the road that led to home.

First medicine gift, Grama Sabbatis said, handing him a cup full of the sweet sap before they began boiling it down in the old iron kettle to make syrup.

Drink it.

He drank. It washed away the last of the darkness stuck in the center of his chest.

Then it was the Moon When Frogs Sing. She handed him his pack. Go. Gather medicines along your way. Help the people. Heal when you can. And when the need arises—as it will—use those other skills you learned at war. You will know when.

He hadn't told her about the letter in his pocket from his old school buddy. A letter he had picked up that morning from the store where mail was delivered. Hadn't mentioned he would be leaving.

But of course she knew.

John Sundown had nodded, shifted the strap of the Winchester over his right shoulder. Then she wrapped her strong old arms around him and held him tight for a long time. An embrace that was, he knew as well she did, the last his fierce old grandmother would ever give him.

So, after two months of steady travel he had come here. He'd traveled some by wagon, some by train, more by walking. Then a week on the waters of the big lake and then upstream on one of its tributaries by canoe to reach Theo Buck's reserve. Theo had been the right end on their team at Carlisle.

He found his old friend sitting on the front step of the trading post, holding a walking stick with a bear's head carved on top of it. Theo had always been good with his hands. Best student in the art classes at Carlisle. Pop Warner, the school's football coach and a lover of art, had bought half a dozen of Theo's paintings.

Theo raised the stick in greeting, pointed with his chin to the steps next to him. John Sundown sat.

You got my letter, Theo said.

Ayup.

Theo cleared his throat, spat.

Remember the stories you told me about your grandmother?

John Sundown nodded.

Turns out, Theo Buck continued, my own grandfather knew her. Turns out a bunch of our old people knew her. Knew about her. Knew that she could, he paused, tapped the stick against the steps, handle things.

That is true.

I have heard, Theo said, his voice cautious, that you can handle some things.

I can try, John Sundown said.

Then Theo had told him about the valley.

Below John Sundown, the next day, the valley was quiet, mostly.

You come.

That voice again. Were the silent words said in Indian or in English? Or neither one?

Setting up his camp took no more than the time for the sun to travel the width of one hand down the sky. He'd learned to travel light when he was a boy. Never carried a tent or all the camping equipment the weekend outdoorsmen seemed unable to live without. Just an oil cloth to stretch over the lean-to frame of straight limbs he'd cut, stripped, and erected against the side of the big boulder that blocked the northwestern wind at his back. If a man had a good knife, he could make about anything he needed from the woods. He'd allowed himself the luxury of a cooking pot, a spoon, and his grandmother's tin cup—which he'd found in his pack. But nothing more in the way of cooking supplies. Left more room for the other things as well that he'd stowed in the heavy pack on his back. Things that might save his life or make a difference. The pot hung now over the small fire he started with flint and steel. His coffee would be ready in another minute or two.

No animal tracks, he thought, chewing on one of the pieces of venison jerky he'd brought.

No birds singing. Not one.

Why am I doing this?

Because I can.

The dark came quick, rippling along the valley like dark water filling in a pool. He'd gathered enough wood to keep the fire going through the night, dry logs laid up so he could just shove their ends further into the fire as they burned. He checked his rifle, making sure it was loaded. A good gun, this lever-action Winchester. Better than those they'd given them to use in Belgium and France. He could get off a dozen shots from it in as many heartbeats. He laid it close at hand on his side away from the fire. He could roll to it and have it up and ready to shoot in a heartbeat. Then he reached under his shirt and pulled what looked like a thin black rope. In the old days, when a man went to sleep in a strange place he would tie a little of his own long hair to a tree root. That way nothing could come in the night and take your spirit. After his years in the boarding school and in the army, where barbers held just as much sway, the hair on his own head had still not grown back much further than his shoulders. But this rope of hair that he carried with him was even better than his own. His grandmother had braided it from strands of her own hair, hair that had never been cut but flowed down, still dark as midnight in the forest, even though she had now seen more than ninety winters.

John Sundown tied one end of the hair rope around his left wrist and then tied the other to one of the gnarled fingers of the venerable cedar tree that had wrapped its roots like an elder's brown hand around one side of the boulder.

I tie myself to the earth, he whispered. I cannot be taken from this place. Something called from the far end of the valley.

You come.

A breathless call. Not a song. Far from that. Nope, John Sundown said.

He wrapped his fingers around his grandmother's hair and slept.

He woke up before dawn. Took a pinch tobacco from his pouch and offered it with a prayer to the rising sun, dropped it into the fire.

Then he checked his gear. He had all he needed. And he was hearing it again.

You come.

I'm coming. But you might not like what I'm bringing.

As he made his way along the trails that were overgrown now, no sign of deer tracks or any other, he thought. Was it new here? Had it come from some other valley that it stripped of life? Or had it been here a long time sleeping, then woke up hungry, ready to eat until it was time for another long sleep?

He leaned back against a big stone

Can I do this? he said to himself.

Don't ask if you can. Just try. That will be good enough.

He grinned at the memory of her words, so strong that they came clearer to his mind than that call—which was not so far away now.

Okay, Nokomis. I try. He straightened up and began walking again.

It'll be a pond or a deep spring. Like in the old stories. I'm almost there.

You come.

Hurry. Hurry.

Don't be late for roll call.

You are going to get demerits in my book, young man.

A ruler across your knuckles will remind you not to be a lazy savage. Quick time, march!

Whoa!

John Sundown stopped himself.

He was so close now that the breathless voice had almost overwhelmed his senses. Not just one voice now but a passel of them.

Using my memories against me, eh?

John swung the gun off his shoulder and squatted down, still a hundred yards from that pool of water that had seemed so enticing just a moment ago. A shiver went down his back at the thought of what lay below the placid surface.

Listen.

He heard it. Below the imagined sound of human speech. A hunger, cold and wet. Deep as dark water, full of its own greedy cleverness, its guile that of the stickiness of a spider's web spun across the paths of insects blundering into that fatal trap.

Cold, hungry, dangerous. And so sure of itself that it is stupid.

He pulled out the other rope from his pack. Not the one of woven hair, but the thicker one that had a woven core of wire within it, strong enough to pull a Model T up a hill without stretching or breaking. He took out the block and tackle. Could be used to hang up a moose carcass, but it could take a much greater weight. He tied it to the trunk of a black ash that looked to be deep rooted enough in the moist soil, threaded the strong line through it. He'd be able to more than double his own strength when he pulled that line. Mechanical advantage. One lesson he was glad he took away from the school shop.

He pulled out the old shirt. Sweat-soaked, it would have his smell. Just in case smell was what drew the thing. A few sticks tied right, leaves stuffed inside to give it shape, stones to give it weight. A passable dummy. Then, last of all, the big three-barbed hook. Designed for catching sharks, he had picked it up in a port town on his way back from France. Just because he'd had a feeling he would need it sometime. The kind of feeling Grama Sabbatis had taught him to always listen to.

A loop in the rope above the decoy's headless body, a long pole through the loop and now he could walk it out in front of him toward the deep pool of water, the weight of the stones in the cloth like the thump of feckless feet.

Keep your mind clear now of any thought of resistance.

Think just that **Yes, Sir,** he'd been taught to say at the industrial school

The same **Yes, Sir,** that had served him just as well in the army. No matter what his soul was saying.

You come.

Yes, Sir.

Come.

Yes, Sir.

Thump, thump of the manikin's stone feet closer and closer to the edge, the rope playing out behind it back to the tree.

No more than twenty feet from the edge now.

Come!

Yes . . .

KER-WHOMP!

It struck so hard and fast that his heart jumped in his throat. Dummy, pole, and line whipcracked forward. Water kicked up into a froth by the big head that arced up with open jaws, and snapped, hurled itself spinning back. Though John Sundown let go as quick as he could, his palms were skinned and he was dragged forward a step.

A death roll like an alligator's. He'd seen that once while sitting at the edge of a pasture a stone's throw from a Louisiana bayou. The big old gator's green head shot out of the water to grab the chestnut foal, yanked it down, tearing flesh and cracking neck bones as it whipped its ridged tail and rolled its massive body. So fast there was nothing he could do to save the young horse. Gone under the weedy surface before he could stand up.

This thing was faster than that gator. So sudden in its attack and retreat that he wasn't quite sure what he'd seen other than gaping jaws and dark shiny skin, maybe pale-bellied like a frog.

He didn't let himself be frozen by the fury of that attack. He stepped quick back to the tree, watching the line that had grown taut, tight as a bowstring. But the tree was strong in the earth. Though the line sawed back and forth as the creature under the surface tried to break free, both the metal-threaded rope and the big swamp ash held against the strain.

John Sundown picked up the Winchester. Gun cradled in his arms, he stood still.

Watching, waiting, slightly disbelieving.

When the sun was in the middle of the sky, the frenzied motion back and forth of the line slowed. He slung the gun over his shoulder. Holding the part of the rope threaded through the block and tackle, John Sundown pulled on the loop to untie the coil around the tree and began to haul in.

No, let go.

Nope.

Let go. Let go. Let go.

Nope.

Though it had swallowed the dummy, lodged the hook somewhere down its throat, it didn't come out head first. It had rolled its body around the rope, tried to pull itself away. What emerged first, covered with mud and weed, was the creature's backside, a snaky tail whipping back and forth. Then short, thick hind legs with webbed feet, a glistening body dark on top and frog white on the belly. He'd been right in what he thought he saw.

Bigger than a gator. But built unlike any alligator or any other critter other than itself.

There were names for this thing in the old languages of the land.

Aglebemu . . . Mannigbeskw . . . The Old One Who Swallows Us. Swamp Caller.

That breathless voice was speaking to him again, still trying to find an edge to confuse him. Draw him near enough so it could get him.

No hurt. Let go. Come here. Help.

John Sundown tied off the rope. Unslung the Winchester. Safety off. It began to turn its head toward him.

Careful. If the old stories were right, now was when the creature would chill the blood of anyone who dared look directly at it. It would hypnotize its prey with terror. It would show John the most fearful and evil visage it could dredge up from his own memories. Then, when its prey was frozen in fright, it would attack, and it would devour.

And, sure enough, the most evil, cold-blooded thing in his memory was there.

That was what John Sundown saw.

And that was why he let out a chuckle as he lifted his gun and blew a hole square between Mr. Asa Poundshaw's eyes.

For over thirty years **Joseph Bruchac** has been creating poetry, short stories, novels, anthologies, and music that reflect his Abenaki Indian heritage and Native American traditions. He is the author of more than one hundred and twenty books for children and adults. The recipient of the American Book Award, the Knickerbocker Award for Juvenile Literature from the New York Library Association, a Rockefeller Humanities fellowship, a National Endowment for the Arts Writing Fellowship for Poetry, the Cherokee Nation

Prose Award, the Hope S. Dean Award for Notable Achievement in Children's Literature. and both the 1998 Writer of the Year Award and the 1998 Storyteller of the Year Award from the Wordcraft Circle of Native Writers and Storytellers. In 1999, he received the Lifetime Achievement Award from the Native Writers Circle of the Americas. His most recent novels are *Dragon Castle* and *Wolf Mark*.

You start to think that you're the only one who has ever seen her.
It's a terrible thing to think, and you hope that it isn't true . . .

ARMLESS MAIDENS OF THE AMERICAN WEST

Genevieve Valentine

There's an armless maiden in the woods beyond the house.

She doesn't wail or weep the way you'd think a ghost or a grieving girl would. Her footsteps are heavy—sometimes she loses her balance—but that's the only way to hear her coming.

It happens in plenty of time that you can grab the bucket of golf balls you're collecting (the golf course buys them back for beer money) and get out of the woods before she reaches you.

If you do see her, it's because you lingered when the others ran, and you hid behind the largest oak, the one you and your dad once built a fort under, and waited for her.

The first thing you see is that her hair is loose. That strikes you as the cruelest thing, that whoever did this to her couldn't show even enough mercy to fasten her hair back first, and cast her into the forest with hair so long and loose that it's grown into corded mats down her back. The knots at the bottom are so twisted and so thick they look, when she's moving, like hands.

(No, you think, that's the cruelest thing.)

But her face is clean, as these things go. You imagine her kneeling beside the creek that runs all the way out past the golf course, dipping her face in the water.

There are dark stains down the sides of her dress, all the way to the ground, where she bled and bled and did not die after they cut her arms off at the shoulders.

The armless maiden has hazel eyes, or maybe brown.

She says, "Hello."

There's no telling what the armless maiden did.

It doesn't matter now. To her father, it was offense enough to warrant what happened. To anyone else, what happened was a crime beyond measure; what happened to her was a horror.

(Where they were when her father picked up the axe, there's no telling.)

• • •

She's been living in the woods as long as you can remember, though no one talks about it much where you are. Live and let live. If she stays off the golf course, no one minds her.

Nobody in town talks about her to strangers, but still, word gets out.

Sometimes one of the news crews from a bigger city would get wind of her and send a crew to do a story about the woman who haunts the woods. Usually it was Halloween, but sometimes it was International Women's Day, or something horrible had happened to a woman where they were from, and they wanted to find as many crime victims as they could to round out the story so it could last.

Once someone came all the way from Indianapolis to write her up; she asked if anyone had caught her, like she was a rabbit or a disease. The station could pay for testimonials, she said. She gave a dollar number that meant Indianapolis was serious about it.

She left empty-handed. The neighborhood didn't like the implications.

The armless maiden has never spoken, that anyone has ever said, and someone would have said. There's no need to tell strangers from Indianapolis about her, but she belongs to the town, sort of, and it's nothing strange to talk about your own.

Suzanne from the hairdresser's talked sometimes about how she couldn't imagine how that poor girl was looking after herself, and how she'd go out to the woods asking if the maiden needed anything, except that it would be butting in. Usually she said this when she was cutting your hair; she said, "I hear she's a blonde," and then there was no sound in the whole place but her scissors, and you watched your hair falling and held your breath.

At least once every year, someone from the PTA stood up in a meeting and asked if she was still of the age where she needed to be in school, even though she'd been in the woods so long that even if she'd started out that young, she wasn't now.

Tommy from the motel told everyone about the time the bird watchers came down to look for some warbler that was hard to find except in the forested region where they were, and ran into her, and got so frightened they left town without paying their bill. But they left most of their things in the room, too, so he sold the binoculars and the cameras and it came out all right.

He told the story like it was funny, how scared they had gotten, like any of them had ever really seen her and there was something to compare.

You start to think that you're the only one who has ever seen her.

It's a terrible thing to think, and you hope for a long time that it isn't true, but in all the stories people tell about her, no one says a word about seeing her themselves. Maybe she's just the kind of person whose privacy people respect, you think.

(But you know already, long before you admit it, that you're the only one who's ever seen her, and that she must be so lonely it makes your stomach hurt.

When she said hello, you've never heard anyone so surprised.)

That year, a researcher comes.

She isn't like the newscasters, with their navy or pastel skirt-suits, and their hair that got blonder the farther south they came from, and their camera crews who said nothing and tipped poorly.

She comes alone, with a roll-along suitcase that Pete from the diner said was mostly just full of notes and books and a laptop. She read papers the whole time she ate, Pete said, and after she paid the bill she asked him if the rumor was true.

"I'm studying armless maidens of the American West," she said. "I hear there might be one in the area. If anyone has any information about her, I'd like to meet her."

Pete said it like she was the weird one, but some of the people he told the story to thought she sounded different.

Meet, she had said, which sounded very civilized, and which none of them, the more they thought about it, had ever really done.

You kind of hate Pete for not asking more about it. You worked Wednesday through Saturday; if she had come in a day later, you would have asked her plenty.

Because it was as though no one heard the part you hear, the part that sends you down to the motel after work Friday to leave a wadded-up note with Carla, who does the night shift, and who would be more likely to actually pass the word along. (Tommy works days, and he'd let it get lost out of spite, because some guys are just nothing but spite, aren't they?)

She had said, armless maidens.

There are more.

There's comfort in an armless maiden.

In the stories about one armless maiden or another, her suffering is finite; because she is a girl of virtue—or was, before her father got to her, but allowances are made—we know she won't always wander the forest, bleeding and solitary.

While she does make the forest her home, angels part the water for her to walk through, so she'll never drown, and drape their heavenly cloaks on her, so she'll never freeze. It's a comfort.

The birds drop berries into her open mouth, and the rain falls past her grateful lips, so that when the prince finds her she won't be starved (princes in stories don't like maidens whose bodies are eating themselves).

The comfort of the armless maiden is how well you know she's being cared for; how easy it is to understand which parts of her are not whole.

When the researcher actually calls you back, you're surprised.

"It was kind of you to contact me," she says. "And yes, I'm still very interested in speaking with her, if it's possible."

You ask, "Why?" like she was the one who left you a note instead.

She says, "I'll show you the structure of the study, if you want. It's very respectful of privacy. It's still at the research stage at the moment—we're a little low on funding—but I hope that we're doing important work."

The guys at the golf course probably do important work, and you hope she's after something besides golf-course money. (You feel like you wouldn't even know what really important work was.)

"Sure," you say.

The armless maiden is alone.

Even in dreams, no one comes near her; even if there are forests teeming with armless maidens, each one is in a world only she knows for certain.

If the woods were teeming with them, the armless maidens wouldn't believe it, somehow; they would pass by and pass by, each thinking of the others, What a lonely girl, how like a ghost.

(In the good dreams, the world of an armless maiden is a world of silence; it's a world filled with rings of silver; it's a world where the axe couldn't hold.)

The researcher comes in on a Thursday night with her rollalong, looking just like Pete described her, and orders a cup of coffee, and asks you to have a seat.

There are some people who stopped off on their way to the antique fair, so you can't right away, but you stop by to refill her coffee about a dozen times, and finally she pushes a document toward you.

You flip open the first page, standing right there at the table because you can't wait any longer to know what's going on.

You scan the page quickly—the corner booth ordered omelets and the toast gets stone cold if it sits out for more than ten seconds.

It reads, "The armless maidens of the American West are not, despite the title of this study, a geographically-defined phenomenon. The concentration on this region merely allows for a reasonable sample size to be defined and, if possible, interviewed."

Then, farther down, "For purposes of this study and in the interests of maintaining privacy for participants, all names have been changed."

Then there are lists of names; there are charts and graphs full of more data points than you ever thought were possible to gather about anything.

(One axis is labeled "Age at Dismemberment." You can't breathe.)

Next to her, there are stacks of paper fastened with clips, with names like ANNA or CARLIE or MARIA written in large block letters across the front, maybe so they're easy to find.

They're not real names; you wonder if she picked them, or they picked their own.

"What happened to them?" you ask, finally, after you've decided there's not enough money in the world to make you pick one up and read it.

(Your fingers are still resting on CARLIE. Underneath her name it reads: AGE 13.)

She considers her answer, like she doesn't want to frighten you.

She says, "Different things."

That's sort of worse—you had tried to take comfort in the old story that only a father did this kind of thing. Your dad was okay; you thought you were fine.

You swallow. "Are they—are they all right?"

"Some of them," she says. "It depends a lot on what happens to them afterward—who they know, how much they feel they have support to rejoin the world. Sometimes their arms even grow back, eventually, depending."

You guess a little bit about what that depends on, but it's not hard; the armless maiden has been around a long time, and nothing has healed, and everybody you know says things about her but never to.

"I'd like to speak with her, if you know where to find her," she says. "It's a good starting point. The more we talk to them, the easier it is to take note of their progress."

Progress.

There could have been progress already, if someone had ever walked out past the golf course and looked her in the eye, just once.

You don't want to talk about this anymore.

"I'll get your check," you say, and fill her coffee cup too full, and clock out for your smoke break twice in a row by accident because your hands are shaking.

You suck the cigarette down to the filter, making up your mind about it.

You go back out to the woods, late in the day, when no one is likely to be on the course.

(You don't like the golfers. They never come into the diner, even though it's right down the highway and they have to drive past it, and it seems more trouble to avoid it than to stop.)

You wait near the tree. You've brought some things that make you feel stupider than you've ever felt, including the time you had to give an oral report on the French Revolution in history and blanked, and Tommy never let you hear the end of it.

(You've brought scissors, a comb, vitamins, a dress with sleeves.

You want to be prepared; when you tell her about the researcher, she might say yes.)

Near dark, just before it's really night, she comes by all the same, with careful footfalls.

When she sees you, she stops.

"Hello," says the armless maiden.

You say, "Hello."

Genevieve Valentine's first novel, *Mechanique: A Tale of the Circus Tresaulti*, won the 2012 Crawford Award and was nominated for the Nebula. Her second novel, *Glad Rags*, is forthcoming in 2014, Her short fiction has appeared in *Clarkesworld, Strange Horizons, Journal of Mythic Arts, Lightspeed*, and others, and the anthologies such as *Federations, The Living Dead 2, After*, and *Teeth*. Two of her stories were nominated for the World Fantasy Award and Shirley Jackson Award. Her nonfiction and reviews have been published by NPR.org, *Strange Horizons*, io9.com, *Lightspeed, Weird Tales*, Tor.com, and *Fantasy Magazine*. She is a co-author of pop-culture book *Geek Wisdom* (Quirk Books).

A cheap graceless ring . . . blue lace agate was supposed to be protection,
but it hadn't even done that much for the girl who had worn it . . .

BLUE LACE AGATE

Sarah Monette

Jamie Keller and his partner hadn't found the shoggoth larva smugglers yet, but his boss, the head of the Bureau of Paranormal Investigation's southeast hub, had other things on his mind: "And, ah, how are you and Sharpton doing, Keller?"

It was a loaded question, and Jamie considered it carefully before he answered. "Me and Sharpton—Sharpton and I, sorry, sir—are doing just fine."

Jesperson's eyebrows went up. He knew it was a lie. But Jamie met his eyes steadily.

"I'm not complaining, sir."

"No, you're not. Another two days and you'll beat the record, you know."

"Yessir." Jamie had been Mick Sharpton's partner for two weeks and three days. He knew why no one lasted longer than that.

"Well, all right then. Be off with you."

"Thank you, sir," Jamie said, and was not surprised, when he got back to the office the six junior-most agents shared, to discover that his partner had already left for the day.

He grabbed his jacket off the back of his chair, turned off the lights on his way out the door. Shrugged into his jacket in the elevator. He checked his watch and booked it to the bus stop, just in time to catch the southbound M that would get him home.

Where Lila would be waiting.

The elderly white lady sitting across from him gave him a funny look, and he knew she was probably afraid his smile—incongruous on a man six-four, black, homely, tattooed, and built like a Mack truck—meant he was high on something and about to start ripping chunks out of the bus. He nodded at her, and she looked quickly away.

He got off the bus at Lindale and Davis and walked another five blocks to the ugly concrete apartment building he currently called home. The guys in 1A had left the front door propped open again, and Jamie sighed, foreseeing yet another unpleasant conversation about why the safety of the building's thirty other tenants was more important than the convenience of their lazy asses. But for now, he just kicked the wedge free and went upstairs.

Third floor, apartment 3B. Lila was on the phone, and after ten seconds and an exasperated eyeroll, he deduced that the person on the other end was her mother. Jamie kissed the back of Lila's neck as he edged past her into the kitchen, and started scrubbing potatoes.

He wondered if there was something wrong with being so happy with this rather tawdry domesticity, and decided he didn't care.

Three days of nothing, and today promised to be more of the same. Mick Sharpton sat fuming in the passenger seat of the Skylark—he didn't drive, and Jamie had decided early on not to ask if "didn't" meant "wouldn't," "couldn't," or "shouldn't."

Jamie drove as an alternative to engaging with Mick's anger. He was, as it happened, perfectly capable of driving and holding a conversation at the same time, but Mick seemed to want to believe Jamie was a big dumb lump, without a thought in his head that Jesperson didn't approve first. And if that was what Mick wanted to believe, Jamie was happy to play along. It made his life easier.

And he didn't want to fight with Mick. He didn't want to compete with Mick, didn't want to threaten Mick. He wanted to keep this job—more than that, for the first time in his life, he'd found something he wanted to do *well*. And having had a chance to evaluate the other junior agents, he knew Mick Sharpton was his best hope of being not merely good at his job, but *remarkable*.

Three years older than Jamie, Mick Sharpton was a sharp-boned, pale-skinned man with long dyed-black hair and long lacquer-black fingernails. The left side of his face bore evidence of reconstructive surgery: the cheekbone that didn't quite match, the skin that responded stiffly when he smiled. Jamie had not asked what had happened, and Mick showed no signs of wanting to tell him.

Mick Sharpton was also a clairvoyant. That was why Jesperson had hired him, had kept him on despite the trouble he caused—why Jamie was willing to put up with a great deal to keep Mick as his partner.

Mick's esper rating was 3(8); most of the time his clairvoyance meant only that his hunches were unusually good, that it was useless to try to lie to him.

But that latent eight meant he was liable to precognitive and retrocognitive flashes, telepathy, rescognition, all the usual occult trappings of seeing ghosts and auras. Unfortunately, the latent eight also meant none of it was under his conscious control, a fact that irritated Jesperson profoundly. Thus far, Mick had refused to take esper training—and made his decision stick by daring Jesperson to fire him. Jamie was just as glad to have missed the resulting explosion; he'd gotten several gleeful eyewitness accounts from agents happy in their schadenfreude that he was the one saddled with Sharpton now.

Jamie parked the Skylark in the lot of the Tree of Life. The next informant on their seemingly endless list was the proprietor: Charlene Pruitt, better known as Madame Anastasia. She used the hippy-dippy froufrou of her store to camouflage a much darker and more serious class of transactions. She was very careful, and therefore never prosecutable—at least, not yet—but her desire to keep on the Bureau's good side made her frequently quite helpful as a source of information.

"Oh, fuck it, Keller. Not here!"

Jamie turned off the engine and looked over at Mick. "She's next on the list."

Mick rolled his eyes and muttered, "Fucking Jesperson," but he didn't argue, and Jamie smothered a smile as he got out of the car.

"Your door locked?"

"*Yes*, the fucking door's locked. Come on!"

Jamie followed his partner's nervy, arrogant stride across the parking lot and into the Tree of Life, where they were greeted by the sweet jangle of a string of tiny bells. Sitar music permeated the air, as strong and characterless as the incense. Mick muttered something under his breath and stalked away to glare at the Tarot decks. Jamie went up to the counter and asked if Madame Anastasia was available.

The white college-age clerk, pierced in eyebrow, nostril, and lip, and wearing enough sandalwood to choke a phoenix, looked up at Jamie, at the broad, unlovely lines of his face, at the octopus tattooed on the shaved side of his head and down his neck, black swirling lines on skin nearly as dark, and said, "I'll, um, go see, okay?"

She scurried off in a flap of Birkenstocks and long shapeless skirt, and Mick prowled over to say, "Charlene sure can pick 'em, can't she?" then began running his fingers restlessly through a basket of cheap silver rings: Celtic knots, snakes, dolphins, pentacles, hearts.

Jamie noticed the bitterness in Mick's voice, and was just deciding, again, that it would do more harm than good to ask, when Mick said, "Hey! This one doesn't—"

Glancing at the ring Mick had picked up—silver set with blue lace agate—Jamie was about to ask what on Earth Mick thought was wrong with it, when he saw the wear on the edges of the band, the brass showing through the thin silver wash.

He looked up, but whatever he would have said died in his throat at the expression on Mick's face. Mick's eyes had gone wide, his mouth a little slack. He said, "We have to go now," in a voice unlike anything Jamie had heard from Mick Sharpton before, the voice of a child who is frightened and trying to hide it.

Jamie couldn't argue with that voice. "Okay," he said and shepherded Mick to the door, calling over his shoulder, "We'll come back later," as the rattle of the beaded curtain announced the clerk's return.

Jamie unlocked the passenger-side door first, which normally would have provoked a sharp comment from Mick about not being that kind of girl. This time, it barely seemed to register; Mick got in and fastened his seat-belt, and then simply waited, pale blue eyes staring a hole in the dashboard, until Jamie, seat-belt buckled and engine started, said, as gently as he could, "Where are we going?"

Mick said, his voice not much louder than a whisper, "She's in the river."

"Oh, *Christ.*" Jamie considered for a fraction of a second telling Mick to call it in, but he didn't think Dispatch would be able to make heads or tails of Mick in his current state. He grabbed the handset and reported November Echo and November Foxtrot en route on a rescog.

Heading west toward the river, Jamie counted. Thirty-four seconds after he cradled the handset, the radio crackled to life with Jesperson's voice: "November Foxtrot and Echo, report!"

"Mick had a flash, sir."

"A flash of what?"

"I don't rightly know. We were in the Tree of Life, waiting for Ms. Pruitt, and he picked a ring up out of a basket. And now we're on our way to the river."

"Latent bloody clairvoyance. All right, Foxtrot-niner. You two go check it out. I'll give Juliet Victor and Mike the rest of the list."

"Yessir. We didn't get a chance at Ms. Pruitt."

"Duly noted. Able out."

Mick gave him directions as they went, leading them to a residential neighborhood: one-story houses, most in dire need of new siding, and decrepit docks sticking out into the muddy river like half-rotted teeth. Everything shabby, faded, cars rusting, grass dying, and the river behind it all like a stain that won't come out.

But there were children playing in the yards and on the sidewalks, mostly white, although some black and some Hispanic. A pair of long jump-ropes were being wielded with professional aplomb by two teenage girls, and the little girls standing giggling in line for their turn were every shade from as white as Mick to as black as Jamie.

All at once, Mick said, "Here!" his voice so urgent that Jamie slammed on the brakes in instinctive response, hard enough to throw them both forward against their seat belts. He swerved the car over against the curb; Mick was already clawing at the door, scrambling out, leaving the door not only unlocked but flapping open. Jamie locked the car and followed him more slowly, knowing that it wasn't going to matter. Not precognition or telepathy—Jamie'd never scored higher than a two on the esper equivalencies—just brutal truth. The woman who had worn that ring was dead, and he didn't need to find her to know that.

But he went after Mick, picking his way through the crabgrass and old Coke cans. Mick was down by one of the docks, up to his knees in river water, tugging at something that seemed to be trapped in the dock's underpinnings, something limp and pale and horrible.

"Mick," Jamie said. "Mick, come away. We need to call the police."

Mick wasn't listening, his breath coming in sobs, but he wasn't making any progress, either. She was well and truly stuck. Jamie's imagination offered him a hideous picture of Mick trying to dive under the dock to get her loose, and that was enough to make him step off the bank himself, to take Mick's arm and say gently, "Come on, Mick."

Normally, Mick reacted to being touched with a sidestep and a snarl. But this time, he let himself be led out of the water and then back to the car, where he sat obediently in the back, his wet feet dripping onto the curb, while Jamie, sitting likewise in the front, called Dispatch and got them to notify the police. For once, Mick wouldn't be sneering at him for doing things by the book.

After a thoughtful look at Mick, he did not suggest that they leave. They waited quietly; Mick's eyes had not regained their customary sharp, shuttered expression, and Jamie knew it was only his own presence in the car that kept Mick from going back down to the dock and the poor, gruesome thing trapped under it.

After a few minutes, he noticed the blue lace agate ring lying on the floor of the car and picked it up. It told him nothing, just a cheap graceless ring—there were probably thousands like it in this city alone. Blue lace agate was supposed to be protection; it hadn't even done that much for the girl who had worn it.

He twisted to hand the ring to Mick. "What else do you know about her?"

Mick held the ring on his palm as if it were some strange, possibly poisonous insect. "She was with her friends. Excited, laughing. They were going to—oh Jesus!" He shuddered, his fingers closing hard over the ring.

"Mick?"

"They figured they'd found a way to live forever. One of them—a boy—had a book. He said it told them everything they needed to know. But they didn't tell *her*."

"What was her name?"

"Don't know. She thought they were all drinking, but they weren't. Just her. And he kissed her—Bobby kissed her, and he never had before. And she was so happy. She thought they were playing when they tied her to the chair. But they weren't. They all had knives, and they took turns cutting her until she died. That was the ritual. Then they each took something of hers, so her death would defend them, and dumped her in the river, chair and all. Please take this ring away from me."

His tone didn't change, nor did his pained frown, so it took Jamie a moment to realize what he'd said. When he did, he came immediately around to kneel in front of Mick, whose hand was cramped so hard around the ring that prying his fingers loose took some effort, even with Mick trying to help. Finally Mick's hand was open, and none of the fingers broken, and Jamie took the ring, wincing in sympathy at the angry red welt where it had dug into Mick's palm.

"I hate this," Mick said, his voice so soft Jamie could almost believe he'd imagined it. And before he could decide what to say—or if he should say anything at all—the police had arrived, in a whoop of sirens and spatter of lights as if that would make some difference to the thing wedged beneath the decaying dock.

It was two hours before Jamie was finally able to get Mick away. Partly that was Mick's own fault—it seemed he could not be satisfied until the body, still tied to an ugly old wooden office chair with all its casters missing, had been pulled out of the river. Then Jamie got distracted by an officer who wanted an account of how two ghoul hunters had come to find a murdered girl, and when he managed to get away, the detective in charge of the case had Mick all but pinned against the police car, snarling questions at him as if she thought she could lever answers out of him by sheer nastiness.

Something seemed to have drained out of Mick with the recovery of the body; Jamie could see the tremor running through him, the unprotected wideness of the pale eyes. Another man might have left Mick Sharpton to be flayed by the police detective. Jamie intervened, patiently, gently, putting his own bulk between the detective and her prey, insisting that her questions could wait, that Mick had told her all he could. Finally, she grudgingly acquiesced, and Jamie dragged Mick to the Skylark before she could change her mind.

Jamie called Dispatch to say November Foxtrot and Echo were emphatically off-duty for the day, and drove to Mick's apartment, which was in a part of the city as shabby as Jamie's own neighborhood, but older, still clutching its fading gentility to its bosom. Mick lived on the second floor of a looming brick monstrosity. Jamie had never been inside.

He found a parking place directly in front of Mick's building and touched the luck charm hanging from the rearview in thanks. He killed the engine, looked across at his partner. Mick was a huddle of long limbs, his head down, and he was still shaking, a fine shiver like a scared cat.

Jamie heaved a sigh. "Come on then, blue eyes. Let's get you home."

He supposed it would have looked funny to an observer: the massive black man and the long-limbed white ragdoll he was trying to maneuver. Mick didn't fight him, exactly, but he was clearly disoriented, confused, and very frightened. He responded to Jamie's quiet-voiced coaxing, though, and was even able, when they at last made it up onto the porch, to fish his keys out of his pocket.

He promptly dropped them and flinched; Jamie couldn't tell whether it was from the sound, or from an expectation that Jamie would whack him one. Jamie picked up the keys, unlocked the door and propelled Mick inside with a hand between the shoulder blades. It wasn't quite a shove.

He followed, made sure the door latched behind him, and then chivvied Mick up the stairs, grateful there was only one flight. Another round with keys and locks, and finally Jamie was able to urge Mick into the apartment, so close behind him he almost stepped on his heels. He locked the door before he did anything else, then turned and examined Mick's home.

It was a studio apartment—one room, not overlarge, with sink and stove and refrigerator and a minuscule amount of counter space along one wall. Nice big windows, at least. There was a futon mattress on the floor, a chair, a card table, a lamp, and a motley assortment of bookcases, cinderblock and plywood shelving, milk crates, and cardboard boxes, some of which seemed to contain clothes, but most of which housed stacks upon stacks of books and CDs. The only thing in the room that looked like it would be worth the bother of stealing was the stereo, and even at that, Jamie thought, any sensible thief would just let himself right back out again and go try somebody else's place.

Jamie steered Mick to the bathroom, which was directly across from the front door. A shower, a toilet, a sink with a mirror. No room to swing even the smallest and most patient of cats. Clean, though, and Jamie said firmly, "You need a shower. Can you manage? Because honestly, I don't think both of us are gonna fit."

A wide-eyed stare, and then Mick nodded. "Good," Jamie said. "I'm gonna use your phone. Okay?"

"You won't . . . leave?" A creaky little whisper.

Jamie smiled at him. "Nah. Won't go no place. You go clean up."

Mick nodded; Jamie hoped this eerie tractability would wear off soon. Then Mick was in the bathroom, the door firmly closed, and Jamie went to call Lila and let her know he'd be home late.

Mick went straight from the shower to the mattress on the floor, long white nude body so skinny Jamie could have counted the knobs of his spine if he'd wanted to. Mick dragged the sheet up over himself, both eyes shut tight, and said again, "You won't leave?"

"Staying right here," Jamie said from the chair by the card table. " 'Til you tell me you want me gone."

"Okay," Mick said and was immediately asleep.

Jamie sat in that uncomfortable chair, one elbow propped on the card table, and read, rather slowly, a book he'd found on Mick's shelves called *The League of Frightened Men*. At five o'clock, he called in—very quietly, although it was clear that nothing short of a tactical nuke was going to rouse Mick—and got an update: the girl's name had been Bethany Timms. She was twenty-two, a record-store clerk; her boss hadn't liked her gothy friends. The clerk at the Tree of Life, who might have known something about the ring, had gone off shift before the Juliet team got there; Charlene Pruitt denied emphatically that she had ever seen the blue lace agate ring before in her life and was not much more helpful on the question of shoggoth larvae.

When it got dark, Jamie turned the lamp on. It was a couple hours after that when Mick rolled over, said, "Fuck me gently with a chainsaw," and sat up, his hair in tangles down his back.

Jamie raised his eyebrows at him. "You better?"

"Yeah." Mick ran his fingers vigorously through his hair, said, "Christ, what time is it?"

"Quarter after eight."

"You must be wanting to get home. Girlfriend waiting, right?"

It wasn't quite a sneer, but the walls were going back up.

"You gonna be okay?"

"Yeah, I'm fine." A hesitation, quite palpable, although Jamie didn't think he was supposed to notice it, and Mick said carelessly, "It takes me like that sometimes, when I get something really strong. No big deal."

"Okay," Jamie said; he didn't need esper to know Mick was lying, especially about the "no big deal" part, and he thought, as he got to his feet and replaced Mick's book on the shelf, that that went a long way toward explaining why Mick was so allergic to esper training.

"See you tomorrow, then," Jamie said to Mick, and Mick, rummaging for clean clothes, ostentatiously preoccupied, said, "Yeah."

And that was that.

In the morning, Mick looked like cold leftover death, and Jamie knew without either of them having to say a word that he hadn't slept. Jesperson noticed it, too, but did not comment beyond a dubious quirk of one eyebrow.

He was bringing them up to speed on what Gonzales and Peters had accomplished the afternoon before, when Mick said abruptly, "What about the Timms case?"

Jesperson gave Mick a dry look over the tops of his glasses. "Not our jurisdiction."

"It was an occult murder. Doesn't that make it ours?"

"She was killed by living human beings."

"Practicing unlicensed necromancy."

"We have no direct evidence—"

"Rescog is admissible."

"Not as hearsay."

"So give me the goddamned ring and a tape recorder," Mick said between his teeth.

Jamie said, trying not to sound like he was intervening, "Have the police caught up with that little clerk yet?"

"No," Jesperson said. "Natalie Vowell didn't go home last night, and didn't show up for work this morning."

"I thought we weren't supposed to listen to the police band, sir," Mick said nastily.

"I don't."

Jamie said, "You could give us another day off from the shoggoths, sir. I did see Miss Vowell face to face, after all, which'll be a help in finding her."

"We don't know the girl had anything to do with it," Jesperson said.

"Why the hell else would the ring have ended up where it did?" Mick demanded.

"If we find Miss Vowell, we can ask her," Jamie said to Jesperson, trying desperately to pretend both to Jesperson and himself that Mick wasn't being unreasonable, trying to forestall another shouting match. But Jesperson's attention seemed to be somewhere else, for after a moment he said thoughtfully, looking at Jamie rather than Mick, "All right. You can have the morning to track this errant clerk. But I go no farther than that."

"Thank you, sir," Jamie said before Mick could get his mouth open. "Come on, Mick," And Mick was sensible enough to see he'd won as much ground as he was going to; he followed Jamie without demur, down to the garage to get the Skylark.

As he was backing out, Jamie said, "Where do we start?"

He had half expected to get snapped at for asking something so stupid, but Mick said, "Tree of Life. Lord knows I don't *want* to do another rescog, but if we can find something of hers there . . ." He trailed off, then muttered unhappily, "Christ, I feel like a fucking bloodhound. Just give me something with her scent on it and watch me go."

"If you think she was one of the people who murdered Bethany Timms, then we want to bring her in. Don't matter how we do it."

"No, I suppose not. Tree of Life, then, and let's hope Charlene isn't there."

Mick's luck was not in. Madame Anastasia was minding the counter, and as soon as they walked through the door, Jamie understood why Mick had been trying to avoid her. "Mitchell, darling!" caroled Madame Anastasia, a big white bosomy woman with her hair dyed henna-red. "How delightful to see you again! And who is your very large friend?"

"Didn't know your name was Mitchell," Jamie said out of the side of his mouth.

"And if you like your balls where they are, you'll pretend you still don't," Mick muttered back, then said with bright, false cheer, "Charlene! Don't tell me I forgot to let you know I'd gone to work for the BPI."

The expensively made-up face of Madame Anastasia fell so fast it was a wonder her foundation didn't crack. "The . . . the BPI? Mitchell . . ."

"We were here yesterday," Jamie said politely, and did not let himself smile at her double-take. A lot of white people reacted that way, as if a man his size and color oughtn't to be able to code-switch. "We didn't get a chance to speak with you."

"I told those two other agents everything I know," she said, rather shrilly.

"Of course you did," Mick agreed, hitching one buttock up onto the counter in a way that suggested he was settling in for the duration. "We're not here to ask you more questions, Charlene. We just want to know if Natalie Vowell left any of her personal belongings lying around."

She stared at him for a long moment; then her eyes narrowed in vindictive triumph, and she said, "I *knew* you could rescog."

Mick didn't miss a beat, just smiled back and said, "Actually, that's my partner. *Things*, Charlene. Did she leave any?"

She looked from Mick to Jamie. "I should ask to see your ID. I know you, Mitchell. I know how far—"

Mick, with a long-suffering sigh, flapped his badge at her.

She was turning red. Fury, Jamie thought, and remembered Mick's bitter crack of the day before: *Charlene sure can pick 'em, can't she?* He wondered how long Mick had worked for Charlene Pruitt, and filed it away with the rest of the questions he was never under any circumstances going to ask.

"I'll go see," she said in a tight voice. Her heels beat a hard staccato rhythm into the back of the store.

Mick turned to Jamie, poised to say something, and Jamie said, "Man, you don't need to tell me how much you hate her."

It was almost funny, watching Mick trip over his own tongue. Finally he said, "Oh. Good." Then a sudden frown pulled his eyebrows together, and he said accusingly, "You're not nearly as stupid as you like to make out."

"Well," Jamie said, grinning, "I guess you caught me."

Mick's jaw sagged, and Jamie would have quite liked to find out what he would have said, but the trip-trap of Madame Anastasia's returning heels brought them both sharply back to business.

Natalie Vowell had left her umbrella at the Tree of Life; after last week's rain, it was hardly surprising. Jamie thanked Madame Anastasia with great politeness, took the umbrella in one hand and Mick's elbow in the other, and marched them out of the store before Mick had time to object. Once in the parking lot, he let Mick pull away and tossed the umbrella at him. "You want to do your bloodhound thing, now's a good time."

"I don't," Mick began, trying for indignation, and then his hands clamped on the umbrella and he said, "*Fuck.*"

"It bad again?"

"Not as much. It's just—God! The people who have touched this thing! Let's hurry, okay?"

"You got it," Jamie said, unlocking the Skylark. "Just tell me where to go."

"She's at the Greyhound station," Mick said, slinging himself and the umbrella into the car. "Panhandling to get enough money for a ticket."

"She getting close?"

"Not very."

"All right then," said Jamie, and put the Skylark into gear.

They had no difficulty in either finding or apprehending Natalie Vowell. She panicked when she saw Jamie looming through the plastic benches and crumpled travelers, and tried to run. Mick caught her easily, shoved her one-handed up against the nearest wall, his long nails threatening to tear the limp cotton of her blouse. "Okay, princess," he said, in a low, controlled voice. "I think we all know why we're here."

"I don't know what you're talking about!"

"Oh, please. You can't lie to me, princess, so don't even try. Tell me about the ring."

She was starting to cry, not the pretty tears girls of her age sometimes used to get their own way, but big, gulping, snotty sobs. Jamie didn't blame her, though he wished she'd be quieter about it. He smiled pleasantly at the approaching station official and showed his badge, which caused both that man and several others to back off in a hurry.

"Mick," he said under his breath. "Not our jurisdiction."

"I want to know first," Mick said, leaning close enough to Natalie Vowell to kiss her. "I want to *know*, Natalie. And you're going to tell me. All about Bethany Timms and that blue lace agate ring."

There was a long moment, queerly intimate, silent except for Natalie Vowell's sobbing breaths as she stared into Mick's pale, fanatical eyes. Then, as suddenly as if someone had flipped a switch, she howled, "It was Bobby's idea!" and the rest of her confession poured out of her. She'd helped murder Bethany Timms, taken the blue lace agate ring. But then she'd had second thoughts, yesterday morning; she'd wanted to get rid of the ring and its load of guilt, and hadn't been able to think of any better way to do it than to add it to that basket of cheap rings in the Tree of Life.

Poor silly bitch, Jamie thought without any sympathy, and Mick said, "Let's find some goddamn cops."

Their afternoon was chewed up by the police and the paperwork and the great disgruntlement of the detective at having her suspect nabbed by ghoul hunters, unameliorated by her officers' steady success at collecting the people Natalie Vowell had named as participants in the ritual, the murderers of Bethany Timms.

Mick kept his composure this time—clearly the umbrella really hadn't been as bad as the ring—although that was a mixed blessing at best. Jamie finally had to invoke Jesperson to dispel the threat of being brought up on charges.

"The Old Man wouldn't like knowing you're taking his name in vain," Mick said, sliding into the Skylark.

"If you tell him, I won't ever give you a ride home before turning the car in again," Jamie said mildly, and grinned at Mick's startled glance.

The same spot in front of Mick's building was free. Jamie pulled in. Mick made no move to get out, and after a moment, Jamie gave him a sidelong glance, eyebrows raised.

Mick was staring down at his hands. "I, um. I need to say thanks."

"You're welcome. What'd I do?"

"Um." He was blushing now—a thing which Jamie had never expected to see, no matter how long they were partners—and he shook his head so his hair fell to shield his face. "You, um. Yesterday. You took care of me. Nobody's ever . . . oh *fuck* I am not talking about this."

"You don't have to. I don't need to know."

One bright pale eye peered at him from behind the curtain of dyed-black hair.

"Mick," Jamie said patiently. "I am not out to get you. I don't care what shit you pull or how hard you ride me. I don't care that you're white, I don't care that you're gay, I don't care that you're a son of a bitch, and I don't care that your fucking esper ratings can kick my ass. You're my partner, and that means we're on the same side. You read me?"

Mick pushed his hair back behind his ears, looking at Jamie strangely. "You really think it's that easy?"

Jamie burst out laughing, a great bass roar that had Mick trying and failing not to join in. "Oh hell no. 'Course it ain't that easy. It's just the way it is."

"Oh," Mick said and grinned at him, nothing held back. "Okay then."

"Get your skinny white ass out of the car and go get some sleep," Jamie said, grinning in return. "We're back to them shoggoth larvae tomorrow."

Sarah Monette lives in a 106-year-old house in the Upper Midwest with a great many books, two cats, and one husband. Her first four novels were published by Ace Books. Her short stories have appeared in *Strange Horizons*, *Weird Tales*, and *Lady Churchill's Rosebud Wristlet*, among other venues, and have been reprinted in several Year's Best anthologies. (Jamie and Mick have, so far, appeared in two other short stories.) *The Bone Key*, a 2007 collection of interrelated short stories, was re-issued in 2011 in a new edition. A non-themed collection, *Somewhere Beneath Those Waves,* was published the same year. Sarah has written two novels (*A Companion to Wolves* and *The Tempering of Men*) and three short stories with Elizabeth Bear. Her next novel, *The Goblin Emperor*, will come out from Tor under the name Katherine Addison. Visit her online at www.sarahmonette.com.

He thought of some presence somewhere beneath me, undefined and huge and with eyes that saw everything, regardless of the dark or the distance.

THE EYES OF WATER

Allison Littlewood

The world above and the world below were divided by a few feet of earth, but out here, it seemed impossible the other could exist. Above, market stalls; brilliant sunshine; a car park surfaced in dust; an ever-present circle of Mexican girls, no more than five or six years old, holding out handfuls of embroidered handkerchiefs. No one wanted handkerchiefs, but they bought them anyway at the sight of the downturned mouths that said, "I'll cry if you don't."

I passed stalls selling lace and dresses, brilliantly colored pottery and carvings. When I didn't stop the women pointed the way to the cave, being helpful. They called out, "Maybe later." I knew this was so they could catch me on the way back, claiming a prior arrangement, but I nodded anyway. It was my first trip to a cenoté—one of the many flooded caverns that fractured the Yucatan Peninsula—and I was already half immersed.

The narrow path led away from the stalls and towards a dark hole in the ground. As I approached I saw that steps had been cut into the stone; the steeper sections were bridged with wooden treads. There was a rope in place of a handrail and a sign bearing the caution,

"Wet stone are slepering." I wondered if Rick had noticed it. He'd be down there already—I'd seen his battered pick-up in the car park—a sign that he belonged, if only in part, while I was merely a tourist.

The sign was right, it was slippery, and I surrendered the macho impulse and clutched at the rope. I couldn't see anything for a few steps, then caught a glimpse of the palest blue below; went on, careful where I placed my feet, until I reached the bottom. I looked up and saw the cave. The water was spot-lit, creating a turquoise glow that darkened to indigo at the edges. Stalactites hung everywhere, save for a brilliant white spot where light speared through a hole in the ceiling. There were vines too, slender and dark, threading down to touch the water; then I realized they were the roots of trees growing above, outside in some other world.

The cenoté was beautiful. It was also empty: no Rick, no tourists. I wondered what it would be like to be here alone in the dark, and shuddered.

A splashing sound: there was someone down here after all. A shape spun out of the brilliant white place where the beam of sunlight hit the water. The shape turned into arms, elbows, a head. It shook itself and the spray sent shockwaves across the water.

"Get in here, Alex," Rick called out. "It's sweet. Wash the sweat off."

I tugged off my shirt as I headed for the pool. The water was clear, and small black fish were swimming in it. I wanted to dip my head into the cold, to dive down and see what lay beneath. I wanted to swim into the circle of light and see what happened.

Rick laughed, his voice echoing. It was too loud, too brash—too foreign, maybe. I didn't like it, and for a split second, I wished him gone; then saw his grin and found myself grinning back. We swam. He told me about his projects, what it was like to really explore, to dive the cenotés, passing from one cave into another. How they had discovered a whole new system. It was infectious, his enthusiasm, always had been. I envied him. His smile was the same as ever: clean, white, broad. His skin was smooth then, and his body was whole.

My mobile rang as I dropped off the dive tanks, and I dug for it in my rucksack. I had been out with a group off Cozumel Island. I hadn't seen much apart from the underwater sculpture just offshore, Christ with his head thrown back towards the light, feet anchored to the seabed. Apparently it was lucky to touch the figure; I wasn't a churchgoer but did it anyway, knowing it was pointless. I could breathe all the time, while the free-divers around me struggled to attain sufficient depth. At least their moment of contact had cost them something.

I found my mobile. I didn't recognize the number and I didn't recognize the voice, bubbly and distorted, as though coming up from the deep.

"It's Kath," she said, and I frowned; I didn't know anyone called Kath, but couldn't say so because she was crying and I couldn't stop her long enough to speak.

Then I caught the word "sister," and my stomach lurched because I did know who it was, after all. I remembered a broad, stocky girl of twelve or thirteen, her hair tied back in plaits that Rick liked to tug when his mother wasn't looking.

Kath must be in her twenties now, a couple of years younger than Rick. I swallowed and stared out across the beach, the waves whipped into white-tops by the steady breeze, and wondered when I had managed to swallow sand.

"Are you there?" she asked, and "Are you hearing me?" She sounded so desperate I wanted to shout down the phone that no, she wasn't alone, I was there. Instead I just croaked, "Yes?"

"They say they found a body. Alex, they say it's Rick. But I don't—"

There was crackling, broken only by the waves and the boats and the sounds of voices shouting on the wind.

"It can't be him," she said. "I'm flying out, but I can't get there yet. Please, Alex, can you help? We have to know it isn't him."

I found myself nodding, my throat closing up. I *knew*. My eyes teared even while I told myself that it wasn't true, couldn't be true. *Twenty-three*, I thought. It stuck in my head while I tried to think of words to say: *twenty-three*. It was so fucking wrong, and I looked straight into the sun, feeling the sting of salt spray in my eyes, blinded for a moment. I remembered a shape thrashing in a brilliant point of light, the head and arms and legs emerging, twenty-three years old and already marked by some fate he couldn't see.

I never doubted my capability to identify Rick until I was standing in front of the body. I had planned to give one simple nod, then do whatever I could to make sure his sister didn't have to see it. The room was filled with the sound of fridges barely ticking over. The smell was at once sweet and unbearable; it couldn't be compared to anything else.

Rick didn't have a face. My mind hadn't got around that yet; the words *twenty-three* were still there, circling like buzzards, and now there was this new thought. My lips pressed together, keeping everything down and in, but inside my head was screaming: *He hasn't got a face.*

The hair was there, at least in part. Towards his forehead—where his forehead should have been—there were only tufts. The skin had been torn away. His eyes were still there but the lids had gone and I couldn't look at them. His nose was a small, soft mound. I found myself staring at it and my stomach contracted. Thank God nothing came up; if it had, I would have vomited over the corpse.

I turned away from it and felt a hand on my shoulder. "Take your time," the attendant said in strongly accented English, and I almost laughed. Time wasn't going to help. The man without a face could have been Rick, could have been anybody. I wondered whether that would comfort his sister.

I turned back, took in the shreds of muscle still clinging to his skull, the places where bone shone through. I forced myself to try and make out what shape the face would have been.

"Are there any other signs?" the attendant said, and I blinked. "What?"

"Signs that you would know. There are no tattoos, but—a scar, maybe. An old scar."

I shook my head. Rick led a charmed life: *had* led a charmed life. As long as I'd known him he'd been into skydiving, zip-wires, rock climbing, anything that gave him a buzz. He'd never broken a bone, never had an injury I knew of. And then I had that image again: a girl with frizzy hair running after us while we rode our bikes, at least until the day she'd grown sick of being left behind and shoved a stick between the spokes of his wheels.

I heard her crying in my mind. "I never knew," she'd said. "I just thought it'd slow him down."

Rick had teased Kath about that scar on his knee for years.

I turned back to the body and pulled aside the sheet. One knee was smooth; the other had a white ridge underlining the patella. The left—had it been the left? I couldn't remember.

"*Señor?*"

I closed my eyes, opened them again. "It's him," I said.

"You're sure?"

"I'm sure."

He nodded, looked happy, then overwrote the expression with sympathy. I didn't care. Kath wouldn't have to see this now. I thought of her horrified expression, back when she'd pulled that stunt with the bike; wondered if it would have made her feel better to know that she had marked him then, claiming him as her own in readiness for a day like this.

"He was found by a surfer," the attendant explained, "in the *ojos de agua*."

I frowned. My Spanish wasn't great, but I knew of a cenoté called Dos Ojos—two eyes. And *agua*—something I asked for every day.

The attendant sighed. He sat back, putting his hands behind his head. "Your friend was diving in a cenoté. It was not on the tourist routes, no? Not safe. This cenoté had many systems. Many caves. Eventually, the caves come out in the sea. The sweet water—fresh water—it come through the cave and goes into the sea. At high tide, it is like—how you say—a bathtub. You try swimming in a bathtub when the plug is pulled?"

I frowned.

"I have felt it myself, in a cenoté near my village. I had to get to the steps and keep hold." He demonstrated, clenched his fists. "So I didn't get pulled down. Your friend, he get pulled down."

"And the eyes?"

"*Sí*. The sweet water, it bubbles up through the sea, like the water boils in that place. It is the *ojos*. The eyes of water."

"But Rick was a good diver," I said. "He wouldn't have gone in alone." I only said this because I didn't want to ask about what was really in my mind: Rick's face.

"It happens." The attendant dismissed my friend with a wave of his hand.

And so I had to ask: "How did his face get like that?"

"He was beaten," the man said. "Sucked down. Dragged against the rocks, all through the tunnels." He sat forward, scraped his chair. "I am sorry."

I wiped damp palms on my shorts, shook hands and left. It wasn't until I stood outside, the sun like hot metal on my head, that I thought about his words: *dragged against the rocks.* And yet—Rick's face was entirely gone; but the rest of his body had hardly been bruised at all.

Kath's flight was due in at 5:00 p.m., but I'd forgotten how long it took to get through customs at Cancun, to have the necessary papers checked and stamped. When she finally appeared it was disorienting to find I recognized her at once. It was the same Kath, the same stocky build, the same hair already frizzing in the heat. She didn't speak to me, just dropped her bags and put her arms around my neck.

I hugged her back. Her skin was cool but heat radiated from her anyway, like a child in a fever.

I tried to explain what had happened while I drove away from the airport. I thought she'd want to sign the papers, get the body home as quickly as she could; and I'd go back to my tour, start trying to forget. So Kath's words took me by surprise.

"When are we heading out?" she asked.

"Out?"

"I want to see where it happened." Her voice was small, but impossible to counter. "I want to see where my brother died." My mind was blank.

"I'm coming with you," she said, as if that was the only thing to be decided.

The village was a small cluster of buildings, some painted pink or blue, but most left dust-colored. "Down there," I said. One of Rick's colleagues, an American, had barked directions down a crackly phone. I turned onto a side street, headed past a small white church. There was a group of men outside it, pulling a crucifix into position, hauling on ropes or steadying the base: no doubt preparing for Easter. They stopped working as we passed, shuffling back, staring. One old man grinned, his face a sudden mass of wrinkles, his eyes impossibly blue. *Eyes of water,* I thought, and grimaced.

Beyond the village we took a narrow track and headed straight into the thorny scrub forest. The Mexican jungle wasn't how I'd imagined. The trees were interspersed with agave and palms, the spaces between filled with thorns and spines, everything parched and brittle.

After a while we saw a *palapas*, an open-sided hut thatched with palm fronds. When we rounded it we found a clearing full of tents, generators, pick-ups, cars. There were stacked crates, bottles of water, barbecue equipment, diving kit, plastic tubs containing what looked like firewood. Two men leaned over a trestle table with paperwork spread upon it. One of them, a slender Mexican, approached, holding out his hand to shake before we'd even stepped out of the car.

"So sorry, *señorita*," he said, and Kath closed her lips tight.

"I am Arturo. You will stay with us tonight. Tomorrow, we show you everything." He waved at the sky; it was already graying, though the humidity and heat remained. "Eat with us." He gestured. People were emerging from a path that led into the jungle, talking and laughing. Some of them carried more of those plastic tubs. I turned to see Kath dragging her bag from the back seat. Heard whistling from the *palapas*. A man with a wetsuit stripped to his waist was stringing hammocks beneath it. I nodded, thinking how much Rick would have loved this.

Arturo bent over the plastic tubs, his eyes wide. The tubs didn't contain firewood. They contained bones, tagged and labeled, darkened to the color of mahogany. "We didn't expect so many," he said. "The Maya used this place. Cenotés were sacred places, then. Not just for swimming." His eyes met mine. "They were gateways to the underworld. Places to offer sacrifice." He waved a hand over the tubs, indicating a femur, a skull. "Many sacrifices."

I took a sip of mescal, vicious in its raw bite. Kath bent low over the bones, peering in. "Is this what Rick was doing?" I asked. "Finding bones?"

Arturo nodded. "The Maya had no water, apart from the cenotés. The god of rain—Chaac—he gave this water. So they give him these *señores y señoritas*."

"Did you know Rick well?"

"In the rich places, Chichen Itza, Dzibilchaltun, they give gold, jade, as well as persons. It was an honor to be given to the gods. It was said that a sacrifice—they would not die." Arturo chuckled. "They did not die, but they did not come back, no?"

"And Rick?" My voice rose. "Did you notice he'd gone? Did you look for him?"

Arturo met my gaze. "Of course," he said. "He was one of us. A good diver. What happened, it was a—freak accident, no? We never had—tides like that before. This is a safe expedition. Organized."

I felt Kath's hand on my arm. "Go on," she said to Arturo. "I want to know everything." I stared at her as Arturo started up again about sacrifices, the way sometimes their beating hearts were torn from their bodies; about how some were simply thrown into the cenotés, cenotés with no stair and no ladder. He opened one of the tubs, took something out. "Another kind of sacrifice," he said. "This one is defleshing. They cut the skull—here, here—and peel the muscle down the face."

I stared at it. The skull was misshapen, the forehead steeply sloping and tall, alien-looking. I remembered reading something about how boards were clamped to Mayan babies' heads, elongating them to show their status. I looked closer. There were cuts across the bone, showing where the muscle had been stripped. I remembered raw flesh tagged with flakes of skin, pale bone shining through from beneath, the soft mound of a nose. Pale eyes washed almost transparent, impossible to read their expression.

"Sacrifice," I said later, as Kath and I settled into our hammocks, pulling mosquito nets over the top. "Strange, isn't it, that they threw bodies into the cenoté. Do you think they knew they were poisoning their drinking water?"

She didn't answer.

"How they demanded blood," I said, "it's hard to understand. A good thing no one does that now."

"Don't they?" she said, quietly. "Remember the village."

I cast my mind back, tried to work out what she meant: thought of the men gathered around the crucifix. I remembered the waters off Cozumel, free-divers plunging down to touch the submerged Christ. Rick, being pulled down into blackness.

"Do you remember that day with the bikes?" I asked, suddenly. "When Rick hurt his knee?"

It took her a while to answer. "I lied," she said. "I knew what would happen. It was the price I wanted him to pay, for always chasing off, leaving me alone."

She fell silent, for so long I thought she was asleep. I listened to the snores coming from neighbouring hammocks, to insects singing in the night. And her voice came again, so low and broken I almost didn't hear.

"I hated him then," she said. "I was his sister and I hated him. I wanted to see him bleed."

I woke in the night. I wasn't sure what had awakened me; opened my eyes and saw heavy shapes suspended from the ceiling, people in their hammocks swathed like pupae. I half-sat, brushing netting from my face, and saw someone standing just outside the *palapas*. It was Rick. I could see it in the tousled hair, the way he stood, the white arc of his teeth. The moon cast a dark shadow at his feet.

I swung myself out of the hammock, looked up once more, knowing he would be gone; but he was not. He raised a hand and waved.

ALLISON LITTLEWOOD

The scar on his knee—had it been the left, or the right? It must have been someone else laid there on the slab. Everything could be well again, made new. I realized I should be calling out to him, but he turned away and walked into the dark.

"Wait," I hissed, and headed after him. Now I couldn't see him anymore. There were only the tents huddled in the clearing, the dark mass of trees. I realized I was standing by the path that led into the jungle and I started down it, pushing past dry, clawing spines.

"Rick," I called. Only the air came back, pressing in close and warm. I went on, emerged into a small clearing. Rick was there, standing at the opposite side, smiling.

"Rick, where the hell have you been?"

He tilted his head, beckoned me on. I started towards him, looked down, and realized what I was about to do. I stopped so suddenly I slid, pinwheeling my arms for balance. There was a hole in the ground. It was a meter across and almost perfectly circular, and when I looked into it, the blackness was so complete it appeared solid.

I looked up, searching the shadows for Rick. The clearing was empty. When I looked back down the path, I saw only my own footprints written in the dust.

My head ached. Last night no longer seemed real. We stood in the clearing, the sun blazing, looking into the hole. Arturo knelt down next to it, gestured. "It looks like a well," he said. "It's only when you lower yourself inside you discover it's a cave. From there a passage leads to another, and another, all the way to the sea."

I peered down but still couldn't see anything, only darkness. Someone brought a spotlight and when Arturo switched it on a little more rock wall was revealed, but nothing more. I imagined being lowered into that hole, thrown down it maybe, and swallowed.

Arturo looked at me. "You can't go in," he said, and my stomach contracted. Then he added: "You can swim on the surface only."

I looked up at Kath, found she was looking at me too. I couldn't breathe. *Of course.*

They dragged a metal structure over the hole. It was connected to a winch and a metal chair hung from it. I started to strip off my shirt, decided to leave it on. I kicked off my shoes and Arturo helped me into the chair, fixed a rope across my lap, put a flashlight into my hands. He nodded and stepped back. They had already started the winch.

I saw the earth floor of the jungle; then there was only rock. The chair bumped against it, and I closed my eyes. When I opened them I saw only the dark. I reached out and found nothing there. I could faintly see my own arm but there was nothing else, nothing I could touch. My heart thudded with the creaking of the winch so that the two things seemed connected.

"You're nearly there." The voice was distorted. "You will want the light, Señor Alex."

The light: of course. I fumbled, switched it on. A bright beam struck out and I saw black webbing wrapped all around; the roots of plants, clinging to the cave wall. It was only a cenoté, like the one I'd visited with Rick.

His face rose before me, pulped and misshapen. I blinked and it was gone.

"Are you all right, Señor Alex?"

I began to shout "Yeah, fi—" and caught my breath as my feet struck cold water.

"*Señor?*"

"Fine. I'm there." I had a sudden image of the chair continuing to sink, fumbled to release the rope that bound me to it. The water was up to my knees, then my thighs. How deep was it? How far to the opening that had dragged Rick under and through? With a grunt I slid from the chair and water took me, splashing my face. I couldn't touch the bottom. They could have warned me, I thought; no one had even asked if I could swim. Resentment rose as I tilted my head, looking back towards the light. It was a long way away.

For a moment I thought of sacrifices thrown into the cave, the way they must have watched that same circle of light until they could no longer tread water and sank into the dark. This time, when I caught my breath, it came with a gasp. *No.* Soon I could swim back to the chair and they would lift me out. I would feel the sun on my face.

I took deep breaths, floated, shone the light around the cave. I wondered if there were fish—blind, white, maybe—and pulled my legs up close. I let the ripples grow silent.

The Maya used this place. Cenotés were sacred places, then.

Arturo's words whispered around the walls.

They were gateways to the underworld . . . The god of rain—Chaac—he gave this water.

I thought of some presence somewhere beneath me, undefined and huge and with eyes that saw everything, regardless of the dark or the distance.

I caught my breath; knew I should leave, now, before panic set in. I swam back to the chair, dragged myself onto it. "Pull me up!" I shouted.

Nothing happened. The chair didn't move. Then I heard a low sound, but not of the winch; it deepened, grew hoarse, reverberating around the cave before tailing away.

Then, at last, the rumble of a distant motor. The other sound had gone.

I tried to remember what it had been like; thought of slender animals with amber eyes that did not blink.

The chair began to swing. I held tight to the sides, letting it take me upwards and out, back towards the light.

"It is unnerving, no?" grinned Arturo. He leaned over me, releasing the rope. "Especially with only one light. Usually we have a group. Three lights each. But this, I felt you should see."

I stared at him. Kath was watching me, her expression anxious. I nodded, letting her know I was fine. I didn't feel fine. My knees shook as I stepped away from the hole. I wanted to sit on the ground, taste the dust on my tongue.

"It is a wondrous place, no? Your friend—he love this place. He wanted to see it alone. We say he should not do this, but he did it anyway. He was like that." Arturo turned to Kath, nodding at her. "We thought he had gone away for a while. I am sorry. Sorry." He couldn't stop nodding. "But cave exploration, it is dangerous. We go together, *si*? Not alone. Much of the caves—it is very deep. No one has been through them all." He paused. "If it is any comfort— your brother, he wish to see everything. And perhaps he did. Perhaps he saw things we will never see."

We ate fajitas and refried beans as the light faded, sitting in our hammocks. We had already packed our bags. First thing tomorrow we would be on our way, back to officialdom and bureaucracy, the task of getting the body home. I could no longer imagine returning to my tour after that, couldn't visualize it anymore.

Kath chewed steadily, staring into space.

The thing that had happened to Rick—I couldn't find a way of looking at it. When I tried, all I saw was that black, empty space; putting out my hand to touch the wall and finding nothing there.

His face had been stripped. The muscles peeled away.

"You heading out?" The voice was loud, chirpy, and I turned. It was the American, the one who'd given us directions to the camp. He came over, waving his hand.

"In the morning," I said. "Early." Kath didn't say anything. "He was a brave guy, your friend."

"You knew him?"

"We all did."

"You all liked him?"

"Sure." He looked at me.

"He seems to have been a wild card," I said. "Arturo said Rick went off alone, into the cenoté. He said he loved the place."

"Wouldn't surprise me. He always liked to push it." He shrugged. "Not sure whether 'loved' is the right word, though."

"Why's that?"

"He was fascinated by the place, sure. Was always talking about what was down there. But he said to me once—Rob, he said to me, there's something wrong with this place."

"Wrong?" Kath spoke at last. "What do you mean? He knew there was something dangerous?"

"Not dangerous, no. He thought he'd seen something down there, once. It freaked him out. There's a place where you go down through the halocline, then through a squeeze, then upward again. He said he saw something in the place you come back up through the halocline."

The halocline. I had heard of that: a place where lighter fresh water meets the heavier salt water beneath. I'd seen pictures of it, a place that blurred and swirled, where light was distorted. In some of the pictures you would swear that the fresh water was actually air; you'd soon find out it wasn't, if you took off your mask. As illusions went, the halocline could be deadly.

"What did he think he saw?"

"Wouldn't say." Rob shrugged. "Probably nothing. Your mind plays tricks on you down there, you know? Look, I'm sorry about what happened, okay? I just wanted to say that, before you go."

I could only nod as the American walked away and Kath went back to staring into space.

I didn't sleep, not at first. I stared up at the rough ceiling of the *palapas*, watched as the shadows deepened. And yet I knew when Rick was there.

I sat up and saw his pale skin shining in the moonlight. I couldn't see his face but his chest was whole, and that made it worse somehow; the shadow that lay above. He didn't beckon or say anything. He just led the way, as he had before, and I got up and followed.

I couldn't hear his footsteps, couldn't hear my own. Even the insects were silent as I went down the path. I didn't need to keep Rick in sight to know where he was going.

At first, when I reached the clearing, I couldn't see him; then I did. He stood off to the side, next to some piles of equipment. When I edged around the cenoté, he was gone; there were diving tanks on the ground where he had been. I didn't want to think about what Rick was telling me. I couldn't do it; but I knew I couldn't go back, either. I had to face this, to see whatever it was he wanted me to see.

I gathered the tanks and grabbed one of the lights. There was a pile of wetsuits; I found one my size and pulled it on. Then I stared at the winch. It was a problem, and yet I could see the solution straight away, as though I'd planned this. I'd winch the equipment down to the water then climb down the cable. When it was done, I'd just have to hope I could climb back up again; either that, or hold on until someone came. In the wetsuit I should be all right until morning, providing nothing happened down there.

I tried not to think about Rick's face as I started up the winch. The motor was loud but I ran it until I thought I heard a distant splash. The equipment was down: it was time.

The hole was a narrow well, leading to blackness. I leaned over it and took hold of the cable, wrapped my legs around it and started to slide.

This time I had switched on the spotlight before lowering it and the surface of the water shone blackly beneath me. The cable hissed under my hands and I tried to grip tighter, to slow my descent. *The cable are slepering*, I thought, and grimaced. It wasn't funny; it was also too late. I already knew I would never be able to climb out. Then I heard a sound, the same cry I had heard before; something like a jaguar, but impossibly close, and in the next moment I was falling.

I hit the surface hard, came up thrashing through water that was dead cold. I couldn't get my breath, just kept gasping at the shock of it. I was trapped. I was drowning. I thought of sacrifices, how long they might have lasted. I forced myself to take steady breaths, reminded myself that I wasn't hurt, that I could float. The wetsuit was doing its job, warming me. Tomorrow, help would come. Now . . . now I could follow my friend. I focused on that, on Rick's grin, the way he would have laughed at my fear.

When I'd retrieved the equipment, I shone the lamp downwards into the water and I dived. It took a while to find the bottom; the cave went deep. I stretched out a hand and found answering fingers of stone reaching upward, their surface almost as dark as everything else. Then something moved. It was a dream of movement, maybe nothing at all, but I headed towards it. The water ahead swirled as though disturbed by a diver's flippers; then it settled and I saw a rope marking the route into the caves. I shone the light along it. There. Something else, swimming ahead of me: Rick.

I followed, ducking through a gap and into a new space. I had no idea how big it was, but it felt endless. I was dwarfed, despite the fact that my world had contracted to only this: the sound of my breathing; the dark; a thin, pale rope.

I kept going for what seemed a long time. I started to wonder if the remaining air would last long enough for this journey and back again; pushed the thought away.

Alex.

I stopped.

Alex.

It was sensory deprivation, that was all. I already knew how sound could seem distorted down here, how the dark could make the mind play tricks. I remembered that noise I'd heard, the cry of a jaguar; closed my eyes. When I opened them, Rick was there. His face was whole this time, pushed up close to mine, his eyes wide open. I started, blinked, and then there was nothing but the halocline blurring and shifting, the light I carried sparking blues and greens from its heart. It was the place the American had spoken about.

I went down through the blurring water, saw where the tunnel narrowed and balked. *There's a place where you go down through the halocline,* the American had said. *Then through a squeeze.*

I wasn't a great diver: I knew this. I wasn't like Rick, who would do anything, go anywhere. The squeeze was a dark hole that didn't get any better when I shone the light into it. It was full of particles that danced and swam and confused everything. It was too narrow for my tanks. I'd have to take them off and push them in front of me, a maneuver I'd heard about but never tried. It was no good. I'd have to go back, wait in the pool until help arrived. Confess I'd wanted to see the place where Rick had died but that I didn't have the guts.

That I didn't have my friend's courage.

I took off the tanks. Without allowing myself to pause, I entered the tunnel.

The tanks were unwieldy, too buoyant, catching on the roof. My breathing quickened; I couldn't seem to slow it down. I knew if they got stuck I'd be trapped down here, tethered to them until the air ran out. The walls touched me, welcoming. Closing in. I was in a tomb, a narrow, dark tomb, and I couldn't breathe.

The tanks moved and I lunged forwards, felt them pull away from me at the other end. I was through. I saw the halocline at once. It was just like before except brighter, as if there was some source of illumination within it; it was turquoise and cerulean and sapphire, all the colors of the Caribbean, the shades moving and passing into each other like veils. Then I saw what was on the other side.

A woman was waiting there. She stood clear of the water on a stone platform that jutted from the cave wall. I craned my neck to look at her. She wore a simple tunic, black stones about her neck and feathers in her hair. Her fierce eyes were turned on me.

I was caught on some surge of water, had to look away. When I looked back I expected her to be gone, but instead I saw someone standing next to her. It was Rick.

I swam towards them, still pushing the tanks. I looked up again into clear air. Their clothes didn't cling; the feathers stuck out from the woman's hair. They were dry. And yet . . . that was what the halocline did, wasn't it? Caused illusions. And Rick, after all, was dead, lying on a slab in some overheated mortuary.

My dive tanks bumped against the platform edge. They were bobbing on the surface; no more water.

I climbed out, knowing that it was all wrong, that there shouldn't be any air down here. And yet when Rick smiled, gesturing towards my mouthpiece, I took it off; pulled in an experimental breath.

I turned to Rick but it was the woman who spoke.

"You traveled through the body of the life-giver," she said. "What gift do you bring?" Her voice was quiet but resonated like the cry of the jaguar. She was dangerous, this woman. I could sense it, see it in her eyes. They were dark and yet liquid: *eyes of water*, I thought.

"The waters are restless. They will have sacrifice. What do you bring, traveler?" I shook my head.

She made a low growling in her throat. Her eyes shone. "My god is a jealous god," she said. "It is the giving time."

My throat felt clogged, as if I wasn't breathing at all. I looked at Rick. It *was* him I'd seen on the slab, I knew that now.

She threw back her head and laughed. "We are the servants of Chaac. Be sure that your gift is enough, or Chaac will take what he needs. The things he desires."

I thought of Rick's face, the remnants of skin, the soft mound of a nose. Defleshed. What had he offered, to have failed so badly? When I looked at him he didn't say a word.

"What does Chaac require?" I asked.

She smiled. It was a casual smile, but it made me want to tear the eyes from my head. She had small, white, pointed teeth. She went to Rick, trailed her fingers across his chest. "Blood," she said.

I looked at my old friend, searching for some trace of the boy I had known. "Rick, help me."

Her laugh rang out, mocking. It echoed around the cave, deepening until my chest ached. "Ask him," she said. "Ask him what he gave. Ask him if it was good enough." Her voice was harsh, peremptory, and my mouth opened of its own accord. "Rick?" I asked.

His head jerked as though he had just woken. He glanced at me, looked away. And I knew, then, even before he formed the word: "You."

"Rick?"

He wouldn't look at me.

The woman waved a hand. "Choose," she said. "What will *you* give?"

I thought, wildly. I had nothing. Some money, back home; I could borrow more, use it to purchase—what had Arturo spoken of? Gold. Jade. But when I looked into this woman's eyes, I knew it would never be enough.

Then I thought of Kath, on the outside, not so far away. Sleeping in a hammock in the warm, close night. I could come back here, bring her with me. Rick's offering hadn't been enough, but perhaps she would be. It was all I could think of. I looked at Rick. He was staring down at the floor, eyes half closed. It would be a fine revenge, to bring her here: his sister. Still I couldn't bring myself to say the words.

"Speak," she said.

I shook my head and her eyes snapped to mine. And I decided.

"I have nothing to give," I said. "I have nothing. I can't make—I can't give you a sacrifice." I wanted to continue, to say something about how that didn't happen, it wasn't done anymore, and forced myself to shut my mouth. She would flay the flesh from my bones. Rip the face from my body.

Something in her look told me I had to continue.

"There's only me," I said, my throat constricting around the words. "It's all I have. I can't bring anything else. I can't offer anyone else." I looked at Rick, saw that other version of him: the faceless one. She would give me to Chaac, to the water, and it would take me down. Flense my body. Eat me and spit out the bones.

"Do it now," I said, and let my head fall. I closed my eyes. "Quickly. Please." I didn't open them again. Didn't have to as the thunder of water filled my ears.

There was cold all around. Other than that I couldn't feel anything: my body was numb, my hands, my face; especially that. I reached up, touched my skin. It felt smooth, but maybe it did, afterwards. I opened my eyes and found I was blind. Then everything started to come back, the light, the air, and I began to shake. My face, though, was warming; I felt the sun on it, the blessed brightness. I was in the water, but something about it was wrong. It roiled and surged like something restless.

When I looked around I could see the coast. In the distance were boats, people swimming. Further inland was the edge of the jungle; it must be a long way to the camp where Kath would be waiting and the others would be wondering where I'd gone. I had no idea how to get back there, or how I would explain. No doubt they'd say I'd pulled some prank, or that I'd delved too far; that I had merely been lucky to survive my fool's dive.

They'd say the changes in pressure had got to me. Made me hallucinate.

I allowed myself to move with the water. Whatever they said, however it happened, I was here, in the eyes, the *ojos de agua*. Somewhere far below, water gushed from a cave mouth that led out of the earth. The dark was waiting there, something that didn't sleep and didn't die.

And I had pledged myself to it.

When I closed my eyes, I saw my friend's face. His whole, complete face. I remembered what he'd done: *you*, he'd said. When I remembered the woman, I couldn't quite bring myself to hate him for it.

Rick had always been the one to go farther, to see things no one else had seen, the one who laughed at what made others fear. But I hadn't betrayed him. I'd been to the place he wanted me to go, seen the things he wanted me to see; but I hadn't given any life but my own.

I wondered when the creature of the cenoté would claim it from me.

I started to strike out for the shore, thinking of the free-divers plunging down towards their crucified god. I thought about how we offered ourselves, wondered if, after all, it was some need we had, to throw ourselves before some idea or thing. Maybe, sooner or later, all of us had something or someone waiting to collect. If so, maybe it wasn't so bad; better than being trapped in the endless dark, unable to go forward, unable to go back. Whatever I had given, for now, it was enough. And the thing in the cave—it was the life-giver, too.

The breeze was picking up and I swam harder. It became easier as the feeling flooded back into my limbs. It felt as though my body were re-forming itself, arms and legs becoming solid, capable, more real; defined by their motion as I swam out of the bright place where the sun struck the water.

Alison Littlewood's first novel, *A Cold Season*, was selected for the Richard and Judy Book Club, where it was described as "perfect reading for a dark winter's night." Her latest novel, *Path of Needles*, was released in May. Alison's short stories have previously been chosen for the *Best Horror of the Year* and *Mammoth Book of Best New Horrors*, as well as featured in magazines such as *Black Static*, *Crimewave*, and *Dark Horizons*. Other publication credits include stories for anthologies *Terror Tales of the Cotswolds*, *Where Are We Going?*, *Never Again*, *A Carnivàle of Horror*, *Magic*, and *Resurrection Engines*. She lives near Wakefield, West Yorkshire. Visit her at www.alisonlittlewood.co.uk.

A place not only unknown to the map,
but unknown to human understanding . . .

THE TALL GRASS

Joe R. Lansdale

I can't really explain this properly, but I'll tell it to you, and you can make the best of it. It starts with a train. People don't travel as readily by train these days as they once did, but in my youthful days they did, and I have to admit those days were some time ago, considering my current, doddering age. It's hard to believe so much time has turned, and I have turned with it, as worn out and rusty as those old coal-powered trains.

I am soon to fall of the edge of the cliff into the great darkness, but there was a time when I was young and the world was light. Back then, there was something that happened to me on a rail line that showed me something I didn't know was there, and since that time, I've never seen the world in exactly the same way.

What I can tell you is this. I was traveling across country by night in a very nice rail car. I had not just a seat on a train, but a compartment to myself. A quite comfortable compartment, I might add. I was early into my business career then, having just started with a firm that I ended up working at for twenty-five years. To simplify, I had completed a cross country business trip and was on my way home. I wasn't married then, but one of the reasons I was eager to make it back to my hometown was a young woman named Ellen. We were quite close, and her company meant everything to me. It was our plan to marry.

I won't bore you with details, but that particular plan didn't work out. And though I still think of that with some disappointment, for she was very beautiful, it has absolutely nothing to do with my story.

Thing is, the train was crossing the western country, in a barren stretch without towns, beneath a wide open night sky with a high moon and a few crawling clouds. Back then, those kinds of places were far more common than lights and streets and motorcars are now. I had made the same ride several times on business, yet I always still enjoyed looking out the window, even at night. This night, however, for whatever reason, I was up very late, unable to sleep. I had chosen not to eat dinner, and now that it was well passed, I was a bit hungry, but there was nothing to be had.

The lamps inside the train had been extinguished, and out the window there was a moonlit sea of rocks and sand and in the distance beyond, shadowy blue-black mountains.

The train came to an odd stretch that I had somehow missed before on my journeys, as I was probably sleeping at the time. It was a great expanse of prairie grass, and it shifted in the moonlight like waves of gold-green sea water pulled by the tide-making forces of the moon.

I was watching all of this, trying to figure it, determining how odd it looked and how often I had to have passed it and had never seen it. Oh, I had seen lots of tall grass, but nothing like this. The grass was not only head high, or higher, it was thick and it had what I can only describe as an unusual look about it, as if I was seeing it with eyes that belonged to someone else. I know how peculiar that sounds, but it's the only way I know how to explain it.

Then the train jerked, as if some great hand had grabbed it. It screeched on the rails and there was a cacophony of sounds before the engine came to a hard stop.

I had no idea what had occurred. I opened the compartment door, though at first the door seemed locked and only gave way with considerable effort. I stepped out into the hallway. No one was there.

Edging along the hallway, I came to the smoking car, but there was no one there either. It seemed the other passengers were in a tight sleep and unaware of our stopping. I walked through the car, sniffing at the remains of tobacco smoke, and opened a door that went out on a connecting platform that was positioned between the smoking car and another passenger car. I looked in the passenger car through the little window at the door. There was no one there. This didn't entirely surprise me, as the train had taken on a very small load of passengers, and many of them, like me, had purchased personal cabins.

I looked out at the countryside and saw there were lights in the distance, beyond the grass, or to be more exact, positioned out in it. It shocked me, because we were in the middle of absolutely nowhere, and the fact that there was a town nearby was a total surprise to me.

I walked to the edge of the platform. There was a folded and hinged metal stair there, and with the toe of my shoe I kicked it, causing it to flip out and extend to the ground.

I climbed down the steps and looked along the rail. There was no one at first, and then there was a light swinging its way toward me, and finally a shadowy shape behind the light. In a moment I saw that it was a rail man, dressed in cap and coat and company trousers.

"You best stay on board, sir," he said.

I could see him clearly now. He was an average-looking man, small in size with an odd walk about him; the sort people who practically live on trains acquire, as do sailors on ships at sea.

"I was just curious," I said. "What's happened?"

"A brief stop," he said. "I suggest you go back inside."

"Is no one else awake?" I said.

"You seem to be it, sir," he said. "I find those that go to sleep before twelve stay that way when this happens."

I thought that a curious answer. I said, "Does it happen often?"

"No. Not really."

"What's wrong? Are there repairs going on?"

"We're building up another head of steam," he said.

"Then surely I have time to step out here and have a smoke in the open air," I said.

"I suppose that's true, sir," he said. "But I wouldn't wander far. Once we're ready to go, we'll go. I'll call for you to get on board, but only a few times, and then we'll go, no matter what. We won't tarry, not here. Not between midnight and two."

And then he went on by me swinging the light.

I was intrigued by what he had said, about not tarrying. I looked out at the waving grass and the lights, which I now realized were not that far away. I took out my makings and rolled a cigarette and put a match to it and puffed.

I can't really explain what possessed me. The oddness of the moment, I suppose. But I decided it would be interesting to walk out in the tall grass, just to measure its height, and to maybe get a closer look at those lights. I strolled out a ways, and within moments I was deep in the grass. As I walked, the earth sloped downwards and the grass whispered in the wind. When I stopped walking, the grass was over my head, and behind me where the ground was higher, the grass stood tall against the moonlight, like rows of spearheads held high by an army of warriors.

I stood there in the midst of the grass and smoked and listened for activity back at the train, but neither heard the lantern man or the sound of the train getting ready to leave. I relaxed a bit, enjoying the cool, night wind and the way it moved through the prairie. I decided to stroll about while I smoked, parting the grass as I went. I could see the lights still, but they always seemed to be farther away than I thought, and my moving in their direction didn't seem to bring me closer; they receded like the horizon.

When I finished my cigarette, I dropped it and put my heel to it, grinding it into the ground, and turned to go back to the train.

I was a bit startled to discover I couldn't find the path I had taken. Surely, the grass had been bent or pushed aside by my passing, but there was no sign of it. It had quickly sprung back into shape. I couldn't find the rise I had come down. The position of the moon was impossible to locate, even though there was plenty of moonlight; the moon had gone away and left its light there.

Gradually, I became concerned. I had somehow gotten turned about, and the train would soon be leaving, and I had been warned that no one would wait

for me. I thought perhaps it was best if I ceased thrashing about through the grass, and just stopped, lest I become more confused. I concluded that I couldn't have gone too far from the railway, and that I should be able to hear the train man should he call out for *All Aboard*.

So, there I was, standing in tall grass like a fool. Lost from the train and listening intently for the man to call out. I kept glancing about to try and see if I could find a path back the way I came. As I said before, it stood to reason that I had tromped down some grass, and that I couldn't be that far away. It was also, as I said, a very well-lit night, plenty of moonlight. It rested like swipes of cream cheese on the tall grass, so it was inconceivable to me that I had gotten lost in such a short time walking such a short distance. I also considered those lights as bearings, but they had moved, fluttering about like will-o'-the-wisps, so using them as markers was impossible.

I was lost, and I began to entertain the disturbing thought that I might miss the train and be left where I was. It would be bad enough to miss the train, but here, out in the emptiness of nowhere, if I wasn't missed, or no one came back this way for a time, I might actually starve, or be devoured by wild animals, or die of exposure.

That's when I heard someone coming through the grass. They weren't right on top of me, but they were close, and of course, my first thought was it was the man from the train come to look for me. I started to call out, but hesitated.

I can't entirely explain the hesitation, but there was a part of me that felt reluctant, and so instead of calling out, I waited. The noise grew louder.

I cautiously parted the grass with my fingers, and looked in the direction of the sound, and coming through the grass were a number of men, all of them peculiarly bald, the moonlight reflecting off their heads like mirrors. The grass whipped open as they came and closed back behind them. For a brief moment I felt relieved, as they must be other passengers or train employees sent to look for me, and would direct me to back to the train. It would be an embarrassing moment, but in the end, all would be well.

And then I realized something. I hadn't been actually absorbing what I was seeing. They were human-shaped all right, but . . . they had no faces.

There was a head, and there were spots where the usual items should be, nose, eyes, mouth, but those spots were indentions. The moonlight gathered on those shiny, white faces, and reflected back out. They were the lights in the grass and they were why the lights moved, because the faceless men moved. There were other lights beyond them, way out, and I drew the conclusion that there were many of those human-shaped things, out in the grass, close and far away, moving toward me, and moving away, thick as aphids. They had a jerky movement about them, as if they were squirming on a griddle. They pushed through the grass and fanned out wide, and some of them had sticks, and they began to beat the grass before them. I might add that as they did, the grass, like a living thing, whipped away from their strikes and opened wide and closed up behind them. They were coming ever nearer to where I was. I could see they were of all different shapes and sizes and attire. Some of them wore very old clothes, and there were others who were dressed in rags, and even a couple who were completely devoid of clothes, and sexless, smooth all over, as if anything that distinguished their sex or their humanity had been ironed out. Still, I could tell now, by the general shape of the bodies, that some of them may have been women, and certainly some of the smaller ones were children. I even saw moving among them a shiny white body in the shape of a dog.

In the same way I had felt it unwise to call out to them, I now felt it unwise to wait where I was. I knew they knew I was in the grass, and that they were looking for me.

I broke and ran. I was spotted, because behind me, from those faces without mouths, there somehow rose up a cry. A kind of squeal, like something being slowly ground down beneath a boot heel.

I heard them as they rushed through the grass after me. I could hear their feet thundering against the ground. It was as if a small heard of buffalo were in pursuit. I charged through the grass blindly. Once I glanced back over my shoulder and saw their numbers were larger than I first thought. Their shapes broke out of the grass, left and right and close and wide. The grass was full of them, and their faces glowed as if inside their thin flesh were lit lanterns.

Finally there was a place where the grass was missing and there was only earth. It was a relief from the cloying grass, but it was a relief that passed swiftly, for now I was fully exposed. Moving rapidly toward me from the front were more of those moonlit things. I turned, and saw behind me the others were very near. They began to run all out toward me, they were also closing in from my right.

There was but one way for me to go: to the left, and wide, back into the grass. I did just that. I ran as hard as I could run. The grass sloped up slightly, and I fought to climb the hill; the hill that I had lost such a short time ago. It had reappeared, or rather I had stumbled up on it.

My feet kept slipping as I climbed up it. I glanced down, and there in that weird light I could see that my boots were sliding in what looked to be rotting piles of fat-glazed bones; the earth was slick with them.

I could hear the things closing behind me, making that sound that a face without a mouth should be unable to make; that horrid screech. It was deafening.

I was almost at the peak of the hill. I could see the grass swaying up there. I could hear it whispering in the wind between the screeches of those pursuing me, and just as I made the top of the hill and poked my head through the grass and saw the train, I was grabbed.

Here is a peculiar thing that from time to time I remember, and shiver when I do, but those hands that had hold of my legs were cold as arctic air. I could feel them through my clothes, they were so cold. I tried to kick loose, but wasn't having any luck. I had fallen when they grabbed me, and I was clutching at the grass at the top of the hill. It was pulling through my hands and fingers, and the edges were sharp; they cut into me like razors. I could feel the warm blood running through my fingers, but still I hung to that grass.

Glancing back, I saw that I was seized by several of the things, and the dog-like shape had clamped its jaws on the heel of my boot. I saw too that the things were not entirely without features after all; or at least now they had acquired one all-encompassing feature. A split appeared in their faces, where a mouth should be, but it was impossibly wide and festooned with more teeth than a shark, long and sharp, many of them crooked as poorly driven nails, stained in spots the color of very old cheese. Their breath rose up like methane from a privy and burned my eyes. There was no doubt in my mind that they meant to bite me; and I somehow knew that if I was bitten, I would not be chewed and eaten, but that the bite would make me like them. That my bones would come free of me along with my features and everything that made me human, and I knew too that those things were originally from train stops, and from frontier scouting parties, adventurers, and surveyors, and all manner of folks who, at one time, had been crossing these desolate lands and found themselves here, a place not only unknown to the map, but unknown to human understanding. All of this came to me and instantly filled me with dread. It was as if their very touch had revealed it to me.

I kicked wildly, wrenching my boot heel from the dog-shape's toothy grasp. I struggled. I heard teeth snap on empty air as I kicked loose. And then there was warmth and a glow over my head. I looked up to see the train man with a great flaming torch, and he was waving it about, sticking it into the teeth-packed faces of those poor lost souls.

They screeched and they bellowed, they hissed and they moaned. But the fire did the trick. They let go of me and receded back into the waves of grass, and the grass folded back around them, like the ocean swallowing sailors. I saw last the dog-shape dive into the grass like a porpoise, and then it and them were gone, and so were the lights, and the moonlight lost it's slick glaze and it was just a light. The torch flickered over my head, and I could feel its heat.

The next thing I knew the train man was pulling me to the top of the hill, and I collapsed and trembled like a mass of gelatin spilled on a floor.

"They don't like it up here, sir," the train man said, pushing the blazing end of his torch against the ground, rubbing it in the dirt, snuffing it out. The smell of pitch tingled my nostrils. "No, they don't like it at all."

"What are they?" I said.

"I think you know, sir. I do. Somewhere deep inside me, I know. There aren't any words for it, but I know, and you know. They touched me once, but thank goodness I was only near the grass, not in it. Not like you were, sir."

He led me back to the train. He said, "I should have been more emphatic, but you looked like a reasonable chap to me. Not someone to wander off."

"I wish I had been reasonable."

"It's like looking to the other side, isn't it, sir?" he said. "Or rather, it is a look to one of many sides, I suspect. Little lost worlds inside our own. The train breaks down here often. There have been others who have left the train. I suspect you met some of them tonight. You saw what they have become, or so I think. I can't explain all the others. Wanderers, I suspect. It's always here the train stops, or breaks down. Usually it just sort of loses steam. It can have plenty and still lose it, and we have to build it all up again. Always this time of night. Rarely a problem, really. Another thing, I lock all the doors at night to keep folks in, should they come awake. I lock the general passenger cars on both ends. Most don't wake up anyway, not this time of night, not after midnight, not if they've gone to sleep before that time, and are good solid in. Midnight between two a.m., that's when it always happens, the train losing steam here near the crawling grass. I guess those of us awake at that time can see some things that others can't. In this spot anyway. That's what I suppose. It's like a door opens out there during that time. They got their spot, their limitations, but you don't want to be out there, no sir. You're quite lucky."

"Thank you," I said.

"Guess I missed your lock, sir. Or it works poorly. I apologize for that. Had I done right, you wouldn't have been able to get out. If someone should stay awake and find the room locked, we pretend it's a stuck doorway. Talk to them through the door, and tell them we can't get it fixed until morning. A few people have been quite put out by that. The ones who were awake when we stopped here. But it's best that way. I'm sure you'll agree, sir."

"I do," I said. "Thank you again. I can't say it enough."

"Oh, no problem. You had almost made it out of the grass, and you were near the top of the hill, so it was easy for me help you. I always keep a torch nearby that can easily be lit. They don't like fire, and they don't come up close to the train. They don't get out of the grass, as far as I can determine. But I will tell you true, had I heard your scream too far beyond the hill, well, I wouldn't have come after you. And they would have had you."

"I screamed?"

"Loudly."

I got on the train and walked back to my compartment, still trembling. I checked my door and saw that my lock had been thrown from the outside, but it was faulty, and all it took was a little shaking to have it come free of the door frame. That's how I had got out my room.

The train man brought me a nip of whisky, and I told him about the lock, and drank the whisky. "I'll have the lock fixed right away, sir. Best not to mention all this," he said. "No one will believe it, and it could cause problems with the cross country line. People have to get places, you know."

I nodded.

"Goodnight, sir. Pleasant dreams."

This was such an odd invocation to all that had happened, I almost laughed.

He went away, closing up my compartment, and I looked out the window. All there was to see was the grass, waving in the wind, tipped with moonlight.

The train started to move, and pretty soon we were on our way. And that was the end of the matter, and this is the first time I have mentioned it since it happened so long ago. But, I assure you. It happened just the way I told you, crossing the Western void, in the year of 1901.

Joe R. Lansdale is the author of over thirty novels and numerous short stories. His novella, *Bubba Ho-tep*, was made into an award-winning film of the same name, as was *Incident On and Off a Mountain Road*. Both were directed by Don Coscarelli. His works have received numerous recognitions, including the Edgar, eight Bram Stoker Awards, the Grinzane Cavour Prize for Literature, American Mystery Award, the International Horror Award, British Fantasy Award, and many others. His most recent novel for adults, *The Thicket*, will be published this fall.

Out there in the sky I see each star again, and like every man dying from the beginning of his days, I regret the things I didn't do, and I regret the things I did.

GAME

Maria Dahvana Headley

15 September 1950
Nightfall.

I write this entry from my tent in Naini Tal, a village in the Kumaon Province of Northern India, shadowed by the snow-tipped Himalayas. I arrived here at 1300 hours, as the sun steamed the dew out of the forest like a laundress pressing an iron on a damp shirt. The whole place hissed, and I closed my eyes to inhale the cypress and cookfire smoke. Much has changed in my old hunting grounds, but were I to depend on my sense of smell alone, it would be as though I'd traveled backward thirty-two years.

A simple glance, however, reminds me of the landslip passage of time. Three years ago, the country dissolved its colonial status and departed from the reign of George VI. The time of the hunter is done, though I warrant that there is still a place for a man such as myself.

The children I met here in 1918 are now grandparents, but to them, I'm not the old man who sits before them. I'm an earlier incarnation, a warrior from a picture book, brought here at their request, a man with mystical powers over their enemy. They need me now, here in Naini Tal. I am their last resort.

My journey originated in Delhi, some four hundred rattling kilometers away. My bones ache despite the care of my porters, and of my colleague, the estimable Dr. K_____, but when the Kumaoni greeted me this afternoon, I felt my heart rise to meet my title.

"*Shikari,*" they cried, all of them in unison. "Welcome, *shikari!*"

Big game hunter. Usually reserved for the native men. For my kills, covered in international newspapers, my kills which inspired other kills, I was long ago granted an exception.

My old partner Henry, also a *shikari,* and native to the Kumaon province, knew this place better than I ever could, but even I can see the changes. The trees were thicker the last time I was here, and the huts were roofed in woven branches rather than tin. Time has not been kind to this place, nor to me. The village now shines bright as a grub dug up slick and blind from beneath a rock, and another addition, a high fence made from a combination of thorn bushes and barbed wire, encircles it.

No one seems yet to have tunneled into the mountains, a mercy, nor taken their tops, but roads have been installed everywhere, and the locally manufactured automobiles known as the Baby Hindustan backfire and sputter their way toward the sky. With Henry, thirty-two years ago, I watched hawks wheeling high above these mountains, but now the air is streaked with machines. I notice a subtle depletion of birdsong. As likely caused by the creatures I come to hunt as by machinery, I know, but I imagine the tragedies to come in the near future, ornithologists aiming their glasses at the heavens in order to identify different species of aircraft.

Given these observations, I will note here that it is immediately clear what has spurred the tigers to their current behavior. Less than a century ago, the cats had limitless forest and limitless game. Now the wild is striated with roads and mines, and armed villagers have beaten the remaining tigers from Nepal into these hills, calling them all man-eaters. Every man and boy in the region has a weapon, a museum's worth of defenses, rusty swords and axes to rifles, but shooting to kill is a skill that must be learnt. Wounding is easier. A wounded tiger is a hungry tiger. Here in Naini Tal, trouble has been brought into town, all in an attempt to keep trouble in the trees. It is an old story.

Untwisting wire to enter through the gate today, I experienced a tremor in my thigh, no doubt caused by the climb, as unlike many men my age, I keep myself in fine form. A porter brought me the customary dish of metallic tea, lightened with buffalo milk and copiously sweetened with jaggery. Even as I sipped it, though, my cup chattered. An involuntary motion in my fingers, like that of a treetop in a fine breeze.

I've been softened by civilization, I admit it. It's been years since I last participated in this line of work, years I've spent writing and lecturing, years of domestic comfort in a house in Kenya, trees of my own, a bed, a wife. As I write this, I'm thinking of my wife's hair, falling straight and black to her knees. Evenings, she sits before me on the floor, and I wrap her tresses round my hands, succumbing, greedy as a nectar-guzzling bat, to this late-life pleasure. I think of how the strands feel running over my fingers, delicate, but when braided together they are strong enough to strangle a man.

Before her, I'd never thought of marriage. All my previous vows were to the creatures I hunted. I've done a good deal of seeing the world at grass level, my universe filtered through golden eyes, my world made of the pugmarks of tigers, the tracks of *ghooral,* the mountain goats of this region, and the creamy camouflaged spots of the chital hind, my ears attuned to the barking of the *kakar* deer, and the hornlike belling of the *sambur,* to the chittering of monkeys and the churr of the nightjar. Before I met my wife, I'd never imagined anything of the world through the eyes of another human.

She's angry with me now. She doesn't want me hunting. She certainly doesn't want me hunting here. As I left our house, she stood in the doorway and shouted: "Old men need not go hunting for tigers! Tigers are already hunting for them!"

She's wrong about that. I'm equal to this, and Dr. Andrew K_____, my taxidermist colleague, is beside himself with excitement. This afternoon, he sat beside me on a stump near the cookfire, knees bouncing, his uniform crisply ironed and starched by his own wife back in New York City. I'd promised him a hunt. He'd read in his boyhood my accounts of the Monsters of the Mountains who'd dragged entire villages into the darkness, leaving only shards of bone behind for the poor Hindu funerary rites that required something to burn.

In certain cases, depending on how long the cat had uninterrupted possession of the dead, there'd be nothing left, the man-eater having devoured the entirety: skin and bones and bloodied clothing. On those occasions, I sometimes removed a fragment of ivory from my own baggage and presented it to the bereaved for burning.

My wife would say that with my substitutions, I've sent elephants to the afterlife, along with rhinoceroses and whales. That I've populated the sky with things that do not belong there. Therefore, I do not tell her. I consider myself to have been, at some moments in my time as a *shikari,* a minister of mercy. I spent my career in these forests. I have my own rules of conduct.

K_____, in contrast, has, according to the vitae he supplied me, spent the bulk of his own career in the bowels of New York City's Natural History Museum, his hands coated in glue, sinew and fragments of stretched skin, refitting the dead for display to the living. Having begged of his institution a paid procurement trip to India, he quivers in anticipation.

Naini Tal's man-eater will be taken to Dr. K_____'s museum and displayed there as a conservationary tale. The teeth and body will be examined for wounds caused by hunters. No tiger turns man-eater of its own instincts. We are not its natural prey. For one such as myself, who has long struggled to reconcile a history of violence with the world's shrinking spectrum of carnivores, the offer of any redemption was too tempting to resist.

Now that we are here in Naini Tal, however, I look at K_____, at his too-gleaming weapon, and at his tapping fingers, with no small degree of suspicion. There is something of the town-raised boy visiting the country in him. Something of the tourist. He carries sharp implements, chocolate bars, and gin in his case. I earlier apprehended a small transistor radio in his belongings, about which he hedged. In case of emergency, he insisted, but I forced him to relinquish it. I'm certainly not convinced he should be armed. The nervous man with his finger on the trigger is as likely to shoot the hunter as the prey, but a man without a rifle will likely need to be defended from the man-eater, given any proximity.

I have less tolerance than I once did. Since Henry's death, I've hunted alone.

Upon arrival, we were given a feast of roasted *ghooral* spiced with the local peppers, and warm cola coddled over rough roads from the city, the bottle recognizable even in the dark. I interviewed the villagers about their experiences of the man-eater, and they answered me vigorously. At first, the Kumaoni tried churchgoing, petitioning Christ and country, but prayer is an inefficient weapon, and the people in these mountains are finished with begging for miracles. Something is stalking them, and they mean to have its head.

There've been sounds in the forests, the villagers tell me, phantom noises of devils. Gunfire, and roars, but they swear no one from Naini Tal hunts tigers. I believe them. It is no longer in fashion, my profession, that of the skilled and specific tracker, that of the *shikari*. These hunters will be poachers. Everywhere now. Every forest, every jungle, the world over. Thieves of tigers and elephants, leopards and monkeys. Recently, an acquaintance of mine saw a tiger in the back seat of a car rattling through Delhi, the cat so recently slaughtered that blood was still seeping out, leaving a trail behind the sedan.

Pillbox hats made of wildcats and leopard skin capes over shocking pink taffeta dresses have lately appeared in Vogue Magazine, igniting a craze for fur. Couture demands man-eaters, and in truth, man-eater is no longer a reason to kill a tiger. *Tiger* is a reason to kill a tiger.

Everyone goes into the forests now, and a man with my history is every man on earth, or so you might believe if you sat down at a bar counter in Delhi and listened to men tall-telling about tigers. Pith helmets and Martini rifles. Waxed cotton tents. Triumphs.

I was, therefore, quite surprised to be personally summoned last month to Naini Tal, the request relayed first by the local version of the *cooee*, shouted village to village, and then by runner, at last arriving to me by phone call, the villager's petition read aloud to me over the wires.

Dearest Gentleman,

We the public beg your kindly doing needful. In this vicinity, which is well known to you, and which has long suffered from famously troubles with tigers, we beg your help in hunting this demon that has turned man-eater since June of five years past. We venture and invite you, shikari, *to shoot this demon, and save us from calamity, for she is no tiger, but an evil spirit, and no one of all the men who have tried to kill her has got near her heart. Please tell us of your arrival, and we will meet you with a cart to bring you to our forest.*

I did not need to consider. I'd been haunted by this place, this village, these mountains long enough.

I've never ceased scanning the news for Naini Tal, even from afar. They've suffered more from man-eaters than other similarly situated villages, or so it seems to me, though I am possibly biased toward that perspective. Naini Tal and Pali, higher up the mountain, have long been plagued by a stream of bloodthirsting strangers walking out from the woods at night. That the village still exists is surprising. Superstition might long ago have caused the citizens to depart, pragmatic, their belongings on their backs. Who, after all, would choose to live in a place claimed by tigers?

From Kenya, I read of this man-eater's five year reign, a factory owner on an exploratory hunt being her most recent victim. The villagers showed me a list with some eight dozen names, the missing and the dead, and for every lost person, there is a story.

Initially, the tiger attacked only men, and those armed, typically game hunters, particularly those who'd come in from outside Naini Tal. Not two weeks ago, however, a young woman, just sixteen, was taken by the man-eater at midday as she gathered firewood, scarcely out of sight of her friends. Her silk sari was left draped on rocks, a trail of blood going up the mountain, and her hair spider-webbed from the bushes. That was when the villagers began counting their coins and mold-velveted paper money, begging their wives and mothers-in-laws for household funds that'd been secreted away, smashing their jars and tithing their tobacco rations.

The men here are gleeful at my presence. I declined a fee, unseemly for a man in my position, though they do not know my reasons. This man, ministering to this village. There is no pay for that. They saved their money for me despite my protestations, and brought it out to show. I complimented them on their hoard, and then ate heartily. In my early days as a hunter, I once found myself faint before a black leopard, having, due to gastrointestinal distress, eaten almost nothing for several days. Tonight, I noticed K_____ pushing his meat around his plate, and admonished him. He took a tiny bite, and swallowed abruptly and unhappily.

As darkness fell, I heard the call of a cat.

"It is a *shaitan* hunts here, *shikari*," one of the men said.

I listened to the tiger call, wondering at the sound of the roars, a scraping sharpened edge to them that I'd somehow forgotten, and I felt the familiar feeling in my stomach. It's an instinct I've long denied, the urge to curl myself into a protective position, and I suddenly found myself nearly not denying it. I am, suddenly, seventy-one years old. My father died at sixty, in his bed.

"The *shaitan* welcomes you home," said another man, and smiled at me, a kindly smile, even for the words he said.

The devil welcomes you home.

I stood and stretched, hearing my left shoulder crack, the bones themselves remembering my encounter with that leopard. My skin, as is true of any hunter who has truly hunted, is a Frankenstein's monster of a canvas, stitched together first with black thread, and now with scars, old wounds packed with chewed leaves, five claw marks stretching from right clavicle to left pubis, the mark of the Widower of Champawat, dead and gone these twenty years. Not the smallest tiger, and not the largest, but one who got close enough that I could see into his throat and feel his heartbeat as he savaged me. I felt that heart stop as I shot him. His shoulder, upon examination, housed an old bullet, suppurating, and his right front arm was darted with porcupine quills. Yellowed, soapy flesh beneath the balding pelt, a withered limb, and thirty-six quills, fat as pencils, broken off at the level of the skin.

I have never blamed him.

"Shall we?" I said.

K_____radiated unease. "It's nearly dark," he replied.

I gave him the look that said *dark is how this is done*, clapped him on the back once, and then walked away from the firelight.

He needn't have worried. We were patrolling the perimeter for signs, but I did not intend to go deep into the trees. The cruelty of this commission was that it was necessary to await an attack. The tiger would have long since scented the roasting *ghooral*, and concluded that there'd be heavy sleep in the village. The man-eater would come to us.

The forest lay before us, black and singing. A hunter listens, and if a hunter does not, then he will not stay a hunter long. Any and all of the animals here will tell tales of a tiger. They'll explain where the cat is, whether it is still or in motion, how fast it moves.

Though I did not say it to K_____, though I would not admit it to anyone save these pages, mute as they are, I too hesitated to walk back into those trees tonight. The last time I entered this forest, I was carried out on a stretcher, mute with loss, the children surrounding me, my hands bloody. The last time I came down that mountain, I vowed I would not go up it again.

After that kill, there was nothing left to bury, nothing left to burn.

The birds are silent now, as I write these lines, and I feel observed. We've returned to our tents to wait for screams.

16 September 1950
Dawn.

I woke three hours ago, blurred by nightmares, having been dream-stalking a man-eater, not the present tiger, but the one from 1918.

With me in my dream was Henry, his elbow in tattered cotton, his silvered beard and long hair, his skin a dark contrast to the yellowed whites of his eyes. I looked over at him once, and saw him open his mouth, but his lips moved, and I heard nothing.

The screams, when they came, seemed a part of the same dream. They were not. At 4:13 this morning, a young man of twenty-three was taken from his hut, and dragged through the center of town. A villager shot at the man-eater, and swears he hit her chest, but she leapt with her victim over the briars and barbed wire, twenty-five feet, a seemingly impossible height, and returned to the forest. Pitiful scraps of the man's clothing hang from the highest thorns.

Dulled by exhaustion from yesterday's travels, by the time I was on my feet and out into the main area, it was too late. In truth, I need not excuse my speed. If one hears screaming, rescue is already impossible. Those left behind can only hope that death will be quick. There's no possibility of pursuing a victim into the dark, not when they've bled so much that the dust is red mud, and the man's wife, having woken to the feel of something heavy and vividly alive brushing past her bed, is already keening in her doorway.

For twenty seven minutes after the attack, we listened to the tigress departing through the trees, heralded by a sound like a kennel of dogs readying for a feeding, though it was something quite different, the kakar barking their alarm, *tiger passing here, tiger coming.*

The man-eater scratched her victim's door, and the scores in the wood are deep. I showed them to K_____, who examined them with interest. There's a slight odor of alcohol drifting about the man this morning, that and a cloying floral cologne, for which I severely remonstrated him. He purged it with a gin-soaked handkerchief. Gin is better than lilies.

The tigress left pugmarks in the dirt, and with them, I'll be able to identify her with certainty. K_____ dutifully cast them in plaster of Paris, and annotated his drawings with measurements. There is no blood trail. It is often the case that a tiger one shoots to kill, even as the bullet seems to have connected, remains strangely unwounded. This is the way things are here, even, in some cases, for a *shikari.*

K_____has arrived with the cast and his rudimentary drawing, and I will examine them, taking notes here, as part of this entry.

Size: Extremely large, at least ten feet over curves, a nearly unprecedented size for a female, and her paws are strikingly unsplayed, unusual in a tiger so immense. Her claws are so sharp as to suggest daggers.

Age: She is, by her prints, young, though her intelligence would indicate experience. This is a tigress who's been terrorizing the villages in this region for over five years, a beast who certainly must at some point have been at least superficially wounded.

Tracks: The symmetry of her tracks shows almost no sign of such wounding. On her left front paw, there is an old scar across the pad.

A clean gash that clearly went deep. Can this—

Break in text

Later. The shape of the scar stopped me as I sat looking at the marks by torchlight. It stops me now that K_____has left, and I sit alone in my tent again. I can't—

After I came down from these mountains, I published a partial account of my exploits. There were photographs of my grin on newspaper front pages, a certain level of celebrity, a short film in which I demonstrated my stalking technique. I had no notion of what was coming for me, of the way this forest would stay with me. I had no idea.

After that film was screened, I borrowed a woman's fountain pen to autograph a photograph for her, and ink leaked onto the pad of my thumb. Without care for observers, for cameras, she took my thumb into her mouth and licked it clean, her tongue turning sepia.

"There," she said, when she was finished, still holding my hand, looking up and directly into my eyes. "Now you won't leave marks on me."

I took her to the coast. We fucked with the lanterns lit, bright enough that all the moths in miles flew to press their bodies against our tent. One night she ran into the dark, and I stumbled after her, calling her name, and waiting for her to show herself. I was tired of tracking.

"You might have found me by my footprints," she said, stepping out of the night, raising one foot to show me the scar on the right arch. "I stepped on a water glass years ago, and didn't get it stitched. Look at that mark. Beautiful, isn't it?" I took her foot in my hand, and then stopped. The mark was a mark I knew.

She looked at me. Her eyes were not yellow, no. She did not change into anything but what she was, a beautiful woman with a broken footprint.

"You'll never forget me now," she said, and her tone was not quite playful. "Did you think you could? But you'll have to follow me, and if you don't, I'll follow you."

I fled the next morning before sunup. She opened her eyes as I pawed my way out of the tent, and said nothing, only smiled. I could see her teeth in the dark.

There were other women after her, and other nights like that, when I ran from imagined monsters. I knew there was nothing haunting me, and yet I couldn't seem to resist the narrative, the tracks of the tigress, broken prints, broken lines. I shunned my own hallucinations, but I kept looking.

I was a drunk, in those days. There are years of my life I scarcely recall. I will say that here.

I will also say that the tigress, the long-ago tigress, the dead tigress, was paw-scarred by Henry's knife. She'd surged up from below him as he leaned over a rock to peer at the place we believed she was lying up over a kill. He managed to roll from beneath her while she licked her wound, and I fired at her, but I missed. A few days later, he was gone, and I was broken.

No one emerges unscathed from my profession. The line between sanity and insanity is imperceptible until you cross it, a mere game trail on a hillside, unmarked and unnoticed, until one finds one's feet pacing that path, higher, higher, into the dizzying thinness of the air.

As I sit here, writing this, I shake my head.

The tracks——- I can scarcely write these foolish lines -—have appeared in various places over the years. In the dust of my stoop in Kenya, a woman's bare feet, scar in the arch. And padding in soft circles around the bed I share with my wife, a tiger's tracks, sliced cleanly across the pads by a knife. There've been times I've seen them everywhere I went. I know that guilt writes its own stories. These prints are true, though, the ones the tigress left here last night.

I leave this entry to page through all the pugmarks I've seen in the last forty years, recorded and coded in my notebook, searching for another explanation.

16 September 1950
Later.

I find myself longing for my old partner. I should never have returned to these mountains. *Shaitan*, my mind tells me, but I should know better. Henry would.

In 1908, when I first met him, he was in his later fifties, but could easily spring shoeless straight up a mountain, fleet as a *ghooral*. I once saw Henry casually pluck a fish from a pool with his hand. I hadn't even seen the glimmer of it in the water. He was a far better hunter than I, for though I was young then, and strong, I was bound by strange decorum, intent upon differentiating myself from the beasts.

Henry's skills had been passed down through four generations, and he had himself functioned as the Kumaon region's chief *shikari* since the year I was born. The hunters did more than simply hunt. They catalogued the spirits in the trees and the devils in the waters, dispersed measured portions of the bodies of man-eaters to the villagers for their good luck charms. The rifles are lighter now, the bullets more destructive, and the ancient ways are being forgotten.

The old *shikari* could track a butterfly on the wing, by the breeze created in its flight. They could find a snake the size of a quill pen, slithering up from a trail, and chart its passage through the streams.

When Henry opened his mouth to speak, it was as plausible that a forlorn tiger's call for a mate would come from it as words in human language. He could mimic anything in these woods. Once, in a moment of triumph, having together slain a leopard after weeks of stalking, he smiled slightly at me, and gave a whistling trill, then another. Eventually, I counted thirty-seven species of birds flocking to us.

I would be remiss if I did not record here that Henry was also superbly mechanical, capable of combining two rifles into something better than either had been. Or of creating a precise and killing snare out of a length of silk thread drawn from a sari, a coil of spring, and razor blade. He mapped our prey with precision, and he knew which tiger might be near from the shape the creature's body left in the grass. For ten years, Henry and I hunted man-eaters all over India, surveying the trees for motion, listening to the sounds of warning coursing through the mountains like ripples on a gin-clear pond.

When Henry and I came to Naini Tal in the final days of 1917, it was our goal to deliver the residents of the monsters they'd made. If a plague strikes a remote place such as this one, and there are not enough villagers left to carry the bodies of the dead down to the water in procession, the rites of burial may be simplified. A live coal is placed in the mouth of the corpse, and then the bodies carted to a cliff, and thrown into the valley below, where the leopards and tigers find them, eat them, and develop their own desires.

We were summoned by a desperate rumor, a *cooee* call from ridgeline to ridgeline until it arrived at us. This place was far from the world, back then. There were no telephones, no telegrams. There were no cars. The village had lost their own *shikari* to a Himalayan bear six months before the plague began.

All the adults in the village were dead by the time we heard of Naini Tal, and only children remained. The tigers had taken over the town. They swept through the narrow passages between the huts, their golden bodies glinting in the starlight, their chins lifted to scent the air. It was as though the cats meandered through a night market, from stall to stall, sampling wares. There were twenty-six of them, and what had been a thriving village had become a place of terror.

Henry and I arrived to a place in shambles, tiger's marks before each door. The children were packed into one hut, and they'd left the rest of the village to the man-eaters. The pond where water was collected was half-dry, and all around it were the marks of claws.

When we arrived, the children came cautiously from the hut. They were all skin and eyes. There'd been no forage, and their livestock were dead. Each of the children had about their neck a locket containing a piece of tiger: red fur or black fur or bone or claw, but the charms had done nothing to save them. I argued to remove them from their village. I'd never imagined so many man-eaters in one location.

Henry, though, had grown up in the region. This was his territory. He knelt at the pond, treading on the tracks of the cats. He searched for a moment in his camp sack, and then brought forth an empty can, along with clockworks from my own recently smashed watch. I hadn't known he'd saved them.

After a few minutes work, he'd made of these materials a tiny creature. As the children came closer, fascinated by the toy he made, trusting him, he finished it, a sharp-edged bird made of metal. He twisted something beneath its wing.

It fluttered, and then, miraculously, took flight into the trees. It circled, swaying and wobbling in the air, and then landed again in his hand. The children looked at him as though he was a god, bringing animals to life out of broken things.

Henry shrugged when I asked how he'd made it, and told me it was nothing, a children's game. I never saw the bird again, though I thought of it often, the part of me that was still a child as enchanted as those children had been.

One by one, over the next months, we stalked and killed each of the man-eaters. At last, there was only one remaining.

I think of how I saw Henry last, his hand raised to protect his face, the choked sound he made—

He'd changed in the months we'd hunted those twenty-six tigers. Begun to drink in daylight, and sometimes at night. At the time, I didn't notice. I was killing tigers too. The night before he died, though, Henry looked over our fire at me, and asked if I thought the tigers deserved to win. I immediately answered that they'd developed a taste for humans, and killing them was all that could be done. I didn't want to talk about anything else.

After all of it was over, I convinced myself that Henry's death had been his own doing, that he'd been drunk, and endangered us both.

But in my mind, Henry looks at me again, mute as he was in my nightmare. I know what he wanted to say, I know.

He'd seen a glimpse of color. In places like this, anything red means tiger.

Anything white means bone. Anything golden means seen, and seen means eyes, and eyes mean death, unless one is luckier than one has any right to be.

The tigress had watched as we placed ourselves, thinking we awaited her arrival, when in fact she'd been crouched patiently in her own blind, waiting for us all night.

In the book that was published all over the world, the book that inspired generations of hunters to come to these woods, I did not say that my courage failed me. When I felt the tigress coming close on me, I abandoned Henry and ran.

She didn't pursue me. No. She took him instead.

I regained my senses too late and followed the trail of her drag, but I found only a pool of his blood, deep enough to dip my hands in, deep enough to cover.

For another five days, I stalked her, sleepless, out of food, my rifle jammed in my flight from her. I talked to myself, and to Henry, talked to the tigers I felt but could not see. I was a coil of rope caught by something invisible and swift, my soul tight between its teeth. I unspooled into emptiness.

At last, I tracked the tigress around a crumbling mountain ledge, the only retreat back the way I'd come. She was there, sleeping in the open, confident in her size and speed, confident in my despair. Her abdomen was exposed, the fur around her teats matted down from suckling cubs.

I brought my pistol from behind my back, and shot her in the chest, my hands too unstable to aim at her head. She was awake and nearly on me then, but mortally wounded. The man-eater leapt over me, lunging through the trees. I shot her again as she retreated, and she lost her footing.

I witnessed her fall from China Peak, her body flipping, twisting, striped gold and black as a wasp, her back certainly broken as she flew.

Irretrievable, the bodies. The tigress fell deep into the straight-sided ravine, and Henry was gone.

I tracked the tigress' two cubs to the place she had hidden them. Not man-eaters. No. Mewling still.

After it was finished, I went down the mountain, eyes full of tears and blood, and I lied to them all about what had happened. I said that it could not be helped, that I had tried to save Henry, but even as I thought I was speaking, out of my mouth came something else, the cries of deer and the dying, the voices of birds and ghosts. One child wrapped my head in cotton while another packed my wounds and gave me, spoonful by spoonful, wild honey and herbs for my fever. They called from a ridge, and a message went forth to another village.

Some men of my slight acquaintance came and carried me from Naini

Tal, hospitalized me in Delhi, and there I stayed for six months, convalescing, writing the book of lies that made me famous.

I wonder now if I'm still in 1918, and all I thought I saw and did since then a madman's dream, because the tigress I'm tracking now, the tigress whose prints I see in the dirt of this village, has been dead for thirty-two years. I killed her.

17 September 1950
Nine in the morning.

"What is it you seek in those mountains?" my wife asked me just before I left. She'd found me at the table, my rifle out for cleaning. "What is it you seek that is not here? Everything is everywhere."

She poured red tea into my porcelain cup, white milk into the tea.

Blood, I thought. Bone. Tiger, I thought.

I thought about the footprints on our stoop. I thought about how every time they appeared, my wife came out with the broom, and brushed them away as though they were nothing. Perhaps they were nothing but dust.

She added an anthill of sugar to the cup, and then stirred it violently with a metal spoon, rattling the saucer.

"Do you want to kill every tiger in the world?" she demanded.

"Not all the tigers," I protested. "*This* tiger. In this village. In my village."

"That isn't your village," my wife said. "I'm your village. Do you see me?"

It was night, and a mosquito had landed on my arm to drink, its beak trembling. A calm came over my wife as she studied it. After a moment, she took the insect between her fingers and crushed its body, my blood smearing her fingers.

"This is a tiger," she said, and she didn't look at me as she carefully placed the mosquito in the flame of the candle, igniting its wings. "This was a tiger."

And now, I'm in Kumaon, making my way up and into the forest toward Pali. Whatever haunts me, I intend to find it. A ghost, a tiger, a woman, a hallucination. Maybe these tracks are left by the wind, but I pursue my old enemy today, and if she finds me before I find her, I deserve what she plans for me.

K_____ and I have been over the nearby parts of the forest, and now we prepare ourselves to enter it. K_____ has perversely over-armed himself, and his rifle is much too heavy. He carries eleven cartridges, far more than necessary, particularly considering that anything we shoot will be shot by me, not by him. Nevertheless, I can't convince him otherwise. I didn't bother to try.

Strapped to his back is a suitcase filled with powdered preservatives and skinning tools. The taxidermist is nervous as a cat, he told me, with some degree of humor.

"Tigers are never nervous," I informed him. "Tigers are nothing like us."

I looped the ropes for the machan around my arm. Aside from the pug and scratch marks, there's no other sign of the tigress in town, nor in the nearby trees. I'd expected to find scat, and other scratching, but I've seen nothing. All I see are her broken prints, familiar to me as my own hands, scarred pad, claws digging strangely unretracted into hard-packed dirt.

Several of the village men traveled with us this morning, and after six hours walk into the forest, we stayed with them to make camp. It is no small thing to have people waiting. A camp plays the role of a wife, tempting the parts of a hunter that do not desire a return home. It's too easy to choose to be lost.

I wasn't always so pragmatic about such things. When I hunted with Henry, we never set up camp. When he slept, if he slept, it was hunched in a tree. I'd be slung up in the machan, imagined man-eaters in my periphery, but Henry slept deeply, and if a tiger came near, he'd shoot. Nearly always, he'd kill his prey without aiming.

Henry's first hunt was when he was seven years old, a tiger that had killed two young sisters cutting grass. Later, their bodies would be found, naked and licked clean of blood, as peaceful as sleepers. Henry believed the tigress sought to replace lost cubs. I thought he was mad, imagining a tiger's heart as a though it were a woman's. Animals, I thought. Beasts. Heartless, I thought.

I wanted, I admit it, to kill every tiger, man-eater or not. I thought of the damage they did to men, and I wanted them to pay.

Henry went to great lengths to avoid targeting cats that had not turned man-eater. The killing of cubs was far astray from Henry's philosophy. He would have taught them about men by firing his rifle near them. He thought that without tigers the forests would disappear. We disagreed in those days. I saw the tigers as enemies. One killed enemies.

Whatever comes tomorrow, a hunter dies hunting.

Now, in our camp on China Peak, I feel observed, but no kakar call to warn us of creatures on the move. Only the trees watch us, I tell myself. And so, we sleep.

18 September 1950

The forest was dark this morning and fragrant, the scent of needles and undergrowth, strangling orchids in bloom up a tree, a constellation of blossoms against a green sky. K_____ and I marched through it, he heaving with exhaustion and altitude, myself with unaccustomed activity. I'd forced him to change his leather shoes for a pair with thin rubber soles, and he was, at least, stepping quietly.

The temperature dropped as we ascended, and I saw a pugmark outlined in dew, another rimed in the light frost that lingers in the shadows long after sunrise. The marks taunted me, orphaned, one here, one miles onward, never two in proximity, not true tracks. High up a tree, a scratch, too high for a tiger, fifty feet, but I looked at it regardless, roped myself up into the branches to examine it more closely. I've never seen a mark like it before. Tiger, but impossible.

On a twig near the scratch, I found a scrap of blue cotton from the shirt of the man the tigress had taken from the village. I lowered myself, painfully stiff from the climb.

It is confirmed. This tiger is not a tiger. We are hunting a ghost.

The tigress walked a dotted line, dancing her way up into the heights, leaving her tracks and signs like breadcrumbs for me. And thus the *shikari* succumbs to fairy tales, imagining a tiger's ghost leading him not to heaven but to some airy hell.

K_____ knew so little about the habits of our prey he didn't think to ask what was wrong. Beside me, he struggled up the mountainside, heaving his bags miserably. He paused suddenly, paralyzed, his mouth a rictus of uncertainty.

"Hear that?" he managed.

I did not.

"That way. Roaring." I listened, and heard nothing, though K_____ heard it twice more. I wondered if I was losing my hearing, along with all else. My fingers ached, and my eyes, and my spine and my heart. Exhausted and too old for this.

He pointed waveringly to the west, and on his certainty, we shifted direction, the forest darker this way, no sun having yet reached this side of the mountain. I led, insisting on lightening K_____'s load by taking his weapon from him, though in truth I was keeping myself safe from any chance of his inadvertently firing.

I'd seen no sign of the tigress in hours. I, who'd tracked the progress of man-eaters by counting single broken blades of grass, by touching bent leaves. I couldn't smell her, couldn't hear her. Wherever she'd slept, there was no sign of it. But ghosts don't sleep.

K_____ stumbled behind me and I heard him retch, a despairing, scavenged sound. I spun, my rifle already cocked, but there was no tigress. No, something piteous instead. The taxidermist had tripped over the remains of the man she'd killed. Shards of rib cage hung with meat, spine crumpled, half his jaw, a few strands of black hair.

I knelt, unfolding the thin sheet I'd brought. We'd wrap him in it and return him to his family, that they might burn him. As I began to wind the sheet about the bones, though, I glimpsed something. I stood and aimed, squinting into the trees, as still as I could manage. Trembling fingers.

"We should go," K_____ said, his voice pinched.

I hissed him quiet. Red. No motion. *Tigress, waiting. Tigress watching.* My only hope would be to fire as she leapt.

My vision focused at last, revealing that the red was no tiger, no blood, but a small building, peeling paint. I let out my breath and stood. No smells of humans. No cookfire smoke. Abandoned. High in these mountains for a hunting cabin, but that, I thought, was certainly what it was. In the trees above us, I could see old bones hanging, their meat long gone. A stake pounded far into the earth, a chain, for what creature I did not know. A dog, perhaps, though a very large one. There was a circle worn in the dirt below the stake, a deep, claw-scarred track, which I chose not to examine. Some brave or mad man had lived here in tiger territory, and someone with a wish for oblivion, too.

I instructed K_____ to follow me to the hut. Door closed. Some part of my mind was certain the tiger would fling open the door and stand upright before me, her belly still stained with undrunk milk, the toothmarks of the cubs she'd lost. I kicked the door open.

And stopped. K_____ gasped and then pushed his way past me.

The exterior of the cabin was wooden, but the interior walls shone. Flattened cans and springs, pendulums and gears, glimmering rocks and iridescent feathers. Rough tools, and some better, nail-hung on racks. Papers nailed up, drawings, writing, but too dark and stained to read. Claws were strung from the ceiling, garlands of teeth decorating the beams.

Against the far wall, a shape, bulky, striped. I shoved K_____ back, aiming my rifle.

"It's stuffed," he said authoritatively, and I realized, to my shame, that he was correct. The tiger was moth-eaten, its eyes replaced with chips of glass, its pelt dull and its pose stiff. "Someone who didn't know the modern techniques. Hadn't studied."

There was a bucket filled with rusting wires at my feet, another of white dust, another of black soil. Another filled with red, old red, dried to nothing now, but I knew what it was.

"A scientist working here," I said, remembering something of the kind. "Long gone, whomever he was."

K_____ was elbow deep in bones, piecing together a skeletal structure. Weapons and traps all over the room. Rifles soldered to other rifles. Triple-barreled here, and here, something rusted and still lethal looking, a bayonet-barreled pistol attached to a chain. A hunting cabin, yes, but a strange one, inhabited by both science and old craft. I opened a jar and sniffed at the contents. Local alcohol of some kind, doubtless poisonous.

What fool had brought this stuffed tiger? I imagined the thing packed up the mountain by reluctant porters years before, the tiger standing on their shoulders, eyes staring at nothing, limbs leaking sawdust. The waste disgusted me, and the light was fading. I saw K_____ thoughtfully measuring the poor beast's ear between his fingers, tugging at the ancient leather.

"We will not be stopping here," I'd just informed him, when something glittered in a beam of sunset shining through the roof.

A metal bird. Perched on the stuffed tiger's back. I did not—

I still do not. Impossible. A plummeting certainty.

Thirty-two years spent in darkness, and now a blinding and horrible light shines on me.

Henry. Alive, Henry, and perhaps stricken somewhere on the forest floor, mere feet from me as I stalked his killer?

If you hear screaming, it is already too late. All one can do is track the man-eater. Henry's the one who taught me that. Was he in the cave where I'd found the cubs? Did he, bleeding, mute, watch as I killed them?

No. Surely not. My mind can only have lost control, ancient guilt mingling with memory. In my book, *I* was the one who'd killed all twenty-six of the man-eaters of Naini Tal. In my book, I killed the tigress that killed him, and I said nothing of how he'd saved me. I couldn't bear to write his name, and so I took his glory. No one knows. Not my wife, unless I've confessed it in my sleep. Not the world. Not the villagers.

But here I am, writing these words, and Henry. Oh, Henry.

I held my head in my hands, feeling my skull spreading in my fingers. In a pouch at my waist, I carry my lucky pieces, my own superstitious version of the lockets worn by natives. Tiger bones, one from each tiger I've killed. I've carried them to Kenya, and to America, and everywhere I've gone, they've kept me safe.

In Henry's house, I opened the pouch and spilled my luck out on the dirt floor. K_____ glanced at me, uninterested.

We found Henry under a coverlet on the metal cot in the corner. Skeleton undamaged, no bones taken, though one shoulder had been shattered and knit badly, the wound of the tigress. His long silver beard still clung to the last scraps of skin. Twenty years dead, longer.

And there, closed in the jaw of Henry's skeleton, a coal, burned almost away. Ash on the ivory. My mentor did his own last rites here, no river, no hymn, no strength.

"Did you know him?" K_____ asked, and I didn't answer. Why did he never return to Naini Tal? What was Henry doing here?

We sleep here, in this strange place, and we keep vigil over my friend's bones, though his soul is long departed.

I twisted the wing of the little metal bird tonight, hoping that it might fly. It opened its beak and sang a single rusting note. Then all was silent.

18 September 1950

The tigress was waiting for us, as I knew she would be. We slept for three hours and rose in darkness this morning, K_____protesting bitterly.

I didn't want to stalk her any longer. I'd dreamed of Kenya, and of my wife sitting at the kitchen table, her tea in hand. I thought about how I would likely not see her again.

I didn't expect to survive a tigress this large, to whom I'd already lost my courage once, to whom I'd lost my pride. A ghost made of hunger and air.

She was out there. The forest wailed her presence. I felt her intentions, her bulk in the trees. I took a small bone from Henry's hand, and placed it in my pouch. I'd burn it, and give him his true funeral, if I made it out from these trees again.

We walked, watched at every step. I felt her in the woods, moving parallel to us, but it was pointless to aim at nothing. One never heard a tiger if the tiger was planning an attack. One might hear a soft sound, as a tiger departed, having decided not to leap. K_____ looked around, uneasy, pale. He felt her too.

The forest felt brittle, each leaf frozen now, each twig K_____ tread on cracking like a shot, and we ascended still higher. At last, something I recognized, a tiger's call, but not that of a tiger.

Henry's version, a human voice, perfectly mimicking a tiger's roar. I heard him do it hundreds of times. It's nothing one forgets. I shook my head, trying to dispel the hallucination.

It was, of course, a tiger calling. A night spent in Henry's company. It was no wonder. Another roar, and this voice was Henry's as well, calling in the tones of a tigress, and a moment later, calling in the voice of a male tiger, and now another, an elderly cat, and a cub.

"Do you hear that?" I asked K_____ and his only response was quick breathing.

"How many are there?" he asked.

"Do you hear *Henry*?" The depth of my uncertainty had overcome me. I was queasy with it.

"I hear tigers," he said.

A flurry of calls, the startling bells of a *sambur*, like automobiles in traffic, squeezing horns. *Tiger here, tiger passing.* All in the voice of Henry. It was as though Henry had become the entire forest, and all its occupants.

I stood still, fighting that old urge, run, curl to protect stomach, meticulously checking my rifle instead. *Tiger running*, shrieked a peafowl, in Henry's voice.

Through the trees, I saw red. And more red. More than one tiger. How many? They were not leaping at us, but running for some other reason. A mass of tigers, in step, all moving at the same pace, flowing through the shadows faster than I could watch. This was nothing tigers, who do not hunt in packs, would do.

At last, I saw her, my old enemy, stepping out of the forest in front of us.

My rifle was already aimed as she leapt. I fired, but did not come close to hitting her. Her spring took her over our heads, and she landed, softly behind us. K_____ shook beside me, and I felt him considering a run.

"Don't move," I hissed. "If you move, she'll have you."

I scanned the trees for the other tigers, but they were invisible. She opened her jaws and roared to me in Henry's voice and I felt the tears of a madman running down my face.

Perhaps this was his last gift to me, I thought, this aural hallucination that reminded me what to do when a tiger had gotten this close. Call her closer. He'd taught me the call, and now I made it back to her. I roared at her, at Henry's killer, at this killer who hadn't killed him.

She stepped toward me, her pelt shining, her eyes golden and glowing, her muscles gathering, and as she launched herself, I fired into her throat, the rifle kicking my shoulder.

The tigress screamed in Henry's voice again, and threw herself into the trees as though they, and not I, were her murderer. I could see no blood on her pelt, but her madness was that of the wounded. The tree trunk cracked as she bellowed and threw herself at its branches, and slowly it toppled, tigress atop it, her growls quietening now, her motions slower.

I shot her once more, this time in the skull, just over her left eye, and she made a sound, a raw hissing, something beyond anything animal. I expected her to disappear, for there to be a cloud of smoke left behind, a ghost gone, but she did not. I edged closer, K_____ on my heels.

The tigress looked up suddenly, pupils fully dilated, and I knew that she was dying. How could a ghost die?

I could smell my own sweat, and a deep, metallic odor too, tiger's blood, I thought, though I'd long since forgotten the smell of it.

Above, the stars blinked on, one by one, and the bats began to hunt. Insects rattled their shells like shields.

The tigress' head dropped slowly onto her paws, and the light went out in her, as a headlamp on a train might go to black when pulled into its end station. There was a sound, a strange sound, which I attributed to bullets against stone, and then she was still.

"*Shaitan*," I said, quietly, a prayer to the devil I'd killed for the second time.

K_____ vibrated behind me. "Is it dead?"

"A man-eater for your museum," I told him, overcome by the sadness I always feel when I kill something large as her, and with this sadness, something more, something darker. Confusion.

"You must know she's not for a museum, old man," K_____ told me, his voice returning, more confident than it had been before. "A museum wouldn't pay for something like this."

I looked at him.

"Everyone wants a tiger," he said. "Everyone wants a man-eater certified by someone like you."

"Who's this tiger for?" I knew the answer already.

"A collector. Already has a table made of elephant legs."

K_____'s wry laugh sounded to me like something from a moving picture, overheard from far down the street, through walls and bodies. Hollow and cluttered, the laughter of something made of less than nothing. My own laughter had, on occasion, sounded the same.

He took his flask from his pocket, sipped, and offered it to me. I refused.

"Don't misunderstand me," he said, kneeling to unpack his case. "I read your book. That's why I do this. I show the world the things they want to see, but don't want to travel to. It's conservation, isn't it? People like that, here, they'd ruin things. You, though, you've killed what? Two hundred tigers? You know what you're doing."

With effort, he rolled the man-eater onto her back, and removed a scalpel from his pack.

"If I don't gut her soon, the skin'll spoil," he said, and then bent over the tigress, parting the fur on her chest.

"An old bullet wound." He jabbed her left shoulder, but I didn't look. I knew the wound. "There's another scar here," he said. "As old as the other."

He ran his finger down the man-eater's pelt, from chest to abdomen. I could scarcely keep myself from tearing the scalpel from his hand. I felt as though she was the only one on earth who'd known my past. I didn't dare think of how she could be here at all, thirty-two years later, did not dare imagine what this all might mean, for it *was* her. I knew her face, her tracks. It was her. A dead, mortal tigress.

"Peculiar," K_____ muttered, cutting into the scar. An echoing scratch. Scalpel on bullet, I thought.

"What in Christ is this?" K_____ whispered.

I wasn't looking at him, nor at the tigress. I was focused into the distance, imagining Kenya, when he shook my shoulder. I turned my head, reluctant to see what he'd done.

A gleam, straight down the center of the tigress' body. K_____ peeled back the flesh on either side of the incision.

There was no blood. No. Only skin, and beneath the skin, metal.

K_____ began tearing at the pelt, pulling it away from the structure beneath, breathing through his mouth.

"What is it?" he asked, looking suddenly, frantically up at me. "Is it a prank?"

I couldn't speak.

Henry, kneeling with a tin can and a watch spring. Henry, wounded, climbing down into that ravine to retrieve her body. Skinning her, hauling her back up the mountain, and bringing her back to life. He'd made a new kind of tiger, one that could resist hunters and poachers. One that could resist me.

K_____'s hands peeled the flesh back still further. I could see solder marks, where seams had been joined.

"The hide isn't dry. How did he get it to heal? What did he use? How does it move?"

He attempted haphazardly to slice into the tigress' chest, denting the metal. He pulled up the tigress' eyelid, his fingernail tapping at her pupil. Glass. I looked at her feet. The strange marks I'd seen in the village had not been made by claws. Henry had given her knives, forged into the shape of talons.

I felt myself half-smiling, an echo of the old enchantment, Henry's genius, Henry as a *shikari*.

"Whatever he's done, however he's done it," K_____ said, his voice scarcely under control, wobbling with joy, "We'll lead an expedition back here. Photographers. Film cameras."

He jabbed the scalpel into a seam between the metal pieces, levering at it. A dark fluid leaked out. Blood? Not blood? Henry never explained himself. I still had K_____'s rifle. I swung it slowly around to the front. When he heard the click, he looked up, entirely startled.

"What are you doing?"

I fired into K_____'s face, approximating the angle he himself would have taken had he stumbled over his own weapon in the forest, drunk on gin, and a fool. I left him where he lay, skull exposed. I used my handkerchief to polish his rifle and put it into his own hands. Took his scalpel.

Anyone who found K_____'s body would imagine he'd been attacked by a tiger, and inadvertently shot himself in the scuffle.

I chopped down two saplings, lashed the tigress to them with my machan ropes, and began a laborious drag. I'd drop her into that ravine. Everything was clear to me now. If the world learned of this tiger, they'd cut down the forests to find more like her, though surely there were no more. This would've taken Henry years to accomplish, however it was he'd done it. Magic. Gears.

Kumaon would be overrun. All the remaining living tigers would be taken, shot, opened like stuffed toys, left to dry in the sun, unused, unburied.

I hauled her through the trees, straining at her great weight, squinting toward the earliest light, toward the place I remembered from 1918. If I threw her off the cliffs here, she would not be found. Dead, I'd tell the villagers, and fallen, just as I'd told them before. My fingers were blue with cold despite the effort of hauling her, and my breath came sharply, each gasp painful.

At last, I found the place, and panting, unlashed her. My heart, by this juncture, was pounding inside me like something independent of my body, a metal bird flying for no reason other than someone else's will.

I pushed the tigress over the edge. I watched her fall for the second time, her golden face and fur, her gleaming, opened breast. I was not watching my footing. Is it any wonder I fell? Not from the cliff, as I might deserve, but over a small rise, and into a clearing, flat rock beneath me.

Hours have passed. I cannot stand. It's cold now, and the light fades again. My left leg, in my trousers, is bent in such a way that I know it would be useless to attempt to place it back in line. I've bled into the ice, and it shines like a glass ruby on an elephant's forehead.

I have this journal, and my pencil, and I write for comfort. What else do I have, after all these years wandering in the wilderness? Tomorrow, I'll burn these words. I write only to tell myself what happened, not to place the story into the world.

Out there in the sky I see each star again, and like every man dying from the beginning of his days, I regret the things I didn't do, and I regret the things I did.

19 September 1950
Dawn.

All night, Henry's tigers paced around me, circling close enough to brush me with their fur. I couldn't count them, couldn't name them. There may be hundreds, or twelve, or a thousand.

Now, the sun is risen, and snow has fallen here at the top of this mountain, over me and around my body. If I could stand, I might look down again onto my own lost village, the teardrop lake at the center of the vista like the eye of a god, wide open for eternity, never freezing, never anything more or less than blue. No passage to heaven from that lake. One needs a river, one needs a fire, one needs bones.

Ram nam satya hai, sing the voices in my memory, a hymn to carry the victims away, shrouded and saved from further sorrow.

What will the tigers leave of me? Will there be bones to send to my wife? Who will find them here? The villagers await the sound of my fire, five shots to come and take the tiger from here, but I won't fire this rifle again. They will assume me dead, along with K_____, and the tigress escaped.

When I turn my head, all I can see in this clearing are pugmarks, tracks circling over tracks, lines and circuits, loops and letters. Each of the footfalls, each of the places where a tail touched the earth, each spatter of blood, each piece of fur brushed onto a tree trunk tells me something.

Coded lines left behind by Henry, placed in the tiger's metal minds, along with the calls he gave them, but I've no key to break them. When the cats move, I hear their machinery now, the sound of gears against gears, metal against metal.

All these years haunted by a ghost that wasn't. All these years imagining tracks around my house, when they were here all along. There are no ghosts but the ones you make.

I lay last night in the dark and heard the tigers dragging their claws through the snow, each one marking my name. That, at least, was mine, but it's become something the tigers use. I can't read it, but I know it belonged to me, just as one knows a book read long ago, the margins scarred with ink, the pages folded down. A possession. This book, this journal, I'd know anywhere. I sought to burn it, but my firestarter is wet, and I can't strike a flame. Perhaps the tigers will take it too.

In my hand, I have a penknife, given to me by Henry, the handle made of something's bones, the blade so thin now that it scarcely exists. Used on pelts, and on tin cans, and on apples, and on birds. Used on tigers and leopards, on man-eaters all over India. Used on tiger cubs. Two hearts eaten, and I thought it made me a man and gave me a vengeance on all the things that take hunters from their lives.

Over my head, high and far away, an airplane tears a line across the heavens, hunting some smaller prey, and I think about a sky filled with roaring ghosts. I feel displaced in time, a traveler returning home after decades spent in a place where years passed at a strange rate. If I came down from the mountains now, an old man, I might find the children I left in this village thirty-two years ago. I might find myself, walking into the woods. I might find Henry, twisting metal into life.

I am well-acquainted with the paths to heaven from this part of the mountains. I do not expect heaven.

Send my bones up in smoke along with those I killed, and let us hunt together, shifting between prey and *shikari*, stalking, killing enemies already dead. The bones in my pouch belong to the dead. Burn them.

A hunter hunts. We are all hunters here.

Maria Dahvana Headley is the author of the historical fantasy *Queen of Kings*, the first volume of a trilogy. Previously, she wrote *The Year of Yes: A Memoir*, which has been translated into nine languages, and optioned for television and film. She has appeared as a featured author and speaker at venues including The Texas Book Festival and Wordstock, and has been interviewed on a variety of national and international television and radio programs, including *The Today Show*, *Countdown with Keith Olbermann*, and many more. Her writing has appeared in and/or been excerpted in a number of literary anthologies, the *New York Times*, *Elle*, the *Washington Post*, and more. As a playwright, she is the creator of The Upstart Crow Project, an organization that will commission thirty-seven female playwrights to adapt all the plays of Shakespeare into contemporary versions. She is a MacDowell Colony Fellow and lives in Brooklyn.

Alone in her apartment she could let down
her hair to slither, unrestrained . . .

PEARLS

Priya Sharma

I sat in the park watching a couple who were like all lovers, only intent on one another. The girl was a beauty ripe for harvest, her hair a golden sheaf. The boy's desire was visible in the way he kissed her. I felt a pang. I, too, had been lovely once and loved.

My hair made jealous noises in sympathy.

A man walked by and I could hear the furious beat that was piped straight into his ears. His curious gaze slid over my sunglasses and cap, then the sketches on my pad.

I loved the park. It had appeared in my work many times. I liked how it muted the traffic's song and softened the steel and glass towers with a shimmering heat haze. I felt sleepy and my pencil made loose, lazy marks on the page, but the coils that passed for my hair were invigorated by the warmth. I hissed at them but the serpents twitched and jerked. They refused to be stilled. They longed to creep and crawl, to enjoy sunlight on their scales.

The young lovers were staring at me.

It was time to go so I packed my things away. Somehow, it was always time to go.

I lived a quiet life, contained within three rooms. Sunshine flooded in through long windows and fell upon the bed, whose sheets were stained with turps and paint. Alone in my apartment I could let down my hair to slither, unrestrained. Without the need for dark glasses, my eyes had to readjust to the light.

My paintings covered the walls. They occupied tables and chairs. They crowded out the clothes from my closet. Canvases were lined up in the plate rack. I filled a crate and sent it to the gallery when I needed funds. The pantheon of my former life was resurrected. Hermes riding the Staten Island ferry. The Graces shopping on Fifth Avenue. Bacchus drinking in a Brooklyn bar. Eros pimping in Harlem, wearing a ridiculous fur coat.

I adored the city but it rarely noticed me. Sometimes I'd hear a long low whistle or the call of *freak*. I'd even been stopped and dollar bills pressed into my palm. Either alms for needy or an invitation to spend a sweaty afternoon in a hotel room. I always declined and went home, filled with difficult wishes, to lie upon the shambles of my bed. When it got too much to bear I'd get up and occupy myself in a fury of oil paint. I'd work until the insomnia and hunger made me weak. Elation made the colors bright and the pictures came alive.

I watched the night retreat from my window. I stood there until the shops' shutters rolled up to reveal their displays. A rainbow of plastic beads. Vintage handbags with creases etched into the leather. Indecent mannequins in wispy lace underwear.

I felt confined. I needed to be outside. I wound a scarf about my head to keep the serpents in check and selected a pair of dark glasses from the basket by the door.

There was a man on the stairs. He stared at me.

"I'm Paul." His proffered hand forced me to stop. "I've just moved in across the hall from you. I wondered when we'd meet."

I took his hand. After all, I'd no reason to be afraid.

"What's your name?"

"I'm Maddy." I'd forgotten the order of social niceties.

Paul peered into my darkened glasses as if trying to see through them. My hair made chattering noises.

"Did you say something?"

"No," I replied.

"This building echoes. I'm not used to it yet."

"Have we met before?"

"Now you come to mention it, you do seem familiar." Paul cocked his head on one side "Where are you from, Maddy? Where's home?"

I was out of world and time. I'd sickened of home, my villa full of torchlight, shadows and statues. The mosaics of my courtyard were obscured by mud, where once they'd been swept clean each day. Broken urns collected rainwater. Fine tapestries rotted where they hung. I kept the remains of a silenced lyre, the strings long since snapped, beside the pile of rags that were my bed.

Home was dangerous. Men came with swords and spears, wanting fame and fortune, to feast and fornicate on the glory of the tale. The battles and vigils exhausted me. Arrows clattered on my breastplate. Javelins struck my shield. Sometimes they used a net as if that could hold me. Tall shadows fell on the walls and reached around corners to find me. There'd be whistles, shouts and the smash of stone as I sent one of them crashing to the floor. The air was fetid with fear. I could taste it on my forked tongue.

The supplicants were worse. They left dishes on milk on the veranda as if I were a pet. Then there was a tribute. A caged mouse. Ravenous, I shoved the wriggling rodent in my mouth and crunched down. Its lifeless tail hung from my lips. A little death compared with all the rest but it caused me so much shame that I ran away. I slithered into the dark, my green tail rattling a warning to worshippers. They fled around me into the trees. More than one stone effigy was found the following morning, immortalized in its own horror.

I sought the safety of the valley, home only to thorny bushes and bony goats. I meant to spend a night or two. To find a shaded hole full of snakes and sleep. To lie down without the stealthy whispers of swords being unsheathed.

I must have been tired because I slept for over a thousand years.

"You ask a lot of questions."

"I'm a curious man." Paul stroked his beard. "Have you ever been to California?"

"No, maybe one day."

We'd progressed to the front step of the building.

"You should. The Pacific's terrific. Would you have breakfast with me?" He didn't pause long enough for me to decline his invitation. "Are you doing anything special today?"

"Yes. No." I was taken aback by my own rashness. "Breakfast would be wonderful."

Paul's grin revealed uneven, ivory teeth.

We walked side by side. Paul had the rolling stride of a man at no one's command.

"What do you do for a living?" I asked him.

"I trained as an oceanographer but I've done a few different things in my time."

"And what about now?"

"Antiquities dealer. Ancient Greece mainly." Paul smiled. "It's a passion of mine. I've quite a personal collection."

I'd thought all the believers, hunters and collectors were dead. That I'd managed to outlive them all. If Paul fell into any of these categories, then we should celebrate. One of us would soon be extinct.

"I like lost things," Paul continued. "I was a bit lost myself for a while. It made me reconsider what's important. Reconciliation. Forgiveness. That life must go on once grief and anger have gone."

"What caused that bout of introspection?"

"A woman. What else?"

I snorted.

"What have you lost, Maddy?"

We stopped at a crossing, the crush of bodies at our back.

"Everything," I replied, "everything that mattered. Some things were taken from me and the rest I threw away."

I awoke in a panic after my millennium of sleep. The weight of the world crushed me. I'd shed my skin while I'd slumbered and it had become a fibrous shroud. I'd regrown legs instead. My tongue was fused, not forked anymore. My overgrown fingernails had curled over on themselves and broke into strange brass spirals as I clawed at the earth. Villagers now inhabited my burial plot and saw me crawl out of the ground and stumble on unpliant legs. I tried to avert my eyes but they got in my way. I left the curious ones with more than feet of clay.

I had to find a means to travel. I had to get away. A traveling show was the only way to go. Home became a shabby caravan. Crowds queued to glimpse my reflection. They saw me in the looking glass, stripped to the waist except for a string of pearls. A mass of writhing serpents hung down from my head and covered my breasts. My eyes shocked them the most though. Yellow, the pupils slits, not circles.

It was a living of a kind. It was a kind of life. I'd have gone on with but for the Lion Man who shook me from my apathy. He knocked on the door of my caravan and asked to come in. He kissed me, unaware of the incompatibility of our species. Or perhaps he didn't care. I didn't either. I had my spectacles on. His mane tickled my face.

"Don't you find me ugly?" I asked.

"You're the most gorgeous gorgon I've ever encountered."

It was my fault.

The Lion Man ripped off his shirt. My glasses fell to the floor. I was thrilled into forgetfulness by his warm flesh and opened my eyes, just for a moment. His erection was stone against my stomach. I was caught in his flinty embrace and had to wiggle free.

I laid him on my bed and covered him with a blanket. I made a bundle of my things. The extra sets of spectacles, spare clothes, my pearls, and an apple I'd saved for supper. It was time to go. Somehow, it was always time to go.

Paul and I ordered breakfast from a waitress who looked timeless in a black dress and white apron. Her smooth, dark hair was twisted into a bun. A waiter was writing the specials on a blackboard while another wiped down the marble counter.

"You never take your glasses off." Paul spoke between mouthfuls.

"I've a rare eye condition. My specialist's told me to keep my glasses on."

"I'm sorry." Paul looked at me as though he could diagnose the fault through my lenses.

"That's nice."

"What is?"

"Nice of you to be sorry." I stirred my cappuccino. The cocoa dust mingled with the froth. It looked like marbled paper.

"I love your style—the boots, the dreds, the headscarf. Where are you from?"

"Here and there. I've traveled a lot."

"Like?"

"Europe mostly." I tore open a croissant, scattering flakes.

"Doing what?"

"Painting. Dancing. Idling."

Paul's eyes were fixed on his empty plate. It occurred me that he might be bored. That he might want to leave and I'd spend another day alone.

"Hey, how about I show you some of my favorite places?"

"Aren't you busy?" He screwed up his napkin in his fist. "You must have things to do. Like painting. Dancing. Idling."

The mood had soured. I felt the unexpected sting of tears and was grateful for my glasses. "Of course. We'll go back."

"No," he covered my hand with his. "You can't go back. You can only go forward. Give me a tour."

I kept moving after the Lion Man. I danced, blindfolded, in a Parisian nightclub. I undulated under dimmed lights, moving in a stupor with all those eyes directly on me. My scanty costume itched. I told fortunes in Prague, my face hidden behind a veil. I was no prophet. I couldn't even see a future for myself but I tried to give solace to the hopeless. London followed with its smog, lamplight, and piecework. I stitched gloves in a garret. I wearied of being treated as if diseased or as a victim. I was backed into an alley by a man with a scalpel. Such a dapper gent to be wreaking havoc on the flesh. I slipped off my specs and gave him a long, hard stare.

I was no stranger to brutality but the old world was depraved. Time to usher in the new. I sold some of my pearls to ensure comfortable passage. It was a long voyage spent confined to my cabin. The ship bobbed up and down in the swell like a bath toy of the gods. I lay on my bed listening as the water thumped the hull. Poseidon's heart beat in my ear.

The Statue of Liberty was as fine as any Titan and it made my heart glad to see her green skin. I slid from the ship into the oily black water, my belongings towed behind me in a sealed oilskin bag. My serpents were limp with hypothermia by the time I crawled onto the banks of the Hudson.

My hate for Poseidon wouldn't abate but it grieved me to sell off his pearls, one by one. Each was a lustrous story. They'd fall from Poseidon's ears, nostrils and mouth whenever we quarrelled. It was his way of getting me to laugh and make up with him.

Paul and I sat in the atrium of the Frick Museum, chaperoned by an angel. She was an impassive creature carved in marble, her wings folded high on her back. Sunlight flooded through the glass ceiling. The fronds of the ferns were delicate under my fingers.

"I love it here because it looks like a home, not a stuffy museum." I remembered the Frick family. A cunning clan of robber barons who'd discovered gentility and art. They'd built this mansion overlooking the park. "I can imagine the Frick women sitting here, gossiping."

"You look sad." Paul was tender voiced.

Sad for my home that was like this, except that my courtyard was open to the elements so that the mosaic floor glistened underfoot when it rained. Water trickled from the dolphin spouts into the central cistern. I'd sit there with my sisters, Sthen and Euryale, sewing and talking.

Sthen would play that damn lyre of hers. She was never very good at it. Euryale giggled as she asked, "What's Poseidon like? Is he more salty than mortal men?"

Sthen tutted and blushed but listened, breath held for my answer.

I took Paul to Grand Central Station to view the crowds from the balcony. It was a grand ballet. People moved with such purpose that I felt tired just watching them.

"Let me show you The Whispering Gallery."

I'd read about it but had no one with which to test the theory. I took Paul's hand and pulled him down the long, low steps. The spot was underground. Not a gallery at all but the junction of four subterranean walkways. The space was marked with four corner pillars that rose to meet at the apex of the tiled dome. I took Paul by the shoulders and put him facing one of the pillars like a child cornered for their naughtiness.

"Don't move." I went to the opposite pillar and spoke to it. "Can you hear me?"

"That's amazing." His voice came back to me. "Can anyone else hear us?"

"No, the sound transmits from one pillar to the opposite one, across the dome."

"You're beautiful." It sounded like we were in bed together and he was whispering in my ear.

"Isn't the acoustic design fantastic?"

"Don't ignore me."

"Easy flattery. How many women are you currently trying to seduce?"

"Just you."

"Directness. Good. Are you doing this for money or sport?"

"Doing what?"

"Hunting vulnerable women in search of trophies. Will you take my head for your collection?"

"It's not your head I'm after. And you're about as vulnerable as a bag of rattlesnakes"

"You say the nicest things."

"You don't cut men any slack, do you? Do you forgive or forget anything?"

I returned home, my tryst with Poseidon in every crevice and pore. There were bloody footprints on my porch as if a battle fresh army had trampled through the house. I followed the trail back to the carnage in the courtyard where I fell to the floor and howled.

My darling Sthen and Euryale. All Sthen had wanted was for Perseus to notice her. I could see her longing looks at his oiled curls and athlete's legs. Strutting Perseus and his friends had given both my sisters their full attention all afternoon. Then they'd cut their throats and laid them out with their arms about each other, like sleeping infants. Their hair, always curled and pinned, was loose about their pallid faces. Blood seeped from their wounded necks onto their tattered gowns.

And all because I said no to you, Perseus. All because you couldn't have me.

I ran to Poseidon's cliff top house. He held me while I screamed and shook. He stroked my hair and the sea below boiled in fury.

"I want him dead. Kill him for me."

"We can't, my love. Perseus is championed by Athena. On Zeus' orders."

"Since when do you care about Athena? I was one of her temple maidens when you seduced me. On her altar, no less."

"Let's not give her another reason to seek revenge."

"You said you hated her. You called her a battle hungry spinster. Why do you care what she thinks?"

"She's Zeus' daughter."

"So? You're Zeus' brother."

"Yes, but Zeus is King of Olympus. There'd be war."

"Zeus would go to war with you over Perseus?"

"Perseus is his son."

"Son." Secrets and nepotism. Zeus, king of philanderers and begetter of bastards.

"We'll have revenge but we'll have to bide our time."

"You haven't seen what they did . . . "

"Listen to me, Medusa. I loved your sisters but we can't do anything. Not yet."

You gods are as treacherous as men. You all stick together. Blood, Poseidon, is thicker than your precious water after all.

So I sought out a goddess where gods had failed me. Hera was Zeus' queen and consort. I threw myself on the ground before her. Hera shushed her sniggering court with a look and stepped down, dainty footed, from her dais.

"Poor dear, your sisters must be avenged." I could see her calculating the gains. A lesson for her errant husband and his illegitimate children. "I commend your loyalty and I think I can see a way. There's so much anger in those lovely eyes. The price would be very high though."

"Anything. I don't care. Just help me."

"Are you sure?" She held my hand, relishing the task ahead. "We poor weak women must do what brave men can't. I'll make them afraid to even look at you."

Goddesses, as treacherous as women. You should have told me to go home, Hera, and bury my sisters.

I didn't care what it cost me. I gloried in what she made of me. A tail replaced my shapely legs. I had snakes instead of locks. Their fangs bit me. I lay on the floor while Hera stepped over my convulsing body. I felt the pain with every heartbeat as waited to become immune. I didn't mind. I felt alive. Best of all was the fury in my eyes. There was no one I couldn't petrify.

It was evening and the summer sky was dark blue and the moon hung low and yellow over the city skyline.

"That one, there." I pointed to a basement bar, the high stools and tables just visible from the street.

We drank whisky from heavy tumblers.

"You don't give much away." Paul gestured to the barman who refilled our empty glasses. "I know you paint. That you can walk me off my feet. Why's a girl like you single?"

"You make it sound like I'm incomplete as I am." I leant back, letting the whisky drain down my throat. It left a combination of peat and antiseptic in my mouth. I decided to stop sparring. "There was someone once."

"What happened?"

"He let me down."

"How?"

"He sided with his family."

"It's a mistake forcing people to chose. Invariably they never chose you."

"Whose side are you on?"

"See? You're doing it now. There has to be a side." Paul snorted into his glass, clouding it up with his breath. "Not everyone has the luxury of choice."

I put an ice cube in my mouth and crunched it up.

"Let's not talk about the past." Paul turned his body towards me. "I've not seen your eyes. I bet they're green. The green of glittering emeralds."

"Guess again."

"Brown, like chocolate."

"Nope."

"Blue, then. But what shade of blue?"

Blue as the deepest part of the ocean. That's what Poseidon, god of all the seas, said to me when we made love. I'd forgotten that.

Oh, Poseidon, you were running water in my hands.

"Do you want to see them?"

My dirty, yellow eyes.

"Oh, yes."

Paul reached out to remove my glasses but I stopped him.

"Not here. Let's go to your place."

My courtship with Poseidon had been steeped in miracles. Marvels were mundane. He took my hand and we dived into the sea, encased in a bubble he'd made. I could breathe despite the fathoms that fell away. I could see the swirling surf above me when I looked up. Poseidon's kingdom was below. Jellyfish pulsed and throbbed. Rays flapped their fins like wings. Sharks stared at us as they patrolled. We were engulfed in a shoal of silver darts that went as quickly as they came.

There was a huge door set in the ocean floor.

"What's that?"

"A jail. It's a prisoner that I guard for Zeus."

"Who is it?"

"The Kraken."

The Kraken was a titan from the start of time who had dared to challenge Zeus. The Kraken appeared at the bars, having heard his name. All I could see was a giant eye. The rest of him was lost in the watery gloom. I smiled in sympathy and raised a hand. The eye blinked back.

"I didn't bring you down here to flirt with him," Poseidon chided. "I wanted you to see the water. It's just like your eyes. The darkest shade of blue that the ocean can possibly be."

Kissing was a distant memory that I associated with gods, lion men, and calamity. Kissing Paul was discovering kissing anew. It reminded me of what I'd put away. Poseidon, a god among the waves but just like any other man in bed. Demanding to worship and to be worshipped in return.

"Come upstairs with me," Paul clutched my hand, "please."

We started to undress in the hall in his flat, amid the unpacked boxes. Paul's shirt lost its shape as he dropped it to the floor, unable to withstand the world without him. I traced the crookedness of his collarbones with my fingertips. The smattering of coarse hair on his chest.

"Where's your bedroom?" I said between kisses.

"There." He indicated a room behind me with a flick of his eyes. I walked backwards, leading him to it. I pulled my blouse over my head and threw it on a chair. Then I saw the picture Paul had hung over his bed. The canvas dominated the room. A fantasy within a Rococo-style frame.

It was one of mine. A self-portrait of sorts. I'd sent it to the gallery as soon as it was finished as I couldn't bear to look at it. I'd remade the city as Arcadia with Bryant Park at its heart. The grass was deep and lush. Trees had conquered concrete and glass. Poseidon and I were postcoital in this idyll. That was clear, not just from our nudity but glow. My head rested on his chest. His arm was around me. He looked down at my head of snakes and yellow eyes like I was the loveliest woman in the world. "Don't you recognize me, Medusa?"

"Poseidon."

"I've been searching for you. I wasn't even sure you were still alive but when I saw the painting I knew I'd found you."

"Well, now you have. What do you want?"

"Forgiveness."

"That won't help my sisters."

"Nothing will help your sisters. It would help us though."

"I was just a plaything to you."

"That's not fair."

"Neither's life. You taught me that."

"I loved you. I still do. Why else do you think I'm here?"

I looked out of the window. Distant lights winked at me.

"It's too late. I'm tired. A tired, old murdering hag."

"And I'm a washed up, has-been deity."

"What became of Perseus?" I surprised myself. I couldn't recall when I'd last thought of him. He'd evaded me.

"Hera chose Perseus' bride as a sacrifice. She demanded the Kraken be released to do the deed. The Kraken was more interested in Perseus," Poseidon gave me a wry smile. "The Kraken liked you. He was glad to oblige."

I should've known to leave the gods to slug it out with one another I felt no satisfaction at the thought of Perseus fixed by the Kraken's slow blinking eye or dangling from its mouth.

I felt nothing.

"Do you really want to see me? See me as I am now?"

A mirror stood against the wall, waiting to be hung. I knelt before it. Poseidon joined me so that we were penitents before ourselves. I unwound my headscarf and took off my spectacles.

"This is me. I've nothing left, not even looks."

"There's still love. Life. We still have those." A pearl dropped from his nostril and rolled to a standstill on the far side of the room. Then another. A third spilled from his mouth. More from his ears. They fell, a percussion of pleading, as they bounced across the wooden floor. "You're beautiful to me. You always will be."

We were reflected in the mirror. A man with a crooked nose and a trimmed brown beard, speckled with silver. A woman with a sinuous coil of dark hair lying over one shoulder. Eyes, blue. The darkest shade of blue that the ocean can be.

"You see? Beautiful."

"Yes," I answered in wonderment, "yes, I am."

Priya Sharma lives in the UK where she works as a doctor. Her short stories have been published by *Interzone*, *Black Static*, *Albedo One*, and *Tor.com*, among others. Her work has been reprinted in *The Year's Best Dark Fantasy and Horror* and *The Best Horror of the Year*. She is writing a novel set in Wales, which is taking a long time as she writes longhand with a fountain pen and then types it up very slowly.

Once she knew he had noticed the oddness, she started covering up the truth—as if she was afraid he might discover her secret.

FORGET YOU

Marc Laidlaw

She came into his life the way his cats crept into his lap. One day he was alone, had been alone for years, his life and his home empty of anyone but himself and a few friends who didn't visit all that often anyway. And then at some point he realized she had been there for a while, in his house, in his bed, in every part of his life, having accomplished the transition so subtly that he could never say exactly when or how it had occurred.

He ran his hand along her cheek in a swift caress, brushing the line of her jaw as he tucked the one stray lock behind her left ear as he often did, and said, "How did we find each other?"

"Oh, you," she said, with that look, as if the question were another of their habitual endearments. "You're sweet."

He traced her other cheek, looked deep into her right eye, then her left, having memorized the stained glass kaleidoscope pattern of her irises so clearly from this practice that he could see them easily when he closed his own eyes.

"No," he said, "I'm serious. How?"

She laughed without a sound, just an exhalation, and mirrored the movement his hands were making, cupping his face in her own palms.

"Just lucky, I guess," she said. "Me, I mean."

"Of course, me too, I just . . . "

She kissed him, and he thought, *Well, that's one difference between her and the cats.*

He asked his friends, when he thought of it, in the very infrequent moments when she was not with him. "How did we meet?" he asked. And they laughed because it was such an odd question that they knew he was setting them up for some kind of joke. And when he said, "No, I'm serious," they grew serious too, and took on a puzzled, questioning tone. "Uh . . . you're asking us? You guys have been together longer than we've been friends."

He went through his photographs, the digital images first, looking farther and farther back through the files, and she was in them all, and he could remember now how she had been there at the time. Beyond a certain point there were no more photos, but that was because of a huge lightning storm, when they'd gone a week without power and his computer had been fried, with everything on it lost. So of course there were no digital photographs from the years before that. He found a box in the closet full of older prints and negatives, in envelopes date-stamped by the pharmacies and photobooths where he had dropped them off to be developed. And it was something of a relief to see that she was not in any of these. He could clearly recall how alone he had been then, but he still could not remember how she'd come into his life. One thing was becoming clear though: It was getting harder to remember life without her. Soon he feared that he would not be able to remember a time when she had not been with him.

He dug out a photograph of himself alone and put it in his pocket to keep with him as a reminder. It was a self-portrait he had taken, just a solitary photo of himself alone in the kitchen looking out the window as if at the emptiness of his life, which had been very empty then. This image had always seemed to him to capture the essence of his loneliness, and looking at it now made him wistful and sad, even nostalgic. He kept taking it out and looking at it, trying to remember how it had ended. Her arrival must have come about sometime in the age of deleted images when everything was uncertain. But when he asked his friends about it, to try and zero in on a date, he couldn't convince them that he wasn't teasing them somehow. And when he started asking her, she began to take offense.

"Why are you always asking me this?" she asked. "What's your problem? It's like you're obsessed. Do you want me out of your life or something? Do you want things back the way they were before we met? Is that it?"

"No, I . . . I just want to remember," he said.

These conversations changed things between them. Or things were changing anyway, and the conversations were a symptom. There was no telling. But he felt he had started something and there was no going back. Just by noticing it, he had started it unraveling. It was as if, once she knew he had noticed the oddness, she started covering up the truth—as if she was afraid he might discover her secret. As long as he accepted the situation and went about his life without questioning it, everything was just fine. But he could no longer pretend to remember. It was driving him crazy. He was convinced she had done something, manipulated reality somehow, folded it around and inserted herself there in his life. Who was she, anyway? What was she? What sort of being had this ability to unravel and reweave the material of existence, working her way into it as if she had always been there?

"Stop looking at me like that," she said. "I don't appreciate it."

"I just want to know how you did it," he said. "I just want to know what you are."

"God!" she said.

It occurred to him that what they were heading toward was the unmaking of what she had made in the first place. Past a certain point, it was inevitable. She would remove herself from his life. She would vanish as if she had never existed. First from the daily routine—she'd be gone from their home, gone from their bed, gone from the parties they had with their friends. Then she would absent herself from the photographs—first from whatever new ones he took, obviously, but then from the older ones as well. If he ever thought to go back through his files, he'd see nothing but photos of himself. When he asked his friends about her, they would look glum to see him filling the emptiness of his life with imaginary partners, and they'd say, "Who?"

Eventually he would have forgotten her completely, and all the evidence in the universe would indicate that she had never existed, and there would be no one to question it because he himself would have forgotten.

This was the way things were heading, and all because he had noticed. He wasn't supposed to, he decided. He was supposed to have been oblivious, and just accept it. She must have done this before, but he was the first to have seen through it. Otherwise she would have done something different to make sure he remained unaware. She would have learned from prior mistakes, which meant he must be the first mistake. He was probably the only one who would see through her, because after this she would know what to do to remain undiscovered. In this way he felt privileged, special. He should feel fortunate that she had come to him, because it had allowed him to learn a very important truth about himself. From now on, even in his solitude, even when the memory of her had removed itself, he would own this bit of self-knowledge. He wouldn't know how he had come by it, but he would cleave to it nonetheless. She had made him more whole, more truly himself. So there was a purpose to her being here after all.

Such were his thoughts on the last morning, as dawn crept into their bedroom, as the air grew bright and she grew dim, as the place where she was lying grew unlaid-in and the cats stretched out to fill it. But the thoughts were fleeting for he was already forgetting her, and he almost didn't notice when, in the final moment, she woke and opened her eyes and turned and looked, but not at him, and said to no one but herself, "Why is this always happening to me?"

Before became one of the creators and lead writer on the Half-Life videogame series, **Marc Laidlaw** was an acclaimed writer of short stories and novels. His novel *The 37th Mandala* won the International Horror Guild Award for Best Novel. A writer at Valve since 1997 (currently working on for the online game, *Dota 2*), his short fiction continues to appear in various magazines and anthologies.

We need souls. We have few left in our world. Come to us, across
the Great Deeps. Restore our world. Become one with us . . .

WHEN DEATH WAKES ME TO MYSELF

John Shirley

—◆—

"Someone's broken into the house, doctor."

Fyodor saw no fear in Leah's gray eyes. But he'd never seen her afraid, and she'd worked closely with him in psychiatrics for almost eight years—ever since he'd finished his internship. She brushed auburn hair from her pale forehead, adjusted her glasses, and went on, "The window latch is broken in your office—and I think I heard someone moving around down in the basement."

"Did you call the police?" Fyodor asked, glancing toward the basement door. His mouth felt dry.

They stood in the front hallway of the old house, by the open arch to the waiting room. "I did. I was about to call you, when you walked in."

They didn't speak for a long moment, both of them listening for the burglar. Wintry morning light angled through the bay windows of the waiting room, casting intricate shadows from the lace curtains across the braided rug. A dog barked down the street; a foghorn hooted. Just the sounds of Providence, Rhode

Island . . .

Then a peal of happy laughter rippled up through the hardwood floorboards. It cut short so abruptly he wondered if he'd really understood the sound. "That sound like laughter to you?"

"Yes." She glanced at the window. "The police are in no hurry . . . "

"You should wait out front, Leah." He was thinking he should try to see to it that whoever this was, they weren't setting a fire, vandalizing, doing serious damage to the house. He was negotiating to buy it, planning to expand it into a suite of offices with various health services—especially bad timing for vandalism. It was a big house, built in 1825, most of it not in use at the moment. The ground-floor den was ideal for receiving patients; the front living room had been converted into a waiting room.

Fyodor took a step through the archway, into the hall—and then the basement door burst open. A slender young man stood there, a few paces away, holding a bottle in his hand, toothy grin fading. "Oh! I seem to have lost all track of time. How indiscreet of me," said the young man, in an accent that sounded Deep South. He wore a neat dark suit with a rather antiquated blazer, thin blue tie, starched white shirt, silver cufflinks, polished black

shoes. His fingernails were immaculately manicured, his straight black hair neatly combed back. Fyodor noted all this with a professional detachment, but also a little surprise—he'd expected the burglar to be scruffier, more like the sullen young men he sometimes counseled at Juvenile Detention. The young man's dark brown eyes met his—the gaze was frank, the smile seemed genuine. Still, the strict neatness might place him in a recognizable spectrum of personality disorders.

"You seem lost," Fyodor said—gesturing, with his hand at his side, for Leah to go outside. Foolish protective instinct—she was athletic, probably more formidable in a fight than he was. "In fact, young man, you seem to have lost your way right through one of our windows."

"Ah, yes." His mouth twitched. "But look what I found for you, Dr. Cheski!" He raised the dusty bottle in his hand. It was an old, unlabeled wine bottle. "I never used to drink. I wanted to take it up, starting with something old and fine. I want a new life. I desire to do things differently. Live! I bet you didn't know there was any wine down there."

Fyodor blinked. "Um . . . in fact . . . " In fact he didn't think there *was* any wine in the basement.

A siren wailed, grew louder—and cut short. Radio voices echoed, heavy boot-steps came up the walk, and the young man, sighing, put the bottle on the floor and walked past Fyodor to open the front door. He waved genially at the policemen.

"Gentlemen," said the young man, "I believe you are here for me. I'm told that my name is Roman Carl Boxer."

Carrying the dusty wine bottle, Fyodor descended the basement steps, wondering if this Roman Carl Boxer could have been a patient, someone he'd consulted on, at some point. The face wasn't familiar, but perhaps he'd been disheveled and heavily acned before. *I'm told that my name is Roman Carl Boxer.* Interesting way to put it.

The basement was a box of cracked concrete, smelling of mildew; a little water had leaked into a farther corner. A naked light bulb glowed in the cobwebbed ceiling, bright enough to throw stark shadows from what looked like rodent droppings, off to his left. To the right were his crates of old files, recently stored here—they seemed undisturbed. He saw no wine bottles. He could smell dirt and damp concrete. A few scuffs marked the dust coating the floor.

Fyodor started to turn back—it was not a pleasant place to be—but he decided to look more closely at the files. There was confidential patient information in those crates. If this kid had gotten into them . . .

He crossed to the files, confirmed they seemed undisturbed—then saw the hole in the floor, in the farther corner. A small shiny crowbar, the price sticker still on it, lay close beside the hole. His view of it had been blocked by the crates.

He crouched by the hole—almost two feet square—and saw that a trapdoor of concrete and wood had been removed to lean against the wall. He could make out a number of dark bottles, down inside it, in wooden slots. Wine bottles.

One slot was empty. The bottle he'd brought with him fit precisely in that slot.

A week later.

"Deal's done," Fyodor said, with some excitement, as he came into the waiting room. He took off his damp coat, hanging it up, sniffling, his nose stinging from the cold, wet wind. "I own the building! The bank and I do, anyway."

"That's great!" Leah said, the corners of her eyes crinkling with a prim smile. She was hanging a picture on the waiting room wall. It was a print of a Turner seascape: vague, harmless proto-Impressionism in gold and umber and subtle blues; a choice that suggested sophistication, and was soothing to psychiatric patients. Still, some patients were capable of feeling threatened by anything.

Leah stepped back from the painting, and nodded.

Fyodor thought it was hanging just slightly crooked, but he knew it would irritate her if he straightened it—though she'd only show the irritation as a faint flicker around her mouth. Surprising how well he'd gotten to know her, and, at the same time, how impersonal their relationship was. A professional distance was appropriate. But it didn't feel appropriate somehow, with Leah . . .

"That police detective called," she said, straightening the painting herself. "Asking if we're going to come to the arraignment for that burglar."

"I'm not inclined to press charges."

"Really? They've let him out on bail, you know. He might com back."

"I don't want to start my new practice here by prosecuting the first mentally ill person I run into." He went to the bay windows and looked out at the wet streets, the barren tree limbs of the gnarled, blackened elm in the front yard. Leafless tree limbs always made him think of nerve endings.

"He hasn't actually been diagnosed . . . "

"He was confused enough to climb in through a window, ignore everything of value, go down to the basement and dig about."

"Did you have that wine looked at? The stuff he found downstairs?"

Fyodor nodded. "Hal checked it out. Italian wine, from the early twentieth century, shipped direct from some vineyard—and not improved with age. Gone quite vinegary, he told me." How had Roman Boxer known the wine was there? It seemed to have been sealed up for decades.

Something else bothered him about the incident, something he couldn't quite define, a feeling there was something he should recognize about Roman Boxer . . . just out of reach.

"Oh—you got approval for limited testing of SEQ10. The letter's on your desk. There are some regulatory hoops but . . . "

SEQ10. They'd been waiting almost a year. Things were coming together.

He turned to face Leah, feeling a sudden rush of warmth for her. It was good to have her on his team. She was always a bit prim, reserved, her wit dry, her feelings controlled. But sometimes . . .

"And," she said a little reluctantly, going to the waiting room desk, "your mom called."

She passed him the message. *Please call. The Psycho Psych Tech is at it again.*

His mother: the fly in the ointment, ranting about the psychiatric technician she imagined was persecuting her in the state hospital. But then she was the reason he'd gotten into psychiatry. Her mania, her fits of amnesia. His own analyst had suggested she was also some of the reason he tended to be rather reserved, wound tight—compensating for his mother's flamboyance. She was flamboyant on the upswings, almost catatonic on the downswings—prone to amnesia. Firm self-control helped him deal with either extreme.

And her intervals of amnesia had prompted his interest in SEQ10.

The doorbell rang, and he went to his office to await the first patient of the day. But his first patient wasn't the first person to arrive. Instead, Leah ushered in a small middle-aged woman with penciled eyebrows, dark red lipstick, a little too much rouge, her black hair tightly caught up in a bun. She wore a pink slicker, her rose-colored umbrella dripping on the carpet as she said, "I know I shouldn't come without an appointment, Doctor Cheski . . . " Her cadences tripped rapidly, her voice chirpy, the movements of her head, as she looked back and forth between Fyodor and Leah, seemed birdlike. "But he was so insistent—my son Roman. He said I had to see him *here* or not at all, and then he hung up on me. God knows he's been a lot of trouble to you already. Has he gotten here yet?"

"Here? Today?" Fyodor looked at Leah. She shrugged and shook her head.

"He said he'd be upstairs . . . "

There was a thump from the ceiling. Squeaking footsteps; brisk pacing, back and forth.

Leah put a hand to her mouth and laughed nervously. Quite uncharacteristic of her. "Oh my gosh, he's broken into the house again."

Roman's mother looked back and forth between them. "Not again! I thought he'd made an appointment! He said he didn't trust anyone else . . . He barely knows *me*, you see . . . " Her lips trembled.

Leah's brows knit. "Did you—give him up for adoption?"

Another thump came from above. They all looked at the ceiling. "No-o," Mrs. Boxer said, slowly. "No, he . . . claims to *not remember* growing up with us. With his own family! I show him photographs—he says they're 'sort of familiar.' But he says it's like it didn't happen to *him*. I don't really understand what he means." She sighed and went quickly on, "He just keeps wandering around Providence—*looking* for something . . . but he won't say what."

Fyodor knew he should call the police. But when Leah went to the phone, he said, "Wait, Leah." *Claims to not remember growing up with us. With his own family.*

SEQ10 was a hypnotic drug for treating, among other things, hysterical amnesia.

Fyodor looked at Mrs. Boxer. She had some very high-quality jewelry; new pumps, sensible but elegant. A rather showy diamond bulked on her wedding ring. She had money, after all. She could pay for therapy. Insurance wouldn't cover SEQ10.

Fyodor took a deep breath, and, wiping his clammy palms on his trousers, went up the stairs.

He found Roman in the guest room right over the office. Roman was sitting on the edge of the four-poster bed, nervously turning a glass of wine in both hands, around and around—he'd put the wine in a water tumbler from the upstairs bathroom.

"Brought your own wine this time, I see," Fyodor said.

"Yes. A California Merlot. Still trying to learn how to drink." Roman smiled apologetically. He wore the same suit as last time. Neat as a pin. "Strange sensation, alcohol." After a moment he added, "Sorry about the door. No one was here when I came. I needed to get in."

Fyodor grunted. He planned to rent the room out as an office, and now this guy was damaging it—the door to the outside stairs stood open, the wood about the lock splintered. There was a large screwdriver on the bedside table.

"Why?" Fyodor asked. "I mean—why the urgency about getting in? Why not make an appointment?"

Roman swirled his wine. "I'm . . . looking for something here. I just—couldn't wait. I don't know why."

It was an evening session, after Fyodor would normally have gone home. Roman's mother had already had the broken door replaced and paid a large advance on the therapy. And Roman was more interesting than most of Fyodor's patients.

Leaning back on the leather easy chair in Fyodor's office,

Roman seemed bemused. Occasionally, he smoothed the lines of his jacket.

"Your mother gave me some background on you," Fyodor said. "Maybe you can tell me what seems true or untrue to you."

He read aloud from his notes.

Roman was twenty-one. An only child, he'd had night terrors until he was nine, with intermittent bedwetting. Father passed on when he was thirteen. They weren't close. Roman had difficulty keeping friends but was likable, and elderly people loved him. He loved cats, but his mother made him stop adopting them after he accumulated four. One died, and he gave it an elaborate burial ritual. Good student in high school, at first, friends mostly with girls—but no girlfriends. Not terribly interested in sex. Bad last year in high school when some sort of Internet bullying took a more personal form. Reluctant to talk about it. Refused to attend the school. Finished with home schooling, GED. Two years of college, attendance quite patchy. Autodidact for the most part. Tendency to have unusual difficulty with cold weather. No close friends "except in books."

"All that sound right to you, Roman?" Fyodor asked, getting his laptop into word processing mode.

Roman looked vaguely about him. "Not very flattering, is it? Sounds like someone I *knew*—but it doesn't feel like it happened to me personally. *Apparently* it's me."

Fyodor typed in his laptop, *Possible dissociation due to unacceptable self-image.*

"But since last year—your memories seem like . . . you?"

"Yes—since last year. All that seems real. I can't remember anything before that unless somebody reminds me, and then it's . . . like remembering an old television episode. Except I can't really remember those either . . . "

Roman's eyes kept wandering to the Victorian fixture hanging from the ceiling. "That fixture's been here a hundred years."

"I would have thought it's older than that, really, as this house was built in the early nineteenth century," Fyodor said absently, adjusting his laptop to make sure Roman couldn't see what he was typing.

"No," Roman said firmly. "Installed early twentieth century. But it was made in the nineteenth."

Fyodor made a note: *Possible grandiosity? Faux expertise syndrome?* "Your mother says you feel your name is not Roman. Although she showed you a birth certificate. Do you feel the birth certificate is . . . "

"Is faked, unreal—part of a conspiracy?" Roman chuckled. "Not at all! What I said was, I *feel* my name is not Roman. I answer to it for simplicity's sake. And as for what my name really is—I truly don't know. Roman Boxer is correct—and incorrect. But don't waste your time asking why that is, I don't have an answer for you."

"And this started when you took a walk on a beach . . . "

"Yes. Last September. We went to Sandy Point. Myself and . . . well . . . *Mother*. She has a little place at Sandy Point . . . so I have learned. My real memories start—really, as soon as I *arrived* on the beach that day. Before that I don't remember much. She's prompted a few memories, but . . . " He cleared his throat. "Well, I was feeling odd from the moment I stepped onto the sand." He smiled dourly. "Not 'feeling myself.' And then—it'll take some telling . . . "

"Tell me the story."

Roman brightened. "Now *that* I enjoy. I've got half a dozen notebooks filled with my stories. But this one is true. Very well: It was a fine Indian summer afternoon. I was in the mood to be alone—this woman who insists she's my mother, even then she often put me in that mood—so I went out to Napatree Point. Big sandy spit of land, you know. The sea looked blue, fluffy clouds scudding in the sky, a real postcard picture. Just me and the gulls. Now, I don't much care for walks on the beach. Rather dislike looking at the unidentifiable things that wash up there. And the smell of the sea—like the smell of some giant animal. I'd rather go to the library. But I keep hearing people talk about how *inspirational* the sea is. I keep looking to *connect* with that Big Something out there. So I was walking on the beach, trying to shake the odd feeling of inner dislocation—I *did* manage to appreciate the way the light comes through the top of the waves and makes them look like blue glass. I shaded my eyes and gazed way out to sea, trying to see all the way to the horizon—and I got this strange feeling that something was *looking back* at me from out there."

Fyodor repressed a smile, and typed, *Enjoys dramatization.*

"All of a sudden I felt like a giddy little kid. Then I had a strange impulse—it just charged up out of my depths. I felt it go right up my spine and into my head, and I was yelling, 'Hey out there!'" Roman cupped his hands to either side of his mouth, mimicking it. "'Hey! I'm here!' I don't know, I guess I was just being spontaneous, but I felt truly very impish . . . "

Fyodor typed: *Odd diction, archaic vocabulary at times. It comes and goes. Possibly clinically labile? Showing agitation as he tells the story.*

" . . . and I yelled 'I'm here, come back!' and it's funny how my own voice was echoing in my ears and a *response* just came into my head from nowhere: *They tolled—but from the sunless tides that pour* . . . And I yelled that phrase out loud! I'm not sure why. But I'll never forget it."

Auditory hallucination, Fyodor typed. *Feelings of compulsion.*

Roman squirmed in his chair, licked his lips, went on. "It was a curious little thing to think—like an unfinished line of poetry, right?"

Use of antiquated expressions comes and goes: e.g., curious. Affectation?

"And as soon as I said it I heard gigantic big bells ringing, like the biggest church bells you ever heard—and it sounded like they were coming from under the sea! A little muffled, and watery, but still powerful. It got louder and louder, the sound was so loud, it hurt my head, like I was getting slapped with each clang of the bell, and each time it rang it was as if the sea, the stretch of the sea in front of me, got a little darker, and pretty soon it *just went black*—the whole sea had turned black . . . "

Hallucinogenic episodes, possible seizure—drug use?—

" . . . And no, I don't use drugs, doctor! I can see you thinking it!" He smiled nervously, straightening his tie. "Never have got into drugs! Oh fine, a few puffs on a bong once or twice—barely felt it."

Fyodor cleared his throat—strangely congested, it was difficult to speak at first—and asked, "This vision of the sea turning black—did you fall down during it? Lose control of your limbs?"

"No! Well . . . I didn't *fall*." Roman licked his lips, sitting up straight, animated with excitement. "It was as if I was *paralyzed* by what I was seeing. The blackness sucking up the ocean was holding me fast, you see. But it was really not so much that the sea was turning black—it was that the sea was *gone*, and it was replaced by a . . . a night sky! A dark sky full of stars! I was looking down into the sea, but in some other way I was gazing *up* into this night sky! My stomach flip-flopped, I can tell you! I saw constellations you never heard of, twinkling in the sea—galaxies in the sea!—and one big yellow star caught my eye. It seemed to grow bigger, and bigger, and it got closer—till it filled up my vision. Then, silhouetted on it, was this black ball . . . a planet! I rushed closer to it—I could see down into its atmosphere. I saw warped buildings, you could hardly believe they were able to stand up, they seemed so crooked, and cracked domes, and pale things without faces flying over them—and I thought, that is the world called . . . " He shook his head, lips twisted. "Something like . . . *Yegget?* Only not that. I can't remember the name precisely." Roman shrugged, spread his hands, and then laughed. "I know how it sounds. Anyway—I was gazing at this planet from above and I heard this . . . this *sizzling* sound. Then there was a flash of light—and I was back on the beach. I felt a little dizzy, sat down for awhile, kept trying to remember how I'd gotten to that beach. Could not remember, not then. The memory of what I'd seen in the sea, the black sky—*that* was vivid. And what was before that? Arriving at the beach. Notions of escaping from some bothersome person."

"Nothing before then?"

"An image. A place: I was lying in a small bed, in a white room, with this sweet little nurse holding my hand. Remembering it, I had a yearning, a *longing* for that bed, that nurse—that white room. For the comfort of it. I could almost hear her speak.

"Then, on the beach, I felt this scary buzzing in my pocket! I thought I had a snake in there, and I was clawing at it, and then . . . something fell out. This shiny, silvery, little machine fell onto the ground. It was buzzing and shaking in the sand like it was mad. I could see it was some kind of instrument—a device. It seemed strange and familiar, both at the same time, right? So I had to think about how to make it work and I opened it and I heard this tiny voice saying, 'Roman, Roman are you there?' It was the . . . it was my mother." He stared into the distance. His voice trailed off. "My mother."

"But you didn't recognize the thing as a cell phone?"

"After she spoke, I remembered—but it was like something from a science-fiction movie I'd seen. *Star Trek*. I couldn't recall buying the thing."

Fyodor made a few notes and nodded. "And since then—the persistent long-term memory issues, your own name seeming unfamiliar. And you had feelings of restlessness?"

"Restlessness. An inner . . . goading." Roman settled back in the chair, staring up at the antique light fixture. "I would have trouble sleeping. I'd go out before dawn for these long rambles . . . in the old section of Providence— with its mellow, ancient life, the skyline of old roofs, Georgian steeples . . . "

Archaic affectations cropping up more frequently as patient reminisces.

"You said you felt like you were looking for something—?"

"Correct. And I didn't know what. Just this feeling of 'It's right around the next corner, or maybe around the next one' and so on. Till one day—I was there! I was standing in front of this house, looking at your sign. It was closed—I took a cab to a Target store, just opening for the day. I bought a little crowbar. Went back to the house—the rest is history. I still don't know exactly what it is about this house. You just bought the place, right? How'd you find it, doc?"

"Oh, my mother suggested it to me, actually. She was in real estate before she . . . " Fyodor broke off. Not good to talk about personal matters with a patient. "So—anything else? We're about out of time."

"Your mother! She was *committed*, right?" Roman grinned mischievously. "The inspiration for your career! And you an only child, too, like me—imagine that!"

Fyodor felt a chill. "Uh—exactly how—"

"Don't get spooked, doc," Roman chuckled. "It's the Internet. I googled you! The paper you wrote for the Rhode Island Psychiatric Association—it's online. Tough childhood with sick mother led you to want to understand mental illness . . . "

Fyodor kept his expression blank. It annoyed him when a patient tried to turn the tables on him. "Okay. Well. Let's digest all this." He saved his notes and closed his laptop.

"No therapeutic advice for me, Doctor Cheski?"

"Yes. Something behavioral. Don't commit any more burglaries."

Roman came out with a harsh laugh at that.

Roman Boxer went home with the woman he doubted was his mother. Fyodor watched through a window as they got into her shiny black Lincoln.

An unstable young man. Perhaps a dangerous young man—researching his doctor's background, breaking into his office . . . twice. He should not be seen here.

Roman refused to be committed. *"I won't take those horrible psychiatric meds. I don't wish to be a zombie. I'll just run off, end up back here again. This is the place. It took me a long time, wandering around Providence, to find it. I know, Mom says I never lived here. But I was happy here once. I have to get help right here . . . "*

Roman and his mother were both amenable to the use of SEQ10, to search out the core trauma, since it was something the patient only took on a temporary basis, with the doctor in the room. There were forms to be filled out, approval from the APA. Fyodor went to his office, feeling restless himself. He wished he'd tucked a bottle of brandy away in the house. But he was trying to keep his drinking down to a dull roar. Too bad the wine in the basement was off. Be crazy to drink the stuff anyway.

He puttered at his desk, organizing his computer files, sending out e-mails to colleagues who might want to rent office space. Making the occasional note on Roman Boxer. The late November wind hissed outside; the windows rattled, the furnace vents rumbled and oozed warm air. He wished he'd asked Leah to work late. The big old house felt so empty it seemed to mutter to itself every time the wind hit it.

About 9:30, Fyodor's cell phone vibrated in his pants pocket, making him jump.

Fyodor reached into his jacket and fumbled the phone out—his hands seemed clumsy tonight. "Hello?"

"You forgot me . . . " It was his mother's smoky voice—a bad connection, other voices oscillating in and out of a sea of static in the background.

"Mom. How did I . . . ? Oh. It's that night?" It was his mother's night to call him. She must have called his home first.

"You bought the house . . . "

"Yes—thanks for the tip. I sent you a note about it. You've got a good memory. So long ago you were selling houses. I'm hoping if I can rent out the other rooms as offices it'll more than pay for the mortgage. . . .You still there? This connection . . . "

"I was born . . . " Her voice was lost in the crackle. " . . . 1935."

"Right, I remember you were born in 1935—"

"In that house. I was Catholic. Lived there till I got married. Your father was Russian Orthodox. Father Dunn did not approve. Father Dunn died that year . . . " Her voice sounded flat.

But it was difficult to make out at all.

He frowned. "Wait—you were born in *this* house? I'm sure you showed me a house you were born in—it was in Providence, but . . . it was an old wreck of a place. I don't recall where I was a kid. . . . But then the agent said they restored it . . . " Could this really be that house?

" . . . *Through sunken valleys on the sea's dead floor*," she said, as the wind howled at the window.

"What?"

The phone on his desk rang. He jumped a little in his seat and said, "Wait, Mom . . . "

He put the cell phone down, answered the desk phone. "Dr. Cheski."

"Fyodor? You weren't at home . . . here you are!" It was his mother. Coming in quite clearly. On this line. "You need to talk to that psycho Psych Tech, he's following me around the ward."

Sleet rattled the window glass. "Mom . . . You playing games with their phones there? You get hold of a cell phone? You're not supposed to have one."

On impulse he picked up the other phone. "Hello?"

"*They tolled but from sunless tides . . . *" Then it was lost in static—but it did sound like his mother's voice, in a kind of dead monotone.

Monotone—and now a dial tone. She'd hung up.

He put the cell phone slowly down, picked up the other line. "What, Mom, have you got a phone pressed to each ear?"

"You sound more like a patient than a psychiatrist, Fyodor. I'm trying to tell you that the 'Psycho' Tech who claims he works here is . . . What?" She was speaking to someone in the room with her now. "The doctor said I could call my son . . . I did call earlier; he wasn't at home . . . " A male voice in the background. Then a man came on the line, a deep voice. "Is that Dr. Cheski? I'm sorry, doctor, she's not supposed to use the phone after eight. I could ask the night nurse—"

"No, no, that's all right—does she have a cell phone too? It seemed like she was calling me on two lines."

"What? No, she shouldn't have one. . . . Oh, there she goes, I have to deal with this, doctor. But don't worry, it's no big problem, just her evening rant, yelling at Norman . . . "

"Sure, go ahead."

He hung up. Picked up the cell phone. Put it to his ear. Nothing there. He checked to see what number had called him last. The last call was from Leah, two days before.

Next morning, a cold but sunny winter day, Fyodor dropped by the ward, at the facility across town. A bored supervisory nurse waved him right in. "She's in the activities room."

His mom wore an old Hawaiian-pattern shift and red plastic sandals, her thin white hair up in blue curlers; her spotted hands trembled, but they always did, and she seemed happy enough, playing cards with an elderly black woman. Someone on a television soap opera muttered vague threats in the background.

"Mother, that house you suggested to Aunt Vera for me—did you say you were born there?"

Mom barely looked up when he spoke to her. "Born there? I was. I didn't say so, but I was. Don't cheat, Maisy. You *know* you cheat, girl. I never do."

"Did you call me twice last night, Mom? Talk to me twice, I mean?"

"Twice? No, I—but there was something funny with the phone, I remember. Like it was echoing what I said, getting it all mixed up. Hearts, Maisy!"

"You remember reciting poetry on the phone? Something about tides?"

"I haven't recited poetry since that time at Jimmy Dolan's. Your Dad got mad at me because I climbed up on the bar and recited Anais Nin. . . .What are you laughing at, Maisy, you never got up on a bar? I bet you did too. Just deal the cards."

He asked how things were going. She shrugged. For once she didn't complain about Norman the Psych Tech. She seemed annoyed he'd interrupted her card game.

He patted her shoulder and left, thinking he must have misheard something on the cell phone. Perhaps some kind of sales recording.

Suggestion. The lonely house, the odd story from Roman.

Auditory hallucination?

It wasn't likely he'd be bipolar like his mother—he was thirty-five, he'd have had symptoms long before now. He was fairly normal. Yes, he had a little phobia of cats, nothing serious . . .

He got back to the office a few minutes late for his first patient. He had six patients scheduled that day; four neurotics, one depressive, and a compulsive finger biter. He listened and advised and prescribed.

A few days later—after Roman signed numerous wavers—Fyodor was sitting beside Roman's bed, in the guest room, with its repaired lock, waiting for the drug to take hold of his patient.

Roman was lying on the coverlet, eyes closed, though he was awake. He looked quite relaxed. He wore a T-shirt and creased trousers, his blazer and tie and Arrow shirt folded neatly over a chair nearby, the shiny black shoes squared under it. His arms were crossed over his chest; his mother had provided the warm slippers on his feet. There was a small bandage on his right arm, where he'd been injected. The furnace was working full-bore, at Roman's request, and the room was too warm for Fyodor's liking.

On a cart to one side was the tape recorder for the session, a used syringe, and the little tray with the prepared syringes for adverse reactions. Superfluous caution.

Leah entered softly, caught Fyodor's eye, and nodded toward downstairs, silently mouthing, "His Mother?"

Fyodor shook his head decisively. No monitoring mothers. Roman was of age.

"I do feel a pleasant . . . oddness," Roman murmured, his eyes fluttering as Leah left the room.

"Good," Fyodor said. "Just relax into that. Let it wash over you." He switched on the tape recorder, aimed the microphone.

"I feel . . . sort of thirsty." His eyes closed; his hands dropped loose, occasionally twitching, at his sides.

"That will pass. . . . Roman, let's go back to that experience by the ocean, a little over a year ago. You said after that, you were remembering a white room, with a nurse. Could we talk about that again?"

"I . . . "

"Take your time."

" . . . She holds my hand. That's what I remember about her. The soft pressure of her hand. Trouble breathing—a pressure, a pushing inside me, crowding my lungs. And then—*my very last breath!* I remember thinking, *Is this indeed my last breath?* Gods, the pain in my belly is returning, the morphine is wearing off. . . . They say it's intestinal cancer, but I wonder. Perhaps I should try to tell the nurse about the heightened pain. She's sweet, she won't think me a whiner. The others here are more formal, but she calls me Howard. I feel closer to her than I ever did to Sonia . . . my own little Jewish wife, ha ha, to think I married a Jewess, and my closest friend, for a time, before he got the religion bug, was Dear Old Dunn, a Mick. . . . I want to raise the nurse's hand to my lips, to thank her for staying with me. But I can't feel her hand anymore. I'm floating over her. . . . There's a voice, an inhuman guttural voice, calling me from above the ceiling— above the roof. Above the sky. *I must ignore it.* I must go away from there, to find something, something to anchor me safely in this world. . . . I want to tell my friends I am all right. . . . I drifted,

drifted, found myself in front of Dunn's house. . . . There is a cat, heavy with pregnancy, curled up under the big elm tree. I love cats. Feel drawn to her. That calling comes again, from the deep end of the sky. I need to anchor. *The cat.* I fall . . . fall into her. The warm darkness . . . then sounds, the scent of her milk and her soft belly . . . light! . . . and I remember exploring. I was exploring the yard . . . the big tree, overshadowing me, days pass, and I grow . . . the sweet mice scurrying to escape me . . . "

Fyodor had to lean close to hear him.

"Oh! The mice taste sweeter when they almost escape! And the birds—they seem happy to die under my claws. Their eyes, like gems . . . the light goes out . . . the gems fall into eternity . . .mingle with stars. . . . I can scarcely think—but my body is my thought as I patrol the night. I pour myself through the shadows. The other cats—I avoid them, most of the time. If I feel the urge to mate, I go into the house . . . this house! . . . through the back door . . . the girl lets me in . . . I know what a girl is, what people are, I remember that much. I know there is food and comfort there. I rub against the girl's legs, climb onto her lap. I will let my embers smolder here. She admires my golden eyes. The girl tells her mother, and Father Dunn, who has come to visit, that the cat understands everything she says. When she says follow, the cat follows. She tells them, 'I think it understands me right now! It is not like other cats . . . ' "

Fyodor shook his head. This was not going as planned. Roman should be incapable of fantasizing under the influence of this drug; the formula was related to sodium pentothal, but more definitive; it had a tendency to expose onion-layers of memories, real memories . . . but a memory of being a cat? Was Roman remembering a childhood incident in which he'd imagined being a cat?

"How . . . " Fascinated, Fyodor cleared his throat, aware his heart was thudding. "How far back do you remember . . . before the white room—and before the cat?"

Roman moaned softly. "How far . . . how deep . . . the nightgaunts. I have come to this house to see Dunn. Of all my friends in the Providence Amateur Press Club, he was the one I trusted the most. Curious, my trusting a Mick—I sometimes sneer at the Irish in the North End, but even so, I love to work with dear old Dunn on his little printing press, in the basement of that magnificently musty old house. I am even tempted to take him up on the wine his father kept in that hidey-hole down there. But I never do. Dunn loves to cadge a little wine from his father's bottles. Makes up the difference in grape juice. The old Irish rogue conceals the bottles from his wife, she doesn't like him drinking . . . wine from Italy, a local Italian priest got for him . . . dear old Dunn! I even ghostwrote a little speech he made . . . ghostwriter, wondrous and most whimsical to think of that term, considering how long I wandered, here, from house to house in Providence, afraid of the

Great Deep that yawned above me when I breathed my last. Gone. Did anyone notice?" He made a soft rasping moan. "What will people remember of me? If anything they'll remember the intellectual sins of my youth. But why *should* people remember me? I'm sure they won't. . . . If I could tell them what I saw that day, on my trip to Florida! Getting out of the bus, on the South Carolina coast, an interval in the bus trip . . .my last real trip, in 1935 it was . . . driver told us the bus would be delayed more than an hour . . . there's time to visit the lighthouse on the point near the station. Determined to get to know the ocean. Wanting to go against my own grain. But you can't grow the same tree twice. Yet I writhe about, trying to change the pattern. I will go to sea, until I make peace with its restless depths. Despite what I told Wandrei—or because of it. I'll show them I'm more than the polysyllabic phobic they think me. Found the lighthouse—tumbledown old structure, seems to have been fenced off . . . a broken spire . . . what a shame . . . there's been a storm, I can see the wrack from the sea mingled with its ruins . . . the breakers have shattered the lower, seaward wall of the lighthouse . . . there, is that a hollow beneath it? I clamber over fence, over slimed stones, drawn by the mystery, the possibility of revealed antiquity. Perhaps the lighthouse was built on some old colonial structure . . . Look here, a hollow, a cobwebbed chamber, and within it a sullen pool of black water—its opacity broken by a coruscation of yellow. What could be glowing, sulfurous yellow, within the water of a pool hidden beneath a lighthouse? It's as if the lighthouse had one light atop and a diabolic inverse sequestered beneath. There, I stare into it and I see . . . something I've glimpsed only in dreams! The tortured spires, the cracked domes, the flyers without faces. . . . I'm teetering into it . . . I'm falling—swallowing saltwater. Something writhes in the water as I swallow it. An eel? An eel without a physical body. Yet it nestles within me, biding, whispering . . .

"Darkness. Walking . . .

"Back on the bus, looking fuzzily about me. How did I make my way back to the bus? Cannot remember. The driver solicitous, asking, 'You sure you're all right, sir? You're wet clear through.' I insist I'm well enough. I take a few minutes to change my clothes in the station restroom. The other passengers are exasperated with me, I'm delaying them even further. I feel quite odd as I return to the bus. Must have struck my head, exploring that old lighthouse. Had a dream, a nightmare—can't quite remember what it was . . . dream of something crawling into my mouth, worming through my stomach, down to my intestines . . . something without a body as we know them. . . . Quite exhausted. I fall asleep in my seat on the bus and when I wake, we're in northern Florida."

Fyodor glanced at the tape recorder to make sure it was going. Had he administered the drug wrongly? This could not be a memory—Roman could not possibly remember 1935. Still, it was surely a doorway into Roman's unconscious mind. A powerful mind—a writer's mind, perhaps. A narrative within a narrative, not always linear; a nautilus shell recession of narrative . . .

Eyes shut, lids jittering, Roman licked his lips and went hoarsely on. " . . . trip to Cuba canceled but still—Florida! Saw alligators in the sluggish green river— seemed to glimpse a slitted green eye and within that eye a sulfurous light shining from some black sky. . . .A great many letters to write on the bus back, handwriting can scarcely be legible . . . oh, the pain. In the midst of my midst, how it chews away. Cursed as always with ill health. Getting my strength in recent years, discovering the healing power of the sun, and then this—the old flaw chews at me from within now. I fear seeing the doctor. Nor can I afford him. Little but tea and crackers to eat today . . . can't bear much more anyway, the pain in my gut . . . I seem to be losing weight . . . R. E. H. is dead! Strange to think of 'Two-Gun Bob' taking his own life that way. He should have been a swordsman, striking the life from the faceless flyers when they struck at him in some dire temple—not muttering about his Texas neighbors, not stabbed through the soul by his mother's passing. We should not be what we are—we were all intended to be something better. But we were planted in tainted soil, R. E. H. and I, tainted souls blemished by the color out of space. I wrote from my heart but my heart was sheathed in dark yellow glass, and its light was sulfurous. So much more I wanted to write! A great novel of generations of Providence families, their struggles and glories, their dark secrets and heroics! I can be with them, perhaps, when I die—I will become one with the old houses of Providence, wandering, searching for its secrets. . . . And I refuse to leave Providence, when I gasp my last. . . .

"The sweet little nurse takes my hand, more tenderly than ever Sonia did. But God bless Sonia, and her infinite patience. If only . . . but it's too late to think of that now. The nurse is speaking to me, *Howard, can you hear me? . . . I believe we've lost him, doctor. Pity—such a gentlemanly fellow, and scarcely older than . . .* I can't hear the rest: I'm floating above them, amazed at how emaciated my lifeless body is; my lips skinned back, my great jutting jaw, my pallid fingers. I'm glad to be free of that body. There's no pain here! But something calls me from the darkness above. Is the light of Heaven up above? I know better. I know about the opaque gulfs; the *deep end* of the sky. The Hungry Deep. *I will not go!* I will go see Dunn! Yes, dear old Dunn. Something so comforting about the company of my fellow Amateur Pressmen. I'll find my way to Dunn's house . . . Here, and here . . . I flit from house to house . . . is it years that pass? It is—and it doesn't matter. I drift like a fallen leaf along the stream of time, waft through the streets of Providence. How the seasons wheel by! The yellowing leaves, the drifting snow, the thaw, the tulips . . . I see other ghosts. Some try to speak, but I hear them not . . . There—Dunn's house! I'll see if he's still within. But no. Father Dunn has moved on. There is the little Irish girl, adopted by the Dunns. And the cat, her cat, fairly bursting with kittens. Oh, to be a cat. And why not? The mice . . . sweeter when they run . . . I speak to the girl . . . she shouts in fear and throws something at me. She chases me from the house!

"What's that? One of the great metal hurtlers in the street! Truck's wheel strikes me, wrings me out like a wet rag . . . Agony sears . . . I float above the truck, seeing my body quivering in death, below me: the body of the cat. But I am at peace, once more, drifting through Providence. Let me wander, as I did once before . . . let me wander and wait. Perhaps next time I'll find something more suitable. Someone. A pair of hands that can fashion dreams . . .

"The Great Deep calls to me, over and over. I won't go! My ancient soul has strength, more strength than my body ever had. It resists. I remember, now, what I saw in the ruins of that old lighthouse—under its foundations: the secret pool, the shamanic pool of the Narragansett Indians. A fragment of a great translucent yellow stone was hidden there—a piece of a larger stone lost now beneath the waves, once the centerpiece of a temple in the land some called Atlantis.

"The cat-eye stone struck from Yuggoth by the crash of a comet—whirling to our world, where it spoke to the minds of the first true men; gave the ancients a sickening knowledge of their minuteness, the vast darkness of the universe.

"It has been whispering to me since I was a child—my mother heard it, she glimpsed its evocations: the faceless things that crawled from it just around the corner of the house. She'd tell me all about them, my dear half-mad mother Sarah. She had visited that place, and heard its whispering. And that seemed to plant the seed in me—which grew into the twisted tree of my tales . . .

"I drift above the elm-hugged street, refusing to depart my beloved Providence. But the call of the Great Deep is so strong. Insistent. I hear it especially loudly when I visit Swan Point Cemetery. No longer summoning—now it is demanding.

"There is only one way free, this time—I must hide within someone . . . I must find a place to nestle, as I did with the cat. . . .Here's a woman. Mrs. Boxer is with child. I feel the heartbeat, pattering rapidly within her—calling to me . . . I go to sleep within her, united with him, the *tabula* rasa . . .

"I wake on the beach, full-grown. I cannot quite speak. I cannot control my body. It moves frantically about, speaking into a little invention, from which issues a voice. 'Why, what do you mean?' says the voice. 'This is your mother, for heaven's sake! Whatever are you about, Roman?' If only I could speak and tell her my name. A voice comes from my mouth—but it is not my voice, not truly. I want to tell her my name. I cannot . . . My name . . . "

Fyodor leaned closer yet. The next words were whispered, hardly audible. " . . . is Howard. Howard Philips. Howard Philips Lovecraft . . . "

Then Roman was asleep. That was the natural course of the drug's effects. There was no waking him, now, not safely, to ask questions.

Stunned, Fyodor sat beside Roman, staring at the peacefully sleeping young man. Seeing his eyelids flickering with REM sleep. What was he dreaming of?

Fyodor had grown up in Providence. Everyone here had heard Lovecraft's name. Young Fyodor Cheski had his own Lovecraft period. But his mother had found the books—he was only thirteen—and she'd taken them away, very sternly, and threatened that he would lose every privilege he could even imagine if he read them again. She *knew* about this Lovecraft, she said. Things whispered to him—things people shouldn't listen to.

It was one of his mother's fits of paranoia, of course, but after that Fyodor was taken with a more modern set of writers, Bradbury and then Salinger—and a veer into Robertson Davies. Never gave Lovecraft another thought. Not a conscious thought, anyway.

His mother, in her manic periods, would babble about a cat she'd had as a small girl, a cat that used to talk to her; she'd look into its eyes, and she'd hear it speaking in her mind, hissing of other worlds—dark worlds. And one day she could bear it no more, and she'd driven the cat into the street, where it was hit by a passing truck. She feared its soul had haunted her, ever since; and she feared it would haunt Fyodor.

A chill went through Fyodor as he realized he had fallen entirely under the spell of Roman's convoluted narrative. He had almost believed that this man was the reincarnation of the writer who'd died in 1937. Perhaps he did have a little of his mother's . . . susceptibility.

He shuddered. God, he needed a drink.

He thought of the wine in the basement. It was still there. Hal said it was vinegar, but he hadn't tested the other bottles. Fyodor had a powerful impulse to try one out. Perhaps he'd see something down there that would spark some insight into Roman.

His patient was sleeping peacefully. Why not?

He went downstairs, to find that Roman's mother, anxious, had gone to see her sister. Leah was yawning at her desk.

He looked at her, thinking he really should take her out, once, see what happened. She's not dating anyone, as far as he knew.

He almost asked her then and there. But he simply nodded and said, "I'll take care of things here. He's sleeping . . . he'll stay the night. You can go home."

He watched her leave, and then turned to the basement door, remembering the agent had mentioned the house had belonged to the Dunn family for generations. Doubtless Roman had found out about the house's background, somehow, woven it into his fantasies. Probably he was a Lovecraft fan.

Fyodor found the switch at the top of the steps, switched on the light and descended to the basement. Really, that bulb was too bright for the basement space. It hurt his eyes. Ugly yellow light bulb.

He crossed to the corner where he'd replaced the cap over the hole in the floor. The crowbar was still there. He pried up the cover of cement and wood— took more effort than he'd supposed.

But there were the bottles. How was he to open them?

Why not be a little daring, opening the bottle as they did in stories? He pulled a bottle out and struck the neck on the wall; it broke neatly off. Wine splashed red as blood against the gray concrete.

He sniffed at the bottle. The smell wasn't vinegary, anyway. The aroma—the wine's bouquet—was almost a perfume.

The bottle neck had broken evenly. No risk in having a quick swig. He sat on one of the crates, put the bottle to his lips, and tasted, expecting to gag and spit out the small sip . . .

But it was delicious. Apparently this one had been sealed better than the one his friend Hal had looked at. Strange to think it had been here undisturbed all those years—even when his mother had lived here. Only once had she mentioned the name of the people who'd adopted her. The Dunn family.

He wanted badly to sit here awhile and drink the wine. Quite out of character—he was more the kind to have a little carefully selected Pinot in an upscale wine bar. But here he was . . .

Strange to be down here, drinking from a broken wine bottle, in the concrete and dust.

It's not like me. It's as if I'm still under the spell, the influence, of Roman's ramblings. It's as if something brought me here. Something is urging me to lift the bottle to my lips . . . to drink deeply . . .

Why not? One drink more. If he was going to ask Leah out he'd need to be more spontaneous. He could call her up, tell her the wine was better than they'd supposed. Might be worth something. Ask her to come and try some . . .

He licked his lips—and drank. The wine was delicious; a deep taste, and unusual. Like a tragic song. He laughed to himself. He drank again. What was it Roman had said?

I never used to drink. I wanted to take it up, starting with something old and fine. I want a new life. I desire to do things differently. Live!

Fyodor drank again . . . and looked up at the light bulb. He blinked in its fierce sulfurous glare, its assaultive parhelion. It seemed almost part of an eye, a glowing yellow eye, looking at him from some farther place . . .

He stood up suddenly, shaking himself, his twitching hands dropping the bottle—it shattered on the concrete with a gigantic sound that seemed to resound on and on, echoing . . . and in the echo was a voice. His mother's voice . . . the part of her mind that had spoken to him through the sea of static. This time it said something else: *We need souls. We have few left in our world. Come to us, across the Great Deeps. Restore our world. Become one with us.*

The room, which should be dull gray, seemed to quiver in ugly colors. He turned and staggered to the stairs. His head buzzed. Then he looked up to see that Roman Boxer was standing at the head of the stairs. "Doctor? Are you well? You are Doctor Cheski, are you not? I believe that was the name . . . "

Fyodor started wobblingly up the stairs. Alcohol level must have gotten very high in the wine. Seeing things. Unable to climb damn basement stairs very well . . .

He got to the third step from the top—and Roman put out his hand to him. "Here—take my hand. You look a trifle unsteady."

But Fyodor held back, afraid to touch Roman and not sure why. "You . . . should be asleep."

"Yes, well—I simply woke up. And everything was fine! Whatever you gave me helped me enormously. The pain in my stomach is gone! I was surprised to be no longer in the hospital . . . Yes. Thought I was a goner. Kind of you to bring me home—if that's what this place is. That nurse—is she here?"

"The nurse? What . . . " Fyodor licked his lips. "What is your name?"

"You really *have* overindulged, my friend. I am your patient, Howard

Lovecraft . . . " Roman smiled widely and once more reached for him. Fyodor jerked back, irrationally afraid of that hand. *The hand of a dead man.*

And Fyodor tipped backwards, flailed, tumbled down the stairs. He heard a sickening crunch . . .

Darkness entered through the crack in his skull. It swept him up, carried him away . . .

He drifted through the darkness—orbiting a far world. Beginning to sink toward that cloud-clotted planet . . .

No. He refused to go.

"In time, you will come. We traded him for you . . . "

Fyodor struggled, psychically writhing, to get back. A long ways back, and an endless time somehow folded within a few minutes . . . Then he was crawling across the basement floor. Someone was helping him up. Roman . . . was that his name?

The young man, quite solicitous, helped him up the stairs to the front hall—and then Leah stepped in the door. "Oh my God! Fyodor! Roman, what happened! Have you hurt him? He's got blood on his head! I knew something was wrong! I was sure of it! Never mind, just sit down, Fyodor, I'll call an ambulance . . . and the police."

How the seasons wheel by. Spring, summer, fall, winter; spring, summer, fall; a year and another . . . And then an early summer day . . . the roses were pretty, quite new, not yet chewed by the fungus. . . .Mom drooped in her chair, across from him, eyes completely hidden in sunglasses. She would want to play cards when she woke up. He preferred the puzzle.

"Fyodor?" It was Leah, speaking from the back door. Smiling. Dressed up rather formally. "We're going out. To the book signing."

"Hm?" Fyodor looked up from his Old Providence jigsaw puzzle. Mother had been grumpily helping him put the puzzle together on the card table, in the late summer sunshine; the rose garden behind the Dunn house. But Mom had gone to sleep, a jigsaw piece in her hand, slumped in her chair. She looked contented, snoring away there.

Roman was so good to take care of her—to care for them both here.

"I said, we're going to Roman's signing—for his book? You sure you won't come? The man from the *New York Times* is going to interview him."

"Is he? That's good. Big crowd?"

"Oh, yes. It looks to be a bestseller. I know you don't like crowds."

"No. Crowds and cats . . . "

He had heard Roman's agent, a pretty blond lady, chattering away over breakfast. "They're framing it as *Roman Theobald, the man Lovecraft might have become . . .* " Then she'd turned to him. "How are you this morning, Fyodor? Would you like some more orange juice?"

Very kind of her. Everyone was very kind to him, since the accident. Since the damage to his head.

Leah had married "Roman Theobald"—that was his pen name. Roman Boxer was his real name. Anyway—the name on his birth certificate. Sometimes, in the house, she used a funny little affectionate name for him. "Howard." Odd choice. Anyway, she was Mrs. Roman Boxer now. She was almost ten years too old for Roman, but Mrs. Boxer had approved. She'd bought the Dunn house as a wedding gift for them. Mrs. Boxer had died, soon after the wedding, of cancer. Buried at Swan Point Cemetery.

Fyodor felt good, thinking about it. Maybe it was the Prozac. But still—it was true, everyone *was* very kind. Roman, Leah, the doctors. And Leah made sure he took his pills in the evening. He really couldn't sleep without them. Particularly the pills against nightmares. He was quite sure that if he dreamed of that place again—the place the bells in the sea spoke of—he would not wake up the next morning. He might never wake up again. And Mother, then, poor old Mumsy, would be all alone. Until they came for her too.

John Shirley is the author of more than thirty novels. His numerous short stories have been compiled into eight collections including *Black Butterflies: A Flock on the Darkside*, winner of the Bram Stoker Award, International Horror Guild Award, and named as one of the best one hundred books of the year by *Publishers Weekly*. He has written scripts for television and film, and is best known as co-writer of *The Crow*. As a musician, Shirley has fronted several bands over the years and written lyrics for Blue Öyster Cult and others. To learn more about John Shirley and his work, please visit his website at john-shirley.com.

Something seemed vaguely odd to her about the meadow
between her grandmother's house and the river . . .

DAHLIAS

Melanie Tem

In Rosemary Farber's dream or waking dream or hallucination or vision, that sunny July afternoon on the couch in the house she'd lived in since her marriage just after the Second World War, on the dead-end street in the little town near the foothills of the Colorado Rockies that had officially slid into suburbia but retained much of its insular small-houses-and-big- trees feel—something was coming. She was no more or less its object or prey than were the rabbit brush or the fox, but it would get her, which she thought not entirely a bad thing.

In Nina Scherer's multi-tasking rush—on her cell setting up an appointment with a client for later that afternoon, juggling the red and yellow dinner-plate dahlias from her yard and the chicken casserole and chocolate chip cookies she'd stayed up late last night getting ready to bring today, checking her Daytimer for when and where she needed to have her son at band and her daughter at karate, trying to remember if there was enough milk at home for breakfast—in the midst of all this getting-through-the-day and keeping-things-running, something seemed vaguely odd to her about the meadow between her grandmother's house and the river. Something out of the corner of her eye about the tall summer grass, about its color or its motion in the breeze. This impression didn't really register with her until she was already on the porch, and it was too much hassle to back out and look again.

When Nina called and pushed open the door, Grandma Rose- mary was under an afghan on the couch. She spent most of her time there now, looking tired and ninety-one years old but not alarmed, not in pain, not otherwise distressed. In fact, looking calmer than Nina herself ever felt.

"Hi, Grandma." Nina set the dahlias on the coffee table and the food on the counter. She bent to kiss the old woman, so dear to her for so long, still Grandma Rosemary but going away from her a little every day, as if pulled down some slope into a place or a placelessness where Nina couldn't follow, wouldn't want to follow, would never want to follow. Although a little rest would be nice.

Rosemary turned her head. "Those are lovely."

"It's been so dry. Our water bills are sky-high, and the garden is still struggling."

"They're so big and bright."

"They grew that way just for you." Nina smiled past a sudden lump in her throat.

"Well, not really. We're in the same world at the same time, is all, the dahlias and me. Nothing personal. I expect I'm a lot more interested in them than they are in me." She chuckled.

Nina's phone vibrated and Caller ID displayed a name of someone who, she decided rather grudgingly, could wait. In the seconds it took for the call to go to voicemail, the worry that not answering it had been a big mistake lodged in her mind where it would cause persistent low-level distress, for in her business there was a commonplace though inaccurate adage that a missed call equaled missed opportunity. In fact the call, and the follow-up text message and e-mail she wouldn't find until much later, were about something that really didn't matter very much, though the client was convinced it did.

One of the cats glided from the couch onto the table and, with that lovely and utterly inhuman pink-tongue flickering, lapped delicately from the water in the vase. Hoping nothing in dahlias was toxic to cats, Nina inquired of her grandmother as she put her cell phone away, "How are you?"

Rosemary said, "Something's moving in and it will take me. I don't have much longer."

When Rosemary was like this, being in a hurry didn't work. But Nina had only about forty-five minutes, fifty at the most, before she had to be back at the office for the team meeting. She knew she'd regret it if she missed this conversation. Really, it was the least she could do, and Grandma Rosemary had always been fun to listen to, with her family stories from as far back as the Civil War, her on-the-spot composition of rhymed and free verse, the sense that she was always engaged with more than one world at a time. Childhood summers spent in this house had affected Nina in ways she wasn't completely aware of, showing her— though she hadn't learned it very well—how not to take herself too seriously in the larger scheme of things and, at the same time, fostering her m.o. of staying busy, filling time to overflowing, by sheer perpetual motion declaring her own significance.

She should have paid attention to Rosemary that afternoon, borne witness and learned something. It wouldn't have made any difference in what happened, but still she should have listened. Instead, "Oh, Grandma," she remonstrated, smoothing her palm across the thin white hair, "don't talk like that."

Rosemary smiled indulgently. "All right, then, what shall we talk about? What's new with you?"

The rocker tipped forward and stayed that way when Nina sat on the edge of the seat. She never knew quite what to say to that question. "Nothing much new, I guess. Same old, same old. You know?"

"How are the children? How's Ken?"

"Good. They're all good. Busy."

"Give them my love."

"I will. They said to say hi." They hadn't, but she told herself they would have if they'd thought of it, which actually wasn't likely.

Anything beyond small talk ran the risk of a longer and deeper conversation than either of them wanted that day. Yet they were both restless, dissatisfied with the chitchat, neither knowing why. Rosemary thought her peevishness was because of her profound, unremitting fatigue. Nina thought hers was from having so much to do.

Outside, the meadow grass undulated, a swath glistening in the high strong sun and bending under the living weight that was moving up from the river, closer and closer to the house though neither the house nor anything else was its particular target. Rosemary knew it was coming. Nina didn't quite yet.

"Are you hungry?" Nina tried.

"I'm never really hungry anymore."

"You have to eat."

This exchange they had almost every time Nina visited. But usually Rosemary didn't say so directly, "Why? Why do I have to eat?"

"What do you mean, why? You have to eat to live." Nina didn't have time for this. Rosemary didn't have much time, either, but the time she had wasn't spoken for anymore.

She did eat a little, a few spoonsful of the casserole, half a cookie, a swallow or two of milk. Nothing tasted good, more a function of her diminished gustatory, olfactory, and tactile senses than of the intrinsic merits of food. Nina ate quickly and quite a lot, sampling, mostly to check on the quality of her own cooking, which she found somewhat lacking. Rosemary said it was good, and it was, because of the companionship and forethought, and also because of the abundance of chips in the cookies, in some places the dough embedded in a melted mass of chocolate rather than the other way around.

They talked—Nina talked—about things that once had aroused her grandmother's interest, often passion: the kids, the economy, the war, religion, politics, family stories. Rosemary reminisced about this neighborhood as it used to be, when at weekly coffeeklatches the women got mending and fancy work done and chatted about mostly inconsequential things made to seem consequential by the sharing. She always pointed out that it hadn't all been placid, there'd been things hidden and not-so-hidden—child abuse, infidelity, illnesses and accidents, a kidnapping. This time how she put it was, "We weren't really friends. But we were friendly. Those get-togethers were like solid ground. Everybody's gone now. Some moved away and didn't keep in touch. Some died. Francine Pollack went to a nursing home last month. So now I'm the only one still left on the street from those days. I'm an island in a rising sea."

"I'm sorry, Grandma. That must be a terrible feeling."

"It's the way of the world."

"Well, we don't have to like it."

"Doesn't matter if we like it or not."

Rosemary saw no point in saying any more right then about what regularly swept through the neighborhood like a viscous transparent tide. It had brought the great love of her life as well as his early death, the Klingmans' house fire and also their glorious roses, Mark Abernathy going MIA in Vietnam and Cheryl Raines becoming a doctor in sub-Saharan Africa, hand-built houses bulldozed for a strip mall and a lovely new creekside park replacing dilapidated and dangerous apartments, both Francine Pollack's deterioration and her good long life—bringing or causing or revealing, Rosemary didn't know, but all of it with the utter indifference she found terrible and reassuring. "I'd like to take a little walk," she announced, and began the laborious process of getting to her feet.

Startled, Nina took refuge in glancing at her watch. "Oh, Grandma, I don't think—There's not enough time—Are you sure you can—?" But she hastened to support the unsteady walker that her grandmother was using to pull herself up.

They made their way out the back door. It was a dry hot summer, and petunias were languishing in their pots. "Do you suppose it would help," Rosemary asked, breathlessness and strain altering her sardonic intent, "if we prayed for rain?"

Nina was praying that Rosemary wouldn't fall, that she would make the meeting, that she had enough gas in the car for all the running around she had to do yet today. Whether she really believed in the efficacy of petitionary prayer or it was only a ritual like a jump-rope chant, it gave her the illusion of calm while actually adding to her tension. Uncomfortable in the heat and her two-inch heels, aware that her cell was beeping with missed calls, she could manage only, "Maybe."

"God," Rosemary panted, "whatever that means, most likely cares not a whit about my dried-out petunias or your drooping dahlias."

"So God hates us? Or the universe or whatever?" Nina couldn't tell whether she should take her grandmother's soft elbow or put an arm around her or not.

"I think we're of no interest to him. It."

"Gee, Grandma, that's cheery."

"Not cheery." Rosemary teetered and Nina grabbed her. "But not *not* cheery, either. Neutral. It just is."

"You're going to fall. It's hot out here. Let's not do this." Rosemary saw or felt or tasted or in some other way took in the gloss moving up over the meadow. Nina probably didn't yet, or didn't know she did. It had oozed around the apple tree now and under the ancient swing set. The tree would live quite a few more years to bear hard little fruit for the crows and squirrels, but the swing set would finally rust through that fall. Nina, realizing her attempt to be helpful was actually contributing to the old woman's unsteadiness, let go of her and just stayed close.

Nina had been having episodes of vertigo and pounding headaches, once or twice with blurred vision, and every now and then two fingers of her right hand went numb. Stress, she was sure. She didn't have time to do anything more than be sure the ibuprofen bottle in her purse was always full. Right now she was having some trouble with her left foot. She didn't mention this to Rosemary or anyone else, didn't give it much thought, her thoughts being busied with many other things, at the moment her grandmother's slow but somehow headlong momentum. "Where are we going?"

"Just down the meadow a little ways," Rosemary said. She was in its path. Everybody was in its path. It was time. Might as well go meet it, see what would happen next. She thought to assure her granddaughter, "It won't take very long," which was true, but what she couldn't know was that it would take the rest of Nina's life.

Frail as she was, Rosemary managed to guide the two of them across the patio and down into the backyard. This meant navigating three steps and the sliding patio door that stuck, requiring Nina to pull hard enough to compromise the balance of them both, individually and together. Clouds were moving in from over the mountains, where weather almost always came from. "It couldn't have stayed pretty just a few more minutes for us," Nina grumbled. The air was humid now, full, as if threatening rain, but it wasn't threatening anything, even if it did rain. And in this case there would be no precipitation all that week, though yards and gardens and the meadow itself could have used drenching.

The meadow looked wet to Rosemary. To Nina, meaning to concentrate on her grandmother but mostly worrying about the time and all the obligations waiting to consume her at work and at home, it just looked big. Maybe it rippled a bit, if that wasn't one of those occasional visual distortions that would turn out to have been harbingers. "Grandma," she said, "we can't go all the way down to the river."

Quietly Rosemary said, "No need." Nina didn't ask what she meant. What Rosemary meant was something like, "It doesn't matter whether we go all the way to the river or stay where we are or go back inside the house and lock all the doors. There's no need to do anything." But even if Nina had asked, Rosemary wouldn't have been aware of all that.

From years of use—horseshoes, baseball, barbecues, dogs, gardens planted and then left to grow over and then dug up again—the ground back here was uneven. When Nina fell, she thought her heel had caught in a hole or on a hillock. In fact, a blood vessel in her brain, weak and bulging for some time without the knowledge of its host, had just burst. Nina might have been aware of pain, thunder inside her head, panic about all the things she was leaving undone, sorrow and guilt about Ken and the kids, the sentient substance that spread over her without any intent at all. But, really, there wasn't much chance for her to be aware of anything.

Rosemary, though, watched it happen. Watched the slime flood the long meadow, claim her granddaughter, and keep right on moving. With great effort and risk, she bent to hold Nina's hand, feel for her pulse, touch her wet cheek. In what for her was haste, she went back to the house, walker rattling, body barely carrying out her desperate orders, after much struggle got the patio door open and found the phone where she'd left it on the coffee table beside the gorgeous, indifferent dahlias and the flicker-tongued alien-tongued cat oblivious to her as it drank from their vase.

Melanie Tem's work has received the Bram Stoker, International Horror Guild, British Fantasy, and World Fantasy Awards, as well as a nomination for the Shirley Jackson Award. She has published numerous short stories, eleven solo novels, two collaborative novels with Nancy Holder, and two with her husband, Steve Rasnic Tem. She is also a published poet, an oral storyteller, and a playwright. Her stories have recently appeared in *Asimov's* and the anthologies *Supernatural Noir, Shivers VI, Portents, Blood and Other Cravings*, and *Werewolves and Shapeshifters*. The Tems live in Denver. They have four children and four granddaughters.

She realized that the darkness had a texture to it now,
the shadows were alive, the shadows wanted her . . .

BEDTIME STORIES FOR YASMIN

Robert Shearman

Mrs. Timothy never wanted Yasmin to be frightened, not of anything, and she made sure that in all her picture books the lions had nice smiles and the crocodiles came with blunted teeth. Mr. Timothy disagreed, and that was predictable enough, since Yasmin's birth her husband seemed to have found a way to disagree with his wife about everything. "You can't protect her from the world," he said. "It's big and it's scary and it's right outside the door!" Mrs. Timothy knew this was true, but it was a scary world Yasmin needn't have to confront just yet—and when it came to kindergarten, and school, and college, and all the other horrors her husband kept throwing at her, then they'd have to see, wouldn't they?—maybe some careful control would be in order. Maybe they could just do their job as loving parents and make sure Yasmin never had to mix with the wrong sort.

When Yasmin was put to bed at night Mrs. Timothy would leave the light on. And she'd read her her favorite stories—about very hungry caterpillars, about beautiful princesses, about kindly folk who would never do her any harm. Mrs. Timothy was not an especially good reader, and her voice inclined towards a flat monotone, so before very long Yasmin's eyes would get heavy and she'd fall asleep. And that was good, that was right, and the final image with which the story would leave her would never put her into a state of anxious suspense.

One night—only a few months ago, was it really so recent?—Mrs. Timothy heard screams coming from Yasmin's bedroom, and she ran to see what was wrong. Yasmin was sitting up in bed, and she seemed to be shrinking away from the sheets, from the windows, from the wardrobe, from everything; she held her little pillow out before her as if it were a shield. "Don't let the giants get me," she said. It turned out that earlier that evening Mr. Timothy had read her a story himself, quite against his wife's instructions, whilst Mrs. Timothy was busy cooking dinner. The story had featured giants galore. Mr. Timothy said, "She seemed to be enjoying it at the time," and Mrs. Timothy opened the book and was horrified by what she saw there: men as big as houses, and stamping upon the little fairy folk, and pulling them apart like Christmas crackers, and eating them whole and raw. It took two readings back to back of *Robbie the Happy Rabbit* to calm Yasmin down again, and even then Mrs. Timothy had had to edit out the bits where Robbie had chewed at his carrots, Yasmin didn't need to hear any more about chewing that night.

It wasn't the incident that caused the break-up, but it hadn't helped. "You don't love me any more," Mrs. Timothy said one day, and Mr. Timothy thought about it, and agreed, as if it were a revelation. "And you don't love Yasmin either," sobbed Mrs. Timothy, "or you wouldn't have frightened her so!" Mr. Timothy said nothing to this, but he didn't deny it, so it was probably true. And that very same hour he left, he didn't even bother to pack, and Mrs. Timothy was left to cry with her daughter and wonder why there was so much wickedness in the world.

Back before Mrs. Timothy had become Mrs. Timothy, long ago, when she'd believed everyone in the world loved her and no one would let her down, she'd had an Uncle Jack who would read her bedtime stories. Uncle Jack would come to her room after lights out and sit on the edge of her bed, and say, "Time for a story, my pretty princess." She didn't want to hear his stories, but the pretty princess always won her over—and she couldn't but help like Uncle Jack, he smelled so unlike her parents, and she couldn't work out why—maybe he smoked a different brand of cigarettes, or drank a different sort of beer—it was a strange smell, a *sweet* smell, as if her Uncle Jack was full of sugar—and sometimes, if she listened to one of his stories without making a single sound, he'd ruffle her hair as a treat. She knew when he began a story she should keep quiet, she mustn't scream or cry out, she mustn't even whimper—if she did, he'd simply stop the story, turn back the pages, and start all over again.

He brought the book with him. An enormous book, when he sat it down upon his lap and opened it up it was wider than he was, and she could only imagine how many stories there must be in there—hundreds, no, thousands, no, all the stories in the world. The pages were thick and heavy and as he turned them they creaked like old floorboards. He didn't turn on the lamp, he read to her by moonlight. Sometimes if the moonlight was bright enough she'd steal a look at those pages; they were dense with long words, and the words crushed tight on to the paper, and there were no pictures.

The stories frightened the girl.

One night he told a particularly terrifying story. And she tried not to, but she kept gasping out loud with fear. And each time she did, no matter how softly, Uncle Jack would hear her, and he'd stop, and back would creak all the pages, and he'd begin once more. He never seemed angry. He never seemed impatient. He read just as before, the same pace, the same wet hiss, the same emphasis on the most disturbing of words. And it was always at the exact same point that she'd gasp—five times, six times now, she could never get beyond the moment where Little Red Riding Hood admired the size of the wolf's mouth. She knew that all that was waiting for Little Red Riding Hood was death, the same horrible death that had befallen her grandmother, and she didn't even know what death was, not properly, only that it was big and black and would consume her, and once it had consumed her she'd be lost and no one would ever find her again.

Six times, seven times, eight. All through the night he read to her the same story, over and over, and each time the girl would jam her fist into her mouth, she'd hold her breath, she'd try to lie in bed stiff and hard and not move a muscle—anything, so long as the story would continue, so that the story would at last come to an end.

She fell asleep at last, for all her terror she was too tired to keep awake. And then she sat up with a start, and it was so dark, and the moonlight had gone, it was as if the moon had been switched off, and she was still terrified, and Uncle Jack was gone. His book, however, was lying on the edge of her bed.

It was her one chance to be rid of it. And yet stretching out her hand to touch it seemed such a dreadful thing. She could feel her heart beating so fast it would pop, and she wondered if that's how her parents would find her in the morning, lying dead on the bed, her fingers just brushing the warm leathery cover of a giant book; she wondered if Uncle Jack would be sad she was gone, or even care.

The book was so heavy she thought she would never lift it. Still, she did.

The house seemed different in the dead of night. The stairs made noises that sounded like warnings as she stepped on them—or maybe they weren't warnings, maybe they were threats—maybe they were calling out to the strange shadows on the wall to turn on her and eat her. The book filled her arms, as she walked ever downwards shifting its bulk from side to side it seemed she was dancing with it. She reached the back door. She unlocked it. She opened it. The blackness of the outside seemed richer and meatier than the blackness of the house, and in it poured.

She dropped the book into the bin. She slammed the lid down, in case it tried to get out again.

And then, back to her room, this time running, as fast as she could, no time to shut the back door, let alone lock it, back to her bed and under her covers before anything could eat her alive.

She had a temperature the next day, and her mother was worried, and kept her in bed. And all day long the little girl looked out of the window and hoped it would stay daytime forever and wouldn't get dark. Because as soon as it was dark, she knew, Uncle Jack would return. And what would he say when he found out she'd thrown his book away? He wouldn't be pleased.

She couldn't sleep that night. She waited for him. But Uncle Jack didn't come.

Mrs. Timothy was worried Yasmin might be disturbed by her father's disappearance, but she seemed to take it in her stride. It was her mummy who dressed her in the morning, who fed her, who read her bedtime stories. "Sometimes things just end," Mrs. Timothy offered as explanation, and Yasmin had nodded slowly, as if she were a grown-up too, as if she could understand such things. But maybe the mistake was that Mrs. Timothy had used the same phrase to explain why the next door dog had vanished after being hit by that car; one day Yasmin frowned at her mother, she had something to ask that had been on her mind for quite a while. She said, "Is Daddy dead?"

"Good god, no."

"Not dead?"

"He's just away. Somewhere else. For the time being."

But Yasmin wouldn't let it go, and eventually Mrs. Timothy had been forced to call her husband. She hadn't spoken to him in a month. *Damn him*, she thought, and she felt lightheaded and girlish as she waited for him to pick up, and she was angry with herself for that, and angry with him too.

She didn't bother with a hello. "Yasmin thinks you're dead, can you talk to Yasmin and prove you're not dead?" She handed over the phone to Yasmin before he could give a reply. Yasmin listened. Her eyes went big. She said, "Okay." She handed the phone back to her mother. Mrs. Timothy put it straight to her ear, but her husband had already hung up. "What did he say?" she asked.

"He's coming back soon," said Yasmin, and smiled, and went to watch something wholesome on the television.

This is all your fault, Mrs. Timothy thought, and gripped the phone tight and hard and pretended Mr. Timothy could feel it, pretended she could make him hurt. *She wouldn't even know what death was without your stupid giants, if you hadn't walked out on us, if you hadn't been someone different to the man you promised to be.* And now he was causing more problems, making promises to Yasmin he wouldn't be able to keep.

She phoned him again, straight away. He didn't answer.

• • •

When the little girl grew up and became Mrs. Timothy, she understood that most of the fairy tales we know today as pantomimes and Disney cartoons were much more violent and disturbing in the original. She read some of the Brothers Grimm, just to see. They were darker, it was true. But they were nothing like the gruesome stories she'd heard from Uncle Jack.

Because he'd told her of Sleeping Beauty, and how when the princess had fallen asleep for a hundred years even the maggots had thought she was dead. And some of those maggots had got sealed fast behind her eyelids, and they were hungry, so they had to feed upon the soft jellies of her eyes, and then when the eyes were gone, they burrowed their way deep into her brain. And when the prince woke her with a magic kiss the princess gazed at him with empty sockets, and her brain had turned to Swiss cheese, and she no longer knew how to speak, or how to think, or how to love. And in the summer months when the weather was hot her brain would start melting and bits of it would dribble out fat and greasy from her ears.

He'd told her of Cinderella, but that she'd had twelve wicked stepsisters, not just two, and that each night they would take turns to beat Cinderella with wire and flay off her skin. And when the prince married her, Cinderella got her revenge. And for a wedding gift she begged for the right to punish her stepsisters by whatever methods she chose. She sought counsel from all the wise men of the land, they would help her devise new tortures never before experienced by man, they would invent machines capable of prolonging each and every agony. And the stepsisters fled; and the soldiers were sent after them; and one by one they'd be caught, and tortured, and killed, and their broken corpses would be hung side by side on the castle battlements for everyone to see. But only eleven stepsisters were ever caught. One got away. And each night Cinderella would lie in bed with her Prince Charming, and she wouldn't sleep for fear that her last sister was coming to get her, that for all the guards she had posted on the door she would find a way in.

He'd told her of Snow White and the Seven Dwarfs. Snow White and the Seven Dwarfs was unspeakable.

One day, as an adult, Mrs. Timothy dared to ask her parents about Uncle Jack. They had no idea who she was talking about. Her father was an only child, her mother had only sisters. Her parents didn't seem very concerned, though. This Uncle Jack, he'd probably been a family friend.

There was a scream that woke Mrs. Timothy up—"Yasmin?" she called—and only then did she realize there was a heavy storm; thunder roared above the house, lightning flashed, and rain battered hard against the windows as if it were trying to break in.

"Yasmin?" She reached her daughter's room, and the room was dark, and she tried the light switch but it was no use. "Sweetheart, it's just a power cut, it's all right, don't be scared."

And as her eyes adjusted she could make out Yasmin, sitting up in bed, quite composed, pert even. "I'm not scared," she said.

"Did the thunder wake you? Did you see the lightning? It's all right, nothing can get at us in here."

Yasmin didn't say anything. Mrs. Timothy felt strangely embarrassed, as if she should leave. Instead she sat down on the end of her bed. "I'll put you back to sleep," she said. "I'll read you a story, would you like that?"

"Yes," said Yasmin.

"I'll read you one of your favorite stories." She took from the shelf the tale of the very hungry caterpillar, sat back down again. Reaching for the bedside lamp she checked herself, remembered that the electricity was out. It didn't matter. She'd read the book so many times she probably knew it all by heart, and besides, there was moonlight. She opened the book, strained to make out the text. Her voice was not only monotonous, it was halting, even Mrs. Timothy could hear how boring she was. Reading by moonlight was harder than she'd ever thought, she wondered how he had ever—and then she stopped herself.

"I don't want to hear about the caterpillar," said Yasmin.

"No. Fair enough."

"I want a different sort of story."

"All right."

"Let me tell *you* a story."

"Yes. Yes. You tell me a story, sweetheart."

Yasmin's story wasn't very good, but her voice was clearer than her mother's, and so much more confident, and she didn't hesitate over any of the words. And Mrs. Timothy wanted her to stop, but she didn't think she could, she froze, and she knew that she had to keep quiet, if she made even the slightest sound Yasmin would start all over—and no, that was nonsense, of course she could make it stop, she only had to tell her to stop, this was a four year old girl, stop, stop, *stop.*

Yasmin stopped.

"Where did you hear that?" Mrs. Timothy asked, trying to sound calm, trying to sound as if everything was normal.

"I don't know."

"You didn't just make it up. You couldn't." Yasmin just stared at her, her mother could almost feel her eyes boring into her. "Who's been telling you this stuff? Who have you been talking to? Was it your father?" And she thought that, yes, maybe her little daughter was making phone calls to her husband, all behind her back, they were ganging up on her, laughing about her, Yasmin was taking sides. It was awful. It was awful. But still so much better than—"I asked you a question, Yasmin! Was it your father?" And she was shaking her, perhaps a little too roughly.

And it was at that moment the electricity chose to come back on. And Mrs. Timothy blinked in the sudden light, and saw herself grabbing on to her daughter, and she let go, ashamed. And she saw her darling little daughter's face, and it was glaring at her.

"Well," said Mrs. Timothy. "Well." She got up to her feet. "Do you think you can sleep now?"

Yasmin nodded.

"Night night, my darling." And—"You have lovely dreams."

Still Yasmin wouldn't say anything, but she did nestle deeper beneath the sheets.

"Night night," Mrs. Timothy said again. And made to leave the room. "Mummy?" she heard, and turned around.

"Mummy," Yasmin said, "I'm sorry about the story."

"That's all right. Never mind."

"I'm sorry about what it's let in."

Mrs. Timothy didn't know what to say to that.

"Please," said Yasmin, "would you turn off the light for me?"

Her mother hesitated. Then did as she was told.

The hallway back to her bedroom seemed longer than usual, and Mrs. Timothy felt cold. A flash of lightning blazed through the house for a moment, it startled her.

She reached her room, closed the door behind her.

She got into bed.

The bed was very cold, and there was a sort of dampness to the cold. It was as if the rainstorm had got in, danced lightly about her bedspread, and got out before she'd returned.

It seemed such a big bed, stupidly big, so empty without her husband, and for the first time since he'd left she wished he was there to help fill it.

She wasn't frightened by Yasmin's story. But nevertheless she decided she'd turn the light on, just for a little while. Her fingers tugged at the cord above her head. Nothing, still darkness. The power must have gone off again.

No, she wasn't frightened, that would be absurd. Indeed, she could barely remember what the story was even about now, it was already fading away like a dream—and she tried to grasp on to the memory of it, and then she made herself let it go, no, let go.

It wasn't the story that was frightening. It was what the story might have *let in.* The words popped into her head like a cold truth, and she didn't even know what that could mean—let what in? Still, it made her shiver.

She pulled up the sheets to her throat. She felt the wetness on her chin, it *was* damp. Disgusted, she threw the sheets off again. They formed a huddle on the floor by the side of the bed.

She looked around the room. She knew the room so well. She'd slept in the room for nearly four years, ever since they'd moved here, ever since she was pregnant with Yasmin. There was nothing to fear from this room. This room was her sanctuary. She had slept in this room over a thousand times, she had never been hurt here, had she? She'd never once been haunted by ghosts, or attacked by monsters, or bitten by vampires, or killed. She wished she hadn't thought of that word, "killed."

The shadows were bleeding out from the corners towards her. She knew why that was. The storm was doing strange things to the light, it was causing it to distort somehow, to break it into weird shapes. If she didn't like it, she could always get up and close the curtains. Get up then, close the curtains. Get up.

She didn't want to get up.

She was frightened of what the story might have let in. What had Yasmin done? She wanted to run to her bedroom, wake her, demand that she take her story back. Unsay it, make it all go away. She should get up and find her.

Oh, but she didn't want to get up, did she? Why didn't she want to get up? Think.

Because there was something under her bed. There was something under her bed. She knew it. She could sense it. If she listened closely, she could hear it whispering to her. Yes, and the moment she put her foot over the side, it would grab her, pull her under and into the darkness. Look at that body on the floor, it whispered. That could be you.—*There isn't a body on the floor, that's just the sheets I kicked off, I did that myself.*—No, it's a body on the floor.

From downstairs she heard a knock against the door.

It was just the wind, of course—but there it was again, and this time there was a rhythm to it, a tattoo of three beats, thump-thump-*thump*. And again.

It must be her husband. And she'd wanted him there only a few minutes before, but now he seemed a very real and present danger, and she wanted him gone, she wanted him off her property—he couldn't just turn up whenever he felt like, he'd made his choice, he'd made his bloody choice, and she'd go and see him and tell him just that—and she nearly got out of bed, this was something *real*, and she was just putting her foot down to the carpet when she felt it brush against her, it was too smooth and too oily, and she realized that the darkness had a texture to it now, the shadows were alive, the shadows wanted her.

She pulled her foot back to safety. The door kept knocking. *You knock away,* she thought, *I'm staying where I am.*

She closed her eyes. She tried not to think of all the darkness in her head when she did that, that the darkness she had within her might be the same darkness waiting for her without.

Thump-thump-*thump*—and then stop.

And nothing. No more of that.

And she kept her eyes closed, and stilled her breath, and listened for the slightest sound.

She heard nothing, but she *felt* it, a new weight on the end of her bed.

Her eyes snapped open, and there was nothing there—it was all right, of course there was nothing there—and she gasped with relief and thought she might even cry—and the door, her bedroom door, had she closed it?—the door was open.

She hadn't closed it. That was it. She could go and close it if she wanted to. She would, just get up and close the door. *Get up. Get up.*

What had Yasmin's story let in?

And at the doorway she saw the darkness harden, and grow denser, and turn into the shape of a person, and she thought her heart would pop—and she thought, this is how my little daughter will find me in the morning, slumped dead against the pillows, my eyes open so wide in fear, oh, Yasmin.

Yasmin?

"Is that you, Yasmin?" she made herself ask.

And the figure said, quietly, "Yes."

She wanted nothing to frighten her, not now, not ever. "Were you afraid of the thunder? It's all right, darling. You sleep with me. I'll protect you. This bed's big enough for both of us." It was *too* big, that was a certainty—and now she'd have someone to hold again, and she'd be brave, and all the ghosts and monsters could come and she'd see them all off.

The figure came in, the figure wasn't bothered by the shadows, or the darkness under the bed, or the sheet body on the floor—and the figure climbed in beside her, and Mrs. Timothy had one last terror, that maybe this wasn't Yasmin after all—but it was, it was, and she could now see her clearly, this was her own little angel.

Mrs. Timothy hugged her. She smelled nice and sweet. "Don't be scared," she told her.

"I'm not scared," her daughter replied. She whispered it in her mother's ear.

"Good."

Such a sweet smell, she recognized that smell. And Yasmin was slightly damp too, as if the rain had got to her. And Yasmin was right by her ear. "Shall I finish my story?"

And Mrs. Timothy pulled away from her, just for a moment, and she saw that Yasmin's eyes were too wide, and her mouth was too big for her face, and then Yasmin pulled her back, she held on to her mother's head tight so it couldn't move.

She told her story. She made her understand that there were so many ghosts, you could never tell who was a ghost and who wasn't. So very many—and some of them want to tear you apart, some of them want to drag you down to Hell—and some, if you're lucky, just want to tell you stories.

The smell wasn't of cigarettes and beer, it was of soft decay. And her touch was moist.

She told her mother her story, and her mother was good, and kept quiet during the whole thing. So she ruffled her hair before she got out of bed. And Mrs. Timothy's mind still had some room to think, to wonder at how much bigger Yasmin had become, why, she looked quite the grown-up.

Yasmin stood there, and they were *both* standing there, she was holding hands with a man without a face who had just leaked out of the shadows, perhaps he'd always been there, perhaps he had been waiting all this time.

They were holding hands, they looked down at the frightened little girl in the bed like they were mummy and daddy.

It was the daddy who said, "Sleep well, my pretty princess," and the mummy who said, "There'll be more stories tomorrow." And they shrunk away into the darkness of the hallway, and closed the door, and locked it.

Robert Shearman has worked as a writer for television, radio, and the stage. Although he has received several prestigious awards for his theatrical work, he is probably best known as a writer for *Doctor Who*, reintroducing the Daleks for its BAFTA-winning first series, in an episode nominated for a Hugo Award. His collections of short fiction—*Tiny Deaths, Love Songs for the Shy and Cynical*, and *Everyone's Just So So Special*—have, collectively, won the World Fantasy Award, the British Fantasy Award, the Edge Hill Short Story Readers Prize, and the Shirley Jackson Award. Most recently, his best dark fiction was collected in *Remember Why You Fear Me*. He is currently writer in residence at Edinburgh Napier University.

I was looking at a hand of glory. Hacked from a murderer
and pickled for use in the blackest of magic rituals . . .

HAND OF GLORY

Laird Barron

From the pages of a partially burned manuscript discovered in the charred
ruins of a mansion in Ransom Hollow, Washington:

That buffalo charges across the eternal prairie, mad black eye rolling
at the photographer. The photographer is Old Scratch's left hand man.
Every few seconds the buffalo rumbles past the same tussock, the same
tumbleweed, the same bleached skull of its brother or sister. That poor
buffalo is Sisyphus without the stone, without the hill, without a larger
sense of futility. The beast's hooves are worn to bone. Blood foams at its
muzzle. The dumb brute doesn't understand where we are.

But I do.

CP, Nov. 1925

This is the house my father built stone by stone in Anno Domini 1898. I
was seven. Mother died of consumption that winter, and my baby brothers
Earl and William followed her through the Pearly Gates directly. Hell of a
housewarming.

Dad never remarried. He just dug in and redoubled his efforts on behalf
of his boss, Myron Arden. The Arden family own the politicos, the cops, the
stevedores and the stevedores' dogs. They owned Dad too, but he didn't mind.
Four bullets through the chest, a knife in the gut, two car wrecks, and a bottle
a day booze habit weren't enough to rub him out. It required a broken heart
from missing his wife. He collapsed, stone dead, on a job in Seattle in 1916 and
I inherited his worldly possessions, such as they were. The debts, too.

The passing of Donald Cope was a mournful day commemorated with a
crowded wake—mostly populated by Mr. Myron Arden's family and henchmen
who constituted Dad's only real friends—and the requisite violins, excessive
drinking of Jameson's, fistfights, and drunken profanities roared at passersby,

although in truth, there hadn't been much left of the old man since Mother went.

My sister Lucy returned to Ireland and joined a convent. Big brother Acton lives here in Olympia. He's a surgeon. When his friends and associates ask about his kin at garden parties, I don't think my name comes up much. That's okay. Dad always liked me better.

I've a reputation in this town. I've let my share of blood, taken my share of scalps. You want an enemy bled, burnt, blasted into Kingdom Come, ask for Johnny Cope. My viciousness and cruelty are without peer. There are bad men in this business, and worse men, and then there's me. But I must admit, any lug who quakes in his boots at the mention of my name should've gotten a load of the old man. *There* was Mr. Death's blue-eyed boy himself, like mr. cummings said.

A dark hallway parallels the bedroom. Dad was a short, wiry man from short wiry stock and he fitted the house accordingly. The walls are close, the windows narrow, and so the passage is dim even in daylight. When night falls it becomes a mineshaft and I lie awake, listening. Listening for a voice in the darkness, a dragging footstep, or something else, possibly something I've not heard in this life. Perversely, the light from the lamp down the street, or the moonlight, or the starlight, make that black gap of a bedroom door a deeper mystery.

I resemble Mother's people: lanky, with a horse's jaw and rawboned hands meant for spadework, or tying nooses on ropes, and I have to duck when passing through these low doorways; but at heart, I'm my father's son. I knock down the better portion of a bottle of Bushmill's every evening while I count my wins and losses from the track. My closet is stacked with crates of the stuff. I don't pay for liquor—it's a bequest from Mr. Arden, that first class bootlegger; a mark of sentimental appreciation for my father's steadfast service to the cause. When I sleep, I sleep fully dressed, suit and tie, left hand draped across the Thompson like a lover. Fear is a second heartbeat, my following shadow.

This has gone on a while.

The first time I got shot was in the fall of 1914.

I was twenty-one and freshly escaped from the private academy Dad spent the last of his money shipping me off to. He loved me so much he'd hoped I wouldn't come back, that I'd join Acton in medicine, or get into engineering, or stow away on a tramp steamer and spend my life hunting ivory and drinking and whoring my way across the globe into Terra Incognita; anything but the family business. No such luck. My grades were pathetic, barely sufficient to graduate as I'd spent too many study nights gambling, and weekends fighting sailors at the docks. I wasn't as smart as Acton anyway, and I found it much easier and more satisfying to break things rather than build them. Mine was a talent for reading and leading people. I didn't mind manipulating them, I didn't mind destroying them if it came to that. It's not as if we dealt with real folks, anyway. In our world, everybody was part of the machine.

Dad had been teaching me the trade for a few months, taking me along on lightweight jobs. There was this Guinea named Alfonso who owed Mr. Arden big and skipped town on the debt. Dad and I tracked the fellow to Vancouver and caught him late one night, dead drunk in his shack. Alfonso didn't have the money, but we knew his relatives were good for it, so we only roughed him up: Knocked some teeth loose and broke his leg. Dad used a mattock handle with a bunch of bolts drilled into the fat end. It required more swings than I'd expected.

Unfortunately, Alfonso was entertaining a couple of whores from the dance hall. The girls thought we were murdering the poor bastard and that they'd be next. One jumped through a window, and the other, a half-naked, heavyset lass who was in no shape to run anywhere, pulled a derringer from her corset and popped me in the ribs. Probably aiming for my face. Dad didn't stop to think about the gun being a one-shot rig—he took three strides and whacked her in the back of the head with the mattock handle. Just as thick-skulled as Alfonso, she didn't die, although that was a pity, considering the results. One of her eyes fell out later and she never talked right again. Life is just one long train wreck.

They say you become a man when you lose your virginity. Not my baptism, alas, alack. Having a lima bean-sized hole blown through me and enduring the fevered hours afterward was the real crucible, the mettle-tester. I remember sprawling in the front seat of the car near the river and Dad pressing a doubled handkerchief against the wound. Blood dripped shiny on the floorboard. It didn't hurt much, more like the after-effects of a solid punch to the body. However, my vision was too acute, too close; black and white flashes scorched my brain.

Seagulls circled the car, their shadows so much larger than seemed possible, the shadows of angels ready to carry me into Kingdom Come. Dad gave me a dose of whiskey from his hip flask. He drove with the pedal on the floor and that rattletrap car shuddered on the verge of tearing itself apart, yet as I slumped against the door, the landscape lay frozen, immobile as the glacier that ended everything in the world the first time. Bands of light, God's pillars of blazing fire, bisected the scenery into a glaring triptych that shattered my mind. Dad gripped my shoulder and laughed and shook me now and again to keep me from falling unconscious.

Dr. Green, a sawbones on the Arden payroll, fished out the bullet and patched the wound and kept me on ice in the spare room at his house. That's when I discovered I had the recovery power of a brutish animal, a bear that retreats to the cave to lick its wounds before lumbering forth again in short order. To some, such a capacity suggests the lack of a higher degree of acumen, the lack of a fully developed imagination. I'm inured to pain and suffering, and whether it's breeding or nature I don't give a damn.

Two weeks later I was on the mend. To celebrate, I threw Gahan Kirk, a no account lackey for the Eastside crew, off the White Building roof for cheating at cards. Such is the making of a legend. The reality was, I pushed the man while he was distracted with begging Dad and Sonny Hopkins, Mr. Arden's number two enforcer, not to rub him out. Eight stories. He flipped like a ragdoll, smashing into a couple of fire escapes and crashing one down atop him in the alley. It was hideously spectacular.

The second time I got shot was during the Great War.

Mr. Arden was unhappy to see me sign on for the trip to Europe. He saw I was hell-bent to do my small part and thus gave his reluctant blessing, assuring me I'd have work when I came home from "Killing the Huns." Five minutes after I landed in France I was damned sorry for such a foolish impulse toward patriotism.

One night our platoon negotiated a minefield, smashed a machine-gun bunker with a volley of pineapples, clambered through barbed wire, and assaulted an enemy trench. Toward the end of the action, me and a squad mate were in hand-to-hand combat with a German officer we'd cornered. I'd run dry on ammo five minutes before and gone charging like a rhino through the encampment, and thank Holy Mother Mary it was a ghost town from the shelling or else I'd have been ventilated inside of twenty paces. The German rattled off half a dozen rounds with his Luger before I stuck a bayonet through his neck. I didn't realize I was clipped until the sleeve of my uniform went sopping black. Two bullets, spaced tight as a quarter, zipped through my left shoulder. Couldn't have asked for a cleaner wound and I hopped back into the fray come the dawn advance. I confiscated the German's pistol and the wicked bayonet he'd kept in his boot. They'd come in handy on many a bloody occasion since.

The third time . . . we'll get to that.

11/11/25

Autumn of 1925 saw my existence in decline. Then I killed some guys and it was downhill in a wagon with no brakes from there.

Trouble followed after a string of anonymous calls to my home. Heavy breathing and hang-ups. The caller waited until the dead of night when I was drunk and too addled to do more than slur curses into the phone. I figured it was some dame I'd miffed, or a lug I'd thrashed, maybe even somebody with a real grudge—a widow or an orphan. My detractors are many. Whoever it was only spoke once upon the occasion of their final call. Amid crackling as of a bonfire, the male voice said, "I love you son. I love you son. I love you son."

I was drunk beyond drunk and I fell on the floor and wept. The calls stopped and I put it out of my mind.

Toward the end of September I hit a jackpot on a twenty to one pony and collected a cool grand at the window, which I used to pay off three markers in one fell swoop. I squandered the remainder on a trip to Seattle, embarking upon a bender that saw me tour every dance hall and speakeasy from the harbor inland. The ride lasted until I awakened flat broke one morning in a swanky penthouse suite of the Wilsonian Hotel in the embrace of an over-the-hill burlesque dancer named Pearl.

Pearl was statuesque, going to flab in the middle and the ass. Jesus, what an ass it was, though. We'd known one another for a while—I courted her younger sister Madison before she made for the bright lights of Chi-Town. Last I heard, she was a gangster's moll. Roy Night, a button man who rubbed out guys for Capone, could afford to keep Maddie in furs and diamonds and steak dinners. Good for her. Pearl wasn't any Maddie, but she wasn't half bad. Just slightly beaten down, a little tired, standing at the crossroads where Maddie herself would be in six or seven years. Me, I'd likely be dead by then so no time like the present.

I was hung-over and broke, and with two of my last ten bucks tipped the kid who pushed the breakfast cart. He handed me the fateful telegram, its envelope smudged and mussed. I must've paid the kid off pretty well during my stay, because he pocketed the money and said there were a couple of men downstairs asking what room I was in. They'd come around twice the day before, too. Bruisers, he said. Blood in their eyes, he said.

My first suspicion was of T-Men or Pinkertons. I asked him to describe the lugs. He did. I said thanks and told him to relay the gentlemen my room number on the sly and pick up some coin for his trouble. These were no lawmen, rather the opposite; a couple of Johnson brothers. Freelance guns, just like me.

Bobby Dirk and Curtis Bane, The Long and The Short, so-called, and that appellation had nothing to do with their stature, but rather stemmed from an embarrassing incident in a bathhouse.

I'd seen them around over the years, shared a drink or two in passing. Dirk was stoop-shouldered and sallow; Bane was stocky with watery eyes and a receding chin. Snowbirds and sad sack gamblers, both of them, which accounted for their uneven temperament and willingness to stoop to the foulest of deeds. Anybody could've put them on my trail. There were plenty of folks who'd be pleased to pony up the coin if it meant seeing me into a pine box.

While Pearl dressed I drank coffee and watched rain hit the window. Pearl knew the party was over—she'd fished through my wallet enough times. She was a good sport and rubbed my shoulders while I ate cold eggs. She had the grip of a stonemason. "You'd better get along," I said.

"Why's that?" she said.

"Because, in a few minutes a couple of men are probably going to break down the door and try to rub me out," I said, and lighted another cigarette.

She laughed and kissed my ear. "Day in the life of Johnny Cope. See ya around, doll. I'm hotfooting it outta here."

I unsnapped the violin case and leaned it against the closet. I assembled the Thompson on the breakfast table, locking pieces together while I watched the rain and thought about Pearl's ass. When I'd finished, I wiped away the excess cleaning oil with a monogrammed hotel napkin. I sipped the dregs of the coffee and opened a new deck of Lucky Strike and smoked a couple of them. After half an hour and still no visitors, I knotted my tie, slipped my automatic into its shoulder holster and shrugged on my suit jacket, then the greatcoat. Pacific Northwest gloom and rain has always agreed with me. Eight months out of the year I can comfortably wear bulky clothes to hide my weapons. Dad had always insisted on nice suits for work. He claimed Mr. Arden appreciated we dressed as gentlemen.

The hall was dim and I moved quickly to the stairwell exit. Elevators are deathtraps. You'd never catch me in one. I could tell you stories about fools who met their untimely ends like rats in a box. I descended briskly, paused at the door, then stepped into the alley. A cold drizzle misted everything, made the concrete slick and treacherous. I lighted a cigarette and stuck it in the corner of my mouth and began to move for the street.

For a couple of seconds I thought I had it made. Yeah. I always thought that.

Curtis Bane drifted from the inset threshold of a service door about ten feet to the street side. He raised his hand, palm out to forestall me. I wasn't buying. I hurled the empty violin case at his head and whipped around. And yes indeed, that rotten cur Bobby Dirk was sneaking up on my flank. I brought the trench broom from under my coat and squeezed off half the drum, rat-a-tat-tat. Oh, that sweet ratcheting burr; spurts of flame lighted the gloomy alley. Some of the bullets blasted brick from the wall, but enough ripped through a shocked and amazed Bobby Dirk to cut him nearly in half in a gout of black blood and smoke. What remained of him danced, baby, danced and flew backward and fell straight down, all ties to the here and now severed.

Curtis Bane screamed and though I came around fast and fired in the same motion, he'd already pulled a heater and begun pumping metal at me. We both missed and I was empty, that drum clicking uselessly. I went straight at him. Happily, he too was out of bullets and I closed the gap and slammed the butt of the rifle into his chest. Should've knocked him down, but no. The bastard was squat and powerful as a wild animal, thanks to being a coke fiend, no doubt. He ripped the rifle from my grasp and flung it aside. He locked his fists and swung them up into my chin, and it was like getting clobbered with a hammer, and I sprawled into a row of trashcans. Stars zipped through my vision. A leather cosh dropped from his sleeve into his hand and he knew what to do with it all right. He swung it in a short chopping blow at my face and I got my left hand up and the blow snapped my two smallest fingers, and he swung again and I turned my head just enough that it only squashed my ear and you better believe that hurt, but now I'd drawn the sawback bayonet I kept strapped to my hip, a fourteen inch grooved steel blade with notched and pitted edges—Jesus-fuck who knew how many Yankee boys the Kraut who'd owned it gashed before I did for him—and stabbed it to the guard into Bane's groin. Took a couple of seconds for Bane to register it was curtains. His face whitened and his mouth slackened, breath steaming in the chill, his evil soul coming untethered. He had lots of gold fillings. He lurched away and I clutched his sleeve awkwardly with my broken hand and rose, twisting the handle of the blade side to side, turning it like a car crank into his guts and bladder, putting my shoulder and hip into it for leverage. He moaned in panic and dropped the cosh and pried at my wrist, but the strength was draining from him and I slammed him against the wall and worked the handle with murderous joy. The cords of his neck went taut and he looked away, as if embarrassed, eyes milky, a doomed petitioner gaping at Hell in all its fiery majesty. I freed the blade with a cork-like pop and blood spurted down his leg in a nice thick stream and he collapsed, folding into himself like a bug does when it dies.

Nobody had stuck their head into the alley to see what all the ruckus was about, nor did I hear sirens yet, so I took a moment to collect the dead men's wallets and light a fresh cigarette. Then I gathered my Thompson and its case and retreated into the hotel stairwell to pack the gun, scrape the blood from my shoes and comb my hair. Composed, I walked out through the lobby and the front door, winking at a rosy-cheeked lass and her wintery dame escort. A tear formed at the corner of my eye.

Two cops rolled up and climbed from their Model T. The taller of the pair barely fit into his uniform. He cradled a shotgun. The other pig carried a Billy club. I smiled at the big one as we passed, eyes level, our shoulders almost brushing, the heavy violin case bumping against my leg, the pistol hidden in the sleeve of my coat, already cocked. My hand burned like fire and I was close to vomiting, and surely the pig saw the gory lump of my ear, the snail-trail of blood streaking my cheek. His piggy little eyes were red and dulled, and I recognized him as a brother in inveterate drunkenness. We all kept walking, violent forces drifting along the razor's edge of an apocalyptic clash. They entered the hotel and I hopped a trolley to the train station. I steamed home to Olympia without incident, except by the time I staggered into the house and fell in a heap on the bed, I was out of my mind with agony and fever.

I didn't realize I'd been shot until waking to find myself lying in a pool of blood. There was a neat hole an inch above my hip. I plugged it with my pinky and went to sleep.

Number three. A banner day. Dad would be so proud.

Dick found me a day and a half later, blood everywhere, like somebody had slaughtered a cow in my bed. Miraculously, the wound had clotted enough to keep me from bleeding out. He took a long look at me (I was partially naked and had somehow gotten hold of a couple of bottles of the Bushmill's, which were empty by this point, although I didn't recall drinking them) and then rang Leroy Bly to come over and help salvage the situation as I was in no condition to assist. I think he was also afraid I might be far enough gone to mistake him for a foe and start shooting or cutting. Later, he explained it was the unpleasant-looking man watching my house from a catbird's seat down the way that gave him pause. The guy screwed when Dick approached him, so there was no telling what his intentions were.

The two of them got me into the tub. Good old Dr. Green swung by with his little black bag of goodies and plucked the bullet from my innards, clucking and muttering as he worked. After stitching me inside and out, he put a cast on my hand, bandaged my ear, and shot enough dope into me to pacify a Clydesdale, then gave me another dose for the fever. The boys settled in to watch over me on account of my helpless condition. They fretted that somebody from Seattle was gunning for payback. News of my rubbing out The Long and The Short had gotten around. Two or three of the Seattle bosses were partial to them, so it was reasonable to expect they might take the matter personally.

Dick's full name was Richard Stiff and he'd worked for the railroad since he was a boy, just as his father had before him. He was a thick, jowly lug with forearms as round as my calf. Unloading steel off boxcars all day will do that for a man. He was married and had eleven children—a devout Catholic, my comrade Dick. Mr. Arden used him on occasion when a bit of extra muscle was needed. Dick didn't have the stomach for killing, but was more than happy to give some sorry bugger an oak rubdown if that's what Mr. Arden wanted.

The honest money only went so far. The best story I can tell about him is that when the railroad boys gathered for their union hall meetings roll call was done surname first, thus the man reading off the muster would request "Stiff, Dick" to signal his attendance, this to the inevitable jeers and hoots from the rowdy crowd. As for Leroy Bly, he was a short, handsome middle-aged Irishman who kept an eye on a couple of local speakeasies for the Arden family and did a bit of enforcement for Arden's bookmakers as well. Not a button man by trade, nonetheless I'd heard he'd blipped off at least two men and left their remains in the high timber west of town. Rumor had it one of the poor saps was the boyfriend of a dame Bly had taken a shine to—so he was a jealous bastard as well. Nice to know, as I'd never been above snaking a fella's chickadee if the mood was right.

A week passed in a confusion of *delirium tremens* and plain old delirium. Half dead from blood loss, sure, but it was the withdrawal from life-succoring whiskey and tobacco that threatened to do me in.

Eventually the fever broke I emerged into the light, growling for breakfast and hooch and a cigarette. Dick said someone from The Broadsword Hotel had called at least a dozen times—wouldn't leave a message, had to speak with me personal like. Meanwhile, Bly informed me that Mr. Arden was quite worried about the untimely deaths of The Long and The Short. Dick's suspicions that the powers that be wanted my hide proved accurate. It had come down through the bush telegraph I'd do well to take to the air for a few weeks. Perhaps a holiday in a sunnier clime. Bly set a small butcher paper package on the table. The package contained three hundred dollars of "vacation" money. Bly watched as I stuck the cash into my pocket. He was ostensibly Dick's chum and to a lesser degree mine, however I suspected he'd cheerfully plant an ice pick between my shoulder blades should I defy Mr. Arden's wishes. In fact, I figured the old man had sent him to keep tabs on my activities.

I'd read the name of one Conrad Paxton scribbled on the back of a card in Curtis Bane's wallet, so it seemed possible this mystery man dispatched the pair to blip me. A few subtle inquiries led me to believe my antagonist resided somewhere in Western Washington beyond the principle cities. Since getting shy of Olympia was the order of the day, I'd decided to track Paxton down and pay him a visit. To this effect, would the boys be willing to accompany me for expenses and a few laughs?

Both Dick and Bly agreed, Bly with the proviso he could bring along his nephew Vernon. Yeah, I was in Dutch with Mr. Arden, no question—no way Bly would drop his gig here in town unless it was to spy on me, maybe awaiting the word to blip me off. And young master Vernon, he was a sad sack gambler and snowbird known for taking any low deed that presented itself, thus I assumed Bly wanted him to tag along as backup when the moment came to slip me the shiv. Mr. Arden was likely assessing my continued value to his family versus the ire of his colleagues in Seattle. There was nothing for it but to lie low for a while and see what was what after the dust settled.

I uncapped a bottle and poured myself the first shot of many to come. I stared into the bottom of the glass. The crystal ball hinted this Conrad Paxton fellow was in for a world of pain.

Later that afternoon I received yet another call from management at the Broadsword Hotel passing along the message that an old friend of my father's, one Helios Augustus, desired my presence after his evening show. I hung up without committing, poured a drink and turned over the possibilities. In the end, I struggled into my best suit and had Dick drive me to the hotel.

The boys smuggled me out the back of the house and through a hole in the fence on the off chance sore friends of The Long and The Short might be watching. I wondered who that weird bird lurking down the street represented—a Seattle boss, or Paxton, or even somebody on Arden's payroll, a gun he'd called from out of town? I hated to worry like this; it gave me acid, had me jumping at shadows. Rattle a man enough he's going to make a mistake and get himself clipped.

I came into the performance late and took a seat on the edge of the smoky lounge where I could sag against the wall and ordered a steak sandwich and a glass of milk while the magician did his thing to mild applause.

Helios Augustus had grown a bit long in the tooth, a portly figure dressed in an elegant suit and a cape of darkest purple silk. However, his white hair and craggy features complemented the melodic and cultured timbre of his voice. He'd honed that voice in Shakespearean theatre and claimed descent from a distinguished lineage of Greek poets and prestidigitators. I'd met him at a nightclub in Seattle a couple of years before the Great War. He'd been slimmer and handsomer, and made doves appear and lovely female assistants disappear in puffs of smoke. Dad took me to watch the show because he'd known Helios Augustus before the magician became famous and was dealing cards on a barge in Port Angeles. Dad told me the fellow wasn't Greek—his real name was Phillip Wary and he'd come from the Midwest, son of a meat packer.

I smoked and waited for the magician to wrap up his routine with a series of elaborate card tricks, all of which required the assistance of a mature lady in a low-cut gown and jade necklace, a real duchess. The hand didn't need to be quicker than the eye with that much artfully lighted bosom to serve as a distraction. As the audience headed for the exits, he saw me and came over and shook my hand. "Johnny Cope in the flesh," he said. "You look like you've been on the wrong end of a stick. I'm sorry about your father." He did not add, *he was a good man.* I appreciated a little honesty, so far as it went. Goodness was not among Dad's virtues. He hadn't even liked to talk about it.

We adjourned to his dressing room where the old fellow produced a bottle of sherry and poured a couple of glasses. His quarters were plush, albeit cramped with his makeup desk and gold-framed mirror, steamer trunks plastered with stamps from exotic ports, a walnut armoire that scraped the ceiling, and shelves of arcane trinkets—bleached skulls and beakers, thick black books and cold braziers. A waxen, emaciated hand, gray as mud and severed at the wrist, jutted from an urn decorated with weird scrollwork like chains of teeny death's heads. The severed hand clutched a black candle. A brass kaleidoscope of particularly ornate make caught my attention. I squinted through the aperture and turned the dial. The metal felt damnably cold. Jigsaw pieces of painted crystal rattled around inside, revealing tantalizing glimpses of naked thighs and breasts, black corsets and red, pouty smiles. The image fell into place and it was no longer a burlesque dancer primping for my pleasure. Instead I beheld a horrid portrait of some rugose beast—all trunk and tentacle and squirming maw. I dropped the kaleidoscope like it was hot.

"Dear lad, you have to turn the opposite direction to focus the naked ladies." Helios Augustus smiled and shook his head at my provincial curiosity. He passed me a cigar, but I'd never acquired a taste for them and stuck with my Lucky Strike. He was in town on business, having relocated to San Francisco. His fortunes had waned in recent years; the proletarians preferred large stage productions with mirrors and cannon-smoke, acrobats and wild animals to his urbane and intimate style of magic. He lamented the recent deaths of the famed composer Moritz Moszkowski and the Polish novelist Wladislaw Reymont, both of whom he'd briefly entertained during his adventures abroad. Did I, by chance, enjoy classical arts? I confessed my tastes ran more toward Mark Twain and Fletch Henderson and Coleman Hawkins. "Well, big band is a worthy enough pleasure. A certain earthy complexity appropriate to an earthy man. I lived nearly eighteen years on the Continent. Played in the grandest and oldest theatres in Europe. Two shows on the Orient Express. Now I give myself away on a weeknight to faux royalty and well-dressed rabble. Woe is me!" He laughed without much bitterness and poured another drink.

Finally, I said, "What did you call me here to jaw about?"

"Rumor has it Conrad Paxton seeks the pleasure of your company."

"Yeah, that's the name. And let's get it straight—*I'm* looking for *him* with a passion. Who the hell is he?"

"Doubtless you've heard of Eadweard Muybridge, the rather infamous inventor. Muybridge created the first moving picture."

"Dad knew him from the Army. Didn't talk about him much. Muybridge went soft in the head and they parted ways." I had a sip of sherry.

"A brilliant, scandalous figure who was the pet of California high society for many years. He passed away around the turn of the century. Paxton was his estranged son and protégé. It's a long story—he put the boy up for adoption; they were later reconciled after a fashion. I met the lad when he debuted from the ether in Seattle as the inheritor of Muybridge's American estate. No one knew that he was actually Muybridge's son at the time. Initially he was widely celebrated as a disciple of Muybridge and a bibliophile specializing in the arcane and the occult, an acquirer of morbid photography and cinema as well. He owns a vault of Muybridge's photographic plates and short films I'm certain many historians would give an eye tooth to examine."

"According to my information, he lives north of here these days," I said.

"He didn't fare well in California and moved on after the war. Ransom Hollow, a collection of villages near the Cascades. You shot two of his men in Seattle. Quite a rumpus, eh?"

"Maybe they were doing a job for this character, but they weren't his men. Dirk and Bane are traveling guns."

"Be that as it may, you would do well to fear Conrad's intentions."

"That's backwards, as I said."

"So, you *do* mean to track him to ground. Don't go alone. He's well-protected. Take some of your meaner hoodlum associates, is my suggestion."

"What's his beef? Does he have the curse on me?"

"It seems plausible. He killed your father."

I nodded and finished my latest round of booze. I set aside the glass and drew my pistol and chambered a round and rested the weapon across my knee, barrel fixed on the magician's navel. My head was woozy and I wasn't sure of hitting the side of a barn if push came to shove. "Our palaver has taken a peculiar and unwelcome turn. Please, explain how you've come into this bit of news. Quick and to the point is my best advice."

The magician puffed on his cigar, and regarded me with a half smile that the overly civilized reserve for scofflaws and bounders such as myself. I resisted the temptation to jam a cushion over his face and dust him then and there, because I knew slippery devils like him always came in first and they survived by stepping on the heads of drowning men. He removed the cigar from his mouth and said, "Conrad Paxton confessed it to some associates of mine several years ago."

"Horse shit."

"The source is . . . trustworthy."

"Dad kicked from a heart attack. Are you saying this lug got to him somehow? Poisoned him?" It was difficult to speak. My vision had narrowed as it did when blood was in my eye. I wanted to strangle, to stab, to empty the Luger. "Did my old man rub out somebody near and dear to Paxton? Thump him one? What?"

"Conrad didn't specify a method, didn't express a motive, only that he'd committed the deed."

"You've taken your sweet time reporting the news," I said.

"The pistol aimed at my John Thomas suggests my caution was well-founded. At the time I didn't believe the story, thinking Paxton a loud-mouthed eccentric. He *is* a loud-mouthed eccentric—I simply thought this more rubbish."

"I expect bragging of murder is a sure way to spoil a fellow's reputation in your refined circles." My collar tightened and my vision was streaky from my elevated pulse, which in turn caused everything on me that was broken, crushed, or punctured to throb. I kept my cool by fantasizing about what I was going to do to my enemy when I tracked him to ground. Better, much better.

"It also didn't help when the squalid details of Conrad's provenance and subsequent upbringing eventually came to light. The poor chap was in and out of institutions for most of his youth. He worked as a clerk at university and there reunited with Papa Muybridge and ultimately joined the photographer's staff. If not for Eadweard Muybridge's patronage, today Conrad would likely be in a gutter or dead."

"Oh, I see. Paxton didn't become a hermit by choice, your people shunned him like the good folks in Utah do it."

"In a nutshell, yes. Conrad's childhood history is sufficiently macabre to warrant such treatment. Not much is known about the Paxtons except they owned a fishery. Conrad's adoptive sister vanished when she was eight and he nine. All fingers pointed to his involvement. At age sixteen he drowned a rival at school and was sent to an asylum until he reached majority. The rich and beautiful are somewhat phobic regarding the criminally insane no matter how affluent the latter might be. Institutional taint isn't fashionable unless one derives from old money. Alas, Conrad is new money and what he's got isn't much by the standards of California high society."

"I don't know whether to thank you or shoot you," I said. "I'm inclined to accept your word for the moment. It would be an unfortunate thing were I to discover this information of yours is a hoax. Who are these associates that heard Paxton's confession?"

"The Corning Sisters. The sisters dwell in Luster, one of several rustic burghs in Ransom Hollow. If anyone can help you against Conrad, it'll be the crones. I admired Donald. Your father was a killer with the eye of an artist, the heart of a poet. A conflicted man, but a loyal friend. I'd like to know why Conrad wanted him dead."

"I'm more interested in discovering why he wants to bop me," I said. Actually, I was more preoccupied with deciding on a gun or a dull knife.

"He may not necessarily wish to kill you, my boy. It may be worse than that. Do you enjoy films? There's one that may be of particular importance to you."

Dick gave me a look when I brought Helios Augustus to the curb. He drove us to the Redfield Museum of Natural History without comment, although Bly's nephew Vernon frowned and muttered and cast suspicious glances into the rearview. I'd met the lug once at a speakeasy on the south side; lanky kid with red-rimmed eyes and a leaky nose. Pale as milk and mean as a snake. No scholar, either. I smiled at him, though not friendly like.

Helios Augustus rang the doorbell until a pasty clerk who pulled duty as a night watchman and janitor admitted us. The magician held a brief, muttered conference and we were soon guided to the basement archives where the public was never ever allowed. The screening area for visiting big cheeses, donors, and dignitaries was located in an isolated region near the boiler room and the heat was oppressive. At least the seats were comfortable old wingbacks and I rested in one while they fussed and bustled around and eventually got the boxy projector rolling. The room was already dim and then Helios Augustus killed the lone floor lamp and we were at the bottom of a mineshaft, except for a blotch of light from the camera aperture spattered against a cloth panel. The clerk cranked dutifully and Helios Augustus settled beside me. He smelled of brandy and dust and when he leaned in to whisper his narration of the film, tiny specks of fire glinted in his irises.

What he showed me was a silent film montage of various projects by Eadweard Muybridge. The first several appeared innocuous—simple renderings of the dead photographer's various plates and the famous *Horse in Motion* reel that settled once and for all the matter of whether all four feet of the animal leave the ground during full gallop. For some reason the jittering frames of the buffalo plunging across the prairie made me uneasy. The images repeated until they shivered and the beast's hide grew thick and lustrous, until I swore foam bubbled from its snout, that its eye was fixed upon me with a malign purpose, and I squirmed in my seat and felt blood from my belly wound soaking the bandages. Sensing my discomfort, Helios Augustus patted my arm and advised me to steel myself for what was to come.

After the horse and buffalo, there arrived a stream of increasingly disjointed images that the magician informed me originated with numerous photographic experiments Muybridge indulged during his years teaching at university. These often involved men and women, likely students or staff, performing mundane tasks such as arranging books, or folding clothes, or sifting flour, in mundane settings such as parlors and kitchens. The routine gradually segued into strange territory. The subjects continued their plebian labors, but did so partially unclothed, and soon modesty was abandoned as were all garments. Yet there was nothing overtly sexual or erotic about the succeeding imagery. No, the sensations that crept over me were of anxiety and revulsion as a naked woman of middle age silently trundled about the confines of a workshop, fetching pails of water from a cistern and dumping them into a barrel. Much like the buffalo charging in place, she retraced her route with manic stoicism, endlessly, endlessly. A three-legged dog tracked her circuit by swiveling its misshapen skull. The dog fretted and scratched behind its ear and finally froze, snout pointed at the camera. The dog shuddered and rolled onto its side and frothed at the mouth while the woman continued, heedless, damned.

Next came a sequence of weirdly static shots of a dark, watery expanse. The quality was blurred and seemed alternately too close and too far. Milk-white mist crept into the frame. Eventually something large disturbed the flat ocean—a whale breaching, an iceberg bobbing to the surface. Ropes, or cables lashed and writhed and whipped the water to a sudsy froth. Scores of ropes, scores of cables. The spectacle hurt my brain. Mist thickened to pea soup and swallowed the final frame.

I hoped for the lights to come up and the film to end. Instead, Helios Augustus squeezed my forearm in warning as upon the screen a boy, naked as a jay, scuttled on all fours from a stony archway in what might've been a cathedral. The boy's expression distorted in the manner of a wild animal caged, or of a man as the noose tightens around his neck. His eyes and tongue protruded. He raised his head so sharply it seemed impossible that his spine wasn't wrenched, and his alacrity at advancing and retreating was wholly unnatural . . . well, ye gods, that had to be a trick of the camera. A horrid trick. "The boy is quite real," Helios Augustus said. "All that you see is real. No illusion, no stagecraft."

I tugged a handkerchief from my pocket and dabbed my brow. My hand was clammy. "Why in hell did he take those pictures?"

"No one knows. Muybridge was a man of varied moods. There were sides to him seen only under certain conditions and by certain people. He conducted these more questionable film experiments with strict secrecy. I imagine the tone and content disturbed the prudish elements at university—"

"You mean the sane folks."

"As you wish, the sane folks. None dared stand in the way of his scientific pursuits. The administration understood how much glory his fame would bring them, and all the money."

"Yeah," I said. "Yeah. The money. Thanks for the show, old man. Could have done without it, all the same."

"I wanted you to meet young master Conrad," the magician said. "Before you met Conrad the elder."

The boy on the screen opened his mouth. His silent scream pierced my eye, then my brain. For the first time in I don't know, I made the sign of the cross.

We loaded my luggage then swung by Dick, Bly, and Vernon's joints to fetch their essentials—a change of clothes, guns, and any extra hooch that was lying around. Then we made for the station and the evening train. Ah, the silken rapture of riding the Starlight Express in a Pullman sleeper. Thank you, dear Mr. Arden, sir.

My companions shared the sleeper next to mine and they vowed to keep a watch over me as I rested. They'd already broken out a deck of cards and uncorked a bottle of whiskey as I limped from their quarters, so I wasn't expecting much in the way of protection. It was dark as the train steamed along between Olympia and Tacoma. I sat in the gloom and put the Thompson together and laid it beneath the coverlet. This was more from habit than expediency. Firing the gun would be a bastard with my busted fingers and I hoped it wouldn't come to that. I'd removed the bandages and let it be—a mass of purple and yellow bruises from the nails to my wrist. I could sort of make a fist and that was all that mattered, really.

I fell asleep, lulled by the rattle and sway of the car on the tracks, and dreamed of Bane's face, his bulging eyes, all that blood. Bane's death mask shimmered and sloughed into that of the boy in the film, an adolescent Conrad Paxton being put through his paces by an offstage tormentor. A celebrated ghoul who'd notched his place in the history books with some fancy imagination and a clever arrangement of lenses, bulbs, and springs.

Didn't last long, thank god, as I snapped to when the train shuddered and slowed. Lamplight from some unknown station filtered through the blinds and sent shadows skittering across the ceiling and down the walls. I pointed the barrel at a figure hunched near the door, but the figure dissolved as the light shifted and revealed nothing more dangerous than my suitcase, the bulk of my jacket slung across a chair. I sat there a long while, breathing heavily as distant twinkly lights of passing towns floated in the great darkness.

The train rolled into Ransom Hollow and we disembarked at the Luster depot without incident. A cab relayed us to the Sycamore Hotel, the only game in the village. This was wild and wooly country, deep in the forested hills near the foot of the mountains. Ransom Hollow comprised a long, shallow river valley that eventually climbed into those mountains. An old roadmap marked the existence of three towns and a half-dozen villages in the vicinity, each of them established during or prior to the westward expansion of the 1830s. Judging by the moss and shingle roofs of the squat and rude houses, most of them saltbox or shotgun shacks, the rutted boardwalks and goats wandering the unpaved lanes, not much had changed since the era of mountain men trappers and gold rush placer miners.

The next morning we ate breakfast at a shop a couple of blocks from the hotel, then Dick and Bly departed to reconnoiter Paxton's estate while Vernon stayed with me. My hand and ear were throbbing. I stepped into the alley and had a gulp from a flask I'd stashed in my coat, and smoked one of the reefers Doc Green had slipped me the other day. Dope wasn't my preference, but it killed the pain far better than the booze did.

It was a scorcher of an autumn day and I hailed a cab and we rode in the back with the window rolled down. I smoked another cigarette and finished the whiskey; my mood was notably improved by the time the driver deposited us at our destination. The Corning sisters lived in a wooded neighborhood north of the town square. Theirs was a brick bungalow behind a steep walkup and gated entrance. Hedges blocked in the yard and its well-tended beds of roses and begonias. Several lawn gnomes crouched in the grass or peeked from the shrubbery; squat, wooden monstrosities of shin height, exaggerated features, pop-eyed and leering.

The bungalow itself had a European-style peaked roof and was painted a cheery yellow. Wooden shutters bracketed the windows. Faces, similar to the sinister gnomes, were carved into the wood. The iron knocker on the main door was also shaped into a grinning, demonic visage. A naked man reclined against the hedge. He was average height, brawny as a Viking rower and sunburned. All over. His eyes were yellow. He spat in the grass and turned and slipped sideways through the hedge and vanished.

"What in hell?" Vernon said. He'd dressed in a bowler and an out-of-fashion jacket that didn't quite fit his lanky frame. He kept removing his tiny spectacles and smearing them around on his frayed sleeve. "See that lug? He was stark starin' nude!"

I doffed my Homburg and rapped the door, eschewing the knocker.

"Hello, Mr. Cope. And you must be Vernon. You're exactly how I imagined." A woman approached toward my left from around the corner of the house. She was tall, eye to eye with me, and softly middle-aged. Her hair was shoulder-length and black, her breasts full beneath a common-sense shirt and blouse. She wore pants and sandals. Her hands were dirty and she held a trowel loosely at hip level. I kept an eye on the trowel—her manner reminded me of a Mexican knife fighter I'd tangled with once. The scar from the Mexican's blade traversed a span between my collarbone and left nipple.

"I didn't realize you were expecting me," I said, calculating the implications of Helios Augustus wiring ahead to warn her of my impending arrival.

"Taller than your father," she said. Her voice was harsh. The way she carefully enunciated each syllable suggested her roots were far from Washington. Norway, perhaps. The garden gnomes were definitely Old World knick-knacks.

"You knew my father? I had no idea."

"I've met the majority of Augustus' American friends. He enjoys putting them on display."

"Mrs. Corning—"

"Not Mrs.," she said. "This is a house of spinsters. I'm Carling. You'll not encounter Groa and Vilborg, alas. Come inside from this hateful sunlight. I'll make you a pudding." She hesitated and looked Vernon north to south and then smiled an unpleasant little smile that made me happy for some reason. "Your friend can take his ease out here under the magnolia. We don't allow pets in the cottage."

"Shut up," I said to Vernon when he opened his mouth to argue.

Carling led me into the dim interior of the bungalow and barred the door. The air was sour and close. Meat hooks dangled from low rafter beams and forced me to stoop lest I whack my skull. An iron cauldron steamed and burbled upon the banked coals of a hearth. A wide plank table ran along the wall. The table was scarred. I noted an oversized meat cleaver stuck into a plank near a platter full of curdled blood. The floor was filthy. I immediately began to reassess the situation and kept my coat open in case I needed to draw my pistol in a hurry.

"Shakespearean digs you've got here, Ma'am," I said as I brushed dead leaves from a chair and sat. "No thanks on the pudding, if you don't mind."

"Your hand is broken. And you seem to be missing a portion of your ear. Your father didn't get into such trouble."

"He got himself dead, didn't he?"

In the next room, a baby cried briefly. Spinsters with a baby. I didn't like it. My belly hurt and my ear throbbed in time with my spindled fingers and I wondered, the thought drifting out of the blue, if she could smell the blood soaking my undershirt.

Carling's left eye drooped in either a twitch or a wink. She rummaged in a cabinet and then sprinkled a pinch of what appeared to be tea leaves into a cloudy glass. Down came a bottle of something that gurgled when she shook it. She poured three fingers into the glass and set it before me. Then she leaned against the counter and regarded me, idly drumming her fingers against her thigh. "We *weren't* expecting you. However, your appearance isn't particularly a surprise. Doubtless the magician expressed his good will by revealing Conrad Paxton's designs upon you. The magician was sincerely fond of your father. He fancies himself an urbane and sophisticated man. Such individuals always have room for one or two brutes in their menagerie of acquaintances."

"That was Dad, all right," I said and withdrew a cigarette, pausing before striking the match until she nodded. I smoked for a bit while we stared at one another.

"I'll read your fortune when you've finished," she said indicating the glass of alcohol and the noisome vapors drifting forth. In the bluish light her features seemed more haggard and vulpine than they had in the bright, clean sunshine. "Although, I think I can guess."

"Where's Groa and Vilborg?" I snapped open the Korn switchblade I carried in the breast pocket of my shirt and stirred the thick dark booze with the point. The knife was a small comfort, but I was taking it where I could find it.

"Wise, very wise to remember their names, Johnny, may I call you Johnny?—and to utter them. Names do have power. My sisters are in the cellar finishing the task we'd begun prior to this interruption. You have us at a disadvantage. Were it otherwise . . . But you lead a charmed life, don't you? There's not much chance of your return after this, more is the pity."

"What kind of task would that be?"

"The dark of the moon is upon us tonight. We conduct a ritual of longevity during the reaping season. It requires the most ancient and potent of sacrifices. Three days and three nights of intense labor, of which this morning counts as the first."

"Cutting apart a hapless virgin, are we?"

Carling ran her thumbnail between her front teeth. A black dog padded into the kitchen from the passage that let from the living room where the cries had emanated and I thought perhaps it had uttered the noise. The dog's eyes were yellow. It was the length and mass of a Saint Bernard, although its breed suggested that of a wolf. The dog smiled at me. Carling spoke a guttural phrase and unbarred the door and let it out. She shut the door and pressed her forehead against the frame.

"How do you know Paxton?" I said, idly considering her earlier comment about banning pets from the house.

"My sisters and I have ever been great fans of Eadweard's photography. Absolute genius, and quite the conversationalist. I have some postcards he sent us from his travels. Very thoughtful in his own, idiosyncratic way. Quite loyal to those who showed the same to him. Conrad is Eadweard Muybridge's dead wife's son, a few minutes the elder of his brother, Florado. The Paxtons took him to replace their own infant who'd died at birth the very night Muybridge's boys came into the world. Florado spent his youth in the institution. No talent to speak of. Worthless."

"But there must've been some question of paternity in Muybridge's mind. He left them to an institution in the first place. Kind of a rotten trick, you ask me."

"Eadweard tried to convince himself the children were the get of that retired colonel his wife had been humping."

"But they weren't."

"Oh, no—they belonged to Eadweard."

"Yet, one remained at the orphanage, and Conrad was adopted. Why did Muybridge come back into the kid's life? Guilt? Couldn't be guilt since he left the twin to rot."

"You couldn't understand. Conrad was special, possessed of a peculiar darkness that Eadweard recognized and later, after traveling in Central America doing goddess knows what. The boy was key to something very large and very important. We all knew that. Don't ask and I'll tell you no lies. Take it up with Conrad when you see him."

"I don't believe Paxton murdered my father," I said. The baby in the other room moaned and I resisted the urge to look in that direction.

"Oh, then this is a social call? I would've fixed my hair, naughty boy."

"I'm here because he sent a pair of guns after me in Seattle. I didn't appreciate the gesture. Maybe I'm wrong, maybe he did blip my father. Two reasons to buzz him. Helios says you know the book on this guy. So, I come to you before I go to him."

"Reconnaissance is always wisest. Murder is not precisely what occurred. Conrad drained your father's life energy, siphoned it away via soul taking. You know of what I speak—photography, if done in a prescribed and ritualistic manner, can steal the subject's life force. This had a side consequence of effecting Mr. Cope's death. To be honest, Conrad didn't do it personally. He isn't talented in that area. He's a dilettante of the black arts. He had it done by proxy, much the way your employer Mr. Arden has *you* do the dirty work for him."

She was insane, obviously. Barking mad and probably very dangerous. God alone knew how many types of poison she had stashed up her sleeve. That cauldron of soup was likely fuming with nightshade, and my booze . . . I pushed it aside and brushed the blade against my pants leg. "Voodoo?" I said, just making conversation, wondering if I should rough her up a bit, if that was even wise, what with her dog and the naked guy roaming around. No confidence in Vernon whatsoever.

"There are many faiths at the crossroads here in the Hollow," Carling said, bending to stir the pot and good god her shoulders were broad as a logger's. "Voodoo is not one of them. I can't tell you who did in your father, only that it was done and that Conrad ordered it so. I recommend you make haste to the Paxton estate and do what you do best—rub the little shit out before he does for you. He tried once, he'll definitely take another crack at it."

"Awfully harsh words for your old chum," I said to her brawny backside. "Two of you must have had a lovers' quarrel."

"He's more of a godson. I don't have a problem with Conrad. He's vicious and vengeful and wants my head on a stick, but I don't hold that against him in the slightest."

"Then why are you so interested in seeing him get blipped?"

"You seem like a nice boy, Johnny." Carling turned slowly and there was something amiss with her face that I couldn't quite figure out. That nasty grin was back, though. "Speaking of treachery and violence, that other fellow you brought is no good. I wager he'll bite."

"Think so?" I said. "He's just along for the ride."

"Bah. Let us bargain. Leave your friend with us and I'll give you a present. I make knick-knacks, charms, trinkets and such. What you really need if you're going to visit the Paxton estate is a talisman to ward off the diabolic. It wouldn't do to go traipsing in there as you are."

"I agree. I'll be sure to pack a shotgun."

She cackled. Actually and truly cackled. "Yes, yes, for the best. Here's a secret few know—I wasn't always a spinster. In another life I traveled to India and China and laid with many, many men, handsomer than you even. They were younger and unspoiled. I nearly, very, very nearly married a rich Chinaman who owned a great deal of Hainan."

"Didn't work out, eh? Sorry to hear it, Ms. Corning."

"He raised monkeys. I hate monkeys worse than Christ." She went through the door into the next room and I put my hand on the pistol from reflex and perhaps a touch of fear, but she returned with nothing more sinister than a shriveled black leaf in her open palm. Not a leaf, I discovered upon receiving it, but a dry cocoon. She dropped it into my shirt pocket, just leaned over and did it without asking, and up close she smelled of spice and dirt and unwashed flesh.

"Thanks," I said recoiling from the proximity of her many large, sharp teeth.

"Drink your whiskey and run along."

I stared at the glass. It smelled worse than turpentine.

"Drink your fucking whiskey," she said.

And I did, automatic as you please. It burned like acid.

She snatched the empty glass and regarded the constellation of dregs at the bottom. She grinned, sharp as a pickaxe. "He's throwing a party in a couple of nights. Does one every week. Costumes, pretty girls, rich trappers and furriers, our rustic nobility. It augers well for you to attend."

I finally got my breath back. "In that case, the furriers' ball it is."

She smiled and patted my cheek. "Good luck. Keep the charm on your person. Else . . . " She smiled sadly and straightened to her full height. "Might want to keep this visit between you and me."

Vernon was missing when I hit the street. The cab driver shrugged and said he hadn't seen anything. No reason not to believe him, but I dragged him by the hair from the car and belted him around some on the off chance he was lying. Guy wasn't lying, though. There wasn't any way I'd go back into that abattoir of a cottage to hunt for the lost snowbird, so I decided on a plausible story to tell the boys. Vernon was the type slated to end it face down in a ditch, anyway. Wouldn't be too hard to sell the tale and frankly, watching Bly stew and fret would be a treat.

Never did see Vernon again.

Dick and Bly hadn't gotten very close to the Paxton mansion. The estate was guarded by a bramble-covered stone wall out of "Sleeping Beauty," a half mile of wildwood and overgrown gardens, then croquet courses, polo fields, and a small barracks that housed a contingent of fifteen or so backwoods thugs armed with shotguns and dogs. God alone knew where Paxton had recruited such a gang. I figured they must be either locals pressed into service or real talent from out of state. No way to tell without tangling with them, though.

Dick had cased the joint with field glasses and concluded a daylight approach would be risky as hell. Retreat and regrouping seemed the preferable course, thus we decided to cool our heels and get skunk drunk.

The boys had caught wind of a nasty speakeasy in a cellar near Belson Creek in neighboring Olde Towne. A girl Bly had picked up in the parking lot of Luster's one and only hardware store claimed men with real hard bark on them hung around there. Abigail and Bly were real chummy, it seemed, and he told her we were looking to put the arm on a certain country gentleman. The girl suggested low-at-the-heel scoundrels who tenanted the dive might be helpful.

The speakeasy was called Satan's Bung and the password at the door was *Van Iblis*, all of this Dick had discovered from his own temporary girls, Wanda and Clementine, which made me think they'd spent most of the day reconnoitering a watering hole rather than pursuing our mission with any zeal. In any event, we sashayed into that den of iniquity with sweet little chippies who still had most of their teeth, a deck of unmarked cards, and a bottle of sour mash. There were a few tough guys hanging around, as advertised; lumberjacks in wool coats and sawdust-sprinkled caps and cork boots; the meanest of the lot even hoisted his axe onto the bar. One gander at my crew and they looked the other way right smartly. Some good old boys came down from the hills or out of the swamp, hitched their overalls and commenced to picking banjos, banging drums, and harmonizing in an angelic chorus that belied their sodden, bloated, and warty features, their shaggy beards and knurled scalps. They clogged barefoot, stamping like bulls ready for battle.

Dick, seven sails to the wind, wondered aloud what could be done in the face of determined and violent opposition entrenched at the Paxton estate and I laughed and told him not to worry too much, this was a vacation. Relax and enjoy himself—I'd think of something. I always thought of something.

Truth of it was, I'd lost a bit of my stomach for the game after tea and cake at the Corning Sisters' house and the resultant disappearance of Vernon. If it hadn't been for the rifling of my home, the attack by The Long and The Short, the mystery of whether Paxton really bopped Dad would've remained a mystery. Thus, despite my reassurances to the contrary, I wasn't drinking and plotting a clever plan of assault or infiltration of the estate, but rather simply drinking and finagling a way to get my ashes hauled by one of the chippies.

One thing led to another, a second bottle of rotgut to a third, and Clementine climbed into my lap and nuzzled my neck and unbuttoned my pants and slipped her hand inside. Meanwhile a huge man in a red and black-checkered coat and coonskin cap pranced, nimble as a Russian ballerina, and wheedled a strange tune on a flute of lacquered black ivory. This flautist was a hirsute, wiry fellow with a jagged visage hacked from a stone, truly more beast than man by his gesticulations and the manner he gyrated his crotch, thrusting to the beat, and likely the product of generations of inbreeding, yet he piped with an evil and sinuous grace that captured the admiration of me, my companions, the entire roomful of seedy and desperate characters. The lug seemed to fixate upon me, glaring and smirking as he clicked his heels and puffed his cheeks and capered among the tables like a faun.

I conjectured aloud as to his odd behavior, upon which Dick replied in a slur that if I wanted him to give the bird a thrashing, just make the sign. My girl, deep into her cups, mumbled that the flautist was named Dan Blackwood, last scion of a venerable Ransom Hollow family renowned as hunters and furriers without peer, but these days runners of moonshine. A rapist and murderer who'd skated out of prison by decree of the prince of Darkness Hissownself, or so the fireside talk went. A fearful and loathsome brute, his friends were few and of similar malignant ilk and were known as the Blackwood Boys. Her friend Abigail, paused from licking Bly's earlobe to concur.

Dan Blackwood trilled his oddly sinister tune while a pair of hillbillies accompanied him with banjo and fiddle and a brawny lad with golden locks shouldered aside the piano player and pawed the ivories to create a kind of screeching cacophony not unlike a train wreck while the paper lanterns dripped down blood-red light and the cellar audience clenched into a tighter knot and swayed on their feet, their stools and stumps, stamping time against the muddy floor. From that cacophony a dark and primitive rhythm emerged as each instrument fell into line with its brother and soon that wattled and toad-like orchestra found unity with their piper and produced a song that put ice in my loins and welded me to my seat. Each staccato burst from the snare drum, each shrill from the flute, each discordant clink from the piano, each nails on slate shriek of violin and fiddle, pierced my brain, caused a sweet, agonizing lurch of my innards, and patient Clementine jerked my cock, out of joint, so to speak.

The song ended with a bang and a crash and the crowd swooned. More tunes followed and more people entered that cramped space and added to the sensation we were supplicants or convicts in a special circle of hell, such was the ripe taint of filthy work clothes and matted hair and belched booze like sulfurous counterpoint to the maniacal contortions of the performers, the rich foul effluvium of their concert.

During an intermission, I extricated myself from industrious Clementine and made my way up the stairs into the alley to piss against the side of the building. The darkness was profound, moonless as Carling had stated, and the stars were covered by a thin veil of cloud. Despite my best efforts, I wasn't particularly impaired and thus wary and ready for trouble when the door opened and a group of men, one bearing a lantern that oozed the hideous red glow, spilled forth and mounted the stairs. The trio stopped at the sight of me and raised the lantern high so that it scattered a nest of rats into the hinder of the lane. I turned to face them, hand on pistol, and I smiled and hoped Dick or Bly might come tripping up the steps at any moment.

But there was no menace evinced by this group, at least not aimed at me. The leader was the handsome blond lad who'd hammered the piano into submission. He saluted me with two fingers and said, "Hey, now city feller. My name's Candy. How'n ya like our burg?" The young man didn't wait for an answer, but grunted at his comrades, the toad-like fiddler and banjo picker who might've once been conjoined and later separated with an axe blow, then said to me in his thick, unfamiliar accent, "So, chum, the telegraph sez you in Ransom Holler on dirty business. My boss knows who yer gunnin' for and he'd be pleased as punch to make yer acquaintance."

"That's right civilized. I was thinking of closing this joint down, though . . . "

"Naw, naw, ol' son. Ya gotta pay the piper round this neck of the woods."

I asked who and where and the kid laughed and said to get my friends and follow him, and to ease my mind the men opened their coats to show they weren't packing heat. Big knives and braining clubs wrapped in leather and nail-studded, but no pea shooters and I thought again how Dick had managed to learn of this place and recalled something about one of the girls, perhaps Abigail, whispering the name into his ear, and a small chill crept along my spine. Certainly Paxton could be laying a trap, and he wasn't the only candidate for skullduggery. Only the good lord knew how strongly the Corning sisters interfered in the politics of the Hollow and if they'd set the Blackwood Gang upon us, and of course this caused my suspicious mind to circle back to Helios Augustus and his interest in the affair. Increasingly I kicked myself for not having shot him when I'd the chance and before he could take action against me, assuming my paranoid suppositions bore weight. So, I nodded and tipped my hat and told the Blackwood Boys to bide a moment.

Dick and Bly were barely coherent when I returned to gather them and the girls. Bly, collar undone, eyes crossed and blinking, professed incredulity that we would even consider traveling with these crazed locals to some as yet unknown location. Dick didn't say anything, although his mouth curved down at the corners with the distaste of a man who'd gulped castor oil. We both understood the score; no way on God's green earth we'd make it back to Luster and our heavy armament if the gang wanted our skins. Probably wouldn't matter even if we actually managed to get armed. This was the heart of midnight and the best and only card to turn was to go for a ride with the devil. He grabbed Bly's arm and dragged him along after me, the goodtime girls staggering in our wake. Ferocious lasses—they weren't keen on allowing their meal tickets to escape, and clutched our sleeves and wailed like the damned.

Young Master Candy gave our ragged assembly a bemused once-over, then shrugged and told us to get a move on, starlight was wasting. He led us to a great creaking behemoth of a farm truck with raised sides to pen in livestock and bade us pile into the bed. His compatriot the fiddler was already a boulder lodged behind the steering wheel.

I don't recall the way because it was pitch black and the night wind stung my eyes. We drove along Belson Creek and crossed it on rickety narrow bridges and were soon among ancient groves of poplar and fir, well removed from Olde Towne or any other lighted habitation. The road was rutted and the jarring threatened to rip my belly open. I spent most of the thankfully brief ride doubled, hands pressed hard against the wound, hoping against hope to keep my guts on the inside.

The truck stopped briefly and Candy climbed down to scrape the ruined carcass of a raccoon or opossum from the dirt and chucked it into the bed near our feet. Bly groaned and puked onto his shoes and the girls screamed or laughed or both. Dick was a blurry white splotch in the shadows and from the manner he hunched, I suspected he had a finger on the trigger of the revolver in his pocket. Most likely, he figured I'd done in poor, stupid Vernon and was fixing to dust that weasel Bly next, hell maybe I'd go all in and make a play for Mr. Arden. These ideas were far from my mind (well, dusting Bly was a possibility), naturally. Suicide wasn't my intent. Nonetheless, I couldn't fault Dick for worrying; could only wonder, between shocks to my kidneys and gut from the washboard track, how he would land if it ever came time to choose teams.

The fiddler swung the truck along a tongue of gravel that unrolled deep inside a bog and we came to a ramshackle hut, a trapper or fisherman's abode, raised on stilts that leaned every which way like a spindly, decrepit daddy longlegs with a house on its back. Dull, scaly light flickered through windows with tanned skins for curtains and vaguely illuminated the squelching morass of a yard with its weeds and moss and rusty barrels half sunk in the muck, and close by in the shadows came the slosh of Belson Creek churning fitfully as it dreamed. Another truck rolled in behind us and half a dozen more goons wordlessly unloaded and stood around, their faces obscured in the gloom. All of them bore clubs, mattock handles, and gaff hooks.

There was a kind of ladder descending from a trapdoor and on either side were strung moldering nets and the moth-eaten hides of beasts slaughtered decades ago and chains of animal bones and antlers that jangled when we bumped them in passing. I went first, hoping to not reinjure my hand while entertaining visions of a sledgehammer smashing my skull, or a machete lopping my melon at the neck as I passed through the opening. Ducks in Tin Pan Alley is what we were.

Nobody clobbered me with a hammer, nobody chopped me with an axe, and I hoisted myself into the sooty confines of Dan Blackwood's shanty. Beaver hides were stretched into circles and tacked on the walls, probably to cover the knotholes and chinks in a vain effort to bar the gnats and mosquitoes that swarmed the bog. Bundles of fox and muskrat hide were twined at the muzzle and hung everywhere and black bear furs lay in heaps and crawled with sluggish flies. A rat crouched, enthroned high atop one mound, sucking its paws. It regarded me with skepticism. Light came from scores of candles, coagulated slag of black and white, and rustic kerosene lamps I wagered had seen duty in Gold Rush mines. The overwhelming odors were that of animal musk, lye, and peat smoke. Already sweat poured from me and I wanted another dose of mash.

That sinister flautist Dan Blackwood tended a cast iron stove, fry pan in one fist, spatula in the other. He had already prepared several platters of flapjacks. He wore a pork pie hat cocked at a precipitous angle. A bear skin covered him after a burlesque fashion.

"Going to be one of those nights, isn't it?" I said as my friends and hangers on clambered through the hatch and stood blinking and gawping at their surroundings, this taxidermy post in Hades.

"Hello, cousin. Drag up a stump. Breakfast is at hand." Blackwood's voice was harsh and thin and came through his long nose. At proximity, his astounding grotesqueness altered into a perverse beauty, such were the chiseled planes and crags of his brow and cheek, the lustrous blackness of his matted hair that ran riot over his entire body. His teeth were perfectly white when he smiled, and he smiled often.

The cakes, fried in pure lard and smothered in butter and maple syrup were pretty fucking divine. Blackwood ate with almost dainty precision and his small, dark eyes shone brightly in the candle flame and ye gods the heat from the stove was as the heat from a blast furnace and soon all of us were in shirt sleeves or less, the girls quickly divested themselves of blouse and skirt and lounged around in their dainties. I didn't care about the naked chickadees; my attention was divided between my recurrent pains of hand and ear, and gazing in wonder at our satyr host, lacking only his hooves to complete the image of the great god Pan taking a mortal turn as a simple gang boss. We had him alone—his men remained below in the dark—and yet, in my bones I felt it was me and Dick and Bly who were at a disadvantage if matters went south.

"Don't get a lot of fellows with your kind of bark around here," Blackwood said. He reclined in a heavy wooden chair padded with furs, not unlike the throne of a feudal lord who was contemplating the fate of some unwelcome itinerant vagabonds. "Oh, there's wild men and murderous types aplenty, but not professional gunslingers. I hear tell you've come to the Hollow with blood in your eye, and who put it there? Why dear little Connie Paxton, of course; the moneybags who rules from his castle a few miles yonder as the crow wings it."

"Friend of yours?" I said, returning his brilliant smile with one of my own as I gauged the speed I could draw the Luger and pump lead into that hairy torso. Clementine slithered over and caressed my shoulders and kissed my neck. Her husband had been a merchant marine during the Big One, had lain in Davey Jones's Locker since 1918. Her nipples were hard as she pressed against my back.

Blackwood kept right on smiling. "*Friend* is a powerful word, cousin. Almost as powerful as a true name. It's more proper to say Mr. Paxton and I have a pact. Keepin' the peace so we can all conduct our nefarious trades, well that's a sacred duty."

"I understand why you'd like things to stay peaceful," I said.

"No, cousin, you *don't* understand. The Hollow is far from peaceful. We do surely love our bloodlettin', make no mistake. Children go missin' from their beds and tender maidens are ravished by Black Bill of the Wood," he winked at slack-jawed and insensate Abigail who lay against Bly, "and just the other day the good constable Jarred Brown discovered the severed head of his best deputy floatin' in Belson Creek. Alas, poor Ned Smedley. I knew him, Johnny! Peaceful, this territory ain't. On the other hand, we've avoided full-scale battle since that machine gun incident at the Luster court house in 1910. This fragile balance between big predators is oh so delicately strung. And along come you Gatlin-totin' hard-asses from the big town to upset everything. What shall I do with you, cousin, oh what?"

"Jesus, these are swell flapjacks, Mr. Blackwood," Bly said. His rummy eyes were glazed as a stuffed dog's.

"Why, thank you, sirrah. At the risk of soundin' trite, it's an old family recipe. Wheat flour, salt, sugar, eggs from a black speckled virgin hen, dust from the bones of a Pinkerton, a few drops of his heart blood. Awful decadent, I'll be so gauche as to agree."

None of us said anything until Clementine muttered into my good ear, "Relax, baby. You ain't a lawman, are you? You finer than frog's hair." She nipped me.

"Yes, it is true," Blackwood said. "Our faithful government employees have a tendency to get short shrift. The Hollow voted and decided we'd be best off if such folk weren't allowed to bear tales. This summer a couple government rats, Pinkerton men, came sniffin' round for moonshine stills and such. Leto, Brutus, and Candy, you've met 'em, dragged those two agents into the bog and buried 'em chest deep in the mud. My lads took turns batterin' out their brains with those thumpers they carry on their belts. I imagine it took a while. Boys play rough. Candy worked in a stockyard. He brained the cattle when they came through the chute. Got a taste for it." He glanced at the trap door when he said this.

"Powerful glad I'm no Pinkerton," I said.

He opened his hand and reached across the space between us as if he meant to grasp my neck, and at the last moment he flinched and withdrew and his smile faded and the beast in him came near the surface. "You've been to see those bitches."

"The Corning ladies? Come to think of it, yes, I had a drink with the sisters. Now I'm having breakfast with you. Don't be jealous, Dan." I remained perfectly still and as poised as one can be with sweat in his eyes, a hard-on in progress, and consumed by rolling waves of blue-black pain. My own beast was growling and slamming its Stone Age muzzle against the bars. It wanted blood to quench its terror, wanted loose. "What do you have against old ladies. They didn't mention you."

"Our business interests lie at cross-purposes. I don't relish no competition. Wait. Wait a minute . . . Did you see the child?" Blackwood asked this in a hushed tone, and his face smoothed into a false calmness, probably a mirror of my own. Oh, we were trying very hard not to slaughter one another. He cocked his head and whispered, "John, did you see the child?"

That surely spooked me, and the teary light in his eyes spooked me too, but not half so much as the recollection of the cries in the dim room at the Corning bungalow. "No. I didn't."

He watched me for a while, watched me until even Dick and Bly began to rouse from their reveries to straighten and cast puzzled looks between us. Blackwood kept flexing his hand, clenching and tearing at an invisible throat, perhaps. "All right. That's hunkum-bunkum." His smile returned. "The crones don't have no children."

I wiped my palms to dry the sweat and lighted a cigarette and smoked it to cover my expression. After a few moments I said, "Does Paxton know I'm here?"

"Yes. Of course. The forest has eyes, the swamp ears. Why you've come to give him the buzz is the mystery."

"Hell with that. Some say he's at the root of trouble with my kin. Then there's the goons he sent my way. I didn't start this. Going to end it, though."

"Mighty enterprising, aren't you? A real dyed in the wool bad man."

"What is this pact? I wager it involves plenty of cabbage."

"An alliance, bad man. He and I versus the damnable crones and that rotgut they try to pass off as whiskey. Little Lord Paxton is moneyed up real good. He inherited well. In any event, he keeps palms greased at the governor's mansion and in turn, I watch his back. Been that way for a while. It's not perfect; I don't cotton to bowing and scraping. Man does what man must."

"Who funds the sisters?"

"Some say they buried a fortune in Mason jars. Gold ingots from the Old

World. Maybe, after they're gone, me and the lads will go treasure hunting on their land."

So, I'd well and truly fallen from fry pan to fire. Paxton wanted me dead, or captured, thus far the jury remained out on that detail, and here I'd skipped into the grasp of his chief enforcer. "Hell, I made it easy for you lugs, eh? Walked right into the box." I nodded and decided that this was the end of the line and prepared to draw my pistol and go pay Saint Peter my respects with an empty clip. "Don't think I'll go quietly. We Copes die real hard."

"Hold on a second," Bly said, sobering in a hurry. I didn't think the Bly clan had a similar tradition.

Blackwood patted him on the head. "No need for heroics, gents. We've broken bread, haven't we? You can hop on Shank's Mare and head for the tall timber anytime you like. Nobody here's gonna try to stop you. On the other paw, I was kind of hoping you might stick around the Hollow, see this affair through."

I sat there and gaped, thunderstruck. "We can walk out of here." My senses strained, alert for the snare that must lurk within his affable offer. "What do you want, Dan?"

"Me and the boys recently were proposed a deal by . . . Well, that's none of your concern. A certain party has entered the picture, is enough to say. We been offered terms that trump our arrangement with Paxton. Trump it in spades. Problem is, I've sworn an oath to do him no harm, so that ties my hands."

"That's where I come in."

"You've said a mouthful, and no need to say more. We'll let it ride, see how far it takes us."

"And if I want to cash in and take my leave?"

He shrugged and left me to dangle in the wind. I started to ask another question, thought better of it, and sat quietly, my mind off to the races. Dan's smile got even wider. "Candy will squire you back to the Sycamore. There's a garden party and dinner. All the pretty folk will be there tying one on. Dress accordingly, eh?"

Candy returned us to the hotel where my entourage collapsed, semi-clothed and pawing one another, into a couple of piles on the beds. Dawn leaked through the curtains and I was queerly energized despite heavy drinking and nagging wounds, so I visited the nearby café as the first customer. I drank bad coffee in a corner booth as locals staggered in and ordered plates of hash and eggs and muttered and glowered at one another; beasts awakened too soon from hibernation. I fished in my pocket and retrieved the cocoon Carling had given me and lay it on the edge of the saucer. It resembled a slug withered by salt and dried in the hot sun. I wondered if my father, a solid, yet philosophically ambiguous, Catholic ever carried a good luck charm. What else was a crucifix or a rosary?

"You know you're playing the fool." I said this aloud, barely a mutter, just enough to clear the air between my passions and my higher faculties. Possibly I thought giving voice to the suspicion would formalize matters, break the spell and justify turning the boat around and sailing home, or making tracks for sunny Mexico and a few days encamping on a beach with a bottle of whiskey and a couple of *señoritas* who didn't *habla inglés*. At that moment a goose waddled over my grave and the light reflecting from the waitress's coffee pot bent strangely and the back of my neck went cold. I looked down the aisle through the doorway glass and spotted a couple of the Blackwood Boys loitering in the bushes of a vacant lot across the way. One was the big fiddler, the other wore overalls and a coonskin cap. The fiddler rested his weight on the handle of what at first I took for a shovel. When he raised the object and laid it across his shoulder I recognized it as a sword, one of those Scottish claymores.

A party and in my finest suit and tie it would be. Goddamn, if they were going to be this way about it I'd go see the barber after breakfast and have a haircut and a shave.

It was as Blackwood promised. We drove over to the mansion in a Cadillac I rented from the night clerk at the hotel. Even if the guys hadn't scoped the joint out previously, we would've easily found our way by following a small parade of fancy vehicles bound for the estate. Bly rolled through the hoary, moss-encrusted gates and the mansion loomed like a castle on the horizon. He eased around the side and parked in the back. We came through the servants' entrance. Dick and Bly packing shotguns, me with the Thompson slung under my arm. Men in livery were frantically arranging matters for the weekly estate hoedown and the ugly mugs with the guns made themselves scarce.

Conrad Paxton was on the veranda. He didn't seem at all surprised when I barged in and introduced myself. He smiled a thin, deadly smile and waved to an empty seat. "*Et tu*, Daniel?" he said to himself, and chuckled. "Please, have a drink. Reynolds," he snapped his fingers at a bland older man wearing a dated suit, "fetch, would you? And, John, please, tell your comrades to take a walk. Time for the men to chat."

Dick and Bly waited. I gave the sign and they put the iron away under their trench coats and scrammed. A minute or two later, they reappeared on the lawn amid the hubbub and stood where they could watch us. Everybody ignored them.

I leaned the Thompson against the railing and sat across from my host. We regarded each other for a while as more guests arrived and the party got underway.

Finally, he said, "This moment was inevitable. One can only contend with the likes of Blackwood and his ilk for a finite period before they turn on one like the wild animals they are. I'd considered moving overseas, somewhere with a more hospitable clime. No use, my enemies will never cease to pursue, and I'd rather die in my home. Well, Eadweard's, technically." Conrad Paxton's face was long and narrow. His fingers were slender. He smoked fancy European cigarettes with a filter and an ivory cigarette holder. Too effete for cigars, I imagined. Well, me too, chum, me too.

"Maybe if you hadn't done me and mine dirt you'd be adding candles to your cake for a spell yet."

"Ah, *done you dirt.* I can only imagine what poppycock you've been told to set you upon me. My father knew your father. Now the sons meet. Too bad it's not a social call—I'm hell with social calls. You have the look of a soldier."

"Did my bit."

"What did you do in the war, John?"

"I shot people."

"Ha. So did my father, albeit with a camera. As for me, I do nothing of consequence except drink my inheritance, collect moldy tomes, and also the envy of those who'd love to appropriate what I safeguard in this place. You may think of me as a lonely, rich caretaker."

"Sounds miserable," I said.

Afternoon light was dimming to red through the trees that walled in the unkempt concourses of green lawn. Some twenty minutes after our arrival, and still more Model Ts, Packards, and Studebakers formed a shiny black and white procession along the crushed gravel drive, assembling around the central fountain, a twelve-foot-tall marble faun gone slightly green around the gills from decades of mold. Oh, the feather boas and peacock feather hats, homburgs and stovepipes! Ponderously loaded tables of *hors d'oeuvres*, including a splendid tiered cake, and pails of frosty cold punch, liberally dosed with rum, were arrayed beneath fluttering silk pavilions. Servants darted among the gathering throng and unpacked orchestral instruments on a nearby dais. Several others worked the polo fields, hoisting buckets as they bent to reapply chalk lines, or smooth divots, or whatever.

Dick and Bly, resigned to their fate, loitered next to the punch, faces gray and pained even at this hour, following the legendary excesses of the previous evening. Both had cups in hand and were tipping them regularly. As for Paxton's goons, those gents continued to maintain a low profile, confined to the fancy bunkhouse at the edge of the property, although doubtless a few of them lurked in the shrubbery or behind the trees. My fingers were crossed that Blackwood meant to keep his bargain. Best plan I had.

A bluff man with a pretty young girl stuck on his arm waved to us. Paxton indolently returned the gesture. He inserted the filter between his lips and dragged exaggeratedly. "That would be the mayor. Best friend of whores and moonshiners in the entire county."

"I like that in a politician," I said. "Let's talk about you."

"My story is rather dreary. Father bundled me off to the orphanage then disappeared into Central America for several years. Another of his many expeditions. None of them made him famous. He became *famous* for murdering that colonel and driving Mother into an early grave. I also have his slide collection and his money." Paxton didn't sound too angry for someone with such a petulant mouth. I supposed the fortune he'd inherited when his father died sweetened life's bitter pills.

"My birth father, Eadweard Muybridge, died in his native England in 1904. I missed the funeral, and my brother Florado's as well. I'm a cad that way. Floddie got whacked by a car in San Francisco. Of all the bloody luck, eh? Father originally sent me and my brother to the orphanage where I was adopted by the Paxtons as an infant. My real mother named me Conrad after a distant cousin. Conrad Gallatry was a soldier and died in the Philippines fighting in the Spanish-American War.

"As a youth, I took scant interest in my genealogy, preferring to eschew the coarseness of these roots, and knew the barest facts regarding Eadweard Muybridge beyond his reputation as a master photographer and eccentric. Father was a peculiar individual. In 1875 Eadweard killed his wife's, and my dearest mum's, presumed lover—he'd presented that worthy, a retired colonel, with an incriminating romantic letter addressed to Mrs. Muybridge in the Colonel's hand, uttered a pithy remark, and then shot him dead. Father's defense consisted of not insubstantial celebrity, his value to science, and a claim of insanity as the result of an old coach accident that crushed his skull, in addition to the understandable anguish at discovering Mum's betrayal. I can attest the attribution of insanity was correct, albeit nothing to do with the crash, as I seemed to have come by my moods and anxieties honestly. Blood will tell."

"You drowned a boy at your school," I said. "And before that, your stepsister vanished. Somewhat of a scoundrel as a lad weren't you?"

"So they say. What they say is far kinder than the truth. Especially for my adopted Mum and Da. My stepsister left evidence behind, which, predictably, the Paxtons obscured for reasons of propriety. They suspected the truth and those suspicions were confirmed when I killed that nit Abelard Fries in our dormitory. A much bolder act, that murder. And again, the truth was obfuscated by the authorities, by my family. No, word of what I'd really done could not be allowed to escape our circle. You see, for me, it had already begun. I was already on the path of enlightenment, seeker and sometimes keeper of *Mysterium Tremendum et fascinans*. Even at that tender age."

"All of you kooky bastards in this county into black magic?" I'd let his insinuations regarding the fate of his sister slide from my mind, dismissing a host of ghastly speculative images as they manifested and hung between us like phantom smoke rings.

"Only the better class of people."

"You sold your soul at age nine, or thereabouts. Is that it, man? Then Daddy came home from the jungle one day and took you in because . . . because why?"

"Sold my soul? Hardly. I traded up. You didn't come to me to speak of that. You're an interesting person, John. *Not* interesting enough for this path of mine. Your evils are definitely, tragically lowercase."

"Fine, let's not dance. Word is, you did for my father. Frankly, I was attached to him. That means we've got business."

"Farfetched, isn't it? Didn't he choke on a sandwich or something?"

"I'm beginning to wonder. More pressing: Why did you try to have me rubbed out? To keep me in the dark about you bopping my dad? That wasn't neighborly."

"I didn't harm your father. Never met the man, although Eadweard spoke of him, wrote of him. Your old man made a whale of an impression on people he didn't kill. Nor did I dispatch those hooligans who braced you in Seattle. Until you and your squad lumbered into Ransom Hollow, I had scant knowledge and exactly zero interest in your existence. Helios August certainly engineered the whole charade. The old goat knew full well you'd respond unkindly to the ministrations of fellow Johnson Brothers, that you'd do for them, or they for you, and the winner, spurred by his wise counsel, would come seeking my scalp."

"Ridiculous. Hand them a roll of bills and they'll blip anyone you please, no skullduggery required."

"This is as much a game as anything. Your father was responsible for Eadweard's troubles with the law. Donald Cope is the one who put the idea of murder in his head, the one who mailed the gun that Eadweard eventually used on the retired officer who'd dallied with my mother. Eadweard wasn't violent, but your father was the devil on his shoulder telling him to be a man, to smite his enemy. After pulling the trigger, my father went off the rails, disappeared into the world and when he returned, he had no use for Helios Augustus, or anyone. He was his own man, in a demented fashion. Meanwhile, Helios Augustus, who had spent many painstaking years cultivating and mentoring Eadweard, was beside himself. The magician was no simple cardsharp on a barge whom your father just happened to meet. One of his myriad disguises. His posturing as a magician, famous or not, is yet another. Helios Augustus is a servant of evil and he manipulates everyone, your father included. Donald Cope was meant to be a tool, a protector of Eadweard. A loyal dog. He wasn't supposed to dispense wisdom, certainly not his own homespun brand of hooliganism. He ruined the magician's plan. Ruined everything, it seems."

I was accustomed to liars, bold-faced or wide-eyed, silver tongued or pleading, often with the barrel of my gun directed at them as they babbled their last prayers to an indifferent god, squirted their last tears into the indifferent earth. A man will utter any falsehood, commit any debasement, sell his own children down the river, to avoid that final sweet goodnight.

Paxton wasn't a liar, though. I studied him and his sallow, indolent affectation of plantation suzerainty, the dark power in his gaze, and beheld with clarity he was a being who had no need for deception, that all was delivered to him on a platter. He wasn't the afraid, either. I couldn't decide whether that lack of fear depended upon his access to the Blackwood Boys, his supreme and overweening sense of superiority, an utter lack of self-preservation instincts, or something else as yet to make its presence felt. Something dread and terrible in the wings was my guess, based upon the pit that opened in my gut as we talked while the sun sank into the mountains and the shadows of the gibbering and jabbering gentry spread grotesquely across the grass.

"You said Augustus groomed Muybridge."

"Yes. Groomed him to spread darkness with his art. And father did, though not to the degree or with the potency Helios Augustus desired. The sorcerer and his allies believed Eadweard was tantalizingly close to unlocking something vast and inimical to human existence."

The guests stirred and the band ascended the dais, each member lavishly dressed in a black suit, hair slicked with oil and banded in gold or silver, each cradling an oboe, a violin, a horn, a double bass, and of course, of fucking course, Dan Blackwood at the fore with his majestic flute, decked in a classical white suit and black tie, his buttered down hair shining like an angel's satin wing. They nodded to one another and began to play soft and sweet chamber music from some German symphony that was popular when lederhosen reigned at court. Music to calm a bellicose Holy Roman Emperor. Music beautiful enough to bring a tear to a killer's eye.

I realized Dick and Bly had disappeared. I stood, free hand pressed to my side to keep the bandage from coming unstuck. "Your hospitality is right kingly, Mr. Paxton, sir—"

"Indeed? You haven't touched your brandy. I'm guessing that's a difficult bit of self-restraint for an Irishman. It's not poisoned. Heavens, man, I couldn't harm you if that were my fiercest desire."

"Mr. Paxton, I'd like to take you at your word. Problem is, Curtis Bane had a card with your name written on it in his pocket. That's how I got wind of you."

"Extraordinarily convenient. And world famous magician Phil Wary, oh dear, my mistake—Helios Augustus—showed you some films my father made and told you I'd set the dogs on your trail. Am I correct?"

"Yeah, that's right." The pit in my belly kept crumbling away. It would be an abyss pretty soon. It wasn't that the pale aristocrat had put the puzzle together that made me sick with nerves, it was his boredom and malicious glee at revealing the obvious to a baboon. My distress was honey to him.

"And let me ponder this . . . Unnecessary. Helios put you in contact with those women in Luster. The crones, as some rudely call them."

"I think the ladies prefer it, actually."

"The crones were coy, that's their game. As you were permitted to depart their presence with your hide, I'll wager they confirmed the magician's slander of my character. Wily monsters, the Corning women. Man-haters, man-eaters. Men are pawns or provender, often both. Word to the wise—never go back there."

Just like that the sun snuffed as a burning wick under a thumb and darkness was all around, held at bay by a few lanterns in the yard, a trickle of light from the open doors on the porch and a handful of windows. The guests milled and drank and laughed above the beautiful music, and several couples assayed a waltz before the dais. I squinted, becoming desperate to catch a glimpse of my comrades, and still couldn't pick them out of the moiling crowd. I swayed as the blood rushed from my head and there were two, no, three, Conrad Paxton's seated in the gathering gloom, faces obscured except for the glinting eyes narrowed in curiosity, the curve of a sardonic smile. "Why would they lie?" I said. "What's in it for them?"

Paxton rose and made as if to take my elbow to steady me, although if I crashed to earth, there wasn't much chance the bony bastard would be able to do more than slow my fall. Much as Blackwood had done, he hesitated and then edged away toward the threshold of the French doors that let into a study, abruptly loath to touch me. "You are unwell. Come inside away from the heat and the noise."

"Hands off. I asked a question."

"My destruction is their motivation and ultimate goal. Each for his or her personal reason. The sorcerer desires the secrets within my vault: the cases of photographic plates, the reels, a life's work. Father's store of esoteric theory. Helios Augustus can practically taste the wickedness that broods there, black as a tanner's chimney. Eadweard's macabre films caused quite a stir in certain circles. They suggest great depths of depravity, of a dehumanizing element inherent in photography. A property of anti-life."

"You're pulling my leg. That's—"

"Preposterous? Absurd? Any loonier than swearing your life upon a book that preaches of virgin births and wandering Jews risen from the grave to spare the world from blood and thunder and annihilation?"

"I've lapsed," I said.

"The magician once speculated to me that he had a plan to create moving images that would wipe minds clean and imprint upon them all manner of base, un-sublimated desires. The desire to bow and scrape, to lick the boots of an overlord. It was madness, yet appealing. How his face animated when he mused on the spectacle of thousands of common folk streaming from theatres, faces slack with lust and carnal hunger. For the magician, Eadweard's lost work is paramount. My enemies want the specimens as yet hidden from the academic community, the plates and reels whispered of in darkened council chambers."

"That what the crones want too? To see a black pope in the debauched Vatican, and Old Scratch on the throne?"

"No, no, those lovelies have simpler tastes. They wish to devour the souls my father supposedly trapped in his pictures. So delightfully primitive to entertain the notion that film can steal our animating force. Not much more sophisticated than the tribals who believe you mustn't point at another person, else they'll die. Eadweard was many, many things, and many of them repugnant. He was not, however, a soul taker. Soul taking is a myth with a single exception. There is but One and that worthy needs no aperture, no lens, no box.

"Look here, John: thaumaturgy, geomancy, black magic, all that is stuff and nonsense, hooey, claptrap, if you will. Certainly, I serve the master and attend Black Mass. Not a thing to do with the supernatural, I'm not barmy. It's a matter of philosophy, of acclimating oneself to the natural forces of the world and the universe. Right thinking, as it were. Ask me if Satan exists, I'll say yes and slice a virgin's throat in the Dark Lord's honor. Ask me if I believe He manipulates and rewards, again yes. Directly? Does He imbue his acolytes with the power of miracles as Helios Augustus surely believes, as the crones believe their old gods do? I will laugh in your face. Satan no more interferes in any meaningful way than God does. Which is to say, by no discernable measure."

"Color me relieved. Got to admit, the old magician almost had my goat. I thought there might be something to all this horseshit mumbo-jumbo."

"Of course, mysticism was invented for the peasantry. You are far out of your depth. You are being turned like a card between masters. The Ace of Clubs. In all of this you are but a blunt instrument. If anyone murdered your father, it was Helios Augustus. Likely by poison. Poison and lies are the sorcerer's best friends."

I took the blackened cocoon from my shirt pocket. So trivial a thing, so withered a husk, yet even as I brandished it between thumb and forefinger, my host shrank farther away until he'd stepped into the house proper and regarded me from the sweep of a velvet curtain, drawn across his face like a cowl or a cape, and for an instant the ice in my heart suggested that it was a trick, that he was indeed the creature of a forsaken angel, that he meant to lull me into complacency and would then laugh and devour me, skin, bones, and soul. Beneath the balcony the music changed; it sizzled and snapped and strange guttural cries and glottal croaks resounded here and there.

A quick glance, no more, but plenty for me to take it in—the guests were *all* pairing now, and many had already removed their clothes. The shorn and scorched patches of bare earth farther out hadn't suffered from the ravages of ponies or cleats. Servants were not reapplying chalk lines; it must've been pitch in their buckets, for one knelt and laid a torch down and flames shot waist high and quickly blossomed into a series of crisscross angles of an occult nature. The mighty pentagram spanned dozens of yards and it shed a most hellish radiance, which I figured was the point of the exercise. Thus, evidently, was the weekly spectacle at the Paxton estate.

"Don't look so horrified, it's not as if they're going to rut in the field," Paxton said from the safety of the door. "Granted, a few might observe the rituals. The majority will dance and make merry. Harmless as can be. I hadn't estimated you for a prude."

My hand came away from my side wet. I drew the Luger. "I don't care whether they fuck or not," I said, advancing until I'd backed him further into the study. It was dim and antiquated as could be expected. A marble desk and plush chairs, towering stacks of leathery tomes accessed by a ladder on a sliding rail. Obscured by a lush, ornamental tree was a dark statue of a devil missing its right arm. The horned head was intact, though, and its hollow eyes reminded me of the vacuous gaze of the boy in Muybridge's film. "No one is gonna hear it when I put a bullet in you. No one is gonna weep, either. You're not a likeable fella, Mr. Paxton."

"You aren't the first the sorcerer has sent to murder me. He's gathered so many fools over the years, sent them traipsing to their doom. Swine, apes, rodents. Whatever dregs take on such work, whatever scum stoop to such dirty deeds. I'm exhausted. Let this be the end of the tedious affair."

"I'm here for revenge," I said. "My heart is pure." I shot him in the gut.

"The road to Hell, etcetera, etcetera." Paxton slumped against the desk. He painstakingly lighted another cigarette. His silk shirt went black. "Father, the crones, other, much darker personages who shall remain nameless for both our sakes, had sky high ambitions for me when I was born. That's why I went to a surrogate family while Floddie got shuffled to a sty of an orphanage. It must be admitted that I'm a substantial disappointment. An individual of power, certainly. Still, they'd read the portents and dared hope I would herald a new age, that I would be the chosen one, that I would cast down the tyrants and light the great fires of the end days. Alas, here I dwell, a philosopher hermit, a casual entertainer and dilettante of the left-hand path. I don't begrudge their bitterness and spite. I don't blame them for seeking my destruction. They want someone to shriek and bleed to repay their lost dreams. Who better than the architect of their disillusionment?"

To test my theory that no one would notice, or care, and to change the subject, I shot him again. In the thigh this time.

"See, I told you. I'm but a mortal, and now I die." He sagged to the floor, still clutching his cigarette. His eyes glittered and dripped. "Yes, yes, again." And after he took the third bullet, this one in the ribs an inch or two above the very first, he smiled and blood oozed from his mouth. "Frankly, I thought you'd extort me for money. Or use me to bargain for your friends whom you've so quaintly and clumsily searched for since they wandered away a few minutes ago."

"My friends are dead. Or dying. Probably chained in the cellar getting the Broderick with a hammer. It's what I'd do if I were in your shoes." I grudgingly admired his grit in the face of certain death. He'd a lot more pluck than his demeanor suggested.

"I hope your animal paranoia serves you well all the days of your life. Your friends aren't dead. Nor tortured; not on my account. Although, maybe Daniel wasn't satisfied with one double cross. I suppose it's possible he's already dug a hole for you in the woods. May you be so fortunate." He wheezed and his face drained of color, become gauzy in the dimness. After the fit subsided, he gestured at my chest. "Give me the charm, if you please."

I limped to his side and took the cigarette from him and had a drag. Then I placed the cocoon in his hand. He nodded and more blood dribbled forth as he popped the bits of leaf and silk and chrysalis into his mouth and chewed.

He said, "A fake. What else could it be?" His voice was fading and his head lolled. "If I'd been born the Antichrist, none of this would've happened. Anyway . . . I'm innocent. You're bound for the fire, big fellow."

I knelt and grasped his tie to pull him close. "Innocent? The first one was for my dad. Don't really give a damn whether you done him or not, so I'll go with what feels good. And this does indeed feel good. The other two were for your sister and that poor sap in boarding school. Probably not enough fire in Hell for you. Should we meet down there? You'd best get shy of me."

"In a few minutes, then," Paxton said and his face relaxed. When I let loose of his tie, he toppled sideways and lay motionless. Jeeves, or Reynolds, or whatever the butler's name was, opened the door and froze in mid-stride. He calmly assessed the situation, turned sharply as a Kraut infantryman on parade, and shut it again.

Lights from the fires painted the window and flowed in through the curtains and made the devil statue's grin widen until everything seemed to warp and I covered my eyes and listened to Dan Blackwood piping and the mad laughter of his thralls. I shook myself and fetched the Thompson and made myself comfortable behind the desk in the captain's chair, and waited. Smoked half a deck of ciggies while I did.

Betting man that I am, I laid odds that either some random goons, Blackwood, or one of my chums, would come through the door fairly soon, and in that order of likelihood. The universe continued to reveal its mysteries a bit later when Helios Augustus walked in, dressed to the nines in yellow and purple silk, with a stovepipe hat and a black cane with a lump of gold at the grip. He bowed, sweeping his hat, and damn me for an idiot, I should've cut him down right then, but I didn't. I had it in my mind to palaver since it had gone so swimmingly with Paxton.

Bad mistake, because, what with the magician and his expert prestidigitation and such, his hat vanished and he easily produced a weapon that settled my hash. For an instant my brain saw a gun and instinctively my finger tightened on the trigger of the Thompson. Or tried to. Odd thing, I couldn't move a muscle, couldn't so much as bat a lash. My body sat, a big useless lump. I heard and felt everything. No difficulties there, and then I recognized what Helios had brandished was the mummified severed hand he'd kept in his dressing room at the Hotel Broadsword. I wondered when he'd gotten into town. Had Blackwood dialed him on the blower this morning? The way things were going, I half suspected the creepy bastard might've hidden in the shrubbery days ago and waited, patient as a spider, for this, his moment of sweet, sweet triumph.

That horrid, preserved hand, yet clutching a fat black candle captivated me . . . I knew from a passage of a book on folklore, read to me by some chippie I humped in college, that what I was looking at must be a hand of glory. Hacked from a murderer and pickled for use in the blackest of magic rituals. I couldn't quite recall what it was supposed to do, exactly. Paralyzing jackasses such as myself, for one, obviously.

"Say, Johnny, did Conrad happen to tell you where he stowed the key to his vault?" The magician was in high spirits. He glided toward me, waltzing to the notes of Blackwood's flute.

I discovered my mouth was in working order. I coughed to clear my throat. "Nope," I said.

He nodded and poured himself a glass of sherry from a decanter and drank it with relish. "Indeed, I imagine this is the blood of my foes."

"Hey," I said. "How'd you turn the Blackwood Boys anyhow?"

"Them? The boys are true believers, and with good reason considering who roams the woods around here. I got my hands on a film of Eadweard's, one that might've seen him burned alive even in this modern age. In the film, young Conrad and some other nubile youths were having congress with the great ram of the black forest. Old Bill stepped from the grove of blood and took a bow. I must confess, it was a spectacular bit of photography. I informed the boys that instead of hoarding Muybridge's genius for myself, it would be share and share alike. Dan and his associates were convinced."

"I'm sorry I asked."

"Does everyone beg you for mercy at the end?"

"The ones who see it coming."

"Do you ever grant quarter?"

"Nope."

"Will *you* beg me for mercy?"

"Sure, why not?"

The magician laughed and snapped his fingers. "Alas! Alack! I would spare you, for sentimental reasons, and because I was such a cad to send The Long and The Short gunning for you, and to curse Donald purely from spite. Unfortunately, 'tis Danny of the Blackwood who means to skin you alive on a corroded altar to Old Bill. Sorry, lad. Entertaining as I'm sure that will prove, I'm on a mission. You sit tight, Uncle Phil needs to see to his prize. Thanks oodles, boy. As the heathens and savages are wont to say, you done good." He ignored the torrent of profanity that I unleashed upon his revelation that he'd killed my father, and casually swirled his elegant cape around his shoulders and used my own matches to strike a flame to the black candle. Woe and gloom, it was a macabre and chilling sight, that flame guttering and licking at dead fingers as he thrust it forth as a torch.

Helios Augustus proved familiar with the layout. He promptly made an adjustment to the devil statue and ten feet away one of the massive bookcases pivoted to reveal a steel door, blank save for a keyhole. The magician drew a deep breath and spent several minutes chanting in Latin or Greek, or bits of both and soon the door gave way with a mere push from his index finger. He threw back his head and laughed. I admit, that sound was so cold and diabolical if I'd been able to piss myself right then, I would've. Then he wiped his eyes and disappeared into a well of darkness and was gone for what felt like an age.

I spent the duration listening to the Blackwood Boys reciting an opera while straining with all of my might and main to lift my hand, turn my head, wiggle a toe, to no avail. This reminded me, most unpleasantly, of soldiers in France I'd seen lying trussed up in bandages at the hospital, the poor bastards unable to blink as they rotted in their ruined bodies. I sweated and tried to reconcile myself with an imminent fate worse than death, accompanied by death. 'Hacked to pieces by a band of hillbilly Satanists hadn't ever made my list of imagined ways of getting rubbed out—and as the Samurai warriors of yore meditated on a thousand demises, I too had imagined a whole lot of ways of kicking.

Helios Augustus's candle flame flickered in the black opening. He carried a satchel and it appeared heavily laden by its bulges; doubtless stuffed with Eadweard Muybridge's priceless lost films. He paused to set the grisly hand in its sconce before me on the desk. The candle had melted to a blob of shallow grease. It smelled of burnt human flesh, which I figured was about right. Probably baby fat, assuming my former chippie girlfriend was on the money in her description.

Helios said, "Ta-ta, lad. By the by, since you've naught else to occupy you, it may be in order to inspect this talisman more closely. I'd rather thought you might twig to my ruse back in Olympia. You're a nice boy, but not much of a detective, sorry to say." He waved cheerily and departed.

I stared into the flame and thought murderous thoughts and a glint on the ring finger arrested my attention. The ring was slightly sunken into the flesh, and that's why I hadn't noted it straight away. My father's wedding band. Helios Augustus, that louse, that conniving, filthy sonofawhore, had not only murdered my father by his own admission, but later defiled his grave and chopped off his left hand to make a grotesque charm.

Rage had a sobering effect upon me. The agony from my wounds receded, along with the rising panic at being trapped like a rabbit in a snare and my brain ticked along its circuit, methodical and accountant-like. It occurred to me that despite his callous speech, the magician might've left me a chance, whether intentionally or as an oversight, the devil only knew. I huffed and puffed and blew out the candle, and the invisible force that had clamped me in its vice evaporated. Not one to sit around contemplating my navel, nor one to look askance at good fortune, I lurched to my feet and into action.

I took a few moments to set the curtains aflame, fueling the blaze with the crystal decanter of booze. I wrapped Dad's awful hand in a kerchief and jammed it into my pocket. Wasn't going to leave even this small, gruesome remnant of him in the house of Satan.

An excellent thing I made my escape when I did, because I met a couple of Blackwood's boys on the grand staircase. "Hello, fellas," I said, and sprayed them with hellfire of my own, sent them tumbling like Jack and Jill down the steps, notched the columns and the walls with bullet holes. I exulted at their destruction. My hand didn't bother me a whit.

Somebody, somewhere, cut the electricity and the mansion went dark as a tomb except for the fire licking along the upper reaches of the balcony and the sporadic muzzle flashes of my trench broom, the guns of my enemies, for indeed those rat bastards, slicked and powdered for the performance, yet animals by their inbred faces and bestial snarls, poured in from everywhere and I was chivvied through the foyer and an antechamber where I swung the Thompson like a fireman with a hose. When the drum clicked empty I dropped the rifle and jumped through the patio doors in a crash of glass and splintered wood, and loped, dragging curtains in my wake, across the lawn for the trees. I weaved between the mighty lines of the burning pentagrams that now merely smoldered, and the trailing edge of my train caught fire and flames consumed the curtains and began eating their way toward me, made me Blake's tyger zigzagging into the night, enemies in close pursuit. Back there in the yard echoed a chorus of screams as the top of the house bloomed red and orange and the hillbillies swarmed after me, small arms popping and cracking and it was just like the war all over again.

The fox hunt lasted half the night. I blundered through the woods while the enemy gave chase, and it was an eerie, eerie several hours as Dan Blackwood's pipe and his cousins' fiddle and banjo continued to play and they drove me through briar and marsh and barbwire fence until I stumbled across a lonely dirt road and stole a farm truck from behind a barn and roared out of the Hollow, skin intact. Didn't slow down until the sun crept over the horizon and I'd reached the Seattle city limits. The world tottered and fell on my head and I coasted through a guardrail and came to a grinding halt in a field, grass scraping against the metal of the cab like a thousand fingernails. It got hazy after that.

• • •

Dick sat by my bedside for three days. He handed me a bottle of whiskey when I opened my eyes. I expressed surprise to find him among the living, convinced as I'd been that he and Bly got bopped and dumped in a shallow grave. Turned out Bly had snuck off with some patrician's wife and had a hump in the bushes while Dick accidentally nodded off under a tree. Everything was burning and Armageddon was in full swing when they came to, so they rendezvoused and did the smart thing—sneaked away with tails between legs.

Good news was, Mr. Arden wanted us back in Olympia soonest; he'd gotten into a dispute with a gangster in Portland. Seemed that all was forgiven in regard to my rubbing out The Long and The Short. The boss needed every gun in his army.

Neither Dick nor the docs ever mentioned the severed hand in my pocket. It was missing when I retrieved my clothes and I decided to let the matter drop. I returned to Olympia and had a warm chat with Mr. Arden and everything was peaches and cream. The boss didn't even ask about Vernon. Ha!

He sent me and a few of the boys to Portland with a message for his competition. I bought a brand spanking new Chicago-typewriter for the occasion. I also stopped by the Broadsword where the manager, after a little physical persuasion, told me that Helios Augustus had skipped town days prior on the Starlight Express, headed to California, if not points beyond. Yeah, well, revenge and cold dishes, and so forth. Meanwhile, I'd probably avoid motion pictures and stick to light reading.

During the ride to Portland, I sat in back and watched the farms and fields roll past and thought of returning to Ransom Hollow with troops and paying tribute to the crones and the Blackwood Boys; fantasized of torching the entire valley and its miserable settlements. Of course, Mr. Arden would never sanction such a drastic engagement. That's when I got to thinking that maybe, just maybe I wasn't my father's son, maybe I wanted more than a long leash and a pat on the head. Maybe the leash would feel better in my fist. I chuckled and stroked the Thompson lying across my knees.

"Johnny?" Dick said when he glimpsed my smile in the rearview.

I winked at him and pulled my Homburg down low over my eyes and had a sweet dream as we approached Portland in a black cloud like angels of death.

Laird Barron was born and raised in Alaska, did time in the wilderness, and raced in several Iditarods. Later, he migrated to Washington State where he devoted himself to American Combato and reading authors like Robert B.

Parker, James Ellroy, and Cormac McCarthy. At night he wrote tales that combined noir, crime, and horror. He was a 2007 and 2010 Shirley Jackson Award winner for his collections *The Imago Sequence and Other Stories* and *Occultation and Other Stories* and 2009 nominee for his novelette "Catch Hell." Other award nominations include the Crawford Award, Sturgeon Award, International Horror Guild Award, World Fantasy Award, Bram Stoker Award, and the Locus Award. His first novel, *The Croning*, was published in 2012; his latest collection, *The Beautiful Thing That Awaits Us All*, is due out this year. Barron currently resides in Upstate New York and is writing a novel about the evil that men do.

ACKNOWLEDGMENTS

"Hand of Glory" by Laird Barron © 2012 Laird Barron. First publication: *The Book of Cthulhu 2*, ed. Ross Lockhart (Night Shade Books).

"Great-Grandmother in the Cellar" by Peter S. Beagle. Copyright © 2012 The Avicenna Development Corporation. First published in *Under My Hat: Tales from the Cauldron* (published in the U.S. by Random Childrens and in the UK & Commonwealth by Hot Key Books).

"Glamour of Madness" by Peter Bell © 2012 Peter Bell. First publication: *The Ghosts & Scholars Book of Shadows*, ed. Rosemary Pardoe (Sarob Press).

"Down in the Valley" by Joseph Bruchac © 2012 Joseph Bruchac. First publication: *Postscripts 28-29: Exotic Gothic 4*, ed. Danel Olson (PS Publishing).

"Bigfoot on Campus" by Jim Butcher © 2012 Jim Butcher. First publication: *Hex Appeal*, ed. P. N. Elrod (St Martin's Griffin).

"Iphigenia in Aulis" by Mike Carey © 2012 Mike Carey. First publication: *An Apple for the Creature*, eds. Charlaine Harris & Toni L.P. Kelner (Ace Books).

"Nightside Eye" by Terry Dowling © 2012 Terry Dowling. First publication: *Cemetery Dance #66*.

"The Bird Country" by K. M. Ferebee © 2012 K. M. Ferebee. First publication: *Shimmer #15*.

"The Natural History of Autumn" by Jeffrey Ford © 2012 Jeffrey Ford. First publication: *The Magazine of Fantasy and Science Fiction*, July/August 2012.

"The Man Who Forgot Ray Bradbury" by Neil Gaiman © 2012 Neil Gaiman. First publication: *Shadow Show: All-New Stories in Celebration of Ray Bradbury*, eds. Sam Weller & Mort Castle (William Morrow/Harper Collins).

"England Under the White Witch" by Theodora Goss © 2012 Theodora Goss. First publication: *Clarkesworld*, Issue 73.

"Game" by Maria Dahvana Headley © 2012 Maria Dahvana Headley. First publication: *Subterranean*, Fall 2012.

"Escena de un Asesinato" by Robert Hood © 2012 Robert Hood. First publication: *Postscripts 28-29: Exotic Gothic 4*, ed. Danel Olson (PS Publishing).

"Welcome to the Reptile House" by Stephen Graham Jones © 2012 Stephen Graham Jones. First publication: *Strange Aeons #9*.

"Fake Plastic Trees" by Caitlín R. Kiernan © 2012 Caitlín R. Kiernan. First publication: *After: Nineteen Stories of Apocalypse and Dystopia*, eds. Ellen Datlow & Terri Windling (Hyperion).

"The Education of a Witch" by Ellen Klages. Copyright © 2012 by Ellen Klages. First published in *Under My Hat: Tales from the Cauldron* (published in the U.S. by Random Childrens and in the UK & Commonwealth by Hot Key Books).

"Forget You" by Marc Laidlaw © 2012 Marc Laidlaw. First publication: *Lightspeed*, April 2012.

"Renfrew's Course" by John Langan © 2012 John Langan. First publication: *Lightspeed*, June 2012.

"The Tall Grass" by Joe R. Lansdale © 2012 Joe R. Lansdale. First publication: *Dark Tales of Lost Civilizations*, ed. Eric J. Guignard (Dark Moon Books).

"Slaughterhouse Blues" by Tim Lebbon © 2012 Tim Lebbon. First publication: *Nothing As It Seems* (PS Publishing).

"The Eyes of Water" by Allison Littlewood © 2012 Allison Littlewood. First publication: *The Eyes of Water* (Spectral Press).

"Good Hunting" by Ken Liu © 2012 Ken Liu. First publication: *Strange Horizons*, October 2012.

"No Ghosts in London" by Helen Marshall © 2012 Helen Marshall. First publication: *Hair Side, Flesh Side* (ChiZine Publications).

"Blue Lace Agate" by Sarah Monette © 2012 Sarah Monette. First publication: *Lightspeed*, January 2012.

"End of White" by Ekaterina Sedia © 2012 Ekaterina Sedia. First publication: *Shotguns vs. Cthulhu,* ed. Robin D. Laws (Stone Skin Press).

"Pearls" by Priya Sharma © 2012 Priya Sharma. First publication: *Bourbon Penn Issue 04.*

"Bedtime Stories for Yasmin" by Robert Shearman © 2012 Robert Shearman. First publication: *Shadows & Tall Trees 4,* ed. Michael Kelly.

"When Death Wakes Me to Myself" by John Shirley © 2012 John Shirley. First publication: *Black Wings II: New Tales of Lovecraftian Horror,* ed. S.T. Joshi (PS Publishing).

"Sinking Among the Lilies" by Cory Skerry © 2012 Corry Skerry. First publication: *Beneath Ceaseless Skies,* Issue #92.

"Go Home Again" by Simon Strantzas © 2012 Simon Strantzas. First publication: *Fungi,* eds. Orrin Grey and Silvia Moreno-Garcia (Innsmouth Free Press).

"The Sea of Trees" by Rachel Swirsky © 2012 Rachel Swirsky. First publication: *The Future is Japanese,* eds. Nick Mamatas & Masumi Washington (Haikasoru).

"Dahlias" by Melanie Tem © 2012 Melanie Tem. First publication: *Black Wings II: New Tales of Lovecraftian Horror,* ed. S.T. Joshi (PS Publishing).

"Who Is Arvid Pekon" by Karen Tidbeck © 2002, 2012 Karin Tidbeck. First publication in English: *Jagganath: Stories* (Cheeky Frawg Books); first publication in Swedish (as "Vem är Arvid Pekon?"): *Jules Verne-Magasinet 513,* 2002.

"Armless Maidens of the American West" by Genevieve Valentine © 2012 Genevieve Valentine. First publication: *Apex,* 7 August 7 2012.

"Everything Must Go" by Brooke Wonders © 2012 Brooke Wonders. First publication: *Clarkesworld,* Issue 74)